The Shroud of Turin

A Novel

The Shroud of Turin

A Novel

A.J.V. Hurston

VANTAGE PRESS
New York

FIRST EDITION

Published by Vantage Press, Inc.
419 Park Ave. South, New York, NY 10016

Manufactured in the United States of America
ISBN: 978-0-533-15683-2

Library of Congress Catalog Card No.: 2006910037

0 9 8 7 6 5 4 3 2 1

Fiction and truth always move in the same footprints.

This book examines goodness versus that of wickedness.

To all who have longed to find God,
but have lost their way;
and to Bob Lewin

The Shroud of Turin

A Novel

1

The Search Begins

On October 5, 1929, the *Imperator*, its bronze propellers stilled, rests in Stettin Bay between Germany and northwest Poland. The aging ship, awash in moonlight and fog, has taken eleven days to arrive from New York. Among the white passengers, making their way down the gangplank into Germany, are a dozen powder-puff Americans, slender women in high-heeled shoes, women adorned with flapper caps and mink coats, their wobbling, pale bodies leaning into the wind. Smoking Cuban cigars, the men—wearing Stetson hats and stylish clothes—walk at the women's sides, steadying them.

Lawrence Winthrop steps from the gangplank and to the curb a few yards away, where he lingers beside stacks of luggage, placed there by young porters.

Lawrence, an American as well, is conservatively dressed and noticeably taller than the other passengers. He's fifty, slender, with blue eyes and has a full head of white hair. With him is his blue-eyed wife, Marilyn. She has recently celebrated her fortieth birthday and still turns heads. Marilyn is holding onto the hand of Sarah, fourteen. The teenager has her mother's blue eyes and blonde hair. She is well-read and intelligently alluring.

"Thanks again, Mother, you and Father," Sarah says, beaming up at them, going on, "for taking the ship out of New York. Times Square! All of those buildings and people. So different from Georgia."

Lawrence forces a smile, his thoughts elsewhere and his expression solemn. "It was a good idea, sweetheart. Your mother and I had business in New York to attend to anyway." Gripping her husband's hand, Marilyn gives him a troubled glance. He goes on, as if trying to convince himself as much as her. "The world won't fall apart before we return home," he tells Marilyn.

Sarah seems aware that something is troubling her parents and watches them with concern but makes no mention of the problems back on their sixteen-thousand-acre plantation. The young girl shifts her attention to an unusual sight behind them: Coming down the gangplank with the white passengers, her face half hidden by the hood of her

weathered coat, her hands covered by gloves and carrying a black poodle—with a rhinestone collar about its neck—is a mysterious-looking
woman. She steps off the gangplank and into the ship's shadow and lingers there, shivering in the night air, while observing Sarah. Dangling
from beneath the woman's hood and over her shoulders are two large
braids, tied off on the ends with strips of leather and strings of Indian
beads, which Sarah recognizes as some she, herself, has collected in the
past. The fog lifts, opening the sky to moonlight, igniting it against the
hooded woman's face. She's black. Her penetrating, brown eyes—reflecting the moonlight—continue watching Sarah. In the current atmosphere of Germany, where only those who sprung from the Teutonic
past are viewed as the superior race, from behind that once
dark-shadowed hood and into the light of the full moon, glows the face
of Naomi Bell. She is dark of skin, thirty-five, part Kiowa, and part black.
With those illuminated eyes, high cheekbones, and sensitive lips—to
Sarah—Naomi has the kindest face she has ever seen; both stand there,
trancelike, observing each other. Marilyn follows Sarah's sights to Naomi and then touches Sarah's shoulder. "Sarah, it is impolite to stare."

Naomi turns her attention to the gangplank and onto the approach
of her employer, a thin, white woman named Stella Fuchs. Stella is several years younger than Naomi and tosses a fox-fur boa over her shoulder
while carrying an umbrella and doing her best to keep her gray, wool coat
closed against the wind. Stepping off the gangplank, Stella hands the
umbrella to Naomi and then follows Naomi's gaze back to Sarah and
Marilyn. Guardedly, Sarah smiles at the drab white Stella, who grunts
and turns away. "Is it so difficult for you to smile at a child?" Naomi asks.

"There's no money in a pretty face," snaps Stella. "I learned that
the hard way, and listen, Naomi, you're among the very rich. Don't try to
shake anyone's hand or make polite conversation with them. They're not
interested in anything you have to say. If they speak to you at all, they
would only be doing it because you're a momentary curiosity to them,
and don't put on airs just because you're in Europe. These people will
see right through you. I'll do all the talking for both of us."

One-by-one, the other New Yorkers gather around their curbside
luggage, a few feet left of the Winthrops. Naomi and Stella wait next to
Lawrence and his family, Sarah chuckling, as the poodle licks its tongue
out at her.

"Would you like to pet it?" Naomi asks, extending the dog to Sarah.

"I'm Sarah Winthrop," she tells Naomi, after petting the dog, then shaking the black woman's hand. Marilyn smiles approvingly, reflecting the pride she has in her outgoing daughter.

"Naomi Bell," replies Naomi.

"Glad to meet you, Sarah." Naomi gestures to Stella. "And this here is Miss Stella. . . ."

"Never mind that!" Stella blurts out.

"Do the two of you work on the ship together?" Sarah queries Naomi.

"I'm so sorry," says Marilyn to Stella and Naomi. "It's because we have colored help at home and she thought . . ." Marilyn turns to Sarah. "They are passengers, sweetheart, the same as we are."

"I'm sorry," Sarah tells Stella, sensing that it is she and not Naomi who is offended by the remark. Her arms crossed over her chest, and tapping the tip of her shoe against the sidewalk, Stella gazes, irritatedly at the night sky. Lawrence and Marilyn are visibly upset by Stella's snobbish attitude. Sarah, however, only momentarily disappointed, presses her face against the poodle's pink nose and radiates her joy up at Naomi when the dog licks her cheeks. "Is this your dog?"

"Oh, no, child. This here dog belongs to Miss Stella."

"What is his name?"

Stella seizes the dog from Naomi, wipes its face with her lace handkerchief and kisses her puppy.

"Did that girl get my baby's face dirty?" The woman glares at Sarah. "She's a 'she,' not a 'he,' and her name is 'Leticia.' " Stella turns to Marilyn and sneers at her, then looks over her shoulder at the other staring travelers, and back at an annoyed Marilyn. "A blind fool can see," snorts Stella in a fit of anger, "that even with you in them style-less clothes, you've never been poor in your life, so don't give me none of your looks."

The other Americans whisper about Stella's behavior. Lawrence, however, remains silent, leaving the matter in his wife's capable hands.

"Come along, Sarah," Marilyn tells the young girl, expanding the space between them and Stella. No sooner does Marilyn turn away with Sarah, than Stella lays into them again, her voice rising: "Listen, you little condescending redneck," she calls to Marilyn, as Naomi stands and watches. "Don't walk away from me like I was dirt. At sixteen, I was married to a man of means." She glares at the wealthier Americans and continues. "And, like the rest of you, I once walked around with my nose in the air also." The woman seems especially interested in Sarah and returns her attention back to her. "And each husband, after my first, was poorer than the last. Now, so that you'll understand," she tells the confused, adolescent girl. "I don't have time for politeness. I looked like you once. Men'll offer you the world now, but you'll grow old fast and be used up before you can blink those pretty, blue eyes of yours!"

Marilyn places a stunned Sarah behind her and faces Stella. "I am sorry you had to marry so young," Marilyn tells the embittered woman. "But, as long as we have to travel together, if you cannot say anything intelligent, please say nothing at all."

Stella fires back, "Your voice, more than those country clothes you're wearing, says you're a grand, refined, southern lady. Southern men might not slap their women folk around, but I've been slapped by the best in New York, and I've survived. Will you? With the handwriting on the wall back home growing worse every day—to save their lands—poor, white, Southern trash marry off their girls to wealthier men before these young souls even know how to pee." Stella nudges her way around Marilyn to Sarah, and the other travelers step completely away from them, as Stella exclaims to Sarah, "My mom never told me, so I'm telling you," the woman hisses at Sarah. "As good as you look, your parents won't have any trouble marrying you off to some rich man in order to survi . . ."

"Then survive this," shouts Marilyn, slapping Stella. Sarah looks away surprised, in shock, ready to cry, at seeing her mother violent for the first time in her life. When Stella seizes a nearby stick to strike Marilyn, Lawrence steps between her and his wife.

"That's enough!" he exclaims, ushering his family to the end of the line.

"The New York Times," Stella calls to Lawrence, flinging the stick aside. "A man like you must have read it. Isn't that why we're all here?" She gestures to the other Americans. "Pretending to be secure and unafraid; we're all afraid. Afraid of what's happening in America. We're all here in hopes of making money to survive!"

A line of cars roll down the cobblestone street and stop at the curb. Men in long, black coats step from the vehicles and open the doors, and the visitors to Germany pick up their luggage and file toward the chauffeured cars. Stella places a leash on her dog and walks it toward their transportation, then looks back at Naomi who lingers as if praying.

"Don't just stand there like a dumbbell, Naomi," hisses Stella, taking her anger out on the black woman. "I'm your ticket home. Or maybe you think that that constant praying of yours can cause you to walk across the Atlantic back to New York?" In the dark of that night, the umbrella helping to conceal her face from the German drivers, and while struggling with their luggage, Naomi follows Stella, the poodle, and the other luggage-carrying visitors to the waiting vehicles. Lawrence, Marilyn and Sarah end up in the back seat of the last car. Sitting next to the door, all thoughts of her mother's fight behind her now, her hair blowing in the wind, Sarah leans out the window, her gaze locked on the chauffeured limousines ahead of them, the well-kept, black cars following a police, motorcycle escort and twisting and turning over the jolting, cobblestone streets, pass medieval buildings, cathedrals, old-world homes, and onto a paved street, and on toward Berlin.

Sometime later, within sight of the Chancellery building, the motorcycle escort pulls into the rear of a hotel, its stone walls flaking, its sidewalk unsteady and cracked, its windows small and dirty. Everyone collects his own luggage and is guided through the hotel's rear door by the men in those black leather coats. Sarah is about to step from the curve to the hotel, when she senses that someone is watching her. She gazes over at a large, polished, black car parked on the opposite side of the street. Besides the chauffeur and another man in the front seat, who appears to be a bodyguard, in the back seat sits a single man—masked in darkness—looking out at her. When their gazes meet, the man in the rear seat motions to the driver, and the car speeds away, led by and followed by guards on official looking motorcycles. Once inside the hotel, and after boarding a freight elevator, the guests are escorted to their different floors and rooms. The Winthrops, and five others, are given door keys and suites on the seventh floor, where the hallway is dimly lit and stuffy.

"Of all the rotten luck," Stella complains, when she notices the Winthrops a door down from her quarters. As Naomi struggles with their luggage, Stella glares at her. The servant woman, amused at Fuchs's obsession with the Winthrops, is smiling. "You people must really like working hard for others," Stella tells Naomi. "Happy all the time. But I guess you can't help it that God made your kind the working class of this world. I'll give you something to smile about with that chuckling grin of yours. You can scrub the floors when we get inside; that way, I'll be sure we're not catching someone else's germs." Stella fumbles with the door key, grumbling on. "Also, I want you to give Leticia a good bath and feed her. Then you can go to bed."

Slowly, Stella looks back at Naomi, who is busily trying to balance the luggage and the dog in her arms. Naomi glances up and smiles at her boss, and then Stella's bitter expression changes. At the same time, Sarah—who is glaring at Stella—takes her father's hand and leads him inside their suite, leaving Marilyn lingering in the hallway, observing Stella, then Naomi. Marilyn retreats into their suite and ponders out of sight by the open door, as Stella unlocks the door to her accommodations, looks about the hallway, then gradually back at Naomi. Marilyn is about to close the door to their compartment, when she hears Stella's act of contrition. "I know you think I'm mean," Stella tells Naomi. "As a Jewish person, whose parents went through the same kind of prejudices as you coloreds, I had no right to say what I did about you being born to work for others. Why don't you ever get pissed off at me? I would if I had a boss like me." Naomi just looks at her with her quiet composure, Marilyn listening, still unseen from her door, as Stella continues. "I'm not heartless. I know you must be tired. I'll wash Leticia. You get some rest."

Just as Stella puts a foot inside their quarters, Marilyn approaches. "Let's begin again," Marilyn says, extending her hand to Stella. Stella rubs the side of her face, as if saying that she's better off by far to be friends rather then risk another of Marilyn's out-of-nowhere slaps. She smiles and gladly shakes Marilyn's hand. "Seems we got off on the wrong foot," says Sarah's mother. "I'm Marilyn Winthrop."

"I'm Stella Fuchs. My friends call me Stell. 'Lucky' would be a better name, seeing that I'm one of the few invited here to make up for what I'm about to lose back home. And you?"

"My family and I, we are here to . . ."

"No. Why are you here? You don't strike me as the kind of woman who needs work. Not yet, anyway. Not with you married to a man like your husband."

"He is a blessing," Marilyn says, a bit confused about what Stella means about Lawrence and her. Going on, Marilyn explains: "I'm a professor and a housewife, and Sarah is our only . . ." Marilyn's focus shifts to the content face of Naomi, who is watching them and seems to be out of place, not only in Germany, but out of place in a world ripe with prejudice. "We're here on school-related business," Marilyn finally says to Stella, but is unable to take her sights off Naomi. Finally, she looks back at Stella. "How long have you and your maid been together?"

Stella faces Naomi. "Oh, her. Just before I was to leave on this trip, at a time when I asked God 'Why me?' I couldn't find anyone to come along to care for my Leticia. Nor did I have the money to pay anyone to do so. Like an angel from God, Himself, but of course, God would never have colored angels. Anyway . . . She arrived at my door. And to top it all off, she said she'd come along for free, just to see Europe. She even had her own passport. A colored maid with a passport, can you beat that? That aside, Leticia has never let anyone hold her but me, but she took to Naomi right off." Marilyn observes that there is something about Naomi, who is standing there without comment. The more she sees of Naomi, the more she likes her. She hardly hears Stella, who rattles on. "And best of all," Stella says, "she never complains. Do you, Naomi?"

Naomi nods with that sparkle in her eyes, as if knowing something no one else in the world knows. Marilyn extends her hand to the maid. "I'm Marilyn, Naomi."

Stella pulls Marilyn's hand away from Naomi. "Don't spoil her," she tells Marilyn. "Next thing you know, she'll be asking to be paid."

Marilyn's shoulders sink. Lawrence, who had returned to the door to see what was delaying his wife, and had been listening, approaches Stella. "Being a doctor," he says, "you would think that I would have known how to prevent seasickness, but when the pills failed to help, we became ill and never ventured out of our cabin to meet anyone." He puts out his hand to Stella. "I'm Doctor . . ."

"A renowned heart surgeon," says Stella. "We all know who you are and why you're here."

"Oh," says Lawrence, lowering his hand. "Are you here on a teaching sabbatical?" He asks her offhandedly, knowing that Stella is too crude to be much of anything, let alone a teacher.

"I don't even know how to spell the damn word," Stella says.

"Then, why are you here?" Marilyn asks. "We thought everyone . . ."

Stella looks from a confused Marilyn to the Winthrops' suite. Watching from the doorway and holding a rosary, Sarah gets everyone's attention. "Father is here to teach Jewish medical students at the University of Berlin," Sarah tells Stella.

"I wouldn't call it teaching them," Stella brags to Marilyn, "unless keeping them students and others in line is teaching. If so, then I'm also here to teach. Some of those fools back home have received letters from Germany about how Jews are mistreated here, and they were told not to come to this country, but don't believe it. I'm a Jew, as I told Naomi, so I know how we Jews are preoccupied with fear and cause rumors to fly. Except for the wealthier passengers on this trip—to protect their aspirin investments here in Germany, I guess, and other investments like that—the rest of us in my group are all Jewish; the only thing we Jews care about aspirins is that they stop our headaches brought on by the sad financial shape of things today. However, we'll be well paid to police our own kind here, with other German-born Jews' help, of course." Stella turns to a stunned-looking Lawrence. "Don't tell me you didn't know?" she tells him. "You're one of the most important among us. Not that you're Jewish," she says, eyeing Sarah's rosary, going on, "or that they'll ask an important man like you or your wife to police anyone. The reason I know this is that word was smuggled out of Germany to some of us by emigrating doctors, who, if you ask me, didn't leave because of mistreatment but because they thought they'd make more money elsewhere. 'Good luck' is what I say to that."

"Emigrating doctors?" Lawrence asks.

"Yes," Stella exclaims. "That's why you and a handful of others here, like you, will be needed in case he or his top people are poisoned, shot, or develop heart troubles or something, since many of the best doctors left the country or can't be trusted."

Marilyn and Lawrence simultaneously ask, "Who is this 'he'?"

"I guess a person who wants to rule the world," says Stella. "Some kind of self-appointed leader from my recollections, but I could care less who he is, as long as I'm paid, and, whoever pays well, in these coming hard times, I'll fall on my knees and worship." When Stella mentions that she'll worship this unknown person, Sarah's young eyes open wide with a surprise look, and—bewildered—the young girl stares at her mother, as Stella goes on. "We'll meet this person tomorrow morning at eight sharp, so write down all the questions you have, then ask him and get a good night's sleep. I'm told his speeches are powerful but long."

Stella follows Marilyn's intimidated gaze down the hallway to their escorts, one of whom is removing his coat, revealing a swastika band around his shirt sleeve.

"Swastikas are ornaments that have been around since the old world," Stella tells Marilyn. "So don't worry like some of those who sent those letters to New York. Even American Indians wore swastikas. It means good luck."

"The Indians' swastikas pointed counterclockwise," Sarah whispers from the doorway.

"Counter what?" Stella grumbles.

"The Indians trusted the first, white Americans and lost their lives and land," Sarah explains. "That man's swastika is clockwise, the opposite of the Indians'."

Naomi is watching the young girl with a look in her eyes that seems to say that she has not made a mistake about Sarah, that Sarah is the right one. Sarah places the tip of her thumbnail against the edge of her even, upper white teeth, ponders for a moment and then bewilders Stella. "I wonder which swastika," the young girl begins, "the clockwise or counterclockwise, will bring luck and which the opposite of luck, since they are in opposition to one another, and whose land will be taken, and from whom, and whose life?"

Stella turns and stares at Naomi. "What kind of child is this that she can ask such a question? Does she think she can predict the future?" She faces Sarah, "Then predict the stock market, young lady!" Once more, she turns to Naomi. "What kind of kid is this . . . again, I ask you?"

"Someone who will help bring hope to the world," Naomi answers, perplexing Stella all the more, but bringing a smile to the lips of Marilyn and Lawrence.

"Sarah has her own mind and is very special to her parents," Lawrence says, going to his daughter and placing his arm about her shoulder.

"Sarah has been home taught at a college level, and at times our child goes a little too far," an elated Marilyn adds, beaming at Naomi. "But we hope she will always have her own way of thinking."

"Oh, she's got that all right," snaps Stella, who then hurries inside her suite. As the Winthrops enter their quarters, Naomi watches Sarah until the teenage girl disappears behind her door; then Sarah suddenly pokes her head out again, smiles at Naomi, then fully enters their suite, closing the door behind her. Chuckling, Naomi enters Stella's unit, calling ahead to her. "I'll set the clock and wake us up real early. We got to be good and ready for that big day to come."

"We?" Stella hisses from within her room. "Don't you dare touch this clock! I'll do that myself. Your job is to care for my dog. Now, get in here and wash Leticia. Hell! Just when you try to be civil toward your neighbors, shit always hits the fan. That little brat. 'I wonder which movement of the swastikas, clockwise or counterclockwise is more un-lucky,'" she says, mocking Sarah, as Naomi—now inside their quar-ters—quietly closes the door behind her.

On the other side of the wall, in their rooms, Sarah showers, brushes her teeth, changes into a nightgown, and climbs into one of two beds in her room. When Marilyn enters, the teenage girl is sitting up in bed and waiting for her. "Mother, was Stella suggesting that God is here, in Germany, and that God is this person, who invited us to this country, when she spoke of falling on her knees before him?"

"Your father and I do not want you to worry about such things, Sa-rah." She tickles her. "Of course, now, if you are 'the hope of the world,' the way that colored lady says, and you can wave a magic wand and make all the world's troubles go away, then I guess we will have to call you a lit-tle 'supreme being,' as well, along with the man before whom Stella wants to prostrate herself, and there won't be any people like Stella or any need for aspirins, because you'll be able to cure all of our headaches, backaches, embittered souls and such. Do you have a magic wand?"

"Of course not, Mother," says Sarah, kissing her mother and hold-ing on tight. "I love you."

Marilyn tucks Sarah in, kisses her and leaves the room, carefully closing the door behind her. While Lawrence runs the water for a bath—preferring that to a shower—and removes his shirt, a wor-ried-looking Marilyn approaches him. "Did you hear what our daughter was asking me?"

"I heard."

"Maybe we should return home on the ship tomorrow, before it sails, instead of staying here for a month. I'm sure the university will un-derstand. The trouble back home, this business of Jews coming here to police other Jews, as if they were talking about inanimate pieces of furni-ture and not their own, beautiful people. Now this talk of a demigod. It's all too much for Sarah, I'm afraid."

"Let's not panic about what was said here tonight," says Lawrence, embracing her with a kiss. "Maybe all of this can be explained to our sat-isfaction in the morning. The *Imperator* won't sail until tomorrow night. There's plenty of time."

10

The following morning, under a soothing sun, and along with the other Americans, Lawrence and family wait in front of the hotel for their rides, during which time, German men and women transverse the winding, old streets around them, people seemingly everywhere, some on foot, some on bicycles, many in cars, a few in horse-drawn wagons, carrying their crops to market. Children race by laughing in youthful exuberance, then flail down narrow alleys, byways, and across tree-lined squares, and out of sight, their joyful voices trailing back. Sarah doesn't miss any of it, admiration reflecting in her eyes for the playful youths. Marilyn wonders why the happy children all appear to be German and not one of them Jewish, whom Stella had said she had come to help control. The escort cars return, streaming around the cobblestone corner and stopping at the hotel.

"Why did they take us through the back way last night and now pick us up in front of the building this morning?" Sarah ponders aloud. She stops, in deep thought, and then goes on. "There was a man in a car watching us when we arrived at the rear of the hotel. Did you see him, Father?"

"I did," says Marilyn. Turning to Lawrence, she adds. "That car last night and the way the man in it was staring at . . ." Marilyn looks at Sarah, and with no wish to frighten her, she takes an indirect approach with Lawrence. "That's one of the reasons why . . . when I spoke to you last night, I wanted us to return home."

Sarah looks up at her parents. Her mother is not smiling, which she often does, whenever Sarah is about, even when she's worried. Sadly, Sarah watches the other visitors hurriedly climb into their waiting vehicles and then their chauffeurs drive them away; Marilyn, however, hesitates and keeps Lawrence from entering their car. The German chauffeur, stands by in silence, holding open the door of that last car for them.

"I don't want to meet this person, Lawrence," Marilyn says. "Please, let's just go home now."

Suddenly, Stella, Naomi closing behind with Leticia, dashes out of the hotel. "Shit!" Stella yells, nudging Sarah and Marilyn into the car and climbing in, followed by Naomi. "I thought I'd missed the last ride for sure. We overslept!" As the females settle in the back seat, Stella looks out the open door at Lawrence. "Well, don't just stand there. We're the last ones. Get the hell in!"

11

Sarah makes herself comfortable on Marilyn's lap, the young girl watching her father, who is looking angrily back at Stella, then with empathy at a troubled Marilyn. Lawrence reluctantly enters the front seat alongside the driver, and off they go to meet Stella's unknown savior, the driver speeding, trying to catch up to the other cars. As their car zooms though the windblown countryside, past green fields—dotted with woolly, white sheep, herding dogs, and an elderly shepherd man—while her parents, from time to time, make eye contact through the rearview mirror at each other, Sarah keeps her sights on the intriguing landscape. Soon, though, when the car swings through a dark tunnel and onto a highway and reaches open land once more, the red barns and thatched-roof farm houses, the white sheets, underwear, socks and shirts hanging from clotheslines and flapping in the wind are left behind.

An hour later, the driver stops next to a gradually rising hill covered with wildflowers, a hill atop which are the other Americans gathered around the figure of a man silhouetted against the blinding sun and blue sky. Her jacket fluttering in the breeze, Sarah steps from the car and races up the flowery slope. Dancing through the wildflowers, smelling their soft essence, the beautiful girl sees an old man sitting on a stone wall at the summit, yards from the Americans. Carrying a wildflower, Sarah strolls to the hilltop and stops beside the elderly man and his wall, which seemingly overlook the world. She gives the flower to him, never recognizing that he is the bodyguard who was in the car from which she had been watched.

Back in their chauffeured vehicle, and having been distracted by Stella desperately searching about the rear seat for her lost passport, Marilyn hasn't realized that Sarah has ventured up the slope, and when she sees her child on the hill she gasps and calls to Sarah; sliding from the vehicle, Marilyn lingers there, when Naomi follows and touches her.

"Let her be," Naomi whispers to Marilyn. "This scant moment of innocent joy is some of the cement that will help strengthen her faith in what's to come in bringing love to the world."

Marilyn, puzzled, gazes at Naomi and then faces Sarah with a disquieted gaze. Sarah is now looking over the hilltop wall, the wind blowing through her soft, golden hair, as she peers down at Stettin Bay. To the highly-intelligent, young girl, the bay is a vast blanket of blue, framed against green trees, fertile land, and the distant thatched-roof houses, adding to a magnificent stage of human achievement under a sky full of seagulls, sweeping low over the *Imperator*, which sits royally at its pier below. Sarah can almost feel the hand of God touching the land with veneration.

In the car below the hill—frustrated—Stella gawks up the slope and leaps from the vehicle, nudging Naomi and Marilyn aside. "The hell with the passport," she says. "It's him! Come on!" Stella rushes up the hill, leaving Naomi behind with Leticia. Lawrence, looking with concern at his worried wife, steps from the car, takes Marilyn's hand and starts to the flowery slope. Marilyn stops and gazes over her shoulder. Lawrence follows her sights back to Naomi.

"You go on ahead, honey," Marilyn tells Lawrence. As he does, she—again—faces Naomi. "Are you coming, Naomi?" Marilyn asks, as if seeking a reason for not going, herself.

"Can fire mix with water and still be fire?" Naomi replies, while gazing at the silhouetted, hilltop man. Marilyn sees a gray shadow form across Naomi's face and tracks a cloud moving across the sky, as well. Marilyn then follows the servant woman's gaze to Sarah. The hilltop is in darkness, engulfing the teenage girl. Marilyn looks at Naomi and is filled with misgivings. "She'll be okay," whispers Naomi. "We must be strong for her, you and I."

Once again, Marilyn is taken aback by Naomi. To Marilyn, Naomi is far more than she lets on. Above them, Sarah observes the other visitors and the man who is lecturing them, a man they truly seem to adore. His dark straight hair is combed to the side of his prominent forehead; his upper lip is marked by a stubby mustache. His words are directed at his guests, but his demoralizing gaze is focused on Sarah. She follows his sights to her open jacket and firm breasts, outlined by her windblown dress. The elderly man on the wall leans over and quietly says, "It's whispered that his mother is a Jew, that he isn't of Nordic blood, but don't believe it. He heard you were coming and was told of your beauty. Your hair, blue eyes, your pleasing body is the Nordic stuff of Germany purity. When you become one with the powers-to-be here, remember me, his old uncle, with kindness." Sarah races off the hill, past Lawrence and into Marilyn's arms, the man on top of his world—and who is adored by Stella and her fellow Americans—following Sarah's frantic flight all the way with his intense, corrupt eyes. Lawrence quickly returns to his family's side. Suddenly, this unrevealed leader screams in agony from his earthen summit. His finger is pointing at Naomi. Leticia barks and struggles to break free of Naomi's arms, when she sees Stella all but being dragged back down the slope by one of the men in black. Releasing Stella, the man storms past the Winthrops and backhands Naomi, drawing blood from her mouth. The hilltop Americans stand in total silence, their gaze on the black woman, as she takes the hit without a whimper.

"Nietzsche had it all wrong and so do you," Naomi tells the German, who is astonished that she, of inferior blood, can pronounce "Nietzsche," let alone debate his intention. Naomi has shocked everyone who has heard her. "Tell that to your leader," she says to the stunned German, "if you want to prove yourself a man, instead of beating up on defenseless women and children. Tell him before he all but destroys your beautiful country and marks its good people in the book of records alongside Lucifer and his fallen angels."

Marilyn turns Sarah's face away, when the man draws back to strike Naomi again. Lawrence, however, grabs the German's hand. A struggle ensues with the German seizing Lawrence by his coat collar. Once more, that powerful, German voice bellows from the hill; in the hilltop shadows, he shakes his finger accusingly at the man in black; he then points at Naomi. Releasing Lawrence, the German returns to Naomi and as he does, Marilyn corners Stella. "What is this about?" she asks the frightened New Yorker.

Stella pushes Marilyn away, screaming. "I already told you. Money!"

The leather-coated German whirls around and lambastes Stella in broken English, while pointing at Naomi. "You should have thought of that before you brought this creature here, this African ape! Isn't it enough that you, yourself, are a Jew? Why did you bring this inferior person here to insult our leader?"

Stella is shaking so badly she can hardly stand, all American eyes are watching her. Marilyn steps toward Naomi to comfort her, but Lawrence takes his wife's hand, forcing her to follow his gaze to the accusatory stares of the others at Naomi. Marilyn eases back to Lawrence's side. The visitors, including the German man to whom Sarah had given the flower, have gathered stones; it's clear they mean to stone Naomi to death. Marilyn quickly tells Sarah to get in the car, which Sarah does, closing the door behind her, but then rolls down the window and urges Naomi to enter the vehicle with her; Naomi shakes her head. Lawrence faces the mystery woman.

14

"Get in the car, Naomi. Now!"

"No. It would endanger the child," Naomi tells him, contemplating a sobbing Sarah.

"My God, Lawrence," gasps Marilyn, "she's saying she'll die rather than . . ."

Her voice trailing off, Marilyn looks from Naomi to Sarah, then back at the black woman in profound wonder. Meanwhile, Stella, her head low, is sobbing on her knees before the German, who towers over her. "I meant no harm, no harm," Stella pleads with the man. Tearfully she gazes up at him. "If I'd have known how you and your country feel, I wouldn't have brought her with me. My dog loves her and can't be left alone."

"Choose between which dog you want the most," the German replies, glaring at Naomi, "This worthless, nothing, African swine of yours or your poodle."

Stella gives Naomi a look of regret, struggles to her feet, grabs Leticia from her maid, and runs up the hill, clutching Leticia in her arms.

The German looks at Lawrence. "I'm sorry you and your family had to see this, Doctor Winthrop. I understand you're concerned about your university position here." He looks up the grade at his leader, the sun—once again—shining mightily, silhouetting the man. Sarah looks up the slopes at him, as well—intimidated—from the car. On this unusually warm day, the heavily coated German begins to sweat, as if in fear of his own life if he displeases his leader. He glances up the hill and then turns to Lawrence, going on. "The German people and our leader want to assure you that you and your family are welcome here and will be able to teach any student you were promised, even those in the Jewish ghettos, with the understanding, of course, that you must be available to him, if he needs to call upon your special skills."

"We were invited here by a taller man, Professor Lester Gorn of the university, not by that smaller man on that hill," says Lawrence, shading his eyes with his hand and viewing the blackened figure. "Who is this person who has such power to have you mistreat women?"

"Someone who hates bad news," forewarns the German. "Adolph Hitler," he exclaims, saluting Hitler, as do all those around the would-be leader. "The supreme being!"

Lawrence, a religious man, is shocked. Marilyn holds onto him, squeezing his hand in fright.

"Are we free to leave?" Lawrence asks, fearing what the Germans might do to Naomi.

"You're free to leave anytime you wish," the German says, choosing his words carefully. "We are not unaware that you have powerful friends back in Washington, Doctor Winthrop."

"She leaves with us," demands Lawrence, pointing at Naomi.

"The sooner the better," the German says, studying the hilltop stone-gripping spectators, then facing Naomi with his eyes of contempt. Dumbfounded, he again, looks up at Hitler, then withdraws a handkerchief from his pocket, his brow heavily perspiring. Lawrence takes the handkerchief from him and wipes the blood from Naomi's mouth, then hands the bloody cloth to the German, who knocks it to the ground, as if Naomi's dark blood were a deadly poison. Lawrence guides Naomi and Marilyn to the car and then looks back at the leather-coated man when the chauffeur makes no motion to open the door for them.

"Please have your man drive us to the hotel," says Lawrence. "Our bags are already packed."

When the man looks away—from within the car—Sarah opens the door and takes Naomi's hand. "Why were you worrying about me?" Sarah sobs. "They were going to kill you. Get in!"

"This isn't the place or time for this woman to die, yet, child," Naomi whispers with a smile, while stepping into the car. "Now hush up them tears, and slide over, so I can sit by you."

Once Naomi completes her entry, the chauffeur holds the car door open for Marilyn. Lawrence rides up front with the driver, who speeds them on their way.

2

Himself of the Most High

After arriving at the waterfront, the Winthrops and Naomi sit on one of fifty rolls of benches in the intriguing, old, pier building, while waiting for the *Imperator*'s gangplank to be opened. All the time, people—carrying cardboard luggage—trickle into the terminal and occupy the benches as well. A young Jewish couple, scarcely past their teens, are among those entering. The female is named Rebecca. She has long, dark, silky hair and tan, olive-colored skin. The young girl is cradling a crying baby, which is wrapped in blue blankets below a white lace scarf that covers the teenage mother's breast, while she tries to get her baby to suckle; her youthful husband, Joel Lewin, also of a similar genetic makeup, is stroking the child and sadly whispering to it, as the couple occupies a seat opposite the Winthrops. After hearing the baby's desperate cries continue, Lawrence approaches Rebecca.

"May I be of service?" he asks. Neither Rebecca nor Joel speaks English, only German; both are terrified of Lawrence. He returns to his suitcase, removes a stethoscope, asks a group of nearby Jews if anyone speaks English, finds an old woman and takes her back to the couple. "Tell them I'm a doctor," he says to the translator, as Sarah and Marilyn join him.

While Lawrence waits for permission to examine the baby, Sarah—looking up at Marilyn—asks, "Who is Nietzsche, Mother?"

"He was a German philosopher who said, among other things, that the will to power was the main motivating force of both the individual and society. He died around thirty years ago."

"Then, how does Naomi know about him?"

"I asked myself the same question, Sarah. I really don't know."

Sarah looks over at Naomi. "Watch our things, Naomi," she calls. "We'll be right back."

After the old Jewish woman explains, in German, that Lawrence is an American doctor, Rebecca quickly hands the baby to him. Upon examining the perspiring child, a troubled look crosses Lawrence's face. He turns to the translator. "This baby is extremely dehydrated, and has diarrhea with serious complications. I've never seen such severe perspira-

17

tion. The child has to be taken to a hospital." Glancing at the ticket counter, he goes on. "The clerk speaks English. I'll ask him to call for an ambulance."

When the woman explains the situation to the Lewins, both implore her in German.

"What are they saying?" Lawrence asks.

"They don't want you to tell the clerk."

"Do they realize that their child is extremely ill?"

Marilyn notices how the other Jews in the building are looking over their shoulders. She faces Lawrence. "They must have their reasons, Lawrence. Isn't there a way to help the baby here?"

He glances out the window at the *Imperator*, and says, "The ship has a general practitioner on board. I'll ask the captain to . . ."

"If the captain knows the baby is this sick, he won't let them board," the translator says. "Their parents must have given up everything they had to give them this chance to reach America."

"They'll be other ships," Lawrence tells her. "There's no lab here. I haven't the right instruments, and I'm not a pediatrician. Without being hospitalized, there's a high probability the baby will die."

"It's up to Adonai, then," the translator explains, then seeing Lawrence's confusion, adds, "Our God." Her voice fades to silence, and she cautiously looks over her shoulder, along with the other Jewish passengers, who now mill about them; then all eyes again, seek out Lawrence. "We must be careful what we say to you," the translator whispers to him. She gets a nod from the crowd and Joel, after someone tells him in German what is going on, a nod that says for the woman to tell Lawrence everything. "As for the baby dying," the woman cautiously continues, once more glancing about. "None of us might be alive to see the next boat that sails, but we thank you for trying."

The Jews sadly wander back to their seats. Lawrence returns to his, with his family unhappily at his side. Lawrence glances at Sarah; it's clear he doesn't wish her to know the full meaning of what he has to tell Marilyn. He then faces his wife. "If these people are right about what I think they're saying," he tells her, "then those young ones have no choice but to board the ship with their baby." He sits on the bench next to Naomi, adding. "And there's little any of us can do but wait for the ship to sail and hope that the baby survives." Sarah sits next to Lawrence, Marilyn next to Sarah. Lawrence's words have sent chills through Marilyn and Naomi, their heads held low, their gaze on the floor, as the baby's cries weaken to a whimper.

"What's needed is a miracle," says Sarah, placing her arm about her father's shoulder, comforting him.

"Miracles come few and far between," Naomi ponders, seemingly unaware that she is muttering her innermost thoughts aloud, going on, "and they can't be wasted."

"Naomi," asks Sarah. "How can saving a baby's life be a wasteful miracle?"

"Innocent children are guaranteed entry into heaven," Naomi, says, never raising her head, as she goes on. "Miracles are best left for adults, who need them the most." Sarah looks away as if knowing there is no hope; Naomi, however, slowly lifts her head, her eyes now on the dying baby.

Later that night, as the terminal clock strikes ten times, Naomi and the Winthrops, lugging their suitcases, climb the gangplank and board the *Imperator* with the Jews and wealthier passengers, including some Americans, all of whom are looking down their noses at the card-board-carrying, emigrating Jews. After the passengers are aboard, the gangplank disabled, and the ship is pulled from the dock by a tugboat, the Winthrops retreat to their quarters for a much-needed nap. Naomi, however, remains on deck and mingles with tambourine-tapping, hand-clapping, dancing, Jewish children, who—up to now—have had to face life in total terror, and who had especially feared strangers; however, fascinated by anything American, anything from the land of the free, every youngster on the deck gathers around Naomi. "American?" one of the teenage boys asks her in broken English, while touching her dark skin. Naomi touches his skin in a playful gesture of tit-for-tat and nods with a warm smile. Suddenly, from the deck, agonizing voices cry out beyond the crowd. After telling the younger children to remain where they are, the Jewish adults rush toward the cries. "It's them," an old Jewish man—on the run—explains to another, both speaking in disconnected English. "The ship's doctor can't help their baby. It's grippe. I'm sure. And if they remove the blankets the child will die."

"No!" the other says, trotting along. "The child will die if they don't remove the blankets, especially if it doesn't suckle."

Sitting in a deck chair, after putting more baby blankets on her child, then taking them off and putting them back on again, the way everyone is telling her, afraid and hoping the night air will help her newborn, Rebecca dries the sweat from her infant with a towel, but the perspiration returns as fast as it's removed. Joel, in agony, stands over his young wife and child, looking down at them. In the confusion of everyone telling them what to do, no one can be heard. The baby turns blue. Joel and Rebecca flee to their cabin with their dying child, sobbing as they go. Naomi, from afar, steps away from the children and watches the fleeing couple, and then she cast a questioning look toward the sky.

Inside their small cabin, standing in the center of the floor, both parents hold onto the newborn and call out to the God of Abraham to save the infant, but the child's cries are all the weaker. They look around and gasp. Naomi is in the cabin, right behind them, her arms outstretched, her white palms upturned, her dark fingers motioning for them to hand the sickly infant to her. Rebecca and Joel look at each other, then at Naomi.

"He's my brother," says Naomi. "Hand him to me." Even though they cannot understand her, Joel nods, and Rebecca hands their only child to Naomi, a woman—they are keenly aware of—who is a total stranger to them.

"He's called Little Joel," Rebecca says, in German, the tears streaming from her eyes.

Naomi nods as if she understands Rebecca and then removes the blankets from Little Joel, hands the several soaked covers to Rebecca, and points at a nearby fresh towel, which the young father hurriedly gives to her, both parents stumbling over each other to help. Rocking the sickly baby in her arms, Naomi chants an African melody, while drying sweat from the gagging little man. She then lifts the naked baby over her head, into the night breeze streaming through the open porthole, along with the deck light backlighting the cabin, her and Little Joel. The newborn stops sobbing. He sweats no more, and Naomi—as if knowing this—lowers Little Joel into her arms once more. His color back to normal, the baby giggles when Naomi tickles his small stomach. The Lewins are stunned beyond belief.

"Dear God," Rebecca says in German to Joel. "Was it how she held him? What did this for our boy?"

Naomi jolts the young couple even more, when she answers them in their Semitic language.

20

"It was a miracle," she says. "Not for this little one, but for the sake of the two of you, by Someone Who loves you very much. He asks only this of you: When you get to America, don't forget the evil that you're fleeing and—in doing so—use that same evil against your brothers and sisters whose skin color is different from yours." Rebecca and Joel are speechless, as she cautions on. "Say nothing of what has happened here to those you have traveled with. They will enter New York and soon forget how persecuted they were, and they will—in their own way—persecute others, while teaching their children to do the same. Words of miracles are not for them."

"We will never forget we're all brothers and sisters, when we reach America," Rebecca begins with a sob, and Joel finishes, crying, saying:

"For as long as we live, we and our children and our children's children will never forget what the God of Abraham has done for us and our baby."

"If you forget everything else," Naomi tells them, "always remember that He's everyone's God and Little Joel is everyone's child, not just yours." With their eyes broadened in a new awareness, their heads nodding in understanding, Naomi hands Little Joel to his mother and he immediately suckles. Looking through another of the cabin's portholes—this one closed and making it impossible for her to hear what is going on inside—is Sarah Winthrop, and even though she can't hear what Naomi is saying inside the cabin, her eyes are wide from what she has been seeing.

On the main deck, long after the *Imperator* has left Stettin Bay behind, the Jews dance under the night sky, the music streaming from the upper deck and ballroom where affluent Americans and foreigners dance away the night, celebrating that they still have their fortunes. The Jews, below, though, are celebrating the sparing of little Joel's life and their renewed trust in their God. During all this time, some distance away, Naomi lingers alone on the ship's bow, her sights penetrating a thin layer of fog, her eyes on the fog-fuzzed stars.

"Since miracles are so few in coming, and Caleb and Flynn are both foretold to be the ones who will be lifted toward the heavens in the hands of their fathers during their births," she whispers, "the same way I lifted up Little Joel and prayed for the life of that precious child, did I use up one of the prayers which might have saved Caleb's life in the future?"

Wrapped in a warm coat and scarf, Sarah quietly comes up behind Naomi. "Hello, Sarah," Naomi says, without turning around.

"Who is 'Caleb' and who were you taking to?" Sarah asks, looking up at the stars shining through the fog and then at the back of Naomi, who continues facing away from her.

"A friend. I was talking to a friend, Sarah."

"What's this friend's name," Sarah asks, "Orion?"

"Martin, child. Martin de Porres," Naomi tells her, turning around and facing Sarah.

"Blessed Martin," delights Sarah. "He's my favorite saint; at least he will be a saint, that is, after he's canonized. He was the son of a Spanish grandee and a Negro woman and died in sixteen thirty-nine. I pray to him sometimes, but no one can just talk to him as if he were standing right beside you."

"I can, and so can you, Sarah. We talk to loved ones through our thoughts all the time. And through our thoughts, they talk back to us." She lowers her head, going on. "Unless, like all humans, we start doubting, and this doubt causes us to speak with our mouth and tongue instead of our heart and mind. The way I just did, as you heard. One of the things that was troubling me was about you being so young, so . . ."

"Worried about me being so young?" asks a suspicious Sarah. "Why?"

Naomi raises her head in the direction of the stars and speaks with such humility now that Sarah is completely disarmed. "Sometimes I worry too much, that's all," Naomi tells her.

"You're strange," Sarah says, then chuckles. "How did you know it was I behind you? You never looked around."

Naomi remains focused on the sky, as if looking for someone to tell her how to answer Sarah.

"It's that nice perfume you're wearing," Naomi says and then looks back at Sarah. "You wore it the day we met."

"A friend gave it to me two days before my parents and I where leaving for Germany. His name is Henry." She beams, going on. "He works for us, and even though it cost him only fifty cents, which is a meaningful portion of his wages, I wouldn't trade it for all of the perfume in Paris and wish to always have it with me until I die." Sarah glances down, then back into Naomi's eyes. "I'm sorry about what that terrible man did and said to you at the hill, Naomi. I saw how young people all gathered around you on the deck. They seem to love you, even if those others didn't."

"Now, they do," Naomi tells Sarah. "But in America, there are those who also say they love Christ, and still they crucify Him every day. Suffering's what we all got to endure before we die, child. That little slap in my face was nothin'. And, Sarah, God loves even those who cast stones."

"God," whispers Sarah. "He has so many wonderful names, at least most of the time, and means so many things to so many people: He Who is all-wise. He Who demands that we love others. He Who is called 'Jehovah,' 'Providence Most High.'" She smiles and gazes at the fuzzy stars. "He and Jesus are also called 'The Light of the World.'" The gleam leaves her eyes and she whispers. "He Who, some say, demands that we kill one another." Sarah turns away, her troubled thoughts on her father.

"What do you feel about your father?" Naomi asks.

"About whom?" Sarah asks, shocked that Naomi should ask that question at that moment.

"About your father. Are he and your mother good people?" Naomi asks, knowing that they are.

"Oh, yes. Mother is a devoted Catholic, but Father . . ." Sarah stares at the deck, momentarily changing the subject. "Our plantation is so large, that no man-made light like the ones in New York diminishes the stars' visible radiation over our fields." She lifts her sights to Naomi and continues. "Naomi, Father doesn't always attend mass, but he loves the stars. He says they are where the angels play at night. At home, he and I sometimes sit at my bedroom window and wait for hours to catch a glimpse of a shooting star, which I pretend is a chariot of fire taking people to heaven. We're always together, Father and I. I wish shooting stars would come more often instead of one or two at a time and few in between."

"Don't worry about your father, Sarah. From what I've seen, both your parents will play with the angels in the stars when they die. But you won't be alone. Even though you can't always see them through the fog or clouds, or light of day, the stars will forever shine over your land." Naomi looks up. "Stars are the windows in the sky for the saints to always look down on us."

"But Father and Mother must never die," Sarah says, "I couldn't live alone if my parents died, no matter how old I was when they died. I saw what you did to that baby in the young couples' cabin. Tell me my parents won't ever die, Naomi." When Naomi fails to answer, Sarah follows the mystery woman's focus back to the upper deck, as drunken passengers stream from the ballroom and into the night air, laughing, smoking and drinking.

"It's sad," the teenager remarks, "how the rich can be so happy for themselves." She studies the distant, dancing Jews, then faces Naomi. "And not be happy for others, and are uninterested in improving poor people's lives, the way Mother and Father want to. God wouldn't take them from me, would He? The German man said that Hitler was the 'Supreme Being.' Father says Germans are some of the brightest people in the world; Einstein is German, so maybe they are the smartest. Maybe there isn't a God among the stars."

Naomi points at the vast body of water swaying the ship. "Men of knowledge, like this here Mr. Einstein, say that these tides are caused by the pull of the moon and even by the wind; and they be right. But who pulls at the moon to keep it from colliding into us, and who controls the stars, and causes space to be endless by increasing its expansion into eternity?" She takes Sarah's hand. "But let's talk about you. This is a world where ghettos rise up faster than good people like your father and mother will ever be able to pull them down; that is the task for His new disciples, twelve of them to eventually come, in a world where babies will be thrown out of windows and into trash cans; synagogues, mosques, and churches will be burned, and millions will leave the holy church and dance with the devil: There will be the slaughtering of millions more in the name of righteousness, turning waterways into blood."

"What has that to do with me?" asks Sarah, extremely ill at ease now.

The fog abruptly thickens around them; the ship slices through the nightdark waters, its foghorn blaring. Sarah becomes even more afraid.

"You're trembling, child."

"That woman, Stella," Sarah begins. "I just realized how wicked she is. The way she spoke against her own kind. Why did you come here with her, if you're not the same as she, since you seem to be saying you're so wise about everything else?"

"There will always be those like Stella who will betray their own kind to fill their pockets with gold, but when the blood waters of despair overtake them, who does such wickedness, they will be pulled down and drown from the weight of their riches. You are the rarest of persons, Sarah Winthrop. I didn't come here for Stella's sake. I came here to be with you. What you saw on that hill in Hitler, that madman of blood and his evil disciples, and in Stella was meant for you to see. All to prepare you for another such man of evil who will come into your life when you return to Georgia. At a time of great sorrow and loss to you, this evil man will overcome your ability to resist him. In the Divine plan of things, it isn't Stella, your parents, you or me who is important. We are helpless to change anything. Only the coming of your sons can do that through their love for each other."

"My sons?"

"Your firstborn will be a beautiful, impressionable, blonde boy, a boy cursed with his father's ungodly seed and steered toward evil by this unholy man."

"I'm fourteen, Naomi. Not a woman to have babies."

"You are not yet the mother of hope, but soon you will be, after you marry Major Cutter."

"Barney Cutter!" shrills Sarah, her eyes wide. "You can't know what you're saying."

"I know he's many years older than you, that his ancestors founded Cutterville—that den of iniquity beyond your parents' land. And I know that many have died because of him and more will follow. Your marriage to this man will be a loveless union; then you will come to know a spiritual one of love. Out of each relationship, a son, separated by a year, will be born to you."

"Are you on dope?" Sarah asks, stepping back.

"Your firstborn will be named 'Flynn,' " Naomi says, never missing a beat. "Flynn will be the sensitive, beautiful one, the future hope of the Klan. Your second son will spring from your womb stubborn and robust. But he will have the seeds of your love and that of another's in him and will be called 'Caleb', named from the Bible. Flynn, with blue eyes, and Caleb, with his eyes of sandy yellow—at the chosen time —will oppose one another. Since humanity has turned its back on Providence—as a final test of man's worthiness—your sons will walk the road of the cross. Either they will walk it as brothers and tear down the curtain of hatred between us, or they will build on this veil of loathing that separates brother from brother, and they will perish with this world."

25

Sarah turns pale and runs away. "You are on something," she cries aloud.

"Don't despair, Sarah. There's no time and much to explain."

"Father and Mother will worry about me," Sarah says, slowing to a walk. Then she stops and looks back. "I will not marry some creature of evil, and you have no right to say that to me."

"Through all that's to come," Naomi tells her. "Barney Cutter will not leave his mark of evil on you, and you will find your true mate and be showered with the greatest love and closeness to godliness in this new person that a woman can ever have on earth. Don't be afraid, Sarah Winthrop. Nothing has been asked of you that you cannot endure."

The fog lifts, revealing the upper deck, where Marilyn is standing outside the ballroom; Lawrence comes up behind her; both look down at Naomi and Sarah on the distance bow.

"Is she okay?" Lawrence asks.

"She couldn't be in better hands, honey. She seems to like Naomi very much and so do I."

Content, Lawrence and Marilyn enter the ballroom. However, on the bow, Sarah is everything but. "Sarah, what do you want most out of life?" Naomi calls to her.

"What I want is for the stars to always shine and to be loved, but not like some woman of the night to a madman! My parents and I despise Barney Cutter!"

"Child, remember how you were once so ill and loved playing in the whirlwind, even though the other kids said not to, because they feared it would suck away your breath and you would die? Your faith was so strong then."

The dancing Jews, a far cry away, are in a world of their own; they are unaware of Naomi and Sarah, as Sarah suddenly gasps when a whirlwind sweeps onto the deck and wraps around her, frizzling her hair, fluttering her coat and dress. Pieces of white paper are sucked off the deck, into the funnel of air and are swept wildly in and out of the powerful vortex. Sarah turns in a circle within the funneling wind, her arms held out, as she laughs with Naomi. "Walk around," Naomi calls to her. "The funnel, it will follow you."

Sarah walks this way and that—closer and closer to Naomi—and the funnel stays with her. Naomi puts out her hand and touches Sarah's outstretched fingers, sending static electricity arcing onto Sarah. As swiftly as it had come, the whirlwind is gone. Out of breath, Sarah runs to Naomi and hugs her, both laughing.

"What was that, Naomi? Did you see it, the way it and the pieces of paper followed me?"

"It was a reminder to you that there are things done and yet to be done that science, even men who are spiritually gifted like Albert Einstein, can't begin to understand or put to paper to save this world."

"Naomi," Sarah says, torn between laughing in the midst of that magical moment, still whirling around in her head, and breaking free of those thoughts, and giving in to the trembling fright of what she is hearing. She steps back, going on, "Einstein could explain that silly whirlwind. Dust funnels. They happen all the time on our land. How can you stand there and expect me to believe what you're saying to me? Maybe next you'll say that the hand of heaven guided that wind to me? We left the fake supreme being back on that hill, so don't imitate him. It was just an ordinary, everyday wind, Naomi."

"There was nothing ordinary about that wind, baby. Don't believe me. Believe the stars." The blackened world above is abruptly filled with an outpouring of shooting stars, many on the ship witness the heart-stopping sight, including the dancing Jews and the captain from the bridge, as well as Lawrence and Marilyn, returning to the upper deck railing—with others—to watch. All music stops, while shipbound human hearts beat in one rhythm, as the unending lines of thousands of Sarah's fiery stars streak across the heavens, lighting up the ocean like silver, then they're gone. Sarah looks around at the mystified passengers, then at Naomi.

"Naomi."

"Yes, Sarah."

"Who are you? You neither look like, nor act like any of our other colored workers."

"I'm colored, I'm Mexican, I'm Indian, I'm Jewish, I'm white, I'm Chinese, I'm all humans wrapped in one, even as whites and blacks must learn, and Caleb must be, the last hope of mankind before His second coming."

"His second coming? Do you mean the coming of Jesus?"

"There they are! The Americans," someone among the Jews shouts from the deck behind them. The emigrates run to the bow, everyone inspired by the stars, urging Naomi and Sarah to join them, as the music, again, flows from the ballroom of the rich. Sarah looks at Naomi and is convinced that Naomi is someone she can never explain to her parents; they would never believe her. Nobody would.

"Are you sure, Naomi . . ." Sarah calls back, as the refugees guide her away, her hand outstretched to Naomi, ". . . that this is what He wants me to do, that I'll find true love, that Barney will not leave a mark of evil on me?"

"As sure as I am here under God's good sky, child. Barney will mark only Flynn with his evil seed." The young girl with the big heart lowers her gaze, crushed at the thought of having a beautiful son, only to lose him to wickedness. "We're all born in sin," calls Naomi to Sarah, as she is quickened away. "It's how we grow out of sin that counts; this is what He wants to see, how Flynn grows, and what becomes of Caleb. The battle between your sons will be a mighty one, because the difference between good and evil is enormous."

"Then, will you stay with me through it all, Naomi, if something happens to my parents?"

"I will suffer, cry, and laugh with you until the end of time."

"Suffer, Naomi?" Sarah says stopping, as do those ushering her away. She and the Jews look back at Naomi, some of them understanding Naomi's words, others not.

"The way all mothers must suffer," calls Naomi, "when their young sons go off to war. Be happy, Sarah Winthrop, for you have been chosen by Himself of the Most High."

While being encircled by the Jewish crowd, a young boy, within their group, tips his hat to Sarah. "May I have this dance?" he asks, dancing off with her.

A heavyset Jewish man approaches Naomi and waltzes off with her, Naomi in perfect step, to the man's surprise. Naomi's eyebrows arch up in response, her eyes aglow, as if to say: "What did you expect, I can do anything."

Lawrence and Marilyn join those with Sarah and Naomi, everyone now dancing to the *Blue Danube Waltz*, Sarah's heart racing, her feet dancing on air, her sights on the stars.

3

The Orange Blossom Special

Fourteen days later, on Thursday, October 29, as the pier clock strikes midnight, the *Imperator* running late and having received permission—offloads the last of its immigrating passengers at Ellis Island and continues up the Hudson to the Port of New York. The lights on Broadway are out, no one is out hustling the other, no one is smiling, no one is shining shoes, no one is buying the wares from the women of the night.

A taxi speeds from the port to Penn Station, Naomi up front with the driver, the Winthrops sitting silently in the backseat, both parents seemingly unwilling to face the recognizable doom: emergency vehicles, sirens screaming, rushing back and forth through the streets, people standing about in despair, the news boy, on the corner, waving his newspaper and yelling: "Black Thursday!"

"Kill me! I want to die," a man, in the midst of others, cries aloud. No one hears. No one cares.

At Penn Station, Lawrence, after the incident with Little Joel in Germany, and the near riots on the streets of New York, carries his doctor's bag to be prepared for any emergency. Arriving at the ticket office, he places sixty-five dollars on the counter and collects four train tickets. Gathering up the change, Sarah gives two dollars each to the black porters, who transport their luggage and then—passing an array of World War Two U.S. Army posters—she walks across the spacious station lobby to a black shoeshine man, his sign saying he'll shine shoes for a nickel. Sarah gives him the last thirty-two cents, lifting Lawrence's spirits when he sees this; for him, it's worth a smile, even in the face of the looming disaster. Naomi, Sarah, Marilyn and Lawrence follow a dozen other passengers to the *Orange Blossom Special*, where Tony, an old, white conductor, checks their tickets and helps, first Sarah, then Marilyn enter into the sleeper car, but when Naomi attempts to do the same, Tony points to the end of the train.

"Miss, the coloreds board down there," he politely tells her. "This is a Southernbound train."

"The hell you say," blasts Lawrence. "This may be a Southernbound train, but this is also America, isn't it, and not Nazi Germany? I purchased four tickets, which is this damn Pullman, and Naomi stays with us. Who's your supervisor?"

"If you think that much of the lady," Tony says. "Hell, why not, because the way things are going now, I'll probably lose this job along with everything else I've dreamed of all my life anyway."

"Go on inside, Naomi," says Lawrence, his focus now shifted to one of the passengers down the line from them, a man reading the *Times*.

"Thanks, Tony, and thank you, Doctor Winthrop," says Naomi. Lawrence doesn't answer, because his intense focus is on the passenger and on that newspaper.

As for Tony—unaware that Naomi is closely watching him—he also has his worried sights on the man and his newspaper. Then, as if remembering Naomi, Tony turns to her and belatedly responds to her "thank you" remark. "You're welcome," he tells her, taking her hand and helping her aboard. "Now, watch that first step," he cautions.

"Your problems are over," Naomi whispers to him.

"They are?" Tony replies, tongue-in-cheek. "You mean just like that, this very minute? Since our elected officials don't know how to do that, repay me for years of hard work and trust in them, as they gaze into their crystal balls and continue to tell us to have faith in 'em, and everything will be okay, that because you say so, my problems are over?" He laughs and goes on. "But then, your tea-leaf gazing can't be any worse than theirs." He looks up at her, as she lingers on the top step. "I'm sorry, Miss. I know you mean well. God knows I wish there was someone who knew the answers about this market business, but it'll take more than platitudes to save me now."

Lawrence is also wondering what will save his plantation and seems to think the answers might be in the newspaper of the man in line to board that adjacent passenger car, a man now growing more aggravated by the minute, as he nervously thumbs though the paper. Naomi glances at the troubled reader and then continues talking to Tony, while giving a nod to the disturbed reader. "Many have tried to enter the gates of heaven with their fortunes intact, and all have failed," she tells Tony. "You won't lose your job."

"Thanks," the busy conductor answers offhandedly, "but I've heard that kindhearted encouragement all day long from well-meaning passengers who don't believe it themselves."

"Next year," Naomi says, "you will retire and pay off that section of land in the Hamptons that everyone says is too risky a venture for you to continue paying for in these difficult times."

Tony leans back, stunned, "The Hamptons . . . How did you . . ."

Naomi continues, "You will live out the rest of your life on that wonderful piece of land with its relaxing waterways, as you've always prayed you would."

"That's some tea leaf you have there, lady," Tony says, recovering from his initial shock and trying to concentrate only on his train. He's sure that Naomi simply made a lucky guess about him.

"You came from a family of five girls," she goes on, "and prayed for a little brother; and—even today—in your marriage, you have no sons, just girls, but you will live to enjoy your only grandson, a grandson who will grow up on that waterfront property, which will increase in value a hundred-thousand fold, making him a wealthy man. More then that, in his manhood, this beloved grandson of yours will become the running mate of yet another man, a man who was raised up in dire poverty among the poorest of whites in Cutterville, a man who—as a boy—was forced to sell newspapers in the freezing snow to help support his family, which nearly cost him his life, but for a blanket given to him by a stranger, and this once-poor boy—after growing into manhood and running for an office with your grandson—will hang that childhood blanket on the wall of the highest office in the land, so that the world will see that even from among the poor, God picks his own."

"Jesus," Tony exclaims. "That piece of land? How in god's name did you know about . . . ?" He suddenly clams up and is more than a little irritated at her. "Who went to all this trouble to coach you about me, and made up this crap about my grandson? Running as Vice President of the highest office in the country? Surely you didn't make up all of this on your own and certainly not just because I let you onto this Pullman? It's not very funny, not to me, a man on his last leg, it isn't."

"Kindness is the rarest of flowers and should always be shown our appreciation of it by any means possible," she tells him. "And He who made your past known to me, did so because you are a special kind of flower in a world of weeds." Naomi focuses on Lawrence, who is so preoccupied with his own troubles and so focused on the man and that newspaper that a train could run over him and he'd never hear, feel, or know it. "This night," Naomi softly continues to Tony, "you will prolong a young girl's happiness for a while longer by saving the life of her father."

31

Tony follows Naomi's sights to Lawrence, and then looks questioningly at Naomi as if she's completely lost all of her marbles, and as Naomi turns and steps into the Pullman, Tony reaches out and nudges Lawrence. "Time to board, Sir," Tony tells him.

When Lawrence sees the puzzled look on the conductor's face, he glances to Naomi, just as she disappears into the sleeper car. Turning back to the old conductor Lawrence says, "I heard you two talking, but paid little attention. If you're confused, as much as you seem to be, over something that Naomi said to you, and have an idea that I might explain her or it to your satisfaction, I can't. No matter what it was she said, that I'm sure of. It seems that Naomi is full of surprises."

"Maybe she read about me in one of those company newspapers," says Tony. "It's no secret that I'm buying that land and want to retire next year, but that I had only sisters when I grew up, and then my grandson. How could she or anyone else but my family, have known about them? As for my grandson, the little fellow and my daughter just arrived from Wyoming this morning." Lawrence shrugs, as if to say that he's confused over what Tony is trying to explain, and once again, Lawrence faces the other man, who is angrily tearing up the paper and flinging it to the ground. Tony looks puzzled from the man to Lawrence. "Your tickets say Cutterville, Georgia," he remarks, regaining Lawrence's attention. "It's a fifteen-hour trip to Cutterville, but I don't guess you or your party will sleep well on your way home, no matter how long it takes." He glances at the Pullman and goes on with a sense of apprehension in his voice. "Sir, that colored woman said something strange concerning you. I could tell it was you by the way she looked at you."

As Lawrence stares at Tony, a harsh voice breaks his and Tony's attention, "Hey, you old fucker," yells the man who tore up the paper. "Are you going to collect my ticket or stand there talking all night?"

"Naomi spoke about me?" Lawrence asks, both he and Tony momentarily ignoring the angry man. "What could she say about me?" Lawrence glances at the angry man down the line and goes on. "Anyway, even more incredible than your reaction to Naomi, my wife thinks Naomi is from God."

"From God, Sir?" asks Tony, his heart racing. He backs off from Lawrence and hurries on down the line checking boarding tickets, all the time puzzling about the interaction back at the Pullman door. Lawrence, on the other hand, having had concerns about how Marilyn might react to bad news, had not purchased a newspaper at the port of New York. He takes one last look at the tattered newspaper now blowing away in the wind, and—with his doctor's bag, now nervously gripped in his hand—he climbs, bewilderedly, onto the train, as a black porter removes the step stool and rushes in behind him.

"The dining car is open," the porter says to Lawrence. "Open all night if you wants to come in later on."

With so few passengers on the O.B.S, the dispirited doctor—who is just about burned out on complications and worries about money—hopes that seeking a quick meal before turning in will be an easy task, and he leads Naomi and his family—who has been patiently waiting for him in the narrow corridor—into the carpeted dining car with its flatware, napkins, chairs and tables spotlessly arranged. There—sitting with his soiled elbows on one of the tables, his shoulders stooped, his forehead resting against the palms of his hands—is a forty-year-old army officer on leave from the service; he's dressed in a lumberjack's shirt and dark trousers. It is none other than blue-eyed Major Bernard Cutter, often called "Barney," a U.S. Army, intelligence officer. An ash tray overflowing with cigarette butts, a whiskey flask, and a crumpled *New York Times* newspaper rest on the table beside him. Also on the table, between Cutter's propped-up elbows, is a glass which contains the last of what was once in his flask. The black porter-waiter—who had removed the step stool—rushes into the diner behind Lawrence and the others. Changing into a white apron, he then hurries behind the serving counter. Major Cutter lifts his head as the Winthrops enter. When he sees Sarah, he smooths back his hair with his hand and eases to his feet. Naomi's dark-brown eyes study Sarah, then Cutter.

"Hello, Doctor Winthrop," Barney says, as Marilyn guides Sarah away, Naomi following, to the most distant table. "What brings you to New York?"

"Just passing through," says Lawrence.

After focusing on Sarah, a look which doesn't go unnoticed by Lawrence, Barney turns back to Lawrence, and has difficulty standing. Seeing the look of disgust on Sarah's face, Barney's tone begins turning sour. "Passing through, you say. I heard you went to Germany. The only country that has the fucking balls to call itself the Fatherland. Where are your balls, that you have to lie to me, Mister grand old Doctor Winthrop?"

"The ladies, Sir. Please watch your language."

Drawing in his shoulders—crouching down and chuckling—Barney points to a poster of Uncle Sam, with his white beard and his red, white, and blue top hat, hanging on the diner's wall. Mimicking the poster, Barney places his index finger against his lips and says, "Shhh."

"I better join the others," says Lawrence, stepping away.

"Why the hurry? Sit down and have a drink with me."

Cutter almost knocks over the glass when he reaches for it. Lawrence, again, moves away.

"I'm not good enough to be in your company. Is that it?" says Cutter, as the train jerks forward, causing him to stumble and Lawrence to catch him. The drunken man sweeps Lawrence's hands away. "Keep your fucking hands off of me! You're not as pure as folks back home think you Winthrops are. I haven't forgotten what you did to us Cutters!"

"What I did was to buy a parcel of your father's land at the fair-market price."

"Fair my fucking ass!" Cutter yells and then glances at a frightened Sarah and whispers. "If you hadn't bought that land, I wouldn't be in here drinking and worrying about my mother's future."

"Take Sarah to our compartment," Lawrence tells his wife. "You too, Naomi. You don't need to hear this man disgrace himself. I'll bring some sandwiches and drinks into you later."

Marilyn hurries Sarah from the diner, followed by Naomi. Cutter picks up the glass of booze and offers it to Lawrence. "Come on. Just one little drink, and let's be friends." Lawrence turns away. "That's right," yells Cutter. "Run away like you told them to do! But I'll get my hands on that succulent-looking daughter of yours one of these days. You won't be around forever to protec . . ."

Lawrence seizes the glass out of Cutter's hand and splashes the drunken man in the face with its contents, temporally blinding the military officer. Blinking in pain, Cutter wipes his face on his sleeve, whips out a Bowie knife and locks his murderous gaze on Lawrence.

The waiter instinctively reaches over the counter to separate them. "You is drunk, Sir!"

With one swing of the knife, Cutter opens a gash in the black man's arm and sends him fleeing from the dining car. The drunken man glares at Lawrence. "I'm going to cut those doctor's hands of yours right out of your sockets," he tells Lawrence. Cutter charges and stumbles, knocking over a service cart. Lawrence drops his medical bag, grabs a chair, and smashes it across Barney's back. The stocky intelligence officer hardly feels a thing; kicking the shattered chair aside, he draws back with his knife to stab Lawrence. The wounded waiter and Tony—armed with a billy club—race into the diner. Tony cracks Barney on the head with the club and then helps Lawrence wrestle the combat-trained man to the floor. It takes all three of them to hold Barney down and disarm him.

"You're drunk, Sir!" Tony yells at the thrashing major. "I smell moonshine all over you." He confronts the black porter. "Why'd you let this man break the law on my train, James?"

"He be white, boss man," says the panic-stricken bleeding waiter, terrified of remaining on Barney and afraid to get off of him.

"It's not the waiter's fault," says Lawrence, looking down at Cutter. "It's his fault, this so-called intelligence officer who's down here on his belly squealing like a pig."

"You guys made your point," Cutter yells. "Get the hell off of me. I can't breathe!"

They release him, gasping for breath, and everyone gets to their feet. Lawrence seizes Cutter's knife from the floor and hands it to Tony, who goes to one of the boarding doors, opens its window and flings the large knife into the night. After Tony returns, Lawrence retrieves his bag and attends to James's wound. Tony glares at Cutter. "Please return to your seat, Sir, or you'll be put off this train at the next stop."

Cutter glares at Lawrence and laughs, while pointing at the crumpled newspaper: "The world's falling the hell apart," he says. "You're in the same boat as the rest of us struggling folks in Cutterville!" Picking up his whiskey flask, Barney nudges old Tony aside and stumbles from the dining car, leaving Lawrence looking over at the crumpled paper when he's not busy stitching James's arm.

"Will James be okay?" Tony asks.

"He'll be fine," says Lawrence, completing the stitching, then wrapping the wound in gauze. "Luckily the laceration is superficial, but by stitching it, it has a better change to heal. Those catgut stitches will dissolve on their own. Just change the bandage once a day." He gives James a shot in his arm. "This will also prevent any infection. Thanks for saving my life, you two."

"My God," says Tony. "She said I would do just that." He looks at Lawrence. "She said . . ."

"What is it?" asks Lawrence. "Who said what? Naomi? Speak up. Are you hurt also?"

"No," says Tony. "Just afraid. Terribly afraid. I've been told my future, and now I believe her. Your servant woman. But this can't be. If it is, then time is running out for us if we're as evil as that man who attacked you. I fear for us all, Sir, for us and my grandson's future, as well." Walking away, Tony says, "I've never been a church-going man. I need to think, maybe even pray."

As Cutter passes down the Pullman's closed-in corridor, he stops at an open compartment door, where Sarah, Naomi and Marilyn are sitting in quiet conversation, while waiting for Lawrence.

"Why does the army let him remain in the service?" asks Sarah, "when he's a known Klansman?"

"It was part of the abolition of slavery," says Marilyn, kissing Sarah on the forehead. "When General Sherman marched through the South in 1864 or so, he not only razed Atlanta and towns in between, with ruthlessness, he also attacked civilians, took their animals, and destroyed their homes and their proud spirits. The South has promised never to forget their defeat and to never forgive the North. It is slowly gaining a chokehold on Washington, and once they have it, they'll never let it go, so the government now looks the other way when it comes to soldiers belonging to those murderous groups of dogs, who are an affliction to all decent people."

"Washington keeps men segregated even in the army," says Naomi, "then asks them to die for their country, this to pacify the Southerners."

"That's not just local politics," Marilyn says, "but the reality all over this world, Naomi."

"The government certainly looks the other way when it comes to lynching people," Sarah adds. "Just like our good-for-nothing Sheriff Richards does. He's a rope which the city bosses pull to make him move, then they pull on the other end to make him stop moving. If I were a man, I'd go to Washington and hurt those lawmakers real bad. Slap them right off of those expensive leather chairs of theirs until they cried."

"Sarah Winthrop," admonishes Marilyn.

"I would, Mother!" Sarah suddenly gasps and points to the open door. Major Cutter is weaving and stumbling about in the corridor and smiling in at her. Naomi goes to the door.

36

"This is not your time, yet, Satan," she tells Cutter, closing the door in his face.

Lawrence never did get those sandwiches to them. As the *Orange Blossom Special* screams through the night, he and Marilyn lie in their compartment bunks, Marilyn on the top asleep, Lawrence on the bottom, wide awake and troubled. Resting on a chair next to his bunk is Cutter's crumpled *Times*. The headline screams out "ALL IS LOST." In the next compartment, Sarah lies in the lower bunk, tossing and turning in her sleep, groaning, as if being chased by the devil; Naomi sits in a chair beside the teenager, her intense brown eyes trained on the locked compartment door. The mixed-blood woman stands and goes to her knees beside Sarah's bed.

"This here innocent child," she whispers. "Is there no other way? This sweet, innocent child."

In one of the nearly empty coach cars, four Pullman cars down the line from the Winthrops, is Horace Tucker, white, fifty, balding, short and stocky, wearing coveralls and cowboy boots; with him is his son, Dane, seventeen. Dane has curly, dark hair, is tall, thickly-built, and also wearing farmers' clothing. He is cursed with unsightly buck teeth, big eyes, a skin rash, and is missing his left ear; someone had bitten it off during a drunken fight in Sue Ann's bar in Cutterville, after his father got into a scuffle, and Dane—who was also in the bar drinking—tried to help his old man. Horace loves Dane all the more for suffering such a blow while trying to help him. Across the aisle from Horace and Dane, Cutter is doing his best to make himself comfortable in his seat, while staring out the window, the train rocking back and forth. Both Dane and Horace watch Cutter warily. Dane nudges his father, and Horace, trembling and unaware that Tony has tossed Barney's Bowie knife off the train, clears his throat and forces himself to speak.

"That money was a loan, Major Cutter," Horace begins and then clams up, afraid, as Barney faces him.

"Fuck you," says Barney, then turns his sights back to the pitch of night outside the window. "You just had to see that damn money. And that's why I didn't want you two to come to New York with me. Seeing that money is making you crazy. It's all here," he says, patting his pocket, going on. "Thanks to one of our members on the Exchange, who alerted me in time to get it all back."

"You said I'd triple it in no time," Horace exclaims, "if I let you invest it fer me fer a reasonable cut of the profit, but things are so bad at home. I need the money back." Getting another nudge from Dane, Horace timidly goes on, "I demand it back, Barney. Now. Tonight. It's my life's savings, not yours."

"Well, cut off my legs and call me shorty," snaps Cutter, glancing over his shoulder at the handful of sleeping passengers and then turns back to Horace "Who suddenly gave you all those balls now, Pops?" He scowls over at Dane. "Who? Good old one-ear Dane over there? With the Winthrops schooling them coons of theirs on Shadow Grove, that's what you should worry about, instead of this goddamn two grand. Look at the two of you! Neither of you got a brain in your damn heads. No wonder that damn Dessen Jew is hiring them tar balls at his tire factory instead of more of you dumb crackers. You want them schooled nigger kids to grow up smarter than white kids and have their factory-working, coon-head dads making more money then you, enough to influence the goddamn politics in my damn town, and it's still my town, no matter what that Jew says!"

"You ain't exactly no Doctor Winthrop, yourself," exclaims Dane, rubbing his earless scar. "Don't got Doctor Winthrop's brains, so how do you think us uneducated whites can do anything to stop what he does? And you got no right to talk about me and my pa like that. No right at all. Instead of school, most of us whites have to shine shoes, like the damn niggers do. Sell scrap metal, work in the fields, or in the factory to help put food on the table. That is, if we're lucky enough to get them factory jobs now. You're the so-called brains. Instead of you leaving town on one of those damn army trips of yours—when we're not even in a war yet—and you staying away fer months and even a year, the way you did last December, and now sitting over there after getting drunk and not getting together a plan. You need to stand up your damn self and be counted." Dane throws up his hands. "Oh, the hell with you. You're nothing but a drunk."

Cutter leans forward on his seat and stares at Dane. "Yes, I'm drunk and a weak, self-pitying fool because of it; this is why you're talking so goddamn bravely, right?" Barney slams his fist through the train window, shattering it, awakening the sleeping passengers and causing Dane and his father to almost jump out of their seats. The Grand Wizard then glares at Dane. "The day will come," says Barney, coldly, "take my word for it. Those words of yours will come back to haunt you in the worst way,

Dane Tucker. Even drunk I can out think a poor-ass-piece-of-trash like you a thousand times over. As for that plan that you're mouthing off about," Cutter says, again patting his pocket, "it's for me to use this money as a down payment. A dowry of sorts to someone I'm going to marry and control, including everything that she owns in time, and along with that, I'll own the souls of every man woman and child on earth, all growing out of one of the largest plantations around."

"God help us," whispers Horace. "You've put us both in danger, Son. He's insane."

"God has nothing to do with it," says Barney. "Satan has, though. He's told me so. Now, go the hell to sleep. That's what you do. Both of you! And don't ever ask me anything when I'm drunk. Not about the money! Not about the niggers!" Holding up his flask, he hisses, "I made a big enough fool of myself tonight in front of Sarah."

Smashing the flask underfoot, Barney makes his way to the dining car, and apologizes to Tony and then to James. After giving Tony twenty dollars to cover the cost of the window, Barney Cutter orders coffee, hands the wounded, black waiter a new, five-dollar bill—from Horace's two grand—and tells James to keep the change. Long after everyone is asleep in the Pullman and coach cars, Barney remains sitting next to the dining-car window, the train, he feels, is his mother, cradling him in her arms, and he whispers, "Mother, she'll soon be mine, and you can do nothing about it."

4

The Triangle

The following morning, Lawrence, Marilyn, Sarah and Naomi enjoy a breakfast of eggs, bacon, grits, milk and pancakes—topped off with butter and Karo Syrup—served by smartly dressed, slender, black male waiters, who now eye Naomi warily, wondering how she can eat with the white family. While Sarah and Naomi laugh and joke between bites of food, at the far end of the diner, sitting at a table with his back to them, is Major Cutter. He's having scrambled eggs, bacon, coffee and donuts, while Horace and Dane, who are sitting at the table with him, are forced to order only water because they have only ten cents between them, and Barney doggedly refuses to give them even a penny of their money. Taking out his anger on the waiters, Dane taunts one of them by dangling the dime at him.

"Look, but don't you even think we're going to be tipping you with this money, boy," he tells the waiter. "Not fer two glasses of water, Pa and I ain't. I bet you tar balls get all the free food you can eat." Dane turns his angry gaze on the Winthrops, and he whispers to his father, "Look at that nigger woman feeding her face with the Winthrops. What's wrong with that white family? Don't they know that's wrong to sit with them spades?"

Neither Horace nor Dane dare mention the Winthrops' name to Cutter. They know that even though he has not looked their way, or said anything about the Winthrops, he knows they're there. After finishing breakfast, Lawrence and his party leave by the door opposite Cutter and his motley followers. Last to leave the diner, Naomi tips the waiter who Dane had denigrated. She then looks back at Cutter.

"That nigger woman's looking at you, Major," says Dane.

Major Cutter slowly turns around. "What you looking at, Aunt Jemima?" he asks Naomi.

"At nothin'," says Naomi, "I'm lookin' at nothin' at all!"

When Naomi leaves, the waiters gawk after her, then at each other, wondering how long it will be before she gets herself hanged.

Morning fades, and at 4:10 P.M., the *Orange Blossom Special* makes

40

a stop at Cutterville's one-room train station, in a town where dusty whirlwinds twist down streets and alleys, and dogs run wild. Lawrence and the tired females alight from the train, Lawrence looking about as if expecting someone. A few yards away, Cutter climbs into the passenger side of a battered, green, Dodge pickup. His middle-aged, stocky friend, half-blind Hank Morrison, has been slumped over and sleeping behind the wheel in the hot weather; he sits up with a smile when Barney opens the door and settles onto the tattered seat. Hank looks through the rearview mirror and watches Horace and Dane pile into the back of the truck with other Klansmen, all carrying rebel flags. Several minutes after the pickup speeds away, a two-team, mule-drawn, two-bench wagon—driven by a sixty-year-old, white-haired, black man—rounds the corner near Cutterville's Pennington National Bank, a small building, a half block away, a bank which Naomi stares at for several seconds with a look of concern on her face. She then faces forward, as the old mule driver arrives at their sides. He is five feet, six inches tall and weighs only a hundred and forty pounds, but makes up for it by outworking half of the field hands on the Winthrops' plantation. Steadying the mules and wagon, the silver-haired man waits while the family and Naomi converse with one another. Finally, easing to the ground, he loads the luggage onto the wagon, including Lawrence's medical bag, then climbs back aboard. Lawrence glances over at him. "We're coming now, Amos," he says, always one to respect the time and kindness of others.

"Andy and I done kept a good eye on the White Dove," says Amos, "like you done asked us to do, Doctor Winthrop. Not one of them curious drunks from Cutterville even got near her out there. Me and Andy and our handy shotguns, we slept in that tent and tucked the silver lady under her tarp like she be a baby."

"I didn't want you to have guns," Lawrence says. "The sheriff was to handle those rebels."

"Just makin' sure the lady be safe," says Amos. "She be cleaned up and ready, I 'spect, with Andy just about now a-pullin' that tarp off of her, now that we got word you was arrivin'." He scratches his head. "But you done come back home so early! What me and Andy gonna do with all them supplies of canned pork-and-beans and canned milk you done gave us befo' you left?"

"Give them to your families," Lawrence says. "It's okay."

As the ladies approach the wagon, Amos tips his hat to them. "Mrs. Winthrop, Miss Sarah."

"Hello, Amos," replies Marilyn, as she, Sarah and Naomi climb aboard the wagon with Lawrence's help. "How is your brother?" Marilyn asks.

"Andy, he be mighty fine, now, you done gave him that cough syrup medicine," the old man says, with a questioning glance at Naomi. "It done cut that cold right out of his lungs like you done said it would."

"Good," says Marilyn, as Lawrence climbs aboard and sits beside Amos. Marilyn takes Naomi's hand. "Amos, this is . . ."

"Naomi Bell, Amos," Sarah breaks in. "She's going to live at our house with us."

"Glad to have you aboard, Naomi," Amos tells her, slapping the reins against the mules, heading them and the wagon into the late-noon sun, while trying his best to steal another glance at the stranger, who is moving into the big house with the Winthrops.

After a twenty-minute ride, just outside of Cutterville, Amos and his mules turn into a dusty field and toward a two-man tent next to an airplane. Even through the dust, it is clear why the Winthrops' workers have named the plane the *White Dove*. The F10, Super, Fokker Tri-motor holds twelve passengers, has three Pratt and Whitney, four-hundred twenty-five horsepower, wasp, radial engines, and can travel three hundred and sixty-five miles in three hours. Its gleaming, spread wings appear to be those of a mighty, white dove. As a worried-looking Lawrence and Marilyn climb from the wagon and gather up their luggage, without waiting for Amos, and head for the plane, Sarah jumps to the ground, grabs up her luggage and follows them.

"Wait, Miss Sarah," Amos calls to her. "Let me carry them things."

"You remain seated there and rest, Amos Fitch," Sarah orders. "I'm not helpless."

Sarah looks back at Naomi, who is standing up on the wagon and admiring the White Dove. Amos watches the black woman's every move, as if asking himself: *Who this black, wicket-looking woman be?*

Naomi winks down at him with a telltale smile that says she knows how he feels and that she's an outsider, and then she turns and calls to Sarah. "Is that your father's plane?"

"Yes," says Sarah, motioning to Naomi. "Come on."

As Naomi and Sarah carry their luggage to the plane, Andy, looking a lot like his older brother, Amos, but stronger, darker, taller, thicker and faster, runs from the nearby tent and insists on carrying the women's bags. He trots away with the suitcases and deposits them on the aircraft. While walking to the plane, Sarah explains more about the *White Dove* to Naomi. "We're not the Lindberghs, and the *White Dove* isn't the *Spirit of Saint Louis*, but the town looks at us as gods, I'm ashamed to say. We own the only plane in the county. We really can't afford it, but it was a gift to Father for saving Mr. Fokker's life: The Fokkers built the *Dove* and others like her."

"It's such a good-looking plane, but so large, child."

"The *White Dove* isn't just for the family. We take our workers for a ride in it, whenever we can spare money to gas it up, once a month or so. Father has a good practice in Atlanta, where he works four days a week, then comes home and helps out on the plantation, but his practice alone can't support the entire Grove. There's too much land for him to even think of doing that."

"The Grove?"

"Shadow Grove," Sarah says, "the name of our plantation. Our workers have so little. Father wants to build them new houses on our land, if he makes enough money on our stocks."

"The market has failed, Sarah."

"So, it finally happened," Sarah says, looking toward the plane, at her parents, and then at Naomi. "It's been on their minds for some time now."

As Lawrence fires up the engines, a troubled-looking Marilyn glances back from the plane.

"Coming," replies Sarah, waving to her mother. She faces Naomi. "I've never kept anything from Mother, Naomi. I want to talk to her about you and what you told me. I still wish to believe you, but I'm so confused. You talked to Martin de Porres, and apparently, the more I think about it, you talked to him about me." The confused teenager struggles on: "Even if I somehow wish to believe you—and I do at times and then I don't—I've never seen a miracle; I'm not Maria Bernadette; this is not Lourdes or Fatima; this is Cutterville, Georgia, a place of evil." She casts an agonized look at her mother and continues on. "It will kill my mother and destroy Father's will to live, if they even thought we talked about me marrying that man." Sarah gazes at the sky. "Why wouldn't God, Himself, tell me and not you, if He wanted me to do this terrible thing? If not me, let Him tell Mother. Then she would understand. Why doesn't He understand? Does He understand, Naomi?"

"Your father and mother . . . their minds are too heavy with worry, now," says Naomi, placing her arm about Sarah, as they near the *White Dove*. "Before this night ends, however, Lawrence and Marilyn will know everything, and they will rejoice in His glorious understanding. Trust me."

At the plane, Marilyn climbs into the copilot's seat beside her man. Sarah and Naomi board the aircraft and settle into a seat next to a window. Now more afraid than ever, Sarah eases close to Naomi. During the *White Dove's* climb into the blue, Amos and Andy—dots against the blowing dust below—wave up to them. The *Dove* circles over Cutterville, as it leaves the brothers behind.

Cutterville covers eight miles of country land and is easily viewed from the air: it has a main street, which is lined with tiny-looking stores, including the bank, and a newspaper office—in the back of which, in a field, is a simple, wooden building, the town's white, segregated school.

Standing out from the other buildings is a red, brick courthouse, which the town's blacks fear. Main Street runs to Town Square, across from which is another building, this one eight-stories high, with a dozen chimneys spewing out black smoke. It is an intimidating-looking building which sprawls out for seven long blocks like an octopus seizing hold of the small town, a building sorely hated, but desperately needed, with the Jewish owner's fluorescent name screaming out from the rooftop: DESSEN'S TIRE COMPANY, a sign which overlooks Sue Ann's bar across the street from it. At the bar, even on Sunday, Major Cutter, as well as Reverend Miller's jobless congregation fill their flasks with moonshine and glare out the bar window at Dessen's hated factory, which—as Barney had angrily reminded Dane and his father on the train—has recently hired blacks instead of more of the whites. To Cutter, filling his flask, at the bar, is not only testing the legality of prohibition, but a time to forget his troubles; to Reverend Miller and his struggling church members, drinking in the bar is just another part of the church's drug-induced ritual of snake worship.

"The factory is a blessing, now that difficult times are surely ahead for the town," says Lawrence, as he flies over the plant, triggering Marilyn's negative reply.

"If Reverend Miller's foolish members don't burn it down."

Reverend Miller's small, white-painted church, with its steeple and hundred-year-old steeple clock, squats just off the squares. Not everyone in town attends that church, however, or lives in squalor, as do those who reside in the shacks scattered around it. Fifty or so elegant homes can be seen looming below on the north side of town, and those residents travel outside of Cutterville to worship in the big cities. However, most of Cutterville's poor live on the south side in hovels, where poor, white women—almost all of them are members of Miller's church—are scurrying in and out of their houses, like so many ants, and into their small backyards with baskets filled with the day's wash, women thinking about the miracles of the snakes, which Miller says will rescue them from poverty and despair, women placing the baskets on the ground and too busy hanging out their "cleanliness-is-godliness" laundry to concern themselves about the *White Dove*, as it flies over them. Their children, on the other hand, whose minds are not yet self-righteously indulged, stop playing in front of the houses, on the concrete sidewalks, and on the paved streets, to wave at the gleaming airplane, and then—with their small arms stretched out at their sides—they run bent over, mimicking the flight of the *Dove*; this is the white side of town, separated from the black ghetto by the train tracks. The train station is on the white side of the community—just barely—by the width of those tracks.

The black community is trash infested, the houses sun blistered and lopsided. In this fifteen-square block hellhole, dark-skinned youngsters play on streets and sidewalks that are twisting pathways of red clay and beaten-down dirt, a good deal of which is blowing away in the wind. This rundown settlement is where emaciated, stray dogs—constantly chased from the white side of town or thrown into the black community—roam the alleys in swarms eating their own droppings in a desperate battle to survive. Not just flies and living things cast an ugly shadow over "Colored Town," as it's called, broken windows, discarded automobile tires, garbage and falling-apart cars and trucks dot the community, especially those strung out around a run-down automobile-repair shop, a constant hangout for out-of-work, booze-drinking blacks, men and women. The ghetto has only two colored-owned businesses besides the car-repair shop: a disheveled church; to some in the community, churches are just that, a business which collects money to fatten the preacher's pocket at the expense of the poor. The community's second

45

black-owned business does not take money from the poor; it's a well-kept, white, two-story house, which draws white males from across the train tracks and out of the white community like bees to honey. This house and well-run business is owned by Ma'am Lana, the color of ebony, thin, mean and sassy. Alone with a judge or two, including white Reverend Miller, Lana has all the customers she and her girls can handle. Barney is extremely careful about keeping his visits to Lana's place from his aging mother.

On the outskirts of Cutterville's south side, a three-story, Victorian house looms, paint-blistered, with its large yard surrounded by a wire fence, a fence posted with a boldly displayed sign. No children play near that house: everyone knows never to trespass on Mrs. Cutter's land, a woman who will do what she threatens to do to children: the same as what she does to shit-dropping pigeons: shoot them in their asses to hell and back and then bake them into pigeon pies, black youngsters and the white ones alike. She doesn't care. She hates them all. Sitting on the front porch with her shotgun, she oscillates in her rocking chair, while smoking a corn pipe. The bent-back, sixty-year-old, badly aging woman swears she'll live to a hundred and two and will die when she gets damn good and ready. Until then, she plans to witness her son kill a dozen more spades, just for the hell of it. When the old woman spots the *White Dove* approaching her land, she stands up and shakes her bony fist at it, then plops back down into her rocking chair, cursing like a drunken sailor.

In the *White Dove*, still agonizing over the possibility of being married to Barney, Sarah looks away from the house below them and makes no mention of it or the woman. Naomi, nevertheless, has noticed the house and continues viewing the old residence with the same look of concern reflected on her face as when she stared at the bank in town. She sees the Dodge that met Major Cutter at the train station roll to a stop by the old house and watches as Cutter steps from the vehicle. Entering the yard, he lingers on the porch beside his mother, both scowling up at the plane. The *White Dove* leaves the Cutters behind, but Barney keeps his sights on the airplane until it disappears into the clouds.

A little over nine miles outside of town, the Cutterville Bridge—named after Barney's founding ancestors—comes into view, an evil-appearing, hundred-year-old, wooden structure with menacing-looking, massive dark-stained arches spanning two rocky cliffs. The bridge's arches are stained dark due to old blood and smoke from the burning bodies that hung from them over the years. It has a set of train tracks running across its top, and also a set of train tracks which curve below it in a graceful, quarter circle heading toward Cutterville. The train tracks atop the weathered structure slope down a six-degree grade to the lower ground where they merge into one with the lower, parallel rails, where they also head toward Cutterville, and then to points beyond the town.

"What bridge is that, Sarah?" asks Naomi, gazing down at it. "It's rather unsettling."

Trembling, and as she had not looked at the Cutter house, Sarah refuses to look at the bridge, a structure she knows will recall chilling images of Major Cutter's mayhem, ruthlessness and murder. Naomi touches Sarah's clenched fists, and as her hand remains there, she seems to get a startling vision and refocuses on the bridge. The structure, she now knows is called the hanging bridge, and she knows far more than that. It's a bridge which expands, contracts and suffers under the blistering sun and in which the living spirit of Satan dwells. Shivering, Naomi faces away from that structure of evil.

When Sarah's thoughts enter the world of travel again, the plane has flown another half mile and is a full ten miles from Cutterville. The young girl quickly looks out the window. "We're over Henry's land, Naomi, the boy who gave me the perfume. Isn't it the most beautiful land you've ever seen? He works so hard to keep it that way."

She and Naomi excitedly study the coastal land, fifteen-hundred feet below them where—under sapphire skies—the chilly, foaming, dark-hued Atlantic splashes its mighty waves against high, seagull-stool-enriched, lime-white cliffs, which overlook the restless ocean and extend along two-thousand acres of golden fields of corn, cotton, wheat, and green, rolling hills. A magnificent deep, blue lagoon—surrounded in part by towering trees and a granite quarry—lies a few thousand feet from a red barn. Close to the barn is a freshly painted white house. The modest house has a small porch, with white railings, and it has an attractive, white picket fence—which circles it—and a large yard, with windblown emerald, green grass—which embellishes it. At the side of the house, Naomi notices two small graves, laid out with flowers.

"Henry's parents must be very proud of him," she says, focusing on the graves, "the way you say he works hard down there."

"His parents are dead," Sarah whispers, then quickly changes the subject. "It's the lagoon," she goes on, as Naomi ponders the tombstones, then turns to Sarah, who continues. "If you're wondering why his land is so green and Cutterville and everything else is so dry . . . Henry's land . . . It's green because of the lagoon. If it wasn't for father, the Klan would have taken it from his parents long ago."

"What happened to his folks, Sarah? Are they in those graves?"

"The sheriff says it was an accident, but it was murder," she whispers tearfully "The Klan. But let's not talk about it. It frightens me to do so."

A short time later, after having flown in two legs of what Sarah calls "the triangle," and now its third and last leg, Sarah glances out the window. "We're home," she exclaims.

Shadow Grove, Cutterville and Henry's land form a perfect triangle to each other: It's ten miles between their individual lands, and it's been a Winthrop tradition, of late, to fly over Henry's land on the way home, doing so enriches their lives with the hope that one day their plantation will also be as well nourished as Henry's place. Unlike Henry's land, the Winthrops' holdings loom ahead under a dusty, murky, hot sunset, a dry plantation spreading out from horizon to horizon, sixteen-thousand acres, a small town unto itself. Centrally located around endless fields of withering corn, cotton, cabbage and potatoes is a general store, an assortment of sheds and a massive, red barn—nearly three times the size of the next largest barn in the county. Also seen from the air are wagons, trucks, horses, chickens, and a hundred and fifty or so small workers' shacks. Field hands, whites and blacks, working side by side across the land, wave up at the plane, as it flies low, dipping its wings to them.

"All of this and those people down there," Naomi asks. "It belongs to your parents, Sarah?"

"For six generations," Sarah says and then teases. "I thought you knew everything about me, since you said it was I whom you came to Germany to find." Sarah goes on. "And that bridge. You have no idea what it's used for. If you had, you would have said it was the work of Satan."

"Are you saying that I should have at least have told you that it was evil?"

"Something like that," says Sarah. "If you are what you may, indeed, be."

48

Naomi smiles at her and says, "There are many things kept from all of us, no matter how blessed we may think we are, so that we might remain humble and hungry for the truth, even as you now are." The mystery woman focuses on cockpit and on the backs of Lawrence and Marilyn, who both have their headgear firmly in place over their ears against the roar of the *White Dove's* powerful tri motors. "Sarah," Naomi goes on, "I wouldn't have been able to come for you but for your extraordinary parents who made you what you are." Naomi continues, her eyes never leaving Sarah's parents, "Also, Sarah, it's not always possible for a person to tell another about what they see in a bridge, for instance, or to warn someone that they're in harm's way, even if she admires them and knows harm is approaching, if it's God's will that she remains silent."

Naomi faces Sarah. The teenage girl has not fully understood a word Naomi has said. She's excitedly taking stock of a three-story manor, a mile ahead of them, a manor perched on a cloudy hill like a gray monolith in the middle of their otherwise lower, sunbaked, vast property. The manor is embellished by sprawling, four-hundred-year-old oak trees. The trees' roots reach deep into the dry soil to suck up life-giving water from underground streams, giving the tenacious, hardwood giants their awesome longevity, as they line both sides of a winding driveway and circle the house with their invigorating shade of windblown, fog-embraced, green leaves. Looming behind the manor is a large greenhouse, which shows through the thinning fog, its glass roof and walls sparkling under the dusty red, setting sunlight, Suddenly, laughing and distracting Naomi's sights from the grandeur of the hilltop property, Sarah waves down at dozens of field hands, who are running after the plane while looking up and waving their arms and hands at her. Eyes wide, a brilliant smile on her face, Sarah watches a certain young runner in blue coveralls, who has taken the lead from the others, his uncovered arms and neck gleaming with sweat, his long legs quickly putting distance between him and those left in his dust.

"That's Henry," says Sarah, "the boy who gave me the perfume."

"The one who owns that land we flew over?" asks Naomi, viewing Henry from the window.

"Yes. Isn't he beautiful?"

"Why is he working for your family? From what I saw, he can make a good livin' off his own land." Glancing at Shadow Grove's withering crops, she goes on. "And why haven't he shared that water of his with your family?"

"After his parents died, he inherited their debts, as well as their land. He only works part-time for us to help pay off the money borrowed against the mortgage to improve his land and to pay off some of his parents' bills." Sarah's face lights up. "Mother treats Henry like the son she and father never had, and Henry loves her and Father and . . ." She beams down at Henry with a warm glow on her face. When Naomi smiles at her, she goes on. "Anyway, Mother makes sure Henry doesn't spend so much time with us that his land suffers, thank God and Martin de Porres, to whom—as I told you—I sometimes pray. It's then that I ask Blessed Martin to watch over Henry. Some like Saint Christopher. I prefer Martin and the Blessed Mother of Jesus, when I feel that God is too busy to hear from me so often."

Naomi, with those penetrating brown eyes, studies Sarah, then gazes down at Henry.

"How old is Henry?"

"Eighteen. Why?"

"This boy, Sarah . . . Do your parents know how you feel about him?"

"We all do," says Sarah. "Feel strongly about Henry. Whenever there's time, our workers help him till his fields. And he does want to share his water with us, but the cost to pump it here is so high. Just like it's so costly to try and drill deep enough to get the water that our oak and citrus trees live off of. Father says there's just enough water in the ground to keep the trees alive. We're always looking for a cheaper way to get the lagoon water to our land; as you can see, we badly need it. Meanwhile, we endure."

The Tri-motor flies over a large gate with a massive, oak trestle that has the name "Shadow Grove" burned into its hard wood, a gate bordered by still more oak trees. Beyond the gate, and within calling distance from one place to the other, lies the heart of the plantation, the manor house, the general store, the barn and still more workers' shacks. Shadow Grove's namesake looms within that calling distance beyond the gate, Manor Hill, on which sits the manor. When the sun is positioned just right in the sky, it casts the hill's distinguished shadow out across a range of citrus trees, which grow at the base of the mound and beyond. Touching the plane down in a grassy field, near the citrus growth, Lawrence skillfully brings the *White Dove* to a stop, as the workers, led by Henry, swarm toward the aircraft. Lawrence is troubled and Henry quickly takes note of it. He puts out his muscular arms, stopping the racially mixed workers, once they catch up to him.

"Y'all let 'em go on home, now, and freshen up a bit before we start fillin' their heads with a lot of questions," he tells them.

The last of the Brooks, at eighteen, Henry is not just tall and strong, he's quite handsome, his un-oiled hair, woolly, clean, and natural, his teeth even and white, his skin smooth and dark; and he has alluring brown eyes. Jumping from the plane with a book in her hand, Sarah sprints to him.

"Did you do it?" she teases, poking the black youth in his side with her finger, her mind, for the first time in days, freed from thoughts of Barney Cutter.

"Did what?" Henry asks, drawing back, chuckling, running in a circle, covering his ribs with his crossed arms, the workers laughing at how ticklish he is, and how Sarah relentlessly pursues him.

"Did you study while I was away? You know what I mean," she tells him.

"Yesum," Henry says stopping and gazing down at her, holding her reaching hands away from his ribs. His sights, then, shift to Lawrence with concern. "Are they okay, Sarah? Your folks? I mean with your stock failures and all."

Struggling against Henry's superior strength, and laughing with the workers, Sarah has no intention of letting bad news spoil her moment of joy, especially if there is nothing anyone can do about it; she simply doesn't answer Henry. On the other hand, Sarah has paid close attention to his English and lets him know it.

"Not 'yesum,' Henry Brooks," she scolds, after he releases her. The word is 'yes.' " She hands the book to him. "I bought this for you before we left, but when you missed seeing us off, I carried it around the entire world just for you, and now, here it is, an easy-to-learn, English book."

It seems that Sarah has been on the workers' cases, as well—the blacks and the whites, all nodding to her when she looks at them, a blend of "Yess" streaming from all of them.

"Well, you better," laughs Sarah. "Study your English. It is so good to be home!"

Laughing, she runs back to her family and climbs into an old Model

T and is driven toward the manor house, Lawrence driving with Marilyn at his side, Naomi and Sarah sitting in the rear seat. Sparkling with joy, Sarah looks back at Henry, as he and the workers go their separate way, their work day at an end. Naomi smiles, while targeting in on Henry, then on Sarah's joyful demeanor. Hanging on the horizon, the sunlight casts its last glowing warmth onto Manor Hill, burning away the mist which diminished its beauty. Weaving its solar light through the driveway's parallel oak trees, with their billions of leaves and countless, massive branches, the sunlight cascades against, bounces off of, around, and through the leaves with its ever-changing, quivering specks of light, competing with and intensifying the black-leaf shade. As the Model T putters under the oak canopy of leaves, Sarah extends her hand out the window and watches how leaf-reflected light and shadows flow up, across and down her arm and graceful fingers, as the car races below the trees, her blue eyes sparkling with delight. She is, after all, safely at home.

Lawrence stops the vehicle in front the manor's grand, wraparound porch, which has twelve Greek ionic columns, a porch furnished with an array of white, wicker rockers, and matching tables along with two wicker swings, all seemingly the color of pink, under the red, setting sun. The large, old house is in need of paint, but still manages to reflect its past grandeur. Sliding from the car and climbing the steps to the porch, Lawrence opens the heavy, oak front door and then follows the ladies into a mahogany foyer, where a small, polished, pie-crust-top, claw-foot table—decorated with freshly cut calla lilies—sits below an elegant, centrally located, crystal chandelier.

"Mother," says Sarah, pointing to the flowers. "They've gathered one of your favorites."

In spite of her troubles, Marilyn takes a moment to smell the soft fragrance of the white flowers and invites Sarah and Naomi to do the same. Naomi does more than that. She touches the table, as if there is something very special about it, as Sarah watches her, puzzled. Nearby, a spiraling staircase, lined with gold-leaf, framed portraits of past Winthrops, leads to the upper floors. To the right of the foyer, through two, large—partly opened—sliding, pocket doors, is a spacious living room. A grand piano; mohair, channel-back couches, empire, wingback chairs, Duncan Phyfe drop-leaf tables, Handel lamps, oriental carpets, and a marble fireplace add character and grace to the elegantly appointed room. Marilyn turns to Naomi. "Please forgive us, Naomi. Lawrence and I have to attend to urgent business. Sarah," she says, "will you show Naomi around the house?"

After Marilyn follows Lawrence through the living room and into his den, she finds her husband staring at an old, wall-hanging, Civil-War sword. "I kept it on the wall as a reminder," he says when he hears Marilyn enter.

"Of the evil that's always lurking in the shadows," Marilyn adds, taking his hand into hers. "It was your father's sword and it saved the lives of many of Georgia's slaves. He changed his ways in time, Lawrence. He changed in time. May God receive his soul."

Out in the foyer, Sarah looks at the table, and then at Naomi.

"Why did you touch that table like that?"

"It just felt like a good place for the Holy Bible to reside, child, just that."

"Oh," says Sarah. She takes Naomi by the hand and guides her down a mahogany-paneled hallway and through the kitchen, all thoughts of evil far from her mind. "This way," Sarah says. "I'll show you to your room. It's through here."

In the spacious kitchen, Naomi runs her hand over a chrome-plated, white, enameled, four-legged, Wedgewood stove. It has an eight-lid cooking surface, two topside food warmers, a side-mounted water heater, and two large ovens. Countless skillets, pots and pans, brass ones, cast-iron ones, hang from the kitchen walls and over a butcher-block table, which Naomi also fingers in delight, as she passes it.

Sarah laughs and says, "You're not thinking of placing a Bible on everything in the house, are you?"

Naomi chuckles. "No, child. Just feeling the beauty of things that I'd long forgotten what they were like."

Oblique-patterned, white and black, diamond-shaped tiles cover the floor. Dishes, cups, glasses—plain and fancy ones—fill two cupboards; off to the side of the kitchen is a well-stocked pantry. A lingering aroma of coffee beans and fresh fruit, on a side table, fills the room. The smell of spices makes Naomi hungry, and the kitchen makes her want to dive right in and start cooking.

Sarah arrives at a flight of rear stairs, just off the kitchen, which leads to the upper floors, as well as to the lower part of the sprawling dwelling. Turning on the staircase light, the young girl descends the steps ahead of Naomi into the basement: a spacious, clean, warm place, with a furnace, a storage room, an assortment of tools and neatly stacked period furniture. "Father is always promising to store some of his parents' things in the attic, but he never finds the time, since they passed on," Sarah comments with sadness. "First grandfather, last year, then grandmother, a week later, in her sleep. She said she could not live without him. It's not the same without them." The teenager steps to a door across from them and opens it. "This is your room, Naomi. It's not very elegant. It's where grandmother preferred sleeping after grandfather died. She said it kept her closer to nature. I hope you don't mind."

When they enter the room, Naomi's eyes light up. The large space has eight windows, all facing out on different directions across Shadow Grove, windows to let in the morning, the afternoon, and the evening sun, as the westerly facing ones do now, filling the room with the last light of the warm red sun, sending its glow spreading across the polished oak floor and onto a double-sided mahogany bed, a bed immaculately prepared with Sarah's grandmother's hand-sewn spread, with two goosedown pillows and an extra blanket resting on an antique cedar chest at the foot of the bed. A brick fireplace, two wingback chairs, and a bedside table—on which rest a Tiffany lamp and an alarm clock—all give the room a beautiful lived-in feeling. After having resided with Stella and Leticia in a cramped, New York apartment, and having had to sleep on the couch, Naomi can't keep from smiling, her eyes taking in every inch of the room; clapping her hands, she exclaims, "Maids don't always get the best places to live, but heaven couldn't have picked out a better place than this, if it looked around for a thousand years."

"Naomi, are you now trying to tell me you're an angel?"

"Oh, no, child. You much too smart for me to try and tell you that. That was a figure of speech. Heaven don't go around looking for rooms for us maids. And angels—from what I'm told—certainly don't break the rules and choose to remain on earth throughout the lives of the ones they've come to be guardians over, when all of the glory in paradise awaits their return."

"The way you broke the rules on that ship," replies Sarah, "when you said you will suffer, cry, and laugh with me until the end of time."

Seemingly trapped by the young girl's remarks, Naomi gets herself out of it by gazing about the room with a huge, clown-like smile on her face, causing Sarah to laugh.

"Grandmother and I did a lot of what Henry calls, 'soul searching' in this room about how coloreds and whites both deserve jobs on our plantation, after the Klan threatened to burn us out for letting the coloreds work alongside our white workers," Sarah tells her. "That's why some of our field hands are armed now. But, I'm sure all of this is humdrum to you after working in New York."

Hours later, Naomi and Sarah are still talking away while sitting in the overstuffed, arm chairs. The only light seeping through the window and into the room is from a dirty yellow moon, which gives Naomi reason to pause; she looks at the alarm clock on the nearby table; it's nearly ten o'clock. Her gaze turns from the clock to the room's open door, as if expecting someone, someone who is late; then she looks out the window and at the moon.

"The sun is gone," says Sarah, following the mysterious woman's sights to the window and into the dark of night. "And the moon looks so frightening."

"That's because this night is racing to its end, Sarah, and I want you to be very brave."

"Brave, Naomi?"

As Naomi reaches over and turns on the table lamp, and again looks toward the door, an anxious Marilyn enters the room.

"Sarah," she says, slipping into a flying jacket. "We've been praying over this for hours."

"You and Father? Praying over what, Mother?"

"We've been praying with Father Haas for guidance to save . . ."

"Father Haas. Here?" Sarah asks, getting to her feet, looking at Naomi and then facing Marilyn. "Naomi and I were talking about something that troubles me, and I want Father Haas to hear what she's been telling me about God and then see what he, then you and Father have to say."

"There's no time, sweetheart," says Marilyn glancing at the clock.

"She's right, Sarah," says Naomi, also looking at the clock. "The night must come to its end."

Surprised at Naomi's remark, Marilyn turns to Sarah. "Your father and I are flying to Atlanta, as soon as he gets a message over the phone. And Father Haas has traveled so far to get here, and he's all talked out."

"But, Mother. It's extremely important. I have to talk with Father Haas about Barney and about what Naomi . . ." Suddenly, seeing how mentally exhausted her mother appears, Sarah retreats somewhat. "I'm sorry, Mother. I know how worried you and Father are about the stocks, but this is so extremely import . . ."

"That's what I came to tell the two of you," Marilyn tells Sarah, then speaks to Naomi, as if doing so will undo the feeling of loss she is receiving when looking at the mixed-blood woman and following her gaze to that clock. "Lawrence was talking to a stockbroker who knows how we can recoup our losses and now he awaits his return call."

"Recoup our losses!" says Sarah now glowing along with her mother.

Sarah smiles at Naomi as well, but Marilyn's expression of joy is completely diluted, when she sees that Naomi is sitting there staring out the window at that ugly moon. Naomi then looks back at her with finality in her eyes. Marilyn's heart races with apprehension. "Between this broker . . ." Marilyn tells Sarah, trying to shake off her feelings of impending doom, then continues, ". . . and between your father, him and me, we might . . ."

"Who is this broker, Mother? Is he Mr. Pennington from the bank in town?"

"Don't ask me who or how, now, dear," says Marilyn, nervously buttoning down her flying jacket, while scrutinizing Naomi, confusion crowding away at her otherwise impeccable logic and filling her with even more affliction. Naomi faces her, and the mixed-blood woman's stoic looks have none of the gleam of soft kindness behind them, only the appearance of fate waiting to fulfill its inescapable purpose. Marilyn turns pale and feels the presence of God entering the equation. She turns to Sarah and—as if surrendering to providence—says, "Earlier, I saw Henry entering Mister Thomas's old place by the south field, sweetheart." Stopping and thinking, as if trying desperately to tie up all the loose ends, Marilyn says again to Sarah. "Henry's sleeping on the plantation instead of taking the long ride home. Go and bring him to the plane."

"Why, Mother?" asks Sarah, causing Marilyn to almost cry, and again, make eye contact with Naomi, as Sarah goes on. "You've never asked Henry to see you and Father off before, even when we traveled to Germany. He's shy about saying goodbye. He won't come."

"He will come this time," Naomi whispers, her sights never leaving those of Marilyn, who trembles. "Tell him I, also, want him there with you and Marilyn."

"But," Sarah says, a bit anxious now. "I still don't understand why tonight of all nights?"

Marilyn then turns to the servant woman, and—although she clearly understands that it is Sarah who has asked the question—she explains the reason for wanting Henry at the plane to Naomi, as if to justify an irrational consideration to her. "To make sure he and Collins can take care of things while we are . . ." Marilyn suddenly turns from Naomi and embraces Sarah. "I'm sorry that I am being so short with you, Sarah. Father Haas is leaving right after we board the plane. But your father and I will talk with you . . ." Once again, Marilyn makes eye contact with Naomi, before continuing and then adds. ". . . when we return. And, honey, this broker is not from around here, maybe from Atlanta. He says for us to wait until near eleven for him to make a final call back to us with the arrangements. That's all I know about him." Marilyn now faces Naomi, the question of her very life, visibly reflecting in her blue eyes, as she asks the faithful black woman, "Will we . . . Lawrence and I. We won't. . . . That is, feel . . ." She looks at Sarah. "I mean . . ."

"Only the fear," Naomi tell her. "After that, only the Light of Love all around you."

Marilyn looks at Naomi in dread, then at Sarah in a panic; then her faith in God stiffens. She turns to Naomi and says, "Have Sarah take you to my closet and pick out one of my nice coats for you while we're away. It's rather cold outside at night, and we don't want to lose you to illness now, do we?"

Naomi's human-side humanity slips her into despair, and she nods and then looks at the clock, Sarah following both womens' gaze to it. "It's only ten o'clock," Sarah says. "Why are you rushing so, Mother?"

"Honey, just get ready and go and get Henry, then meet us at the plane. There is so much paperwork your father and I have to complete to take with us before we can leav . . ." Marilyn stops short of finishing the word. In those seldom realized, difficult steps toward life's true worth, she is awakened to the fact that it is all a waste, those important papers. Ever so slowly she faces Naomi, her kind, blue eyes begging for the unvarnished truth, but afraid of putting it in recognizable words with Sarah there; are she and Lawrence going to die and is it God's will? Is Naomi a real angel, and would Naomi come out and tell her so? "Don't forget about that coat or anything else you might need of mine, Naomi."

Both women know full well that none of Marilyn's streamlined clothes will fit Naomi, who sits there gazing up at Marilyn with admiration and love. "Our attire and our needs are always simple, even if the coat would fit," Naomi explains. She then faces the window and the moon.

"I understand," Marilyn tells Naomi.

Naomi springs from the chair and hugs Marilyn. Taking Naomi's hands into hers, Marilyn kisses them. She then kisses Sarah on her troubled face and hurries from the room. Sarah turns to Naomi. "Mother is afraid, Naomi," Sarah says, trying to be brave. "She and Father are really afraid. But this family will be okay now. No matter what God lets happens to me, He won't do anything to harm my parents will He? The stars are still shining brightly for Father and Mother, aren't they, Naomi? Now that this unknown man is trying help?" Sarah looks out the window and goes on. "Even with that ugly moon outside, it isn't a bad sign, is it?"

Naomi embraces Sarah, and they both stare out the window into the pitch black night. "I was wrong when I said the stars will always shine for you, Sarah. There are no open windows in the sky tonight," Naomi whispers. "Events that impact our earthly lives don't always come from the hand of God, child. Often they come from Satan, whose hand is all-powerful in helping people who accept him as their god, people who refuse the Lord, and will destroy those who are in the way of what Satan wants. The angels are on the run and afraid of this dark presence that only comes this way every million years or so. In the dark of this very night, when the clocks all over the world strike eleven, our time, depicting the times Lucifer sinned against God before he was driven out of heaven, the dead will turn over in their graves and pray that Lucifer does not win in the struggle between your sons, and thus they—the dead—will be dragged into hell with your sons at the end of time if they should lose. It now begins, Sarah, evil massacring the heart of God, creating the final path to the birth of Flynn and Caleb."

5

Chariots of Fire

A few miles away, south of Henry's land below old Cutterville Bridge—that Southern, coastal landmark of horror—the hands of the evil are massacring the heart of God in a barbaric act against five black teenagers. One of Cutterville's most important citizens, forty-year-old Charles Pennington—the son of Pennington National Bank's president—is there with his dog to witness his first hanging. In his white Ivy League sweater, dark trousers, dark-blue tie and polished shoes, he's the only one dressed in street clothes. Lingering wide-eyed in the shadows, behind the Klansmen, Charles is trembling with excitement, while holding onto and left-handedly stroking his young, female Saint Bernard. Charles, who knew Henry's parents before they died, and always treated them with respect, whenever they entered his father's bank, professes to be a friend of Henry's, but by willingly witnessing the killing of the black youngsters, he's anything but a friend. There is something that Charles has not counted on: he will see something out of the future this night, something that will twist his stomach into knots. Under the watchful eyes of the Grand Wizard, in his flowing white robe and silken white hood, a dozen sheet-covered Klansmen with burning crosses cheer as a young girl's and four black, teenage boys' bodies burn while hanging from Cutter Bridge by their necks. The hanging ropes burn through, dumping the bodies on the ground. "You're not God's beloved children, not His heart—you dumb, uneducated coons—like your coconut-head preacher tells you people," a Klansman yells at the bodies.

Among the Klansmen are Horace Tucker and his one-eared son, Dane, who removes a wool cap from his back pocket, carefully slips it under his Klansman's hood and onto his head where he pulls the inner cap down over his forehead while grimacing in pain.

"What's wrong with you, boy?" his father asks.

"Nothing," Dane lies. "I just bumped my head when I fell off my horse, earlier, that's all."

It's far more than a simple bump, that pain on Dane's forehead. It's a horrific nightmare that was born during the rape of the now-dead girl; this night—as it will young Pennington—will haunt Dane Tucker for the rest of his life. He and his father receive a nod from the Grand Wizard and stand over the bodies. Dane—his Klansman's hood revealing the area around his missing ear—in one hand carries a handful of moth-eaten books and yells at the human remains. "No tar-ball ink spot from across the tracks will ever attend school in Cutterville! You want to learn to read and write?" He tosses the books on the bodies, then pinches off his nostrils against the stench, backs off and goes on. "Then, learn in hell while you burn!" He faces his father. "Did I say it right, Pa?" Dane asks, removing his hood, but not his cap. "Will killing them coons help save our land?"

Horace glances at the Wizard and says, "Saving our land, Son. That's in my hands, now."

Horace removes his hood, as do the other Klansmen, and he approaches the Wizard, who also unmasks; he's Major Cutter.

"I can't wait like you ask, Barney. I'm losing my land. My boy's hungry. Him and his ma."

"That's your problem," exclaims Cutter. He guides Horace to an old Chevy pickup, out of earshot of the others. At the truck, Horace rebels.

"Don't tell me it's my problem, and don't try and separate me from my son and the others, thinking you can intimidate me over here alone," he hisses at Barney. "You put the fear of God in them stinking, burned spades and the other men out here, but not me." With his squeaky voice, Horace is a chipmunk jawing up at a bulldog, but he feels that he has an ace in the hole and unwisely goes on with the intent of using it. "Give me my money!"

"I don't return money to dirt."

"Dirt!" exclaims Horace. "I'll show you dirt. I know how you set up that fake phone call. How your man in Atlanta is stalling a certain party over the phone until you can get out there tonight to kill them." Cutter is taken aback and turns a deeper shade of pale. "Who's afraid, now, Mister Almighty Major Cutter? The Winthrops have enough political might to fuck you up real bad." As Barney glares at him, Horace chuckles. "And now," he hisses, "you're wondering how I know about your plans to murder Sarah's folks. I'll tell you how. While we were all drinking in Sue Ann's place, and you were smoking your Lucky Strikes like you was the king of the world, I kept my eye on you. We was supposed to be planning this nigger killing fer tonight, but you were hardly listening, just had to use the phone. I followed you into Sue Ann's storage room and listened behind her moonshine crates, as you set up your plans over that storage-room phone. You ask me where I got my balls on the train. I certainly didn't get them from your small-dick, dumbass self. Yes, I said 'small dick, dumb ass.' You see, you're not as smart a intelligence officer as you think."

"I'm impressed," Barney says after the initial shock, causing Horace to start to wonder if he's bitten off more than he can chew, as Barney coolly goes on. "But surprise and failure are like husband and wife in my trade, where one has to be prepared for the unexpected. You and Dane have big dicks, Horace. Did you ever wonder why?" As Horace turns pale, Barney goes on. "That's right. I know all about your dicks, but it's not the length of a man's dick, but the thickness of it, and mine's going right up your ignorant ass."

"You have nothing up your sleeve," Horace says, trying to bluff his way out of trouble. "Go back to that army base of yours and play soldier boy and draw that monthly pay. At least you and your mother won't starve. You—with a mother smelling like that, who sits on her bedpan all day—got the nerve to talk about my boy. Go away, Barney, and let Dane run the Klan. He's always wanted to and can't be any worse at it than you." Horace looks over his shoulder, then back, trembling even as he attempts to compromise Barney. "I haven't told anyone about your plan to kill the Winthrops, not even Dane, but I will, including telling the Winthrops, if you don't give me my two grand, and do it now!" Cutter eyes Horace up and down. Even more uncertain of himself after that look of death, Horace struggles on, for he knows he's gone too far to try and turn back now. "I'm not afraid of you," he squeaks out. "It's time you knew who you're dealing with, Barney Cutter. Me! Horace Tucker, not one of your frightened coloreds!" He holds his breath. If Barney had what he thought he had on him, it would come out now, and how Horace silently prays that Barney is only bluffing.

Barney leans back, laughs, then grabs Horace by the throat, drawing the attention of the Klansmen; even so, no one dares to step forward to stop Cutter, not even Dane, who watches, helpless and afraid, out of hearing range with the others, as his father is slapped about, during which time, young Pennington looks about as if wanting to get out of there, so does Horace, but that's now impossible, as Barney continues. "I've known for years about you, ever since you got off that cotton train

61

from Texas," Cutter hisses, his voice kept to a whisper, "and how you've hid it from the rest of the men and that damn boy of yours. The reason I let you live this long is that I've been using you, but—as you say—you're broke; so here and now you must die."

"You've lost you mind," Horace says backing away. "You can't just kill me out here in front of the men. Slap me around, maybe, but the men won't stand by and watch you kill me. You got no reason. I'm one of you, you know that."

Cutter removes a snapshot from the truck and shows it to Horace. "Does this look like you're one of us?" he asks. Horace slumps back against the pickup and cries, knowing that what he's done over the years, the rapes, the castrations, the beheading, dragging, whipping and burning is now being revisited upon him. How many times, he ponders, as he leans against the truck shivering and glaring at that photo, have blacks gone to their graves begging him and Dane and the others for mercy then, getting none, falling on their knees they ask God to welcome them into heaven? How will God look upon him after his death, if Barney has him killed? His brain goes numb, as he listens to Cutter's ongoing, insane ranting.

"That fucking ugly son of yours with his degenerative, one-ear body! He and your wife don't know about you. I'll give you that. But there's room in that fire for the three of you. Your family dies, too."

Horace gawks at the bodies. "Don't do it, Barney. God will have mercy on you if you have mercy on others." He lowers his head, whispering. "We're all sisters and brothers."

"Run that by me again," says Barney. " 'Sisters and brothers?' You're asking me to let you live to say, 'Please don't do that, we're sisters and brothers?' "

"I want to live, Barney. Just keep the money, and don't tell my boy about me and don't let the men hurt him or his mother. I'm lowdown trash. I admit it, and I'm sorry I said we're all sisters and brothers and lost my head by mentioning God's name before you. Okay?"

"How quickly do we back away from God, when our feet are in the fire," smirks Barney.

"Please, Barney. I'll serve you and still kill niggers. Just let me live. Dear God, let me live!"

"You're a church-going man, aren't you, Horace, a worshiper of the

Savior? That's why you can't stop calling on God's name, even though you know you piss me off when I hear it."

"I am a Christian, as all of us Klansmen are. You know that."

"I'm not!" Barney exclaims. "And you make me sick standing here begging God to save you. God has nothing to do with this. God didn't create you white inverts, Satan did! He made you to serve men like me in hell and on earth."

"Yes. Anything you say. I'm dirt under your feet, but please don't kill me. My boy and wife need me."

"I'm not laying a hand on you, Horace," Barney tells the petrified man and goes on. "Some say that all Klansmen worship the devil, not God and why not? They should worship Satan, so tell me that you will worship him and piss on the name of God and follow me as your savior, Horace Tucker, and I will let you live."

"My God. My God. Don't ask me to do that, Barney, not that. Not to massacre His heart by trading in the safety of my physical body over that of my soul."

"What the fuck you think you been doing all this time by killing those coons, who say that God loves them as much as He loves you?" Turning his gaze on a terrified Dane, Barney—once more—glares at Horace. "Since there are so few of us Klansmen left, and the nigger population is growing stronger every damn time a white man turns around, I might even let old, one-ear Dane live. It'll be a good laugh to watch your boy killing niggers. It's all up to you. Remember, though, that all of that sick blood of yours I want to destroy, runs in your son's body, as well. And since you won't give allegiance to Satan and swear off of God, you know what to do, if you want to save your son and wife." Barney withdraws a revolver from his shoulder holster, removes all but one bullet, and hands the weapon to Horace. "And don't try aiming that thing at me. I'd have that gun out of your shaking hands and stuck clean down your throat before you can blink those inferior eyes of yours. Do it or we'll burn you and your boy alive, here and now. Do it and you'll always be a good old Klansman to the others, and Dane will go on living. You got my word on it."

Convulsing, Horace puts the gun barrel in his mouth.

"Pa! Nooo!" Horace hears Dane's sobbing cry. His teeth clicking against the cold, steel barrel, Horace sees Dane racing toward him. A shot rings out.

"Ahhhhh! Pa!"

As Dane runs screaming to his father, Charles Pennington sees something far more startling than witnessing Horace's head spattering from his body: a young boy is standing over the black students' burning corpses. Pennington looks at the other men. The boy—having come out of nowhere—is right in their midst, but no one seems to see him. Granted the men all are looking at Horace's headless body and at Barney, but that small, poor soul is wailing down at those students' remains so loudly that someone should have looked toward him. Even Barney—who is so callous that he would not give Horace a second look, but would have noticed a stranger suddenly appearing among them—doesn't seem to see or hear the youngster.

Pennington looks from Cutter and the others, and gawks at the lad. He rubs his eyes, and gawks at him again. *Was he losing his mind*, he ponders. The sobbing youth is white with red hair and has a gap between his front teeth, and he's curtained by a thin layer of fog, as if half in their world and half in a much darker place. To Pennington's dismay and for reasons he will never understand, he suddenly knows the gapped-tooth boy's name, it's Marcus. Then, Pennington's eyes widened in horror; from out of the fog comes a massive albino sidewinder with black and red, diamond-shaped markings along its thick, scaly back, and it opens its huge mouth and swallows up the screaming boy. Pennington sees a shadowy man made of ice standing in the fog and pointing his accusatory, icy finger at him. Gagging and vomiting, Charles Pennington and his frightened dog run for home, the image of the boy being eaten by the snake and the icy man burned into his mind and following him all the way. What the future banker does not know is that Marcus is a boy who is not yet born, that he will not leave his mother's womb until after the birth of Flynn and Caleb, to further complicate their lives.

Major Cutter—his work completed—pockets the photo, slides into the truck and speeds into the night, removing his robe as he drives toward Shadow Grove to complete still another mission of death to simplify his life.

Thirty minutes later, a little before eleven o'clock, the major arrives at the plantation, turns off his headlights, looks about, then motors under Shadow Grove's trestle gate, through the citrus groves, and stops alongside the *White Dove*. Dressed in coveralls, he climbs from the truck and into a world of a billion crickets ringing the night air with their mating calls. Barney surveys the far-off workers' shacks which surround the fields. Kerosene lamps glowing against those many window panes are the only witnesses to his diabolic intent, as he steps to the *White Dove* with a tool box. The crickets go deadly silent, and time stands still.

Sometime later, the sound of clunking, spoke wheels and voices are heard breaking the deadly silence, as a mule-drawn wagon, moving out of the darkness, approaches the aircraft and stops sixty feet or so from it. Henry is driving the team. Naomi is also in the wagon and wearing her weathered coat. An emotionally distraught Sarah, however, continues to sense that there is something terribly wrong with her parents, and as she sits between Naomi and Henry—even with her coat on—she is shivering. Henry lifts a blanket from the rear of the wagon and wraps it around the women. Minutes later, the Model T arrives. Lawrence and Marilyn leave the car, as does Father Haas, a fifty-year-old Franciscan priest, wearing his brown robe. Marilyn hurries to the wagon and kisses Sarah and breaks down and sobs, causing Sarah to cry.

"What is it, Mother? What's wrong? Tell me. I have a right to know."

"Honey," calls Lawrence, firing up the plane, this is the first time he's never said goodbye to Sarah.

Looking back at Lawrence, Marilyn then faces Naomi. "Have Sarah keep warm and maintain her studies until the five of us meet again," she says, her sights sweeping over all of them with love and stopping on Henry. Her gaze lingers on him until Sarah's voice breaks her concentration.

"Are you sad because we may still lose everything, Mother?" Sarah asks, reaching out to her. "Is that why you're crying? If we lose it all, we will still have each other."

Marilyn nearly breaks down. She turns pale, stumbles over, reaches in and hugs Sarah close to her and gazes at Naomi for strength. Then, from out of the night sky, a white dove flies over them, and Naomi looks from it to Marilyn. "He has made the rarest of exceptions and has made it known that you don't have to go on this trip, Marilyn."

As the dove disappears into the night, Marilyn steps away from Sarah and sobs. She gazes back at Lawrence, then at Naomi. "I can't let him go alone," Marilyn sobs, inching away from them and the wagon, as Sarah looks confusedly at her and Naomi. "Explain to Sarah that I love him too much not to go with him."

"What is she talking about, Naomi?" asks Sarah. "About us losing everything?"

"Your parents will gain everything, not lose it," Naomi tells Sarah and then faces Marilyn. "In the blinking of the eye, we'll all be together again, you, Lawrence, Sarah, Henry and me."

Watching Marilyn backing off toward the plane, neither Henry nor Sarah understands what is transpiring between the two women.

"Take care of my child, Naomi, you and Henry."

"With my life," Henry calls to Marilyn, he also now tearing up.

With cold chills racing over her body, walking backwards to the plane, her arms at her sides, her thoughts racing, Marilyn can't take her sights off Naomi, who mouths to her that she'll be all right. Marilyn opens her arms toward the black woman in a distant embrace. She then boards the *White Dove*, and Lawrence roars the plane across the field, Father Haas making the sign of the cross as the plane lifts off; all the time, Marilyn and Naomi keep their gazes locked on one another, Marilyn gazing down, Naomi up, both women's lips moving as they silently pray, a horrified Sarah—her blue eyes wide—watching the two women, and then, as the grandfather clock in the manor strikes eleven, the *White Dove* explodes. As parts of the plane, engulfed in a ball of fire, fall from the sky into the field, and the cries of horror fills the air, Sarah holds onto Henry. Recovering from the initial shock of seeing the plane destroyed, Henry leaps from the wagon and—followed by Father Haas—races toward the burning aircraft, leaving Sarah in total disarray and numb. Naomi holds onto Sarah and mutters half aloud: "Satan has destroyed their bodies for the sake of that man, but not their eternal souls, child. Not their souls."

From every direction—with buckets of water, shovels and blankets—the workers race from their homes and into the field toward the combusting wreckage. Even though the *White Dove* has crashed a good distance from the wagon, Henry is one of the first to reach it. Those who have arrived before him can only stand by, shielding their faces with their hands and arms against the searing heat and flames. Henry runs up to those workers who are cowering near the plane, then glimpses the oncoming field hands with their splashing buckets of water. "Come on!" he cries, urging them on, frantically tucking his shirt into his trousers, anticipating entering the fire; some of the men around him tremble in fear, but seeing Henry tuck in his shirt, do the same with theirs, their eyes lock on Henry, trusting that his judgment will not get them killed. When the first of a half-dozen workers arrive, tossing water and dirt onto the flames, Henry dumps one of the pockets of water over his head and body and cautiously moves within touching distance of the burning aircraft; the wind is his ally, blowing the flames and smoke to the east, away from him and the workers, but even at that, Henry is driven back by the heat. Six more men join Henry, tossing water over his body and over each other, desperately trying to protect them from the raging fire and still be able to enter the *White Dove*. As more men, women and children with buckets swarm toward the wreckage, Father Haas and others, form a bucket brigade which stretches across the field from a distant water well to the *White Dove*.

"More water!" shouts Father Haas, as Henry and the six men with him take advantage of a strong, easterly wind and jerk and pull at the twisted cockpit door, the field hands frantically tossing water onto the forward men and the door.

As Father Haas prays for God to intervene and stifle the raging blaze, Henry and those with him manage to rip off the battered door, and an army of workers, one after the other, flood the fire and exposed cockpit with water; with walls of rapidly flung water, bucket after bucket and prayer, the brutal flames are beaten back.

"Thank You," whispers the priest, facing the heaven.

Henry is first to enter the smoldering plane, and as he does, several hundred yards behind him and the rescue teams, Sarah is screaming and trying to reach the wreckage and her parents. When she attempts to jump off the wagon, Naomi seizes and holds onto her. Father Haas quickly makes his way back to the wagon to help Naomi restrain the frantic teenager.

"You'll only get in their way," exclaims Naomi, wrestling with the distraught girl. "Talk to her, Father," Naomi says, as Sarah reaches out for the priest when he arrives. "Now is the time to tell him what you wanted to tell him and your mother. Now, Sarah," says Naomi. "Vent your sorrow and your anger toward me by telling him everything."

"Father," cries Sarah, looking back at Naomi. "She could have saved my parents. When we were flying here from Cutterville, she as good as said that they would die in their plane. Now I realize it, and she did nothing to stop them. And the way Mother and Naomi looked at each other as the plane lifted off. Naomi knew. She knew they would die. Ask her, Father! Ask her why she let them die?"

"They are not yet dead, Sarah," Father Haas tells her. "Purgatory awaits us all, and only then are they dead if He says they are hell-bound, child."

Naomi touches Sarah on her shoulder. "Satan is trying to turn you against me, Sarah. Touch me and know that I am love, not evil."

The mixed-blood woman's voice is so calming, her touch so eternal that Sarah stops sobbing and looks at her, mesmerized, then hugs Naomi and cries in her arms; as for Father Haas, he stands there in disbelief, studying both of them for several moments. He knows that whatever it is that Sarah has to tell him, it is something that completely and so profoundly changed her from a shrieking child, in the face of her beloved parents' death, to such a sudden and serene state, that it has to do with Naomi and Naomi alone, the mystery woman who Marilyn had said came so dramatically into their lives.

"What's wrong, Sarah?" a frantic Father Haas asks, with a wary eye on Naomi, feeling Naomi's awesome energy stemming from her, not knowing if Naomi is from God or from hell.

Father Haas, capable and tall, continues to lock his sights on Naomi, sights that demand that she explain herself.

"Jesus gave His disciples their own powers of knowledge in the matter of good and evil, Father," Naomi tells him. "I am but a woman. You, as one of His present-day disciples and having devoted your whole life to Christ, must seek that holy awareness from your heart, not from my lips as to who I am."

Stunned, Father Haas asks himself if Naomi has actually read his thoughts. Trembling, he scrutinizes Naomi.

"You are still not convinced as to what I am, Father, or if I'm someone deadly to this child's very soul," Naomi tells him, going on. "So that you will know that we are both right, and that God is in me, as He is in you, this night, before the flames of that plane are completely out, Lawrence—who will be found by Henry—will be carried toward us by one of Shadow Grove's strongest and most trusted white workers, a weeping, red-haired giant of a man called Collins, and Marilyn—who will be found and lifted off the ground by this same weeping, red-haired man—will be carried in the arms of Henry, as is God's will, so that those who witness this will know that both colored and white are here equally to take care of one another." She sweeps her arm and hand from left to right as if across the heavens, going on, "And both Lawrence and Marilyn will rise up across this night sky to their place of temporary rest accompanied by a legion of angels in what, you, Sarah, call 'chariots of fire.' "

Father Haas, his mind racing, climbs into the wagon. He sits alongside Sarah, and with his eyes wide, he listens to her tell him about Naomi, while she sobs in his arms. Father Haas's perplexed eyes never leave the woman, an enigma, the bush drawing its strength from the tree.

At the *White Dove*, inside the cockpit, under a continuous cascade of bucket-tossed water, Henry locates Lawrence's body and lifts it from the twisted debris. Lawrence's snow-white hair is blackened and burned, and having seen this, from the eyes of every last man, woman and child—who continue passing buckets of water—tears flow as wet as the tossed water. "Where's Marilyn?" Henry sobs, repositioning Lawrence's body in his arms, in order to easily hand the gentle man's remains through the twisted cockpit doorway. Again Henry calls out, "Where is Marilyn?"

"She's here, Henry!" someone calls from outside and from the far side of the plane.

Henry transfers Lawrence's body to other outstretched hands to fulfill Naomi's prophesy that a red-haired man will carry Lawrence. Yet, the man who takes Lawrence at the end of the line is bald, and—though filled with grief, he is without tears. Muscling his way out of the mangled plane, Henry runs to the other side of the smoldering aircraft and stops. Marilyn is lying faceup some distance away from the wreckage, after having been thrown into a field of calla lilies. A huge, weeping, red-haired white man is bending down over her and lovingly lifts her limp body free of the debris scattered around them. The red-haired man is Marilyn and Lawrence's trusted field boss Keith Collins, thirty-two, with a freckled face and kind, green, tearful eyes. Henry stops running and walks now, tears streaming down his cheeks, as he moves toward Collins and the lifeless body of the woman he had loved as much as his deceased mother.

"I didn't think they'd live too long outside of the greenhouse," Collins, so gently carrying Marilyn, says while looking back at the calla lilies, then returning his focus on a stunned, slowly-approaching Henry and going on. "I replanted the calla lilies in this field for her to see the minute the *White Dove* got in sight of them, on their way home from Germany, Henry, but I didn't expect her to die in them. I don't mind if you want to carry her, Henry," he continues, sobbing, as Henry falls in step with him. "I know how much you loved her."

As Henry's tears flow, and Keith Collins hands Marilyn's body to the young black youth, two struggling white men, carrying Lawrence's body, falls in step with Henry and Collins, and the exhausted men hand over Lawrence's body to the field boss, who continues—without missing a step—at Henry's side and toward the wagon, both with the late masters of the land royally in their powerful guardianship, a line of workers wailing along behind, as the flames continue flickering in the mangled aircraft, and a stunned Father Haas—from the wagon—after witnessing the sight of the giant and Henry carrying the bodies, as Naomi had made known, looks back at Sarah and then at Naomi and makes the sign of the cross, his own tears now flowing, as he humbly kneels and asks Naomi to pray for him. Henry glances ahead at the buckboard and at the mules. Even the animals of burden seem to sense the death of their masters, as they restlessly move about.

He sees Naomi, Father Haas and Sarah standing in the wagon, their sights fixed on the sky. Henry follows their gaze. The sky is lit up by two shooting stars.

"Chariots of fire," whispers Sarah, holding onto Naomi's hand. "There's going home in chariots of fire."

6

On the Wings of a Bird

Beyond Shadow Grove's trestle gate, not a bird sings or a butterfly is on the wing. The leaves of the mighty oak trees are laid still; the trillions of parched blades of the grass are motionless in their thirsty quivering for water, and the blue sky is placidly clear, warming the land with the power of the sun. On a sunbathed promontory—a quarter of a mile from Manor Hill and the citrus groves, as viewed by the mule drivers Amos and Andy from the massive, trestle gate—is the plantation's cemetery; not only is it a place of final rest for the Winthrops' ancestors, entombed there, but it is also a place where many of Shadow Grove's past workers are buried, blacks and whites side by side in the Winthrops' tradition of hope that God will accept the gesture as a sign that not all whites are evil.

Today, the cemetery is filled with the living, not just the dead: wealthy citizens from all over Georgia and beyond have arrived to show their respects, as well as fifty-year-old, bald and pale Harry Pennington, father of Charles Pennington. The elder banker is dressed in his appropriate, dark chairman-of-his-national-bank suit; and, there, standing beside him, is his ill-at-ease son, Charles, with his dog, the only friend he has ever trusted or wants near him, especially after witnessing those horrific burnings and killings of the school kids, that sobbing, ghost-like, red-haired boy, and the death of Dane's father. Pennington's bank holds the notes on most of the businesses in town, as well as on Shadow Grove, and on Henry's land. As the stocky banker nervously shakes the hands of wealthy mourners and politicizes with them, standing twenty feet away, Sarah's interracial make up of workers—dressed in their everyday, ordinary clothes—form a wide circle outside the freshly dug grave. It is a sobering sight, this deep, single hole in the ground, inundated by transfixed gazes, old and young ones alike, brimming with sadness—a grave site where male workers stand in silence, resolving not to cry and stoically resisting the wearing-down effects of that all-present, profound feeling of abandonment and despair which has taken hold of the women and children. The men do, nonetheless, set their sights on Sarah as the only hope now to shepherd them through the hard times. When it's the adult workers' time to view Lawrence and Marilyn's closed caskets, the women's tear-soaked, white handkerchiefs are waved at the caskets, as they file by, and each woman—in turn—embraces Sarah, trying to re-kindle the Winthrops back to life by rocking their young daughter lovingly in their arms; it is a place where young boys and girls have offered to file by the caskets last in order to continue crying in private for a while longer, as they cling to each other, as well as hold onto wild flowers picked from the land while sobbing and crystallizing the effects of the pounding sunlight from their eyes with their river of tears. After the last embrace of the women, Sarah—dressed in black—seems completely traumatized, as she lingers beside Father Haas and Naomi, next to the calla lily covered, bronze caskets of her parents.

Back at the gate, Amos and Andy—whose task it is to direct the visitors to the cemetery—nervously linger beside their mule and a horse. They're watching a battered old truck moving toward them. Riding in the back of the worn-out Dodge are a dozen, motley-dressed white men, including one-ear Dane, now wearing an old 1913 Brooklyn Dodgers baseball cap sideways on his head, while guzzling moonshine from a canning jar. The rusty pickup—driven by half-blind, bifocal-wearing old Hank, comes to a brake-squealing stop, nearly striking the gate. Armed with a bouquet of red roses and wearing a dark suit, his white shirt neatly ironed, his shoes highly polished, his flannel hat firmly on his head, Major Barney Cutter steps from the passenger side of the pickup, then, after brushing off his suit and the black brothers tipping their hats to him, he walks by them, through the great gate and flags down a nearby fieldhand, driving a horse-drawn wagon. He climbs aboard and leaves the gate, the truck, and the Klansmen behind. Dane glares down at the black brothers, then spits on them. Amos and Andy mount the mule and horse and quickly ride away.

Remaining in the truck cab, along with Hank—and using a small hand-held mirror to replenish her lipstick—an attractive, pale-looking, white, eighteen-year-old female runaway, has the men gaping through the truck's shattered, rear window at her. Her name is Betty, but she prefers to be called "Lilly", because of her soft, Easter-lily-colored skin, clean, pure and white, at least that is how she sees it. Far from being concerned over Lilly, Dane Tucker is prancing about on the truck bed, as if a trapped animal. He scowls past the gate at Cutter and the wagon clunking its way toward the distant cemetery. With Dane is his boyhood friend Chad Travers, nineteen, short and all of three-hundred pounds, a pit bull without mercy and easily driven to madness. Chad is wearing a bullwhip on his belt and has a Klan hood stuffed half out of his back pocket. He reaches for Dane's moonshine. "That won't bring your pa back to life," he tells him. "And take the damn cap off. It makes you look like a clown."

Dane sweeps Chad's hand aside. "What the fuck do you know about what will or won't bring my pa back or why he shot himself like that? So pipe your ass down, okay!" Dane squints toward Cutter, going on. "But he knows. Barney knows why Pa killed himself. It was something he said and what he showed to Pa, and if it takes ferever, I'm going to find out what it was, even if I have to kill that old fucker."

At the cemetery, as Father Haas sprinkles holy water on the caskets and Sarah completes the sign of the cross with him—as do many of her workers—the calla lilies are removed from the coffins, allowing a dozen, stalwart men to dutifully stand the caskets on end, facing one another—as Sarah had instructed. Using ropes and the strength of their arms and hands, they lower the erect caskets into that same deep grave and shovel in the dusty earth, creating a half-egg-shaped mound, on which is implanted two identifying, waist-high, marble tombstones. When the gravesite is finished to Naomi's expectations, young people, having been too afraid to view the boxes of death, drying away the tears on their sleeves, come forth and lay their collections of wildflowers on the grave, as well as assisting Sarah and others in replacing the calla lilies on the two-part, final resting place. After the last calla lily is positioned on the mound, Sarah searches about the gathering with her desperate, blue eyes. She's looking for Henry, but he's nowhere to be seen. However, she spots Barney Cutter at the back of the mourners, standing head and shoulders over a line of women, his roses gripped in his large hand, a demeaning smile on his unattractive face. Sarah turns away in despair. Everyone knows that Cutter is the Grand Wizard and that City Hall protects him and his Klan. Most of Sarah's field hands have been careful to stay clear of Cutter, especially the blacks. Today, however, no one seems especially disturbed by the Major's presence, only Sarah, as she, once again, looks at him from a far, agony in her eyes. How strange and unreal it seems to her, this unwanted intrusion into her life: the Klansman, Barney, the image of evil itself. Standing beside Major Cutter is a thickly built black woman and her eleven-year-old, woolly-haired son, who is holding onto a bunch of dying dandelions and waiting his turn to approach the grave. Also at the woman's side is a freckled-faced, white boy, age thirteen. Both boys are holding each other's hands and clinging to those limp dandelions.

"I told you two to get real flowers," the black woman scolds them. "Y'all can't put them there dead weeds on the Master's grave and embarrass me like that."

"Mamma, don't make fun of us," the woman's son says, pointing at a distant tombstone in the cemetery behind them. He goes on, as the white boy begins crying. "Kevin took 'em off his ma's grave." The boy's large, brown eyes refocus on Kevin, and he places his arm about his whimpering friend's shoulder, sadly explaining on. "The other kids picked all the nearby wildflowers. And, Mamma, his ma's dandelions was the only things we could find in time fo' the funeral."

The woman hugs the white boy and kisses him on his wet cheek, then her son on his. Teary-eyed, she tries to make a more suitable arrangement of the drooping dandelions in their innocent hands.

"It's not in the freshness of it or the cost of it," she tells them. "God knows it's in the love of it, and I thank you two fo' remindin' me of that. These weeds say as much of your love to the masters and to God as any flower." Noticing that Cutter is watching them, the woman locks gazes with him, as he takes the dandelions from the boys, cradles the drooping weeds under his arm, and separating the roses into two bundles, he gives a bundle to each boy. When the woman's son smiles up at him, Cutter brushes his hand across the boy's woolly head of hair, then across that of the white boy's. Smiling, he taps them on their butts and nudges them toward the Winthrops' grave, then notices that Sarah has been watching him through it all.

"This can't be the man who folks done said hanged them po' kids at Cutter Bridge," exclaims the black woman, turning to other workers, the black ones and the white ones around her, either being dangerously stupid, or too spiritually inspired to know that she is being foolish to think that Cutter is suddenly worthy of sainthood, while going on. "Is God touchin' yo' heart this sad day," she asks Cutter, "that you done run yo' hand through ma child's hair and done offered these two boys them beautiful, red roses, when the Klan all along done been tryin' to separated the races?"

"God moves in mysterious ways, indeed," someone whispers from the racially mixed crowd.

More akin to a politician than a Klansman, Major Cutter places the dandelions aside and shakes a few of the white workers' hands, ignoring the outstretched ones of the blacks. From the grave site, not only does Sarah continue watching, but Naomi also watches the Klansman. "That's right, Satan," Naomi with her squinting eyes and nodding head whispers. "Work your devil's magic on them po', unschooled, white and colored workers with your forked tongue and self-serving, wicked, hand-shakes of false gestures."

And, indeed, Cutter does work his magic. "Some say," Cutter quietly begins to the whites, "that you have to teach kids to hate. They say that left alone, children will save the world with their innocence and un-prejudiced love for one another."

"That be true," whispers a black man.

Cutter puts his finger against his lips, signaling that the black man must remain silent, while at the same time, he begins drawing the mis-guided attention from other blacks, all seemingly feeling that the Winthrops' death has touched the Klansman's heart with understand-ing; their hopes are soon dashed, when Cutter—absolutely sure of his grip on Sarah, now, with the help of Satan—continues, placidly address-ing the whites: "Not only do mostly blacks say that children will learn to love each other in their own way if we adults stay out of it, they then say that blacks need to learn reading and writing." He stops and stares at Sa-rah, then continues verbally preparing her workers—blacks and whites—for the time when he will run Shadow Grove. "But if you give a dog a bone," he smiles as he goes on, "it will want the entire ham next."

"We sho' will, and that's the truth," an old, black woman—condi-tioned all of her life to serve the white man before arriving at Shadow Grove under the Winthrops—says, as she stands with an umbrella over her head and giving black teenagers the evil eye, daring them to dispute her.

Among the black teenagers, one of the boys gently kicks the old, umbrella-carrying female on her ankle. "Ouch! That hurt," she exclaims.

Barney continues, "And being schooled will make them want more out of life than there is to give." He turns to the blacks. "Unlike your Reverend Harris—in his storefront church in town—who says this world and your problems are caused by the hand of Satan, I say this: Harris's

75

own hands are reaching deep into your pockets to take your hard-earned money in the name of his God. Satan doesn't do that."

Again, the black woman says, "That be true," and again she's kicked in her ankle. "Ouch!"

"It's people like you," the kicker exclaims to the old woman, "who give us a bad name. That man just belittled Reverend Harris and God in the same breath, and you say, 'That be true.' The world is sho' 'nough screwed up!"

A week ago, the boy and his parents had arrived in Cutterville from Akron, Ohio, the rubber capital of the world, where jobs were also lost to the Depression. His father had sought work at Dessen's tire company—and having failed to get a job there—he and his family had recently settled down on Shadow Grove. Someone then whispers in the boy's ear that Barney is the Grand Wizard.

Barney steps over to the youthful, black kicker. "You folks believe in God and don't like it when I say there are forces in the world more powerful than your God. Right?" he asks the boy, "And that's why you kicked that woman?" As the boy and others with him nod in agreement, Barney lowers the hammer on them, pleasing more than a few of Sarah's white workers.

"Well, then, you might say that your so-called-mighty God bested the devil, when He made only certain men masters of this world. You do believe God made man master here, don't you?" The old, black, woman—truly born to agree with everything white—again nods. Barney goes on. "And those men that your God made masters of this world were not you people. Your God made the white man masters over you. So this world is fine, contrary to what your kind thinks. Satan hasn't ruined it or us whites. You folks did with your big eyes and open hands reaching out for your welfare checks and government food handouts. Your colored religions and your attempts to climb into the Tower of Babel and steal the white man's knowledge has rendered you folks lower than apes. Education is not for you. Remember that the next time you pray for the downfall of the Klan. We're here to stay."

Again, someone whispers into the boy's ear, telling him about the recent deaths of the school kids, and the brash kicker swallows hard and says, "Yes, Sir."

Meanwhile, the two rose-carrying boys—devoid of all hatred—persist in their mission of love toward the grave site. From her place at the grave, Sarah cannot hear what Cutter is saying to her field hands, but she watches him and them with more than a little interest; she fears that Barney's evil influence will corrupt everything that her parents have worked for. Cutter now speaks equally to the white and black workers around him, but more to soothe those of Sarah's white workers who are shocked at his unvarnished message of hatred. "I'm a soldier," he tells them, "fighting to save this country, not a killer of children, but who are our children? Not those who turn against the good of society." He points to the rose-carrying boys, happily going on their way. "Look at them," chuckles Cutter. "Like two peas in a pod. At their young age, the black one only dreams about playing with his white friend, not about climbing the Tower of Babel. . . ." He points toward the whites and goes on, ". . . the tower of these good, white people's base of intelligence, their library of heaven, after blacks were warned to stay away from it by their God. Isn't that what your Bibles tell you?" he asks the agreeable, ignorant, black woman. "That man tried to steal others' knowledge from God's Tower?"

"That be right," the woman answers, giving the teenage kicker the evil eye, while drawing back her umbrella to whack him, daring him to try and kick her again. "We is at a funeral, boy! Not at some kickin'-on-ma-leg wrestlin' match. Even Reverend Harris says the Bible done said that about the Tower."

"It's true," one of Sarah's white workers adds. "It does say that, and I bet it was black folks who tried to steal God's knowledge from that tower, if you ask me, not us whites."

"Well, then," Cutter interjects. "Should those two boys be allowed to play together? The late Doctor and Mrs. Winthrop said they should, and I'll go along with that." He faces the kicker. "Neither I nor my men will ever harm anyone who knows their place and doesn't try to read books, which endangers the stability of the world order, where your God has ordained that only the white man should read."

Total silence grips the blacks and many of the white workers; they've heard talk that Barney doesn't believe in God, only in the devil, and that he can talk the stripes off of a zebra without the zebra knowing it, and they have heard rumors that he will marry Sarah. Perplexed, they can only stare at each other, then at Cutter, not knowing if they should join him or run from him to save their jobs on Shadow Grove. Back at the gate, Dane stands on the truck bed, he and the men gawking at the two boys as they drop, then stop, pick up, and fumble with their roses.

"Look at them pigeon-toed, butter-finger, fucking kids," growls Dane, greedily guzzling the last of the moonshine. "What the fucking hell does the major think he's doing over there? He said he wanted to marry Sarah to drive the niggers off her land, to take the nigger Henry's land from him, and makes us all rich by selling that coon's land, and sharing the money with us. Said he wanted to strengthen the Klan, now that that ink-spot-loving, heart doctor is dead. He didn't say he wanted to be some kind of nigger-loving, butt-touching, asshole himself."

"Do you think Barney killed the Winthrops, Dane?" one of the men asks. "Some think so." Dane spits toward the cemetery, only to have the wind blow it back in his face. Wiping his face on his sleeve—as Chad inches back from him and the slime—Dane raves on. "You all saw it. Saw how the major rubbed that coon kid's tar-ball head and gave him and that white boy them roses, like he was they daddy or something. Playing like he's God on earth. That ain't no way to separate the races, is it!"

"Major Cutter has found something he can't resist," says old half-blind Hank, squinting through the broken rear window at those on the truck bed, then focusing on the cemetery and Sarah, going on. "Barney has to win over her and her workers in his own way. And if he wants to play God on earth, as far as I'm concerned, that's okay and we all better get used to it or, like that little girl Sarah, there will be hell to pay, and only God in heaven can save us. Barney is possessed with the idea that he's protected by Satan."

At the cemetery, handing Sarah the roses, the young boys, then point to Cutter, indicating that it was he who gave the flowers to them, all the time, Sarah keeps an eye on Naomi and doesn't know if she should hold onto the roses or throw them away. She looks at Barney, who tips his hat to her with a smile. After all is said and done, and the funeral is over, Sarah's workers voluntarily go back to the fields to save what crops they can. When most of the mourners have departed, Barney moves toward Sarah. Terrified, she drops the roses. She gazes about for Naomi, as the towering Klansman steps up to her, removes his hat, picks up the roses, and places them on the grave, his blue eyes beaming with admiration at Sarah's beauty. "You'll need someone to help you run this place," he says, his sights sweeping about the vast land. Then—as if wanting privacy—Barney glares at Naomi, who seems in no hurry to leave Sarah alone with him. Cutter removes most of Horace's appropriated, two-thousand dollars from his pocket. "I know it's not enough to feed your workers for long, but, with your crops dying, this money will be helpful. I just didn't want you to think I came to you looking for a meal ticket in these hard times. I'm still employed by the army and make a living wage. I want you to be my wife, Sarah, and give me the son that I've envisioned and . . ."

Stunned by even the thought of sleeping with the monster, as well as by Barney's belittling act of flashing his money at her, as if she were a prostitute, Sarah steps away from him and glares over at Naomi, a look that demands that Naomi come to her rescue and put an end to that living nightmare with the five little words of: "God has called it off." Naomi, however, turns her back on the two of them and begins rearranging the gravesite calla lilies, covering over the roses with the white flowers. Sarah silently asks God to take this impossible task away from her or give her a sign to show that He truly loves her, and that she's not alone as she now feels she is with Naomi turning her back on her. The young girl sees a darkened figure in one of the fields. Her blue eyes reflect an immediate flood of joy. Behind Cutter, in that field, this side of the departing workers, Henry is standing, tall and divine. As Sarah watches him, her eyelids open wide. A dusty whirlwind is spinning about Henry, just as one had about her on the ship. Seemingly impervious in the funnel of air around his powerful, slender body, Henry—his long eyelashes red from the blowing dust, his lips parched, his straw hat tilted to one side of his head—has his sights riveted on Sarah. How her heart races with exaltation, revealing to her that she does and always has loved Henry, and now with all of her strength she prays that Henry is the one with whom Naomi says she will find the greatest love that a woman can ever have on this earth. The whirlwind suddenly vanishes from Henry. Sarah goes limp. Cutter looks at her. She quickly looks away from Henry, who continues lingering out there looking up at the cemetery and at her, as she stands in Barney's shadow. Now Sarah prays that she can keep the Klansman's attention on her and away from Henry.

"I know your parents loved your workers, the blacks and whites." Barney tells Sarah, trying to conceal his two-fisted toughness. "I also know about this boy Henry and how you need money."

"Henry," Sarah whispers, her heart pounding in fright.

Cutter misreads her look of distress and thrusts the wad of dollars at her.

"Take it, Sarah. It'll keep Shadow Grove afloat for a while until we're married and . . ."

Sarah wards the cash off from her sight with her raised arms, with her turned-out palms and delicate wrists moving back and forth across her face. "Don't you dare offer that to me," she hisses at Barney. While a disappointed Barney momentarily looks down and rubs the scuff marks off his shoe against his trouser leg, Sarah flashes a glance beyond him to Henry, her thoughts going in all directions at once on how Henry is unaware of the danger he's in by standing out there in the open watching her and Barney. When the major pockets the cash, and starts to follow Sarah's gaze to Henry, the young girl distracts him.

"What about Henry?" Sarah asks, looking angrily at the Klansman. "What is it that you think you know about him? He's a worker, my parents' worker!"

"I'm told that and that he's a well-trained dog," Cutter says. "Never causes trouble the way his ma and pa did before their unfortunate demise." Sarah's eyes glare with catlike anger, as Cutter continues. "I know Henry promised to give your father all the lagoon water Shadow Grove needed, before the doctor died." He glances at the grave. Minutes of silence follow before he finally speaks. "It would be a shame," he warns, turning back to her and giving up on trying to be tactful, "if some hooded men mistakenly took your black workers out here for the trouble-making, job-stealing coloreds in town, or they begin to feel that your workers are like the colored kids who wanted to go to school and were hanged from the bridge." Sarah now faces him with clenched fists, but the major is only attracted to her all the more for it and continues threatening her. "Without someone to control them, no telling what the Klan might do to your black workers, even to the white ones, if they get in the way, now that the man of the house is no longer here to use his political muscle to protect them and this place." Again, he looks at the Winthrops' grave and then at Sarah. "Not that you don't have the same pathway to those political connections, because you do. And that's the main reason I want you on my side. I know you believe strongly in God, Sarah, but those who are Divine to you, and motivate you on this earth to go on, can help us humans only so much. Power and violence moves and shapes this world, not soft words of love to some so-called angels or

80

saints. You're a teenage woman in a man's world, Sarah." She turns her back on him, and he blares. "If I have to, I'll burn your black-ass workers to death, all of 'em, including that coon and his place out by that lagoon, and I'll take that water for Cutterville alone and let Shadow Grove dry rot to hell and back, and no goddamn judge in the entire state of Georgia will ever raise a finger to convict me for it, now that Lawrence is dead. Sarah, you're all alone! All alone!"

Sarah whirls about and faces him, her tearful eyes locked on Henry, then, horrified, she turns toward Naomi, who walks away, straight to Henry, and guides him back into the crowd and field with the other workers, Sarah watching them as they go. This time, Cutter is determined to see what is so interesting to her, and he follows her gaze. He sees only the plantation workers spreading out across the cabbage field, where Naomi and Henry have been absorbed. The Klansman angrily squints at Sarah, who is trying to hold back the tears.

"Tell me that the Klan won't kill my workers," she begs. "That they won't go after that lagoon water and hurt . . ."

"I'm just a man, Sarah. A man who only wants a son, a son with the combined surnames of 'Cutter-Winthrop,' a name that will make waves in the world, even as a certain individual in Germany wants to do, to create a new world order. Make no mistake about it, I will get this land—one way or another—and that lagoon water, as well. No colored should hold that much power over whites, drought or no drought. But, if you agree to be my wife, then I will honor the covenant that your father had with this boy, pet-dog servant of his, and this boy's lagoon; because—with this Henry willing to share that water with us, as promised—through a pipeline your father planned to build, Shadow Grove will come though the Depression and drought in good shape and be a bright beacon for our son's base of operation to spread his wings over Georgia, then over the world with the help of a powerful source to which I'm devoted. I've worked it all out." Cutter notices the white boy and his black friend riding by on a white mule. His eyes reflect his inner rage, and his bitter words reflect his true intent, as he exclaims. "A son who, after he reaches manhood, will no longer play with his dogs or his toys, no matter how much he thought he once cared for his childhood property."

It's all Sarah can do to keep from telling Barney that her father and mother loved Henry, that Henry is not a piece of property, that he, Barney Cutter, is the dog and a wicked, old man. Sarah notices Henry and

Naomi in the middle of still another field. It's clear that Naomi does not want Henry looking back at Sarah, but Naomi does look as Henry walks away from her, the old woman's spiritual eyes on both the young girl and the major. Cutter spots Naomi making her way from the field toward them. He sees how Sarah is watching her, and how she is filled with love for the black woman.

"Sarah," he says coldly, "I will kill anyone who stands in the way of me marrying you, or anyone you depend on more than you do on me, because I want all of your devotion—not necessarily your love, because I can live without that from you. But I demand all of yours and that of your mother and father's immense genius—their scientific minds, their musical ability. I want these things passed on to the son you will give me as my wife."

"Are you God to be so sure you'll have a son or any child at all?" Sarah asks, bitterly.

"In my position in the military," the Klansman softens his approach, ignoring her question and going on, "there is no limit to what a motivated officer can do. I have future plans, Sarah, monstrous plans with which I could marry a thousand women one day. My plan will give you and our son more wealth than you will ever dream of, enough money to enrich this plantation many thousands of times over. It's the reason I've remained in the service so long. That's all I can tell you now. As you pray to your God, I also pray to mine, and he has heard me by bringing me to this point with you. I don't need an answer today, Sarah, about a marriage between us. But soon."

"Who, Barney Cutter, who do you worship? The devil? Naomi thinks so."

"Naomi also thinks that she is godlike, from what I'm told," he says with a smile. "Surely no one believes anything that woman has to say, not even most of the coloreds that I know."

He reaches out and touches her arm, and as he does, a cloud passes overhead, diminishing the light of the world. Cutter sees the shadow of fear flash across Sarah's blue eyes. "Don't be afraid of me, Sarah, or of Lucifer. Just last night I had another dream, a dream with fire all around me, and a voice in that fire said, 'The name of the son you will father from Sarah shall be called Flynn.' "

Sarah simply sits down on the ground with a wide-eyed glare and sobs. Naomi had said her son would be called Flynn, but now hearing it from Barney it is as if a mountain has fallen on her.

Barney has Sarah just where he wants her, at his feet, and he makes no attempt to help her up. "Flynn will be a mighty soldier," he says, "a soldier who will put out the flames of all my enemies."

Pushing herself off of the ground, Sarah stumbles back, her hand pressing against her pounding heart, her legs nearly taken from under her once more. Everything that Naomi has heralded about her having sons who will walk the road of the cross, has now placed Sarah's feet on that same road. The major tips the hat to her and leaves.

After reaching the trestle gate on foot, Cutter stops and glances over his shoulder at Sarah; once again, Naomi is at Sarah's side. When Cutter continues toward the pickup, Dane, who is angrily gripping the empty moonshine jar to the point of shattering it, glowers down at Barney with a look that is as deadly as any razor. "That motherfucker," Dane whispers to Chad. "He showed Pa's money to Sarah. He still has it, and I'm gonna get it back, and I mean right goddamn now."

When Dane attempts to climb from the pickup's bed, Chad grabs him. "You dumbass damn fool!" Chad says, shaking Dane, going on, even as Cutter closes in on the vehicle and sees them arguing. "You're drunk. You heard Hank. Barney is like a god, now. If he did have something to do with your pa killing himself, or him taking your pa's money, like you say—with the Klan as short of men, as we are, and the major needing every white man he can get his hands on to stand up against them damn coons—Barney must have had a good reason fer doing what he did to your pa."

Once Cutter reaches the truck, Hank jumps from the cab, races to the passenger-side door and opens it for his god, then circles the battered vehicle, cleans his thick glasses on his shirt sleeve, and slides behind the steering wheel beside Lilly. Hank is eager to drive everyone out of there and into town to get falling-down drunk. The young whore smiles at Cutter and taps her hand on the seat for him to slide in next to her warm body, but Barney doesn't enter the cab. He motions for a glaring Dane to come to him; Dane pushes Chad aside, bounds off the Dodge and stares at Barney, his hands on his hips, his bloodshot eyes filled with hatred. Chad and the men leap to the ground, and Chad stands by his friend.

"Spit it out," Cutter tells first Dane, then eyes Chad, who inches back from them.

Dane slams the empty jar to the ground, shattering it. Inside the truck cab, Lilly looks into the rearview mirror and spit-fingers her eyelashes, as if only her appearance is of interest to her, not a potentially deadly showdown between Barney and Dane. She's seen enough killings to last a lifetime. While Lilly again studies her image in the mirror, Cutter looks at the shattered glass jar on the ground alongside the truck, and then, smiling, he focuses in on Dane. "Breaking canning jars won't solve the problem between us now, will it?" he tells Dane.

"You're the problem!" hisses Dane, shaking his head. "You and Pa's missing two grand!"

"Two grand," says Lilly, her eyes popping open, as she now takes notice from the truck, those money-hungry, snake eyes fixed on Dane, a seductive smile on her sensual lips.

"What two grand?" she asks Hank, who waves her off, his attention on Dane and Barney.

"Up there kissing up to Sarah," hisses Dane to Barney. "She ain't one of us with her educated, perfumed pussy, which got your nose quivering in the damn air around it like a hound sniffing at a bitch in heat. And you, who went away fer months, last year, and left the real business of running the Klan to Pa! What you never knew is that while you was away, Pa let me runs things. Who's gonna run it now when you rejoin that precious army unit of yours?" Barney slaps him, but it doesn't stop the drunken Dane. "What did you say to him? What did you say to cause my pa to blow his head clean off? What did he do to you to cause me to have to hold his bloody, headless body in my arms and beg God to wake me up from that hellish nightmare, that night and every night since? What did you say to make me beg God to make my pa not be headless and dead? What!"

When Dane stops sobbing and yelling, and catches his breath, the other Klansmen look at each other, wondering if Dane's head will be the one blown off next.

"You begged God?" asks Barney.

"Yes, I begged Him, damn you, but He never answered, goddamn Him now, as well!"

"Only fools seek help from a powerless God," Barney hisses, "and only a drunken fool would dare talk to me this way in front of my men."

In a flash, before Dane can blink, Cutter whips out another, recently purchased, Bowie knife from his waist and plants the cold, steel blade against the side of Dane's neck.

"I told your pa I'd let you live, boy," Cutter tells Dane, that icy blade microscopically sliding over Dane's neck sweat, sending electrifying shock waves through the one-eared boy's entire body, the razor-sharp, knife edge peeling away Dane's epidermis. "This is a Bowie knife," the major tells Dane, the others watching in horror and fearing for Dane's life, while Barney coldly goes on. "Sharpened to a military edge, and it can cut through your neck as easy as it can through air, as it's doing now through the thinnest layer of your skin. Do you feel it?"

When Dane, gritting his teeth, can only shake and groan, Barney delivers a quick slice across the one-eared Klansman's cheek, drawing blood, causing the men and Chad to recoil in alarm, with Dane yelling: "My God, Yes! I feel it! Ohh!"

Major Cutter gives him a glaring once over, seconds away from taking Dane's life.

Then someone butts in, and in trying to save Dane's life, says, "Dane was just saying what we all want to know, Major, about how friendly you seem to be to Sarah and her niggers. We're just worried that you will break your promise of getting control of her land and giving us all a share."

"You've corrupted my men, Dane," says the Major. Cutter is enraged all the more and goes on, the blade, again, finding its mark against Dane's neck. "This blade is now resting against one of the most vital parts of your body. No, not your penis, where you do most of your thinking, but against the side of your neck, under which is your carotid artery. Do you know what that is, Dane?" Dane's bulging eyes turn downwards in an attempt to see the blade of the knife, which is once more ever so slowly parting the top layer of his skin and is now stained with his oozing, capillary blood.

"Well, do you?" Cutter asks. Dane blinks in rapid succession. "I take that to mean you don't know," sputters Cutter. "On the train, you said I wasn't as smart as Sarah's father. Remember? Don't move. Just keep blinking your eyes if you do."

As Dane blinks, Cutter slams him to the ground, while inside the cab, Lilly wiggles herself to a climax, squeezing her crossed legs together, and squealing excitedly as she watches Barney looming over Dane exclaiming, "Your carotid lies on both sides of your dumbass, fucking neck! It's the main vessel carrying blood from your heart, and it's under so much pressure that even a puncture as small as a pin prick and your blood will explode from your worthless ass, and you'd be dead before you hit that ground. You want to die, here and now? I run the Klan. Me and no one else!"

Dane shudders helplessly, and after those diabolic, chilling words of Barney, not even a whisper comes from any of the other men, or a sound from the prostitute goggling from the truck window. Sexually excited for a second time, she watches Barney reach down and wipe the blood from his knife onto Dane's fly, then plays with the blade there momentarily before flipping off one of Dane's fly bottoms. The teenage boy crawls beneath the truck, a move which really angers Barney.

"Get back here," he yells at Dane. "Don't you try and escape from me!"

He knows that if Dane gets away from him, there will be more challenges from the men. Knowing that he has to put the fear of the devil into his followers to maintain control of them, Barney does what he had not wanted to do in public, not yet anyway, and that is to reveal just how much power Satan has given to him. Everyone is shocked by what happens next. Major Cutter reaches down with one hand and lifts the truck, tilting it on its side and maintains it there a foot off the ground, and then—with his free hand—he jerks a screaming Dane from under that old vehicle by his leg. Barney releases the Dodge, which comes crashing down onto its passenger-side wheels, scaring the wits out of a bounced-about Hank and Lilly.

Focusing on the tossed-away, broken, moonshine jar, beside which Dane now lies and mutters in trouser-wetting dread, Barney stows his knife and yells down at him. "Take off your shoes, Dane Tucker!" When the petrified boy—after seeing all of that power that's in Barney—is slow to act, Barney rips off Dane's shoes and socks, flings them across the ground, where a horrified Chad quickly picks them up and—in turn—tosses them onto the truck bed to save the precious shoes for his friend. Barney jerks Dane to his feet with one hand, as easy as lifting a baby, and he walks the sobbing, one-eared Klansman barefoot through the glass. "If we have to walk as if on glass until I gain Sarah's trust," Barney chastises his men, "then, by the power of Satan, we will walk on goddamn glass!"

"He's not a god," Chad whispers to the others, while backing away from Barney. "He really is Satan."

All of the disapproving looks fade from the disgruntled men's faces.

"You're our leader," one of the men tells Cutter, while facing down a bleeding Dane, as if blaming him for causing the shaky relationship between them and Barney, a man now seemingly with the power to lay the world before their feet, as he had done with the truck.

More than willing to let his men have a free hand with the one-eared, sobbing boy, Barney returns to the Dodge and slides into the cab, where the prostitute purrs, "I've never seen anything like that in all my life. You're like Samson!" She cuddles up to him. "Now, what's this about two thousand dollars?"

"This long-haired Samson praise of yours," Barney responds coldly to her, "is a waste of your talents." He slaps her. "You see, I have no long hair, so you might as well go fuck yourself, because you're not going to get a cent of this money. You goddamn conniving bitch!"

"I'd rather fuck you, not masturbate," she says, undaunted. "Come to Mama."

He slaps her, again, this time across her mouth. "Don't you ever tell me to 'come to Mama!' Ever! Anything but that."

In a rage, Lilly slaps him again and again. Then Barney slaps her, and they violently and passionately kiss and groan, grappling at each other's bodies; as they do, the Klansmen push Dane into the back of the vehicle and climb in behind him. Having kept out of Amos and Andy's sight, a thirty-year-old man called "One-leg Trout"—with his peg leg, after being helped onto the truck bed—attempts to comfort a sobbing Dane. "Keep away from him, Trout," one of the men yells. "He's a fuckup!" Not one to wish for trouble, Trout hobbles to a neutral corner and remains there, as Chad, the last to climb aboard, scolds his friend:

"Are you insane?" Chad asks Dane, once aboard the truck. "Don't ever do that again. I'm not walking on glass, and not ready to die with you. Did you see how strong that man is? Did you?"

The only one willing to help Dane now is Hank, who's disgusted at the sight of Barney and Lilly's ravenous lovemaking. He slides from the cab, then climbs onto the back with the other Klansmen. Adjusting his wire-rimmed glasses, Hank locates one of his oil rags on the truck bed, and with it wipes the blood from Dane's feet and the vomit from the one-eared boy's shirt. "Why are you helping me?" the angry, frightened boy asks. "The others wouldn't."

"Yeah, Hank," exclaims one of the men. "He got what he damn well deserved."

"It's what that woman did fer Christ in the Bible," says Hank. "Washed the feet of Jesus. Isn't that what Reverend Miller preaches fer us to do? Dane's white and our brother. Not some coon. Don't you guys get me wrong about Barney. He's my best friend, but . . ." Hank looks through the rear window into the cab at the wrestling grunting pair, then toward the empty cemetery, whispering, he goes on, ". . . he's in that cab, a second after leaving the cemetery and still at Sarah Winthrop's front door. Seems to me that's a godly sin, but we all saw him and that unnatural strength of his. Barney no longer believes in God. I'm just playing both ends against the middle by helping Dane here just in case one or the other wins out in the world, God or the devil. I have never seen God, but damn ifin' we all haven't gotten a good look at the power of Lucifer; he lives in Barney." Hank sees Dane's shoes on the truck and gives them to him, then gives him a warning. "I'll speak to Barney fer you out of respect fer your dead pa, Dane, but you better watch that drunken mouth of yours and listen to Chad or you'll end up losing that other ear of yours or worse. The major knows what he's doing when it comes to running the Klan, anyway, if not his outlook on God."

Still too stubborn to listen to anyone when it comes to him hating Barney, Dane looks through the rear truck window and whispers, "If loving Satan gave him all that strength, then I'll also worship the devil. Fuck Barney and his offer of this so-called land-grab money; he will never give us anything, him and that fucking Sarah Winthrop. I hate her too with her stuck-up ass."

One-leg Trout leaves his neutral corner of the truck and looks into the cab at the groaning couple, then at the cemetery, and then at Dane. "I've worked fer that sweet girl's family fer more years than you were born, Dane Tucker, and never had a finer family fer a boss. Doctor Winthrop desperately loved Sarah and Marilyn, in part because of their kindness, especially about how they loved the stars in the sky, and that whole family worshiped our Lord." Again he looks in the cab, then whispers to Dane, "You're lucky to be live, so don't push it by tempting God to strike you down with lightning, by saying you'll worship the devil, like he's doing in that truck, and lay off of Sarah. She's done you no harm." He faces old half-blind Hank. "Now, if you don't mind, Hank, tell Barney to please button it up, and let's get out of here befer one of the workers comes along and sees me with you guys and destroys any chance I'd have of holding onto my job out here, especially if Barney fails to marry that child."

Hank returns to the truck cab. The lady of night quickly adjusts her lifted dress. She glares at Hank and then faces Barney. "Enough of this playing around," she hisses. "Will she or won't Sarah marry you?"

"I hold all of the cards," Cutter says, closing his fly. "She knows it. End of conversation."

"After you marry this young chicken, will you forget about me?"

"Now, what do you think?" Barney says, kissing her, both wildly sucking at the other's lips. Hank switches on the ignition, grinds the gears, and the chattering truck is quickly driven away.

That night, Sarah resides in her grandmother's quarters in bed with Naomi and cries herself to sleep in the kindly woman's arms. In time, Naomi also falls asleep. As the hours pass, Naomi is awakened, not by the sound of a grandfather clock striking four in the morning in a distant wing of the manor, she awakened from sensing that something is wrong. Sitting up in bed, her eyes adjusting to the dark, she sees Sarah at the westerly window, in her nightgown. The young girl is aglow in moonlight and gazing at the twisted remains of the *White Dove*, her faithful field hands and several of Sheriff Richards' investigating deputies—thinking that those residing in the manor are fast asleep—are as silently as possible loading the plane wreckage onto a flatbed truck. They then haul it away. Naomi picks up two housecoats, slips into one and moves in behind Sarah with the other and places it about the teen's shoulders. Without looking around, Sarah whispers: "I was thinking about killing myself."

"I know," whispers Naomi.

"At the cemetery, the major asked me to marry him."

"I also know that," Naomi again whispers.

Sarah locks gazes with the mystery woman, crosses her arms over her chest and shivers while sadly scanning the room with fright reflected in her eyes. "Grandmother and Grandfather are gone. And now, Mother and Father are as well. This place is so suddenly cold." When Naomi stokes up dying embers in the fireplace, Sarah steps close to the crackling oak logs, going on. "About the major, Naomi, even the Hunchback of Notre Dame can appear handsome if a person tries hard to see him that way," she reasons to Naomi, clearly never believing a word of it, while trying to convince herself into believing that she could be marrying an even worse man than Barney, the tears flowing from her disappointed eyes. After waiting for Naomi to expand on the subject and she does not, Sarah continues. "He's the leader of the Klan. Henry says Barney killed his parents and I believe him." Naomi still remains deadly silent. "You were groaning in your sleep, Naomi. Where you having a bad dream? I was."

"Yes, Sarah. I was dreaming, but not a bad one. It was a dream like no other."

Sarah, tearfully looking up and about, whispers, "I dreamt I was standing at an altar of snakes and married to a monster, and after I married that man, I was standing under one of our oak trees, where I often had stood with my father, and one of the oak branches fell off and crushed me. I never said goodbye to my father. Did you know that, Naomi? And now, even you can see that I'm not strong, not worth this attention from heaven. How can I go on? To run this place and make sure our colored workers are taken care of the same as the whites? How can I have hope? Even mother acknowledges that this is a man's world.

"Powerful men like Barney start wars, kill at will, and the sheriff and our court look the other way. Naomi, the only solace that I can expect from life as Barney's wife, the only hope I would ever have to overcome my fears of him and the trepidation of living in this huge house without my mother and father is to live every moment of my life thinking that Father is still here with me in this house and . . ." Her voice trails off, and then she continues. "To me, my father could stand as tall and be as strong as any of our beautiful oak trees with his incorruptible goodness, but Barney is possessed, some say, as you yourself have as good as said in the past, that he has the power of Satan in him. The workers even whisper that Barney is a man who can tear down this land's mighty oak trees with his bare hands, if Satan chooses him to do so, and they are so afraid of him."

Naomi raises her hand and the young girl becomes voiceless. A few minutes pass, and Naomi looks at Sarah.

"Do you still trust me, child?"

"Oh yes, Naomi."

She guides Sarah into one of the wingback chairs. Naomi then sits down in the other chair, in front of her. "Then listen carefully, child. Everything that is in all of creation is blended into everything else, the air, the mountain, the rainfall, the deserts, the stars, everything on this earth and beyond. Nothing is unto itself or has a sharp paper-edge line that keeps everything else out. As evil as Barney Cutter is, he cannot shut out the fact that God is real and Barney, in spite of himself, will always struggle with that fact. Sweetheart, a bush is only a small tree, a tree is but a towering, giant bush, and man is somewhere in between. You need not fear either one of them, the tree, the bush or Barney." Naomi strokes the side of Sarah's soft cheek.

"Now, I'm going to tell you about the dream I just had. It's both frightening and glorious. It's about your folks." As they talk, Sarah takes Naomi's strong, reddish-brown hands into her delicate white ones, sometimes sadly holding on, sometimes joyously, sometimes afraid, sometimes in tears, the young girl leans forward in the chair, her eyes intense, the moonlight streaming through the windows onto them, as Naomi infuses her charge with the courage to go on.

7

Embedded with the Daughter of Lucifer

While Sarah is being empowered with the will to go on, the Dodge—driven by old Hank—rattles through Cutterville, that town of iniquity founded by Barney's ancestors and now controlled by Dessen, the despised Jewish factory owner: Cutterville is a place not only in a rage because of the number of factory jobs that have been given to blacks, it is deeply divided between the unemployed whites and those whites who work in Dessen's factory alongside the scorned non-whites. As Hank drives through the town in his old Dodge, Barney slams his fist against the dashboard, startling the old driver and the intoxicated, hot-dog-eating Lilly riding along with them.

"Fucking bitch witch!" Barney explodes. "Who the hell does she think she is? You're a filthy, monthly-blood-gushing, piss-ass woman!" The drunken prostitute thinks Major Cutter means her, but soon realizes that he's talking about Naomi. Cutter raves on, aggravating Lilly. "Fucking, bitch servant to kiss my white ass if I ask you to, and those smart-ass, goddamn, so-called, all-seeing, nigger eyes that them other cotton heads say you have, better see that Sarah is not your fucking business and stop sniffing around her all the time, Naomi, fucking bitch, and I mean real soon, or I'll cut out those big, snooping eyes of yours and have my men stick their dicks up your nose, in your ears and in that big mouth of yours so fast, you'll wish you were dead."

"Enough, Barney." Lilly screams, breaking in on top of Barney's degrading verbal flow of disgust. "Up her ear? Her nose? I don't like that kind of talk. Maybe up her butt, but not that other."

Barney continues, inadvertently taking his clue from Lilly. "And then I'll give you a butt whipping that you will never forget! This is a white man's goddamn world, not the fucking jungles of Africa, you fucking, black, nigger fool!"

Cutterville's streets are like a jungle, with few streetlights and no traffic lights, dark and gloomy. When the truck approaches Sue Ann's Main Street bar, Lilly has had enough of Barney's filthy ranting and raving.

"Why are you looking at me like that, bitch?" he shouts at her.

"Because I want to, and if you don't shut up I'll keep my legs closed tonight good and tight, when you drop by, until I'm good and ready to open them, and not when you're ready all the time. I own you with this fine, slim body of mine and you know it!"

"Bitch! Not even that pussy of yours is made of gold! Until it is, close your damn mouth."

"You go to hell, Barney Cutter. Whatever that black woman did or said to you, maybe she had a right to. You should learn to treat women with respect and go to church more often. Devil worship my rear end. You were raised a Baptist by your saintly mother, and a zebra can't change its stripes and neither can you. You believe in God the same as I do. The only thing you worship more is yourself. You make me crazy sometimes. You even defame God, so let me out of this damn truck."

"She's right, Barney," pleads Hank. Hank was once a college professor until he drank himself out of his tenure, as well as out of his mind. His hair to his shoulders, his bifocals like Coke bottles, his eyes hard and unfeeling, he seems to respect no one but Barney, the only exception he makes is when it comes to Lilly. He sees her as the child he never had. With his front tooth missing, he gums his words and spread spittle when he talks. As Barney glares across Lilly at him, Hank doesn't back off.

"Our friendship or not, Barney, I'll say it again, Lilly's right," sputters Hank, even though he's still fearful of Barney, remembering the way he lifted the truck and what he did to Dane, and so would Lilly be afraid of Barney, but for the fact that she's been drinking moonshine and is half out of her mind. She giggles as Hank goes on, cautiously spelling out his case. "You used to be a gentleman; and now this business about the devil and . . ." Barney swings his leg over Lilly's ankles, slams his foot on the brake, bringing the pickup to a dipping, screeching stop, which sends Lilly smashing against the dashboard and Hank onto the steeling wheel.

"Open the damn door," yells Cutter when the truck stalls, "and get the hell out! Both of you!"

"Wait a damn minute, Barney. This is my damn truck!" Hank hisses.

"Now, dammit! Out!"

The disheartened old man opens the driver's-side door and steps onto the night-dark street.

"I'm not going anyplace until I'm good and damn ready," an angry Lilly hisses.

"Good," says Barney. He puts his back against the passenger's-side door, lifts his leg, and kicks the young woman past the steeling wheel and out the door and onto the street.

"You ready now!" Barney yells, going on. "You got a lot of balls, you little witch, coming between me and Hank that way. The Klan doesn't take advice from some ignorant whore who says I'm making her crazy, a bitch who hasn't brains enough to know that I'm a man who loves a woman like you only as long as I'm burning up with desire and packed with sperm, and once I ejaculates them into someone like you, I sees you as any other bitch, as just so much meat. On top of that, you bitch, telling me to go to church. Churches are for fools searching in the dark for a god to light their way around Satan, a god that's not and never will be there for you. Yes, I worship myself. Who else will do that if not me? You, who lives only for sex? Don't ever tell me what to do or question my motives. Ever! I'm doing that enough to my own goddamn self with this Sarah business and my mother's reaction."

"Okay, Barney. Now, calm down," says Hank helping the stunned whore off of the street.

Wobbling on her high heels, her head tilted to the side, her suggestive green eyes unafraid, threatening, yet sassy and inviting at the same time, Lilly squints at Barney. "I came between you and Hank, yes, but you also did something to me too, tonight, that you shouldn't be proud of." She tells him and then turns to Hank. "He kicked me out of that truck like I was nothing but a sack of nigger potatoes to him." Her bedeviling eyes refocus on Barney. "But that's okay, Barney Cutter. I guess it's just part of the business of bedding down with a white cracker like you to survive in this one-horse town. Maybe a black man across the tracks would treat a white woman better. They certainly have bigger dicks. I need a drank."

She brushes herself off, lights up a cigarette, and wobbles toward Sue Ann's nearby bar. "I'll return your truck tomorrow, Hank," Cutter tells his friend, without taking his sights off of the swaggering whore, as she opens the bar door, then leers back at him. Hank follows Barney's glaring gaze to the well-proportioned female until she disappears into the bar, then he looks at Barney.

"Lilly, she didn't mean what she said about them coons across the tracks, no matter how drunk she is or how much money some of them darkies are making in that factory now. She was just mad at you and kidding, that's all. Wasn't she, Barney?"

"I know that."

"Barney, did you mean it about God not being with us? Do you really believe in the devil, now, like you say or are you just jerking our chain? Or were you just mad all of these months, like Lilly was when she said that about the coons' dicks? Barney, you as good as said God ain't shit. Please tell me you really don't mean any of that devil-worshipping stuff. It was a drug of some kind from Miller's church that gave you the strength to lift my truck, wasn't it, and not the devil?"

Cutter just stares at him, then slides behind the wheel, restarts the motor, closes the door in Hank's face and drives away.

"Drive careful, Major Cutter. That's my livelihood," calls Hank, as he's left behind in the dust. Hank faces the bar. "I need a drank," he says, making his way to his and the prostitutes' daily bread, the liquid answer to their prayers.

Cutterville's prostitutes have a saying that by using their heads and what they have between their legs, they will make it through the night with or without prayers. However, with half of Cutterville's whites in danger of losing their homes, not everyone feels they will make it through the night or through the day. They fill Reverend Miller's church every Sunday and pray that God will save them and their homes, but if the truth be known, every one would gladly sell his soul to Satan for rain or for the price of a drink. Drunken white men, guzzling brain-numbing moonshine from canning jars, stagger through the dusty streets and wave to Cutter, as he drives by them, a few blocks from Sue Ann's bar. Gathered near the men are a dozen young white boys, who also are moonshine-gulping from jars.

"Hey, Major," one of the boys calls out. It's Chad, Dane's best friend. He continues calling to Barney, who slows the truck to a creep and focuses on the boy. "Major, did you hear? Some Yankee brothers with Catholic-sounding names—from that nigger-lovin' California—are getting the jump on the end of this Yankee law that puts us in jail fer making moonshine. The radio says them California brothers are coming out with a cheap wine to sale to the ghetto niggers up North to tie up the wine market. Ah!"

With no desire to go home to face his mother, Barney stops the truck across from the boys.

"And guess what, Major?" Chad goes on, momentarily relieving Barney of thoughts of what awaits him at home. Chad flaps his arms as if he were a bird. "Their wine's called 'Thunderbird,' and they even gave it a jingle." Even with all of his three-hundred pounds of body weight, Chad manages to jump up and down and lift his moonshine jar toward Barney, smiling in drunken giddiness.

"Guess what else?" one of the other besotted boys says. "We made a better jingle out of their jingle." He then delivers their inebriated limerick, all of the boys' jars held high. "What's the word? Thunderbird! What's the reason? Grapes in season. What's the price? Thirty twice! How are they drinking it? By the cup. What will it do? Fuck you up!" Giggling, arms stretched out, the boys spin in a dizzying circle. "We can fly," they all yell.

No one flies out of Cutterville. They end up staying there all their lives. This night, the boys end up with half of their numbers falling down, as they spin and laugh themselves silly. At least one of their group, however, seeing the futility of it all, sits down on the sidewalk, his collectable Dodgers baseball cap pulled tightly onto his head, his legs bent to his chest, his arms embracing his knees, as he rocks back and forth, crying like a little girl: He's none other than Dane Tucker, still holding onto the memories of cradling his bloody, beheaded father in his arms, and haunted by the thing of his nightmare hidden under his cap.

"Pa! Pa!" he wails, giving his friends pause to wonder, then they, too, begin crying.

Barney Cutter gazes back at Dane, then turns away and looks straight ahead. In spite of having a reputation of being a heartless bastard and a killer, Cutter is profoundly troubled, but not out of compassion for Dane Tucker. Sympathy for Dane had passed the second Barney had discovered that photo of Dane's father. Barney would have killed Dane with Horace to protect family members of the Klan, but for the fact that Dane is so unsightly with his one ear, buck teeth, big eyes and skin problems that none of the local white girls or the white prostitutes will let Dane get near them; only an occasional black whore from across the train tracks will sleep with him and only then for the right price. For this reason, Barney is in no hurry to expose Dane to the others, so that they can tear him apart.

Mayor Cutter has yet to determine how to use the boy for the good of the sheeted organization; he will, however, in his own good time, personally take care of Dane after the others get their turn at him. Naomi had hinted to Sarah that Barney cannot totally dismiss the fact that God is real, and that Barney will always struggle with that nagging feeling. As Cutter sits in the truck, parked next to Main Street Square, he finds himself troubled with thoughts of having killed Lawrence and Marilyn. Even the blacks across the tracks rarely killed or robbed other blacks. But he, Barney Cutter, after sabotaging their plane, had lingered among the citrus grove and had watched the Winthrops and the *White Dove* explode and burn, had seen Marilyn fall flailing from the plane and had watched her land on her stomach, then rebound, from the impact, onto her back, spilling out her blood onto the white flowers. He had witnessed how devastated Sarah was as she stood up on that wagon beside that priest and that evil black woman, Naomi, all of them looking up at the sky as if asking their God why He had let Sarah's parents die.

Can whites go around killing whites? Barney ponders, *without ending up in a lower caste than the blacks? Did he, Barney Cutter, kill them because he is pure evil?* Barney shivers. He dreads the thought of what his mother will tell him once he gets home, that he's absolutely evil. But that's okay, he forces himself to believe. He's been promised by the guardian of the most divine force on earth, hatred, that he'll become the most powerful man alive, and that has to be worth it at any cost.

On the other hand, Barney thinks about the future of Cutterville's young people drinking themselves into insanity. He himself drinks too much. He knows that and he knows something else: Nothing stays the same. History has proven it. Even in the South, even with the Klan's relentless killing of the blacks, how long can the Klan survive if young whites and young blacks become too friendly, like the white and the colored boy at the funeral with their dandelions? The military is slow to change, but change it also will. Cutter feels that he should be a full colonel by now, and that promotions have been withheld from him by the general staff because of his connection with the Klan.

His troubled sights shifts to an alley across from him, near the drunken white boys. An anorexic dog, searching for morsels of food in the darkened passageway, is occasionally returning to and sniffing a passed-out, hopelessly drunk, pale man and his urine-and-feces-soaked clothing. Again, Barney Cutter shivers. He turns away in alarm. After having been assured it would never happen, he fears that without a war, the service will eventually discharge him and others like him, a discharge that might even happen before he can pull off his devil-inspired intelligence *coup d'etat* and make his fortune with the double-dealing army paying the bill for his success. Failing that, if he is discharged, as he dreads, he feels that the same fate awaits him and his mother as the alley dog—that he and she will become homeless and be forced to live off welfare or eat garbage, especially if the coloreds aren't eliminated from the factory jobs and even from Cutterville.

Staggering from the alley, the dog drifts toward Barney. Glancing at the rest of Lilly's half-eaten hot dog, which she has left on the seat, Barney—still upset with Lilly—seizes the hot dog and flings it at the four-legged creature and quickly rolls up the truck window. As the dog wolfs down the tossed food, mustard and all, a rumbling sound permeates the air and quivers through the street and the truck, a sound stemming from Dessen's factory, from his expensive, massive, rubber-crushing, churning motors and machinery, which vibrates everything within a block and a half of the building. Accompanying the vibration are clouds of blue smoke with the acrid smell of newly cooked rubber tires about it.

Cutter bitterly sizes up Dessen's eight-story, redbrick factory, a stone's throw away. To Barney, the plant is telling the world that blacks are as good as whites, the irritating smoke spewing from the roof's many chimneys irritating his lungs, adding to the insult. Barney shakes his fist at the sprawling factory and at the bustling workers inside the building, whose shadows occasionally pass by the towering windows.

"Work, you spineless, white-bastardized pigs. You'd be better off out here with real white men facing a million hardships rather than remain in that damn Jew's factory alongside the niggers!" Slamming his foot on the gas pedal, he roars away, nearly running over the fleeing dog.

After squealing hairpin turns and a straightaway down a dark, bumpy road, Cutter eases the steam-spewing truck to a stop next to a wire fence—a posted fence, which reads: CUTTER PLANTATION KEEP THE HELL OUT. Sixty yards beyond the wire fence is the three-story Victorian—which Naomi had viewed from the *White Dove*, and at which Sarah had refused to look. A wall of Italian cypresses blanket themselves around the house, twenty such ghostly-looking trees, some with a spread of six feet and a height of forty feet, trees bending in the wind and brushing their thickly packed dirt and spider-infested branches against the old house's windows. The aging Victorian is silhouetted against a dog-piss-yellow moon, a dirty, earthen color of distortion brought on by Georgia's best countywide topsoil eroding in the wind. Cutter climbs from the truck, opens the gate, drives onto his mother's property, stops, alights, closes the gate, springs back into the Dodge and dips the old pickup to a stop at the house's porch. He somberly slides from the cab, makes his way up the squeaky steps, and enters the home he hates and can no longer maintain on his officer's pay.

To save money on the electrical bill, Barney uses as little electricity as possible, and he turns off the chandelier and wall lights once he's inside the residence and instead, fires up a kerosene lamp. Sadly gazing about as the lamp floods the room with its weak, yellowish illumination and pungent, kerosene smell and smoke, Barney Cutter would rather be anywhere else, at this moment, than in the house of his mother.

At first glance it's difficult to understand why the house is so revolting to him. Even with the poor lighting—unlike the house's exterior—the interior structure is a stunning example of what life was once like for the Cutters. A fourteen-foot-high ceiling and beautifully carved crown moldings loom overhead. Centuries' old oriental carpets line the hardwood, oak floor, and glorious hand-painted pictures of the whitest of white, rosy-cheeked cherubs—winged-head ones, including full-bodied, winged, naked ones—elegantly beautify the fresco walls.

The once-breathtaking house—especially constructed after those in San Francisco and graced with channel-back, mohair couches and fine Chippendale—was once the pride of Georgia and visited by only the most influential families, including the Winthrops from time to time. The guests drank and dined like royalty. Now, the frayed, burgundy draperies lining the bay windows alone woefully testify that time has passed the old place by, as Major Cutter has always feared it would. Of late, the front room has been turned into sleeping quarters, because of the large, wood-burning, marble fireplace there, which is a great benefit to his mother.

Mixing with the smell of the kerosene there is a thick, sickening stench of urine and feces in the air. Barney looks across the room irritably at a walnut, four-posted, Duncan-Phyfe, canopy bed with a matching footstool, a high and low, claw-foot dresser set, a freestanding peer glass, and an antique wash basin. The bed canopy is slid aside by bony fingers, exposing a frail-looking, pale, white-haired woman, the same woman

99

who Naomi saw sitting on the porch and glaring up at the *White Dove* with Cutter. A blanket over her lap, she is sitting up in bed on a bedpan.

"You're late," she says, "and you know I don't like the dark. Turn the lights back on."

"I'm here, now, Mother and the lights remain off. We're not made of money."

"Why are you being so nasty, and why are you late? You know it pains me to sit here and wait for you to return."

"Please, Mother, let's do this and get it over with. Are you finished with it?"

"No."

She coughs into a handkerchief, makes herself more comfortable on the bedpan and says, "Now, you wait, as I had to wait." She leans back against the carved headboard and scowls at him, reflecting her displeasure at his tardiness. "You've been to the Winthrops' place spying on that young girl again, haven't you? Is that why you went out and bought this?"

She tosses a black tuxedo, shirt, shoes, and bowtie from the bed at him. They end up on the floor at his feet with Barney looking down at them. "You've been in my room again."

"This is still my house," she exclaims. "And you, wanting to strut around in that expensive-bought party suit when the town is struggling to put food on the table. Why spend good money that way? Never mind. Just quit the damn military, you hear, and you ferget this foolish scheme of yours of getting your hands on millions from those northern generals and white, political crackers." She then tosses one of his deceased father's pin-striped suits, along with the dead man's hat and old shoes, at Barney.

"Wear those clothes, and be thankful to have them, if you're so worried about saving money by turning off the lights, not that expensive black thing and shoes, and as fer your get-rich plans, there isn't that much money left in the whole country to hear the government tell it."

"Oh, there is, Mother, and at the right time, the right place, and under the right conditions a mountain of military funds has to be available during catastrophe events or a war. If a person is real lucky, a world war, with thousands of soldiers waiting to be paid in cash. I've thought it all out."

"With your mind, you can do better by thinking as an engineer and

100

rebuild this place. The drought and effects of the Depression will end soon. Our Lord won't make us endure more than we can handle."

"Don't be a hypocrite, Mother," he says. "God left this house a long time ago. And as for God, the coons have been saying He will make a way for them to be free since they were shipped here from Africa in chains. They're free all right. Now we rent them instead of owning then. Forget about God like I've told you to do a thousand times over."

"No, you ferget about that," she yells pointing at the tux. "Buying that suit, hoping that young girl will see how handsome you look in it. Is that it?"

"I'm renting it, Mother, not buying it."

"Why? I'm not dead yet."

"Not for a funeral. For a wedding."

Her heart skips, and she pretends not to have heard him mention marriage. "Sixteen-thousand acres weren't good enough fer that family," she says, changing the subject from talk of marriage. "They as good as killed your pa by stealing his plots out there and joining them to theirs now."

Barney closes his eyes in disgust. She knows why: marriage. Also knowing he'll keep bringing up the subject, she decides to attack him head-on about it. "During this Depression you're talking about going to a wedding." Her voice trails off. Shifting about on the bedpan, she prays that the talk of a wedding is about someone else's and not that of her son's. She continues. "This is a time when we need all our money and energy to be used on us, not on fancy clothes for someone else's shotgun mistake."

"Not someone else's," he says. "And I've not gotten anyone pregnant. I'm getting . . ."

Putting up her hand and fanning it across her face, she's telling him that she doesn't want to hear anymore; now it is she who closes her eyes and holds her head stiffly in place in a show of disgust: everything is coming too fast for her to handle.

"Okay, Mother, no talk about renting that suit," he tells her, "but the word is 'bought' when it comes to Sarah's father. Lawrence bought those plots. He didn't steal them. And I'd have been a lot more civil to him on that damn train in front of Sarah if I hadn't made such a drunken fool of myself. What's laughable, I actually think I could have learned to like the man, but what's done is done. He had one of the most brilliant minds you'll find in all of Georgia, maybe in this country. Think of the genius offspring that family's bloodline will create in this world of halfwits. As for father, he was a bigger fool than I ever was to sell that land in the first place, this Depression or not."

"Stop calling him, 'father.' He was your pa, not some Catholic priest!" She throws a pillow at him and gestures to a nearby table on which rests a large Bible. She reaches out, seizes the Bible, kisses it, and replaces it on the table. "The Good Book says call no man 'Father!' And don't you ever talk about your pa like that again! He wasn't the educated parent like Mister god-almighty, rich, doctor-trained L. T. Winthrop—or whatever his full name was—or like that college-professor wife of his was. Your pa knew nothing about selling land and got taken in by those people. He wanted that land to go to you, Barney."

"I know, Mother. You've told me often enough how he spent his whole life trying to improve our land for you and me. How he—"

"Not fer me. Fer you! Your pa is in his grave, and I won't live ferever. Now all you think about is Sarah Winthrop and improving yourself to impress her and not about this house and me."

"Look at this place, Mother. Our ancestors would die all over again if they knew that the last of their line to inherit their land where no more than dumb dirt farmers, left only with this house and thirty acres and a mule, the same as promised their freed damn slaves by the goddamn Yankees!"

"Your pa and I didn't work our fingers to the bone to send you to that goddamn academy so that you could become an intelligent officer and compare us to slaves and call him a fool. No, Sir!"

Barney throws up his arms in disgust. "We're called, 'That white trash family' even by those black apes across the train tracks, because—even with this house and pitiful piece of land—from where we once were and now are, to them tar babies, we're no better off than they are!"

"Then say it! You want to be like the Winthrops, not like me! The town says even as young as she is, this Sarah is some kind of genius. Evil is what I call it. Can speak and read Latin like them evil priests of old, and only Satan knows what else that Catholic girl can do. But you. Can you even understand a word of Latin? No! And you never will, no matter how much you want to, or how you been promoted to major of intelligence." She shakes her finger at him.

102

"Stay away from her, son. This Depression is making you demented. I know we don't serve fancy dinners or have guests in the house like the Cutters in the past, but these hard times aren't called a Depression for nothing. It's also knocked half of those so-called higher-class folks in this country down to our level, including the Winthrops. You'll always be white trash to those people, since we fell further from the social graces than the others."

"It wasn't that, Mother and you know it. Those friends of yours found out what you did in this house and what it turned me into."

"Reverend Miller says that young girl is damned just by being a Winthrop," she says trying to change the subject.

"The hell with Reverend Miller and his damn church of snakes."

"You didn't say that as a boy, when you adored God in his church and received his blessings of love with the other kids, most of who are still attending his services today as adults."

"Those drugged-up, drunken white fools going to that idiotic church with their moonshine jars in one hand and praying for work, while their other hand is shelling out their hard-earned pennies to Miller in the name of some unseen god. Miller doesn't love them, me or you, only money, and he's doing a damn good job in getting the little those uneducated white dummies have left. But if it takes what he's doing—standing with one foot in his God's yard of obedience and poverty, and the other foot in the devil's yard of wealth and power—to get his congregation to join the Klan, I'll keep going to that church, and I'll kiss a snake's ass if Miller'll hold its head. And, whether you admit it or not, Mother, you're the same as I am—walking in Satan's shadow—and we both know what I mean. So stop taking as if you're a damn saint. But you taught me one thing. It takes godless powers, not god-full love to control people, the way you controlled my father and me."

"Control your pa? Unseen God? What's wrong with you? You have lost your mind!"

"The Winthrop name carries that kind of power recognition and more, enough to conquer the world without so-called Divine intervention."

"There is Divine power, son. And we have a chance to return to God's embrace no matter what happened in this house. Have faith."

Hearing only his own thoughts, not her empty words in which even she doesn't believe, he says, "The race to control this planet is already underway. A German called Hitler is trying hard to do just that. Conquer Europe first, then the world. Our department has tracked this Adolf person for years." Barney faces the cherub wall. "And I'm quite sure this Hitler isn't planning on conquering the globe with a bunch of naked, winged angels guiding his footsteps. Mother, don't let plaster and little, painted people and some invisible Savior of yours guide you through life or tell you that your sins are all forgiven, when you know better than I that that's impossible." A profound silence falls over his mother. "I guess I better empty that bedpan now before you develop another bedsore," he tells her as she sits on the enamel pan, sadly regarding her wall of cherubs.

"Did you kill them, Barney? That girl's mother and father, to get to her? Is that what makes you act this way, your conscience?"

He has a love-hate relationship with his mother. Now—under the kinder side of their up-and-down bond—Barney is ready to say anything, to lie, steal or kill to keep her from suffering, with the belief that he murdered whites. "It was an accident," he says. "The coroner and Sheriff Richards said it was accidental. That fancy plane of theirs, it just—bang!—Blew up."

"Good," she says. "Then whether you know it or not, you still believe in God. Kill coons, yes. Kill them all if you feel they're out to harm whites, but never kill your brothers and sisters. Now, don't tell me anymore, Barney. I don't want to be escorted to heaven by the angels, when I die, and then have to face my God and explain that many details to Him about you. And He will ask you, too, when you die, so make sure you can righteously justify all of your killing in His name." She relaxes against the headboard, inhales and closes her eyes. "Now, let's talk no more of religion or of marriage. Okay, son?"

"Mother, I didn't tell you earlier, because of your attitude toward Sarah, but tomorrow I have to rejoin my section, and I've arranged for a six-week leave, because after the six weeks, our department will be relocated to New Mexico on another of those damn top-secret projects."

"No! You can't go! And leave me alone again? You know how sickly and weak I am."

"I have my orders. We're about to be dragged into the war in Europe—regardless of what those political fools in Washington and that big, polio cripple who wants to be President says. What I told you is not to be repeated. Our team may be away for as long as a year, and before I

104

leave for that godforsaken desert, Sarah will be my wife. There are tremendous benefits in such an arrangement for me and you and—"

Eyes popped wide, arms flailing, spilling its contents, Mrs. Cutter bounds off the bedpan, her wrinkled, red buttocks exposed, staining the sheet brown. Her so-called weak body and legs are a blur as she barefoots down the step stool, sails through the air and ends up spread-legged on the carpet in front of Barney, her spit spraying him in the face.

"You truly have lost your mind!" she yells. "Isn't it enough that you run off to that damn, military unit of yours fer months on end? Now you say you'll marry the damn enemy and—I guess—leave me here to die alone, while you sleep in Doctor Winthrop's bed with his young daughter as a bonus to your reproach against heaven, God and your father's plan to destroy Jews and all dark-skinned people in this damn county, not just the niggers, and that includes Catholics! Son, as a boy, you cried when animals were hurt, and crying was a godly thing to do, but back then you also spoke fondly of Satan and struggled between good and evil. Don't let evil recapture your soul now."

"One Reverend Miller in Cutterville is enough, Mother. I also cried when Father whipped me for—as you say—being evil. He wasn't like that until he joined Miller's goddamn church. Among other things, he beat me, because one day he walked into the bathroom when I was sixteen and saw that I had an erection. He saw a clear liquid dripping from my penis. I had no idea what it was. He shouted that I was too old now to be around you, Mother, and after that he broke all the mirrors in the house and made me wear gloves and a blindfold whenever I took a bath or urinated. And Mother, he also forced you to blindfold yourself when you bathed, after he said God told him not to have sex again, that he was a disciple and had to remain chaste for the remainder of his life. But him! He sat there and watched you and never blindfolded himself. I saw him, many a night, sitting in the hallway outside the bathroom door watching you with his hungry eyes, at the same time, softly sobbing and praying to his phony God to forgive him for having weak flesh. His erection, Mother! And his sperm! All over the place!"

"We never told you this, your pa and me, but at night, when it was dark in this house, he and I cried." She glances about the room. "Something lives in this house at night, something evil. Your father didn't want to hurt you, son. He said he had to save you from Satan, and now these things are in this house."

"Things?" Barney says, fed up with her. "Maybe you put them there with your mind. Stop reading that Bible and stuff." He glances at her Bible.

"You're outside their reach, Barney. They fear he which dwells in you."

"Outside of what? And whatever dwells in me, you put there. You, Mother, put it there!"

She closes her eyes, her lips quivering, her eyeballs darting about under her squeezed-shut eyelids, her legs quaking. Opening her eyes, she reaches out and attempts to kiss him, the smell of excrement on her, and he steps back.

"I know your pa tied you up and beat you, but befer he died he asked fer your fergiveness."

"I will never forgive him to the day I die."

"Don't say that, son. Barney, you've hardened yourself against all love, even mine."

"Love!" he hisses, turning his back on her.

"Yes, even my love," she exclaims. "That's why you can't marry that child."

"Mother!" he says facing her. "You know I love you, but only as a son to his mother. But you changed all of that when I was only ten and younger."

He attempts to get her half-exposed body back in bed. "After I'm married, I'll look in on you with some money from time-to-time and—"

"You keep your money," she says, slapping his face.

"Mother! I've had all I can take thinking about that Naomi bitch tonight! Stop this and get your ass back in bed!"

"No!" she yells, slapping him again. "Don't you dare talk to me that way. Your pa would roll over in his grave if he heard you talk of marrying that Winthrop, little bitch. Yes, she's a whore, if the likes of you want to marry her. You've been sexing her, haven't you? Don't lie to me. You finally learned what that erection of your was meant fer after your pa saw it in the bathroom. How long has this been going on? This business of you and Sarah?"

He starts to slap her, but lowers his hand. "The hell with Pa and you, Ma! That's none of your damn business. I'm a man, not a boy anymore."

"Now he's 'Pa' and I'm 'Ma!' Not 'Father,' since you lost your false pretense in anger of me. Did you also lose your sperm inside that Winthrop girl, the way you accused your pa of losing his?"

"Whatever you call him or whatever you and he did to me, Pa wasted his life digging and crawling around on this dirty land like some common, nigger sharecropper. He hated this place and wanted to sell it to the Winthrops with the other plots and move to California, but you made him stay here, working his heart out, and it killed him."

"Your pa loved this place. I couldn't let him go to California where them niggers run wild in Los Angeles, and men act like women in San Francisco. He died of a heart attack after he sold our land to them Winthrops. He was a living saint and is in heaven right now, no matter how many times he beat you, and he's looking down at us even as you assault his memories. He took good care of me and never once complained like you of late. Why can't you be more like him and care fer me?"

"Took good care of you! Pa hated emptying your bedpan day in and out, and he hated you, because he knew you weren't as sick as you pretend to be. You drove him into a sex lunatic. You were never a wife to him, never gave him intercourse. That's why he masturbated at the bathroom door, then cried like a baby when he saw me watching him, and asked me and his God to forgive him."

"Liar!"

"When I move out, I'll hire a niggra woman to come here to do the washing and cleaning. They work cheap and are kindhearted and gentle to us whites when they have to be."

"How dare you! You'd do that . . . invite one of those people into your pa's house, knowing how he despised them! At age eleven, you kissed the deadliest snakes in Reverend Miller's church, then bit its head off when it hissed at you; you spat that snake's head, fangs and all, onto the altar and laughed." She shakes with apprehension, going on. "Then, as if drawn to those altar candles, as if the devil himself was motioning to you to come to him in those flames, like a moth to fire, you put your hand into that flickering affliction and refused to withdraw it, even as you cried from the awful pain and Reverend and others rushed toward you, begging you to pull your hand from the fire; you ended up badly burned, but—just like that—you suddenly stopped crying.

"The next morning your hand was healed. Healed, Barney, if you can call it that; and fer some strange reason, you were never afraid of anything after that, not even of your pa when you displeased him and he laid into you with his belt, that is until you turned sixteen and—as young as you were—you hit him and knocked him out. Then you laughed. I often wondered why you did that. Spit that creature's head on Miller's holy altar and touched the flames and laughed at your frightened pa, once he became conscious again. Why, son?"

"Because of you, dammit! That's why. Because of what you did to me!"

Her ears perk up. Ever so slowly she turns her head toward the howling wind at the window.

"She's out there in the wind," his mother whispers, "out there on a mission as the forerunner of a child, a child to be born, a child who will enter this world and has to destroy this house and you, Barney and you. And I was wrong, son. All this time I was wrong. I didn't know it until this very minute. That dream I've been having. It isn't Sarah who can destroy you. Baby boys, Barney. Two of them, son. Far out in space on their long seventeen-and-eighteen-year-old journey befer they reach us. They're carried on a blanket of rocks, of air and of shedding ice, ice that shines like diamonds, brighter than the sun; and fog, son, ice and fog, all around them two boys, including fire, as they approach through the beyond."

"You're drunk," he says as she seizes his wrist and attempts to hold onto him.

"What fog," he asks, leaning back from her. "What's gotten into you? What boys are coming?"

Her wild eyes locked on the window, she exclaims, "One of them is in the priest's can, a silver tin can encrusted with jewels. The other boy is outside of the can and wrapped in fire, and oh, how that can and those boys soar through space, as if the planets themselves back off and make room for them boys to pass. You, Barney. God is sending them after you."

"Mother, let go of my hand; I don't want to talk about your childish dreams."

"The boy in that can . . . Barney, in my dreams, he's always reaching out of that can and trying to hold onto the heel of the other, a year ahead of him, both coming this way to enter the womb of a white girl, whose face is covered with stardust, concealing her features from me and curtaining off the boy inside that flying can as well as the one outside the can. Why, God? Why? Why am I not allowed to recognize who they are, in order to save my son from them, only that they are coming?"

She attempts to kiss him, and Barney pushes her aside, causing her to stumble and fall. "You've been smoking reefer again, hasn't you?" he tells her, as she slowly rises to her feet once more and spits on him.

"Don't ever spit on me again, Mother," he yells and then seizes the bedpan to empty it.

"And don't you ever again disrespect me by knocking me down," she blares back at him, while grappling the bedpan from him and splashing him in the face with its contents.

Gagging, Barney slaps her. She drops the bedpan and stumbles back against the bed, sobbing and screaming, "May you burn in hell, Barney Cutter!"

"No, Mother! May Satan burn you and your goddamn God in my place! Do you still believe in God, or that He loves you after our sickening encounters? Do you!"

"Noooo," she bellows, "never speak of that! He has forgiven me. I know He has!"

Barney is devastated for having attacked his mother. At the same time he is gasping for air and trying to exhale the stench from his nostrils. To show her how much he truly loves her, sobbing, he approaches her with open arms. "Mamma! Kiss me, Mamma."

"Don't you come near me unless you accept God, Barney Cutter."

"Never!" he stops and says. "And only Satan will accept you, as he has me. You marked us both!"

"I will never embrace the devil," she screams. "God is the only one who is all powerful, not Lucifer!" The window suddenly explodes, scattering glass across the floor and the bed, and carried by a howling wind, a thick, black fog rolls into the room through the shattered window, like a monster, the wind whiplashing the worn drapery. Barney's elderly mother watches him standing there, as if that demonic wind is talking to him, and she jumps into her bed and lies there on her back, frozen in fear, her head turned to the side, her eyes opened wide and staring at her son and at the fog, her locked elbows and arms at her side, her fingers clenched, pressing her fingernails into her flesh. She shuts her eyes and cries aloud, "Go away, Satan!" The wind rips the blankets off the bed, and Mrs. Cutter kicks and screams, and just that fast, the howling monster is gone. Only the fog remains.

"My God! I can't be left alone in this house! I can't ever be left alone! I know what I did to you was wrong, son! But don't let Lucifer take me."

Barney goes to the window to close the drapery; he sees Naomi at the posted open gate, a gate now closing on its own, as the black woman walks away into the night. Pulling the drapery closed and diminishing the fog, Barney examines the palm of his left hand. After he had burned it as a boy in Miller's church, on that same night before he went to bed, he had prayed to Satan telling him how much he loved him, and in the morning his hand was healed of all signs of ever having been burned, but something else had appeared in its place. Barney looks toward his mother. She's sitting up in bed sweating and glaring at his palm and at a thick, quarter-size layer of scarred-over flesh in the shape of bull's head, with a star-shaped section between the horns, a star the color of blood.

"Who are you?" his mother whispers.

"I'm your son. Let's put this behind us, and then wish me luck in my marriage. Won't you?"

"Ever since you touched that candle fire," she tells him, "something protects you at just the right times. Fer your sake, I pray it always will. May the Lord help you."

"Have mercy on me? Why? Because of two unborn boys? I'm not afraid of a child, one *or* two of them. And that's what Sarah is, as well, if now you want to go back to telling me that it is she who will destroy me. Sarah Winthrop isn't even enough woman to cause my blood to run hot or cold."

"Hot, you say. And cold. Like those shameful women of the night who do you? Have you no shame, if not fear of God? You haven't believed a word I've said about the approaching boy babies."

"I don't and I never will. Will you at least welcome my children here to visit you, if not Sarah, after she and I are married?"

"No children of yours with even a drop of Winthrop, Catholic blood in them—no matter how smart or beautiful you might think Sarah's precious body will cause them to be—will ever set foot in this house. Why, for God's sake? So that every time I set eyes on them, I'll be reminded of her being close to you in your bed? And neither will you, Barney, ever be allowed in this house again. Go ahead! Leave me sick and dying here alone. I don't need you! I don't need anyone! Get out!"

He picks up his feces-soiled tuxedo from the floor. "Get this shit to the cleaners and off of my suit before I get back tomorrow night." He tosses the suit at her and storms from the house, slamming the door behind him. Stunned, his mother sits frozen in bed, her hand covering her mouth, her regretful old eyes focused on the front door in disbelief. This time, he actually left and no doubt for good. She hears his truck tires shrilling from the yards and toward town, and she gawks down at the thousands of broken-window glass slivers, not only across the floor and on the bed, but also in her slippers. Then, she hears it—the train—her lonely ghost, sending chills down her back, the wind wailing once more, and again whiplashing the draperies, the tree limbs reaching into the room and scratching against the windows, as the sound of her far-off, nightly ghost—roaring along the tracks from Cutterville—looms closer. Wide-eyed, she watches the lamp's wick suddenly flicker and die from lack of kerosene. In the dark house with glass everywhere, the old, bare-foot woman—unable to walk to the wall lights—slides under her sheet and pulls it over her head and wails for dear life.

Everything goes deadly quiet, even unto the train's ghostly cry, and she hears their cotton-soft footsteps—the others—coming across the floor and glass toward her bed. Shivering below the sheet she prays, "The Lord is with me!" she cries out, haunted by her and her husband's participation in tossing blacks under the wheels of that ghostly oncoming and other trains, or having known about it and the lynchings at the hand of her son and having done nothing to stop it.

"He leads me beside the still waters!" she sobs. "I see them when it's dark, son," she whispers, surrounded by the lingering, ghostly fog. "See burning bodies hanging from trees and butchered under the light of the burning crosses. See them beside the train tracks in the swamps. Can hear the engineer laughing as the coons cry and beg for mercy. I see their arms, their legs and heads ripped from their black bodies under the train wheels. I could never tell you or anyone else of this nightmare of mine for fear of being called a nigger lover." She listens. More footsteps are heard moving toward her bed.

"Lord," she cries. "Now, they come in my weakened old age and in the dark and stand over me, their burned-out, grayed-over eyes haunting down at me. Why don't they go away? Why don't they speak? Say anything, but don't just stand there with their rotting flesh. My God, why do You let them torture me so, these blacks from the dead? I go to church. I give money to the poor when I can." When God does not answer her, she knows that she is doomed, and she decides to attach her fate to that of her son, and she calls out his name as her god.

"You and I are the last of the Cutters, Barney, and I love you. But if it's Satan that's in you, it's my doing, as you said, and I destroyed you, not your father who knew all along that it was you who I lay with in bed and gave of myself after refusing him and could never refuse you. I love you so. May God have mercy on us both. Where you go, I will follow, even into hell."

She slowly uncovers her head and looks up at the side of the bed. Those shadowy bodies are looking down at her. She screams, "Come back, Barney, I can't live this way. Please come back."

8
The Wedding

Seven days later, the tower bell in Reverend Miller's church steeple rings without end, calling the faithful to come and witness a miracle. Even the hopeless town drunks lingering around Sue Ann's bar—a half block away—on Main Street watch in awe, as the congregation and nonmembers continuously stream toward the church, drawn there by the possibility of seeing Sarah, a Winthrop, being married to one of their own. Across the train tracks, the blacks line up along the rail line and also watch. Under that unusually warm morning sun, in the whites-only church, stands ash-pale Reverend Miller, short, stocky and wearing his black toupee and his best Sunday-go-to-meeting dark suit. Miller is forty years old, with the squinting, brown eyes of a dishonest car salesman. Before him—in a near catatonic state—stands Sarah. She's dressed in a flowing white wedding gown and holding a large arrangement of red roses, roses that Barney had purchased and insisted that she carry. As Sarah stands with her gaze toward the floor, at her side in his spotless tuxedo, is a smiling Barney Cutter. Behind him and Sarah, laid out on the altar between flickering candles, are locally grown firethorns: poisonous, thorny plants with green, paddle-shaped leaves and red berries, a few also contain white berries; also on the altar are jimson weeds. The seeds of the jimson weeds and the firethorn plants have been successfully mixed with other drug-producing herbs and made into a potent narcotic by the church members, members who are packed wall-to-wall, with people sitting, standing or jostling about, their excited eyes locked in on the young, land-rich girl, their white hands spasmodically stirring the suffocating, hot air with paper, Jesus-faced fans.

More than a few members of the church are holding live snakes, and having mastered the art of surviving poisonous bites, Reverend Miller kisses the head of a snake, which is extended to him by a woman from the congregation; then, as the woman returns to her seat, Miller waves his Bible at the faithful.

"The late Doctor and Mrs. Winthrop," he begins, "may God have mercy on their souls, were devoted Catholics, and now God has softened Sarah's heart and is wedding her to our Grand Wizard, which everyone in the county knows he is, including the blacks, so I'm not giving away any military secrets here in our church family by saying it."

A series of chuckles spreads throughout the house of God. Glowing with pride, Miller tables his Bible. "Just to forewarn everyone," he lectures, "there won't be any smoking in honor of Sarah's presence here. Besides, we don't need the plants to glorify this day." The applause fills the church. The reverend continues. "With the mighty name like that of the Winthrops joined to that of the Cutters, and with us having an understanding state senator, a politically savvy banker like Harry Pennington in town and others among us . . ." He beams at Sarah. ". . . all of this should put Cutterville on the road toward a renewed and grand and better way of life for every white man, woman and child in our community." Again the applause rings out.

Barney grows impatient, as Miller leers at Sarah and goes on, "The Klan didn't hang those kids from that bridge, Sarah Winthrop. I know your family and others believe that they did. Some numbers runner maybe. I'd bet my life on it. Them poor, unfortunate boys and girls were hanged and burned after they stole the collection money from one of them godless, colored, number runners and were later caught by them. That's what Sheriff Richards says, and all of us here believe him. He's the law, you know." Miller faces his flock and grumbles. "Trying to enter our schools fer God's sake. What will the coloreds think of next?"

Sarah cannot believe what she is hearing from this Christian man of God. Her world whirls.

Naomi, where are you?

Outside, several yards from the church, the Winthrops' Model T has been washed and decorated by Naomi and covered with wildflowers long before it arrived at the church. Naomi had refused Barney's offer to use his store-bought roses, opting instead to decorate the car with the wildflowers, which were among Marilyn's favorites. Just beyond the car, lingering in front of the church, the spill-over crowd—rice in hand and puffing on corn pipes—have grown excited at hearing those inside the building exuberantly calling out, "hallelujah," which is more in tune with a Sunday church meeting rather than a wedding, and those waiting under the sun clap their hands with the increased applause coming from the church. With the ringing of the steeple bell above them, the outside whites prance about in a primitive-looking frenzy, unknowingly in a limited, but unshakable style of their African, drug-induced ancestors, while connecting with their white peers inside the church by also calling out "hallelujah!"

One of those outside is Chad Travis, carrying a large snake. He and his two sidekicks, one-ear Dane Tucker and a young boy, nicknamed Tiny, yell and then charge after a frightened teenage girl, Chad viciously thrusting the snake at her, as she flees from the three boys, the crowd laughing as if the chase is but an everyday occurrence and of no great consequence.

Barney's marriage to Sarah is of great concern to him, and he glares at Reverend Miller, who is bouncing about with childlike joy over the wedding. "Let me hear you say hallelujah," he calls out to the congregation.

"Hallelujah," the members resound.

Barney had agreed to let Miller marry them in his church, instead of having a civil service. He had done so hoping that his mother would have attended the ceremony as a catharsis in her struggle with her conscience. After looking about the church and not seeing her, he turns to Miller and says, tersely, "Get on with it and leave the 'hallelujahs' out of it."

"Of course, Major," says the abashed preacher. "Major Bernard Cutter, do you take . . ."

While Miller goes on, the major, having convinced Sarah to marry him, thinks he has also persuaded her that her dependence on Naomi is wrong in her God's eyes and suggested that she fire Naomi, but Sarah will have no part of that, and even though she has told her white workers not to attend the wedding, and is totally aware that coloreds face severe punishment if it's known they even look as if they wish to enter the white place of worship, Sarah knows that Naomi will back away from no one, and Sarah looks about the church for Naomi to show up and save her.

"You're looking for that Naomi woman, aren't you?" whispers Barney, as an irritated Miller stops his monologue and waits for Barney to stop whispering. "Naomi wouldn't dare to show her face around here," Barney tells Sarah. "No coloreds ever have and never will."

Outside, under the bright, sunny sky, Chad, Dane and Tiny suddenly break off their snake pursuit of the girl. Dane—following the stares of the crowd—pulls down the brim of his baseball cap to block out the sunlight for a better look at the unbelievable sight of what's approaching the church. The three boys' sunburned, pink faces—and those of the crowd—are firmly fixed on: Naomi, riding bareback on a donkey, daring to approach them. Wearing a gray maid's uniform, over-laid with a white apron tied about her waist, the black mysterious woman stops the donkey on the edge of the crowd near Dane, Chad and Tiny and is immediately confronted by Chad and Dane, with Tiny bringing up the rear. Dane steps over and seizes the donkey's reins. An intimidated Tiny stops in his tracks and lingers in the background with the angry crowd.

"What you doing here, Mammy?" the one-eared boy asks Naomi. "In that fancy maid's outfit?"

"You should be on the rich side of town taking care of them wealthy, white folks and them rich, Jew kids," Chad hisses, to the delight of the crowd.

"Yeah," Tiny adds his two cents' worth, keeping his distance, fearful of all blacks, women or not. "Put the fear of God in her, Chad."

"A nigger would rather be boiled in oil than to face a snake," says Dane. "Do it, Chad, like Tiny says. Pa always said it ain't no sin to scare or kill a coon."

The crowd watches with stimulated gazes, just waiting for the boys to send Naomi screaming on her way, just like blacks in the movies run away from spooky places and anything eerie that they happen upon. Grinning, Chad thrusts the deadly reptile at Sarah's faithful maid. Naomi doesn't move or flinch. The donkey does, though, hee-hawing all over the place, shuffling this way and that because of the snake. Only Dane's firm grip on the reins keeps the domestic ass from breaking free and trampling them. As Naomi sits cool and collected, Chad—assured that Naomi is one of the dumbest tar-ball spooks he's ever seen and just too stupid to know what a snake like the cottonmouth can do to her—decides to teach her a lesson she won't forget. He presses in against the mule and eases his snake within inches of Naomi's thigh.

"This here snake is a water moccasin, a dang cottonmouth, you dumbbell. Who are you and who do you work fer now that Sarah is a Cutter, so Pa can call them rich folks up and tell them to fire you fer step-ping out of your place and showing your face around here? You better thank God the Klan ain't around to take you into them swamps, where you'll never come out live again, you ignorant mammy!"

When she still doesn't move, the white boy projects his snake up-ward toward her face; Naomi smiles down at him with a mother's love. Chad steps back, baffled, his shoulders drawn up, his neck and head pro-

116

jected forward. He blinks in wide-eyed confusion at her; no one has ever looked at him with such love before. Inching back to Naomi, his snake held up toward her, Chad—as if to ask what he should do next—glances over at Dane, Tiny and the crowd, who are all puzzled, especially by Naomi's next move. Unflinchingly, she leans forward from the donkey—eye to eye with the open-mouthed, extended serpent of death.

"Make it strike her in her head, Chad," calls an elderly, drugged woman from the crowd, the defiant crowd now inching toward Naomi. "Even if it kills her," the elderly woman shouts. "Strike her good with that venom snake. She's asking fer it! They know they're not wanted here!"

Chad begins to fear Naomi, her lips clenched, her left hand holding onto the reins. Dane, however, thinks that Naomi is holding tightly to the reins so that she can have a quick getaway. However, even when a stone is hurled through the air, just missing her and striking Dane instead, Naomi continues sitting there, a lightning strike away from that snake and death. Chad's eyes pop open, as Naomi suddenly seizes the snake about its neck with her free hand—the terrified girl who had been chased by the boys cheering as Naomi, in the blinking of the eye, turns the snake's venomous fangs on Chad, who slips, losing his grip on the cottonmouth. Naomi flips the snake away from her, and the whiplashing serpent strikes Chad on his arm. Dane stumbles back as the snake falls to the ground and attempts to escape; it's recaptured by Chad's father. Screaming, Chad leaps into the arms of his father, who, while holding Chad close with one hand, the snake with the other, yells at Naomi.

"What'd you do to my boy? Who the hell are you?"

The whites are extremely suspicious of Naomi, a black woman who has power over their snakes. Chad could care less about the crowd or anyone else. He cries allow, "It bit me, Pa!"

"Hush up, boy! You've been struck before and will live."

"No, Pa! It's different this time. I can feel it!"

Naomi causes a profound hush to fall over the congregation when she climbs off the donkey and walks by Dane, Chad and his old man to the Model T, straightens out a few flowers attached to the old car, and unencumbered, makes her way past the contemptuous sea of frozen white stares and to the church, causing the whites to step back from her.

"What's she doing?" the whispering begins, as she continues to the church.

"Stay away from our church," someone calls to her.

"I'm not here to enter that house of wickedness," exclaims Naomi pointing at the church.

The crowd gasps. No one has ever called their place of worship wicked or evil. No one! Naomi goes to the side of the building, where she lingers below one of the dirt-stained windows, the crowd's eyes and heads, in machine-like oneness, following her there. Stacked below the window and against the structure's blistered clapboards, are several wooden delivery crates containing pint-sized, empty milk bottles. They're from Miller's free, milk-and-cookies treat for the children. The whites watch as the black woman climbs onto three of the stacked crates, wipes the soil from the window on her apron tail and peers into the church. Most of Miller's congregation has heard about an occult, black woman who is said to know witchcraft and also recently came to live with Major Cutter's new wife-to-be, Sarah; they've never seen Naomi before, but by now everyone outside the church has guessed that the woman they now see is she.

"She's the woman who prophesied the coming of a boy to destroy their town," one of the white women says to the others. And no one among them—standing there with open mouths gawking at Naomi—seems willing to challenge her further. From atop the milk carton, Naomi answers their troubling thoughts.

"No one here has heard such a thing from my lips. I came here not with news of destruction, but to help, but not for your sake, you who are beyond help. I'm here for the sake of another."

Naomi again takes note of the church's interior, and as she does, the youthful, red-haired, gapped-tooth boy Marcus—whom young Pennington saw crying over the dead children and is yet to be born for another eight years—appears in the midst of the crowd. He's wrapped in that same thin layer of fog and is visible only to Naomi, who is gravely puzzled after noticing him.

Charles Pennington had looked at the boy during the killing of the school children and had felt his heart beating when he saw Marcus, but young Pennington had no compassion, only fear of Marcus and ran away. Naomi's heart, on the other hand, bleeds for Marcus, a boy that God has forbidden her to approach. Unlike Caleb and Flynn, who are to be born before him, Marcus represents mankind whose hatred of another is used but for one thing only, to cover up man's fundamental need to recognize the indisputable truth that all humans are brothers; and if not rescued in time, young Marcus's future will be one of devastation on the streets of Cutterville, when he's born, and he will touch everyone's lives, especially those of Caleb and Flynn's. Then, like dust blowing in the wind, Marcus is gone. Naomi looks at the sky and then gazes back at the spot where the boy stood, the whites following her sights and grumbling about her and the place she's staring at. Naomi then faces her primary task, the immediate needs of Sarah.

Inside the building, as Miller finally pronounces them man and wife, Major Cutter stares at his teenage bride, his sinister eyes daring Sarah to disobey his present and future controlling commands of her. He then places a dispassionate kiss on Sarah's pale lips. Those inside the church rush to the altar and embrace Sarah, welcoming her into their "family of God," and as teenage girls wait impatiently for Sarah to toss her rose bouquet to one of them, Barney goes into the seated area of the church, shaking hands and hugging a group of women, ladies of the night, who Miller preaches deserve a chance to be "saved", and with the other female church members streaming to the altar to congratulate Sarah, Reverend Miller and what seems like half of Cutterville's male population follow Major Cutter's lead of giving an especially warm welcome to the young prostitutes by using the church-encouraged practice of hugging all lost souls. Barney embraces one of the youngest of the night-walkers, pressing his body firmly against hers, while slipping several bills into her hand, as he whispers in her ear. She's Lilly. She glances over her shoulder at Sarah and then runs her hand across Barney's fly.

"You don't need that young chicken tonight, do you?" she asks, as she purrs in Barney's ear. "You can make that special baby you want anytime. Come to my place after the wedding. I'll be waiting to pay you back for kicking me out of that truck, just the way all you tough men around here like it, especially you and me. In my butt."

"You're not afraid of God, are you?" Barney asks and then mischievously glances toward the ceiling as if looking for God. "God might strike you dead talking like this in His house."

"Hell no, I'm not afraid of Him. If Satan protects you, I guess he protects me too. This day belongs to the devil, as far as I'm concerned. Bring your ass to me as soon as you drop Sarah off."

Barney fingers her dress and through it her breast, then glances back at Sarah, but Sarah's sights are elsewhere, her eyes lit up with hope.

119

The older man follows her gaze to the side window, where he sees Naomi looking in at Sarah. It's at that moment, watching Sarah's longing reaction to Naomi, that Cutter fully realizes that with Naomi's unshakable hold on the young girl, and Sarah's connections to her father's powerful friends, it will be difficult to fire Naomi, kill her, or even get rid of the blacks who work on Sarah's land, as he had hoped, not now, anyway, not until he gains Sarah's absolute trust and obedience to his will. He returns his attention to Lilly. "As soon as I drop her off at the manor, I'll come back to you. At Sue Ann's bar. Be there."

Barney returns to the altar and the crowd of women around his bride. Embracing Sarah, he smiles at those admiring her innocent beauty, then whispers to his wife. "I know you're concerned about your workers, Sarah, and I understand. For now the coloreds can remain on Shadow Grove, but segregated, as befitting your new status. Also, I know how upsetting it will be for you on this our first time together, so I'll be out with the boys all night, a belated bachelor's party you might say, to let you get accustomed to being Mrs. Cutter first."

When Sarah looks back at the window, Naomi is gone. Outside the crowd gives out with a thunderous roar when Sarah and Barney step from the building into the sunlight, followed by the joyous, fan-carrying women. Sarah is still holding tightly to the roses, but not out of love of them—for after all they came from Barney. She fears them and what they symbolize, a marriage to a madman. The frightened girl, nonetheless, clings to the roses out of a need to have a lifeline to her mother, who loved roses as much as she had wildflowers and calla lilies, a fact Barney was aware of when he purchased them. Try as she might, though, roses or not, Sarah cannot evoke the image of her parents, only the maddening touching of hands and blurred faces and voices of those crowding in around her. Under a bombardment of tossed rice from those outside, who have waited so long to catch a glimpse her, Sarah looks about for Naomi without success. She gasps when Chad—his father having told him that when you fall off of a horse you get right back on or get an ass whipping, his arm, gray and swollen, where the snake bit him—stands before her and extends the killer snake for her to stroke. Sarah backs away. Barney waves the boy off, including Dane.

"Get out of here, Dane Tucker, you and Chad, with that damn thing. Can't you see she's afraid of it? Everybody, please give us some room."

After everyone shuffles back, Sarah sees Naomi riding toward the road to Shadow Grove on her donkey, the church and Sarah, now, a good distance behind her. Just as Sarah feels abandoned and is about to run screaming after Naomi begging her to save her, she hears Naomi's voice:

Suffering's what we all got to do before we die, child. Remember . . . you have not been given more than you can endure. Keep remembering that. You will not be soiled by Barney and will find a love that's pure and unmatched in this entire world.

Up the road, Naomi stops and looks to her left. Henry is concealed from the whites by a large magnolia tree and is gazing across a dry, grassless field at the church. Under the blooming magnolia tree and in its shade, and tall in the saddle, Henry skillfully handles the reins on his powerful, prancing filly, "Clara." For moments at a time, as the graceful horse dances partially in and partially out of the tree's cast shadows, only the horse is clearly seen, while Henry—his ebony skin absorbed in the tree-speckling sunlight and leaf-cast shade—is as if invisible, but for his sad, brown eyes fading in and out of sight, as the wind moves the leaves back and forth over his head, letting in, then cutting off the sunlight. All the time, Henry keeps his intense eyes fixed on Sarah, as she and the major travel southbound in the Winthrops' flowered Model T, dragging tin cans behind them and sending back a line of swirling dust. In the car, as an impatient Barney drives with his eyes focused on a sharp curve in the road and his thoughts on Lilly, Sarah silently prays.

God, where are You and Henry?

As Barney shrills the tires into the curve, and the Model T's angle changes on the magnolia tree, Sarah sees Henry sitting on the vibrant horse and looking like a young warrior. When their sights meet, he raises the English book over his head and nods. Tears flowing, Sarah returns the nod; they will carry on, and neither will give up hope, is what both of them innately know the other's gesture is saying. The roses fall from Sarah's hands, and the Model T is swallowed up in the dust. Henry then notices Naomi in the distance. She looks away from him and turns her sights upwards to the sky and then, just as quickly, she gazes downwards, her head remaining low.

"I don't deserve to raise my sights to You, Jesus," she whispers. "In my weakness like Henry, who loves that innocent child as much as I do, I still have so many concerns about Sarah. But Henry, Lord, if you can, please gladden his young heart so he can be a good person and not become wicked like the man he now scorns. And there is Lawrence and Marilyn," Naomi goes on. "Marilyn was so worried about Sarah before Satan killed them in that plane. If she and Lawrence are still waitin' to enter heaven, and they don't already know, would You please tell them that after my dream was explained to her in her grandma's wonderful bedroom, Sarah now understands that her folks are heaven bound, and soon, they'll be with You, God and the angels. Please, somehow, let Sarah know that her folks are at peace about her marryin' that man, and I just know she'll feel better, but Your will, not mine be done, Jesus."

Henry looks up and sees an earth-brightening object streaking across the sky, an object which is seen all over the world as it circles the globe. The fast-moving projectile is the thing Barney's mother feared in her dreams; now—after traveling at the speed of light, and slowing as if commanded to do so—it looks like an elongated, silver, tin can, a can encrusted with jewels. It's far from being that, this can-like streaking body from space, this rocky substance, made also of fire and ice, disintegrating as it goes—worlds above Naomi's bowed head—exploding off the jewels that Barney's mother also dreamed about and feared. It's ice, not jewels, an ocean of icy crystals, filling the sky with zillions of glacial, celestial diamonds and burning gases, sparkling brighter than the sun to all who see it, its tail of fire streaming out a million miles behind it, as it glides silently in an arch of grace through the cloudless blue and disappears off the side of the world.

The difference between the way Mrs. Cutter saw the futuristic image and the way Henry sees it, is that Henry sees the object awash in sunlight, not in fog. He also hears something that the major's mother was not permitted to hear: something that opens wide his eyes, as he listens in awe to the sounds of crying babies, two of them, their wailing voices clearly distinguishable one from the other, voices of both hope and fear intermittently trailing back from the comet among the drifting ice crystals, and down to those who have ears to hear and the goodness to listen.

At the church, Reverend Miller and his congregation's eyes are riveted on the sky.

"Was that Halley's Comet?" Chad asks Dane.

"Can't be," says Miller. "Haley came in 1910 and comes only once every seventy-five years or so."

To the church members, the unusual sight is a sign that only good will come from the marriage between Sarah and the major, a man who will—they are absolutely now sure—reclaim Cutterville from the Jew factory owner and his deep pockets and return their town back to them.

"Marilyn . . . Lawrence," Henry whispers to the sky, inspired by the streaking object, "I couldn't save Sarah from Barney. Will you ever forgive me?"

As the comet's fiery tail fades, something draws Henry's sights back to the field, and there, where nothing, not even weeds, grew before, calla lilies thrive by the thousands. Slipping the English book into his saddlebag and kneeing his horse, he gallops through the field, leans low from the saddle and plucks up calla lily after calla lily, then he races the horse on to Shadow Grove in order to place the white flowers on Marilyn and Lawrence's grave, he and his powerful horse passing Naomi and disappearing into sunlight, as had the comet in the sky. Naomi and her donkey continue on their way, her sights on the heavens and the decomposing comet's icy diamonds.

"Welcome, Flynn, and you, Caleb, you who follow on the heels of your brother," she whispers. "We'll see you soon, Flynn, and you, Caleb, a year from now."

9

A Time to Love

One year later, 1930, under a blue, warm, sunlit sky, the manor house, the greenhouse—reflecting the sun's rays in the large house's sprawling backyard—the massive red barn, the many sheds and the general stores are still central to surrounding fields and workers' shacks. On this dusty, summer day, however, the heart of Shadow Grove has been cut out: The blacks and the white field hands pick cotton and work the fields segregated from one another, and Sarah seems helpless to change it. Riding in a red, horse-drawn wagon, Sarah—appearing downhearted—hurriedly drives the horse and wagon from the barn's rear door. Wearing a straw hat to help disguise her, she glances about, lashes the horse through a distant, seldom-used back gate, and leaves the plantation behind.

Ten miles later, at a place which seems to be part of heaven and graced with two-thousand acres—where the blue skies, the sprawling lagoon, the corn fields and the rolling, green hills overlook the restless Atlantic, while being nourished by fresh water and clean air, where birds sing so sweetly that all broken hearts are mended—next to Henry's modest white house, with its bleached picket fence and white porch railings, Sarah is happily kneeling on her knees, while weeding, and placing flowers on the graves of Henry's parents. It's been almost two months since she and Henry have been alone together, and she wants to make the best of it. Smiling as she leans against the fence to rest, she watches a ladybug land on her hand.

"Ladybug, ladybug fly away home. Your house is on fire and your children will burn," she says, giving it a puff of her breath. As the ladybug takes to the air, Henry—dressed in work jeans and also sporting a straw hat—leaves his nearby barn with Clara, his faithful saddled horse. He ties her to Sarah's wagon, into which he and she then load firewood from Henry's plentiful wood pile. While Henry continues stacking wood, Sarah stops and listens to the sounds of the restless ocean crashing against the distant rocks below the promontories.

"I'm so ashamed," she says, continuing an earlier conversation she's had with him, since her arrival. "When I kneel in prayer at my bed, I find myself asking, 'Why, God?' "

"You were young, then, as you are now," Henry tells her, "and he took advantage of you." Henry puts aside the wood and lifts her chin. "Now you're the mother of a six-month-old, beautiful, blonde boy. Live for Flynn and for me, not for Barney. Okay?" He points to his saddlebag. "If I can suffer through that book all last year, then surely you can make it through this time in your life. Everything will work itself out. I promise."

"I'll show you suffering," Sarah teases, tickling him. "And that English book did you a world of good. Listen to you. In another year or two, you'll sound as if you're a college professor."

"I still can't read very well, but in time," he says, grabbing Sarah and tickling her in return. After expressing their mirthfulness, Henry resumes loading the fireplace wood. "Sarah, why did you wait so long to tell me about what happened to you on that ship from Germany?"

"Because I didn't want you to think—" She goes silent and stops him from his work, then continues. "Always stay close to me, Henry," she whispers. "I'm so afraid of Barney."

"I promised your mother I would," he says, holding her in his arms and then asks. "Sarah, your reason for not telling me about what happened on the ship . . . I've put off asking you this long, because of what you've been through. Now, tell me. You didn't want me to think what?"

"That I was childish, the way girls are, who dream of soaring among the stars."

"You who knows more languages than I have fingers and now carry the burden of your workers and Shadow Grove on your shoulders—regardless of Barney's claims that he's the man of the house now—Childish? Never," he tells her. "But just because Naomi and you were caught up in some kind of strange wind funnel doesn't make that woman a saint, Sarah, unless there is more than just that whirlwind business on the ship than what I've been hearing through rumors." Teasing, he goes on. "Such as that the ship broke down and Naomi walked on the water to fix the propellers or some other crazy thing that your workers are saying about her?"

"That was my fault, Henry," Sarah responds with humbleness. "Naomi didn't tell the workers about the shooting stars and that enigmatic wind and cause it and her image to balloon out of proportion, I did, even though most of those blabbering about her don't realize how close to being right they really are. She may not be a saint, Henry, but Naomi is a gift from God, and she and I felt His presence all around us, and I think He actually spoke to Naomi."

Henry just stands there, pondering for almost a minute. What could he do or even say to someone who thinks they were in the presence of God?

"Enigmatic, Sarah?" he finally asks. "What does that mean? And just make it simple to understand, more than it is for me to understand this thing of you and Naomi being around God, okay?"

"Okay. For now, just think of it as meaning somewhat of a puzzle."

"'Enigmatic.' I like the sound of that word. But this ship business, even though I don't understand it, in the future, if you want to talk, you can tell me anything. I thought you knew that."

"Dear Henry. I know that, but most of all, I never told you about what really happened on that ship, because I know how skeptical you can be about things you can't touch, hear, smell or taste." She looked around at his beautiful land. "Like your corn, or the clean air, or the sound of the birds that seem to serenade clearer and with more joy on your land than on Shadow Grove. But that ship, and my parents' death challenged my own ideals about creation and blind trust in faith alone. Then I glimpsed that magical, rarely seen, elevated side of life, as Naomi said I would, but it sometimes is still difficult for me to accept what has happened and still happening."

"Sarah, no person in his right mind that I know believes in stuff like magic. That kind of thinking died out when the slaves gave up on the witch doctors who tried to use tribal magic to free their African brothers and sisters from the white man's chains. You don't believe in magic, do you?"

"Don't you, Henry, even come close to believing in miracles, after our talks about Naomi?"

"No. Naomi's just like you and me."

"Those in Jesus' time didn't believe in Him either, even when He rose the dead."

"Are you now trying to tell me that Naomi actually did walk on the water during that trip?"

"Of course not, silly."

"Sarah, I have my doubts about many things, but I know that if you believe in something—as bright as you are—something that helps keep people from stealing, robbing, and killing each other, then that's good enough for me. Only a fool would argue about that," he says with a shrug. "I hope there is a God. I think most people do as well. And I live every day of my life thanking my lucky stars that there is goodness and people like you in this world, which is 'enigmatic.' There, I've used my new word." Henry proudly struts about the plush lawn, his arms bent toward his chest, a cocky look of self-approval on his face. Sarah strolls up to him and gives him a light kiss on his lips.

"That's for being so smart, you devil. That English book did you a lot of good, but don't get so cocky. Strutting about as if you were Einstein and just solved the law of gravity."

"Cocky, you say!" he laughs, jostling with her.

She goes on after they settle down and once again load the firewood. "In the guestroom, where I sleep, on a clear night I watch the lamplight in your window through the telescope. A military general gave it to Father as a Christmas present, and as far as ten miles away, I can still see your flickering light. When I can't keep my eyes open any longer I go to bed."

Both look at the unlit lamp in Henry's window. "That's why I keep it burnin' all night . . . for you. Sarah, do you still lock your bedroom door when you go to sleep?"

"Yes."

"And he still hasn't kicked in the door or asked you to unlock it?"

"Once in a while he knocks, if he's not too drunk to walk from the master bedroom, and demands entry into my quarters, then—when I don't open it—he leaves the house to be with Lilly." Her eyes widen and she excitedly exclaims, "That's what I mean about Naomi, Henry. It's as she said it would be. He hasn't touched me since the day after our wedding night, when Flynn was conceived. I had no climax and felt nothing but pain that horrible night, Henry." She sadly gazes at Henry as if to apologize for letting her husband near her. She goes on. "He's leaving today on one of his desert missions again, and this time he won't be back for a year. I think it's what he really wants—besides Flynn—more than wanting me or anything else except the excitement of being a soldier, and his dream of ruling the world. Now, with the real possibility that the United States will actually be drawn into a war in Europe, Barney's consumed with thoughts of a world war and so busy packing and thinking about making his fortune in the service, that he doesn't know I'm alive. That's why I dared come out here today. Your place, here on the coast, so green and peaceful. Henry, Barney says I should sell my land while it's still worth something. The bank refused to loan him any money to buy irrigation pipes."

"If your workers and I have to dig those pipe ditches night and day, we'll get my water to Shadow Grove, with or without pipes or money."

"Naomi says the two of us praying together can make miracles happen. Will you pray for rain with me?"

"Why would God listen to me, Sarah?"

"Because you're beautiful, and you're brown like Him." She kisses his hand. "I wish I were as dark as you."

"And I wish I was lighter like you," he says, returning the kiss to her soft hand. "But what's this 'brown like Him' stuff?"

"Someone was to arrive here to say a few words over your parents' graves, then over that of mine on Shadow Grove. He's better qualified to tell you what I meant by 'brown like Him.' "

"Well, this someone isn't here, whoever he is," Henry says. "So let's get you home before you're missed. I can bring the rest of the wood tomorrow, once the major's left town."

When they climb aboard Sarah's wagon, Henry notices a firethorn plant growing in the dirt just beyond the wagon. Sarah watches him leap to the ground and angrily kick the plant out of the soil and trample on it, then climb back into the wagon. "I told Mom not to make jelly out of them berries. Now, she's buried next to Papa."

Sarah glances at the two graves alongside the house. "Henry, firethorns aren't usually harmful unless pesticide's been sprayed on them."

"With so many ladybugs around, we never used pesticides, so why did the berries kill her?"

On Shadow Grove, Barney has discovered a little-used section in the attic of the sprawling manor, and after having located a suitable room in that isolated section of the attic, he has carefully prepared the room for future use, a room with no windows, a room with solid, wooden walls and an impenetrable oak door. After changing the door's lock, Barney hides the key under a manipulated attic floor board. Satisfied, he retreats down the back stair steps from the manor and into the greenhouse. Once there, he slips into a full-length apron and sprays pesticide on his favorite plants: firethorns. The greenhouse is filled with the thorny plants. Barney stops spraying and carries a pot-less plant to a nearby workbench and places it alongside several other pot-free fire-thorns. Also on the bench is a framed photograph of Adolf Hitler, and next to Hitler's photo is a crude drawing of Jesus wearing a crown of thorns on His head. Barney hurriedly cuts, and then forms a thorny crown out of the firethorn branches. Removing his apron he checks his gold pocketwatch, tears up the drawing of Christ, tossing the torn pieces in a nearby trash can. With the thorny head piece, he leaves the green-house and walks with quick steps to the manor, accidentally pricking his finger on the sharp thorns. As he sucks away the blood, his evil mind is at work. He couldn't care less about Christ or His crown of thorns as a sym-bol of good versus evil. Barney has made the crown of thorns to reverse their holy symbol to that of evil besting good. That hideous firethorn crown is designed to fit Flynn's head, to inflict on him so much pain that he will forever hate even the thought of Christianity. Keenly aware that he will not get all of the Klansmen to forsake God and Christ, Bar-ney—in order to convince, if not all of his men, then as many as he can to accept Satan as their savior—plans to put his own twist on mankind's belief in the love of God by using his son as the supreme example of the anti-Christ.

Below Manor Hill, a half dozen plain-clothes Klansmen leave Sa-rah's general store with coffee and donuts. One of them is old Hank with his uncombed, shoulder-length hair and his dirty, thick glasses. Sliding behind the wheel of his run-down Dodge truck, Hank waits while a handful of the men climb into the back of his battered pride and joy. Now that his best friend Barney seems fully in charge of the plantation, Hank openly flaunts his praise for Barney and that of his membership in the brotherhood of the Klan. Two of the Klansmen remain on foot, one-eared Dane and Chad, the overweight boy who tried to stop Dane from confronting Barney at Shadow Grove's gate when Barney walked Dane barefoot through glass. After having been bitten by the cotton-mouth at Sarah's wedding and having run screaming to his father and swelling up from the poison, and nearly dying, Chad still has not fully learned his lesson. Now, Chad goes out of his way to stick by Dane, to prove he's Dane's best friend and just as tough. Chad is wearing a bull-whip in his belt loop and has a Klansman's hood dangling half out of his back pocket, as is the custom of the young, lower-ranked members of that group, this to put the fear of God into any tar baby—who might happen upon them— and—by seeing the dangling hood, is made aware that the young men are feared Klansmen and not to be fucked with. As Chad struts about, sixty-year-old Ben, one of Sarah's elderly, white workers, leaves the store and attempts to skirt around the cocky young Klansman.

"Old Timer," says Chad, grabbing Ben by his arm and giggling. "Have you seen Sarah? Dane here is asking about her."

"Are you two drunk or just crazy?" asks Ben. "Sarah wants no part of you, Chad. Especially when it comes to you, Dane Tucker, with your ugly face."

Dane kicks the elderly man in his buttocks and then holds onto him, as he staggers about.

"Don't talk to me or my friend that way," Dane warns. "You fucking old cracker. You'll find yourself with a rope about your neck, the next time we catch you alone in the swamps. Now, you can just kiss my lily-white ass to apologize, the way you whites out here kiss up to your nigger-loving Sarah's. Whites willing to work with the coloreds. This place ain't no better'n that Jew factory in town."

Dane draws back to slap him, but Ben breaks free and flees, looking over his shoulder at them he yells, "Stay away from Sarah, Dane, or I'll tell Major Cutter, and he'll cut off your balls."

Chad decides to back off at the mention of Barney cutting off their balls, but Dane lingers behind as if he has a spare set of balls to give away, while kicking at the rocks as if hating the world.

"You coming, man?" asks Chad. "The Major's expecting all of us at the house. Now, I went along with you this far, but I'm not going to get on Barney's bad side while he's still up there on that hill with his knife, while you stand down here kicking dirt like the danger ain't real. It's a long walk up to that house and Barney hates you enough, ever since your pa died, as it is. Why take chances?"

"You go on," says Dane. "I'll stick around here fer a spell. Besides, old cripple Trout took the guys to them close-by swamps fer a quick fill-up from his moonshine still. There's time."

"It's your funeral," says Chad, calling back as he climbs the hill. Dane watches his friend walk about twenty or so feet, then stop and return to the front of the store.

"I thought you were leaving," Dane says, pleased that Chad has returned.

"What are friends fer?" says Chad. "I won't die fer you, but I'll wait here as a lookout fer you by the store. Now, go on and try and find that girl befer I change my mind and really leave."

Unnoticed at the Grove's entrance gate, Henry and Sarah have arrived in the wagon, Henry's tethered horse, Clara, following behind. Sarah sits up in the seat and stares at the area beyond the gate where the *White Dove* went down, then turns away, fighting back the tears. "Do you mind if we visit my parents' graves before you go to work in the fields?" asks Sarah. "He may be there."

"Who, Sarah?"

"The person who was to meet us at your place."

Henry drives through the gate and surrounding trees, to still another line of trees concealing them from the workers and, to some degree, from the hilltop manor house. At the cemetery, with the wagon parked nearby and in blowing dust, Sarah and Henry walk the short distance to the grave site of her parents. The grass there is brown, but the grave is adorned with dusty, but freshly cut flowers. Henry stares down at the raised mound and whispers. "I can't get used to the idea that the two of them are buried standing up down there."

"Neither can I, even though it was my idea," Sarah replies. "I thought it would please Mother." She surveys the cemetery. "The Major wants to get rid of the coloreds that are buried here."

"How? Dig 'em up and truck 'em away? To where? To Africa? It's a bit too late for that. America is our home, especially in death, after we've worked all their lives to help build it."

"I don't think he's thought about how to do it. Just that he wants to."

"I hope you told him to go to hell, because—before Mom and I buried him—Papa said the town certainly put your great-grandparents through hell, when they first decided to integrate this place long before Barney Cutter and his crazy mother were born. That's why Papa and Mom said they didn't want to be buried in that dump of a colored cemetery in town, and instead wanted to be buried on our land, where they feel only love from the earth and not the hatred of the town against coloreds and whites being buried together or alive walking together on top of the ground visiting the graves."

"Your folks, at your place and mine here on Shadow Grove, are together now, heaven-bound." Sarah wipes away the wind-blown dust from the tombstones and flowers and looks up at him. "I missed my last three times," she says returning to Henry's side.

"You did!" Henry exclaims, filled with discrete joy, while glancing toward the manor. Immediately, his jubilance turns to fear. "The major. My God, Sarah. You said he doesn't sleep with you, only with those call girls. If he finds out! This baby. You should have told me. We could have made plans earlier than this . . . maybe even had time to head for California, where they say coloreds and whites can legally get married to each other."

"I'll never leave here, Henry, and neither can you ever leave your land. Shadow Grove is to be left to Flynn and now . . ." She places her hand on her stomach, ". . . to our son as well."

"Our son? Are you sure? A boy?" Henry squints at the manor house. "Sweet Jesus. We're so lucky that the major's leaving. For a year, even. Thank God."

"It wasn't luck. I knew for months that Barney was leaving. Time enough for me to have this child. I didn't tell you about the baby because I wanted to be sure that I had conceived."

Henry is filled with love for her. He glances about and reaches toward her stomach, then quickly withdraws his hand, while keeping an eye on the manor house. "I wish I could feel it," he says.

"There's nothing to feel this early. It's the boy you've always wanted, a boy with my brain, as you so proudly put it, who will be well educated, good looking and strong in order to survive."

Henry goes deadly silent.

"What is it?" asks Sarah. "What's wrong?"

"Barney, Sarah. Isn't that why he wanted to marry you? For the same reasons. Your mind and music skill, so that Flynn will have these traits? Both of the boys with the same traits, but each with a different mission in life, to kill or be killed."

Sarah's young eyes focus on his, and she desperately attempts to change the subject of the boys killing one another, as—over the long months—Naomi has hinted that they might. "This baby will enter the world and bring about love, Henry, but not just for the coloreds. Our son must also help the whites, too, including Flynn. That's what I came to realize on that ship when Naomi told me what she did about Flynn. You have to help me watch over Flynn as well, Henry, you and our new baby.

132

You both must love Flynn as much as you love me, and never let Flynn go the way of Barney."

"Flynn will be my son as well, but are you sure? This baby is ours, and not Barney's?"

"Oh, yes. On the ship, Naomi said I would have two children and both would be boys."

"You mean Naomi said that, that I'd be the papa of our boy?"

"I'm sure of it."

"How, Sarah? I wasn't even sure you'd accept that perfume I gave you before you and your folks left for Germany. That's why I gave it to you in private the day before you left. Now I'm standing here talking about a baby we're having, when you hardly noticed me in the past."

"That's what you think, Henry Brooks. I had my eye on you since I was twelve."

Henry blushes at Sarah when she says that she has wanted him since age twelve. Then Henry returns his discussion back to Naomi. "She actually told you that you'd have my baby back then on that ship? Well, I'll be . . . I'm beginning to really believe in that woman, Sarah."

"Not only that. She said that I'd find the greatest love a woman can ever have, and I've found it and had hoped all the time that she meant you, and it seems she did."

"Jesus, Sarah . . . that Naomi . . . so strange. I've never heard of a colored person like her: stiff and strict about things and so damn sure of herself, and I mean all the time. It's a wonder those people didn't kill her when she insulted them at your wedding in town last year by going to that church."

"Naomi's not stiff and certainly not always serious. Last week, she crawled on her hands and knees like a horse with Flynn riding on her back laughing his head off, while I held him up straight, and he pulled on her braids like reins with his small hands. But then, as unpredictable as ever, after the back ride, Naomi cradled Flynn on her lap and told him a story."

"What's wrong with that?"

"She told him the strangest story, one about the baby you and I are having. Of course she wouldn't have dared told it to him if Barney had been in the house, but he was in town as usual."

"What did she say to Flynn about our child?"

"That our baby's—" she says, glancing into his eyes a bit stupefied,

133

now. "That his placenta will reside in a silver can, that the blood that drains from the placenta—"

"Placenta, Sarah?"

"The baby's afterbirth, Henry."

"Oh. Go on."

"She told him that our newborn's blood will drain from the placenta into that accursed word 'can', which Miller's congregation is always saying to defame the Catholic Church. What that really means, I don't know, but Naomi went on to say that the placenta blood will turn the leaves and an oak sapling into a mighty red tree as a symbol of man's hope for a better world."

"A tree of blood and a can?"

"She also said the can was in the sky over the church the day I married—"

Sarah abruptly stops talking when Henry looks as if he's in shock. In truth, he's wondering if he and Naomi saw that same thing in the sky last year, when Sarah was married to Barney. Feeling that Sarah has enough on her mind than to be burdened down with nonsense, and fearing for her health, he decides to deny everything about Naomi and her so-called powers from God.

"She's lost her mind!" he tells Sarah. "Why do you suppose she told Flynn such a story?"

"She said it was to give him a head start in order to run from Satan. She also said our baby would come into the world early, riding on the wings of a dead raven, while fleeing from death and from the hand of Satan and Chad."

"For God's sake! Chad, Sarah? How could she say such a thing when it might harm Flynn by hearing such talk?"

"Because she is from God, Henry, if you ever believed in me, do so with her now. She is from God."

Deeply pondering, Henry, almost in a whisper, says, "Sarah . . ." He says no more, as he looks puzzled, up at the sky.

"Last year," he goes on, "when you rode off with Barney in the Model T, after your marriage, did you see something in the sky that looked like a can and . . . maybe heard babies. Two of them and—" Again Henry clams up, while shaking his head in denial.

"Go on, Henry. Why did you stop?"

" 'Cause babies don't come into the world in cans, silver or not and

134

they don't ride on the wings of dead ravens, and a one-year-old child like Flynn doesn't know how to pee yet, let alone think about killing our son the way Naomi says." Lowering his voice, Henry recalls how he just said he was beginning to believe in Naomi, and he whispers, "It's too confusing to think about or talk about it now, even if she is right."

Suddenly, the caw of a raven is heard. Sarah looks at a distant treeline, between them and the manor. She sees a raven flying from the branches and retrieves an arm full of firewood from the wagon. Henry tries to help her with the wood, but she again looks at the raven.

"No, Henry. Have one of the other workers bring the rest of the wood to the house. The major or Dane might be watching."

"Dane Tucker? He knows he's not welcome here. Him or Chad."

"Dane came into the store this morning before I left. He was with Chad and the Klan. They bought coffee before going to the house to wish the major Godspeed."

"Godspeed? I don't know about the rest of these sheet-wearing punks, but Dane hates God as much as he hates the major, and we both know how much Barney hates God. And Sarah, what Naomi said about Chad, stay away from him. Naomi has been right more than she been wrong, even as crazy as it seems she is at times."

"I will," Sarah exclaims, just as Father Haas—in his brown robe—arrives on horseback and calls to them, then ties his stallion to a thicket.

"I'm sorry I missed you at the Brooks' place, Sarah," he tells her. "However, I said a prayer over Henry's parents' grave and came here as fast as I could, knowing that you might be visiting this hallowed ground."

"Sarah and I were just leaving," says Henry.

"I'll just be a minute," Father Haas tells them, while removing a vessel from his saddlebag and sprinkling holy water from it on the Winthrops' burial site, at the same time discreetly listening to Sarah and Henry and admiring the tall, black youth.

Meanwhile Sarah is letting Henry have it. "You're not to lay a hand on Chad or Dane Tucker, Henry Brooks. They're no danger to me. I ignore them. You want those men to hang you?"

"Sarah," Father Haas says, "you and Henry . . . sit a moment and rest. I'm almost finished."

"Sitting around won't plow my fields or yours," Henry whispers to

Sarah. She nudges him with her elbow, puts aside the firewood and sits on the ground. Henry sits next to her. The priest finishes his task and approaches them.

"Father, this is—"

"The young man who carried your mother's body in his arms so magnificently under that sky of those shooting stars," the priest says. "How could one ever forget him? Hello, Henry Brooks. It's good to see you again," he exclaims, shaking Henry's hand.

"You're the priest who helped fight the plane fire that night," a surprised Henry replies, never thinking he'd see the priest again.

"I am, and now that I'm being sent to a mission in California, Sarah asked me to speak with you before I leave."

"Why?"

"Henry," Sarah explains, "I told Father that unlike my land—which has not a blade of green grass on it—that your land makes you special, but you keep saying you're dirt to whites."

"He's right," says Father, smiling at Henry. "He's something I've sought to be all my life."

"You want to be dirt?" asks Henry, sitting back more comfortably and crossing his legs Indian style, his total attention now given to the priest.

"Yes, Henry. Dirt. The soil of the earth. Without it and water, even with the sun, all of mankind would vanish from the world. Did you know that the Franciscan order granted Little Shadow Place to your Freeman ancestors, Henry?" Father asks.

"They did?" remarks Henry in surprise. "Papa and Grandpa once said the church gave our land to our people, but I didn't know they meant the Catholic monks did."

"We're all monks in one way or the other, Henry, clustered or not, but the Franciscans seek out our sisters and brothers in need in the outside world."

"I heard Grandpapa talking about it once, when he was alive," Henry says with a smile in remembrance of his grandfather. "He said it was given to his ancestors out of some kind of remorse from the church at seeing the sin of white men enslaving colored people."

"He was right, Henry, but the enslavement list goes on and on: our American Indians, our Mexicans, our Chinese, including our more recent brothers and sisters from Africa, and our kin from the Middle East, to name a few."

"Henry gets upset sometimes, Father, because—as beautiful as he keeps his place—people like Reverend Miller, in town, preach that blacks are lazy and will destroy the value of white property if they're allowed to move into white neighborhoods, and attend white schools, and not kept in ghettos the way the Jews are kept in Germany."

"Whenever I pass by your land, Henry, it's as if passing the land where the Soul of God lives," says Father, "especially that magnificent lagoon and quarry. As for being black," he says, beaming at Henry with a look of profound wisdom about him, "we were all black once, my son. I wouldn't say that Jesus was lazy. He was possibly as dark as you."

"White men are black men turned white?" sarcastically asks Henry. "Even Jesus! Come on, Father! Is that what he just said?" Henry asks Sarah, "Christ was black?" Sarah, who had at first smiled and nodded to Henry, quickly changes that smile to a teenage frown, as Henry continues. "Boy, Father, you better be careful. The Klan will stretch your neck as fast as they will mine if you're heard saying Jesus was black or whichever way you said He was just now."

"I only said that Jesus was possibly as dark as you, not that our Lord was ever white." Father goes on, "Two thousand, six hundred years ago, after the destruction of the First Temple, a priestly, black, African Tribe, rooted in Judaism, carried what is believed the Ark of the Covenant out of Egypt and into Yemen."

Henry slaps his hands against his thighs and laughs, that is, until he looks at Sarah. "I'm sorry, Sarah," he scoffs, choking on laughter. "Next he'll be saying that people live out in space on planets like ours, and that Jesus is out there still dying for those people, even now, the way He died for us on earth." Henry shrugs at the priest. "Sorry, Father. That's just the way I feel, that's all."

"Henry Brooks!" snaps Sarah.

"That's one of the most interesting things I've heard all week, Henry," replies the priest. "That part about Jesus in space."

"Father," Sarah exclaims, "if God did scatter people from the Tower the way the Bible says . . ." She pauses, returning to Henry. "After some of the things I've seen Naomi do, just maybe, Henry, you and that unpredictable mind of yours may be onto something."

137

"I'm not onto anything, you two. Especially if it'll get me noticed by the Klan."

"Is God capable of that, Father," Sarah asks, "maybe even having created as many worlds of living souls as there are stars in the sky?"

"Capable, yes. But dear God, is Jesus to be forced to be crucified over and over thousands upon thousands of times more, maybe even without end in outer space? Would God put His Son through that?"

"No," says Sarah. "I guess that means we humans are alone in all of creation. But, Father, I've read the Bible through more than once after Father and Mother died, and it does speak about the Tower. It clearly does."

"Sarah, have you read *Homer* or the *Odyssey*, which I sometimes read in my travels?"

"Yes, I have."

"Now there's a fascinating book, in that it, in some ways, parallels the Bible by making us profoundly consider the creation of man here on earth or in space. I think it will lift mankind's spirits if we all read it, though many would disagree."

Henry just looks at them in controlled disgust. "Stop making fun of my remarks about Jesus not being colored, you two. And your Bible, Sarah, that Tower might be in there, but there's nothing in the Bible about a black Jesus, otherwise every church-going colored person in the world would be jumping up and down and tilting the earth to one side with their joy. Bibles aren't written by God: they're written by people and only a child would believe this priest about Jesus being black."

"I'm sorry, Henry. Father and I didn't mean to offend you," Sarah says, touching Henry.

His left eyebrow slightly rising, Father Haas knows there is more than friendship in that touch between them. He looks toward the manor. Sunlight is reflecting off of a military .45, over the treetops from the sprawling house's second-floor, where the major has just approached the window and is cleaning his weapon, while trying to observe them. Father Haas turns to Henry. "God doesn't always send His messages through the white man's Bible, Henry. God might send His message by a dog, a deer, a bolt of lightning, or through the stars. He may even send it by the lowly crow, or by a child. But you must be able to hear it as a child to be delivered from the dangers around you. Now, my children, I must leave."

138

"May I have your blessing before you go?" asks Sarah, kneeling.

Father Haas makes the sign of the cross, not about Sarah's head, as she lowers it, but in the direction of her abdomen. Sarah looks up at him. Father Haas smiles and mounts his horse.

"Father," calls Henry. "I'm sorry about my attitude. I didn't mean to disrespect you. I'm indebted to your order for giving my family Little Shadow Place and, Father, most of the world doesn't believe in Jesus. The proof of Him just isn't there."

"I know, son," Father says. "Sarah Winthrop has taught you well." He deliberately called Sarah, not by her "Cutter" name. "Shadow Grove is legally yours and Flynn's, Sarah. It was always your parents' intention that this land would never fall into the major's hands and that you'd find yourself a protector one day. God watch over you, Henry Brooks, you and Sarah and the blessed, unborn child."

As Father Haas rides away, he looks back. "The proof is in the shroud, Henry," he says. "Look for it there." Sarah and Henry look at each other in shock. "The baby, how did he know?" Henry asks, Father's shroud a distant memory, neither of them aware of sunlight breaking through the dust onto Father's saddlebag. An object, wrapped in a purple cloth, is mysteriously moving upward from the goatskin bag, and it drops onto the dying brown grass, exposing what's within it, a silver, jeweled chalice, a chalice which Miller's congregation named the "Tin Can." Aware only of each other now, Sarah and Henry continue their conversation. "Henry, Father Haas said you must be able to hear it as a child to be delivered from the dangers around you. Did he mean Barney?" Sarah asks, almost afraid to hear Henry's reply, "Do you think he killed my parents? The major? Naomi thinks so."

"I know it's hard to stop grieving, Sarah, but they've passed," he says, gently. "And, Sarah, as for the two of us praying for rain, this land is bone dry, because nature works that way, on its timetable, and nothing can change that or turn this place green, not even praying for the hand of God to reach in and do so, because—seems to me—the law of nature is the law of God, and if He wanted to He would have made it rain by now."

Behind them, a brown hand reaches from the thicket and picks up the chalice, the hand of Naomi, her hair in long braids, her forehead adorned with Indian beads. She looks at the distant priest, as he travels alone on his own personal road of the cross, while reading the book of Homer. Naomi gazes down at the grass. The circle of dying brown grass where the chalice had lain has turned green, water bubbling from the ground around the chalice's grassy impression. During Henry and Sarah's conversation, the young girl suddenly touches the side of her face and gazes skyward.

"What is it?" ask Henry, following her upward glance.

"Rain, Henry. I felt a drop of rain."

"I felt nothin'."

While Henry examines the heavens, Sarah slowly turns around and sees Naomi holding the chalice in her hands, the light of days sparking from it and from Naomi as if it were gold. Wide-eyed, Sarah looks from the holy vessel and locks gazes with the enigmatic woman. Naomi then reenters the underbrush with the chalice. Sarah quickly gathers up the firewood and faces Henry.

"Naomi thinks it's dangerous for us to be seen together, Henry." She hurries away, leaving Henry feeling lost and alone.

"One day," she stops, looks back and says, "after some lucky girl marries you, she'll make you happy."

Henry looks at a wedding band on Sarah's finger. "The one I love belongs to someone else. I'll never marry, Sarah. We'll always belong to each other."

Watching Sarah continue sadly on her way, Henry then leaves as well.

When Sarah reaches the tree line, Dane is just arriving on the foot trail which leads from the store below the grade. He steps in front of the teenager, startling her. Waiting for Sarah to catch her breath, Dane squints across the treelined, distant field at Henry, who is traveling away in Sarah's wagon. Suspicious at first at seeing Sarah coming from the direction of the black youth, Dane then sees the wood on the wagon and that which Sarah is carrying, and then his angry suspicions subside.

"Let me carry that wood," he tells Sarah. "I've been looking all over fer you."

"No, Dane," she says, stepping back from him. "I can carry my own wood."

"Sarah, I know some of your workers say I'm a bad influence, some even say I talk against you. That's a ball-face lie. I respect you fer helping the niggras, so why won't you look with a little more favor on me, like you do your trained, bone-fetching dog Henry? And as fer that old man you were forced to marry, what a mess. Just give me one little kiss and I'll prove I can make you happy."

Sarah drops the wood and runs away while a frightened Dane calls to her. "Don't tell the major on me! He'll kill me if you tell. Please, Sarah!"

In the manor's third-floor guestroom, where Sarah has chosen to sleep away from Barney, Major Cutter   in his army uniform but for his shirt—is looking through Sarah's telescope at Henry's distant lagoon, then returns to the master bedroom. His officer's shirt is lying on the bed, one of the sleeves dangling close to the floor.

"All of that damn water out there on that spade's land," he mutters. "Where's the justice in that no matter what I told Sarah?"

"In God's hall of records," he hears the answer and whirls around. Naomi is cradling a blanket-wrapped Flynn lovingly in her arms, Sarah and Cutter's blonde, blue-eyed son.

"What the hell are you coming in here for without knocking, woman?" hisses Barney.

"The door was open," Naomi says, nodding back at the open bedroom door.

"What'd you want, Naomi? I don't have time for you," he says as he searches about the room. "I can't find my Bowie knife. Have you been snooping about in here and moved it?"

"I haven't seen or have the need of such weapons to kill this world. I came in here thinking you might want to change your mind about Flynn and that thing." Her anguished gaze targets the crown of thorns on the bed beside Barney's luggage. "The hall of records is where all our sins are carefully stored," she goes on. "And maybe your knife is stored there, as well."

"Spare me your damn play on words, woman."

Naomi gently bounces Flynn in her arms and whispers to him. "You are one beautiful child. Don't grow up to be one of those whose hall record is in the bottommost drawer. You weren't born under the North Star, Master Flynn, as he to come will be, but you can be a blessing on earth if you learn to walk at his right down the chosen road of life and not at his left with the goats and snakes."

Cutter flings aside a chair and storms across the floor at Naomi. "You are not . . . I repeat . . . not Flynn's goddamn mother, not his fucking teacher, not a goddamn thing to him, but a black-ass mammy.

141

Sarah and I do the teaching in this goddamn house. Now keep that big mouth of yours shut, and stay the hell in your place, or I'll put my foot up your black ass! Do you understand me?"

Naomi fires back, "Yes, Sir, Major Cutter, Sir!" As Flynn coughs, Pancake, a black-and-white puppy, darts into the room and rumpuses around Naomi's feet.

"Pancake," she hisses, her anger meant for Barney, not for the dog, "get away! I don't have time to play with you now!" She jostles Flynn into the blanket, trying to subdue his coughing.

A sarcastic Barney glares at her and says, "That's strange, you yelling at the dog. I thought angels never got angry. Isn't that what you have Sarah thinking you are, an angel? The word's gotten around about you, Naomi, about those so-called miracles of yours. And that blanket around my son. I wouldn't think you'd need that to stop the boy from coughing. Just wave your magic wand or call on your God, and Flynn will be cured, the way folks say you cured that baby on the boat, just like that," he says, snapping his fingers.

"Would I pray for this sweet child if he was really sick enough to need it? Yes I would. Would God answer my prayers or yours if you also prayed for your son? Maybe. But all children catch colds and usually heal with love. Major, how long do you think you'll be gone this time?"

"Ah! That's the quickest damn turnabout I've ever seen," he says. "You went from smart-ass mouthing off at me to your motherly woman talk about how long I'll be gone. Why do you care? You'd just as soon see me out of this house for good, but don't press your luck, old woman. You're not my mother, and your neck will fit a rope as easily as a man's."

"Just trying to stay in my place and be civil and ask the right questions like all good mammies should, when the daddy of the child they takin' care of is going away," she says, "and if you think what I say and do is disturbing to you, and think that you can make me back off, there will come another who will make what I do and say seem like child's play, Major. Someone who—as he grows older—will not back down from you or from Satan."

"Are you threatening me, you black bitch? Is that what you think you're doing?" He slaps her.

"Hitler's man slapped harder than that," Naomi defiantly hisses without a flinch.

Barney draws back to whack her again, then lowers his hand when he glimpses Sarah from the window. She has returned to the firewood and is retrieving it as fast as she can, then runs with it toward the manor. Barney notices Dane making his way from the trees. He is keenly aware that Sarah cannot manage Shadow Grove, not without Naomi's help, and knowing that Naomi has all the balls needed to keep Dane and young men away from Sarah and the manor while he's gone, he faces the black woman. "You're always on your toes, aren't you, Naomi," he tells her. "I'll give you that much. A nigger with a quick mind. You know just how far to press the white man and when not to." Barney takes Flynn from her and kisses Flynn, as the young boy coughs. The Grand Wizard looks at Naomi. "Get one of the older men to plane that warped window in Flynn's room. I don't want the boy sleeping in that night draft any longer."

"Yes, Sir."

Barney hands Flynn back to her and reaches for his shirt. He sees a sleeve sticking from under the bed and yanks it into the open, dragging sleeve-chewing Pancake along. He throws the dog across the room, Naomi hurriedly covering Flynn's eyes. Cutter brushes off his shirt, slips into it, tucks it into his trousers and fastens the bottoms. He then picks up the crown of thorns and angrily takes Flynn from Naomi, who frowns at the crown. Cutter, carrying the young boy and the crown, followed by Naomi, struggling with the heavy luggage, descend the spiral staircase into the living room. Naomi places the suitcase on the front porch and returns, as Sarah enters the room from another door with the wood. Her face and clothing soiled, Sarah timidly approaches. "Barney, while you're away, I want . . ." She stops. Major Cutter follows her hesitant gaze to Naomi.

"What, Sarah? Don't look at Naomi. Finish what you were going to say, and Naomi, you stay the hell out of it."

"It would be nice to build a school, that's all," Sarah replies, "for our workers. The adults and young people. One of the workers has done quite well just by studying an English book, and all of the workers could do much better if we built them decent houses and—"

"Money, Sarah. Where do you think the money will come from, the trees?"

"Father had put aside a little lumber for a school, and as a memorial to him and mother—"

"We're still in the effects of the Depression!" exclaims Cutter, glaring at her. "If those poor, white crackers learn to read and write, they'll ask for higher wages. And I know you weren't planning to include the coloreds in that dumb school idea of yours. And that wood. Look how dirty it's gotten you. I told you to let the niggers do the dirty work for you, otherwise, why do you keep them around? What were you going to do with that wood, anyway?"

"It burns cleaner than our oak wood," Sarah tells him, crushed, looking down at the floor. "I'll burn it in Flynn's fireplace. You were worried about that draft in his room, and—"

"That chimney hasn't been cleaned in years. You want to burn down the house? You do nothing! I've told Naomi how to handle it."

Sarah is near tears.

Naomi stamps her foot. "This is your wife, Sir."

"Then let her grow up! In my absence, who'll run this damn sixteen-thousand-acre, dust-bowl, pain-in-the-ass land until I return or until my son is grown if I should—" Barney was going to say, if he should die, but lately he's had the feeling that he will never die, that nothing can harm him. After these thoughts subside, he again attacks Sarah. "She's nothing but a child!"

"Yes, she's fifteen, and you should have thought about that before you took advantage of her and married her and—" The minute she utters those words, Naomi clams up tight. *After all*, she tells herself, *God had placed that evil man and Sarah together to prepare for the second coming of Christ.* Nevertheless, she takes a different approach and hammers on. "You might be a big man in army intelligence, Barney Cutter, but you don't know nothin' about bein' a father or a husband."

The black woman quickly leaves, slamming the front door behind her. Major Cutter leers at Sarah. "You see what I put up with for you, Sarah? My ancestors would have tarred and feathered that black witch of a bitch the second she opened her black mouth like that."

"Let me have my baby," Sarah says, "and please don't speak of Naomi that way."

"One of these days," Barney says, "I'm either going to fire Naomi's black ass or hang her."

"No, you won't!" screams Sarah, slapping his face, and as he looks at her in total surprise, she slaps him again.

"That's the best sex you've given me since our marriage," he tells her, rubbing the side of his face, smiling while holding onto Flynn.

"Seems there's hope for you yet. Now I'll have something to come back to."

Outside, the workers watch a military command car, with only the driver aboard, pull up to the manor and stop. An army corporal steps from the vehicle and picks up the luggage from the porch, ignoring Naomi as she sweeps around it. He places the suitcase in the car and slides behind the wheel, just as the hoodless Klansmen and Hank's Dodge pull in behind him and the car. Chad is now driving Hank's truck, he and Dane having climbed into it at the general store, after a drunken Hank stopped to pick them up there, and then vomited and passed out. An angry, vindictive Dane is sitting next to Chad, guzzling moonshine from a jar and can hardly sit up straight. Hank, however, while still gripping a moonshine jar, is sprawled out in the back of the pickup at the feet of the other lowly Klansmen; all of them who can stand, do so respectfully, as Cutter leaves the house carrying Flynn, with Sarah close behind. She grabs Cutter's arm, stopping him on the porch.

"Don't put those firethorns on him," she begs. "If those men are Christians, they will understand a mother not wanting her son to suffer, so that you can change theirs and Flynn's belief in Jesus." Surprised, Barney stands there, stunned. He had no idea that Sarah could have been able to see through his systematic plans to condition Flynn against Christianity through pain. "Isn't it enough that you don't believe in God or Christ? Why are you doing this to your son, Barney?"

The major sweeps her arms away. Sarah falls. Naomi rushes forth and strikes Cutter across his back with the broom, snapping the broom handle in half, and causing an uproar from the Klan. Barney bashes Naomi with the thorny crown, and when she drops to the porch, he stands spread-legged over her, while she groans on her knees and bleeds about her mouth beside Sarah. Cutter's eyes of fire glare down at both Naomi and Sarah, who is in a fetal position and terrified, Sarah holding onto her surrogate mother and crying. Barney leans down to Naomi.

"In front of my men you'd do that, you fool. Strike me with that goddamn broom, knowing I'd have to retaliate?" He looks at his sobbing wife, while exposing a .45 to Naomi, the deadly weapon mounted in his waist. "Sarah needs you, Naomi, goddamn bitch, if not for that I'd blow your goddamn head clean off right here and now, and no court in the land would convict me."

145

"Beat Sarah, Major," one of the Klansmen, in a red, rebel's baseball cap, on the truck yells. "She's the reason that Naomi is so uppity."

Barney whips out the .45 and fires two rounds at the Dodge, blasting the hat off of the insolent Klansman's head, causing those standing on the truck bed beside him to duck, as well as the command-car driver, who sinks down behind the steering wheel.

"Who brought this fool out here to insult the mother of my son?" yells Barney to those in the truck, while slipping the weapon back into his waist and one-handedly straightening out the crown. "Who, so I can kill the asshole with my bare hands and the one who brought him here."

Having been awakened by the shots and told about the insult, Hank stumbles to his feet—as do the several Klansmen who had hit the deck. Hank wobbles in front of the trembling heckler.

"It's not Clarence's fault, Major. He's just drunk." Hank looks about the men and throws up his hands and exclaims. "Hell, all of us is drunk. No jobs or a way to pay the rent. We need Clarence even with his big mouth. Ain't but a handful of us Klansmen left."

"Most of our members swore off the Klan to get them factory jobs," the heckler adds, shuddering, trying to get back in Barney's good graces.

"And in town that Jew factory owner," Hank adds, "he's hiring even more of them coloreds in his plant, instead of giving us out-of-work Klansmen them jobs. Said we'd be a bad influence on his whole damn crew in there, since the rest of us didn't swear off the Klan with the others."

Cutter looks at the black smoke spewing from the factory's chimneys on the horizon in the town that was once his family's domain. As he stands there musing toward Cutterville, at that same time, down the hill, on the edge of the cabbage fields, while the white workers are lined up and watching Sarah, the Klan and Cutter, Henry stands with the black workers. He looks at Naomi and Sarah, then his eyes of vengeance lock on Barney.

As Sarah and Naomi help each other to their feet, Henry takes a hoe from the black man next to him. Perplexed, the other blacks—feeling that Henry is going to try and attack the armed Grand Wizard with the hoe—hold onto him, but Henry jerks free of them and eases his way up the slopes to a place near the Klansmen's truck and begins hoeing the bone-dry ground and dead weeds, all the time sizing up and listening to the Klansmen and Barney. On the porch, holding his son close, Cutter regains his composure and faces his drunken men.

"Every two thousand years or so," Barney begins the diabolical dialogue of his plan to keep his men's feet to the ground and loyal to him by using his son, "our Nordic doctrine says a savior is born, a genuine, living Christ type to guide you. I'm going away for a year in order to seek my fortune and secure my son's future and yours." After Barney includes them in his plans, the Klansmen cheer him and whistle. Barney then raises his hand and silences them, his sights of displeasure on a drunken Dane as he sits slumped over in the truck. "There are those among you who say that I'm away too much to be of worth to you, but Master Flynn, this small boy, will be my living symbol while I'm gone. I've instructed Sarah on how to raise him during my absence. It's only through our children, my mother always says, that tomorrow can be secured for us. And now I have a son, as I prayed he would make possible, he who protects me, as he will you, in time, if you believe as I do. Soon, the world will be at my son's and my feet and at yours."

The sky suddenly explodes, with thunder shaking the land, drawing all eyes to the heavens, and those in the truck trembled, some fearing, others feeling that the abrupt thunder is a sign that Barney is indeed a god.

Ten miles away in Cutterville, Barney's elderly mother crawls under her bed to escape the house-shaking thunder. As she peeks from beneath the bed frame, her eyes all-encompassing against her filthy, soil-blackened face, her nappy hair slicked across her head from her body waste, her dress tattered and urine soaked, she clings to her bedpan and to a butcher knife, viciously stabbing out at the shadows.

"Go away! Leave me in peace! I don't want you in this house," she cries.

Back on Shadow Grove, not knowing what to expect, the Klansmen and Sarah nervously watch in disquietude as Barney places the firethorn crown on the crying child's head, then lifts Flynn high in the air.

Naomi's sights are not on Flynn, nor on Sarah, Barney or on the Klansmen. Standing on that porch of hell, she sees herself back on the bow of the *Imperator* talking to God:

Since miracles are so few in coming, she hears herself asking God, *and Caleb and Flynn are both foretold to be the ones who will be lifted to-*

147

ward the heavens in the hands of their fathers during their births, the same way I lifted up Little Joel and prayed for the life of that precious child, did I use up one of the prayers which might have saved Caleb's life in the future?

When Barney raises Flynn to the summit of his reach, Naomi screams, "Nooo!"

With Barney glaring at her, the mysterious woman snaps out of it. Barney goes on without missing a beat. "Here is the blood of my blood," he exclaims, holding Flynn aloft. "Pure and white! I give you my son Flynn! Your next Grand Wizard and your god!"

The Klan rocks the truck with exuberance, everyone, that is, except Dane, his awakening eyes of loathing on Barney, who hands his sobbing son to Naomi. Sarah reaches in and also holds onto her traumatized boy, both she and Naomi immediately smother the wailing child with kisses, while trying to remove the crown of thorns.

"Let him be," says Barney, "he has to learn to become hardened-steel and razor-sharp."

Naomi—feeling Flynn's pain—glares at Cutter and holds Flynn even closer, careful not to aggravate the thorns into the blonde boy's tender scalp more than they have been already. Moved by his young wife and the black woman's compassion for his son, a kinder Cutter shows itself. "Take the crown off now, if you wish," he quietly tells Naomi. He steps close to her. "And Naomi, stay here and look after my family."

"As if a slap from you would make me do anything less," she says trying to remove the crown. "Me! Leave Sarah and Flynn? No, Sir! That will never happen. I raise both of them kids, Sarah when she was fourteen and lost and Flynn since these very hands delivered him from that young child's body, when your Doctor Schmidt's pure, white hands didn't show up in time. But these black hands—that you didn't want to be the first to touch your son—did just that, delivered Flynn, in spite of you, and I will never abandon him."

Barney scowls at Naomi and then turns to Sarah, who is sobbing. He strokes the side of her face, turns sharply about and calls to the Klansmen. "While I'm away, check with Hank, who I've arranged to work in the store here with one-leg Trout, in order to make sure this place continues to keep the blacks separated from Shadow Grove's white workers. I'll stay in touch with you by mail, those of you who can read." He faces Naomi and says. "Keep Dane and Chad away from this house."

"Now, go on about your business and let me tend to mine," Naomi scolds. "Nobody's coming in here to do Sarah wrong. If they try . . . be warned," she says to Barney, "they will have to do it over ma dead body."

The major enters his chauffeured command car and is driven away. He never looks back. Inside the Dodge cab, a drunken, half-awakened Dane nudges Chad.

"Did you hear what the nigger woman said about her dead body, Chad? I'll not only grant her that wish, I'll put my dick right up her black, dead butt, where I always wonder what it was like to fuck a dead woman. And that major, damn, Barney Cutter saying that about Flynn. Now, Sarah, there's a real goddess fer you. One day I'll own this spread and I'll destroy Mister Barney Cutter fer whatever he said to pa that night and made him put that gun in his mouth." Dane notices some of Sarah's workers digging a ditch in a nearby field and again nudged Chad. "Poor fools. They'll never reach the coast by digging those irrigation ditches by hand, no matter what Sarah and that curly-head spade Henry Brooks tells them. And even if by luck they do reach Henry's land, I'll kill him too. If Sarah gets that coon's water, she won't be as easy to pull off that high horse of hers and be made to submit to me. The bitch actually threw down that wood and ran from me as if I was a nigger or something, like I was a pile of shitty-ass shit with eyes! And I won't ever ferget that, Sarah, you bitch!"

The minute Barney's car fades in the distant dust, the ditch diggers stop working, and this time, Chad nudges Dane when he sees what those workers are doing. "I see them, dammit, Chad! Stop jabbing on me!" Both watch the workers run to a tree-shaded area of the central field and then sweep away a scattering of fresh-laid hay, uncovering a concrete foundation. On the porch, Naomi is carefully removing the last of the crown from Flynn's tangled hair, and he's reduced to a whimper by the black woman's Afro-Indian soothing voice, a nervous Sarah, all fingers, doing her best to help.

"I'll take care of Flynn, Sarah. You're no good here. Go help 'em build that dream of yours before them workers start thinking about Barney returning and firing them and that he's the real boss here and not you. Show them, by example, that this is yours and Flynn's land and not that monster's."

Sarah kisses Flynn's small feet. She then backs off the porch, suffering for her son as she goes. Once off the porch, she turns and runs into the field, drying her eyes on her sleeve. After reaching the workers, when she looks back and sees Naomi smiling approvingly, Sarah shouts to the women who are standing idly around and watching the men work. The teenage plantation owner leads her female workers into the nearby barn. Minutes later, yelping like drunken cowboys and angrily waving their straw hats, to show their disapproval of Barney, the fired-up females drive wagon loads of lumber from the end section of the massive barn, several of the wagons carrying A-frames. When the exuberant ladies and their wagons join up with the foundation workers, Sarah rolls up her sleeves and, surrounded by plantation children, she hammers a pole sign into the ground at the foundation site. It reads: OUR SCHOOL. A wave of cheers fill the air, and Sarah is swamped with kisses and hugs by the young people and the women. Field-boss Collins with those kind, green eyes and powerful arms and hands, that carried Lawrence's body from the plane, now takes charge. He gives directions to the men on the ins and outs of raising the walls and A-frames to the roaring delight of whites and blacks alike. Naomi—having removed the crown from Flynn's head and hair—is far from content.

"One of the babies is reactive and easily influenced," she says in the wind, while cradling Flynn, going on, "the other still to come will be stubborn and difficult to convince like his daddy. May God have mercy on the two of you, Flynn Cutter, you and your brother who is even now in your mamma's womb waiting to enter this world."

In the truck cab, while the men on the truck's bed watch the workers feverishly building the school, Chad, sitting angrily behind the wheel, looks at Naomi. "What the hell you think that bitch witch is sayin', Dane?" he asks. "Over there talking to herself."

"Who cares," hisses Dane. "Now that it's whispered that Barney'll be out of the picture fer a year or more, I'm making my move."

"You're nuts, Dane! Flynn's the next Grand Wizard. You heard the major."

"Fuck you, Chad!" yells Dane. "When things got bad in Cutterville, my pa was the Big Hat Walk to them poor, white crackers, not Reverend Miller, not you, not Barney, so don't you give me that I'm-in-charge bullshit now by trying to tell me to lay off making my move on the Klan and on Sarah. Barney'll be away fer a whole year. Didn't you hear him? What better timing could I ask fer? Besides, you want in Sarah's pants as much as I do, and I've always known it." He violently nudges Chad back into the seat. "As fer Flynn becoming the Grand Wizard, I'm not going to sit around growing old waiting fer a snotty-nose kid to grow up and play god. Not even Sarah is safe from my revenge now because of the way she insults me."

"You're drunk and as crazy as the major and his devil worship, Dane. You can't—"

Dane grabs him by his throat. "Don't you ever talk to me like you just did! Never! I'm not crazy!" Dane head butts Chad, knocking him half unconscious, then whips out Barney's knife and presses it against Chad's neck. "Remember this? How Barney put this knife against my throat last year?" he hisses. "I stole it from his greenhouse, and I'll cut anyone's throat who's against me, and God be damned."

"With you! We're all with you!" mutters Chad.

"Damn well better be," says Dane, putting the knife on the seat between them and opening a bottle of moonshine and guzzling it dry. When he finishes, the bottle slowly slips from his hand, and he topples over on the seat and passes out, his knife lying there with Chad staring down at it. Chad slowly turns his head and glares at the men who have been watching through the rear window.

"What you guys looking at?" he yells, causing the men to turn away. "Ain't you ever seen a man pass out befer?" Burning rubber and oil all the way down the driveway, Chad speeds them for home, his free hand reaching for Barney's Bowie knife. When the dust settles, Henry is standing in the old truck's tire marks. Beside him is a thick-bodied, sandy-haired, freckled-faced teenager named Jeffery, his pale lips and his clenched, white knuckles reveal the tension that rages within him. It's clear that both boys have heard what Dane has said about taking over Shadow Grove and possibly harming Sarah. Jeffery runs screaming into the field, alerting the workers, a few of the women groaning in dread and going to their knees in prayer.

Henry yells at them, "You can't help Sarah by crawling on your knees every time there's trouble. Get up! Praying won't help!"

The barn doors abruptly begin opening and slamming shut; the sunny sky turns gray; laundry is ripped off of clotheslines, and workers' straw hats are blasted off their heads in an abrupt, breathtaking upheaval; yet not a blade of drying grass is disturbed, nor a tree limb swayed, for there is no wind or even a whisper of a breeze to cause the marvels. Sarah's workers all gaze about, a few of their groans filling the air in profound fright, and as many of their co-workers are knocked off

151

their feet, even more of the workers drop to their knees in prayer. Sarah manages to hurry back to the porch to Naomi to draw courage from her. Henry, however, is forced backwards, as he attempts to go to a terrified Sarah. Finding himself more than a little terrorized by the force upon them—and gasping for breath—Henry somehow remains standing. In the face of the buffeting might, his eyes turn to the sky, and he begins talking to his unseen God.

"Sir, I know a lot of folks misunderstand me 'cause I don't go to church and never pray for Your help in anyway. But it ain't because I don't believe like they think I don't. I just feel You got bigger things to do than to worry about someone as small and unimportant as this human. Your Son died on His cross—even for the ones who find it hard to believe in Him or in You—to show us all how to love. Sarah has shown me such great love that I'll even start going to church, 'cause Sarah just might be right about that Babel Tower, and that through all the killin' and hatin' in this world, that You surely made others worlds and folks, colored and white, far out in space, better'n the ones You made here on earth, and if it'll help keep Sarah and our unborn child safe from Dane and Major Cutter and the Klan, I'm willin' to die to prove I love Sarah more than my own life."

As abruptly as it had started, the opening and closing barn doors subside; everything is stilled, and the hats and laundry slowly fall back to earth. Henry looks around. Most of the black workers are kneeling, while most of the white workers have gotten off their knees and now remain standing, looking at the coloreds, then about and at each other, the creatures of the field, the cows and sheep, all gazing up. Slowly, Sarah's white field hands do as the blacks are doing and ease back to their knees before that unseen force. Henry sees Sarah on the porch observing him in awe, while holding Flynn close in her arms. Naomi is holding Father Haas's chalice. She lifts it over her head and loudly exclaims: "God has heard your cry, Henry Brooks! Stand brave, stand fast, and stand strong, for it is on your feet that you will be the most help to Flynn and Caleb. He will arrive at the height of winter and you will be here long enough to be your son's guiding light!"

The days turn into weeks, and weeks into months. The light of the sun soon fades, leaving the land darkened and cold and the plantation in apprehension; cotton fields are laid bare; the leaves fall from the trees, and soon the height of winter is upon them.

10
Winter's Night of the Raven

Late at night in Cutterville, the day before Christmas, during the height of a fierce snowstorm, a young, white newsboy— age twelve—is standing on Town Square selling the Cutterville *Sentinel* for five cents each to a scattering of customers. The oldest of six children, he hopes to help raise money for his family's rent: An excellent student in school, he's always telling his parents that he wants to be President of the United States. Waving a newspaper about from his windblown, weighted-down, stack of papers, he coughs between yelling out Major Cutter's name, his shivering voice reverberating through the howling wind. Suddenly, seemingly appearing out of nowhere, he sees Naomi standing before him, startling him. She's adorned with an Indian headband and is wearing a beaded Indian necklace, a necklace with an eagle's feather dangling from it.

"Hello, Adam," she says, smiling down at the news boy, the falling snowflakes covering him faster than the boy can brush them off.

"How did you know my name?" he asks, stepping back, bumping into his stack of papers and accidentally knocking off the paperweight.

"Oh, I know many things," she tells him, while watching the wind lift the edges of his newspapers, threatening to blow them away without the paperweight to anchor them down. She hands Adam a heavy wool blanket and a hundred dollars, all in one-dollar bills. The young boy's eyes widen, his mouth opens, his young heart gallops in disbelief as he holds onto that money. He stares down at it, more money than he or his family has seen at one time in a year; looking up at the black woman, he asks, "This money. . . . For me?" She nods and he goes on, even more in shock. "Why? I'm white and you're colored."

"A beautiful young girl had been saving that money and a little more, since she was about nine," Naomi tells him, "and today she unfolded it and gave it to me, so that I might buy myself a present; 'spare change' she insisted, when I told her I couldn't accept it, that it was far too much money for the likes of me. She playfully put the money in my pocket, regardless, and told me to spend it anyway I like. This is the day before Christmas, Adam, a time for sharing. It doesn't know that you are white and neither will he, when he arrives."

"He? Do you mean Jesus?"

"Not Jesus. Not yet. He who is coming will be called 'Caleb', and he will be born a minute before twelve, this very night."

"Who are you?"

A powerful wind explodes Adam's newspapers skyward, and he drops the blanket and the hundred dollars and attempts to rescue his wayward papers, grabbing at them this way and that—to no avail—Naomi looks at the headline of one of the journalistic printouts, which the boy desperately catches and re-anchors with the paperweight: "Colonel Cutter Captured," the headline screams out in bold print. Naomi again faces the worried young boy, a boy trying to save a stack of papers that has a total value of less than three dollars, papers, however, that he's come to depend on for three years and something that he's trusted will be there for him to help out his family, and now he's worried that he'll be fired.

"The money," he says, all eyes, looking up at her, after he reaches into his pocket and realizes he has dropped the money, and it has also been lost to the wind. His innocent eyes watering up, he stands there. "I lost the money," he whispers to her.

"God has a future plan for you and does not want any of His beloved children to die in the cold. Go home now, and stay warm." As the tears flow down Adam's ashen face and freeze on his cheeks, he retrieves the blanket from the sidewalk, looks at his one rescued newspaper and again turns to Naomi, as if to say that one newspaper won't help much. Naomi wipes away those frozen tear drops, and as he closes his eyes against the sting, she whispers, "Live long, Mister President." She takes the blanket from him and wraps it about his small body. He opens his eyes, and she's gone. He slowly walks away in dismay. He hears Naomi call to him.

"In your pocket, Adam. Look there." Reaching into his pocket, he withdraws the neatly folded one-hundred-dollar bills. After looking this way and that for Naomi, he runs for home, through the falling snow, with the money safely tucked away in his pocket. At the same time, even as she seemed to have vanished before the boy's eyes, Naomi is blocks away, near the black side of town and crossing the train tracks in a horse-drawn wagon and heading back to Shadow Grove. She's wrapped in a blanket, with several more piled in the bed of the wagon, blankets which—along

154

with a paper-wrapped package—she had earlier purchased with some of Sarah's money and has been giving away to the needy. The paper-wrapped package is resting on the seat beside her, and as if to signal its importance, Naomi taps the package with her hand. The mysterious woman suddenly stops the horse and wagon right on the train tracks and stands up. She stares down the snow-covered rails into the blinding snow where human forms are seen moving toward her through the cold maze and wind. A barefoot black female—carrying firewood on her head—walks out of the distant blizzard and into view along with her three scantily-dressed children at her side, two teenage girls and an eleven-year-old boy carrying buckets, two of which are half filled with coal that has fallen from passing locomotives, and the girls and the boy have collected from alongside of the tracks, as they've been making their way home.

"Mamma," the oldest girl, named Goldie for luck, is sobbing, "you' feet gonna freeze."

"May I be of help?" Naomi calls to them once they neared.

"Do you have any snow to be shoveled?" the young boy asks, running ahead of the others and to the wagon. "My name is Bootie," he tells her, "and I'll do it fo' a quarter."

"If you do got snow to shovel," the woman says, approaching with her girls, "we knows that a quarter is a lot of money, but all ma kids beside these three, a older boy and three other older girls, at home, will chip in and shovel you' snow fo' the same price, a quarter. We on welfare relief, and a quarter'll buy oatmeal and maybe a can of Carnation milk that I can water down fo' us to have a bit mo' of it to eat that way."

"Your husband," asks Naomi. "Does he work? Or did he abandon you to the drinking of alcohol, like so many other husbands have around here?"

"Oh, no!" the youngest girl sadly replies. Instead of coal in her bucket, she is carrying water. She continues. "Papa, he died from T.B. from workin' in that tire factory. He knew he was sick, but kept workin' there 'cause he had no choice, in order to keep us warm and fed. We already lost two of our brothers from the cold. Kenneth. He would have been the oldest in our family. And Carl would have been somewhere between me and my sisters."

Naomi—with those penetrating brown eyes—looks at the woman,

a woman who, Naomi senses, needs to tell the world the truth of how she feels.

"Their father was a hard-working man, but he was a mean man," the woman says, not knowing why she would reveal such intimate family details to a stranger, as her children nod in agreement. "He dragged me down the steps by my feet, bumpin' ma head off of each step, and he beat me and the children whenever he got drunk, but in his own way, he loved them and me."

Naomi glances over her shoulder at the shabby houses across the train tracks behind her and says, "I don't live in Colored Town, so I can't hire you to shovel my snow."

"Then, where do you lives?" Bootie asks. "Colored Town is where all coloreds lives, unless they be lucky enough to live out yonder on God's Little Acres." He sees that Naomi is bewildered and thinks he has confused her and adds. "Shadow Grove. That what we in Colored Town calls God's Little Acres, where only blessed coloreds live and not here, in spite of Major Cutter, thanks to a young girl called Sarah and—"

The youngest girl breaks into the conversation, "Folks say that some magic colored woman called Naomi lives out there, right, Mamma?" she says turning to her mother.

"Ifin not here in Colored Town, wherever you live," Bootie again controls the conversation. "We'll go there."

As the woman nods in agreement, Naomi tells them, "I live on Shadow Grove, ten miles from here, too far for you to walk." She then notices the woman's bare feet.

"Where are your shoes, child?"

The shoeless woman gazes down at her feet, then up at Naomi. "They fell apart on the way home," she says. "Did you say you live on Shadow Grove?"

"Yes, I live there, but your feet. Let me drive you home."

"We there already," says the woman, pointing at a shack just across the railroad track. As the family starts for home, Naomi digs in her pocket and gives the boy the last of Sarah's savings: two-hundred dollars. As had the news boy, Adam, the penniless family stares disbelievingly at the cash. As they gawk at her with wide-open eyes, Naomi gives the children several blankets and addresses their mother, "That money'll help fill your stomachs with butter beans and biscuits through the winter and the blankets will keep you and yours warm. This summer, good fortune will come your way, and you will recover as a family."

Taking off her fur-lined boots, Naomi hands them to the barefoot woman, who gasps, "Oh, no! I can't take you' boots. You've already given us so much. What will you do to keep warm?"

"He who watches over me will see to that," Naomi tells the woman, who takes the gift, and with tears flowing down her face, she places the firewood on the ground and slips her cold feet into the warm boots.

"God'll bless you," she says, again lifting the wood onto her head and sobbing. "God surely will. He will bless you fo' this."

"He already has," Naomi says. "He's given me a warm place to live and enough to eat."

"Who are you?" the woman asks. "I has never seen nobody like you, who would give the boots off her feet, and even give away all that money, or talk to us or look like you."

While the oldest girl continues to remain silent, her younger sister, who seems to have profound faith above and beyond the others, looks at Naomi and asks, "If you live on Shadow Grove, do you know the woman called Naomi, who folks say lives out there and gots God's blessin' and says a colored baby is to be born in the world to help us poor? And is she really real? If she is, tell her I love her."

"You have just done so yourself, child. I'm Naomi."

Dropping her wood and going onto her knees before the wagon, the woman gazes up at Naomi. "Lord, is you really her. Really the one blessed called 'Naomi?' "

"Please don't bow down to me," Naomi tells her. "This, even Caleb would not ask of you."

"You're Naomi," sobs the woman, as her children gape up in wonderment at the mixed-blood woman. Looking at her children, she says, "Show you' respect fo' her." Lowering their buckets to the ground, the older girl and the boy also go to their knees beside their mother. The youngest girl kneels as well, but she holds onto their precious bucket of water, as her mother goes on talking to Naomi.

"You is truly her, the one they say come to live with young Sarah Winthrop, who was forced to marry that wicket Klansman?" When Naomi nods, the woman cries aloud. "My God. Some of us coloreds say you come with a message of hope fo' us about this baby boy, and that you knows everything there is to know."

157

"If I knew everything," Naomi tells them, "I would have known that you wore no shoes long before I saw you, and I would not have to have been told that your husband died trying to feed you and had not abandoned you. God does not tell us everything, only some things, that we will not just be His puppets and that we will sharpen our own insights into this world. 'Caleb,'" she says. "This baby boy who you mentioned . . . He will be called Caleb. Now, please stand up."

"Will Caleb be born, or will the Klan kill him?" the youngest girl asks, extremely worried, carefully holding onto that bucket of water, as they again stand up.

"God willing, he will be born, child. As to where, I don't know—maybe on the Grove—just that it will be soon, now, and he'll change our lives forever, one way or the other," Naomi says. "And yes, Jesus sent him and another. And if these two special boys clear the pathway to God, there will be ten more like them to help share their burden in preparing the world for the second coming."

"The second coming?" whispers the woman in excited exaltation to her young ones.

The young girl hands the bucket of iced-over water to Naomi, who looks at the bucket, then at the smiling young girl.

"What's the water for, child?" she asks the young girl.

"It's from a pure stream blessed by Reverend Harris to be used as holy water to baptize us. It's all I can offer you," the girl says. "Now it's a Christmas present for you."

Naomi looks about. "Where is this Reverend Harris now?" she asks.

"After he blessed the water, he went to check on one of our sick church members and told us to take the water home and bring it to church on Christmas, tomorrow," the children's mother says.

"But, it's for your baptisms?" says Naomi.

"My youngest is full of love, and each family brings their own blessed water," their mother says, "and I let her speaks fo' us all, when it comes to Jesus and what's important to our souls."

The girl looks at her mother, sister and brother, all nodding in agreement, and she goes on.

"We already been baptized by desire, when you said a colored boy is being born and sent by God. That's all the hope we need."

Now nearly in tears, herself, Naomi feels that it's one of the best, most-loving Christmas gifts she could ever want. She places the bucket on the seat beside her.

The family crosses over the train tracks, all of them looking back over their shoulders in awe at Naomi, who had magically appeared out of the snow in her wagon with gifts from God.

That youngest of the girls calls to Naomi. "And will Caleb make life different fo' us?" she asks, then gazes at the desolated black community, then back at Naomi. "Will God cause Caleb to be born in one of our shacks just like Jesus was in a stable, if I pray that he will be, so that I can see him? If not, tell him I also love him."

"What's your name, child?" Naomi calls to the young girl.

"Briana," she calls back.

"You will see him, Briana, when your young son points him out to you, as he rides by on a magical horse with the vision of God reflected in his light-brown eyes and the wind at his back. He will be with Flynn. And he will be able to cast out hatred where it eats away at us like a cancer and replace it with love. Then you will know that Caleb is, indeed, worthy of your love. Pray for Caleb and for the boy named Flynn that they will not be destroyed by Satan." Naomi drives into the storm and disappears from their view.

On the edge of town, she stops her wagon next to the Cutters' wire fence with its no-trespassing sign. The three-story Victorian looms dark and foreboding beyond the gate, the Italian cypress, the wind and the snow trumpeting against the aging, godless-looking dwelling, slamming window shutters back and forth. Without warning, a pale Mrs. Cutter jerks open the front door.

"I see you out there!" she screams. She balls up a section of newspaper and hurls it across the snow-covered lawn at Naomi, screaming, "My curse on you and Barney." She steps back into the house, closing the door behind her; moving to the front-room window, with a kerosene lamp in her trembling hand, she eases aside those tattered, burgundy draperies and stares out of that boarded-over shattered window at the black woman. Naomi focuses on the tossed, wind-blown newspaper, as it tumbles across the snow toward the gate, where it sails over the fence and into the black woman's hand. It's an out-of-town newspaper, and the headlines also mention Barney: "Cutter missing on secret mission behind enemy lines!" Naomi faces the shivering woman behind her glass-fractured window of protection and that of her glowing lamp.

"Do you want me to pray with you that God might have mercy on you and your son?"

The demented old woman yells, "Go away! You're not from God! May Satan fry your black ass and destroy Sarah Winthrop, who stole my son from me. That's what I say, you false-talking bitch. I don't need you or your God, who has abandoned me! Kill her Chad! Kill that child, bride Sarah and Naomi. Kill them all!"

"Chad!" Naomi gasps. Releasing the periodical into the wind and in a panic, Naomi fingers the eagle's feather hanging from her beaded necklace and quickens the horse on its way. "Sarah," she whispers. "Satan is after my baby girl."

11
The Birth of Hope

Two hours later, after she and the horse battle against the raging wind and snow, Naomi passes through trestle gate and approaches the barn. She's wrapped in several more layers of the blankets from her feet to her head, the package safely on the seat beside her and covered with snow. Suddenly, she stops the horse. One side of the huge barn door is open and swinging back and forth in the stiffening wind. She feels the presence of Satan all around her.

"Sarah," she whispers, lashing the horse while looking worriedly toward the well-lit manor house. Removing the eagle's feather from her necklace and placing it in her hair, she races the horse through the open barn door, jumps from the wagon with the package, and closes the heavy two-sided door behind her, shutting out the wind and snow. Just as she is about to rush back outside and toward the manor, Pancake appears, barking at a darkened corner of the stable across from her.

"What's wrong, Pancake?" asks Naomi. She then faces the corner. "Who's there?"

Wearing a maternity gown and shivering, while draped under a horse blanket and strips of burlap material—which the workers use to bundle up weeds and carry them away—steps Sarah. The moonlight suddenly appears through the snow and filters through the barn window onto her, her stomach enlarged, her eyes reflecting profound terror, as she gazes about in a panic, then at Naomi.

"My God, child!"

Catching her breath and exhausted, Sarah reaches out for Naomi and then collapses in a sitting position on the straw-covered floor. Naomi drops the package. "Sweetheart, are you hurt?" She sits next to Sarah and wraps her arms about the trembling girl. "Sweet Jesus, Sarah, you're freezin'!"

"Naomi, Chad . . . He—" Sarah abruptly stops and clings to Naomi, who rocks the teenager back and forth in her arms, adding warmth to her body.

"What about that boy! If he or Dane Tucker hurt you, I swear I told them all that I'd kill 'em, and may God forgive me for saying it, but He knows I will kill 'em."

As Sarah shivers and looks about, Naomi hurries to the wagon, retrieves a blanket from the others there, shakes off the collected snow from it, quickly returns to the frightened girl, and drapes the blanket around her and in doing so, accidentally knocks over the package. Naomi follows Sarah's gaze to the wrapped bundle and places it on a hay bale next to them.

"Your package, Naomi. I caused you to knock it over. I'm sorry."

"It's just the diapers, baby, that's all, infant blankets, sterile scissors, extra long ones used for horses is all I could find in that town. Just stuff to have ready. I'm sorry I can't get you to Atlanta to that colored doctor friend of your family in this storm." She again sits by Sarah. "Now, tell me . . . What about Chad, Sarah? Did he touch you?"

Sarah holds onto Naomi, whispering, checking out the barn. "He was drunk and—"

"Jesus, child. Drunk! Why'd you ever let him in the house or even lay eyes on you, knowing I had gone into Cutterville for these supplies, so as not to draw attention by getting them here from your store? I knew I should have asked Mrs. Smith or one of the other women to look in on you while—" Naomi raises both hands, dumbfounded by her own stupidity. "What am I sayin'? We can't let no one see that you with child, not with Barney being away all this time and after us making all these excuses why you haven't been seen about the plantation these last few months. Did he see that you are pregnant, child? Stop and think. Did Chad get a good look at you?" Sarah is gripped in fright and doesn't respond. "Did Chad notice that you're with child? Try and answer me, Sarah."

"I thought he was Henry, Naomi. Henry was coming here to help me trim the Christmas tree, because you've been too busy taking care of me to do so. Henry was to stay with me while you were in town. I was standing inside in the dark and never let Chad in the house, just on the porch by the slightly opened door. Chad said he had come to tell me about Barney. Maybe he noticed. He just grabbed at me and tried to kiss me, but Pancake bit him, and I was so afraid, Naomi. I didn't think of calling out for help. Instead, I ran out the back door and hid here in the barn. I used a horse blanket and burlap to stay warm, but it wasn't

162

enough with the wind coming though these walls. The wind. It's so cold."

"This evil work, Sarah, was brought on by Barney's mother. The work of Satan."

Naomi looks about the cold barn, her breath frosting up. She retrieves still another blanket from the wagon and wraps it about the young girl and then, again, sits beside her, both of them listening to the wind howling through the barn walls. "Is God still with us?" asks Sarah.

"He is, Sarah. Otherwise with this wind as loud as it is, if you would have stopped and tried to call for help, instead of running, no one would have heard you in this storm. Thank God that boy didn't get to you before you reached this barn. Do you know if he left for town?"

Sarah suddenly doubles over in agony, her arms across her stomach, her fingers tearing at her gown. "Oh, God! Naomi, my water . . . it broke when I was running! The pain!"

"My Lord," exclaims Naomi, her eyes wide, amazed at the way the prophecies from time in memorial have always been fulfilled and are inexplicably fulfilling themselves now.

"It was meant to be. All of this, Sarah. It's not your fault that you spoke with Chad. It was prophesied that Caleb would come into this world fleeing from the hand of Satan." Squirming about, her teeth clenched, her back arched, Sarah grabs at Naomi's arm; as the kindly woman eases Sarah onto her back, Pancake dashes about, wildly barking at them as if trying to help.

"Then it's over?" Sarah says, desperately trying to ward off the painful contractions and her fear of Chad, as Naomi slips one of the blankets under her. Sarah goes on, in pain. "Those warnings that you saw ahead of us. Caleb is safe now, isn't he, Naomi? Isn't he, now that Chad has failed?"

"No, Sarah," Naomi says, again looking about, then feeling for her feather, making sure it's still there. "It was you who ran from Chad, not Caleb, Sarah," Naomi tells her. "Your unborn child's race from Satan's grip of death is still at hand."

Pancake looks up at a nearby hayloft and barks; bits of straw is drifting down from it. While the young girl lies in discomfort alongside several hay bales, the cows and sheep watching the teenager from their pens, Naomi strokes Sarah's perspiring forehead with a towel. Slowly, Sarah's quivering legs are made steady by Naomi continuously stroking and encouraging words of love. The midwife-experienced woman hurriedly lights a nearby red kerosene lantern. As she does, the two-sided barn doors are blown open in the storm and cold air and snow rushes in.

"It's Chad!" Sarah screams and sits up. She glances about. "He's followed me here!"

"Then Satan is leading him to you, in order to kill Caleb," Naomi says. Terrified, Naomi—once again—fingers that feather in her hair, then picks up a hammer from a horse-shoeing anvil and cautiously goes to the doors with the lantern, muttering: "In case the power of Satan isn't in you, this hammer will be. Right in your skull, Chad Travers." Following her, and looking back at the hay loft, is Pancake, wagging his tail and barking. Naomi squints into the frigid night, ululating wind and snow, then closes both doors by propping a board against them. She puts aside the hammer and hurries back to Sarah. "I guess I didn't close that door as good as I thought," she says. "It was only the wind, honey. I'll have the workers fix the locks on them doors after Christmas."

Positioning the lantern on the hay bale next to the package and hurriedly opening the wrapped bundle, Naomi removes a baby blanket and spreads it over yet another close-by hay bale. Besides scissors and baby blanket, the embellished chalice, wrapped in its purple cloth, is in the package. Naomi spreads the sacred, purple cloth across the bale as well, and then places the chalice on the purple vestment. Sarah, ignoring her pain, is captivated by the jeweled goblet. "It's magnificent, Naomi. Father Haas's chalice."

"Not to all. To them who worship a god of hatred it's called a 'can,' the same as 'Jack-in-the-box, Jack-out-of-the-box' makes fun of the Holy Sacrament that is taken from the chalice by Father Haas in his travels," Naomi tells her.

" 'Can', Naomi? That's what you were talking about when you spoke of a 'can' to Flynn."

"Yes, Sarah. It's to house your afterbirth, which is now beatified by our Lord, and under the attack of Lucifer; because if it survives his attack, it will nourish a mighty tree, which will symbolize—with its spreading roots and lofty elegance—the love of Caleb, instead of that of Flynn's hatred, which Satan wants to champion."

Upon hearing her describe Flynn's hatred Sarah cries. Suddenly she again screams, "Naomi," and lies back down. "The baby's coming out!"

Naomi kneels, and as her wristwatch reaches one minute before midnight and Christmas Day, a male child is delivered from Sarah's body into those angelic, white palms and dark fingers. Covered with a coat of delicate downy hairs, the newborn is white from his hair to his toes and laced with Sarah's bright-red blood. Its chubby arms and legs are like tied-off sections of bloody sausages. With the view of Naomi and the newborn blocked by the hay bale, Sarah faces to the side, where the lantern-cast shadow of her infant and that of Naomi looms twenty feet high against the barn wall. The teenage girl watches the faithful woman's shadow place the baby on one of the uncluttered, blanketed stacks of hay, scissor through the infant's birth cord and then tie it into a knot. Sarah marvels at the sight of Naomi's dark image, as she stands with the child in one hand, the afterbirth in the other and lowers the fetal membrane into the chalice. Next, while holding Caleb by his feet and giving him a backside whack, Naomi seems to have given a powerful meaning to Caleb's presence, as he announces his entry into the world with a full-bodied cry. As the baby cries, tears flow down Sarah's cheeks, all thoughts of Chad and Dane temporarily removed from her mind.

"You and Henry have a beautiful son," Naomi says stepping up to Sarah with her newborn.

"Caleb," exclaims Sarah. "We've waited so long to see you since the night Naomi named you from the Bible on that ship. I'll teach you and Flynn to love one another as brothers, not just to be friends, no matter what Barney does or says."

"Flynn and this child must never know they're brothers," cautions Naomi, as Pancake watches still more bits of hay drifting from the loft. "If anyone besides the three of us knows who Caleb is, blood will flow. Now, I have to wash this child to see what he looks like, under this white curtain of humanity. Lord, our little man is coated with it from head-to-toe."

"All babies are covered with it, Naomi. It protects them from the amniotic fluids."

Naomi recalls the bucket of water given to her by Briana, and she quickly takes the water from the wagon, removes a small towel from the package, breaks through the thin, iced-over surface and dips the towel into the blessed water. She then removes the towel and one-handedly squeezes out as much of the cold liquid from it as possible and places the towel over the lit lantern and waits for the lantern's heated surface to take the chill from the cloth, so that Caleb can be lightly washed in relative comfort. All the time, still unnoticed, even more straw trickles down though the loft's gapped floorboards. The falling pieces are followed by the wind slamming against the barn windows and doors. Then, as still more straw falls through the floorboards, a ghostly caw emanates from the cold darkness outside, the call of the raven, heard even over the storm. Naomi withdraws from the bucket of water and holds tightly onto a yet-unwashed Caleb.

"What is it, Naomi? What's frightening you?"

"Hush, child. It's trying to warn us. Can't you hear it? The cry of the raven."

Naomi—cradling the crying infant close with her right hand—lifts the towelled-over lantern high with her left. On the loft, above them, is Chad. Like a wild animal, he's crouching and rocking back and forth, his knees bent, his left hand gripping the edge of the loft's floor boards; in his right hand is Barney's Bowie knife, and his killer, satanic eyes are locked onto Caleb.

"Ahhhh!" he screeches, leaping off the loft, swinging the razor-sharp blade at Caleb. As Sarah screams, Naomi throws up her arm to protect the wailing newborn, and she receives a gash across on her dress sleeve and into her arm. She lets the lantern fly, then crushes it when she trips over it, shattering the globe. Blood streams from her arm, but she holds fast to Caleb when she goes down. A lantern-caused fire breaks out in the straw and races across the floor. Chad seizes Caleb from Naomi and then kicks Naomi in her head, as she flails about, yelling up at him and grappling at his legs. Chad kicks her again, laying her out on her back, blinking up at the barn's ceiling, which seems to be spinning dizzily about her. Desperately fighting against the urge to lapse into unconsciousness, Naomi can hear Caleb and Sarah's frantic cries, as the dark world of oblivion closes in on her. She sees images of Sarah during happier moments whirling in the wind on the ship, sees herself promising Sarah that she will be with her until the end of time. Try as she might to protect Sarah and Caleb, Naomi cannot speak, cannot open her eyes and cannot rise to her feet.

When the screaming Klansman charges toward Sarah with Caleb, Pancake goes on the attack, ripping and pulling at Chad's trouser leg. Chad kicks the small dog through the air and across the barn. Sarah leans forward on the blanket and grabs Chad's leg and sinks her teeth into his ankle. He reaches down and slaps her, then towers over the teenager, holding her wailing child above his head. "I was wrong to care fer you! You ain't shit! Die with this nigger baby of yours. Nigger lover!"

Chad slices down at her with the knife. The young girl ducks. "Naomi!" she screams.

Chad sees Naomi sit straight up, her gaze of fire targeting him with mortal finality. He recalls how the witchcraft woman threatened to kill any Klansman who attempted to do harm to Sarah, and at first, in great distress, he stands there and watches as she struggles onto her knees, but only for a second. Chad runs yelling at Naomi, his knife slicing the air as he closes in on her, a wailing Caleb helpless in the Klansman's grip of steel.

"You ain't magical," Chad calls out as he closes in on Naomi, trying to convince himself that the terrifying stories he's heard about the black woman is just a bunch of tar-baby talk.

"I'm going to cut your nigger head clean off, then I'm going to fuck you and Sarah in your asses like Dane says it feels so good to him." He arrives at Naomi's side before she can completely get to her feet and towers over her with his massive weight. "Then I'm taking this black baby to Dane and we're going to hang it by its neck and burn him." While Chad shakes Caleb, trying to silence him, and with the flames sizzle crossing the hay strung floor toward him and Naomi, Sarah crawls toward Naomi, the fire, Chad and her son.

"No, Chad!" she yells.

"Stay back, Sarah," Naomi warns. "God has promised that you will not be soiled by evil, not just from Barney, but also from creatures like this boy. His vile blood will splatter on you!"

Naomi's caution to Sarah accelerates Chad's fears of her. He wonders what trick she has up her sleeve to be that confident about splattering his blood; feeling that he has to get her first, before she gets to him, he lifts Barney's Bowie knife above his shoulder and is ready to plunge it into the top of her head. Backing off, Naomi reaches up to her headband and jerks out the feather, snaps it in half and throws the two pieces at Chad. They land at his feet. Shocked at such a bizarre and unexpected move by the half-breed, Chad gapes down at the broken feather, then at Naomi, followed by another disturbing look at the broken feather, a feather which begins an eerie, horrifying metamorphosing into a large raven, its plumage as black as night, a raven the size of a large, mad, housecat and ten times as fierce looking. Chad trembles in fear. The bird's blackness appears as a dark river, drowning out everything white in the world to the Klansman; when those beady, achromatic, bird's eyes stare up at him, Chad stumbles back. Surrounded by the burning hay and fire, the fierce-eyed bird begins flapping its wings to balance itself, as it hops about on its long, garish legs and caws up at the stunned Klansman. Chad—even with his Klansman's mentality—senses that the raven is trying to protect Caleb, that Caleb is the key to the weird events now going on around him, and to save himself, he feels that he has to kill Caleb on the spot.

"No matter how many tricks you have, you witch," he yells to Naomi, "I ran from you when that snake bit my arm, and I almost died, but I'm not running from you anymore." He lifts the knife toward Caleb, and—when he does—the raven rockets off the floor and launches an all-out cawing attack on the Klansman, flying about his head, pecking at his eyes. It takes only that brief moment for Naomi, bleeding from her arm, to stumble forward, grab the scissors from the hay bale and baby blanket and stab Chad in his back.

"Ahh!" he bellows in extreme agony. "I'm running! I'm running," he cries out to Naomi, who chases after him a few steps then collapses onto the floor. Sobbing in unbearable pain, and in a desperate attempt to reach behind him and pull the scissors from his back, Chad drops Caleb but Sarah is there, on her belly, and catches her embattled son.

Outside under the winter sky and bundled against the storm, Henry and his faithful horse are galloping toward the manor's drive, when over the wailing wind, he hears Sarah's screams coming from the barn. Sprinting the young horse full out toward the massive, red structure, Henry envisions everything imaginable, including the death of Sarah. Inside the barn, Chad stumbles about shrieking in pain, the raven flying about his head continuously attacking his face and his eyes. Chad seizes the black winged bird and crushes it, and then—driven by Satan—he again goes after Sarah even though he's now half-blind and those excruciating scissors are still anchored in his back. "I'm dying, Sarah," he blares, the blood trickling from his mouth. "But you're going with me!"

Sitting petrified on the floor, holding onto Caleb and unable to stand and run, Sarah scoots backwards away from the crazed, forward-stumbling Klansman, but she ends up with her back against the barn wall. As Chad looms over her, and Sarah lets out a bloodcurdling cry, the barn doors are powered open. Covered with snow, his horse lingering behind him, Henry looks at the fire, at Sarah, at his newborn and at Chad, who glares across the barn at him.

Henry turns into a roaring and bellowing, wounded bull, a bull that seems to throws itself through the air onto Chad. Henry delivers a lightning blow to Chad's jaw, shattering it, sending the Klansman crashing facedown onto the floor and losing the knife, exciting the animals.

In one gruesome, angry sweep, the near-insane black youth pulls Chad off the floor, lifts the three-hundred-pound, stunned Klansman over his head and hurls him backwards against the barn wall, a few feet away from Sarah, who screams as the impact sends the horse scissors jamming its way through Chad's back and out the front of the wailing Klansman's chest. Chad, his chin against his chest, looks down at the bloody scissors' tips sticking out of him, then turns his sight away from the bloody scissor tips and toward Sarah, his frightened eyes locked on her, and he begs for her help and panics when his heavy body begins to slide downward, and the scissor's looped handle snags on a wall hook, forcing the sharp instrument's tips to spread open and become jammed in his sternum, and as he continues sliding, the jammed scissors begins ripping a hole in his chest and painfully breaking his ribs and his spine. Then, his body slides off the scissors, leaving them stuck on the wall with a trail of blood following along behind him. As he comes to a rest slumped between two hay bales, Chad looks over at Sarah once more. "Please," he whispers. "I don't want to die in sin," and then his world slowly goes dark, as he watches Henry beat out the fire with his coat then hurry toward Sarah and Caleb.

"We're okay," Sarah sobs, holding Caleb close in near shock, her sights locked on Chad in disbelief, then on Naomi. "See about Naomi! Hurry! She's hurt!"

The dark-complexioned Henry hesitates, his sights on his baby, his eyes questioning the newborn's color. Caleb is white, not brown, not tan, but pure white. Henry screams within, certain that Sarah has made a terrible mistake and that Barney is the child's father. Walking backwards toward Naomi, Henry's confused sights never leave his newborn son.

"I'm cut, but I'll live," whispers Naomi, when Henry reaches her. Exhausted, gasping for breath, she looks over at Sarah and with great effort gets to her feet and exclaims, "And so will your family, Henry, be okay. Thank God." When Henry moves to the young girl once more, Naomi stumbles over to Sarah. She takes Caleb from Sarah and tells the

169

young girl to lie down, and when Sarah does, Naomi covers the anxious girl's face with the blanket. Blocking Henry's path when he attempts to get to Sarah, Naomi warns: "The Sarah you knew is dead, for all of our sakes, Henry."

"Then let me die too, God!" Henry exclaims. "I don't care what Sarah and I agreed on."

Sarah slides back the blanket and sits up, tears flowing down her cheeks. Henry rushes into her outstretched arms, and on his knees, he kisses her moist cheeks, her forehead and her hands. He gently runs his fingers through her soft, blonde hair and tries to untangle it. Overwhelmed with grief for her, he presses his face against her breast and sobs, "I'm so sorry I wasn't here when you needed me. If Chad had of taken your life, I'd have killed myself to follow—"

Crying, Sarah takes his face into her hands and lifts his chin. She kisses his lips. "Remember how you raised my chin on your land when I talked of how I feared Barney, and you gave me courage to go on? You would not have killed yourself, Henry Brooks; you would have lived on to raise our son. You're that strong, my love. But we have to keep our promise and live only for the sake of our child now." She tenderly guides him under the blanket alongside of her, and while Henry and Sarah lie side-by-side, holding onto the other's hand in the hay, their hearts beating as one, Naomi—cradling Caleb in a blanket—sits back on a bale of hay in semi-darkness, opposite the barn windows, the faithful black woman's gaze fixed on the stars as the moonlight floods through the snow and the window onto her and the newborn. Behind her and Caleb, Chad—still firmly wedged between the hay bales—seems to stare beyond Naomi and Caleb, and out of that same window, his unseeing eyes seem to wish for the hope and love and peace which mankind believes is beyond the stars, while, also, as well—in death—he seems to be seeking absolution from his God.

Much later, Naomi carries Caleb to Sarah.

"It's time, Henry," Naomi says, handing Caleb to his mother. "Caleb needs nursing and—" She looks over her shoulder at Chad's blue-blackening, moonlit face. "It also be time for that poor soul to be taken out of here and put to rest. May God have mercy on him."

While Sarah parts her gown and lets Caleb suckle, Henry kisses them both and quickly gets to his feet in the shadowy barn. He attempts to fire up the lantern, but has trouble doing so—and fearful that if he or

Naomi ventured out of the barn to the plantation store for one of the lamps there, that they would attract attention, possibly even bringing field hands hurrying to the barn and discovering Chad's body and Caleb—Henry patiently works at repairing the battered lantern; finally, after nearly an hour, and straightening out the lamp's wick assembly, he awakens a weak, flickering lantern light.

"Henry," remarks Naomi, as Henry adjusts the light. "Barney wasn't just talking to Chad or the Klan from town when he told them to keep an eye on Shadow Grove while he's away; he was also talking to some of Sarah's Klan-minded field hands who are his eyes and ears just as much as Chad was." As Sarah listens and cradles Caleb, Naomi goes on. "We can't bury Chad here on Shadow Grove without someone seeing us. Will you bury him on your land?"

"No. Not where Father Haas says the soul of God dwells and where my god-fearing folks are buried. Not some Klansman's evil remains. Not there, Naomi."

"Then what will we do with him, Henry?" asks Sarah, timidly glancing over at the body.

Henry lays out several strips of burlap beside Chad's corpse, the same burlap that Sarah had earlier wrapped about herself to keep warm. He lifts Chad's body up and places his remains onto the burlap, then looks around and retrieves the anvil and places it on Chad's chest. Bundling the body and anvil in the durable burlap, Henry ties everything together with ropes and finally wraps a heavy chain about the burlap and Chad's remains. Grunting, he lifts the weighed body onto Naomi's hitched wagon and faces Sarah, then Naomi. "It won't hurt Caleb if I hold him, will it?" he asks.

"You wait until I separate some of this water for the child's bath," Naomi says, pouring half of Briana's holy water from her bucket into still another one, then going on, nudging the other bucket toward Henry. "Now you wash them hands good," she tells Henry, while pouring antiseptic soap from her package on his hands and into the water. Naomi retrieves one of the worker's shirts and a heavy coat from a wall hook and scolds on, "Make sure you remove Chad's evil blood from them hands and arms, and then take off that shirt and get into this one before you touch that baby, and I mean for you to even take off them trousers if you got any part of that evil man's blood on them."

"Jesus, Naomi," Henry exclaims, "I killed a man, not an exploding pack of germs. My trousers are okay." After he takes off his coat and shirt and washes his hands, his face and his muscular chest to Naomi's satisfaction, Henry shivers from the cold and slips into the worker's garments and makes his way to Sarah and the infant. Naomi, unnoticed several feet behind them, places the lantern on a wooden crate, spreads iodine on her wound and wraps her bleeding arm with a diaper, while silently thanking God that Caleb was not killed. Meanwhile, under the dim light filtering through the moonlit window, as well as the light flickering from the distant, damaged lantern, Henry cradles his and Sarah's well-bundled son in his arms, Henry—hoping against hope—tries to examine the newborn's complexion, the weak moonlight making the examination all but impossible.

"Are you okay, Henry?" asks Sarah, gazing up at her man and at their son.

While Henry's mind goes on reeling this way and that about the color of Caleb, Naomi, having successfully stopped the bleeding, uses the lantern to sort out the extra blankets in the wagon. Her housekeeping complete, she retrieves the dropped towel, shakes it off, dips the end of the towel into the clean bucket of water, removes it, drapes it over the lantern and moves with lantern and towel to the couple's side. Positioning the lantern on the hay bale next to Henry, she takes the newborn from him and wipes Caleb clean with the moist part of the cloth, then thoroughly dries him with the dry end, and—once again—wraps him in his blankets. When she moves into the full light of the lantern, the flickering illumination jackets itself about Caleb, and Henry bursts into laughter and kisses his boy's small hand: Caleb has turned from white to a sparkling tan.

"He's the color of gold, Sarah! Naomi! He was so white before! He's mine! Part of me, part of his mother. The bridge between us, Sarah. Our boy! His skin is like gold!"

"Babies all look white when they are born, Henry Brooks," says Naomi and then chuckles at Henry's surprised delight.

"Epidermal vernix caseosa," Sarah remarks, then smiles with a chuckle.

"Epidermal what?" asks Henry. "Ver . . . caseosa?"

"Dead epidermal cells," says Sarah. "Skin cells," Sarah lovingly explains, while watching Henry finger Caleb's hair. "His hair," Sarah goes on, "it's an oily secretion called 'sebaceous' that puts that beautiful gloss on it."

"Wouldn't surprise me at all if God Himself was golden," says Naomi, admiring Caleb.

"Then, you've never seen Him, Naomi?" says Sarah. "With your powers. Never seen God?"

"No one of false pride looks upon His face and lives, Sarah."

"You're loving and humble," says Sarah. "Without false pride or anything else that God would disapprove of, otherwise you wouldn't be—"

"An angel, Sarah? I'm far from that. If it was not so, I wouldn't have gotten angry and cursed at Barney and those like him or stabbed Chad. I'm still learning. No. Mine is not the face to look upon God, not yet."

"Is that why you've been able to stay here with me so long, because you're still learning?"

"Jesus, Naomi," Henry interrupts. "You and Sarah . . . and that Father Haas. You're starting to sound just like each other. This is a time for joy for me, not a time to frighten me with talks of God, not after I've broken His commandment and killed," he says glancing back at Chad's wrapped body. Trying his best to remain elated over Caleb's birth, he faces Sarah. "What name will we give him, Sarah, our son?"

' "Caleb', Henry."

' "Caleb?' " Henry ponders. "Does the name 'Caleb' come from the two of you and that wind funnel, when you said some kind of voice contacted you from God on that ship?"

"Yes," says Naomi. "From God and the Bible."

"Then that's good enough for me," says Henry. "Caleb's' a fine name," he says, kissing his son. "When you grow up, you'll be too smart to be ashamed of what you are, part colored, part white, because you'll be as smart as your mother and twice as stubborn as me."

"He will never be ashamed of his bloodline, Henry, " Naomi says. "He'll know that most of the world will soon be awash in the same golden skin, and you killed Chad, not murdered him. There is no sin."

"I'll teach Caleb and Flynn musically, academically and philosophically," says Sarah, reaching out for her son. "And I pray that they will both love God and help others to conquer ignorance."

"Both of you listen to me," says Naomi, "especially you, Henry, because Caleb will spend almost all of his life with you. When Caleb and

Flynn are old enough to think on their own, and this especially goes for you," she says, eyeing Sarah. "Don't insist that they embrace God. It's what we all want, but these special boys must go their own way in life, and there's little anyone can do about it."

"He's our son, Naomi," exclaims Henry, "and Sarah and I will—"

Laughing, Sarah pushes aside all feelings of discomfort and sits up and enjoys the sight of the two people she now trusts and loves more than anyone else in the world. "You two sound like Father and Mother when they debated about my education, and I turned out okay. Now, that's enough. Stop it. Both of you."

"Sarah," Henry says, momentarily holding Caleb away from her reaching hands. "I have to take our boy out to my place."

"In this storm?" asks Sarah, as Naomi remains silent and sees the wisdom in Henry's words.

"Even in all this snow," Henry tells Sarah. "It was an added promise I made to God, the day Barney left, and everyone was blown around on a day when not a leaf on a tree was stirred, not a blade of grass moved, and no wind was to be felt or heard. Now I'm sure it came from the hand of God, and on that strange, windless day when I was blown around, as we all were, I promised God that I'd dedicate our son in the hour of his birth to Him on my land, Caleb's Freeman ancestors hope for a better tomorrow."

"Go with him, Naomi, if he promised God."

"But, child . . . You need me here. I have to get you in inside the house where it's warm."

"I'll be okay. I don't want my man to have to make an extra trip to bring Caleb back here in the snow, not when he has to get up in the morning and return anyway to help us with planning that irrigation pipeline for next summer, on paper with Collins, now that Barney has left. And remember, Barney has said that I'm too easy on the coloreds, especially on Henry and has ordered his men here to make sure Henry never sleeps in one of the empty workers' shacks or be here overnight." Sarah glances about. "On this curious night," she exclaims. "I feel sure God will protect you and Caleb through this storm."

"Well, come on, Henry Brooks; extra blankets is what I got a plenty of on that wagon. It's the day Christ was born and seconds before Caleb came into the world. It's Christmas, everyone!"

Naomi places extra blankets under and over Sarah and then she,

Henry and Caleb, wrapped in woolen covers, leave in the wagon, Henry's faithful horse, un-tethered, following close behind. As the wagon, Henry, Naomi and Caleb leave a sleeping Sarah farther and farther behind, the snow stops falling, and a light from a bright star shines down from a crystal clear starry sky onto the barn, causing the large structure to glow. When the three of them pass a line of workers' shacks—the workers inside fast asleep, warm in their beds, the wagon wheels and the horses clumping alone—they come to the trestle gate and open land beyond. Then Henry notices the plantation's animals, the pigs, the woolly sheep, the cows, the chickens, the horses and the mules, moving toward them over the heavily laden snow. He is stunned, and at times afraid and keeps the wagon moving, as the cadre of silent domestic creatures all press in around them and the wagon, their animal eyes, large and small, all looking in at Caleb, the pigs and sheep glancing upward, the chickens from the backs of the cows horses and mules. Unlike Henry, his attention absorbed by the animals, Naomi, holding onto Caleb, has her focus straight ahead. She's looking for things yet to come.

Ten miles away, with the snow no longer falling, and in the dark of night, with the stars and the moon sparkling overhead, and the air crisp and clean, Naomi remains in the wagon with Caleb nestled close to her warm body, while Henry shoves Chad's body over the cliff into the raging Atlantic and continues into the cold night, as the mighty ocean does its job and pushes Chad's remains out to sea, then plunges his remains downward into the deep.

Once on his land, Henry places an earlier-carved headstone on a false grave alongside the house, next to that of his parents' burial sites, as Naomi faithfully rocks Caleb in her arms and patiently waits: "When Caleb's old enough to visit his mamma's grave, he won't have far to go," she tells Henry.

Once again the snow begins to fall, and Henry lovingly takes Caleb from Naomi and lifts him, blankets and all, over his head toward the stars. "God, even as the major lifted young Flynn up to Satan," he says, "I dedicate my son to You, that he be humbled and led down Sarah's road of love, not in the hatin' and killin' ways that Naomi says Barney Cutter will have Flynn follow, and may these two boys find a lasting friendship and rescue each other from the evil that will follow them."

When Henry lowers Caleb into his arms, he kisses the sleeping child and hands him to a beaming Naomi. She tells him, "Caleb'll need a real, living mother for a spell, Henry, not some cold, empty coffin." Naomi scrutinizes the fake grave, and adds. "It's a well-known fact that the white masters' beds creates half-white babies with their colored slaves and still do with their colored maids and harlots, so no one will disbelieve me when they ask and I tell them that Henry Brooks' young wife worked in Atlanta for a rich, white family, after she left Henry in the first few days of their marriage, and she became the mother of this rich man's child, and when the white man's wife kicked her out, and she returned here to your land, Henry, here on Little Shadow Place, to give birth to this blest child, Caleb; she did so, died and was buried alongside your folks. I'll swear it on a stack of Bibles if need be—which is one of the reasons I'll never be able to look upon the face of God. I'm too quick to lie. For now, though, I'll raise Caleb like my own at the manor. A year at the most, while Barney is away, and when this child no longer needs Sarah's milk of love, then he can come home and live with you out here on the soil where the Soul of God dwells."

Back on Shadow Grove, upon passing though the massive gate and holding onto a peacefully sleeping Caleb, Naomi is exhausted. The snow has covered over all of the animal's tracks, and inside the barn—as Sarah sleeps—the chalice begins to glow, as Caleb arrives. The light from that brilliant Northern star is shining through the barn window onto it. When Naomi approaches the barn, she's surprised when she sees the door, once again, open with Flynn standing by it, dressed only in pajamas and cotton slippers. Sarah's year-old, blonde son is sprinkled with snow and reaching out in Naomi's direction. She wastes no time in driving into the structure and clambers from the wagon. She looks down at Flynn, still reaching up to her as if for something which only he can see. Naomi glances over at his sleeping mother, then back at him. "What in the world are you doin' down here in this cold and out of the house and your bed, Flynn?"

Cradling Caleb in her arm, she uses her free hand and gently moves Flynn away from the open door and closes it with the strength of her back. As she turns up the battered, red lantern, her eyes light up; some of the afterbirth blood has flowed from the chalice and has puddled on the ground, where the lantern's kerosene fire has scorched the earthen floor black. Naomi notices blood on Flynn's hands.

"Your hands. You had 'em in Caleb's blood." Using water from the bucket out of which she bathed Caleb, and while holding onto the newborn, she one-handedly washes Flynn's hands. He lifts her coat and dries them on her dress tail, then again reaches out, but not for her. He's reaching up for Caleb. "Baby, your little arms and legs ain't strong enough to carry this child." The red lantern's light—which was only a weak glow when Henry had finally managed to light it—now streams from that battered red vessel brighter and brighter. Naomi squints away from it, as if away from something she's not permitted to gaze upon; she places Caleb into Flynn's arms; supporting both of them with one hand, while easing the remaining blankets from the wagon, she helps Flynn make his way to his sleeping mother with Caleb. Naomi assists Flynn as he sits down on the extra blankets, while he trustfully holds onto the newborn. She hurriedly unbridles the horse, rubs it down and places it in a stall besides other corralled horses. Returning to Sarah, Naomi gently nudges the sleeping, young girl. "Sweetheart," she whispers. "Let's wrap you and Flynn up real good and get the three of you going on up that hill to the manor where it's nice and warm. I'll run ahead and get the car."

"I'm awfully tired, Naomi, and you scarcely know how to drive and will wreck in the snow. Did you say Flynn? Is he here?" Sarah mutters slipping back into restful sleep. "Caleb . . . is Caleb oka—"

Naomi places Flynn and Caleb between her and Sarah and spreads the blankets over the lot of them, including over Pancake, asleep at Sarah's side.

Hours later, after the lantern light flickers and dies, in the dark, with Flynn, holding onto Caleb, Naomi's voice is heard:

"Yes," she says. "I understand."

Flynn's eyes stare up at a ray of Light melting through the barn roof above them. With the strange Light entering through the roof, he can clearly see all around them, as if it were daylight. Once again, Naomi begins talking. He looks over at her. She's talking in her sleep. "Because man has gone too long without loving the Light. . . . The circle of Light from yesterday, today and tomorrow, man no longer believes in Jesus or in God." The mysterious woman goes deadly quiet, not even the sound of her breathing is heard, as the Light continues melting through the roof and intensifying, placing the barn in an eerie glow of sparkling, magical luminescence. Once more, Flynn glances at Naomi, as if wanting to awaken her, but then again, he pursues the Light coming through the barn roof; the year-old boy's eyes of blue follow the endless passage of Light as it sinks into the barn, seemingly drinking up the world with its dazzling brightness, as it now centers only on and around the area of the afterbirth and chalice.

"By the Light of day," Naomi again mutters. "Yes, angels of God, as He instructs . . . Bury the afterbirth. Bury it with the red sprout, as He says." Flynn sits up on the blanket with Caleb, his eyes open wide. A red sprout appears out of the blackened, bloody soil within that dazzling circle of blinding Light. Then, Naomi—in her sleep—repeats words spoken by several more angels, as well as words of her own. "*From this time on,*" the angels say in a distinct tone of voice through Naomi's lips, "*the word 'can' of damnation that refers to this holy vessel, graced by blest wine and the symbol of our Lord's sacred blood, will no longer be tolerated, and we understand how you desire our blessings to attack at will all those who would defile its holy name, but this act of vengeance is to be left up to Caleb, as the chosen warrior of Jesus in this matter.*"

"I understand," says Naomi to the spirits, which then again speak:

"*The chalice was called that accursed tin-can name to fulfill the prophecy that today's enslaved countless millions of Satan willingly spit on the tradition of Christ's churches—symbolized by their wanton renaming of His holy chalice as something which they urinate into during their drunken orgies of dance, sex, drugs, snake worship, rape, torture, burning and lynching of God's children, their brothers and sisters, and in so doing made clear that they have only one god, and he is Lucifer. All that was foretold has been made ready now that the chalice is here. The Holy Spirit now again nears. It comes without beginning, middle or end so that Caleb and Flynn might also have a better chance—by Its presence—in their journey to show man the way home and not into the fires of hell.*"

"What is this Light?" ask Naomi, transfixed in her deep sleep.

"*The Mandorla, Naomi, blessed servant of God. The Light of Love,*" The voices begin to fade away now. "*Light that only their innocent pairs of eyes are allowed to see or enter.*"

The barn doors swing open. Flynn struggles to his feet with Caleb and walks toward the open doors, and he and Caleb are swallowed up into the Light.

12
The Letter of Doom

Seventeen years later, during the summer of 1946, the droughts have come and have gone time and time again, but the attempts of Shadow Grove's workers to reach Henry's land and water have run into a hard bed of rocks with their hand-held trench tools and they are still more than two miles short of completion. Today—with the land needing less water and attention—Sarah's faithful field boss, Keith Collins, graying of hair, but still with his freckled face and kind, green eyes, eyes which had shed tears of sorrow when he carried Lawrence's body toward Sarah's wagon, alongside Caleb, after the plane crash, now, those eyes and Keith are gleaming with contentment and satisfaction as to the condition of Shadow Grove; Collins has assigned a dozen male workers to paint the old barn. Driving up to the structure in a well-used Chevrolet pickup, he faces the opened barn doors. "Flynn! Caleb! Where are you boys?"

Wearing paint-splattered blue jeans—with Caleb riding piggyback on him—Flynn trots out of the barn and trips, sending both him and Caleb tumbling to the ground, laughing. Now eighteen, and six feet tall, Flynn is compassionate, sensuous and slender. He has Sarah's blue eyes and silver-blonde hair. Caleb—also slender—stands over six feet with his golden complexion, his light brown eyes, and his curly, glossy, black hair buffeting in the breeze. Naomi's hope for the world is seventeen, is well muscled with Henry's good looks as well as those of Sarah's. At times Caleb, unlike Flynn, is completely fearless when he wishes to be, which is not very often.

"The barn's looking good," Collins says, as the boys smile up at him from their sprawled-out position on the ground. "I think the others can get along without you guys for a while, and, now, if you two are finished horsing around, might I interest you in getting on your feet and working in the fields with the men? I'm sure Sarah would appreciate it." As Caleb and Flynn gather themselves off the ground and trot off toward the distant field, still laughing about their fall, a worried Collins looks toward one of the manor's bay windows.

Inside the manor, standing behind that den window is Sarah. She's now thirty-two, slender and absolutely stunning. Holding onto a letter, she looks over at Henry, who is thirty-six and approaching thirty-seven. Henry is still as strong as a bull and still maintaining his handsome appearance and his patience, as he waits for Sarah to read aloud Barney's correspondence to him.

"This is his last letter after the army rescued him and before his promotion to Colonel," Sarah says, then reads: "Dear Sarah, Hitler's crusade has failed. It's now up to us to keep his dream of a superior race alive in America, or the blacks and Jews and Mexicans will overrun our great country." Sarah looks at Henry in dismay. Henry shakes his head in disgust. "It gets worse, much worse," she tells him, continuing on. " 'I've grown old in this war, and I've sent a portrait of me to you, so you won't be too disappointed when we meet again. Sarah, about my long absence from Shadow Grove, even before I was captured, I can only say I haven't been a saint in this matter, and I must be totally honest with you and say that—' "

Sarah gazes up at the portrait hanging over the fireplace. Colonel Cutter's sinister-looking eyes glare out in space, his hair white, his brow wrinkled. Henry follows her intimidated glance to the portrait. "You can skip that private part, Sarah. I can guess what he's tryin' to say. That not only has he been captured for a spell, as we all know, but he's had another woman all this time. But I don't, Flynn don't . . . Nobody understands how or where he was captured, or for how long, or when he was rescued, or who he lived with all this time when he wasn't captured."

"The army wouldn't say, Henry, due to his secret clearance."

"I know I was against it a first, Sarah, but why don't you divorce him? Caleb says the law's on your side, since Barney's been gone so long, beyond his capture time. I'm sure God would understand."

"I'm Catholic, Henry—of which, thankfully you reminded me—and I made an oath to God 'until death do us part.' " She ponders and then goes on, "Long ago, Naomi said I would not be asked to bear more than I could endure. Barney's being away has been enough of a blessing, and I live in a glass house and cast no stones."

"Of course not. But he hasn't been back in seventeen years. Why now? It's even been years since he was rescued."

"Flynn, Henry. He wants to be with his son," she says, then reads on. "The day I left, I promised myself that you would never have to worry about money again. Toward the end of the war, before I was captured and the Japanese defeated our little two square miles of hell, a worthless

180

Philippine island called Corregidor, during those last days, I was in charge of a critical mission, which turned out to be the break I dreamed of all of my life, the very key to all my plans over the years, and I have my special guardian to thank. That's all I can tell you now, but our son will soon be one of the richest, most powerful men in the entire South.' "

Sarah walks to a bay window, the letter dangling in her hand. She gazes down at Caleb and Flynn as they laughingly jostle each other about while making their way to join the other workers.

"Do you have any idea what he's talking about when he speaks of a special guardian, or what would cause him to say it was the key to his plans, Sarah? Plans to make Flynn into what, a monster? He has no rights to that boy."

"This key business . . . No I don't. I wish I did," she says watching her sons. "Brothers, Henry. They've been inseparable since that night Flynn carried Caleb from the barn and into that snow and strange light that Naomi told us about. My God, how I wish I could tell them who they are to each other, but Naomi is right. That would put us all in danger and now this letter from the man who would kill Caleb and me at the drop of a hat."

"What else, Sarah? I'd read it myself if I knew how. Caleb never could get readin' through my thick skull. Please go on."

"You would be able to read," she says, facing him, "if you hadn't worked your heart out for me and Flynn, while keeping up your own land. Thank God Caleb is more than able to help you now. And Flynn doesn't always say it, but he loves you for being here for us as much as he loves Caleb."

"The letter, Sarah."

"It's ugly, Henry. You don't want to hear the rest."

Henry motions to the letter and, dispirited, Sarah gives in: " 'I understand, my dearest, why you never wrote me, and I'm deeply grateful that you didn't stop Flynn from writing as well. Those Red Cross letters from him saved my life while I was detained behind those terrible lines, living off bread and water. Our son's intelligent, incisive letters were worth more than gold to me then and after my rescue. Even so, in his correspondence, Flynn continuously praises a colored boy, Caleb Brooks. I never told Flynn in my letters to him, but his relationship with this boy Caleb is unacceptable and dangerous to the cause. My first priority,

181

when I return—after getting to know Flynn better—is to drive Flynn and Caleb Brooks apart.' "

"Barney will be here in five days," Sarah says, fighting back the tears. "It'll be difficult for Flynn and Caleb to remain friends now, and you and I will have to be careful not to be seen together. Henry, I want Caleb and Flynn to be with each other as much as possible in the few days that are left before Barney arrives. Will you see to it?" Henry leaves the room, nodding in agreement.

Despondent, Sarah walks through the backyard to the greenhouse, a place where she's always found peace. Inside the glass house of flowers, all of Barney's firethorns are gone. Under the dazzling, warm sunlight streaming through the glass roof and walls, Naomi—working at the far end of the sprawling nursery—is planting colorful flowers among her and Sarah's favorites, the buttermilk-white calla lilies. Now completely gray of hair, Naomi is aerating the dry potting soil with her hand tools, sending billions of the sun-reflecting, lighter-than-air, dust specks rising into the atmosphere around her. While she works, the soul-stirring sound of the "Gregorian Chant" is playing on a nearby gramophone. Occupying a table by the greenhouse door, where Sarah enters, is the chalice, resting on its purple, vestment cloth. Sarah—drying her eyes on her sleeve—begins cleaning the sacred vessel with a soft white feather duster. As she does, Naomi comes up behind her and touches her on her shoulder.

"I brought it out here for one last look at it," she tells Sarah. "And even though I stabbed Chad to save our lives, I alone must attend to this chalice as my penance, before God."

"We were in it together, Naomi, and it was Henry who, in the end, put that Klansman out of his misery by killing him, not you, and may that evil boy continue to roast in hell."

Naomi carefully washes her hands with a water hose and dries them on a towel. She then reverently wraps the chalice in its cloth and slips it into a nearby leather carrying case.

"Naomi, about Caleb . . . Now that Barney is—"

"There is no guilt in what God has put a man and a woman on this earth to do, child," Naomi explains, interrupting Sarah. "Caleb came from God. Remember that when that Klansman returns. Now let's put this holy chalice in a safe place where Barney's eyes of evil will never look upon it."

Naomi turns off the gramophone and embraces Sarah, then points to a section of the greenhouse where a red, twenty-foot, tall tree is growing. "That slow-grownin' oak tree was a sprout when I woke up in the barn and found Caleb and Flynn out in that storm so many years ago now; them boys were standing out there with the snow melting around them and the grass, green as you please, was springing up under Flynn's feet. Sweet Jesus . . . It was back then, when I was comin' back inside the barn with the two of them, that I took a closer look at that sprout and it—like the grass under Flynn's feet—was a-strugglin' up out of that scorched earth and yo' chalice blood as if the devil himself was after it. Then, once I replanted it in this greenhouse, it slowed down its growth, as if knowing Satan couldn't touch it here near where this holy chalice of God is housed."

"But why did you plant the sprout and afterbirth among the Colonel's god-forsaken firethorns?" Sarah asks. "You never did explain it, and I can still almost feel their evil presence."

"Remember how them plants refused to be destroyed and how we tried pullin' them up, and they kept growin' back, even when we put that weed killer on 'em? Well," Naomi says, puzzling at the red tree and going on, "once that tree sprout grew stronger and stronger in here, the way it is now, them firethorns upped and died. God, Sarah . . . that's the way He operates—like that red tree—a little at a time to give us all a chance to repent, even the Reverend Millers of the world need time to change their corrupt ways. But in the end if we don't grow stronger in the way of the red tree, and kill the evil around us with our love, then the evil will kill us. God and Jesus didn't guide this family through harm's way to abandon you now, the mother of their hope, just because Barney's returnin': Caleb is the embodiment of Jesus' long-lost disciples. Whatever happens to the boys now that Barney is comin' back is up to Flynn and Caleb, and all the worryin' and guilt feelin' on earth won't change that." A shadow falls over the land and reflects down through the glass roof. Naomi gazes up through the glass at the darkening sky. Sarah follows her sights and whispers:

"A three-headed monster is coming this way: the Colonel, Dane and the devil."

Suddenly, a clanking bell, resounding from the field, signals the lunch hour. In the field of rising dust, where men drive mule-drawn plows over the parched land, an old black bell-ringer continuously rattles the pole-mounted brass gong. The mule drivers leave their plows where they drop and join other workers along the roadsides under shade trees, where they eat their paper-bagged lunches, everyone now fully aware that Barney's on his way back home, whites on one side of the road, blacks on the other.

Apart from the rest of the field hands, Flynn and Caleb rest with their backs against a sprawling, four-hundred-year-old oak tree. Lifting his arm, Caleb examines a woven rope bracelet about his wrist. "Remember when Papa first made these for us?" he asks Flynn.

"And every few years since," chuckles Flynn, examining a similar-looking one about his wrist. "At times, when I'm bathing," he says, lying on his back and gazing at the blue sky, "and have taken mine off, I forget to put in on again and wake up at night looking for it."

Smiling, Caleb runs his fingers through a law book, while Flynn, content, lies on the ground with a straw in his mouth, his crossed arms pillowed under his head, a book of poetry and a pair of work gloves on the dry earth by his side. Running through the dusty field toward them is an attractive sixteen-year-old black girl. She dashes up to Caleb, kisses him on the cheek and hurries off again. "Claretta," calls Caleb to no avail. "Stay and talk awhile."

"You better go ahead and sleep with that girl to keep her happy," Flynn teases, reaching over and nudging Caleb. "She's one of the prettiest girls around and wants you, man."

"I'm not sure Claretta want to marry me or anyone else."

"Who said anything about marriage?"

"Papa. He talks about it all the time. Says he wants to have grandchildren while he's young enough to enjoy them, but I don' think he likes Claretta very much. He thinks she lives only for—Anyway, I know that can't be true. It just can't be."

"Why, because she goes to church in town?" teases Flynn. "Anyway, Henry is usually right about these things. He's been after me to be careful as well. Boy, has he ever. Isn't it miserable to lie in bed and think about it all night long?"

"Everyone has to be wrong about Claretta. She's just a little wild, that's all, and likes to tease."

"Regardless, Caleb, it's okay for men to do it, but girls are young ladies and are not—hypothetically speaking—supposed to act like boys.

184

But you, you want to wait until you're married to get it. Why, for God's sake?"

"It seemed the right thing to do. Besides, you're Catholic and are supposed to wait, as well, so clam up about it."

"Remember how Henry and Mother insisted that we pray before going to bed? And you, Mister-want-to-be-virgin, on Little Shadow Place and I here, on Shadow Grove, praying to be 'good' without the slightest notion of what we were praying for, or what praying really meant, or—in fact—why Henry and Mother were so repetitive about wanting us to pray all the time. Mother and your father, some characters."

"I'll make you a wager," Caleb says, then laughs and tosses a clump of brown grass at Flynn, "that I'll get some before you ever will, even if I have to marry Claretta to do so."

Flynn glances to the road, where Claretta is climbing into Amos and Andy's mule-drawn wagon. The brothers are taking her and other girls into town on this, Cutterville's once-a-month-coloreds-only day to see a movie in the town's theater, the only one around for fifty miles. Then, as Flynn turns his sights away from the road, he glimpses his mother's colored workers eating their lunches under the distant road-side shade trees; one of the workers—light complexioned, freckle-faced, sixteen-year-old Billy Joe Maddox, as thin as a broomstick, and better known as B.J.—is far from handsome, but he attracts girls like bees to honey. His hungry sights are on Claretta and the wagonload of girls. Flynn's left eyebrow arches up. Just as he turns toward Caleb to tell him about Billy Joe's roaming eyes, seventeen-year-old Peter Scott, with his red hair, runs across the field with two brown bags, while calling to Flynn. Peter's father—Jeffery—was the boy eighteen years ago who stood near Hank's truck by Henry, and heard Dane and Chad discussing killing Barney and harming Sarah and then raced screaming into the fields warning everyone about it. Now, red-haired Peter is the man of his father's house. Last year Jeffery died of T.B. Peter places the bags on the ground between Caleb and Flynn.

"Naomi said fer you guys to eat them vegetables in there," he explains, "not just her sweet 'tader pie or you and Caleb won't hear the last of it."

"Thanks, Peter," says Flynn.

Following in the distance behind Peter, with baseball bats, gloves

185

and a ball, a dozen or so teenage boys are running with their gloves covering their heads as a flock of gray pigeons fly over them. Caleb—out of the direct line of the birds—opens his lunch bag and nibbles on a sandwich and then returns his attention to his book. Flynn, on the other hand, returns his attention to B.J., who is sprinting across the field toward him and Caleb and the approaching boys. When B.J.—puffing and gagging for breath—catches up to the other boys with their ball and bats, Flynn watches how the freckle-faced, black boy studies Caleb, then sneaks a gander at Claretta and her girlfriends once more, Claretta and the girls well on their way down the road toward Cutterville.

Flynn knows what the girls all see in B.J. He's heard about it many times from the other guys: B.J. can take it out and put it in his back pocket. Having never seen Billy Joe do that, himself, Flynn finds it hard to believe, but then, as Billy Joe continues looking toward Claretta, Flynn notices the boy's fly rising with the unmistakable proof that every girl on the plantation both fears and worships. When B. J. realizes that Flynn is looking at him, the boy looks down at his fly, then quickly turns his back to the others and presses down on his crotch and embarrassed—and thinking of nothing else to do—he gazes up at the sky as if to ask God why he was made so large, and unfortunately for him, it's just at that moment that the swarm of pigeons changes its direction and flies over the boys and B.J.

"Look out!" someone yells, but too late, a pigeon's dropping hits B.J. in the eye.

"Dee birds flew by and somethin' white hit me in thee eye," B. J. says, wiping away at his eye, "I'm just glad elephants don't fly." When the others hear that, they laugh themselves into a tizzy at him, B.J., even more embarrassed, looks back at Flynn and adds, "I ain't feelin' so good, Mas'ta Flynn. You think Sarah would mind ifin I went home to wash out my eye and rested a bit? Musta been them chittlins I ate dat done made me sick."

"Ohhhh!" hisses one of the white boys, pinching off his nostril at the mention of the smelly eatables. "It's the pig's ass and holds pig shit. I wouldn't eat that stuff if I was starvin'."

"Go on home, Billy Joe," says Flynn, glancing away and trying to hold back the laughter, as B.J. takes off running. "I don't think Mother would mind."

"Come on, Caleb," Peter says. "You and Master Flynn before lunch time's over. We'll even let you two play on the same side and still beat you."

Flynn sees Caleb scrutinizing a nervous B. J., who continues trotting away, looking back at them. Flynn watches how Caleb looks down at his book. Flynn has no doubt that Caleb, who never misses much, knows that B.J. is after Claretta, and that Caleb is fighting hard not to believe what his keen awareness tells him. After watching Caleb, Flynn sits up and looks at Peter. "It was the colonel's idea to call me 'master,'" he tells Peter. "I know he's coming back, but you guys call mother 'Sarah', so just call me 'Flynn' like always. Okay?" He nudges Caleb. "Come on," he tells Caleb, getting to his feet. "Let's teach these guys a lesson and kick their butts and forget these books. Eyeing B.J., he goes on, "And everything else?"

"In your dreams," Peter shouts with a smile. "And Caleb, Flynn is right. Naomi says you best put that law book aside, or she says she'll take them books away from you guys. Said fer you and Flynn to have fun and not sit around on your lunch breaks like two old men reading all the time." Caleb saves his place in the book with a paper marker and closes the cover. What he says next, half out of frustration over B. J.'s attraction to Claretta and out of being fed up with the South is clearly meant for Flynn's ears.

"The colonel's last letter, I'm told, said we're not to work in the same field with each other, let alone play ball together. Is it wise for us to do so now that the man is coming back?"

"You and Flynn are always together," Peter says, as Flynn unappreciatively scrutinizes Caleb.

"Besides," says one of the blacks, "maybe the colonel's done changed from the way our folks say he felt ta-wards coloreds back when they was young like us and he was even old then. Old people fo'get a lot. Mamma said so. She should know, because she's old and fo'gets all the time."

"The way it's told in the papers," Peter adds, "colored boys fought alongside us whites in the war. So let's all play together. We're as good as them soldiers, ain't we?"

Caleb again opens his book and begins to read. Flynn shrugs to the disappointed boys, sits back down, crosses his legs Indian style, opens his lunch bag and removes a bottle of milk. "You heard the man," he quips and then gives Caleb a wicked look and adds, "The hell you did!"

187

Putting aside the milk, Flynn springs upwards, takes the book from Caleb and pulls him to his feet. Caleb attempts to shake him off.

"I'm not playing any ball!" says Caleb, laughing at Flynn's persistence in spite of himself.

"Play ball," comes the familiar echoing call from Sarah's workers, the whites and the blacks alike, who continue eating their lunch while excitedly gathering around the field, watching the boys at play. Flynn hits the ball over the head of the white outfielder and rounds the bases trying to stretch it to a triple. As his teammates cheer him on, the outfielder fires the ball to the black third baseman. Flynn dives head-first for the plate, hurting his shoulder and is called out.

"Out!" yells Flynn, impervious to his pain and leaping to his feet. "I was safe!"

"He was out," one of the white boys, on the opposite team, pleads to Caleb.

"You know white boys can't run," teases Caleb, next in line to bat and highly amused, "I would have driven you in. You were out by a mile."

Just like that, the game is over. Flynn storms off the field, glaring back at Caleb. At their shade tree, Flynn looks away when Caleb catches up and steps over to him, sits and settles with his back against the tree trunk. Caleb then broods and looks over at Flynn. "The war's over, in case you haven't heard. Or is this your way of preparing for Barney's return? Practicing to be the way his letters have forewarned you to be, unreasonable and stubborn? You know you were out. What were you told in those letters from him that seems to worry Papa and Sarah so?"

"Why don't you go to hell, Caleb? With that so-called brilliant mind of yours, you may easily grasp what Mother and those private instructors teach us, but I'm not one of those who worship the ground you walk on or prostrate myself to whatever you have to say."

Caleb is shocked speechless. Flynn has never reproached him that way before.

"Maybe they're right, Flynn. Maybe Barney has changed and you're worried for nothin—"

"No one knows a damn thing about the colonel, including you. And what gives you the right to even suggest that I'm worried about anything? Naomi might think that you're God-sent, but you can't read minds, so shut up about that man!"

" 'That man?' You really are afraid of him. Most educated white boys would have said 'Father.' "

At the end of that heated exchange, as Caleb flings aside the page marker and angrily flips though his book, a dozen workers' children march up to Caleb and Flynn, surrounding them with song: "Tramp, tramp, tramp the boys are marching, here comes Hitler at the door, if I had a piece of pie, I would bop him in the eye, and there wouldn't be a Hitler anymore." The racially mixed group of children giggles and nestles about Caleb. One of the white girls looks up and touches him.

"Will you tell us a story, Caleb?" she asks. "Momma says if the colonel comes back, it might be the last time us white kids can ask you to read to us or tells us stories."

Flynn follows Caleb's gaze to the workers and sees how everyone is smiling when Caleb puts aside his book and gives his full attention to the children, then begin telling them the story of *Uncle Tom's Cabin.*

"Once upon a time," Caleb begins, as the children wiggle in close, giggling all the more with excitement and fairytale expectations.

After the story is concluded, Flynn watches all those bouncing, ponytails, cowlicks, afros and innocent faces, smiles and young bodies skipping along back to their grandparents, who watch over them while their mothers and fathers work in the fields, the children's small hands waving back over their shoulders at Caleb and Flynn. Once the children leave, Flynn faces Caleb.

"Sometimes, I think the workers empathize more with you than they do with me, Caleb." Their troubled gazes lock. Flynn clears his throat. "As much as you like kids and read, Caleb, virgin, Mister Brooks," Flynn says, his displeasure of Caleb fading fast, "Why haven't you ever read Walt Whitman? He has a real feel for the plight of foolish humans."

Caleb smiles and then delivers a deadly sounding comeback. "Reading Walt Whitman won't win court cases." After a moment of Flynn looking at him, puzzled, Caleb speaks in even clearer terms: "Flynn, with thousands of colored soldiers coming home from the war and expecting a fair break from this country, what will you do when your father arrives? Will you keep the workers segregated the way he insists through those letters to you—the ones you tell me about?" Caleb points to the workers, who have returned to their shade trees to finish their lunches. "Will you, Flynn, keep them segregated the way Collins feels it's best to do now that Barney's returning, segregated the same way this country will treat its returning colored soldiers? Or will you do away with that barbaric inhumane practice that robs people of their dignity as we discussed, you, Naomi, Sarah and I?"

"The workers seem happy enough at this time," Flynn says, toying with his work gloves. "You better finish eating now, Caleb. We have but a minute or two left before we have to return to work."

"Everyone knows how you love poetry and playing the piano," Caleb says as Flynn slips on his gloves, "and how you hate getting your fingernails and those soft hands of yours dirty. One day you'll own this place. Sarah says it's in her parents' will as such. Remember? Besides, Papa wants us to be together as much as possible, so, so what if we're late returning to work once in a while? As easily as it is for you to get sick, and need your strength, you sit there and take off those gloves and finish eating your lunch."

"Who are you, my mother, now?" asks Flynn, sitting up, laughing.

Flynn does what he's told and begins wolfing down his lunch. "Naomi's always saying how you were born special, Caleb," the sensitive blonde boy says between bites, as Caleb also hurriedly eats. Flynn goes on. "But you've never said what you really think about that or want. To be a lawyer, maybe a doctor the way grandfather was, a famous heart specialist? Rich or saintly poor, Caleb, like that nagging Naomi thinks you'll be and be blessed by it for helping the blacks?"

"No, both Sarah and Naomi," Caleb says with a chuckle, more than willing to patch up their differences, "say I have to help the whites and the coloreds. Naomi just seems to have us coloreds more in mind, because of all the killing and beating we have to put up with in the South. Do I want to be a lawyer all my life? I don't know. And I certainly wouldn't want to be poor—saintly or not—no matter how many times I've been told that I was born on the wings of some bird. That's just silly talk, Flynn, as damn right silly as Billy Joe . . ." Caleb, struggles on, trying to hold in his laughter about B.J. " 'Something white hit me in the eye. I just glad elephants don't fly.' "

They laugh themselves silly until slowly, Flynn stops laughing, his intense, blue gaze locked onto Caleb's light-brown ones, Flynn's inner soul looking and groping, seeking understanding, desperately wanting peace between him and his best friend in the face of Barney's return. "Billy Joe's dumb remark was no more ludicrous than mine, Caleb. Arguing over that childish game and the colonel. Right?" When Caleb reaches over and touches him in agreement, Flynn gazes at the sky . . . to him, a blue ray of hope accommodating dozens of birds which are seemingly dark spots against endless space. Flynn is sitting a bit straighter now. As the boys talk, two lofty, spread-wing white doves fly among the other birds, two doves that seem to be listening to them. Caleb follows Flynn's sights to the white birds, but when the blonde boy whispers, they both forget about the doves, and Caleb faces his friend.

"I'm not cut out to be the master over this land or any other land with its cows, smelly pigs, dusty soil and its ever-present-heartaches," Flynn tells him. "All I want is to be free to soar."

"Like the colonel, Flynn? That's what he's done since you were born. Run away to soar."

"I know," Flynn again whispers. "And that's what frightens me."

"Same here, Flynn. All of this talk about me helping others is okay for those who have a calling for it, such as that Father Haas who Papa and Sarah told us about. I want to soar free as well." Neither boy is aware that the white doves are circling in the sky directly above them, now as Caleb continues. "But I love Papa too much to tell him that."

"Caleb . . ."

"Yeah?"

"The colonel's been sending duffle bags home with his letters."

"So?"

"They're locked and he told me not to tell anyone about them. They were almost too heavy for me to carry from an out-of-town warehouse where Barney arranged to have them sent, a few at a time, until Mother and I could go and get them. Some weighed as much as seventy-five pounds. Over a hundred and eighty bags during the last few months."

"Did you look inside to see what your father has in them?"

"No. That would dishonor him. And Caleb, each has a U.S. Senate seal on it."

"A senate seal?" asks Caleb, more than a little interested now. "With a seal like that, one could get through customs or just about anywhere else without the usual hassle, I imagine, and rather quickly. These bags, what does Sarah say about them?"

"Mother wants nothing to do with him or his bags. Even so, she told me to honor his wishes and lock them away, as he asked, until he gets here."

"Force one open and see what's inside, if you're that curious about what they're all about by mentioning them to me. I would."

"I couldn't do that. Didn't you understand what I said? It's a matter of honor." Flynn guardedly goes on. "Caleb, would you do it? Take Cutterville and us to court to force desegregation of this place and the school in town the way the workers are whispering that you will, if he returns and demands that Shadow Grove remains segregated? Is that why you study that law book so judiciously? If so, that would put you at odds with the Klan and the colonel, and what would that do to our friendship?"

As Flynn worries over their situation, Caleb springs to his feet. "No more talk," he says, "about your father . . . or anything else. I'm not a lawyer. Not yet. If Naomi thinks we're like two old men, let's show her and run with the wind and finish working on our boat before your father arrives."

"With the wind," shouts Flynn, tossing aside his gloves.

The two of them race, laughing, across the field, their hair blowing in the breeze, the workers cheering them on, the boys looking back at the applauding field hands with their joyous, smiling faces, all of them inspired by simply seeing the loving friendship between the two boys. Naomi, peering at them from her kitchen window as they run side by side, returns to her ironing, a smile on her face as well.

After taking a detour on the way to their boat, and with their truck parked down the road to their rear for a quick getaway, Flynn and Caleb crawl on their bellies and crouch behind a growth of shrubbery; they gaze through the thick growth and down a slight grade to the spooky, Victorian house of Flynn's grandmother. In dread and in absolute, total silence, they watch Barney's weary old mother—her shotgun on the nearby rear porch—as she hangs out her dingy white laundry on the backyard clothesline.

"I told you we shouldn't have come here," whispers Caleb, more than a little afraid. "She has that shotgun on the porch again. Remember what happened the last time we knocked on her door and you said hello. She took one look at you, then at me and threw that stuff from that bedpan on us."

"As if I could forget it. I had to sit in the tub for nearly an hour washing myself before I felt clean again, but she is my grandmother, Caleb."

"I know, and Papa says grandparents are as loving as real people, but just a little crazy at times, the way she is. I wonder what made her like that. She's nothing like Papa says your grandparents on Sarah's side of your family were."

"I wish I could have met the Winthrops," whispers Flynn. "Mother is always talking about how Henry and others risked their lives to try and save them, and just this morning, at breakfast—if one can ever believe anything she says—Naomi said that you and I will meet them."

"Meet whom? The Winthrops?"

"Yes. Mother's parents."

"For God's sake, Flynn."

"Naomi said we'd see them. I'm not lying."

"What she means is that when we die, Flynn. Not in this life."

Flynn pales, puzzled at Caleb and his standoffish viewing of God, life and everything in between. "No, Caleb. She said soon. At any rate, I'm not ready to die from some buckshots, so let's get out of here."

At that moment, a white dove lands on the bush next to Caleb and flutters onto his hand.

"Jesus!" says Caleb, startled, and draws back.

"Where did it come from?" exclaims an astonished Flynn. "It's not afraid of you."

"Then it shouldn't be afraid of you," Caleb tell Flynn. "Here. You take it. Remember what happened to B.J."

Flynn extends his hand, and the white dove flies over and lands on his upturned palm.

"Caleb, it's beautiful. Maybe it's someone's homing pigeon. A white one. Did you know that that was the name of my grandparents' plane? The 'White Dove?' "

"There's one more," says Caleb, pointing at another one circling overhead in the azure sky.

"I hear you out there spying on me!" Barney's mother yells to the boys and runs for her shotgun. "Don't ever come back here and tell Barney not to either, when he returns, or I'll blow his brains out as well! And take them dirty, fucking, goddamn shit-ass pigeons with you! I hate birds! Hate them as much as I hate you. You're no grandson of mine, you Catholic, statue-worshiping pig!"

"Run," screams Caleb, as the buckshots fly over their heads and the doves fly away.

The boys reach the lagoon in record time. They have not only decided to work on their boat, but have retrieved their hunting rifles—which they often carry with them—from the old plantation truck. Caleb jokes that it's to practice shooting back at Mrs. Cutter if she ever came after them with a weapon again. Caleb hits all of his cans, Flynn only half of his. As the sound of their rapid fire echoes through the air, the door to a tin shack opens and closes in the wind. The shack holds tools, old newspapers, tar and several paint-stained shirts, which are scattered across the floor. Next to the shack is the boys' rowboat, propped up by logs near the pickup. Just beyond the truck, Flynn and Caleb stop firing their rifles at the cans and listen to the sound of their gunshots wildly echoing off the water, the trees and the land. Flynn laughs, exclaiming, "I'll never get used to the way the echoes bounce around out here."

"At times, under the right conditions," Caleb says, "it can continue for nearly thirty seconds."

They store the rifles in the truck, enter the shack, slip out of their clean shirts and into the stained ones and begin working on the boat.

Unknown to them, some distance away, concealed in the lagoon's cattails, three white teenage girls from Cutterville are on the prowl for puppies, as they call them: boys. Their fingers against their lips and softly giggling, the Hill sisters—with only their faces showing in the warm sunlight—peek out of the cattails at Flynn, then pull back, closing the floral curtain behind them. Jayne, the oldest of the sisters, sixteen, slender with cat-like, dark eyes and curly, sandy hair, takes another look through the cattails, her sights on Caleb as the boys step from the shack, on his hair, on his golden skin, and on his muscular body, as Caleb slips into his shirt. Her sisters pull her away.

"You were looking at that nigger, Jayne Hill," says the younger sister. "I saw you."

"Why would I look at a nigger when Flynn is so beautiful?"

"Because blacks have larger penises," says the youngest girl, who is nine.

"You!" the other two exclaim, as they chase after her.

After an hour of working on the boat, the boys are more than pleased with their progress. "I can't wait to try it out again," Caleb says.

"Are you sure it won't sink the moment we put it in the water? It came close to doing that the last time, you know."

"Everyone on Shadow Grove is betting it'll float this time. Have faith and it shall be done."

"Ah! 'Have faith and it shall be done?'" teases Flynn. "Bible paraphrasing. This from someone who won't set foot in a church to save his life, and if it wasn't for reading the Bible to Henry, you'd never even know that Jesus was ever born, and that He went around talking the way you were just doing. 'Have faith and it shall be done.' That's one for the books. Do you get even a tenth as much from reading the Bible to Henry as he does having you read it to him?"

"Bibles keep people from killing each other as often as they would without it, and because of that, Bibles have merit. Lately, however, Papa believes in that Book as if his life depends on it, Flynn. But what about you? You're controlled when you and Sarah attend mass in Atlanta or during that priest's visits on Shadow Grove to offer the sacraments to you guys and your workers."

"And you don't want to be controlled, right? Nobody controls me, Caleb. And yes—Just in case that quick mind of yours is thinking about bringing it up, the colonel and his mother attend that preacher Miller's church in town, where he and Mother were married. And yes, the colonel does believe in the Bible and in God. At least he did, I'm told by his best friend old Hank, regardless of the rumors that he now worships the devil. And neither you nor anyone else can prove my father went to that church to worship Satan like Naomi says those other whites do, or that all churches are evil, not to me you can't prove it, anyway. Like you said, Bibles keep—"

"Whoa! Naomi may have said that Miller's church is evil or that your father went there, but I've said nothing about the man or about his worshipping anyone, devil or God."

"What's with you, Caleb? That's what you're thinking. I know you, Caleb Brooks."

Not wishing to be dragged back into the heated colonel debate again, Caleb looks away from his friend and toward the nearby lagoon. "The next thing we need to build is a good, strong dock for our boat," he says. "Okay?"

"Okay," replies Flynn, also more than willing to let the matter drop, and ashamed of being so sensitive when it comes to his father. He nevertheless can't resist something else on his mind. "When the workers go into town," he explains, "That one-eared Dane tells them it's against the best interests of whites for you and me to build this boat or anything else together."

"I'm not surprised. He's as crazy as ever. All these years . . . still blaming you and Sarah along with Barney for his father's death. He's one of these examples of so-called Christian-church goers. Fakers are what they are. If there is a God who knows everyone's heart the way people say, then how can people hate and pretend God doesn't know how false they are and will punish them for it? They hate because they don't believe even for a minute that there is a Divine Spirit, or that there is everlasting life after death for them. Don't listen to anything Dane says that spreads his venomous Klan ideology, and don't listen to the colonel when he returns. He and Dane are branches from the same poisonous tree."

"Dammit, you don't know anything about the colonel, only what you and I have heard, and don't always tell me how to think, Caleb. I also have a brain."

The girls' echoing laughter captures their attention. Caleb and Flynn look at each other and make their way to the water's edge. They ease aside the cattails, and their eyelids pop open. The Hill sisters are totally naked.

"Look at that!" Flynn whispers, all smiles.

The sisters' sleek, water-glossed bodies glow in the warm sunlight, their young breasts pointed and pinked tipped—the older ones, that is— their pubic hairs clinging to their young crotches, as they leave and enter the crystal-clear water. "If that Jayne is only half as sweet as those white guys in town say she is," whispers Caleb, "I wouldn't mind a taste of that honey myself, right now."

"They're white, Caleb!" hisses Flynn, pulling Caleb back to the boat. "That kind of talk is dangerous. Dane considers Jayne Hill his personal property. He's been trying to get in her pants for years! You're out of your cotton-picking mind to even think about having sex with a white girl!"

"Oh, and you aren't out of yours. I can't watch them on my papa's land, but you can? And what the hell are they doing here on our land like that anyway?"

"I didn't mean that I could look and you couldn't, and you know it,

196

and I don't know why the hell they came out here and got nude like that."

"We shot off enough rounds to wake the dead," Caleb exclaims. "They knew we were here, unless they're blind, deaf, and dumb. They wanted us to see them, especially Jayne. I have eyes and know how she looks at me whenever I go into Cutterville. The hell with Dane and the Klan! They don't own the right to have sex!"

"Let's get out of here, before those girls accuse you of doing something that'll get us both killed," says Flynn, taking off his work shirt and slinging it into the shack and then seizing his clean one from the shanty and slipping into it, the sisters, all eyes, watching them from the cattails, especially Jayne, her eyes on Caleb, who angrily rips off his soiled shirt, accidentally tearing it in half, revealing his flat, muscular, stomach strength and powerfully built upper body. Caleb flings the shirt to the ground, retrieves his clean one from the shack and slams the door shut. The door swings open again. Caleb closes it once more with an angry bang, causing Jayne to blink from the impact of tin against tin, sending the feel of exciting chills down her back.

"Killed for what?" yells Caleb. "Are you sure you also have a mind and can do your own thinking? Sounds to me as if it is Miller's church of snakes and Dane talking through you. That's why I don't attend some damn-ass church or fall on my face before a Bible, to be told that God will reward us in heaven, in effect to render us into becoming sheep. Jesus, Flynn. You never get it. Churches and Bibles are as bad as the Klan if used as a weapon of racial control, instead of a guide to unite people. Don't talk back. Be good, because the Bible says God will reward you. The Klan's Bible as good as professes that it's wrong to protest against being de-balled of every man's constitutional right to live without being lynched and burned alive for everything from looking at a white woman to having reciprocal sex with another human being who happens to be white, including being killed for having sex with someone of your own race, if that person is attractive and a white man wants her!"

This time, when the shack door swings open, it is Flynn who slams it shut.

"I'm getting tired of your bitching about white people all the time, Caleb!"

"And I'm damn tired of all the shit we go through! I can't drink water from any goddamn fountain in town I want—just the ones with those 'colored-only' signs on them. Organized religion could stop this hateful business tomorrow if it wanted to instead of using their energy trying to outcongregate each other. It's all bullshit just like the colonel and you are if you don't get it! Pretending that God made whites better than the rest of the world and that the Klan can kill with impunity. You know you're upset over those letters that that man's been sending you. What did he tell you to do, organize the Klan and lynch a handful of niggers by the time he gets back?"

"Jesus Christ, Caleb," yells Flynn. "It might have been a mistake for Mother to have taught you so well. You're much too bright to be colored. With the way you're trying to save your manhood for marriage, you'll never be killed for having sex with a white girl or a colored girl. It's your brains. That's what will make them fear you. They'll hang you because of your highly educated, white-man's-way-of-thinking that you're every bit as good as they are and—no doubt—a damn site better."

Flynn storms to the truck. He looks back when Caleb doesn't follow.

"Are you going to stand there like God Himself gave you the right to condemn His church and all of those who go there that you happen not to like? Reverend Miller may be a bit eccentric with his damn snakes, Caleb. . . . He is that and more, but he and his congregation are God-fearing people, unlike you, it seems, who as good as says there is no God. Henry has enough on his mind without him having to worry about the two of us fighting like this. Now, are you coming with me or not!" From the cattails, the nude sisters watch as the boys drive for home. Slipping into their clothes, they climb aboard a mule-drawn wagon and head back to town. "Did you hear what that Sambo said about us whites and God," says the younger sister to the next oldest. "And the way he as good as said he has a right to have sex with us. My God. What's this world coming to? May God strike him dead."

While her sisters focus on Flynn's departing truck, Jayne can't take her sight off the two halves of Caleb's torn shirt—a viciously stimulating sexual drive stirring her blood to boiling. Her sister talks about how the Klan will take care of a tar baby like Caleb. Jayne, however, has her own private plans for Caleb goddamn Brooks, to kill him in order to free herself of those unclean desires, for, to her only the devil could cause her to even look at a nigger.

13

The Black Exodus

With the sun ebbing lower on the horizon, Naomi looks out her open kitchen window at the workers, which includes Sarah, Henry and fieldboss Keith Collins; nearby in a wheat field, Caleb and Flynn can also be seen. Flynn—his work gloves protecting his hands—and Caleb, without gloves, till the land side by side, laughing and from time to time jostling with each other, as if never having had an argument over the Hill sisters just a few hours earlier.

"Lord," Naomi whispers. "How well we'd all get along together—the good folks of this earth—if Satan would only leave us alone." When Naomi returns to her ironing, a harsh caw is heard behind her. She glances over her shoulder. Perched on the window ledge is a raven with one whitened wing; it's looking into the kitchen and at an open kitchen door across the room, a door which overlooks the hallway and the open den door and Barney's portrait, his shadowed face and evil eyes highlighted by the Tiffany lamp aglow on a nearby table. The lamplight eerily reflects off the fireplace and gold-leaf frame and onto the painting. Naomi looks away from the portrait and turns, contemplating the black, white-wing bird, as it hops about on the ledge looking up at her with those black eyes and that cawing, jet-black beak; then upward the raven flies into the twilight skies and is gone. Naomi quickly puts aside her ironing and hurries from the house. Outside, she spots several workers who are digging up a dying bush by the porch. "Come with me," she says leading them toward the greenhouse, "and bring those shovels."

A short time later, elderly white men and women, who are chaperoning their grandchildren and earlier had permitted them to go to Caleb so that he could tell them a story, sit in the front yards of their plantation shacks and quietly watch over those children, whose mothers and fathers are voluntarily working late in the fields in a desperate effort to save Sarah's crops. Looking down the road, the old people see Naomi driving fast toward them in a horse-drawn wagon, sending out a trail of dust behind her from that late-evening, sun-baked road surface. The temperature of the red-clay road is a 114, so hot that the rising heat from its searing surface is creating a distant, quivering illusion that Naomi, her wagon and her horse are traveling on air, a foot or so above the road. When she, her wagon and horse thunder past their shacks, the elderly men tip their hats to the mystic woman, and the old women nod with respect, Naomi never looking left nor right, only straight ahead, driven by her anxiety. Lying in the back of her wagon is the red tree of fire. Caleb and Flynn watch as the galloping horse, wagon and Naomi leave a dusty trail, as she swerves the wagon and horse off the road across their section of the field and on toward Sarah, who is a short distance away with several buckets of water on the ground at her side. Next to Sarah, Henry is clutching a wood-handled pick, and Keith Collins, next to Henry, is holding a shovel; a freshly dug hole is at their feet. Naomi stops the horse beside them and stands up in the wagon, then gazes back into the wagon at the red tree.

"Thanks," she says, turning back to the others, "for coming."

"If I'm not needed anymore," Collins says. "I best get back to the trenches with the men." He tips his hat to Sarah and departs, leaving the shovel behind.

"What's so important that we have to stop workin' on Sarah's pipeline to meet you here with that tree, Naomi?" asks Henry. "You know we've hit solid rock in the trench, and it'll take all of us to break through it."

"The raven, Henry," says Naomi in despair, a sign that she's becoming more human-like then ever as time goes on. "A white-winged raven," she exclaims to Sarah, their attention locked on Caleb and Flynn, now. "It appeared at the window. A warning is what it was. That if this tree dies, it will mean Caleb has been morally defeated by Barney and Lucifer." A deeply troubled Henry looks at the red tree, its earthen-bound roots wrapped in burlap. Without a word, he lifts the heavy tree from the wagon and lowers it in the hollowed earth and holds it in place, while Sarah pours in the water and Naomi shovels in the dirt. The tree firmly planted, Naomi climbs back into the wagon.

"Naomi," Sarah asks, "now that Barney is old and frail, is Caleb still in danger of him?"

Naomi warns, "Woe unto those who underestimate the power of Satan to rescue his own, to personify Barney to any level, enabling him to pick up not one truck, but two, and to kill all of his enemies, including Caleb."

200

"He'll win out over Barney with his goodness," Henry says, truly worried. "You'll both see."

"Satan was powerful enough to misguide a multitude of Jews, God's chosen people, into condemning Christ to the cross." Naomi stops talking and faces a darkening sky, and then whispers. "Even now, the evil soul of doom approaches to give Barney godless powers."

Henry, looks from Naomi to a terrified Sarah.

Naomi nods to them, and, as she glances at that darkening sky, she paints an even grimmer picture: "Because this land was the birthplace of Caleb, who will confront Flynn—besides what Barney may do to you, Sarah—this day is the beginning of Satan's plan to destroy Shadow Grove, starting with your workers. They will unknowingly be tempted by him and guided toward more money than you can pay them, until all of your workers are gone, and in this way Satan plans to take Shadow Grove apart, until it becomes a vast wasteland."

"But God, Naomi," asks Henry. "Will God stand by and let Satan destroy this land and maybe all of us?"

"The workers—like all of us—have the power to refuse or to accept Satan's temptation, Henry, but Satan knows that money is also a powerful god to man, and that money usually wins out. That's what happens when we have been given a free will to choose by God, and He will not take that freedom to choose away from us, now that He has given it to us." Naomi leaves in the wagon.

Passing a cluster of workers' shacks, she notices Bruce Johnson and waves to him. Bruce is forty-eight and dark; he's standing by his shack, next to their sheet-wrapped belongings and is looking at a heart shape, which he's carved in the front door along with the word "love" and his wife's initials, "C. J." With him is his loving wife, Carrie, thirty-nine; also there is Bruce's youngest daughter Earlene, fourteen—the pride of his life—and then there is the pain in his heart, his second to the oldest child, sixteen-year-old, attractive, wild and unpredictable Claretta, wearing red trousers outlining her shapely body. Last of all is nineteen-year-old Brick, Bruce's mentally handicapped son, lagging behind as usual, and carrying a can of dollars. Brick is lingering at the back of their shack—a shack where he and his siblings were born. The boy runs his fingers over another heart carved in the rear door by his mother. The word and initials there are "Love" and "B.J."

"You love this place too, don't you, Brick?" a voice calls out to him.

He turns and sees Naomi, who has stopped the wagon on the road behind him. "You, a man in a child's body," she tells him. "Be careful after you leave here and move to that town, for Satan has placed his evil eye on you."

At the front of the house, Bruce leaves his family and approaches Flynn, who has joined up with Sarah by the red tree. "Can we talk private, Master Flynn?"

As Flynn walks a few feet away with Bruce, Brick watches Naomi ride away, and then the frightened boy runs from the rear of the house and follows his father to Flynn.

"What's wrong with you, boy?" asks Bruce. "You look like you seen a ghost."

"Naomi says the devil gots his eye on me, Daddy."

Flynn and Bruce follow Brick's intimidated gaze toward a distant Naomi and her wagon.

"She's always saying things like that," Flynn tells Brick. He rubs the top of the boy's woolly head of hair. "I wouldn't worry about it."

"I'm rich, Master Flynn," Brick exclaims, free of all fear now that Flynn, the master of the land, has spoken. "But don't tell nobody, 'cause Claretta and Billy Joe needs money to rent a house together, but I got the money. Lots of it. Not ma sister. I ain't loanin' ma money to them now that I finally got it. They can just live with our cousins in town, ifin they wants to be together, til they earns they own money, 'cause I'm buyin' a car."

"Hush up," warns Bruce, lightly whacking Brick on the rump, knowing that Caleb is sweet on Claretta, and Flynn is likely to tell Caleb . "I done told you about talkin' so much, and put that money in your pocket and throw away that can befo' someone robs you in town."

Flynn looks across the field at Caleb, who's having a difficult time conversing with Bruce's attractive daughter, Claretta. The determined young girl is shaking her finger at Caleb. Flynn stares at Brick as if trying to figure out what the boy had been telling him. He gazes at Brick's can of money. "His grandpa left him that money," explains Bruce. "Now, he wants to be the first colored boy about these parts to own a car."

"What did you want to talk about, Bruce?"

"We is leavin' Shadow Grove, Master Flynn."

"You're leaving?"

"Didn't want to hurt Sarah and mention it in front of her," Bruce says, glancing over at Sarah. "Me and Carrie came here as a young, married couple long befo' you was born, Master Flynn, and it was then that we carved our initials on them doors, but now, suddenly, we got them jobs in town. It's like a blessin' from God, and Master Flynn, it ain't just us."

"Who else?" asks a stunned Flynn. "How many?"

"Mister Dessen done hired more than a third of yo' best colored help. Says we ain't like the coloreds in town, who smokes reefers and drinks too much to be good workers in his plant."

Flynn follows Bruce's gaze to the fields. Blacks near and far are putting down their cotton bags and picking up their belongings in sheet-wrapped bundles at their feet. Balancing the bundles on their heads, they make their way to Bruce and line up behind him and Brick, as Sarah looks on in dismay.

"Mr. Dessen done sent a truck fo' some of us to start work Friday, today, Master Flynn. The rest of them who was hired gonna sleep on the side of the road and walk to the town and start on Sunday."

"On Sunday? That's your day of rest."

"That factory done got itself some kind of real-big tire contracts now that the war be over."

"It's Friday. Why are they leaving now and willing to sleep outside? Our crops—"

"They afraid of the colonel comin' back," Bruce says, eyeing the stormy-looking sky, his trembling voice reflecting his own fears as well. "Can't you feel it? Strange things gonna happen around here. Everybody feels sleepin' on the road be much better."

Disturbed about leaving Shadow Grove, Bruce quickly walks toward the main gate with his family, the deserting blacks following. Claretta leaves Caleb and runs to Flynn and kisses his cheek.

"I'll miss you, Flynn. Tell Caleb goodbye for me."

Flynn looks over at Caleb, standing with his hands in his pockets, his head low. "You were just talking with him, Claretta. Are you saying you didn't tell him goodbye or anything?"

"I tried to, but he was arguin' about me and Billy Joe. Says I encourage his attention."

"Go back over there and tell him yourself! You do encourage B.J. You're going to live with him! Don't get me involved in your betrayal. You know Caleb sees only stars when he looks at you."

Crushed, Claretta slowly walks away. Many workers cry as they look back at Flynn. Then, breaking into subdued song, they leave Shadow Grove, the only home most have known. While Sarah stares at her bolting workers, Collins—having witnessed them leaving—returns to her side.

"What's going on, Collins?"

"Damned if I know, Sarah. But Flynn . . . He was just talking with Bruce. He must know."

At the last minute, Billy Joe runs across the field, lugging his belongings in a blanket and joins the exiting blacks. Flynn sadly watches them leave and then moves to Caleb's side. "The whites in Cutterville were expecting those jobs," Flynn says to Caleb.

"Dane Tucker," says Caleb, his voice filled with concern now over Claretta, not anger. "Trouble, right? I tried to warn Claretta. She wouldn't listen."

Flynn follows Caleb's sights to Billy Joe, who catches up to Claretta and walks beside her. "Caleb," he says, "there is something you should know about Claretta and—"

"Hey, you two!" calls Henry from his wagon. "Time to go home." He sadly faces Flynn, feeling that Barney's return will change their relationship forever. "Seems you'll finally get to meet your father, son." As Flynn views the churning sky, Henry goes on, "Caleb and I would be pleased to have you spend the night with us, that is, if you'd like to before Barney returns."

That night, in the Brooks' house, half-heartedly Henry, Flynn and Caleb prepare a sweet potato pie, both boys' favorite. After the pie is baked, eaten and the kitchen cleaned, Caleb paces about and lets out his frustrations. "All hell will break lose now that the colonel's returning."

"You don't know that, Caleb," Flynn exclaims. "Nobody does. So shut up. I have my own troubles to worry about, and they don't involve the colonel, at this minute, if you don't mind."

"Don't tell me to shut up, whitey!"

"Stop it, you two. Don't let me ever hear you call him that name again, Caleb Brooks," says Henry. He places his arms about Flynn's shoulder. "And Flynn," he lovingly tells the blonde boy, "if losin' your workers is what's worryin' you, we'll find you and Sarah some more help.

There are plenty of godfearin', decent, out-of-work folks in Cutterville who'll gladly come and work on Shadow Grove."

"I'll go into town and try and recruit some help tomorrow," Flynn says, "then I'll stop by and talk with Mister Dessen. I don't think he realizes the danger he's putting our workers in."

"I'll go with you," says Caleb, tapping Flynn on the chin, bringing a smile to Henry's face.

"Now you two turn in," he tells them.

In Caleb's room, as Flynn sits dejected on one of the twin beds, Caleb stands on the matching one, while reattaching his handmade dragon kite to the ceiling. After finishing, Caleb hits Flynn with a pillow and the battle is on, both throwing pillows at each other. Henry enters. They toss the pillows at him and wrestle him to the floor. Upon having a good laugh, Henry tucks Caleb into bed.

"Papa, I'm too old for this now."

Henry kisses Caleb on his forehead and then tucks Flynn in as well, Flynn chuckling as the kindly black man also plants a kiss on his forehead. "You two'll never be too old to be tucked in," Henry teases with a smile. "You'll always be my little boys." He moves to the bedroom door and hesitates. "If you still plan to go into town tomorrow and talk to Mr. Dessen about your workers, Flynn, I won't try to stop you or Caleb, but be careful, especially you, Caleb. Flynn has the Cutter name to somewhat protect him from those mad dogs in town, you have only mine. With the colonel returning, them Klansmen will be insane with drunkenness and celebration."

Henry leaves the room and is closing the door when he hears Flynn whisper to Caleb. "Get up! We forgot something."

Caleb and Flynn climb out bed and kneel on their knees, saying their prayers, as had been taught to them from earliest childhood, a habit not so easily broken, even by Caleb, who does it mostly to please his father and Flynn. Henry closes the door. Normally, he would have done so sporting a huge grin, but he has other things on his mind. Is Caleb, unknowingly, being infused with Naomi's powers, and what will it do to him if he's unprepared to handle it?

14

The Death of Lilly

The following morning—under the same ugly, gray sky, from yesterday's approaching dark clouds—Cutterville's houses and businesses on Main Street appear to be deserted. It seems the entire town has gathered in the square, several blocks on down the road, across from Dessen's eight-story, sprawling factory. Flynn drives down the deserted street in Henry's wagon, which is pulled by two mules and carrying the workers who had been left behind to walk, including Claretta, her brother Brick, and Billy Joe. Wearing a denim jacket, Caleb rides alongside the wagon on his father's spirited horse, Old Clara, which Henry has given to him. Caleb has renamed her "Old Clara," which is a misnomer, because Old Clara is a horse that seems to be magically growing younger, not older, with Caleb now her youthful master. Suddenly, from one of the street-lined houses, a disgruntled white woman tosses garbage out a second-floor window onto the blacks and wagon. Flynn stops the mules and yells up at her, "Hey!"

"They're not wanted here, you young fool," the woman yells down at Flynn, while pointing a pistol at the blacks. "If you weren't your father's son, I'd shoot you and them. But you are his son! Act like it!"

Instead of going directly to the factory with Flynn, to ask about their starting time, the blacks leap from the wagon and run across the nearby train tracks to houses where other blacks mill about a white man in Dessen-tire coveralls. After arriving on the colored side of town, with their belongings, Claretta, Brick and Billy Joe move to the front of the crowd around the Caucasian, as he hands out the tire company's long-sleeved, dark-blue coveralls to certain people in the crowd. He smiles at Claretta. "I saw young Flynn Cutter drive you into town, and how that woman threw trash on you guys. Saw you run across the tracks." As the other workers from Shadow Grove ease in behind Claretta, the white man asks. "Are you all part of that Shadow Grove group that's due here tomorrow?"

"Yes, Sir," says Claretta, delightfully charming. "Ma brother and ma—"

The man tosses coveralls to Brick, to Billy Joe, to Claretta and to all of the ones from Shadow Grove. "Okay, you three," he tells Claretta, Billy Joe and Brick and then points at other blacks wearing the same type of coveralls and waiting on a nearby large flatbed truck. Bruce is one of those lucky ones in the vehicle and is all smiles when he sees his children walking toward the truck and then climbing onto it. He is doubly happy that they are assigned to the day shift as he, in order that he might keep an eye on them.

The white man faces the other ex-Shadow Grove workers. "Those of you who arrived with Flynn Cutter just now, and are from his place, will start to work at your assigned time, tomorrow. For now, until you get your first pay envelope, and can pay your own rent," he tells them, "I'll show you where the company has paid your first month's rent and where you will live while you're employed by Mister Dessen." He tells the disappointed locals, "You others will have to wait a bit longer to be hired."

Back in the white section of town, sitting alertly on Old Clara—after he and Flynn have traveled a half block away from the angry white woman's house—Caleb watches as Sarah's jubilant ex-workers are driven away in the truck. Reassured after seeing how Bruce had become a protecting shadow over Claretta, Brick and even over Billy Joe, Caleb, then Flynn continues on toward the factory. More than a little upset about having his workers taken from him, Flynn is determined to personally talk with Dessen before trying to recruit, possibly, no more than a bunch of drunks from the streets of Cutterville.

Jerry MacDonnell, thirty-eight, is sweeping the sidewalk in front of his Main Street newspaper, the Cutterville *Sentinel,* and when he sees Caleb and Flynn pass by his office, he drops the broom and quickly picks up a notepad, and follows the boys on foot toward the center of town and Market Square. The square is packed with desperate whites. Among all of that desperation and gloom, four teenage boys strum banjos on the gazebo next to a group of people roasting potatoes and baking homemade bread over barrels of fire or in crudely made brick ovens; elsewhere, throughout the entire square, people are cooking meals in the out-of-doors or trying to sell their belongings. The choices are many: stacks of old records, socks, sheets, blankets, trousers and dresses, as well as chairs and tables, dishes, pots and pans, bicycles, scooters, skates, even unwanted dogs and cats, but no one buys. After becoming frustrated with their impossible-to-sell pets, some of those in the crowd fling the animals off the square and into the street; a few of the four-legged creatures, too thin and too hungry and too weak to walk, crawl back to their human masters and lie down beside them and make no attempt to flee even when their handlers kick them and try to force them to leave. Most of Cutterville's adults are drunk and the boys in the band toss in the towel and begin packing up their instruments, when the crowd's frustration and anger grows to the point that people begin pushing each other about.

Then, the straw that breaks the camel's back happens: an unemployed white woman spots the trucked-in, black factory workers—escorted by armed guards—being off-loaded at the factory's side entrances, and the crowd swarms toward that side of the plant, just off the south end of the square, and as the blacks climb from the truck, Claretta and B.J.—looking afraid—remain close to Bruce and the guards, but Brick has caught sight of a car lot beyond the crowd and square. He removes his money from his pocket and meanders in the direction of that lot, counting his cash as he goes, his excited eyes constantly shifting from his money to an old yellow Hudson parked among other vehicles on the crowded, small car lot. Having safely tucked away his money in his pocket—as Bruce had told him—he now flaunts it, grins and then re-pockets his cash. He's now king of the world, almost as if one of Reverend Miller's drug-enslaved congregation, unable to resist the temptation of the snakes, in Brick's case a car, even in the face of great danger. Brick looks over his shoulder at his father and the others and continues toward his wildest dream. Moments later, whites swarm around the plant and confront the newly hired blacks. A line of wooden barricades and the guards, however, stop the angry crowd in its tracks. In the excitement, Bruce realizes he's lost sight of Brick and begins anxiously looking about for him. As the guards hurriedly line up the workers and clock them in, Brick is well into his dream world of owning a real honest-to-goodness automobile, an automobile on a lot with its owner's name displayed on a high pole: "Dane Tucker's used cars."

With most of the crowd now held in check about the black workers at the factory's side door, Flynn stops his wagon near the gazebo and gives the packed up banjo players a few dollars, and as he does, MacDonnell overtakes him and Caleb.

"There's a parade planned for Barney," the editor-publisher-owner says as he steps to the wagon and Flynn. "Folks aren't excited about that right now," he says glancing across the square at the angry whites swarming about the factory's side door, then goes on. "Seems they're more interested in stopping those coons, which is old news. But after it sinks into their uninformed heads that I'm a damn good reporter, and that the *Sentinel* is better than those big Atlanta newspapers, and well worth the price of a nickel, those stupid fools—barking at the wind over there—will realize that the real news is that your father is really coming back and it's not just another rumor. When he gets here, this crowd will bow down to him as if he was a god, praying that—unlike Dane Tucker—Barney will be able to get those factory jobs into the hands of the ones who pay their lawful taxes, the ones who are decent, law-abiding citizens." He eyes Caleb and continues, "And who do not forever keep their hands stretched out for government food stamps and welfare checks."

"As if poor whites don't receive welfare and those stamps," mutters Caleb, as Old Clara prances about, drawing a glance of admiration from Mac.

"What a beauty," he tells Caleb. "Is this the old horse that everyone is talking about living forever? Is she really as old as they say?" he asks Caleb.

"She's never told me how old she is," Caleb mutters. "Maybe she'll tell you."

MacDonnell angrily faces Flynn and snaps, "Let's get down to business. Is it a fact that the colonel's not only arriving, he's actually arriving a day or two earlier now? Hopefully you can be more civil than your colored friend."

Flynn's eyes widen upon noticing Brick at the south end of town heading straight for Dane's car lot, a good block away. "I'm talking to you, Flynn," says Mac. "Don't ignore me, boy."

Flynn faces MacDonnell, as Caleb studies the newsman with contempt.

"I don't have time to talk now," Flynn tells MacDonnell, trying to keep an eye on Brick.

"In other words," Mac hisses, "the colonel doesn't feel he needs to tell you anything."

"He didn't say that. You did," exclaims Caleb.

Search as best he can, Flynn cannot relocate Brick. As an upset MacDonnell rivets his sights on Flynn for turning away from him, Caleb looks at several starving dogs, then at the newsman and lambastes him.

"Don't you think you should go find a starving-dog story or something worthwhile to write about? Clearly, you see that Flynn doesn't wish to talk to you."

"I never did like you, Caleb," Mac says. "Now I know why. Good old Caleb Brooks. Still thinks the *Sentinel* and I are pro-Klan, instead of just gathering the news."

"When you refuse to have a balanced presentation for fear of those guys, you're as iniquitous as they are," Caleb tells him.

"Iniquitous," says Mac, taken aback, surprised that Caleb knows the meaning of the word.

"Did you expect me to use a plethora of four-letters word that were easy for you to spell?" Caleb says. "How about sinful as shit?"

"You heard him, Flynn," says Mac, angrily facing Flynn. "The way he expressed his disgust for the Klan. You're a Cutter, and your father is the Grand Wizard, the last time I checked, anyway. Besides that, what is all this business of Caleb speaking for you? Can't you talk for yourself?"

"Only when he lets me," Flynn says, grinning at Caleb, then at MacDonnell.

"Don't get smart with me," says Mac. "I don't get it. You and Caleb. . . . Friends. How can that be around these parts? But I'll have to leave that question up to the colonel when he gets here, won't I?" The news-man smiles at Caleb and then looks up at the gathering clouds. "Seems we're finally going to get some badly needed rain," he quips. "Have a good day, you two."

After MacDonnell leaves, the air turns cold, and the first of two whistles shrills from the factory's roof, bringing a stream of white men and several women in Dessen coveralls, from different sections of the white community and across the square, nudging their way through the few protesting whites remaining there.

"Nigger lover," the unemployed whites exclaim to their working, white neighbors.

As a second factory whistle blares, under the watchful eyes of still more guards, the white employees enter the factory alongside the newly hired blacks, as those ending their shift leave the plant in a parallel line from the same doorway, an arm stretch away from on-coming day shift and new arrivals, the crowd booing the coming and the going workers and tossing rocks at them. A guard fires a shot in the air, and the protestors quickly back off.

Taking a shortcut through the car lot is none other than Lilly, an aging, haggard-looking Lilly, far from resembling the young girl who Barney kicked out of Hank's truck eighteen years ago or the sexy girl he rubbed up against at his and Sarah's wedding. Lilly has a tattered, soiled blanket draped about her shoulders as she wobbles along. She carries that blanket with her wherever she goes, because on many a night she has to sleep on the street. Ironically, it's one of the blankets which Naomi gave away Christmas Eve on that winter's night just before Caleb was born. Lilly had taken it off a drunk's body when she stumbled across him in an alley frozen to death. She is as if sleepwalking, pale-white and yearning for peace of mind. Smoking in between sips of moonshine, she suddenly flips the cigarette aside, lowers the glass and eases into the shadow by Dane's small, office building. She is unaware of what looms over her. Because he has no outside water line and the only water in his small office is that which flushes his toilet, Dane has brought buckets of water from home to use to wash his cars. There is hardly even enough room in his office for him, let alone for all of that water. On top of that, he fears that the homeless people and the stray animals will drink the buckets dry if he stores them outside on his property. He's placed the heavy containers of water on the edge of his office roof, in order to easily get to them with the use of a ladder; all the time the buckets are clicking against one another in the stiffening wind.

Continuing to linger beside Dane's office, Lilly watches the one-eared Klansman with extreme curiosity. About thirty feet away from her, Dane is now in his thirties and as ugly as ever. He's still wearing that same old, now-faded and dog-eared Dodger's baseball cap and standing next to the yellow Hudson. He has his foot resting on the running board, while he scribbles on a piece of paper and from time to time glares down at Brick, who is anxiously watching him from within the car.

Brick Johnson, ponders Lilly. *What in the hell is he doing at that car, him and Dane?*

While sitting behind the wheel of his dream car, Brick keeps glancing back at the factory and hurriedly pays Dane with most of the inherited money, causing Lilly's eyes to pop open and focus in on the black boy and on him alone. "Sweet, fucking Jesus," she whispers. "Look at that boy with all that goddamn money. I could fuck all night and not make that kind of cash in a month. I'd be in heaven if I can only get my hands—" The wind sweeps across the car lot, knocking one of the buckets of water off the roof, splashing water over the old whore. "Shit!" she hisses. She's dripping wet, including her blanket, which she flings to the ground and draws back into the shadows, as Dane looks about to see what fell.

At the car, Brick beams up at Dane: "I always wanted a car just like the white boys on the rich side of town, 'cause white boys there, with they motor wheels, gots a real good chance to get all them girls, colored ones and white ones, po' ones and rich ones. I want all the girls I can get, too."

"And all this fucking country wants is no more monkeys like you," shouts Dane. "We got all the coon babies in America that we can stand, let alone have some grinning, backward, tar baby like you bringing more of your dark-skinned kind into this world, through all them nappy-head girls you plan to fuck in the back seat of this car." Grimacing, Dane hisses. "And who'd have thought a retarded dummy like you could come up with fifty bucks."

"I ain't retarded! Pa said I ain't."

"Shut up!" Dane yells, counting the money. "I should have asked fer more." He glares down at a sheepish-looking Brick, who's grinning again. "Wipe that smile off your ugly face, boy! They say I'm ugly to look at, but you take the cake. Am I ugly as you, boy?"

"No, Sir. You ain't near as ugly as you think."

Dane, at his wit's end, throws up his hands, lifts Brick out of the car and head butts him. "Get out of here until this car is ready fer you. And don't you go around blowing that horn at white girls."

"No, Sir," says Brick rubbing his forehead, near tears. "No honkin' at no white girls. Only at colored girls. They all seem to like red. Ma sister Claretta likes red and told me if I ever had a chance that I should buy a red car. That's befo' she knew she'd need to ask me to barrow the money to her."

"Loan the money to her, dummy."

"That's what I just said, dilalie, 'barrow the money to her.' "

" 'Didn't I,' asshole, not 'dilalie!' "

"Anyway," says Brick, a little afraid of Dane now, "my sister use to like Caleb Brooks, 'cause Caleb and Henry's got lots of land, but sis, she says white folks will only take the land from us coloreds, anyway. And she changed to likin' B. J., 'cause he got a factory job and they gonna buy a house, 'cause white folk won't take a nigger's house from him ifin' he lives in it across the tracks in Colored Town. So paint the car a nice red, like I said, and give me that receipt." Brick nervously glances at the factory, "Would you please hurry with the receipt? Caleb say we should always get receipts when spendin' our money."

"Caleb Brooks told you to say that, did he?" Dane seizes the car keys from Brick. "Well, I say what money, you talkative fool? You gave me no money, and you get your black ass out of here while you still can. You'll get no receipt from me. You're too dumb to have this car or this money."

When Dane hurries off to a white couple on his lot, he accidentally drops the receipt. The stunned wide-eyed boy has enough sense to scoop it up. As he does, the last of his money falls from his hand to the ground: five one-dollar bills. From out of nowhere, Lilly stumbles up to him. A drenched rat could not appear more gruesome to Brick, as he gawks at her. Looking more dead than alive, her face is thick with makeup and make-up-trapped water bubbles are embedded in it; her thin lips are painted thicker, her fake eyelashes are falling off and sliding down her cheeks, and to makes matters worse, as she removes the lashes from her face, she inadvertently smears the black dye from them around both of her eyes, making her appear to be a stand-up vampire with two black eyes. "I saw what you gave Dane," she tells Brick, lusting down at the five bills. "At forty-two cents a pound, I could buy a lot of T-bone steak with the rest of that money. Eat like the rich folks fer a change."

With her glass of moonshine in her left hand, she crouches, reaching for Brick's five dollars with the right. Brick squats, covering his cash with both hands. Lilly looks around, then at Brick and spreads her legs.

"I'll let you see my flower garden, if you give me that money."

"Go away befo' God strikes us both dead," hisses the terrified, black boy, grabbing up his cash. "You one of them holes. God don't want me to sex with no hole or even look at yo' dirty stuff. It be a sin."

Lilly deposits her glass of courage on the ground and rises up, slapping Brick, causing him to stumble backwards. "God don't care about you or me. Now, give me that damn money!" she says grabbing the cash.

Rushing her and wailing, Brick shakes her by her shoulder, drawing the attention of the crowd. "God does love me. Naomi says so!" he screams at the once-beautiful whore.

The disheveled prostitute sees Dane running toward them from between the cars.

"You little fool! You don't know what you've done," she hisses at

213

Brick. "Not even God can save you now. Let's hope He can save me." She stuffs the money into her blouse and tries to make herself more presentable. Brick sees Dane approaching and runs. The one-eared Klansman stops in the midst of the enraged, white crowd—now rushing onto his lot, all wanting to kill Brick—and he fires a .38 repeatedly in the air, sending the crowd scrambling for cover. Brick stops in his tracks, hands raised, his back to Dane, who races up to him, as the factory guards watch from their distant posts.

"You tried to use your money to get your way with this white woman," Dane blares at Brick.

Fearing Dane virtually as much as Brick does, Lilly cowers before the one-eared man.

"He put his black paws on me, Dane. I didn't go to him. He came to me."

"Where's that money I saw you take from him?" Dane yells.

"What money?"

He rips her blouse, seizes the five bucks and then slaps her, causing the crowd to gasp. "She offered herself to this retarded, raccoon brain!" Dane tells the crowd, as Lilly ties her blouse together and covers her exposed, compressed breast. Dane sees Brick gawking at Lilly's breast, and he backhands Brick, buckling the boy's knees, then pockets the cash. Suddenly Bruce's voice is heard sobbing and calling out his son's name. Pushing his way past the angry whites—who had returned to the car lot, after Dane stopped firing off his revolver—Bruce runs up to Dane, grappling with him.

"Please don't hurt ma boy, Mister Dane. Been lookin' all over fo' him. We gotta go to work."

" 'We gotta go to work,' " Dane mimics Bruce, his spittle flying. "Not in my fuckin' town!"

"This ain't yo' town or the colonel's no mo'!" yells Brick. "Pa says it belongs to the Jew Dessen and his factory now."

As Dane's eyes of madness swallow up Brick and then Bruce, the spectators beseech the Klansman to kill both of them. Back on the square, following the trailing whites, Caleb and Flynn inch their way toward Dane's lot as the enraged car salesman knocks Bruce down, almost losing his cap, so hard did he hit him. Dane frantically adjusted his cap on his head and looks about to see if anyone had noticed the part of his forehead that had been exposed when the cap all but fell off. Feeling that no one had noticed the cap or his forehead, the one-eared Klansman continues yelling at Bruce. "This is my town, now that Cutter's been away. You tell that to that piece of shit you call your son!" Bruce staggers to his feet once more, dazed and groaning, only to be grabbed and shaken by Dane. "If I ever see you or your nappy-head, mindless boy near that Jew's factory again, taking jobs away from whites, I'll cut off your balls and make you eat 'em, you and your whole damn car-buying family." Dane slips his gun into his waistline and kicks Bruce in his crotch, sending him to his knees, the regrouping whites cheering Dane on. "You see. . . . You hear them," Dane yells at Bruce. "This is my town, not that Jew's, not Barney's anymore. Mine!"

From his church, just across Main Street and the square, Reverend Miller nervously puffs on his pipe which contains a mixture of several drugs, including the deadly jimson weed. Having built up immunity to the drugs, the badly aging kisser of snakes is coldly looking out the rectory window onto the square and watching the events unfold. Miller then turns away, closing the curtains behind him.

Someone on the square throws a rock at Caleb.

Flynn panics. "Let's get out of here, Caleb," he yells.

"Why?" hisses Caleb, glaring about, looking for the person who threw the rock, ready to do battle with him, as he yells on at Flynn. "Because Dane is white and Bruce and Brick are colored, and that Bruce—as strong as he is—could easily kick Dane's ass, but knows that'll only get him and his entire family lynched, and that makes it okay for you to say 'let's get out of here' and let Dane kill them?"

"No! Because I'm about to piss in my pants, damn you! We're also in danger here!" Flynn says, watching the whites around them begin arming themselves with rocks and sticks, even a chair or two, and some with pistols. "Come on, Caleb, before they kill us."

"That pig Dane won't be allowed to hurt Bruce or Brick. Not if I can help it. Go on, Flynn. Get the hell out of here! This isn't your fight."

"Dammit, Caleb! God's not going to protect you, like Naomi says, if that's what you're counting on to save us. Let's go! Now!"

Gasping, Flynn attempts to turn the mules around, but the nervous creatures are now boxed in by a wall of screaming white bodies. To Flynn, the yelling mob is more like a vicious pack of wolves, reaching into the wagon while clawing and grabbing at his legs, feet and arms.

"Get out of that wagon, nigger lover and stop dishonoring the colonel," yells the same old woman who tossed the garbage out of her window onto them and had followed them to the square with her revolver, and is trying to untangle herself from the crowd in order to aim the revolver at Flynn. When several other rocks are hurled at Flynn and Caleb, and one of them lands in the wagon at Flynn's feet, he picks it up and slams it against the old woman's head, as she untangles herself from the crowd and is about to shoot at him; she falls backward, firing the gun in the air. In the panicked rush that follows, she's trampled under the scattering crowd's feet.

Suddenly, Lilly screams, "Somebody help me!" Her cry for help sends the whites around the boys, racing toward the car lot.

"You filthy whore!" Dane is squalling at and slapping Lilly. "Me, a white man asked you many times, but you offer yourself to this nigger boy! I'm too ugly fer you. Is that what you think?"

Dane slaps her again, as she continues screaming, while scratching at him with her poorly painted fingernails. "Don't just stand there," Lilly yells to the throng of angry whites on Dane's place of business. "Don't let him beat me like this! Help me!"

"They listen to me, not you," Dane says, whacking her again.

"What about Brick?" Lilly pleads to the crowd. "He touched my private part."

In total despair, still on his knees in unbearable pain, Bruce—fearing for his son's life—calls to Brick, "Come to me, boy!"

Brick runs wailing into his father's arms. When Lilly sees how the crowd—with absolute loathing—watches Brick sobbing with Bruce, to them, one baboon wailing to the other, she feels she has gained the upper hand and can turn all attention onto the two blacks. She causally picks up her glass of moonshine and sips from it, the relieving thought that she has turned her troubles with Dane around whirling about in her mind. Removing a lighter and cigarette from her pocket, she lights up the cigarette and relaxes and ponders about making a daring move. She knows that Dane is totally unpredictable and once again may suddenly turn on her. Taking the cigarette from her mouth, she looks at it and then studies the lighter and then Bruce. Stepping to the black man's side, nudging Dane aside with her wet hip, she puts her bold plan to work by pouring half her drink on the frightened, black man, causing the crowd to laugh. On the square, no longer blocked in by hordes of whites, Flynn is absolutely terrified when he sees Lilly pour her drink on Bruce and wants more than ever to get out of Cutterville, but remains in spite of his fears. Flynn knows the history of the Klan and is keenly aware what is coming next for his ex-workers, and so does Caleb, who angrily noses his horse toward the car lot, nudging the scattering of trailing whites aside. Flynn excitedly bounds straight up in the wagon and points across the square. "Caleb!" he cries out. Three white men—armed with shotguns—have entered the arena of battle, their weapons trained on Caleb. Beyond the armed men, just off the square, Deputy Sheriff Reggie Snodgress—twenty-seven, full-bellied and pale—watches from his patrol car. He quickly turns his car around and drives away. After the gunmen see Snodgress leave, they cheer.

"Burn them apes, Lilly," one of them calls to her. "Show them they can't take our jobs!"

Bruce staggers to his feet, his arms flailing at Lilly, now the darling of the crowd. Lilly is not going to give that up by letting Bruce leave. She kicks him down again, unscrews the cigarette lighter and splashes the fluid on both him and Brick. Dane laughs, as Bruce pushes Brick away.

"Run, boy!" he yells. "They gonna to burn us alive!"

"They're tryin' to burn Pa!" Brick screams as he runs. "Naomi, help us!"

Thunder rocks the sky from that days-long approaching storm and darkness suddenly falls over Cutterville. Lilly looks up at the storm clouds directly above them, and cold, tingling fear takes hold of the aging prostitute. Soaked to her skin from the bucket of water which fell onto her, she begins searching over her shoulders, this way and that, in profound concern, after hearing Brick cry out for Naomi to help him and his father. The old whore's hands begin to shake, as she looms over Bruce with the lighter.

Dane glares at her. "Burn him, you bitch. What are you waiting for?"

"He called on her," Lilly whispers to Dane. "Brick did. Called out to Naomi, the one the coons say puts a curse on folks. The one they say sent Colonel Cutter off to war and got him captured. Brick, he called her name. And now this dark sky. The sky! It's like the sudden darkness that fell over that Biblical town when they crucified Him. Christ, Dane. When they crucified Jesus!"

"Naomi," hisses Dane—after seeing the negative affects Lilly's raving is having on the crowd, putting the fear of God in some of them. He puts his pistol to her head. "You're not telling me, you—a white woman—are afraid of her! A nigger. You burn that coon, or the Klan burns you!"

As several Klansmen take off chasing after Brick, Lilly flips her lit cigarette on Bruce. It bounces off his trembling body and sizzles out in the spilled drink. Bruce gawks down at the cigarette, then across the square. "Thanks, Naomi, blest female of God!" he cries aloud.

Lilly follows Bruce's gaze across the square. Naomi is standing in high relief against a scrubby, old, Judas tree and illuminated by the factory's, reflected, window lights in the obscurity of the storm. The Judas tree has always been looked upon as a bad omen by the town—a tree that is whispered to have been there for over a hundred years, grown there when a raging storm carried its unwanted seed into Cutterville, and no one dared cut it down for fear of Satan; for it is he, who the citizen thought placed the tree there to honor the first Cutters, who are said to have worshiped Satan and butchered over a thousand rebellious slaves who had refused to embrace the Master of Darkness. Suddenly lightning strikes the old tree, exploding it into a fireball, but Naomi—unflinchingly—stands firm, the crowd glancing about at one another in wonder. Then, as suddenly has had the lightning struck, another anomaly occurs: the earth shakes, rattling the town.

"Earthquake!" screams the garbage-tossing woman, getting off the ground and forgetting about her gun or about killing anyone as she races for home.

When the shaking stops, everyone looks at Naomi. "It's her," someone whispers. "That woman who came to the wedding—years ago—and turned the snake on Chad. She's older, but I'll never ferget her if I live to be a hundred. She caused the earth to shake. Satan is in her as he was even back then in the first Cutters."

"He almost died, Chad did," says another of the bystanders. He waits in fear of another earthquake and then goes on. "Chad, after being bitten time and again and always getting over it, just upped and almost died. And now, no one's seen Chad since. Naomi's evil like they say."

"But what destroyed that evil tree?" an elderly man asks with one eye on Naomi. "If not the woman you call Naomi, then who did?"

The old man follows Naomi's intense gaze back to Caleb, and—he thinking that the power that destroyed the tree came from Caleb (and that Caleb's power is even stronger than that of Naomi)—runs for home, passing up the old garbage-tossing, pistol-packing woman as he does. At the gazebo, where a scattering of the crowd gawk at Caleb and Flynn, the gunmen—who at first had their sights on Caleb—now cautiously advance toward Naomi, their weapons at the ready. Flynn flops down on the wagon seat, gasping and fighting to catch his breath, his sights fixed on Naomi and that burning tree and on those men stalking toward her with their weapons of death. Flynn has heard many things about the black woman from his mother and others all of his life, but nothing he's heard could have prepared him for what he's seeing and feels. Even Caleb's reaction to the bizarre moment confuses Flynn. Caleb is sitting in the saddle, trance-like, as if unaffected by the earthquake or anything else at the moment, not even by those men with their weapons of death, who—after having decided to go after Naomi—once again are trying to decide who is the most danger to them and now have their killer's eyes on him and Caleb once more. Flynn is captivated by Caleb's lack of reaction. His best friend seems to be focused on Naomi, but not actually looking at her or even seeing her, as she now stands by that burning tree gazing at Lilly and at Bruce in the car lot. Then, as Caleb continues focusing on her, Flynn sees Naomi slowly turn her glaring eyes back toward Caleb and Caleb alone, as if she is transfixed by his very presence.

The whites on the square and on Dane's car lot follow Naomi's sights to the golden-complexioned young man, who continues sitting there on his horse as if in a world that no one else can enter. Naomi seems unable to look away, as if some unshakable force from Caleb is melting the two of them together, Flynn watching both now in foreboding, as the lightning intensifies and rages on. Lilly is especially knee-knocking terrified of the thunder and lightning, and—as for the crowd of whites—there is absolute, eerie quietness among them that Caleb's presence has caused. Lilly—finally realizing that everyone is looking at Caleb—fixes her gaze on him as well and then guzzles her drink. There's a glow all about Caleb and Old Clara.

"He is truly from God," she whispers and then looks about in fear, wondering if anyone had heard her. As the whites around her and Dane whisper about the lightning, about the burning tree, about Naomi and about Caleb, Bruce eases to his knees, and it seems that he will escape harm, but one look from Dane freezes Bruce in place with bone-cold chills. Lilly looks from Bruce to Dane, and she cries aloud, "Brick called her name and she appeared, Dane. The cigarette. It didn't burn Bruce. It went out." When Lilly looks again Naomi's gone; only the burning tree, the thunder, the lightning and Caleb remain as a symbol of the eerie feeling she has, the lightning flashing, silhouetting and illuminating Caleb and his horse.

"See! I told you. Just like that she's gone again!" Lilly again cries aloud, and now pointing at Caleb. "And now there is Caleb! Didn't you see how it fits? How he glows now that Naomi gone?"

"He ain't glowing," says Dane, after looking at Caleb then at her, "Unless it's going to be your ass after I kick it up and down this block, bitch."

"He made her leave, Dane. Can't you feel it? He has king-like powers even over Naomi now."

"You damn drunk," says Dane, taking out a match. "Let's see just how magical this black witch of yours is—or Caleb—in putting out matches."

He removes a piece of dry paper from his pocket, lights it and flings it on Bruce's fuel-soaked coveralls. Flames roar across the horrified man's heavy, long-sleeved uniform. While most cheer, some whites in the crowd—who have been touched by that night as much as Lilly has and have never seen a man die by fire or by any other means—watch in repulsion, as Bruce flees screaming across the square, feeding the flames all the more. "Get Brick!" Caleb yells to Flynn, after seemingly snapping out of his trance-like state. "I'll try for Bruce."

"Shit," exclaims Flynn, having no choice but to go into action. He zeros in on Brick, who is flailing along in circles and chased by those Klansmen who had earlier gone after him. Flynn then sees the other gunmen running toward Caleb and aiming their guns at him. "Go!" he yells to Caleb. Lashing the mules, Sarah's delicate son plows through the gunmen, running over one of them and continues after a distant, screaming Brick. While Caleb is sprinting Old Clara toward a flaming, wildly, running Bruce, Flynn manages to overtake a hysterical Brick—who runs back toward him—on the far end of the car lot. Flynn drags the boy into the wagon, lashes the mules with everything he has and leaves the gunmen, Dane's property of horror and the square behind. Brick looks back from the bouncing wagon and shrieks "Jesus, if You really is You, save ma daddy."

More than ever, now, resembling a running torch, his incredible speed causing the flames to flare back away from his face and hands, Bruce sprints toward the factory, to him, a beacon of safety, but in his confusion, instead of running to the side door and the guards with their fire extinguishers, he crashes into the loading dock, the flames, now engulfing the legs and sleeves of his coveralls. The crowd stones two guards who venture out to help Bruce, and the guards retreat behind their barricade. Dane and Lilly are hot on Bruce's heels, and Dane catches up to Bruce. He kicks him to the ground by the loading dock. While holding onto her glass of liquor, Lilly laughs down at Bruce, now that—to her drunken reasoning—Dane has proven that God is not with Naomi and certainly not with Caleb, but with them. Otherwise, why would Bruce be burning, if not by the will of God?

She screeches when she sees Caleb and his horse suddenly upon them. Caleb smashes the powerful horse into Dane. Lilly's glass drops from her hand. Dane also goes down hard, losing his gun, but not his cap, which he manages to hold onto his head with both hands. Caleb leaps from the saddle and rolls Bruce across the ground, covering him with dirt, the armed men now closing in on him and Bruce. With unbelievable strength, Caleb lifts Bruce off the ground and onto Old Clara, then springs on behind him.

"Nigger," shouts Lilly, spitting at Caleb and clawing at Old Clara, trying to block Caleb's escape route. Caleb reaches down with one hand and throws her aside, then knees Old Clara.

"Go!" he shouts.

One of the gunmen gets a shot off at Caleb as he, Bruce and Old Clara disappear around the side of the plant. When Caleb races Old Clara pass a group of rioters and comes into the view of the tire workers—blacks and whites—looking down on Market Square from the factory's towering windows, the workers cheer Caleb's escape. Among the factory workers, at the window, is a short man of fifty dressed in a brown suit, white shirt and necktie.

"Who is that boy?" he asks one of his white-shirt supervisors at his side.

"Caleb, Mister Dessen. Caleb Brooks," says Krause, Dessen's foreman.

Back on the loading dock, the gunmen approaches—one of them being half-blind Hank—as Lilly is pulling a dazed Dane to his feet, while he holds onto his cap with one hand, keeping it in place on his head.

221

Once Dane is on his feet, Lilly is again having grievous doubts about whom God loves and doesn't, while eyeing the sky.

"That black Naomi woman should have been fried by the damn lightning," Old Hank says, holding onto his thick wind-blown glasses. He had been watching the action from a side road, and has joined his friends only after Caleb and Flynn have cleared out. Hank—now thick of body and face—didn't want Flynn to see him and possibly fire him from his job at the plantation store. "What in God's name saved that bitch like that?" Hank asked, adjusting his eyeglasses, while gazing at Lilly with fatherly concern for her. As thunder and lightning rocks the town, Lilly—frightened even more—loses any convictions she has had that God is with her and Dane. She desperately looks around for her drink. Glaring down big-eyed at her broken glass on the ground, and—with just the bottom rim of the glass remaining intact, and with some of her liquid courage remaining in the jagged, razor-sharp bottom—trembling, she seizes the broken depository of her life's blood and sips the moonshine from it.

"What we did to Bruce and the coloreds is wrong," she whispers, blinking up at the lightning, causing Hank to fear for her safety, as Dane glares at her, while shaking his head and trying to recover his senses. "We're all going to die because of our sins," Lilly tells Dane. "I can feel it in my head, in my arms and legs and in my bones and in my pussy. Maybe God'll let it rain. The rain. Enough of it might wash me clean."

The gunmen are now joined by Crippled, one-leg Trout—a wrinkled, tired-looking white-haired specimen now. Trout had come to town with Hank for a drinking binge. He looks at Lilly, at the sky, and at the men, all eyeing each other with uneasy glances. "You gonna stand fer this, Dane?" Trout asks. "Let that coon get away with this, while Lilly got everybody thinking the end of the world is upon us whites?"

Dane jerks the broken glass from Lilly and hurls it onto the loading dock. "You goddamn, weak-ass, spineless, white, pussy bitch!" he yells shaking Lilly. "I'm going to rain down pain on you if you keep talking like this. As good as telling these good Klansmen that God's gonna kill them. We're in a fucking drought! Clouds or not, lightning or not, like always, it'll never rain. Nothing will wash you clean."

Suddenly, it rains buckets, extinguishing the burning tree, sending the firemen—who had responded to put it out—scratching their heads

222

and driving back to their firehouse. The gunmen gawk at one another then at Lilly and finally at Dane.

"My wife's at home alone, back on Shadow Grove," says Hank, covering his ears against the thunder and flinching from the exploding, cracking and sizzling lightning. "She's afraid of storms. I better get back home and be with her and the kids."

When Hank leaves, Trout follows, and the others also leave. Soon—it seems—not a living soul remains in the square or in sight, only Dane and Lilly by the loading dock. However, in the building's dark shadows, not ten feet away, someone is watching them in horror; it is Charles Pennington of Cutterville's Pennington National Bank. He's the bank's president, now. His father and dog have died. Eighteen years older and even more afraid than he had been—as a young man—during the murder of those school kids, when he had turned and run away, he stands there with yet another dog, wetting himself as he listens to Dane and Lilly speaking about God and punishment.

"I'll kill that sambo fer knocking me down," Dane bellows, prancing about in the downpour, shaking both of his fists at the sky. "So help me, your goddamn God, I'll kill him with my bare hands."

"There's something about Caleb, Dane, him and Naomi. They scare me. You should be afraid, too. There was a raven watching us."

"A raven! Just admit you think I'm totally insane, bitch. Colonel Cutter ruined my pa. And just now Caleb goddamn Brooks knocked my ass down in front of the whole, goddamn, fucking world. My goddamn mamma just died of a broken heart, 'cause she couldn't live no longer without Pa. She's in Wilson's Funeral Home as we speak, with cotton stuck clean up her ass to keep her from shitting on herself after death. Her fucking neck on a block of wood to keep her head from tightening back. Now you tell me a motherfucking raven was watching us? I ought to slap the goddamn living shit out of you. You as good as told the men that God's on them darkys' side. Run away before I kill you. Run away, Lilly!"

"You'll shoot me in the back like your pa and Barney did those colored kids, after the Klan told them to run away, then left them burning from Old Cutter Bridge."

At the mention of the incident of killing those school kids, Pennington begins inching away. Dane's reaction to the gruesome reminder causes him to pull the cap brim down even more about his forehead.

Lilly goes on, "Please, Dane, let me walk away from this. I know I never let you bone me, but let me live to do some good in my life, so God will fergive me fer being wicket. I want to go to Colored Town. To beg their fergiveness. To teach their kids how to sew, how to read, how to love us whites, how to—"

"Nooo! You damn bitch! Nooo!" Dane yells, sobbing, then slapping her. "God or no God, no! A thousand times no! Now you beg, but I also begged for some pussy from you. Remember? You always said, no! You will not kneel before them coons, now or ever!"

Sensing her demise she begs, "There are other girls that you can have. Spare me."

"So you can go into nigger town and spread that lie—by being an example to them—that Jesus was a nigger like that goddamn Catholic priest spread around when the Winthrops were alive. Hell no! I'll kill you befer I let you do that."

Lilly sees a soaked old Hank and Trout standing in the downpour on the square a few yards away. A guilty look crosses Hank's tired old face in the pouring rain. He could not go home without trying to help the elderly whore whom he has always looked upon with a father's love.

"Get the fuck out of here, Hank," warns Dane. "You and Trout. Befer I kill your old asses."

Hank lowers his head in shame, as Trout leaves him alone. Slowly, he lifts his troubled sights to Dane, as if to ask him to spare Lilly. Then sensing that it would mean his own death, for him to oppose the one-eared madman, the old man runs sobbing into the night and is gone. Lilly spits in Dane's face, as he drags her up the steps onto the loading dock out of sight of the factory windows and workers. When Dessen sends a handful of his guards toward the loading dock to see what Dane is up to, shots are fired at them from a scattering of Klansmen in the shadows of distant houses and stores across the square, and the guards retreat back into the factory. On the dock after throwing Lilly onto a stack of used tires, wooden pallets and poles, an enraged Dane grabs a fragment of her shattered moonshine glass from the dock floor and cuts her throat, missing her vocal cords. With the rain hammering off the dock's tin roof and all around them, Lilly slumps into a sitting position against the factory's steel cargo door, her hands about her throat, as Dane towers over her. "The others say you was the best pussy they'd ever had after Barney fucking Cutter left town," he tells her. "But you despised me. Me! Because to you I'm ugly!"

"I was a good person once. Oh! Oh!," she cries and gags in pain, spitting up blood and gurgling on, her hands trembling slipping and sliding about her bloody throat, slowing the flow of blood. "I studied the Bible all my life until men like you and Barney Cutter, the devil himself, came along." Fading fast, her voice failing, she fights through the pain. "I'll die knowing you'll never get in my flower garden."

"You always did underestimate me," Dane tells her and drags the groaning, dying woman by her feet away from the door and drops his trousers and shorts, rips off her underwear and straddles her. As Dane gasps and groans in pleasure and thrusts about on top of her, Lilly holds her hands even tighter about her throat, her blood spurting, her voice gushing forth from Dane's vicious, up-and-down, wild, sexual ride on her, a lifetime masturbator, exploding out all his pent-up sexual needs at once. Suddenly, galloping full out on Old Clara, from the far end of the loading dock, Caleb closes with lightning speed on Dane. By the time Dane realizes what is happening and leaps to his feet and tries to raise his trousers to reach his pocketed revolver, Caleb leans down, sweeps up a dock pole and cracks Dane on his crotch.

"Stick that in your pants, pig!"

"Not again!" shrieks Dane, one hand between his legs, the other holding his cap on his head, as he stumbles backward and topples off the four-foot-high dock onto his back, groaning in pain, his cap of shame having been successfully held onto his head, and now both hands grappling at his testicles. Lilly locks gazes with Caleb when he approaches on Old Clara, and gazes down at her sending Charles racing away.

"You came back for me. Hank didn't, but you did," she wheezes, her hands covered with coagulating, thick, red blood, her fingers slowly slipping downwards from her throat, as she talks. "You are what Naomi and the others say you are. I can feel it now as clear as I can see that Light glowing all around you, Caleb Brooks."

Caleb is more afraid of Lilly's hair-raising death statement of a light that she sees around him than anything Dane can ever do to him. "Don't talk," he tells her, "I'll get help for you and—"

"You came from Him," Lilly forces herself to say, grimacing. "This pain. This awful pain," she sputters half aloud. "Ask God to take away this pain. Please, Caleb."

"Someone . . . if anyone can hear me phone for a doctor," Caleb cries aloud.

Deputy Snodgress is flagged down and informed of Caleb by several of the fleeing whites. Snodgress races his patrol car down Main Street in the pounding deluge, then rumbles the car across the square and dips the light-flashing vehicle to a stop at the dock. Snodgress sees Dane wailing on the ground with his hands between his legs, and Caleb on his horse next to Lilly. Trembling, the deputy leaps from the car with his revolver drawn.

"Get the hell away from her and off that horse and hit the deck, boy, or I'll blow you off of that goddamn critter, and I mean right now!" he yells. Then Snodgress notices how Lilly's covered in all of that blood. He leans over and vomits. Caleb glances at the heaving deputy and sidesteps Old Clara closer to the dying prostitute, who now smiles up at the gentle horse she earlier spit on and cursed. Leaning down in the saddle and with profound compassion, sickened by her pain, Caleb attempts to reason with her, as she continues begging him to have God take away her pain. At the same time, a befuddled, gagging and almost paralyzed Deputy Snodgress, now violently regurgitating—to the point of nearly being paralyzed—can do nothing more than helplessly watch Caleb and Lilly, realizing that Caleb could not have harmed the prostitute, not in the way the two of them are talking to one another. Snodgress glares down at the disabled Dane, who is groaning at the lawman's feet.

"You're confused," Caleb tells Lilly. "I have no power except the power of pity for you. I'll take you into the factory. They have a doctor there and—"

When she attempts to rise up, her blood explodes from her throat and out between her fingers, and she sinks back down. "I'll be dead before you can get me off of this dock," she tells him, then screams, in agony, her blood flowing all the more. "Naomi, the Bible says Jesus fergave that other one like me, that Mary Magdalene. Why not me? Please, Naomi, you or Caleb, let me die and take away this cup of pain from me. My mother said God'll do anything for His beloved Son's chosen ones: Peter, Paul and the others." She faces Caleb. "Everything about this night, the thunder, the lightning, the burning tree, they all say that you, Caleb, you also, have the power, even more than Naomi, like Jesus promised that His disciples would have. Caleb Brooks, come close. Let me touch you and die."

A frightened, black drifter—searching through the factory's trash cans not ten yards away from the dock—peeks out at the racket and sees something that causes his eyes to widen in astonishment. As Lilly proclaims that Caleb is from God, she reaches up and touches Caleb's boot and then slumps over and cries no more. The rain, the thunder and the lightning stops, and a night bird sings. Even the roaring motors from the tire factory seems to be muted, as Caleb scrutinizes the dead woman; her lifeless eyes are frozen toward a cross atop Miller's nearby church. Caleb follows her gaze to the cross, as does the drifter. Deputy Snodgress—no longer vomiting—wipes his mouth on his sleeve and also follows Caleb's sights to Miller's church and cross. Caleb turns Old Clara and sprints away.

As Dane—fighting off his agonizing affliction—grabs his revolver from the ground and stumbles to his feet, he yells at Snodgress, "Why does that half-breed prevail over me? Does God love the coon more than He loves us whites, who worship Him?" The one-eared Klansman points at Miller's church. "I worshipped Him in His holy church with every week that passed when I was a boy! Now I know why I hate God, because He hates His own church, otherwise why would He let folks say He loves Caleb and treat me this way?"

A howling wind rips the fire-damaged tree out of the ground, hurls it airborne, exploding it against Miller's church tower, damaging the rooftop cross. Snodgress turns pale white and drops his gun. He looks at Dane, all eyes, and he groans. Again, he faces the church, sobbing up at the damaged cross, his only thought is to also run for home. "What in God's name is going on, Dane?" begs Snodgress. "Dear God, what is going on?"

The black drifter gawks about and runs back across the tracks to Colored Town. "He's from God," he yells. "She said Caleb's from God."

"What's going on?" screams Dane at the petrified deputy. "I'll tell you what's not going on! You didn't shoot Caleb dead! That's what the hell should have gone on! Why didn't you shoot his ass! Now you get rid of Lilly's body and tell Sheriff Richards to make it look like a nigger killing. Caleb Brooks, you've opened the gates of hell! Now, we barbecue all you coons fer killing Lilly!" Once more it rains.

15

The Factory Workers' World

In an alley a few blocks away, a massive discharge pipe protrudes from the back of Dessen's sprawling tire factory where the factory and the alley ends. A ten-foot, high fence keeps trespassers from getting to an ominous man-size pipe which projects over a deep, forty-foot wide, fast-moving river. The pipe has a narrow walkway welded to its side with steel rungs from the walkway to the surface of the turbulent, dark water. Sealing off the entrances into the pipe is a locked six-foot-round, rusty, grilled gate, on which hangs a corroded tin sign: *EXTREME DANGER KEEP AWAY* After having their wagon blocked by a roaming white crowd on Main Street, and having to run away on foot, Flynn and Brick have wandered into the alley and have found themselves trapped, with a swarm of Klansmen and white citizens looking for them. In the pounding rain, the two of them race toward the river and take their chances with it and the fence. They desperately climb up, then over the fence, splash into the choppy water and chaotically swim through it, Flynn from time to time having to help Brick along. Crawling out of the water onto the opposite bank, the boys stumble to a metal factory door. Just as Flynn is about to pound on it, the door is pushed open, and there—smiling out at them and holding a broom—is Billy Joe. He sticks his head out and looks around, then hurriedly motions for the two boys to enter. B.J. quickly secures the door behind them. While Flynn and Brick bend over, gasping for breath, B.J. worries down at them. Flynn gazes up at B.J. "Thanks, man," he tells him. "How did you know we were out there?"

"I saw Dane's men a-watchin' the front of this here factory. Saw 'em stop yo' wagon, and I saw you and Brick a-runnin' into dat there alley, then I run-did as fast as I could, and I found this here door." B.J. puts aside the broom. "I ain't never seen nothin' like it in ma life, Mas-ta Flynn. Dat there storm, dat there lightnin'. Saw it from the window with them other tire workers. I had to help you, after seein' Naomi and dat burnin' tree and how you and Caleb risked everything to help po' Bruce and then Brick here."

As Brick looks up at B.J. with tearful eyes, thanking him, Flynn glances about. "You haven't seen Caleb, have you?"

"Seen only you and Brick; that's all I seed."

Flynn shakes B.J.'s hand. "I apologize for laughing at and not respecting you in the past."

"Shucks, dat okay, Mas-ta Flynn," B.J. says, gladly shaking Flynn's hand. "Everybody laughs at me. I gets used to it, but they never gonna believe that you done shook ma hand, man-to-man like this."

Flynn and Brick gaze at the impressive plant, as B.J. leads them though the factory, seemingly unnoticed by the other workers, who have returned to their tasks and away from the windows, in a world of fine, floating particles of dusty tire fibers, of nearly unbearable heat, of frantic movement and noise. The boys—including B. J., this his first ever having a non-plantation job—marvel at the thundering, massive machinery, gawk at the forklift drivers noisily zipping by them, lift drivers carrying pallets of honey-colored, four-by-six-foot slabs of thick, heavy, raw rubber to gigantic, rubber-flattening machinery.

Flynn, Brick and B.J. watch with open mouths as men toss lampblack powder onto the tan sheets of raw rubber, and as the sheets are squeezed between twenty-ton, sizzling-hot, steel rollers and emerge out of the other sides of those rollers black as night, blistering hot and smoking, the tremendous, downward pressure from the rollers explodes trapped air from the super-heated, blackened layers like gunfire, causing Brick and B.J. to flinch. Lamp-blackened-faced white and colored men are identifiable only by the rings of un-blackened oval-shaped flesh around their constantly wiped eyes.

As the boys continue walking, they see other men in different section of the factory feverishly keeping pace with the machines around them and profusely sweating, still other workers are cutting cooler slabs of the blackened, pressed rubber into narrow, tire-size strips and then fix the strips onto fiber tire casings. After the strips are glued to the casings, thick, inflatable, industrial inner tubes are inserted inside the casings and held in place by two-piece interlockable, steel rims. The uncured tires and rims are then loaded into blistering-hot Lodi F1 and F2 tire molds. It takes two men to close each of the chain and pulley-assisted mold lids and then turn the spindles by hand and lock the lids in place. Finally, the inner tubes are aired up and expanded under tremendous pressure, forcing the flexible casings and newly placed, smooth, treadless rubber surface against and into the high-relief, tread designs of the molds until the tires are heated to a skin-peeling point and cured. Men

229

often get badly burned on the job, but continue working, swiftly going about pulling out cured, smoking tires from still other molds and placing them on ascending hooks that raise up through six-foot-wide opening in the floor with thousands more smoking tires on them, hooks and tires from other workers on lowers levels. Clunking along, the hooked automobile and truck tires continue rising through still more openings to higher floors or twist, clank and turn, this way and that, across the factory ceiling. To Brick, gawking up at them, the tires appear to be an unending march of wobbling, black, rubber donuts across the factory.

Above the plant in the thirty-foot-high, first-floor ceiling, where steam pipes crackle and ping, is an office; it's nestled among the rafters and connects to the main floor by way of long flights of steel stairs steps from two sides of the sprawling building. Inside that office in the sky—as Brick now sees it—Sidney Dessen is talking with his supervisors now that the workers have left the windows and are back to work. Dessen faces his foreman, pale-skinned Douglas Krause, forty-one. With them are several young plant supervisors in their spotless, white, rolled-up, long-sleeved shirts.

"Doug," says Dessen, "Caleb Brooks brought the new man Bruce Johnson into the infirmary. Check on them for me and then phone Mayor Sipple. Keep him informed. Burning people! There's no doubt in my mind. Not anymore. Dane Tucker is not losing his mind; he's lost it, and our sheriff's department—which should have brought this madness to a quick end—is absolutely worthless."

Dessen spots Flynn from the office window. Claretta, carrying a push broom, is hurrying across the factory floor to him and Brick.

"Isn't that Flynn Cutter down there with the new girl?" asks Dessen. He and the supervisors descend the steel steps and then split up at the bottom of the rungs, where fork-lift drivers load pallets of smoking, acrid-smelling rubber onto a bank of freight elevators. When Dessen moves to Flynn's side, he sees the trail of water from the door to the boys' dripping clothes, but makes no mention of it, to B.J.'s relief.

"I'm Sidney Dessen, young man," the plant owner tells Flynn. "Surely you didn't come here seeking work, as much as there's to do on Shadow Grove."

"No, Sir," says Flynn, shivering. "You hired our workers, and that puts them in danger."

"This plant is the biggest employer in the county, now," Dessen explains, "and even though the sheriff and I . . . let's just say . . . doesn't always see eye-to-eye, if I call upon him and his deputies to aid my plant security—and I will put his ass to the fire if this unacceptable business outside continues much longer—you can bet your life he will do just that and make no bones about it. It's all about politics, isn't it? Your father was one of the best at getting city hall to go along with him, son. He ran this town with an iron hand. But even though we do our best to safeguard the workers, as well as this plant, there are those who still get hurt." He places his arm about Brick's shoulder, "Like Bruce Johnson and his boy here. Thank you for looking after him. We saw it all from the office windows. Those mindless animals." Near tears, Brick muscles himself up, his arms taut, his fists clenched; inspired by Dessen's talk, in his mind, Brick is already beating the tar out of Dane, Colonel Cutter and the entire Klan all by himself.

"As for your colored workers, Flynn . . . Not that your grandparents, you or your mother were ever or now unfair to them," Dessen says, "but because they've traditionally been barred from obtaining decent jobs and have waited so long to work at a job that takes them out of the fields, they're hungry to learn and have turned out to be excellent employees, as I surmised they would. That's why I pay them the same wages as the whites working alongside them. Would you have me not hire the coloreds and take away their chance to make, not just a living, but a pretty damn good one?" Flynn recognizes some of his ex-workers being trained to operate the complicated machinery, and he gazes at the floor.

"You no doubt had heard," Dessen tells him, "that I was only interested in making money, no matter who died in here. Yes, some of our workers die from time to time, and we're working to stop this trend. Not all Jews walk around with holes in their shoes, so that when we step on a coin we can tell if it's a penny or a dime. I've heard that all my life. Cutterville, like the world, lives off misinformation. The way it's said that you want your father to return to reorganize the Klan. After seeing what you did for Brick here, and how you worry about your help, I find that almost impossible to believe."

"It's true ain't it?" asks Brick. "That you got a Ford contract to keep us colored workin' long enough fo' ma sister and Billy Joe to buy a house and me another car?"

"Everyone in town thinks I won the Ford contract," Dessen tells them. "We did win a big one, but not that one. Mister Ford hates blacks

231

and Jews, as far as I'm concerned. There were many who attempted to blackball my company—people in the South and in the North—into not hiring coloreds. I don't take orders from German sympathizers or from those who are isolationists in the face of millions being slaughtered." He turns to Claretta. "Get these two to Doc and have him shower them down and given dry clothes. If you can't find the way, ask someone where the infirmary is. Caleb Brooks may still be there. Brick, you and Bruce take a few days off after you shower and see the doctor. I don't want you and your father working after all you've been through outside and end up thinking about it and fall into one of our machines and get crushed."

"Take care of Brick," says Flynn, as Brick is led away. "I'm okay." Flynn then anxiously addresses Dessen. "Caleb. Is he hurt? You said he was at the—"

"He's fine. But if you don't wish to wait for dry clothing or a blanket, an armed guard will walk you and Caleb out the front gate. The agitators there have been persuaded to move on for now." When Flynn steps away, Dessen sends chills down his back. "You were born of an evil seed, but God must have been watching over you and Brick, Flynn Cutter." Flynn muses back at him and Dessen looks up at the pinging ceiling pipes. They're far more widespread across the humongous factory than Flynn had first noticed. The pipes, all of which are at least three feet wide, are all bolted securely to the ceiling and up and down the walls, while jerking and knocking with the sound of accelerating fluid surging through them, as if a racing train.

"If the emergency pumps would have kicked in," Dessen explains, "with all that scalding fluid surging through those pipes and sending that boiling water racing into that main conduit and dumped it into that river while you boys were crossing it—" Dessen stops as if not wanting to visualize the horror of it, then goes on, as Flynn's cocked head and questing eyes tell him to. "If the force from that exploding water into that stream didn't shatter your bones or rip your flesh from your bodies, the superheated water that would have run through those pipes to the river from all of these presses—Dear God, if even a splash of that boiling water would have hit you, you would have been cooked, the two of you, alive."

Flynn shuddered. He turns back around and makes his way toward the plant hospital, following Brick's wet footprints. He sees Claretta, B.J.

and Brick walking ahead of him. When they near the hospital wing of the plant, they and Flynn sees foreman Krause, the white-coat plant doctor, Caleb and Bruce talking together beside stacks of glossy-wrapped new tires. Bruce's uniform is scorched black about his sleeves, chest and trouser legs. His left hand is wrapped in gauze, and he has a band-aid on his right cheek. Brick runs to his father and hugs him. After Bruce and Brick kiss each other, Bruce tearfully gazes at Flynn, as he brings up the rear and appears worn out. "Doc here says these coveralls and Caleb saved ma life, Master Flynn," calls Bruce, "and it seems you saved ma boy's, and I'll never fo'get you and Caleb fo' as long as I live, and there ain't nothin' in this world I won't do to help you. And I mean nothin' ifin you ever need my help." Bruce breaks down crying. "And God knows I mean it, Master Flynn," he says running to Flynn and hugging him and then tearfully returns to Caleb and the others.

Flynn is so overwhelmed by Bruce's humility and with his blue eyes watering up, he can only nod his "thank you" to Bruce and linger next to a stack of tires and catch his breath. Caleb—also with a band-aid on his hand—joins Flynn.

"Your hand, Caleb," says Flynn, then gives Claretta and B.J. the once over, as they go arm-in-arm into a door marked "infirmary," with a shivering Brick, Bruce anxiously following them, along with Doc.

"It's only a minor wound," says Caleb, his disappointed gaze also on Claretta and B.J. He then faces Flynn. "Doc says my hand will heal in a day or two. What about you, though?" asks Caleb, frowning at Flynn's wet clothes. "You know how easily you get sick. How did you . . . Oh, no. Don't tell me you and Brick swam across that river. That damn, dirty river!"

"Then I won't," says Flynn, his teeth chattering. "Besides, the dirt in it isn't the half of it," Flynn says. "Mister Dessen seems to think Brick and I could have ended up on somebody's dinner plates as cooked meat if the pipes had discharged its water on us." Caleb takes off his jacket and gives it to Flynn, who quickly slips into it.

"Flynn Cutter," calls Claretta, running back to them from the hospital room with a towel, a pair of socks, and coveralls. "You get yo'self behind one of them stacks of tires, Master Flynn Cutter and dry yo'self off and into these coveralls and things. Don't care what you told Mister Dessen. Do it or I'll put you in them maself. I ain't lettin' you go outside while you soakin' wet. You gonna die from a cold. Caleb, you make him do it," she says handing the items to Caleb, going on. "Nobody else seems to be able to."

Shivering, Flynn steps behind stacks of tires. Caleb follows with the clothing and towels. Flynn is shaking so badly that Caleb has to help him dress, including helping him into the socks. When they again step from behind the tires, Caleb is carrying Flynn's wet clothing wrapped up in the towel. Flynn—wearing the dry coveralls, socks, his soggy shoes and Caleb's jacket—is quickly returning to normal. However, Claretta has returned to B.J.'s side, as well as that of her father and a dried-off, sneezing Brick. Flynn follows Caleb's sights to B.J. and Claretta, as she takes Billy Joe's hand and holds onto him, while listening to Doc explain about Brick and Bruce's conditions before sending father and son home.

Flynn and Caleb are escorted to the factory exit by an armed guard and Caleb keeps looking back at Claretta, Flynn also glancing back, while keeping step with his friend.

"I need to talk to you about Claretta and Billy Joe," Flynn tells Caleb.

"I saw how she took to him," Caleb says. "She only feels sorry for him, that's all. Let's just talk about something else, okay? Such as how you should never have crossed that river." Flynn only now fully realizes how dangerous it was to swim across that river, and he looks at Caleb. The thought of being cooked alive turns him a lighter shade of pale, both of them a little unsettled at the thought of either of them dying that way. "Or," says Caleb, "you and I can talk about you never again trying to stretch a double into a triple."

Any other time they would have laughed at Caleb's last remark, but they settled down into silence, with the plant guard grinning back at them. The silence doesn't last long. Flynn turns deadly serious.

"Caleb, back on the square. The way you looked at Naomi and she at you." While they continue moving down the long corridor, Flynn clams up. Putting out his arm, he slides his fingers against stacks of new tires lining the walkway just before the exit door. Then he continues. "What did you see out there?" he asks Caleb. "I mean, besides Naomi and that tree. Did you see how that earthquake sent glowing dust up around you and her? It glowed like an electric light and still seems so unreal to me."

"I certainly didn't see God, if that's what you mean," says Caleb, catching the attention of the guard, who—although he doesn't look around at them—has heard about Caleb, and for the first time realizes that the boys whom he is escorting is none other than Caleb Brooks and Flynn Cutter. Caleb goes on, "For God's sake, Flynn. According to Sarah and Naomi, you were the one who carried me into that so-called-magical light that night, if that's what you're somehow getting at, so you're as much as affected by this light stuff as I am."

"It did enter my mind."

They see the guard looking back at them, and after that, they walk with their hands in their pockets and in absolute silence behind him. "We're here," the guard says with a smile. "The rain has stopped. Good luck, you two." He leaves—looking back at Caleb—as still another guard outside the front door opens it for them. When Caleb and Flynn step into the fresh air and sunshine, suddenly, the local train roars down the train tracks that separate the two sides of town, the train's ghostly whistle drowning out the boys' renewed and touching conversation.

On the edge of town, blocks away, Barney's emaciated mother covers her ears against the train's disturbing cry and continues fixing lunch in her dated, Victorian kitchen. Draped out on her husband's overstuffed chair—which it took her five minutes to drag into the kitchen—is the deceased man's pin-striped suits, along with his Stetson hat and alligator shoes that she had attempted to force Barney to wear, instead of buying that tux. The arms of the suit coat are stretched out along the length of the chair's arms and held in place by straight pins, the way they might appear if a man's arms were resting in them; Mister Cutter's shoes are placed under each of the dangling trouser legs, which droop to the floor, and his old hat is perched on the back of the chair, the way it would have been worn on the dead man's head. Tobacco smoke slowly rises from his old, chewed-up pipe, which is resting on the table beside the Cutterville *Sentinel*, headlining the return of Barney.

"Okay, you insist on reading about him," she says facing the suit. "Now he's coming back, but we don't need him. I only bedded down with your son because I smoked those evil drugs from church. Tell me you forgive me, sweetheart, and how many lumps of sugar you want in your coffee?"

Back across town on the square, Dessen's security team has rounded up Old Clara, the mules and wagon for Flynn and Caleb. Climbing into the wagon, the boys then look about the square. Not an angry white face is in sight: they're all across the street in Miller's church, filling the air with their joyous singing and praising God that they came through the storm with as little damage as had been inflicted on their church. The cross atop the church has been temporarily repositioned on the damaged tower and it sparkles under a fresh coat of white paint, the ladders and ropes that help them remount it are still in place alongside the building.

After scrutinizing the church and cross, the boys sit close together, in the wagon, and head for home, Old Clara, unfettered, following behind.

Hours later, on a magnificent bluff—far from town—sits the wagon, Flynn and Caleb watching heaven's ball of orange fire light up the sky, the water and the ground, painting the world of the boys reddish-orange: The sun; they cherish its warmth, as it slowly sinks below the horizon, encompassing the mighty pride of Caleb, his body and soul, the hopeful face of Flynn, willing to follow wherever Caleb goes: The setting sun. They sit there under its zeal, Caleb and Flynn, two friends wishing the day would never end.

In time, the cool darkness of night looms over Little Shadow Place, which Henry reverently calls his land out of love for Sarah, Marilyn and Lawrence. While Henry is sitting on the porch in his rocking chair, listening to the sound of the crickets and anxiously waiting for Caleb and Flynn to return, Naomi arrives in a horse-drawn wagon. Alighting, she approaches the house and places a covered pot on the porch near the steps.

"I dropped by," she says, "with some fresh-baked biscuits that the boys like so much. It'll go fine with your fried chicken and them beautiful collard greens you grow out here and I smell slow cooking on your stove."

"The boys aren't home, Naomi. I thought you were them. Old Clara returned hours ago, but not Flynn and Caleb. Did you happen to get any feelings about them?" he asks, his face reflecting anxiety. "They went in town to speak to that factory owner about Flynn's workers and—"

"My ability to see things has all but left me, now, Henry."

This does not sit well with Henry, and he leans forward on his chair and says, almost in a whisper, "Sarah and I have always depended on you to know if the boys are okay. To know if—"

"Henry Brooks, you won't let me deny you anything. I do have some feeling left that tells me them boys will be here soon." She laughs, picks up the pot, and hands it to him. "Tell them two I said hello and that they better eat all of them greens and not pick over them if they knows what's good for them."

Henry sits back down, squints at her and cautiously says, "You didn't come all the way out here to just bring these biscuits, Naomi," he says, glancing at the pot and then back at her. "In spite of that laugh of yours, what's wrong?"

A look of finality appears in Naomi's eyes. "Time is coming fast, Henry, that I won't be able to tell you anymore about Caleb. Only he'll be able to do that. All of us need to get used to that." She momentarily ponders. "Henry."

"Yeah?"

"I saw that Light in him tonight."

"What light?" asks Henry getting to his feet. "On who? On Caleb? Tonight? Was it in town? Did you see them there?"

"Yes. In town. The Light was the same Heavenly Energy that Flynn carried Caleb into that winter night of Caleb's birth. Even with the rain and lightning and thunder, even with my eyes closed, I knew what it was. The Mandorla, the Light of Love that only their innocent eyes or those chosen for God's expressed purpose are allowed to see, and all those who saw it who are evil will die. Now after living passively in Caleb all these years it has awakened. Lilly saw It shinin' all around Caleb, Henry. Do you know what that means? God's purpose is truly a wonder. By permitting Lilly to see the Light about your blessed son, even if Caleb himself didn't, God has shown us that He is a forgiving God. Then He permitted me to look upon the Light, once I open my eyes, Henry. God did! As my reward for helping you and Sarah watch over Caleb throughout all of the hard times which confronted us."

"Then the Light," whispers Henry. "Here in Georgia? Tonight in town? It's happening too fast, Naomi." He stares at her in disbelief and then continues. "This Lilly, Naomi? Lilly, the wayward harlot woman from town? Don't tell me she tried to accommodate them boys with her diseased self."

"No, and she will never infect anyone else again. But you see, Henry.

You're doing it and we all do, judging her and those like her, even after you've been told how God has forgiven her. If you, a good, religious man, who feels no hatred against Lilly or whites, but have a hard edge on your voice when speaking about her as a whore, how much more difficult is it for religious whites who hate us without realizing that the Lord turns away from them and us coloreds for such un-godlike revulsion? He wants us to be what we were intended to be when His hands first molded us into life, sisters and brethren. If Lilly had been born of your mother's womb, would you have spoke of her in the same way that you just did? Death, Henry. It's the equalizer of us all." She stops talking and looks at him in dread.

"What is it, woman?" Henry asks, stepping to the porch railing and resting the pot on it, while leaning toward her. "You're trembling."

"It's that old-timer, Hank," she replies. "Be wary of him, Henry. Be very wary of him. Satan has chosen a very special way for you to leave this world by that old man's hand. He's Judas Iscariot, Henry, old Hank is Judas Iscariot of our time, and God let me know this to help you face the road of the cross, but it was not revealed to me just how Hank will harm you." Tears flow down her cheeks, and she turns away to hide them from him. "Lord, Lord," she says, drying her eyes on her sleeve. "Excuse me for doing that, Henry. This old woman is becoming more human every day now, and now, I got to get back and fix supper for Sarah and me." Climbing aboard her wagon, she looks back. "Get ready, Henry. This night, when Flynn calls you 'father' and hands you a gold coin from the devil and Caleb asks you about his mother's photograph; it'll be time for you to pray. May God be with you through it all."

An hour later, under a full moon, Caleb climbs from the wagon next to his father's well-kept yard and picket fence. Henry's white chickens are pecking about on the lawn. "You guys' chickens have gotten out of their coops again," says Flynn.

"Papa must be asleep. I'll put then back before we turn in."

Flynn follows Caleb's longing gaze to his mother's grave at the side of the house, a grave aglow under the moonlight and adorned with fresh flowers. "We might not be able to be friends, once your father arrives," Caleb says, facing Flynn.

"Are you asking me to turn my back on him, Caleb?"

"Papa's been more of a father to you than Barney has. You only know Barney through his letters and mostly speak of him as 'him,' or 'the major' and now the 'colonel,' rarely as 'father.' "

"You've never had as much as a letter from your mother," Flynn says, looking at the grave. "Yet, you place flowers on her tombstone, and the few times Henry talks to you about her, as if she's still alive, you act as if she is as well by keeping up her resting place the way you do, so you've never seen her either, not physically and never will, not in this world anyway, unlike the fact that I'll soon see the colonel."

"Don't mention my mother again, Flynn. I don't share thoughts of her with you."

Flynn removes Caleb's jacket and hands it to him.

"Hey! What I said to you doesn't mean you have to return the jacket and catch a cold."

After Flynn slips back into the jacket, he climbs off the wagon and hands Caleb two coins.

"They're made of gold," says Caleb, antiques and jewelry being some of his vast interests.

"I know," says Flynn with a smile.

"Flynn . . . they're exquisite. Where did you get them?"

"The colonel sent several of them to me from Germany. I want you to hold onto those two. One of them for you and the other for me."

"You want me to hold onto one of these for you? Why?"

"Just in case . . . With things the way they are at home, well, I might lose it. This way, I'll always know you'll have both of ours on you and will remember that it's mine no matter what might happen next. I have one for Henry, too."

"Is this your way of saying goodbye?"

Flynn looks at him, turns away, and—without a word—heads for the house. The Brooks' front room is neatly kept with three wing-back chairs—one for Henry, one for Caleb, and one for Flynn, who spends a good deal of time with them. Also in the room is a comfortable overstuffed couch, a scattering of straight-back kitchen-type chairs, a hand-crank Victrola with a neatly stacked pile of seventy-eight-inch plastic records on a small end table next to it. A Cathedral-type radio adds manly character to the house. Hanging all around the walls are pictures of the Brooks' ancestors, stern images mostly in shades of black and yellowing white mounted in oval-shaped, convexed-glass-covered picture frames, some of the photos dating back a hundred years or more.

The hardwood floor is highly polished, and next to the porch-side window is an old, upright piano. On top of the piano is an open, violin case, in which rests an old violin. When the boys enter, Henry is sitting in his chair, his focus on the door.

"You're late, you two," he says, getting to his feet. "Was there anything wrong in town?"

"Nothing that we couldn't handle," says Flynn, beaming with pride at Caleb.

"Good," says Henry, not willing to bring up the matter of what Naomi had told him about the vision and about Lilly or about his time being near.

"Papa. There was a little trouble. Flynn got some of that plant's waste water on him. He was given coveralls by Mister Dessen's factory, and his soiled clothes are in the wagon, but he needs to wash himself before he starts to itch, he swam across that old river."

"That filthy river is no place for you boys to be playing around," exclaims Henry, hurrying Flynn into the bathroom and filling the tub with buckets of water from the kitchen and the old Wedgewood stove's water warmer. He hands Flynn a bar of the Brooks' homemade soap. After Flynn washes and Caleb gives him some of his clothes to wear, Caleb tosses out the water, refills the tub and takes a bath as well. Later, they gather in the front room and talk.

"Naomi dropped by with some of her biscuits," Henry tells them. "Now, that you two are cleaned up, go in the kitchen and have your supper and then right to bed."

"The chickens are out again, Henry. Caleb and I have to put them away before turning in."

"I'll attend to that and your wet clothes," Henry mandates. "Now go in the kitchen and eat and then off to bed, like I said, okay?" He playfully taps Flynn on his rump.

"Why so early, Papa? You, Flynn and I should spend all the time we can together. Isn't that what you said Sarah wants?"

"Sarah, son. She needs us to help with the pipeline early tomorrow. And—" Henry abruptly stops, then smiles at Caleb and adds. "You're right. With Barney returning, Sarah also wants you and Flynn to spend time together. She didn't ask for any of us to help with the line. I did."

"Papa, you should also stay here tomorrow; this might be the last time we can all be together—you, Flynn and I—to fish and go hiking in the swamp and woods, to—"

Both Flynn and Caleb stand dejected. Henry puts his arms about the two of them. "You and Flynn stay right here tomorrow, and do all of these things, and I'll be with you in spirit," he tells them. "Sarah's workers and I can handle it. Sometimes I forget you are just boys, not grown men. Next time, though, Flynn, you and Caleb, phone when you're going to be late. That's why Sarah went to all that trouble to get that fancy talking box put on our kitchen wall."

"I will, Papa," says Flynn, catching himself too late. Stunned, Caleb looks at Flynn, Flynn at Henry. "I didn't mean to call you that, Henry," says Flynn.

"It was one of the most beautiful things I've ever heard," Henry exclaims; he embraces Flynn. "Now don't try and take it back."

"This is for you," says Flynn, handing Henry the other gold coin.

Henry's heart races out of control; he recalls Naomi's warning about receiving that gold coin and Flynn calling him "Papa."

"If Mamma was alive," says Caleb, completing Naomi's prophecy of bending doom, as Henry stands in double shock, looking on, "Flynn would have two mammas and two papas." Sadly, Caleb focuses on their pictorial wall. "Papa, why don't you have a picture of Mamma on the wall? I know you don't like talking about her and have told me more than once how beautiful and intelligent she was, but lately, when I dream about her, I can't remember what you said she looks like anymore."

"God!" gasps Henry, heading for the door, trying to hold back his tears. "Excuse me, boys."

After Henry steps into the night, Flynn looks at Caleb. "Did I say something wrong, Caleb?"

"It was I, Flynn, not you. He always gets like this when I press him about Mamma. I'll read to him. The Bible always makes him feel better, almost as much as our playing for him does."

Outside on the porch, under a starry sky and inundated by millions of singing crickets, Henry slowly undulates in his rocking chair, thinking about the road of the cross and how swiftly its come upon them. At times, he considers asking God to lift the burden of the boys killing one another from him, but when Caleb leaves the house with the Bible, Henry dries his eyes on his sleeve and all thoughts of asking God to take the coming burden from him are dismissed from his mind. "Read that passage of Cain and Abel to me, son," he says.

"Why that one, Papa? That's the story of two brothers, one killing the other."

"Read it, Caleb. Read it nice and slow, so I can understand God's will."

While Caleb stands on the porch, paging through the Bible, and Henry rocks slowly back and forth in his chair, within the house, Flynn walks to the upright piano and sits before the keyboard; his distinguished-looking shadow outlines the porch-side window curtain, and reflects his poised fingers above the ivory. When Caleb leans against the porch railing and reads the Bible to Henry, the air is filled with Flynn's very soul, as he superbly plays Ludwig van Beethoven's *Fur Elise*, silencing even the crickets into listening from the surrounding, dark woods, the music quietly overlaid by Caleb's biblical reading of Cain and Abel to his beloved father.

16

The Return of the Jackal

Early the following morning, Flynn is already up and around and wearing his own clothes—which Henry had washed the night before and left hanging outside for the hot morning sun to dry. He's busily fixing breakfast at the stove when Caleb enters and—just as Caleb does—the wall phone rings.

"Hello," Caleb says, answering it. Flynn sees an uneasy expression on Caleb's face as he listens and hangs up. "That was Papa calling from Shadow Grove. Your father's arriving early. Today, Flynn. And Papa took Old Clara and the mules and wagon with him to the plantation to help with the work. You have no way out of here." The boys hear a distant train's horn. The local train is coming their way from Old Country Road, where the train tracks cross the dirt road. Putting together bacon and egg sandwiches, they gulp down their glasses of milk, remove the skillet from the stove and run from the house, eating their sandwiches on the way.

A few miles from them, as the Cutterville-bound locomotive passes Old Country Roads and negotiates a steep grade, and slows, as it climbs the one-mile-long incline toward the aging, Cutter Bridge, Private Joe Metcalfe, forty-two—a black veteran recently discharged from the army—is concealing himself in the bushes alongside the tracks. Metcalfe has gold front teeth and is still in his uniform, which has Quartermasters Corps' shoulder patches. When the rumbling locomotive goes by, and he feels he can't be spotted by the engineer, Metcalfe runs alongside the slowly moving train, forces open the sliding door of an unsealed vented red boxcar and climbs aboard, closing the door behind him.

Old Amos steps out of the darkened shadows and opens the opposite-side sliding door, letting in the light. Going bald on top, with far more gray hair, Amos, nevertheless, looks much the same as he did eighteen years ago, when he picked up the Winthrops at the train station. The smelly vented boxcar is carrying cows, and there are several broken, ventilation boards scattered across the scorched floor, where hobos have ripped them off the boxcar walls and burned the broken pieces on the floor to cook or to keep warm during their cold night travels.

Amos stands there holding his straw hat in his hand and watching Metcalfe stagger about, attempting to retain his balance and stand erect in the side-swaying boxcar. After Metcalfe braces himself against the wall, he and Amos size up one another.

"What the hell you looking at?" hisses Metcalfe.

"Nothin'," says Amos. "Just wonderin' what you lookin' fo' in yo' travelin', solider, work? I'm goin' to town—like a lot of our workers—to be there when the parade welcomes ma boss's husband's return from the war. He like you, a soldier, that we all proud of, 'cause you and soldiers like him fought fo' our country. I works on Shadow Grove. Ma older brother Andy and me started workin' there fo' Doctor Lawrence and Marilyn Winthrop since we was teens. I can get permission fo' you to sleep in they barn if you wants, and come sunrise, I maybe can get Sarah to give you temporary work on a pipeline they been fo'ever diggin' out there. She can't pay you much, maybe a good, hot meal and a few dollars to get you on yo' way again. Want-a come along to town and meet ma boss's husband and ride back to Shadow Grove with me on this train's turnaround trip later on, that is ifin you want a job, 'cause you never did say what you is lookin' fo'."

"Colonel Cutter," says Metcalfe, "been going up and down these damn lines throughout this poor-ass state for days, looking for his place. Heard it's someplace in this part of Georgia. Have you heard of him and know where the motherfucker hangs his hat?"

"Did you just say he was a motherfucker?" The old black man drops his hat and steps back, looking about. "Does you know who belongs to that name you just cursed?"

"Damn right I know! And what you looking around for?" asks Metcalfe, following Amos's gaze. "Ain't nobody in here but us."

Amos eases forward, his finger against his lips. "Shhhh. The coyotes howlin' at the moon go silent when that man's name is mentioned. The leaves on the trees stops tinglin' in the wind. They know the white man's ears is everywhere. Folks in town worship the colonel and Flynn as gods."

"Hey! What the fuck kind of silly-ass talk is this? The colonel got wives in every port. A fuckin' god, you say! God ain't no heartless killer! That man's the devil himself. He shot some of his own soldiers in the back, colored soldiers on a goddamn, secret mission with him."

"The army don't kill its own men. Why should anyone believe you or that?"

"Because I was the only lucky-ass bastard to get away alive of all the others who was with that white asshole that night." Metcalfe jerks open his shirt and points to several scars on his chest, going on. "And I got these bullet wounds to prove it! To this day, he thinks he's killed us all."

"Then why is you lookin' fo' him? To let him finally kill you?"

"We all look alike to them damn white officers, specially in the dark, the way it was on that island of hell the night them Japs kicked our ass. No, Colonel Cutter had just met us and quickly put the team together and wouldn't know me from Adam. He'd be lucky to remember the number of guys he's killed or all them so-called live-in wives he's had."

"He did that? Killed his own men? And he got that many wives? I thought he was a church-goin', heartless killer man, but not what Reverend Harris calls a adultery man."

"What's going to church got to do with a man's dick? All you dumb-ass Southern Uncle Toms! That's the kind of thinking that keeps you stupid down here. 'Leaves on the tree.' 'Coyotes' my ass! What you need is for me to take your stupid old ass back to Detroit where they'll kick the living shit out of you up and down the block, and then you'll learn to grow up with some damn backbone."

"We're not stupid down here. Sarah taught us to read a little and speak better, and—you—if you hate that man so much, stand in line. And as fo' me, I don't got nothin' to say to you, now that I know you just-a boilin' over to get yo' self killed and me too if I gets involved." Amos steps up to him and whispers. "So be warned, brother. You said it yo'self. You lookin' fo' a killer. The devil himself, and you can't win."

"I eat the shit out of the devil's ass for breakfast!" Metcalfe shouts, pushing Amos aside, his eyes rolling in rage. "Sit your dumb butt down, you old fool, before I kick your ass off this train. Whoever taught you to speak is dumber than you. I'm not your brother. Money's my brother."

Metcalfe flips out a straight-edge razor to clean his fingernails, but before Amos takes time to discover what the ex-soldier is going to do with it—a razor that old Amos sees as that Detroit weapon of death that will kick shit out of his ass up and down the block, then slice him up and down as well—he grabs his hat and jumps off the moving train, as it closes in on Cutter Bridge.

Sixty feet below the bridge, as the locomotive nears the old span, a quarter mile away—with the red boxcar some fifty cars or so behind

245

it—Caleb and Flynn, running along, glance up and see the silhouette of old Amos sailing out of the boxcar and through the air against the blue sky. The boys then leap over a narrow section of stream water and across a set of train tracks, both of which—the stream and the tracks—run under the bridge in the home stretch to Cutterville.

Sprinting up the slopes, and wondering why someone would leap off the train, the boys reach the top of the bridge at the same time as the locomotive does, the engineer blowing his horn warning them to be aware. In one of the passengers' cars, Colonel Cutter, in full-dress uniform, is sitting by the window and looks out when the engineer repeatedly activates the horn. Colonel Cutter sees Flynn and Caleb scrambling alongside the passengers' car, an arm-length away, toward the end of the train and those boxcars. When the boys disappear from sight, Barney Cutter—unaware that Flynn is his son—reminisces at his gold pocketwatch. The watch contains a photo of Sarah and a year-old Flynn. Barney turns his sights back toward the direction where Flynn had disappeared. Puzzling, he then—once again—ponders the boy in the photo.

Out of Barney's sight and no longer running recklessly across the bridge, Flynn and Caleb are carefully stepping their way along the outside edges of the rail ties—the stream and lower train tracks looming dizzily below them. Within brushing distance of other moving passenger cars, the boys know that one misstep in bumping against the train, or stepping into one of the open spaces between the rail ties, and they'd end up with one leg dangling through a tie up to their crotches or worse, they'd end up falling off of the bridge. In a skilled balancing act alongside the seemingly endless line of passenger cars, where the white travelers and soldiers look out at them, finally they complete that treacherous section of the bridge and sprint full out toward the train's oncoming boxcars. Running alongside dozens of locked boxcars, they come upon the red, cattle car and spot the slightly ajar boxcar door. The door is suddenly slid fully open, and Metcalfe—with his gold front teeth gleaming in the sunlight and smiling down at Caleb—reaches out, as Caleb seizes hold of a steel rung, and pulls him aboard. Metcalfe glares with disapproval as Caleb, in turn, reaches back and pulls Flynn into the odoriferous, live-stock car.

Suddenly, the boxcar rocks side to side and Metcalfe stumbles against one of the cattle corrals and goes into an ad-lib, arm-waving dance to balance himself and finally is able to regain his footing by holding onto the corral posts. Neither Caleb nor Flynn make the connection that this is the boxcar out of which old Amos had leaped, nor that the person jumping from the train was Amos or had anything to do with Metcalfe. Caleb turns away from Metcalfe and grins at Flynn, both boys amused by the soldier's previous, extemporaneous equilibrium dance. After the train settles down to a smoother run over an even sector of tracks, Metcalfe pushes himself off of the corral, and Caleb shakes his hand. "Thanks for helping me aboard." Flynn extends his hand to the black man as well.

"I don't shake no peckerwood's hand," snorts Metcalfe. "Last time I did, fucking white folks tried to hang me. And you, nigga!" Metcalfe says to Caleb. "Don't you be laughing at me. You—who hangs out with this white boy—I guess like the other poor-ass niggers down here, who's too afraid to even mention the man's name, I expect you don't know where I can find Colonel Cutter either, do you?"

Flynn's eyes pop open at the mention of his father's name, but unlike Flynn's eyes, Caleb's eyes squint down in anger. "What did you just call me, Mister?" he asks Metcalfe.

"I called you a goddamn nigger! And I'm not a goddamn 'mister' I'm a damn United States soldier. Where's all that respect some old fool told me you colored folks had for colored soldiers down here in the South?"

"Go to hell, old man! I don't give a damn who you are or what you did in the army," exclaims Caleb. "I'm not a 'nigger!' That's a remark given by the old masters to people like you."

"I've been to hell and back!" Metcalfe says, flashing a wad of cash. "Money is the way to get out of hell or anyplace else. Tell me where I can find that monster and some of this bread is yours."

While Flynn looks at the atypical black soldier, Caleb—now amused—walks around Metcalfe smiling, looking at the ex-soldier up and down. Metcalfe pockets his cash and grabs Caleb, and now, no longer a laughing matter, Caleb pushes the war veteran away. "Get off of me!"

In the adjacent boxcar—sitting among the cows—is One-leg Trout. Seventeen years ago, after Barney had lifted Flynn into the air and proclaimed that Flynn was God, Barney had given Trout a job in the store with old Hank, so that Trout could help keep an eye on the black workers. Trout was the only Klansman who had attempted to befriend Dane in the back of Hank's truck and then stood back, while old Hank used a rag to wipe the blood from Dane's feet, after Barney had walked Dane through glass. Trout, now bald, with his walking stick propped between his stub and his good leg—and unable to hear what's being said—is squinting through the vent slots of his dark boxcar into the broken slots of the red, sun-lit boxcar. By now, Flynn is showing sign of extreme anxiety and moves to the opposite, opened, sliding door—from which Amos had leaped—and leaning out, he pales, gasping for his breath.

"You gonna jump, too?" asks Metcalfe laughing at Flynn.

"That man who we saw jump from this train. . . . Was he jumping because of you?" asks Caleb and then getting a nod and a grin from Metcalfe.

"We need some air in here," says Flynn opening the door wider, while fighting for his breath.

Metcalfe, believing that Flynn is saying that he stinks, blasts, "Go to hell, punk!"

While their boxcar slowly approaches the bridge—which looms only a just few hundred yards ahead of them now—the locomotive, having already traveled downhill, is merging with the lower train tracks. Caleb joins Flynn at the open door and leans out, but Metcalfe gives chase. Again, Caleb and Flynn walk away, and again Metcalfe stalks them.

"Have any of you punks heard of a Colonel Cutter? That's all I'm asking, and I'm asking you for the last goddamn time. Answer me, or I'll throw you two damn fruitcakes off this train!"

The boys refuse to even look at him now. Metcalfe steps in front of them and grabs Caleb about his throat. Flynn tries to pull the enraged man off of Caleb, but Metcalfe—a powerful man—holds onto Caleb with one hand and easily one-arms Flynn away, then reaches for his pocketed razor.

"Stay back, Flynn," Caleb says jerking free. "This guy is shell-shocked."

"I'm shocked that's for sure," says Metcalfe stepping back, disregarding his razor now, and feeling that he has nothing to fear about being overpowered by two country boys, boys who seem passive and indecisive. The ex-soldier continues with his verbal assault on Caleb. "Shocked that you, a colored boy, would protect this white trash. He's got to be white trash to hang around with you, a poor nigger. Look at his white-ass skin and the way he's shaking in his shoes. Like you coons do whenever you hear the Klan's name mentioned down here. What do you do, boy, live on some white man's plantation like a trained dog and lick the master's boots?"

"He doesn't lick anyone's—"

"Shut up, white boy. I ain't talking to you." Metcalfe, then, goes on nagging Caleb, "Is that it? You been trained to protect white folks like this blue-eyed honky or be hanged for not doing so?"

"As if you wouldn't piss in your damn pants," says Caleb, "if one of those wild animals even as much as looked at you with their burning crosses and their cut-out, eye-hole stares of death."

"Fuck the Klan, boy! I just came back from a real killing circus of death, a damn United States of America army war, nigga! And I might add a war where our enemy was treated better than the nigger soldiers, even though them Germans slaughtered all them poor-ass, so-called, white Jews, babies, mothers and dads, stacked them rotting bodies up like one-story buildings. Legs, arms, assholes, eyes and heads like so much damn garbage. Never been so sick in my life. The stink alone would kill you, and I'm still here to talk about it." He lifts up his shirt and points at his bullet-caused scars and goes on. "I'm not afraid of any god-damn man alive, especially not of some Klansman who's afraid of me enough to hide under a fucking sheet and think that's enough to scare the pants off my black ass. No, Sir!"

Totally frustrated, Caleb glances at Flynn, while asking himself:

What am I to do to get this madman away from us?

"His son, Flynn or to his wife Sarah," Metcalfe goes on. "Maybe you know them."

"Flynn and Sarah?" Caleb asks, as stunned as much as Flynn is now.

"You ain't got no cotton in your ears, boy. You heard me."

"What do you want with them?"asks Flynn.

"I have something that belongs to—" Metcalfe clams up and scowls over at Flynn. "I told you to shut up, white boy. I'm not going to tell you again. This has nothing to do with you."

"Then tell me what it is," says Caleb, "this thing you have that's theirs."

"A gold watch encrusted with rubies," the veteran exclaims. "One with a pretty young girl and a small, blonde boy's photo fitted in the cover."

"Let me see that," says Flynn, highly excited, knowing that the picture is of him and Sarah and that the watch belongs to the Colonel, a watch and pictures he's never seen. "Did you steal it?"

"Keep it up, whitey and I'll cut out your tongue," warns Metcalfe, reaching into his pocket.

"You wouldn't dare!" says Flynn. "I'm the son of—"

"Hey!" Caleb yells at Flynn, silencing him, then faces Metcalfe. "You don't have that watch, do you?" asks Caleb, looking from Metcalfe's pocket to Flynn, a look telling Flynn to back away.

"No I don't," yells Metcalfe, his hand now deep in his pocket, "but I've seen it and so have you two. The white boy gave it away. Should have kept his mouth shut, while he was still ahead."

"I will not keep my mouth shut, damn you," hisses Flynn, "you old fool! What do you really want? Is it to hurt the Colonel, his wife, his—?"

"Did I say I wanted to hurt anybody to this white boy?" Metcalfe asks Caleb. He grins at Flynn. "But I would like to get next to that good-looking girl in that watch of his. Put ma black dick right up her white ass . . . and that sweet-looking, golden ass of yours, too," he tells Caleb.

In a blur, Caleb lifts the surprised, screaming man off his feet and slams him against the boxcar wall, in much the same manner that Henry had—that winter's night of the raven—slammed and killed Chad. Caleb's sudden and violent action sends Flynn stumbling back in shock, as well as stunning Trout, witnessing it all from the other boxcar. Caleb again picks Metcalfe up and slams him down. This time, it is Flynn pulling Caleb off of Metcalfe. When Metcalf hits the deck, his wad of money falls from his pocket and rolls across the floor. Through the vent slots, Trout's old eyes eagerly follow the rolling, green stuff of dreams. "Please don't fall out the door," mutters Trout, the wad ending up behind a pile of trash next to the open door. "Stay put like a nice little ball of money," the old man whispers, all eyes and wishes.

Metcalfe rebounds with his straight-edge. Broad-eyed and insane with rage, his teeth clenched, he wildly slashes at Caleb, then at Flynn. Caleb grabs one of the vent boards from the floor and knocks the razor out of Metcalfe's hand, but the bayonet-skilled veteran grapples up the blue blade and flings it underhand at Caleb, who ducks. Just missing his head, the deadly weapon ends up slicing into the wall. Flynn and Caleb pounce on Metcalfe and pound him to the floor, causing the cows to kick up a fuss as the ex-soldier and boys crash against the cow pens. Then, as their boxcar clears the bridge and starts downhill, the boys carried the cursing, thrashing black man by his legs and arms to the door and toss him off the train. They watch him roll yelping down the slope and end up in the low-lying stream, where he scrambles to his feet, cursing and ranting at them. The boys sit with their backs against the cattlecar wall, both shaken from the frightening experience. They look at each other and smile.

At Cutterville, as the engineer creeps the train through the freight yard and toward the small train station, Caleb and Flynn jump from the boxcar, as does Cripple Trout—from his—with his large walking stick, almost falling on his face. Hobbling speedily along with the stick, Trout frantically reaches into the moving, red, cattle car, snatches up Metcalfe's money and limps down the tracks, where Dane Tucker suddenly steps out of a sidelined boxcar, a place he sometimes sleeps, when he's too drunk to make it home. He stands there looking down at the shorter Trout and then at the money in Trout's hand.

"Well, what do we have here?" Dane exclaims, zipping up his fly. A shabbily-dressed, young, white girl jumps from that sidelined boxcar and races away, looking back over her shoulder at them. Trout grins at her, but his grin disappears when Dane grabs the money from his hand.

"I got it off a nigger soldier on the train, Dane," says Trout, reaching for the money. "It's belongs to me. I'm going to buy a pair of them new-fangled crutches in O'Neal's Department Store."

Dane smiles and gives Trout a fatherly tap on the cheek. "Now, where were we," he asks. "Oh, yes, you said this was your money, and you wanted to buy some crutches. But you were coming here to meet me in this freight yard. Right? So that we could talk about Barney's return, and that means that if I hadn't asked you to meet me here, you'd have never been on that train to get this money, so you see, it really belongs to me. Just pretend I'm old, returning, Colonel Cutter, and you're here to offer me this money as a welcome-home gift." Dane's eyes squint. "The motherfucker who has never left my thoughts and never will."

Caleb and Flynn—their thoughts on Barney, as well—stroll through the train yard, both wanting as much time together as possible before Flynn reaches the station and falls under his father's control.

"Caleb, did you believe that man?"

251

"About your father being a killer?"

Flynn's eyes say he wants Caleb to state he didn't believe it, and Caleb knows that Flynn is aware—as much as anyone—that the entire town whispers that the colonel is a ruthless killer, a terror to the blacks and a joy to the whites, but Caleb also feels for Flynn. He also knows that Flynn is so desperate to have a father to call his own that he would welcome one even if it were a snake.

"What do you want me to say, Flynn?"

"Nothing if that's all you can say. 'What do you want me to say, Flynn?' It wouldn't be wise for us to be seen together now, Caleb."

And with those words, both boys sadly go their separate ways. Back in the freightyard, as Dane and Trout anxiously count Metcalfe's wad, members of Bruce Johnson's family short-cut through railroad property on their way home after working in the homes of wealthy whites. Walking along with them, Bruce's attractive, young daughter, Earlene and Carrie—his wife—is Reverend Miller and a thirteen-year-old, black boy named Jimmy—who lives next door to the Johnsons in Colored Town.

"Did you earn any money from those rich Jews and white folks?" the reverend asks Carrie.

When she looks at him as if its none of his business, Miller—never too proud to beg—turns his sights on the industrious boy, Jimmy, who has earned two dollars today with his shoeshine box and is going after more. He has departed from them and is now walking up to Dane, with Miller and the others following. The young boy stands there, all eyes and open mouth, gawking at the money in Dane's hand, as does Miller, licking his chops.

"Shine, Mister Dane?" asks Jimmy.

"Did you retire to the monkey farm, Reverend Miller?" asks Dane. "Walking with those living dead? Ain't that what they call these black zombies you walking with? 'The living dead?' "

"Sorry you feel this way, Dane," says Miller, nudging Jimmy aside. "Your ma's death had nothing to do with us not praying for that dear sister. God alone took her home, not our members, son."

"I ain't your son, "says Dane, glaring at the blacks. "Are you recruiting coons now, Rev?"

"It's not like they've been invited into our church just because I happened to run into these people and walked with them," Miller replies, angering Carrie as he goes on. "Besides, God came to me in a dream right after that terrible earthquake shook the town and my church, and right after that lightning struck that tree, God told me to go out and collect money among the unclean to rebuild His church as big as any of them Catholic cathedrals in the big cities, and that's why I'm walking with—"

"Ha!" Dane exclaims and next glares at Carrie. "Old Miller here is only interested in getting money from you dumb-ass coons." When Carrie draws back from him in revulsion, Dane spits on Jimmy, leaving the small boy wiping his face in tears. "You ain't getting shit from me, boy, even if it means you end up starving." Dane shakes Metcalfe's money at Miller. "You or this phony preacher, who I won't have to beg to eat in his religious soup line now that I have this money and soon maybe a whole lot more."

"You'll always need the church, Dane Tucker," Miller says. "The same as your pa and ma both did."

"The hell you say! If you preach to their kind or even walk at their side, even fer all the money in this world, I want no more part of you or your goddamn church and neither does the Klan from now on! I'd worship dirt first." He spits at Carrie and Earlene and pushes Jimmy away. "Get lost, you dark ink spots! And take that preacher man with you," he says, whipping out a gun, going on, "befer I blow off his head and yours."

Miller hurries away. Carrie and those with her also quickly head for home, looking over their shoulder at Dane, who returns to counting his money.

"Like I was trying to tell you, Dane," pleads Trout, "that razor coon was yapping about the colonel, befer he was slammed against the wall and lost that money. You know how Barney always said he'd return with enough money to revitalize the Klan and make his son a god. That parts's a laugh, but that money I took off the train isn't. Must have been stolen from Barney. Otherwise where would a darky like that soldier boy, right out of the war, get his hands on two hundred dollars? That's why the black bastard is here looking fer the colonel, to get more from him. I'll bet my life on it. Barney did it, Dane. He finally realized his dream of having lots of money."

"Keep your mouth shut about this to the fellows," Dane warns, glancing over his shoulder and about. "You and I will look into this and maybe split whatever Barney has between the two of us and leave the boys out of it, including Barney. He might even have as much as two or three thousand, the amount he stole from Pa."

"How can you do that . . . Leave Barney out, if whatever it is he has belongs to him?"

"Kill him, of course, stupid. Now, go buy them fancy new walking sticks from O'Neal's," he says, giving a meager portion of the money to Trout, then raises his arms. "It begins! Finally. My chance! It begins!"

At the train station, Colonel Cutter steps off the passengers' car to a marching band, and hundreds of white citizens are there cheering his arrival, including a few blacks. Twenty minutes later, Sarah arrives in her used 1940 Chevy car—the old Model T now a part of history. When she slides from the Chevy, Flynn is waiting nearby and trots over to her. "I was held up by one of our workers' sick children," says Sarah. "How long have you been here, Flynn?"

"About five minutes, Mother." Flynn looks across the way at Barney. "I know he's my father, but I don't know how to approach him. I didn't think it would be like this. It's like looking at a stranger and . . . How will he know us, Mother. He's distracted by those people"

Sarah looks over at Barney and the mayor. "Surely you knew that he would be greeted by Mayor Sipple."

"He's not how I pictured him."

"He looks like his portrait, Flynn."

"I was hopping that he would look different, that's all and even be like . . ."

She embraces him and quietly asks, "What would you have him look like and be, Flynn?"

"I don't know. Maybe a little like Henry."

Profoundly concerned, she takes his hand. "There's no need to explain," she says. Sarah kisses Flynn on his forehead and places her arm about her son's shoulder. "I told Barney what kind of car I would be driving, and the color of my dress."

Leaning back against the car, both nervously watch Colonel Cutter, seventy or so yards away, as he reviews the parade and from time to time glance over at them; then, shaking top-hat-wearing Mayor Sipple's hand and thanking him for the reception, Barney—carrying a briefcase and a heavy, black, leather coat across his arm—approaches his family. He's shocked by Sarah's electrifying beauty and—for a second—stands there staring at her. When Barney next studies his son, both Flynn and Sarah notice how his unsteady hands tremble.

"I'm sorry we arrived too late to be with you at the parade, Barney," Sarah tells him.

"That's quite okay," replies Barney, following their sights to his trembling hands. He controls the trembling and goes on. "Unlike me, Sarah, you seem to have grown younger, not older. Look at you. Both of you. Grace, elegance and radiance all in one."

"This is Flynn, Barney, your son," Sarah tells him.

"So you're Flynn," Barney says, facing Flynn and shaking his boy's steady hand. "Most of your correspondence and the photos you sent of yourself never reached me, son, or they became victim to the mildew and humidity in my cell. The only one I have left of you and your mother is years old, and I keep it in my watch, which I—by the way—had to bribe my captors with as much as half of my Red Cross packages in order to hold onto it."

"You had to do all of that just to keep our photo?" asks Flynn, extremely impressed.

"Yes."

When Flynn beams at his father, Barney lovingly taps him on the chin. "You have your mother's hair and eyes. A fine-looking young man. And the other boy . . ." Barney quickly adds, "the one I saw running along with you on the bridge, Caleb Brooks. Is that who he was?"

"It was he, Sir."

Flynn follows Barney's gaze across the square and sees Caleb watching them from afar. Turning and walking away, Caleb never looks back.

"We're a family, again," Barney tells Flynn. "It won't take long to get things back to normal."

Sarah looks toward Caleb, as he disappears behind the gazebo, fear reflecting in her eyes.

Much later, in blowing dust under the midnight moon, Sarah stops the Chevy next to the barn and sits behind the steering wheel of the idling car and listens patiently while Barney converses with Flynn in the back seat. When Barney finally climbs from the car, he causally carries his briefcase, but holds onto that long, black, leather coat as if onto a deity.

"Let me carry that coat for you, Sir?" Flynn says, stepping from the car behind Barney. "It looks heavy."

"That's because it is heavy and very special," says Barney. "But I brought it this far, and I'll manage to carry it a little farther, but thanks."

"Special, Sir," says Flynn, looking at the well-maintained coat.

"It belonged to Hitler," replies Barney, who then faces a shocked Sarah. "Thanks for the tour," he tells her. "I'd forgotten how large Shadow Grove was." Turning to Flynn he asks. "The key, do you have it?" Flynn removes a chain from around his neck and hands the chain and key to Barney. "Good," says Barney. "You've kept it close to you as I had asked. Do you have any idea what is in those duffle bags—you or Sarah?"

"No, Sir," says Flynn, Sarah shaking her head as well. "But I piled hay barrels in front of the hiding places' door to conceal it." Cutter hardly hears Flynn; he's looking at the manor. From a second-floor window, Naomi is staring down at that coat, her terrifying eyes of doom then focus on Barney as if a warning to him to keep that coat away from Flynn. Flynn follows his father's gaze to the window, and Naomi slowly lowers the shade. It's then that Flynn takes another look at the coat, a coat adorned with Hitler's ribbons, swastika and all. He looks at his father.

Barney looks back at Flynn, both Flynn, Barney and Sarah are ill at ease. An explosion of laughter comes from the general store, a hop skip and jump away. Colonel Cutter scrutinizes the well-lit building, as white and black workers enter and leave. "Son, go enjoy yourself with your white friends. I'm sure your mother has many things to say to me and I to her."

When Flynn approaches the large mercantile building, he glances back at his mother, knowing, to her, her marriage to Barney is in name only and is her worst nightmare.

"I know this is not easy for you, Sarah," Barney tells her, "my returning this way, and I want you to know that I won't force myself on you. Take all the time you need to get to know me again."

"I appreciate that," Sarah tells him with a look of relief.

After several moments of silence, with Barney impatiently studying the barn doors, Sarah interrupts his intense thoughts and stares. "Is that it," she asks. "That's what you wanted to tell me?"

"That's it," says Barney. "Goodnight, Sarah. I'll walk to the house."

Sarah drives off and Cutter hurries into the barn. Quickly removing the bales of hay from the west wall, he exposes a tarnished metal door. Unlocking it with the key, he enters into the Winthrops' old wine cellar and closes the door firmly behind him. Switching on a lightbulb hanging from the ceiling on a single electrical cord, he sees his duffle bags piled by the spiderweb-covered wine racks containing hundreds of dusty, bottles of wine. Nervously unlocking one of the duffle bags with a military-issued key, he excitedly shakes the bag and out tumbles paper-strapped U.S. dollars onto the floor.

When Flynn arrives at his mother's store, he is quickly surrounded by the Hill sisters and his many white admirers. The blacks have been cautioned to be patient and to stay away from Flynn by field boss Collins, now that Barney has returned. Jayne Hill and her giggling girlfriends have no such restrictions, and they waste no time in tugging Flynn to a table and sitting with him by the windows, Jayne—her dress up well past her knees—nestles in close to Flynn as the merrymaking goes on. Not all is bright and cheery on Shadow Grove, though. Shriveled plantation crops are piled in bins along the walls, a painful reminder to many of the elderly that the hard times and the drought have returned. That aside, in celebration of Barney's return, it seems that all of the field hands in the spacious store—either warming themselves around the potbelly stove, or enjoying the free snacks, ham sandwiches, watermelon, cookies, soda pops, including donuts and coffee—are in heaven, with the coffee fast running out. Not to worry. A strong aroma of fresh-ground coffee beans fills the air, as old Hank skillfully turns the handle of a large gold-leaf wheel on a red and olive-green, four-foot high, antique, coffee grinder. Spinning out of it comes the rich, delicious-smelling coffee granules to refill the workers empty cups with the dark drink of choice. Hank has never seemed happier in his life. His lifelong friend has returned home, and he can't wait to get together with Barney to bring each other up to date about Shadow Grove and—of course—Barney's long absence.

The rustic store has floor-to-ceiling shelves filled with straw hats, socks, dresses, trousers of all shapes and sizes. An assortment of tools, nails, nuts and bolts are situated in barrels which sit in zigzag patterns across the hardwood floor throughout the building. Sarah has also made arrangements for all of her workers to receive clothing without charge to celebrate the return of Flynn's father.

Near the brass, multi-drawer, cash register and the store counter, is a white enameled barber chair with a sign: HAIR CUTS ONE CENT. Sitting

257

in the chair and fast asleep is the store's old white barber; no one is in the mood for a haircut, not tonight. Off in a corner is a raised platform and piano, welcoming anyone who wants to perform. Old timers are playing checkers, next to the potbellied stove and patiently waiting—like all the others—for several black youths to finish setting up their stage equipment, which includes a drum set, a base and a lead guitar as well as the store's piano.

When the black band finally begins to play, the workers, whites and blacks, clap their hands to the energizing, rhythmic beat, Flynn sitting with his admirers, tapping his foot on the floor and clapping his hands together as well. Henry makes his way through the crowd, carrying a red five-gallon can of kerosene in one hand, while dancing a little softshoe routine to the band's staccato beat. He sees Naomi approaching, and when she steps closer and before she can make a move, he lowers the can of kerosene to the floor and dances off with her, until she wiggles free of him and moves on, shaking her head: "None of that young-folks dancing for this old woman, Henry Brooks," she scolds, causing him, Flynn and the joyful crowd to laugh. The wall phone rings. Trout, using his new crutches, limps over and answers it, as the music blares.

"Who the hell is this?" he asks, covering one ear. He quickly changes his tone. "Oh," he says looking over his shoulder, whispering. "It's you. You shouldn't call me here. He just got home. There's nothing to report yet. What? Okay. I said Okay! Don't get mad all the time. I'll be there."

He looks back at Flynn, regretfully and leaves the building, followed by Henry.

Stepping into the night with the kerosene, Henry sees Caleb standing back in the shadows and looking through the window at Flynn.

"Son, you should have come inside. Barney certainly can't object to you shopping in the store while Flynn is in there. Anyway," he says putting the kerosene in the wagon and both climb aboard. "Let's go home, so I can refill those cave lanterns before we turn in."

"Papa, you'll get bitten by one of those bats up in that cave one of these days, yet, if you don't stop going there. There's nothing in there but deposits of coal. And we keep spending money on kerosene and lanterns to light up that place, when we have our mortgage payments to think about."

"God and I will take care of that mortgage. And you, young man, re-

258

member that I'm the papa of this family and you're the child. I'm not afraid of bats. I enjoy going in there."

"Is that why you always go in that cave at night, when the bats have left?" Caleb teases.

Smiling, Henry balls his fist and shakes it at Caleb. "One of these days, boy, bang," he tells Caleb, "right between your eyes. Again I'm the 'Papa' here."

Laughing, Caleb exclaims, "Okay, Papa. Let's go up in the hills and fill those lanterns and we'll see who passes out from exhaustion first. I'm a man, not a boy. You've told me that since I was twelve. Remember?"

As father and son laughingly head for home in their wagon, and Henry ponders over Caleb's remark—that he, Henry, has told him that he was a man since an early age—at the same moment, to the rear of the store, Trout looks around, climbs into a plantation truck and speeds pass them and into the night, Naomi's eyes of doom watching him all the way from the store window.

Twenty minutes later, on a moonlit plantation road with the wind-stirred tree limbs shadowing over them, Trout—his store-bought, new crutches on the truck seat beside him—is talking truck-to-truck with Dane Tucker. "Find out all you can about him, where he goes and who he talks to," Dane orders.

"I don't know about that, Dane. He doesn't seem worn out or inca-pable of running the Klan again from what I saw of him, when he and Flynn and Sarah was talking together at the parade and then by the barn tonight. And I kind of like my job here now and have grown to like Sarah. She's been real good to me, even though she knows Barney left me there to spy on her. If I go along with you and lose this job, what will happen to me? I'm too old to look fer work now, and who would hire a one-leg old man, anyway? Nobody."

Dane leans outward from his vehicle and into Trout's lowered win-dow and stuffs a bit more of Metcalfe's money in the old timer's hand. "Does Sarah pay you this well? Play along with me, and think only about Barney's money. Maybe more money than we'll ever see in our lives again."

The sound of Henry's wagon is heard approaching from the general direction of the store.

"It's Caleb and Henry," exclaims Trout, squinting down the road at the distant wagon. Trout quickly drives away, passing face-to-face with Henry and Caleb, as he heads back to the celebration.

Dane, however, waits in the shadows, and when the wagon rattles by him, he screeches his tires on the moon-lit road, and roars his truck at the rear of Henry's wagon; he hammers on his horn, intimidating the Brooks and narrowly misses their wagon as he speeds by, sending Henry's mule and wagon off the road. Speeding through the plantation gate and laughing, Dane is on top of his world.

"Damn fool! Dane Tucker," shouts Henry, driving the mule and wagon back onto the road. "You'll draw no blood from this family tonight! See there, Caleb. You worry too much about the wrong things. It's folks like Dane that should concern you, not that cave."

Caleb looks up at the sky. A swiftly-moving, zigzagging, line of shadows are quivering against the moonlight and multiplying by the hundreds of thousands across the horizon, creatures with wings of death flooding out of the cave above their distant land, a good ten miles away. On the road ahead of them, Dane looks up and sees these nimble, winged creatures now covering the face of the moon in their endless search for animal and human blood, and he pulls off the road and stops, trembling in dread, the blood draining from his face, rendering him grayish-white. "Whoever is in charge of my life, God or Satan," he whispers, "if I should die, please don't let it be alone around them bats! You must know how I fear 'em, you who have the power over my life. They're like him. Like Barney! They'll sweep down upon you like he did my pa and suck out your blood, leaving you cold and dead. No matter who you might be, like me or like Caleb damn Brooks, he will kill you. Barney Cutter will kill you, even his own son."

17
The Cathedral

Barney and Flynn are seen everywhere, riding on horseback, walking together through Cutterville, playfully jostling about on Shadow Grove, strolling through the meadows and through fields of workers, who tip their straw hats to them; even with Barney's trembling hands and crippling pain, no distance seems too far or near for them to reach, as they search out new areas to explore. The stream that flows under Cutter Bridge dries up more often than not, but at times—after a heavy rainfall—it contains durable catfish; father and son laugh while snagging the vigorous fighters on poles that they've made from tree limbs. They ride their bicycles for miles down tree-lined country roads, picnic in the woods and pursue rare butterflies, one of Flynn's favorite hobbies, and each day Flynn sees Barney less and less the way he did at the train station and more alike to Henry: kind, patient and fatherly. As if their love will never catch up to where it should have been over those lost years, between them, they walk through the occasional downpour, their trousers rolled up to their knees. Those happy, bare feet—even the arthritic ones of Barney—stylishly dance through the rain puddles. Barney—who has fathered only Flynn—has never felt more alive in his life than he has now since returning home to his son.

For weeks after the rain stops, neither seems troubled about the lack of the life-giving water, including about their once-again-slowly-drying-out land; they sit at a table by the bay window and play chess, at peace in the unspoken silence between them, knowing that the other is across from him, fulfilling his need for love. On clear, windy days, field hands see them atop Manor Hill, Flynn and Barney, flying their red and yellow kites high against the patchy blue sky. After coiling in their kites, Barney stretches out on the grass and gazes at the white clouds. Flynn lies down next to his father and does the same, the clouds never seeming more beautiful. "I wish it would rain down buckets every other day," Flynn says, again facing the reality of the draught and going on, "as it did in town that day lightning exploded and burned that tree. Then our land would look like Henry and Caleb's. Did you know that Caleb and I wit-

261

nessed Naomi and —?" Flynn suddenly clams up. He timidly glances over at Barney.

"It's okay, Flynn. But, again, try not to mention this boy Caleb's name or Naomi's. I know she works here, but those two no longer exist as far as we're concerned. And I've heard about Naomi, the burning tree, the rain and how they say Dane murdered Lilly and the way some of our white workers and blacks seem to feel that these droughts, the earthquakes and the damage to Miller's church are signs that God is against certain people, mainly the whites and the Klan and against me."

"I was just hoping our land will turn emerald green again," Flynn apologizes, "and didn't mean to suggest anything about the morals of the Klan one way or the other, Sir."

"It will. This grass. It and all of Shadow Grove from horizon to horizon will soon be emerald green, as that poetic mind of yours wants it to be. We now have the means to make it so. Enough money to buy all the land we desire, even land owned by others, land rich with water. Soon, now, after things cool down in D.C. I'll make my move."

"That money you showed me in the barn . . . You never did say how our family got it, Sir. There must be millions of dollars in those bags. And why does Washington have anything to do—"

"What's important now is that you never mention that money to anyone. Since the market crash, we can't trust the banks, especially Pennington's small bank in town, now that old Harry Pennington's dead and Charles is running the bank. At the right time, I'll tell you all you need to know."

"That would be so great," says Flynn again facing the clouds. "Our land with water on it. Then, Caleb and I would have two places to row in our boat." Too late. For the second time, Flynn has made the mistake of mentioning Caleb's name. Cutter eyes Flynn, knowing that the battle for his son's mind will have to take time before victory can be declared, even as it took time to try and win over Sarah, so he takes another approach.

"This boy, Caleb. Tell me about him."

"There isn't much to tell. We've played and at times argued together since our first steps."

"Is Caleb unusual?" Barney asks, the sound of uneasiness in his voice, as he goes on. "I mean from your point of view, not from that of ignorant whites here or some dumb crackers in town."

262

"What do you mean by 'unusual?' " asks Flynn.

"Do you think he has these so-called special gifts that people whisper about?"

"If he has, I've never seen anything about him which would make me think so," Flynn lies, eyeing his father, nervously going on. "Why do you ask, Sir?"

"Anyone who has the respect of my son, piques my curiosity, that's all. I don't want you running about diminishing your intelligent mind by picking up habits from ill-bred workers."

"Oh, Caleb isn't uninformed. He's brighter than I. He speaks Latin, is an excellent violinist, outstanding in everything he does and is well respected by our white workers. He and I built a rowboat—which I might add—sinks more than it floats, but we'll fix that, and we even plan to build a dock on his father's lagoon for our boat one day." Flynn looks to the side. "That is we were."

"You said he's even brighter than you? Seems he's quite the fellow. Who taught him?"

Once again Flynn has said too much. Barney would not appreciate hearing that Sarah taught them both. Flynn has never lied to Naomi or Sarah. Now he has to out and out lie to his father, but Barney is much too wise to press Flynn into perjuring himself and feels that Sarah, as she has done for all of the workers, has taught Caleb, never knowing that he would have turned out as gifted as Flynn has described. Barney sits up. "I've heard enough. Seems you're quite the pianist, yourself. I've heard you playing in your room, and I want you to know I couldn't be prouder of you. However, I also want you to continue practicing playing. Every day, mind you. We can't have you trailing behind Caleb. From what the workers have told me, you hate getting your hands dirty, so—"

"Even at that," says Flynn, "I'll do my share of work to keep this land afloat."

"From now on, son, no more working in the fields like some commoners," says Barney, "Which of the old masters is your favorite, son?"

"Beethoven, Sir."

"Excellent! He's also mine."

What Flynn fails to tell his father is that from the pictures he's seen of Beethoven, that Beethoven, with his curly locks, his sturdy-looking facial features and ruddy complexion, reminds him of Henry, and his playing is similar to the way Caleb interprets the violin with such force.

Standing up and pulling Flynn to his feet, Barney also has a reminder for his son, not a musical one, but a harsh racially motivated one. "Leave that dirty, difficult work to the poor whites and especially to the coloreds, since Sarah insists on keeping those darkys on here for now." Amazed, Flynn stands there staring at Barney's hands. "What is it, Flynn?"

"The way you pulled me to my feet. Your hands. They no longer shake, and you haven't complained about your arthritis lately. Are you taking medicine?" He gazes at Barney, up and down, "And you seem younger to me."

Barney just smiles at Flynn and places his arm about his son's shoulder, and they start for home, carrying their kites with them, Flynn marveling at his fathers, a man who seems young in appearance, and in stamina, and again Flynn wonders if Barney is visiting his doctor and is taking medicine and if that is the miracle which has enlivened his father. It's far more sinister than that—Barney going to a doctor and taking medicine. He won't dare tell Flynn the truth for fear it will drive Flynn away from him. Barney has entered into a covenant with Satan and has been given one last wish in exchange for his and Flynn's soul. Barney chose to be a god, to truly and finally be one.

At the manor, Naomi watches from the window with Sarah, as Flynn and Barney happily approach. Sensing that Barney has all but taken full control over Flynn, Sarah looks at Naomi, terror reflecting in her eyes. "There is nothing, Sarah," says Naomi. "Nothing we can do. Barney is far too strong for you or me to diminish his powers now, and no, your eye aren't deceiving you. Barney is younger. He walks with Lucifer at his side."

During the next few days, Flynn remains in his room practicing on his baby grand piano, the bright, morning sunlight streaming through the window onto him, onto his golden hair, and onto his sheets of classical music, the sun, with all of its joyful essence of warmth, letting Flynn know that he has a wonderful life and a father, finally a father. Barney has been traveling back and forth to Cutterville in secret meetings with the mayor and some unnamed U.S. Senator, and Flynn has seen little of his father and yearns for his presence. He hears someone driving up to the house and blowing the car horn. Looking out the window, Flynn is enraptured. Colonel Cutter, wearing a short-sleeved shirt, white trousers and tennis shoes, is driving a brand-new red Cadillac convertible. Cutter looks up from the large, shiny car—which he had had especially painted to please Flynn's young taste. He waves for his son to join him. Flynn dashes down the spiral staircase pass Naomi and Sarah, who are in the living room sewing, having moments earlier gazed out the window at Barney. "Where you off to in such a hurry?" calls Naomi.

"With Father!" Flynn yells, one of the few times he has addressed Barney as 'father.' "He's bought a Cadillac. A new Cadillac, Naomi. And it's red! See you later, Mother!"

Entering the luxury car, Flynn is greeted by that special smell found only in new cars. He slowly settles onto the rich, leather seat and listens to the stimulating, certified, solid sound that comes from closing a General Motor's car door. With the wind blowing through their hair, father and son ride down the winding driveway, under the shade trees, pass the general store and gawking plantation workers, whose young children run alongside the breathtaking car, all of whom are gaping up and waving and smiling at the Cutter men, the "Big Two" of Shadow Grove. Waving back, Barney then speeds away, sending a trail of dust and leaves the plantation behind, including Henry and Caleb, toiling with other blacks digging a final link to one of several large irrigation pumps, which Barney recently purchased and spread across the wearisome plantation. Irrigation pipes are now only a half mile from the lagoon. Barney has hired outside contractors to speed the line along, as well as prepare a surprise on Henry's land for Flynn. Henry—removing his straw hat and wiping his brow with a white handkerchief—lovingly regards Flynn, who appears to be extremely happy and fits well in the new car, but Caleb refuses to look at Flynn and continues with his chore. In the car, Flynn looks back at Caleb, then focuses on Barney, who is keenly aware of that momentary, unspoken tug-of-war between him, Flynn and Caleb, and he is pleased that his son has—for the moment—chosen to look to him instead of to Caleb.

"Where are we going, Father?" Flynn excitedly asks. Barney is deeply moved by Flynn calling him 'father,' and he reaches over and touches his son's arm.

"Sit back and relax, we'll be there soon. I have a surprise for you."

Ten miles later, the slick, sassy, red car rolls to a stop at Henry's lagoon, where a dozen white construction workers, along with their trucks and tools, are leaving. One of the departing vehicles stops alongside the Cadillac. "It's all completed as you ordered, Colonel," he tells Barney. "In less than a day. The quick-dry concrete and those special pilings made it possible after we dammed off the water. But now the blockage has been removed and water levels about the dock are back to normal and we're on our way. Thanks. We certainly needed the business."

Once the truck leaves, Flynn looks at Barney. "Why were they on Henry's land and what dock was he talking about?"

Colonel Cutter steps from the car and gazes toward the lagoon and at a brand-new wooden dock, which extends out into a muddy section of water, where the construction crew has been working. "The water will clear up in a few days after the sediment settles to the bottom," Barney tells Flynn, who is staring dumbfounded at the dock and at a new aluminum rowboat tied to the pilings. Flynn races from the car, sprints across the dock, climbs down the rungs and steps into the boat. He touches its smooth-cold surface, while beaming up at his approaching father. Laughing, Barney crosses the dock and stands at the rungs, grinning down at Flynn. Almost immediately, the smile fades from Flynn's face.

"This boat . . . The dock. Did Henry give us permission to build it and store the boat here?"

"I didn't ask him."

"But we have to."

"Why? The dock, even the boat improves the value of his land. And as far as I'm concerned, this dock and that boat belong to him and Caleb, when we're not using it. Okay?" Cutter descends the rungs and steps into the boat. "Now, let me see how well you can row this thing."

Once on the lagoon, within view of the tar shed and his and Caleb's rickety boat, Flynn avoids looking at them, at anything which reminds him of Caleb, and he skillfully rows his father about the vast stretch of water and away from those area of recent memories. Instead, he concentrates on the opposite shoreline trees, on the rich green hills, the swaying cattails by the thousands, the butterflies, the dragonflies and the leaping fish and the blue sky. All of this accelerates the lust for life in Barney and in Flynn, as Flynn now rows them along with gusto.

Flynn then studies his father, knowing that Barney's full measure of happiness depends, in part, on Sarah. Flynn asks. "Have you and Mother slept together yet?"

For a moment, Cutter's face reflects discontent, then he observes

266

Flynn in awe of his courage to ask such a question, and Barney quietly explains, "Not since my arrival, but let's give her all the time she needs, okay? Son, there are so many things I must make up to you for staying away so long. I want you to know that other women were involved in my life and—"

"I know that," says Flynn. "Mother told me. I think that's why she refuses to look in the wine cellar or know about the money there, even now."

"Your mother, Flynn. She's isn't concerned about me having another woman. If she refuses to know about that money it goes deeper than that. Another man possibly and also—"

"There's no other man in her life, Father. She'll come around. There is something that has always troubled me." With concern for others—which loving Caleb has instilled in him—which Barney knows he must destroy, Flynn goes on: "It's the war, Sir. Those people in Hiroshima, the ones who witnessed it, did they suffer much from that bomb?"

"The atomic bomb?"

"Yes, Sir."

"Some did, of course, but many didn't feel a thing. They were vaporized in a flash with all of their belongings, including entire parts of their cities. Others will suffer for years to come, with their offspring sharing in the pain as well. I was held captive there when that bomb went off. Japs cooked and ate their prisoners and deserved to be, themselves, cooked."

"But, you, Father. You made it out alive. How?"

"By prayer, to a powerful patron."

"It's the war. It caused a lot of people to pray as you did to God. Some say wars are the work of the devil." If Barney is offended by Flynn's statement, he doesn't show it. Flynn goes on. "The way Mussolini died when his people killed him, then hanged his body upside down. And that animal Hitler, no telling how he died before his men burned his body. What about those Jews, Father? Were millions of them exterminated by the Germans, the way we're told?"

"Millions of people die of starvation, of bullets, and disease in all wars, but there are those, even some of our generals and captains of industry, in this country, who say that Hitler did not murder millions or exterminate anyone. There just isn't enough proof to personally tie him to

267

that, and, son, even here in America, you either destroy your enemy, or they'll destroy you. And that business of this country imprisoning all of the yellow-skinned Japs, into those desert camps, has nothing to do with Satan, wouldn't you say, only the need to survive?"

"I realize that from the newsreels. But, Father," says Flynn, his white knuckles tightly gripping the oars. "Must we always kill?"

"Yes," answers Barney, his sights on Flynn's nervous hands. "If that person is your enemy."

"There was a colored soldier in one of the boxcars that Caleb and I were on," Flynn says. "He told us that he was looking for you, and later—after I left you and Mother at the barn, Amos, one of our old workers, told me that he also ran into this colored soldier, that this person was raving on about you and a secret mission."

"What did you tell him, this colored soldier, about me?" asks Barney, his eyes squinting with more than a little anxiety.

"Neither Amos, Caleb nor I said that we even knew you. He was a crazy man and made no sense, and I think Amos feels the same way. But—" Flynn goes deadly silent.

"But what, son?"

Flynn looks Barney in his cold, blue eyes. "It isn't I so much as it is my friends on the plantation who are always asking about you. Some of them say that since your health is getting better all the time, that you must have the special powers, just like they say Naomi has, that you know everything that will happen before it does."

Barney respects Flynn's forthright honesty and says, "I have no such powers to know what is going to happen. However, my health is, indeed, getting better all the time, and that's to both of our advantage and our enemies' disadvantage."

"Oh," Flynn says looking about. "We're here. The cathedral." The young man rows through the opening in a quarry wall and into a section of the lagoon where the towering walls majestically surround a confined world of still, deep, dark-blue water on three sides; that thirty-foot opening into it leaves the sounds of the outside world behind, a quiet place, which Flynn has named "The Cathedral." The insightful, blonde boy lifts the oars so smoothly that not a ripple disturbs the serenity and silence there, which does not go unnoticed by Barney. He follows Flynn's lead and sits back in total esteem. Colonel Cutter, his eyes caressing the view, looks about in absolute amazement.

268

"I had no idea this was out here," Barney whispers, leaning forward, his hands reaching up to touch the sky. "One can almost touch the face of his god in here," he whispers to Flynn.

"Don't tell Caleb that, because—as much as I think I know him—I'm not sure he believes in God, or in angels, but certainly not in churches."

"Neither do I," says Barney, maintaining his focus on the sky. "So you see, Caleb and I think alike in some ways, it seems. Wouldn't you say?" What Barney is getting at is that with Flynn respecting Caleb as much as he does, then by suggesting that Caleb's ideas about God is the same as his, then it will be much easier to convert Flynn into devil worship. Barney goes on. "Churches are not where my god lives, and I'm not even sure he lives in the sky."

Flynn is stunned into silence, and he dare not ask his father who his god is, but Barney sees the shock in Flynn's eyes and reads the stiffening state of his son's body.

"During my imprisonment, I was tortured and starved," he begins his task of brainwashing Flynn. "Once I actually called on the Supreme Being, including Greek and old Roman deities and others, but my prayers fell on deaf ears. When all else failed, to save my sanity, I went back to him and prayed to him, and he came to me and helped me get through it, even through that hellfire of that bomb to end all wars. I offered him nothing. He did all of what he did out of love for me."

"I don't know why Caleb agreed to let me call this place our cathedral," Flynn say, fearing what he hears from Barney.

Colonel Cutter looks at his baffled son. "This Caleb . . . You say he doesn't believe in God. That's highly unusual for a colored boy."

"He doesn't believe in churches. I'm not sure that he feels the same way about God," Flynn says, attempting to undo some of the damage he feels he's caused.

"What I'm not sure of," says Barney, going on, "is what Caleb wants from you?"

"Caleb is mixed up and doesn't know what he wants. He's going to make an excellent attorney one day, though, and—"

"The violin, Latin, and now he's into the law," Barney replies, them gazes about the quarry land. "Son, what do you think about me approaching Henry about selling his land to us?"

"Henry would not want that and neither would I."

Barney eyes Flynn: "This Caleb, son. The whites in town say that Naomi claims that he was born into this world as a savior and will take her place—whatever that means."

"But Caleb could never be a savior for coloreds," Flynn says. "Not the way Caleb dislikes churches and the colored love them. Caleb knows that the colored would stone him if he even thought about mentioning to them that he was their savior, him, a non-church-goer." Flynn looks pleadingly at Barney. "And as I said, about Caleb, he's confused. So if the Klan is concerned about him leading coloreds through the Red Sea against them, they need not worry. I don't want Caleb hurt, Father."

Barney lovingly strokes Flynn's hand. "Move aside and let me row now, son," He tells Flynn. "I don't want the hands of such a gifted pianist rowing a boat this tough to handle through troubled water, not when your father's on board to do it for you. Sit back and leave this to me. Everything well work out okay, as my god is my witness. I'll smooth out the rough waters, so that it'll be easy sailing for you and soon."

Barney trades places with Flynn, recovers the oars and begins to row, while gazing at the magnificent surroundings. "This place will be my body," he whispers. "This so-called cathedral of yours, son. My body and my soul. From now on, it will be your Holy Grail and your sanctuary from all harm, where we can maintain our relationship as father and son, a place where we can come and talk and be together for as long as we live—and as long as we love one another."

The deer and the beavers watching them from shore, the butterflies fluttering overhead and the frogs perched on the water lilies all seem to have heard the threatening tone in Barney's voice, even toward his beloved son. Those creatures of the land and water seem, also, to be warning the world, through their intense stares that, although Barney seems to truly love Flynn, Barney is the devil's Grand Wizard and is fishing for Caleb in order to slaughter him, and Flynn is his deadly bait.

18

The Porch of Wisdom

In Colored Town, the sun beats down on a community with all of its heartfelt pain. It's warm, yes. It turns darkness into light, yes. But it's also a reminder to blacks that there is no milk and honey on the south side of Cutterville's railroad tracks which sunlight clearly makes it possible for them to see only so far, because unlike the whites under the same inviting rays, over the blacks, no matter how poor the whites are or are not, the whites' way of life across that deceiving, finger-high, steel, rail boundary, clearly offers them equal justice under the law, something blacks only dream of; many blacks feel that instead of living under God's free sun, they are imprisoned under Lucifer's punishing snowstorm of hatred. However, Colored Town's rainbow-colored people—sun-ripened, inky, golden-yellow, as well as near-white—are mostly enduring, and over the long haul, they have adjusted and always will adjust to their difficult way of life by reaching out—through their Bibles and churches—to touch the face of God. Dust blows everywhere and noon temperatures rise to 113 degrees, driving the fires of hatred between blacks and whites to a new boiling point. But there is joyful singing to be found here on these agonizing hot days, also, a gladness that depends on a merciful God to lead His people onto "the road that calls up yonder."

Entire families sit out on the porches of row after row of rented, bedraggled, paintless houses. In the precious shade, those full-bodied women—sitting there with their pig-tail-braided children at their feet—hunker down to face the long, sizzling day. They've worked under oppression all their lives, while giving their young ones Bible lessons to soften their youthful hearts and pains. These porch-dwelling, God-thirsty women—thick of skin, scarred from head to toe—have unshapely, callused, bone-hard hands, pale, colorless palms, raven fingers and broken fingernails; they faithfully hold onto paper fans from Reverend Harris's Baptist church as if their lives depended on it, fans with large, white faces of Jesus imprinted on them.

Two blocks down the road lives another kind of woman, in a different kind of world and house. Three young neighborhood girls jump rope on the new sidewalk of the much-talked-about residence, a well-painted, now lavender-colored, two-story, wooden residence which is financially sound and the best show in town for the three sex-starved girls. Forty-year-old Madame Lana lives in that house. From her fancy, canopied veranda—perfumed and colored mahogany—Lana surveys her kingdom, her plush lawn, her white picket fence, and her peach trees along the side of her old Victorian, one of the few such houses left standing in good repair after the upper classes moved from that area to the far north side of town and the blacks gradually invaded. Heavy-set and robust, her hair tied up in large, pink rollers, Lana's wearing a satin, white robe, fluffy, yellow slippers and is relaxing in one of several, naturally-colored, tan wicker chairs next to a glass-top table, from which she serves tea to her girls.

With her delicate fingers and painted fingernails, she mimics the British upper class and daintily lifts one of her fragile eggshell china cups from the table and sips her favorite, ice cold jasmine tea. Sitting on the porch next to her is one of her best money makers: Mellow Yellow, eighteen, breathtakingly stunning and as sleek and slender as an alley cat on the prowl. Lana's house is far better furnished and maintained than many of the rich, tasteless whites on the wealthier, north side, so whether the sun shines warm or cold matters not to Lana, nor does the black community's opinion of her and her girls. For privacy, heavy burgundy drapery covers the downstairs windows of the whorehouse, and for comfort—to the envy of the poor whites—a large porch fan stirs the air over the crafty businesswoman and the girls' heads.

Representing the only law in Cutterville, chalky-white, potbellied and on the easy side of fifty, Sheriff Leopold Richards strolls out of Lana's place, looks at the three teenage girls and says, "Y'all hurry up and grow up, you hear?" He picks his teeth with a broken matchstick, climbs into his patrol car and drives away. He and his deputies control Colored Town with an iron fist, judge, jury and executioner. The sheriff's brother heads Cutterville's planning commission. He and Richards gave Lana a precious gift, that real, honest-to-goodness, cement sidewalk, the only one in Colored Town that is not broken up by tree roots or old age and carted away. Not only has the sidewalk been extended to Lana's porch, it stretches the full length of her property and points due north toward the white community—according to the blacks— it does so in order that Lana's well-paying white night-sneaking clients won't get their polished shoes muddy, when they leave their fancy cars in whitey's community and walk to Lana's place, so as not to be identified by their fancy cars, as would be the case if they parked them in front of the whorehouse and in doing so would expose them to their unsuspecting wives. Sheriff Richards, on the other hand, doesn't give a damn as to who sees him or his car. Pussy is pussy. As he drives across the train tracks into White Town with a big smile on his face, the rope-jumping girls' large eyes lock in on the local jive-cat Crazy Walter, as he sidles from a group of bushes and approaches the whorehouse, while keeping an eye on Richards' distant car.

Walter struts onto the porch as if he owned the world, even though—as Mellow Yellow fondly tells him—he hasn't a pot to piss in. The attractive yellow-skinned teenager offers the happy-go-lucky man a seat on one of the rocking chairs, and once he plops down in it, she rests lazily on his lap, her legs spread. Tall and well-muscled, Walter's ebony skin looms in sharp contrast to his long, prematurely-graying, wiggly, Jamaican hair and mustache. He jerks his head to the side, brushing his hair from his eyes, as he laughingly reaches around Mellow Yellow with both hands and fondles the easily aroused female's breast through her robe, the young sidewalk girls pretending to swoon. Suddenly, sprinting toward the whorehouse is sweaty and dark Reverend Harris, screaming at the teenage girls as he runs. Harris is forty-eight, thin and full of fire and brimstone and forever ready to spread it around. "Look away from that house of damnation," he yells at the girls, as he bounds onto the sidewalk, "or God'll strike you blind."

"Naomi say Caleb Brooks will be our road that calls up yonder," says a girlfriend of Claretta, nicknamed Pumpkin. "Not you, Reverend, who always says God will burn us in hell."

"Caleb Brooks can go straight to hell, too!" shouts Harris. "He ain't even a churchgoer." He points his finger at Pumpkin. "And you, young lady, you're from one of them families who just moved here from Shadow Grove so your family can get one of them factory jobs, so shut up when you're spoken to, and this Naomi you talkin' about is a voodoo, witch fool from one of them jungle countries where they eats dumb little girls like you alive, for God's sake."

"Naomi say God got nothin' to do with blindin' folks, Reverend. Only you does!" Pumpkin fires back. "God's good."

Laughing, Walter rises to his feet, leaving Mellow Yellow sitting spread legged on the rocker.

"Little old missy got you there Rev.," teases Walter. "Didn't she? As young as he is, Caleb Brooks is one of the damn-dest-intelligent niggers, including Booker T. Washington, I done ever heard of or seen. And I seen a picture of Booker T. in a book once when them white folks was tryin' to run him out of town, so don't say I ain't never seen nobody worth something like you always do.

"Now, folks around here, they say Caleb not only reads the Bible to his pa, but he understands the meanin' of all them fancy Latin, holy-than-thou words, not the pig ears, and the intestines, and pig guts, and pig feet, and pig noses that you make of the Bible and force feed to us ignant, po', black folks. That is what you call us who don't attend yo' church, ain't it? 'Ignant.' Even as young as he be, we'd be better off with someone like Caleb leadin' us rather than a money-hungry man like you. Less colored churches in this world and mo' colored business to hire mo' dumb niggers. That's what I say. So open up a business Rev. Harris and I'll be first in line to come a-callin' on yo' black ass fo' a job."

"Walter," says Lana. "He's a man of the cloth."

"Tell that to his congregation," says Walter. "The ones he paints the way that white preacher Miller paints his whites: all in sin. Harris ain't got sense enough to be his own man. So like Miller, he tells his followers they gonna go to hell even if they look at they naked bodies when they take a bath, that we gots to put on blindfolds when we naked and facing a mirror so as not to look at thy own self. And God help us ifin we touch our self in the wrong place or shake it one time too many after we pee, like Barney Cutter's pa caught him doing. No wonder Barney worships the devil. Churches drove him to it, churches and his ma who boned him, or made him bone her."

The young girls—on the sidewalk—and the prostitutes, on the porch, break into robust laughter.

"Strike him dead, Lord. Please strike this backslider blind and dead fo' blasphemy and fo' acting in a way that teaches these young girls that it's okay to look upon the half-naked body of a whore, or on themselves with lust and become masturbators of sin."

Laughing, Walter drops to his knees and spreads Mellow Yellow's legs. "Blind, you tell them young girls and me," exclaims Walter, "that God'll strike us blind fo' just a-lookin' this way? If so, then I just got to

274

take a chance on one of these eyes going blind." He covers his right eye and looks under Mellow Yellow's robe, then withdraws and snickers at Harris. "I didn't go blind, and what a beautiful young tunnel of love Mellow Yellow has, even smells good. Want a look, Reverend Harris?"

"Get him, Lord! Get him with yo' lightnin' rod of justice!"

As Lana, then more of her girls—who have run outside to listen—laugh themselves half silly, Walter continues embarrassing the angry preacher. "Talk is God even fo'gave that murdered, white woman, Margaret Lilly, who tried to steal Brick's money on Dane Tucker's car lot. I just wish Lilly had offered me a look. Call it what it is, Reverend, Pussy! Say it. It's something pretty, not ugly like you make it out to be. Her flower garden is what that dead white woman called it. I say praise the Lord fo' pussy. Even that white woman's dead one. Somebody had to enjoy it while she was alive."

The sidewalk girls' eyes open wide in astonishment, yet not one of them walk away, their eyes sparkling with never-before-felt excitement, as they smile at one another and at Walter, their legs crossed, relieving their pent-up frustrations, as they wiggled about and against one another. Once more Walter covers one of his eyes and lifts the young whore's robe. "I just got to take another chance on losin' this other eye," he jokes, looking between the young woman's legs, then winking at the giggling girls.

Chuckling and gagging on her tea, Lana accidentally drops her expensive cup, shattering it. "Dammit!" she hisses. "Get out of here, Walter."

While the sidewalk girls goggle at Walter, Lana—attempting to remain upset with him—can't restrain her hilarity, when she sees Mellow Yellow pointing at her and breaking her sides laughing at the expression on the young sidewalk girls' faces, at their legs, which are crossed even tighter. Following Mellow Yellow's sights to the young girls, Lana and her other ladies of the night burst into simultaneous, roaring laughter.

"That's enough, Walter," Lana says, wiping away the tears from her eyes, desperately wanting not to insult the exasperated, large-eyed Harris anymore, knowing that he can make her life a living hell by forming a picket line of holier-than-thou, man-less females around her place with the wave of his Bible. Somehow Lana manages to contain her outrageous elation and faces Walter.

"Now, Walter," she struggles on, holding in her giggles, "you get

275

your crazy ass out of here before one of ma white customers sees you and thinks yo' black ass is spoiling the merchandise."

Holding onto his fly and ragging Harris, Walter bounds over the railing and off the porch, sending the rope-holding, youthful girls stumbling back from him. The fastest pair of feet in town, in a flash, Walter whirls in a circle and runs backwards by Harris, sticking out his tongue at the preacher and leaving a trail of backwards dusty and size seventeen footprints in his wake. The enraged preacher seizes a twig from a close-by, prickly tree and strikes the young gawkers.

"Now get like I told ya!" Harris yells, chasing them back to the houses of the fanning women. "And no more sinful rope jumping. It gets men excited when they see you young girls breasts also jumping up and down and moving this way and that and all around without you wearing a bra." He leaves the girls under the church sisters' severe, authoritarian gaze. Defiantly Pumpkin and her girlfriends resumed their child-like play, pigtails bouncing, their jumping ropes turning up the dust, their worn shoes slapping rhythmically against the hardened earth, their angry tears flowing down their cheeks, due to the blisters rising on their buttocks where Harris had lashed them with the switch. The girls refuse to give him the satisfaction of not jumping, no matter how painful it is to do so now. After Harris is out of earshot, sobbing and sticking out their tongues at him, the young females break into a well-rehearsed jingle: "The Klan come a-vis-sit-tin' 'till Lana drains they manhoods thin. White man don't like a nigga in the bed behind him. So crazy-talkin' Walter go a-hiddin', 'cause he wants to save his skin. Our old preacher climb a tree, tells us girls what he see in Lana's upstairs bedroom window where thin curtains hang free and all the lovin' be. The Klans in the whorehouse havin' fun, Reverend Harris yells down to us girls three. They all in there gettin' some 'cept you and po' old, Bible-preachin' me." The girls break into laughter.

"Stop that," demands one of the fan wavers from the porch of wisdom. "We saw you down at Lana's place. No wonder Reverend switched ya, and ifin he tells yo' mammas and daddies you girls'll sho' 'nough get another switchin' when you gets home."

"Satan's in his kitchen boiling the stewing water in a big pot to put you girls in once you end up in hell with you talkin' about evil sex like that," scolds another of the manless church sisters, this one in a drab, washed-out, red dress and with a shape and face that only a dog would love.

"But Naomi say God made sex good and man made it ugly," Pumpkin says.

"You girls sho' 'nough gonna burn in hell like that murdered white girl Lilly," the red-dress woman yells to them, "ifin' you don't change yo' ways," After that stern warning of damnation, she faces her two nephews sitting at her feet. "No matter," she begins, looking back and forth from the rope jumpers to her nephews, "ifin' any of you kids believe Naomi or Reverend Harris or even that Caleb Brooks boy, that folks whisper about, it still means that God's eyes is on all of us. He's a-warnin' us that He'll attend to the wicket and the—" When the girls laugh at her and run back to Lana's house, the woman in red sobs, "Please, Lord, please, please let it be soon. Let somebody come and save our children befo' it's too late."

A sudden murmur rises from the crowd of blacks on the street, and all heads turn to the east side of Colored Town; someone on the street is pointing in that direction, pointing at something glowing under the morning sun and slowly moving their way.

"My God, Marlene, it's his daddy and him, that boy," says one of the porch women to the one in red, "The boy everyone's talking about. Look fo' yo'self."

The oncoming image of Caleb and Henry gleams under the sunlight, which seems to be wrapped all around only them. Henry's wagon is loaded down with his and Caleb's bountiful assortment of vegetables, including their golden corn and ice-packed fish. The wagon is pulled along by what the blacks now call Caleb's miracle horse, Old Clara. With a growing number of people turning and staring at them, Caleb—more than willing to be understated—sits next to his beloved father and marvels at the man who commands the love of Flynn and Sarah, and now seemingly the crowd. On the other hand, Old Clara can never be understated, not with it rumored by many blacks that the old horse will never die and that God also blessed it with everlasting strength, as He has Caleb, in order that she might forever serve her new, young master. Nevertheless, for now, in the driver's seat, Henry holds the reins, but Caleb sits at his father's side with such presence that there is no doubt, by those watching, about his important place under the sun.

"Papa, I know it would mean we'd have to sell everything, but what

277

would you say if Flynn and I moved away, maybe to New York or to California, where we could remain friends and you and Sarah can come along with us. Possibly even Claretta and B.J. for a better life?"

"You would do that for B.J., son?"

"Yes."

"Our land, Caleb? Slaves were promised thirty acres and a mule and never got it. That's why the priests gave it to our ancestors. Two-thousand acres, son, an eighth as large as Flynn's place and with all the water in the world, compared to Shadow Grove. You would leave that because a friend has seemingly turned his back on you? That's what this is all about? About Flynn deserting us?"

While Henry guides Old Clara toward the center of the black community, praying as they go—and Caleb, his shoulders stooped, his eyes closed and wishing he had never been born—word quickly spreads through the community that the Brooks are coming, and the blacks stream from their disheveled houses and hurry to the colored section's main byway to catch a glimpse of Reverend Harris's disreputable, nightmare family. Even so, elderly men tip their hats to Henry and Caleb, and aging, god-fearing women wave as father and son pass by, not however, the paper-fan women on the porch of skepticism. They frown at the Brooks, as Henry lifts his straw hat to them and to the crowd, and Caleb graciously follows his father's lead by nodding his head in a show of respect to those whom Henry has said are their brothers and sisters.

Caleb smiles when he sees an old friend among the growing crowd waving to them: It's Bruce Johnson, free of his bandages. Bruce runs to the wagon and Henry brings Old Clara to a stop. Shaking Henry's hand, then kissing that of Caleb's, Bruce causes a murmur in the crowd of onlookers, all having heard how Caleb risked his life to save that of Bruce's. The good-natured man tearfully sobs, while exclaiming to Caleb, "I can't never thank you enough fo' savin' ma life, son. Got only a few scars to show for' it. And, my God, Caleb, is you healed okay from the burns on you?"

Caleb—embarrassed by Bruce's kiss—looks at his hand, and as Henry listens to the two of them in amazement, Caleb replies to Bruce, "Not even a scar is left, and I have no idea why."

"God, Caleb," says Bruce. "He's making you whole in ways none of us understands. I felt it when you put out that fire on me. Listen, y'all," Bruce calls to the crowd. "This is the boy who fought the devil and won over Dane Tucker and the Klan, and he the boy who saved ma life. I can't say it enough"

The old man who had been searching through trash in the alley behind the factory and had witnessed the death of Lilly, yells to the crowd: "And he's the one that Lilly called a godsend befo' she up and died, as I told everybody. This here Caleb Brooks is from God, and ifin I'm lyin', I'm flyin'. He's from God!"

Dozens from the crowd swarm in and shake Caleb's hand, crowding Bruce into the background, where he's met by his faithful wife Carrie, who gratefully waves to Caleb. Bruce's youngest daughter Earlene throws a kiss at Caleb. Bruce's son, Brick, lagging behind as usual, catches up to his father and yells "Hello, Caleb!" However, the pain in Bruce's heart, his second to the oldest, wild and attractive and unpredictable, Claretta is nowhere to be seen. Caleb searches over the crowd for her to no avail.

"Caleb," calls Brick, pushing through the river of people to Caleb and the wagon. "Pa is always sayin' that you bested Dane Tucker. Can you help me? Dane won't give me ma car, even when I done paid fo' it and Billy Joe and I done went back twice to beg him fo' it."

"Don't trouble Caleb with that nonsense," Bruce shouts at Brick. "You shouldn't never gone to Dane Tucker in the first place and spent yo' grandpa's hard-earned money on that car. Now let Henry and Caleb go on about they business. They gots to make a livin' too. You'll never get that money back. Never. Now come on back over here, you hear?"

Once Henry continues on his way, and Bruce and his family fade to the sidelines, Caleb settles back onto his seat and ponders about Claretta.

"Claretta's well, son, I'm sure of it."says Henry. He relaxes the reins and gives his full attention to his troubled boy, permitting Old Clara to slowly go on at her own pace, passing still more waving blacks. Henry touches his boy's arm. "You love Claretta very much, don't you?"

Filled with grief, Caleb looks over at his father. "It doesn't matter, Papa. But, Papa, why are they waving at us? We're not important, at least I'm not. If I were, I'd still have friends and a girl."

"Some of them feel you are, son. Even though at this time you don't."

Suddenly running after the Brooks, young, frail-looking children fall in step with the slowly moving wagon, their sights on the delicious-looking crops, but their hearts are with Old Clara, and they forget about their growling stomachs and stroke the side of Caleb's gentle horse as if to rub off some of her perceived magic, while she walks along. Henry watches Caleb, who once again has a smile on his face, as he views the children crowd about Old Clara. "I know I spoke against it, son, but do you and that girl Claretta still have eyes for each other?"

"Claretta wants to marry Billy Joe."

"That poor, backward boy? I don't believe that, Caleb. Why would she . . . unless. . . ."

"Believe it," says Caleb watching the children, who, after stroking Old Clara, reach up to shake his hand.

"Son, those other girls jumping rope and eyin' you back there. What about them?"

Caleb faces Henry. "They're just infatuated with childish passion, Papa. You know that." Caleb turns away once more and seeks sanctuary in his own thoughts.

"You have to forget about Flynn, Caleb, now that the colonel's home." He gently tugs on Caleb's ear, causing the youngsters alongside the wagon to laugh. Then, their hungry sights lock in on the fish and corn, as the Brooks continue talking. "I want to see my grandchildren before I die, son."

"You're never going die, Papa. I won't let you."

"That's almost what Sarah told Naomi about her parents, that they should never die. That she couldn't live if they did. Death, Caleb, awaits all of us. I know you dread it when I talk like this, but it has to be said. You're older, now, and I won't be around forever to watch over you."

Caleb glances from Henry to the children—still staying alongside after six, long blocks; he can see that the children are tired and hungry, but he can't ignore his father's last comment and returns his focus to him, "You've never talked this way before, not about dying. Not this way, Papa," he replies, keeping his voice to a whisper, as not to frighten the young people with words of death.

"It's those kids, who were burned to death all those years ago? Right?" asks Henry. "And that's how you see death, as painful and something to run from?"

"Somebody has to keep their deaths fresh in all of our minds and see that justice is done."

"Do you remember those killings because we're all brothers and sis-

280

ters, or is it Barney? Do you want to punish him, because you feel he murdered those kids, or because he took Flynn from us? You were born to be Jesus' disciple, son, to love, not to hate." Henry sees the fear on Caleb's face. He also sees that trepidation pass away, when Caleb returns his attention to the young children and concentrates on the hunger reflected in their eyes; Henry smiles when Caleb reaches out to the young boys and girls with ears of corn and with fish, seemingly putting aside his own troubles and shouldering theirs, and Henry is reassured that, indeed, as the Bible says, the little children will lead the way, hopefully down the road of the cross for Caleb, making it more sufferable for his son, all the time Caleb pressing a day's meal into the young people's hands, as Henry's heart goes out to them as well.

"Naomi, Caleb. If she's even half right . . . and God wants you to walk this road of Christ, I'll make a trade. Take your place, if I thought, you, ma only son, would die before his old man."

"What did you say?" replies Caleb, breaking off contract with the boisterous children. "I didn't hear you. Did you say 'make a trade?' What trade?"

Henry looks down at the last of the young toddlers still trotting alongside of the wagon and trying to keep up with Old Clara, who has broken into a fast trot, after the others have run for home with their fish and corn. The young boy is called Pee Wee, and Caleb has unknowingly forsaken him in favor of addressing Henry. Now Pee Wee is left with outstretched hands, pleadingly reaching up for some corn and fish, and Henry clearly sees that even as hungry as the young boy is, Pee Wee has no intention of grabbing some of their crops and running off with them. Beaming down at Pee Wee—who, to Henry, resembles Caleb and looks as if the world has left him behind even as Caleb now does—Henry's heart melts, and he reaches over, slows Old Clara to a walk and hands the boy twice as much as had been given to the others. Smiling for joy, Pee Wee runs for home. His mother, who has entered the streets looking for him, sees him coming her way and runs to meet him. "Food, Mamma! The Brooks, they has given us food!" Pee Wee shouts running into his mother's arms.

After hearing the emotional exchange between Pee Wee and his mother, it is then that Caleb and Henry fully realize just how destitute the community really is. Sadly, Henry surveys the bleak-looking neighborhood: Colored Town with all of its rats, roaches and garbage-lined allies, Caleb is doing the same, both wishing they could do more to help and plan to do so.

"Papa," Caleb says, "remember the newspaper story I read to you? The one about that colored man in Atlanta who the courts put to death after they alleged he killed a white woman?"

"The colored man who was strapped to the electric chair and called out, 'Joe Louis, Joe Louis, save me, champ!' "

"Yes. That man. All of us coloreds, including me, are looking for a Joe Louis and successful coloreds like him as our little gods. I know that without heroes to worship we feel we're nothing. The coloreds here are starting to see me as their Joe Louis, and, in doing so, are beginning to feel that they are nothing. I'm not anyone to be worshipped, praised or pampered like Harris or Miller. When I die, if I'm real lucky and there is a heaven, and somebody there hands me a broom and says, 'hence forth, you are now called 'Sweeper,' that'll be the happiest day of my life, because, then, at least, I wouldn't have to end up in that other place, that people like Reverend Harris calls hellfire, to be burned for eternity. Forever, Papa! Can you imagine that? If God caused us to suffer that horror . . . to burn forever, that would make Him worse than the devil, wouldn't it?"

"Caleb, I don't want anyone puttin' pressure on you about this business of what you were born for or not for, okay? 'Cause that's only for me to do, as your pa. Not Naomi, not Flynn or Barney Cutter. God hasn't given me even a hint that you are what Naomi and Sarah seems to want you to be, so don't think of God or the devil with thoughts of Flynn so heavily on your mind now, but, son why didn't you tell me that you and Flynn saved Bruce and Brick's lives?"

"That would be bragging, Pa, and Naomi's not saying anything I can't handle," whispers Caleb, worried "Did you know that Flynn doesn't want to run Shadow Grove? That all he wants to do is to soar free."

"No, Caleb," says Henry following Caleb's sights to the sky. "I had no idea. Is that what you want also, Caleb, to fly like birds? Because I'll not stand in your way, even if it means we have to sell the land and move away from here."

"Pa, I don't really want us to sell our land. What I want, beyond having you always at my side, is to be with my friends and return things as they were and not be troubled."

"Sweet Jesus, you and Flynn . . . So fretful. And Naomi . . . I know about her. Once she gets an idea in her head, not even a dead man can escape her wagging tongue. Son, I love Flynn like he was ma own child, but even Flynn will have to feel my anger if he's sided with that animal and turned against you now."

"He just wants to soar, Papa. Soar like a bird."

The sweet sound of music, streaming from a radio at the nearby pool hall, catches their attention. In front of the disheveled green building, men work on a rundown truck, around which are other junk cars: Packards, Studebakers, Fords, a rusty Cadillac, and a junked-out Chevy truck. In the background, the radio—resting in the pool hall's open window—is playing Billie "Lady Day" Holiday's greatest. Suddenly, a black announcer interrupts the song, the radio volume turned up. The fanning porch women are all ears. Teenage boys turn from their clanging, horseshoe game and listen. Not one jumping rope is zipped though the air or turned, nor a young girl's feet bounce against the hardened ground. All eyes and ears are fixed on the radio. Henry pulls the wagon to the side of the road near the old pool hall and stops, as the radio message slowly sinks in: "Them white folks across the tracks," the radio voice goes on, "are stockin' up on bullets to keep us from gettin' them well-payin' factory jobs. Brothers and sisters, protect yourselves out there in Colored Land."

A muffled, thumping sound clouds the radio's reception, much as if someone's hand has been abruptly placed over the struggling announcer's mouth and the microphone jerked from his grip, his voice hushed, causing a suffocating gloom to hang over the community. "Mamma may have, Papa may have, but God bless the child who's got his own," Billy Holiday's voice once again rules the airwaves.

"Listen to me," Crazy Walter shouts, coming out of nowhere and climbing atop the rusty Caddy. He glares angrily out at the community, which has always been starved for leadership and, at that moment of fear, gladly welcome his; and they quickly gather around him and the old car. "Radio Jake took a big chance on tellin' us what he just did," says Walter—who is not the bravest soul in the world when it comes to being lynched—sheepishly glancing over his shoulder. "I'm sho', by now, that white station owner done fired Radio Jake and our good old Sheriff Richards is a-draggin' po' Jake into the back of his police car at that crosstown local radio station, and he and his deputies is a-whoppin' him good.

Beatin' him all upside his head and everyplace else on his body, a-speci-ly a-cause his proud manhood made him wake us all up."

Many among the blacks groan and lower their heads, some in anger, but no one dares to speak out and awaken the wrath of the Klan as Crazy Walker is doing; all the time, from across the tracks, several whites are gathering and listening now with their own fear, fear that the sleepy black community is awakening.

"I knows I ain't respected much," Walter says to the crowd, "and I knows some of you thinks I'm a clown, but let's embrace each other as brothers and sisters and stand strong and keep goin' after them factory jobs like grownups, fo' what Jake done did fo' us."

Ranting and raving, Reverend Harris shoves his way through men, women and children and towers between them and Walter with raised hands and out-turned palms. "Stay away from this fool," the preacher bellows, many of his church members among the spectators. "You'll only embrace the whirlwind, not them factory jobs that this here trouble-maker don't got sense enough to know that them jobs belong to them white folks and not to us. What you gonna do with all the Jew man's money ifin you get them jobs, Walter?" Harris shouts, now facing Crazy Walter, "buy my people mo' caskets with it? We don't wants to make them whites madder than they already be, especially with the colonel back. You got fast legs, Crazy Walter, the fastest in town, but you can't outrun them there Klan with they trucks, cars, horses and guns, you damn moron. They is gonna catch you and cut off yo' feet and burn you alive like they did them school kids yonder, years ago."

"And still do, Walter," someone calls from the crowd. "Come a-ridin' in the night and dragging us off fo' talkin' like you doin' now, and we never seen again. Get off that car and hush up like Rev. Harris say."

Walter has no intention of backing down, and he shouts over the grumblings, "I'm not afraid. I'm a man!" Nevertheless, he again looks about with concern written on his face, as does everyone else, targeting the growing crowd of whites across the train tracks. From Lana's porch, Mellow Yellow glares scornfully at the whites and then motions to Walter to go on, and he does, getting into a rhythm. "Like that white man said on the radio last year about the evil of whiskey, 'ifin the Klan cuts off ma feet and I can run no mo' . . .'"

"We can't hear you, Walter!" yells a man now feeling the strength of the community's numbers behind him and less afraid of the whites

284

because of Mellow Yellow's abrupt move pushing Walter even more toward leadership of the community.

"... And I can run no mo'," Walter says slightly louder, while still looking about, his courage now fluctuating, after eyeing the crowd of angry whites.

"Look at that fool! He's an idiot," someone bellows from among those in the white community.

"Remember ma warning, Walter," hisses Reverend Harris, "about them feet of yours. You hear them white folk across them tracks same as we do."

"Come on Crazy Walter," Mellow Yellow calls from the porch, knowing that she and her kind have the protection of Sheriff Richards to keep them safe. "Us girls are all behind you!"

Walter's voice rises with confidence and power. "Ifin the Klan cuts off ma feet, and I can't run no mo', I'll hobble on ma ankles, and I'll ankle them Klans to death; and ifin they cuts off my ankles, and I can't ankle 'em to death no mo', I'll jump around on ma footless legs, and I'll leg 'em to death; and ifin they cuts off ma legs to ma knees, and I can't leg 'em to death no mo', I'll use ma knees, and I'll knee 'em to death; and ifin they cuts off my upper thighs to ma crotch, and I can't stand up and upper leg 'em to death no mo', I'll fall on ma back, and I'll use ma hands, and I'll choke 'em to death."

In the wagon with Henry and sporting a wide grin, Caleb nudges his father, then continues listening to Walter with great surprise and admiration for the man.

"And ifin they cuts off my hands, and I can't choke 'em no mo', I'll use ma lower arms, and I'll arm 'em to death; and ifin they cuts off ma arms all the way to ma elbows, and I can't arm 'em to death no mo', I'll use ma elbows, and I'll elbow 'em to death; and ifin they cuts off ma upper arms to my shoulders, and I can't elbow 'em to death no mo', I'll use ma mouth, and I'll bite 'em to death; and ifin them damnable Klansmen pull out ma teeth, and I can't bite 'em to death no mo', I'll use my gums, and I'll gum 'em to death; and ifin they sew up ma mouth, and I can't gum 'em to death no mo', I'll use ma eyelashes, and I'll blink 'em to death; and ifin they plucks out ma eyelashes, and I can't blink 'em to death no mo', I'll use ma eyes, and I'll look 'em to death; and ifin they pokes out my eyes with a stick, and I can't look 'em to death no mo', I'll use ma brains like Caleb Brooks—no matter ifin, he's from God or

285

not—and I'll think 'em to death 'til they go back to their home in hell, and you—out there in Colored Town—go to your home in heaven, and I go wherever men like me who go nowhere, not even to church, end up going wherever they go after we dies."

Caleb is stunned to hear his name mentioned, but more than that, he's amazed to see what happens next: mass courage. Oblivious of the whites all around them, the blacks go wild, and the cheering is deafening. However, the whites have gathered in full strength along the train tracks, their angry eyes and ears targeting Colored Town, ready to explode onto them. Moved by Walter's speech to the point of religious insanity, the fan women pounce off their porches; and with one hand fanning their dark faces, the other on their hips, they chicken strut down close-by mule trails, their children following, imitating their movement, their thumbs tucked under their small arm pits, their elbows flapping, wiggling their way as if closer to "my God to thee," crowing as if chickens, the wall of whites, gawking across the train rails as if at out-of-control zoo animals.

"Let's all go to the church and pray," says Harris, taking note of the fuming whites and shouting loud enough for them to hear that he, at least, should not be visited at night by the Klan, when he's done his best to defeat Walter's way of thinking among the blacks. "God will show us how to survive without them factory jobs," Harris yells on. "He always has. All we need to do is practice His teachin' of patience, peace and love and He will continue to provide for us."

When the blacks finally recover from their momentary lunacy and take close notice of the whites, who abruptly boo and heave rocks at them, the crowd about the Cadillac and Walter quickly leaves him and follows Harris to the church. Walter, though—now in a frenzy and seemingly unaware of the loud "boos" and the flung rocks, or the white storm which has built alone the train tracks and ready to pounce on him—loudly exclaims to the withdrawing blacks. "Reverend Harris wants you to keep bendin' over, while them K.K.K. keeps stickin' they white dicks up you' tight, dumb, black asses. You won't end up in hell with Satan, like Harris says, ifin you fight fire with fire. The devil's right here in Cutterville. Wake up befo' it's too late. Get guns and kill the bastards befo' they kill us."

On the whorehouse porch, along with Lana and the dozen other scantily-dressed, young females, Mellow Yellow watches Walter, her chest swollen with pride. "Remind me to give Walter some free pussy the next time I see him," she tells Lana.

"Ifin he lives that long," Lana cautions, spotting Hank's pickup scattering the line of whites and speeding across the train tracks into Colored Town, a truck hauling several armed men on its bed. The battered vehicle squats down to a shrieking, dipping stall near Henry's wagon. Crazy Walter sees it, leaps from the Caddy and into the swarming black masses.

"You got a lot of balls, boy," yells Dane, exiting the truck cab. "Come back here, Walter, so I can cut off them big balls of yours, then them legs, teeth and them big lips and eyeballs!"

The men leap off the back of the truck, firing their revolvers in the air while running after the petrified Walter. Old Hank—much too elderly to run now—knows that no white man can catch Walter in a foot race, and the aging Klansman sits calmly behind the wheel of his junky truck, cleans his thick eyeglasses and patiently waits for his peers to return. He's been told by Barney how to catch Walter and will so instruct the others. The slippery, county-smart Klansman looks toward the square. Behind the wall of silent whites, just off of the empty square, sits Barney in his Cadillac, and with him, as if being given a dry run on survival of the strongest, is Flynn, his posture slumped over, his head held low. Barney—with a single gesture of his hand—has silenced the white crowd and has freighted their feet to the ground on their side of the train tracks, instead of permitting them to go storming into the black community and causing an all-out, out-of-control race riot and putting Cutterville unfavorably in the news across the country. Old Hank is religiously watching Barney's every move, as his sights now shift to Lana's place, and then Barney sets his sights on his old sidekick Hank, the crowd turning their heads as one and also looking at Hank. Barney nods to Hank and drives away.

Hank, smiling, continues nodding at the car as it fades from sight, his aging eyes and nodding head saying that he is fiercely loyal to Barney. Once the Cadillac disappears completely from sight, ever so slowly, the pro that he is, Hank puts on his clean bifocals, scrutinizes Lana's house and zeros in on Mellow Yellow, as Barney had indicated him to do. Yes, he would so instruct the rest of the Klan that Barney is now in charge and back to stay, with Flynn being well groomed to become the next Grand

Wizard over all of Georgia and then over all of America, first as a United States Senator, then as President.

Barney had calculated that Crazy Walter was not only crazy, he knows that Walter is a sex-starved animal, and that Walter would be drawn back to Mellow Yellow like the bees to flowers, but Barney had not counted on Lana's years of savvy about dealing with the white man. She watches the dust from Barney's car fade and then locks her gaze on Hank and his well-known truck.

"Get word to Walter," Lana tells her black handyman, watching also from the porch. "We all know where he's going to hide. Right? Tell him to never come back here . . . that Barney's set a trap for him through one of our girls. He'll know who that is." She ends up eyeing Mellow Yellow, who nods that she understands and is in agreement.

From the wagon, Caleb watches Lana's handyman race from the porch, bound onto his old bicycle and pedals off—as fast he can go—in the direction that Walter had run, swinging clear of the angry, out-of-breath, returning white gunmen as he does. Wanting nothing more than to leave that lawlessness behind, Caleb faces Henry. "Shouldn't we turn back for home and try selling the corn and fish at Sarah's store?" he asks Henry, eyeing the returning Klansmen.

"Sarah has her own troubles and we got us a mortgage to finally pay off to the bank, son."

Henry picks up the reins, stoically faces the whites and gently lashes Old Clara, who pulls the wagon, lumping it over the train tracks into the white community and through the line of silently leering whites who are still obeying Barney's call for cooler heads. While crossing the tracks, the Brooks are unaware that some of their crops are toppling from the wagon as they go.

Hungry, white children scoop up the dropped vegetables as Henry focuses on the town monster that started all the trouble: Dessen's sprawling tire factory. Once they pass beyond the whites and their railroad line of defense, the Brooks continue on toward the train station.

Henry abruptly stops Old Clara. Just ahead of them, a dozen white women in their flimsy dime-store, floral-patterned dresses and patent-leather shoes, are spread across the street, near the factory and blocking Old Clara's path.

"Who told you goddamn Brooks you could come into my neighborhood, after what that tar baby Walter said to insult us? Who? Damn you!" one of the women yells.

As the females glare at Caleb and Henry, their barefoot, thumb-sucking children—standing at their sides—gawk at the Brooks, as well. A couple hundred feet away, the husbands of many of the angry females are milling back and forth in front of the plant employee's entrance and yelling, "Get rid of the niggers and give us them jobs." One man out of desperation throws a rock at an armed factory guard, who is looking down at them from his position atop a high wall.

The guard is struck in his face, and an angry security team sweep from the building with wooden clubs, scattering the protesting men—including the street-blocking women and their children—who run screaming for home, only to immediately return when the guards retreat behind the factory wall, and Dane, who comes out of nowhere, ordering them to stand their ground.

Henry turns Old Clara toward the train station, just off of the square, the only place coloreds are permitted to sell their wares in White Town; the dark barbeque smoke and the smell of honey and molasses and slow-cooked ham is rising in the air from the stationhouse grounds, a place where the powers-to-be—the railway companies and others like them—have demanded that Cutterville allow blacks to cook for and service the train companies' clientele outside on the station's grounds, just a short distance away from Henry and Caleb now, where a half dozen blacks wait for the arrival of the next trains, those which lack dining cars. They now wait to shine the white layover passengers' shoes, to serve up carry-out, brown-bagged, fried fish, chicken, cooked grits, greens or fresh corn—which are all purchased from Henry's wagon. The blacks also serve hot biscuits, buttered cornbread, peach and apple pies and frosty, cold milk, packed in tubs of ice. As Henry heads Old Clara and the wagon to the stationhouse, the blacks there are extremely nervous; Packing up their gear, black businessmen keep an eye on the returning white women and their children; one of the women and her young ones are racing alongside Henry's wagon screaming and spitting at him, while Dane laughs.

"You coons got all the jobs we gonna let that Jew give you! Now get!" the woman yells, looking back at Dane as if for instructions.

The black businessmen at the train station watch as the woman and her children reach into Henry's wagon and steal his merchandise, followed by an onrush of other hand-grabbing whites, fighting each other to be first to plunder the Brooks' goods. At the same time, the train-yard blacks see the whites who had remained at the train tracks now running and screaming toward them. The blacks at the stationhouse take what they can carry of their belongings, and run with them across the tracks into the black community. Caleb takes the reins from his father, who doesn't protest and, instead, watches Caleb take his first step into manhood, as he lashes Old Clara and heads him and his father out of there, as the whites swarm the train station and seize all of what the black men have left behind. Henry and Caleb's livelihood would have to wait another day, and as they retreat across the tracks, Caleb stands up in the wagon.

"God dammit!" he yells. "Enough is enough!"

19
The Potentate Awakens

The following day, Caleb and Henry agreed not go to Shadow Grove and work under Colonel Cutter, for Sarah yes, but not for that butcher of Cutterville, who has now seemingly taken over the plantation, including Sarah and Flynn. On this day long before the butterflies, singing birds, and the soothing sounds and swells and smell of the ocean's spray permeates his land, Henry has gotten up at four in the morning and has harnessed two of his plow horses to their wagon of replenished corn. He had tossed in a fishing pole and left for the lagoon. Because of Caleb's outrage when they were forced from the train station by the whites, Henry—having never seen Caleb so angry—had told his boy to remain behind and rest for another hour, and to let Old Clara do the same, then meet him at the lagoon if he wishes. Caleb agreed, but his heart wasn't in it. It's been nearly an hour since he promised Henry he'd remain home, and Caleb moves about in discomfort, his arms pillowed under his head as he lies there—fully dressed on his bed—listening to the alarm clock ticking away. He notices a ladybug crawling across the ceiling; standing up on the bed and carefully lifting the guardian of their crops onto his fingertip, Caleb releases the small insect out the window. From the window, he watches the first light of dawn creeping over the eastern horizon. Then, again, he lies on the bed, pillows his arms under his head and watches the hands of the tabled clock slowly inch around the wind-up time piece. Caleb is deeply troubled, because—even though Henry was eventually able to speak with Sarah about it, and Sarah has said not to worry, that she will make sure the colonel does not use the dock and new boat as a first step to seize their land—Caleb feels that Barney will somehow manage to take everything from them, even as he knows that Flynn is slowly being taken away from him and Henry by his menacing father. Suddenly, the wall phone rings. Rushing into the kitchen, Caleb answers it.

"Hello!"

"Caleb. This is Flynn."

"Where are you? Something is wrong. I can hear it in your voice. What is it?"

"I'm on the highway, not far from your place, at Jowers' gas station. I left the plantation on foot by a back road and hitchhiked, so as not to be seen using one of our horses or trucks. Can we meet? We need to talk. Mr. Jowers said he's coming your way in about fifteen minutes and will drop me off on Old Country Road, about a mile from your place. I'll walk the rest of the way through the woods and meet you at the lagoon. It'll take a half hour or so."

"Where on Old Country Road, so I can come and get you on Old Clara? It's dangerous to walk through the woods this early when there's not much light to see where you're stepping."

"No, Caleb. I'll be okay. There will be plenty of daylight soon, and I need to walk and think. Just be at the lagoon when I get there. Okay?"

"Okay."

Caleb hangs up the phone, races from the house and then stops in the middle of the front yard. He looks over at Old Clara, peacefully grazing in the meadow under the first gray light of dawn. He thinks about going after Flynn anyway and using Old Clara to get there in a hurry. He decides in favor of Henry's wisdom, that Old Clara deserves a rest.

Caleb makes up his mind to catch up to Flynn in the swamps before he reaches the lagoon, which will give them more time to talk together, as they walk. He then sprints back into the house and into his room and hurriedly slips off his low-cut shoes and into his buckskin boots. The section of the swamp where Flynn wants to cross is about forty minutes away; if he's lucky, Caleb tells himself, he'll be there before Flynn arrives. He races headlong across the yard, through the fence gate, across the pasture, past Old Clara and through the woods about their land, accelerating with the elated anticipation of being with Flynn again; it's difficult to see the joy in Caleb's alluring, light-brown eyes or the smile across his golden-tan face. The bright morning sunlight finally breaks over the horizon and streams through the treetops revealing only moments of Caleb's classic features with him moving so fast. It's far easier to make out his clothing, his patched, blue coveralls and snake-bite-resistant, buckskin boots, as he takes his shortcuts through the ominous swamp. Immune against the gadflies and waterbugs, Caleb loves that quagmire swamp part of their world, which touches their land on three sides with simmering heat and beautiful, endless flagrant bloom; Henry has protected him from the Klan, thanks in part to the swamp's cosmos of snakes. The Klan speaks as if belonging to Reverend Miller's church, but actually never go there for fear of Miller's snakes; they also fear the swamps for the same reason: snakes. Caleb knows that the surrounding cape of fear—which most outsiders must use to get to their land—and his father will go on watching over him as long as it and Henry lives and survives the onslaught of Barney's land-grabbing hand of greed. The snakes alone should be enough to keep Colonel Cutter away, to say nothing about what the disease-carrying mosquitoes would do to a frail man of his age.

There is only one problem: Caleb is not aware of the stunning development in Barney's health. While he runs, thoughts of his father comes to mind. Barney isn't half the man that Henry is, Caleb thinks, sprinting past a towering, pine tree reminding him of his father's strength. *What a remarkable man,* he muses. To him, Henry's only weakness is that he puts too much hope in the Bible. Though Caleb feels he will never put his trust in the Bible, he knows that the confidence others see in him stems from Henry's love of the Good Book. Even with his undying love for his father, Caleb is troubled about some of Henry's ideas. On the one hand, Naomi, Sarah and Henry are always saying that God is with him, Caleb, and will protect him, but when it comes to the side of churches where Christ's disciples were told to go out and preach against evil, even unto giving up their lives in some cases, Henry often cautions him about speaking out against racially-motivated rules of iniquity. In Georgia it's dangerous to talk about such things, Caleb knows that. But where is Henry's faith when it comes right down to God's protection for him, Caleb, if Henry has to worry so about his and Caleb's life?

In spite of Henry's warnings, Caleb has begun speaking out against segregation to anyone who will listen, more so after he saw his father humiliated, embarrassed and driven out of Cutterville, which motivated him to call out: "Enough is enough!"

Birds sing to Caleb from the trees, and billions of blades of grass crunch under the heels and soles of his boots, as if welcoming his crushing might against their green brows. Again, Caleb thinks of moving away: to California. Yes. He will ask Flynn to do the same when they meet. Suddenly, from out of the blue, a series of ghostly, young voices cry out to him: "Caleb! Caleb. Don't move away! Don't move to California! Help us!" The sky is immediately eclipsed by hundreds of clamoring parrots. The winged creatures begin mimicking those young, human voices between their piercing caws. Stopping in his tracks, Caleb knows that the voices are those of the mutilated black school children, the ones who were burned before he was born, the ones he dreams about. Caleb watches the parrots explode into a towering white cumulus cloud, leaving behind a deafening silence, sucking in at his racing heart. Then, another awareness is suddenly upon him; he hears the sobs of the boy who cried over those mutilated black children, the sobs of the gap-toothed boy Marcus, who a powerful Spirit had revealed to young Charles Pennington—as he had stood with his Saint Bernard dog and witnessed the killing of those children. Convinced that he's imagining things, Caleb forces himself to dismiss all thoughts of voices calling him from the dead or from anywhere else. Then he looks over his shoulder. He's shocked and nearly passes out from the horror; his shadow has separated itself from him with a path of bright sunlight marking the shadowless grass between him and his full-length, black image behind him. Blinking in disbelief, testing his logic against the insanity of that heartstopping sight, Caleb stands there with an open mouth, as the shadow points to the shadowless grass between them.

When Caleb thinks he's seen it all, a gray sheet, flapping in the breeze, with a human head, rises out of the grass between him and his darkened reflection, and the sheet monster glares at him.

"So that you will know the power that's in me," the head says, "I am he who has commanded your shadow to stand back from me and from you. Follow me, Caleb Brooks, and you will rule even over Barney Cutter, over all whites north of the equator and over all brown souls south of it, leaving the rest of the poles to Barney."

Caleb wants to turn and run, but is immediately locked to the ground by the creature's might and can only stare back at the ghostly-looking figure in dread, its face as black as night itself. "Maybe, by the fear I see in you, you are not he who was prophesied as the one who would fiercely battle against Barney Cutter," the evil specter says. "The one who was prophesied would be one who would fight like Samson and not fear me, would pull down the pillars of fear that bind him as Samson did the pillars of the palace of the Philistines. If you are the chosen one, Caleb Brooks," the ghostly head goes on pointing to a large, moss-covered tree, "go there and pull down that tree, that I might know who you are, and I will double my offer to you with an added gift of a mountain of gold."

The stench of cooked flesh suddenly permeates the air, as—once

294

again—the frightened cries from those long-ago murdered, school children cry out, "Run from him, Caleb, or he will capture you for eternity, as he has us! He's Satan."

"Get behind me, Satan." says Caleb, not knowing why he chose those words.

"You are he!" shouts the figure. "Otherwise they would not call to you. But not yet with your powers to destroy Barney!" The specter charges at Caleb with a huge scythe then stops as Caleb steps back. "I have many horrific faces to force mankind to do my bidding, Caleb Brooks, but one which is so beautiful that men like you, as well as women, gaze upon my flesh with lust in their hearts. Look upon my godly body and lie down with me." Satan changes from a sheet with a head into a sculptured, breathtaking, nude man of beauty. The swamp is immediately engulfed in fog, and the sound of thundering horse hooves are heard shaking the ground as they approach. The devil steps back from Caleb and fades into thin air. Caleb sees why the evil spirit vanished when a powerful, white stallion gallops out of the thick haze toward him. The mighty steed prances about Caleb as if on a mattress of air, and on that invincible horse—straddling a blanket, instead of a saddle—the black practitioner of fear's eyes of fire glare down at him. It's Naomi. Adorned in deerskin garments and boots, the glorious-looking woman is also enriched with Indian beads and a red headband, within which has been placed those two pieces of broken black feathers one on either side of her head, in the manner of owls' ears. Caleb knows about that feather and how it was said to have been broken in half and flung on the barn floor to save his life. He looks behind him and sees only the fog, but he can clearly see that separated, free-standing shadow of his, and he knows that the sheeted creature, with the scythe, unseen as it may be, is still lurking nearby in that curtain of gray mist and watching them. Had Naomi now arrived in that troublesome moment to save him, or had she come to destroy him for not embracing God, as had not the walking sheet from hell—which had tempted him with sex—because it had thought that he had chosen God over evil?

Naomi just sits there on that glorious dancing horse, as if waiting for a sign to bring more misery down on him or, indeed, to kill him in the name of God, the Herculean horse moving her body in oneness with its powerful gyration from those graceful, prancing legs, feet and unshod hooves. The four-legged creature's mighty breath, escaping from its nostrils, scatters the fog about Caleb and its massive head with a thunderous exhaling of fire, while continuing to toe dance in place. Caleb has never seen Naomi this way. He knows she considers her visions both a gift and a curse, and he sees that the one she carries with her now gives her no joy.

"What do you want, Naomi?" he asks in consternation, back stepping and bending down searching for a rock to hurl at her, while—at the same time—looking behind him for the sheeted one.

Naomi closes her eyes, her face grimaces, her body quakes, her arms tremble, stretched out to her sides. She's in the grip of two forces, each tugging at her, a bizarre sight, as she struggles in one of her unpredictable spells. When they take hold of her Naomi, herself, has said it's because her faith has weakened, and that the devil is trying to lure her away from him—Caleb—and from God. Abruptly, she begins speaking, "So that you will see and believe, Caleb Brooks," she tells him, her eyes still shut against her pain, as she goes on while being tugged this way and that, "God has willed that you should witness the forces of good and evil." His eyes opened wide, Caleb sees that gray sheeted figure jerking on Naomi's right arms and a winged angel pulling on her left. Then they fade away, and only the horse, Naomi and her violent jerking and pulling motions are left. There are those who warn that to speak to her, now, would be to chance being turned into a frog from the powers in those pieces of broken feather. Then a soul-shaking vision wrenches at Naomi's guts, ready to pour forth, and Caleb studies her with apprehension. He sees a rock and seizes it. Naomi opens her eyes and turns her barbaric sights on him. "Put that damn rock down, Caleb Brooks," she scolds.

It's the devil controlling her, he tells himself, and the rock falls from his hand.

"Woman!" Caleb shouts, no longer willing to give in to his fear, taking his second step toward manhood, "have you lost your mind or been smoking jimson? You're disturbing me shaking like that." Naomi turns her head toward the horizon, and the fog lifts. On the skyline, ten mile away, Caleb sees Cutterville glowing white in the grips of the dazzling dawn. Suddenly, astonishing blackness of night swallows up the faroff town. Caleb finds that he can actually hear the cries coming from the citizens of Cutterville in dismay over that abrupt darkness in their town. Yet, at the swamp it remains day-bright, but then, the darkness sweeps toward the swamp, sending birds fleeing through the countryside ahead of it, and—in seconds—it gobbles up the birds and turns the sky over the swamp and Henry's land into night. Caleb nearly sinks to his knees in dismay. With the swarthiness all around them, Naomi now speaks to him in a ghost-like tone of voice: "Those young children, Caleb, the ones you dreamed about off and on in your young life, you've told yourself that they are dead and cannot be harmed by man again. But the souls of those innocent kids who were raped and burned, are still hanging from Cutter Bridge," she exclaims, pointing to the distant bridge of doom, "They are held there by the hand of Satan, just as surely as you and I are now under his powerful spell of darkness."

Her chilling words rekindle Caleb's pulsating dread, especially as she reveals even more of those young lives to him. "Before these kids' spirits can be freed to enter heaven from that bridge—that living, wooden structure—its evil heart has to be cut out and destroyed by you, Caleb." Caleb looks at the bridge.

"Look you well, Caleb Brooks and know this, this mighty horse is my only protection from Lucifer, and it and I have but a limited ability to protect you for a while longer. But the Light of your life is ready to shine down on you and protect you from Satan's evil presence here, even though you refuse to seize onto Its mighty power. Take the power, Caleb, for even now, an innocent boy and girl's blood is about to flow in the streets of Cutterville, set in motion by Satan, when he used God's Holy Bible to harden that town's heart, and now is here, trying to reach into you and into me." Immediately, a wailing winds roars into the swamp, as if to drown out her voice, but Naomi goes on, exclaiming over its might.

"The Klan and the Bible must be made to part company," she says, the wind hammering away at her. "No, Satan!" she cries aloud. "He has not yet the power to fight you, and you cannot force me to leave him to you."

Caleb's baffled response echoes through the chilly darkness and over the howling wind: "Nobody will ever separate the Klan from that Book of Burden. It's their holy justification to murder."

"Your views of the Bible are well known, Caleb Brooks," Naomi calls to him, the wind threatening to topple her from the horse. She endures, though, exclaiming on. "But the Holy Book—be it written in man's mind, or residing in mosques, cathedrals, synagogues, tabernacles, temples, basilicas, churches or placed in houses of prostitution—is a double-edged sword, and—as it is with all of man's sacred writings, which evil invades and attempts to destroy—there is the good side and there is the other, the evil side."

"If it is a double-edged sword," Caleb demands, feeling less threatened by the dark now, the more he goes on, "why is it that poor coloreds keep hanging on the good side of the sword when our fingers bleed with such pain from it? The Klan hangs on the evil side of that Bible and never bleeds? That's what makes me so afraid, people and the way they will follow any church and any preacher who waves his angry Bible at them. If the preacher is evil, then his Bible is evil, and those who worship in his church are evil, because they have not been told the truth and worship an evil lie."

"It's your mind, Caleb. Ain't that really your double-edged sword? Your God-given intelligence, a thing the devil knows you're afraid of, as much as you are of that freight train that passes near here and where them kids—who only wanted to attend school and learn—were hanged and burned, afraid that you too will be killed because of your knowledge?" Caleb turns toward the sound of the Grim Reaper: the far-off train, a train as if calling to him, as it speeds toward the swamp. He whirls back toward Naomi with a blistering defense:

"The Klan has tossed many an uppity one of us under the wheels of that train. What are you afraid of, Naomi? There must be something that frightens you, if I'm afraid, and you say I'm so special. What? What, then, frightens you—you who has lost much of your power. This so-called devil thing out here with us? Are you afraid of it?"

"Devil thing' you say and persist in your disbelief. You've just faced him with his scythe, Caleb, and you still refuse to believe your own eyes. The Mandorla, son. The Light of Love. That's what I fear, that like the wife of Lot, I will be turned into a pillar salt for daring to look upon the Light of pure Love for a second time without being invited to do so by God, which the devil is trying to tempt me to do, even now. The Light, it still lingers, Caleb. Through you! It lives in your thoughts waiting for you to call upon It with love and humility."

Naomi squeezes her eyes shut and turns her head away from him, as immediately, an explosion of Light erupts in Caleb's head and he sees a year-old, silver-blonde boy, sprinkled with snow, reaching out in Naomi's direction; he sees the boy struggle to his feet from blankets on the barn floor, while carrying a newborn; he sees the barn doors swing open, sees the boy and the baby being swallowed up into the Light. The Light that only their eyes were allowed to see.

"What does it mean!" he cries out to Naomi, his hands frantically brushing away that burned-in image of the boy and the infant against his eyes. The morning sun abruptly returns, and once again daylight enters the swamp. When Caleb opens his eyes, he sees the beauty of a blue sky and white clouds over Cutterville as well as over his father's land. Naomi stares down at him from her horse, and he jumps all over her: "Now, don't you dare try and tell me that what just happened makes me like you. If you're so worried about the Klan, Naomi Bell, use that powerful brain of yours, and you destroy them, and you and God leave me alone, and that horse. Did you train it to move about like that to confuse me or did God? You've made me late, woman, and now I'll have to run my ass off directly to the lagoon to get there in time."

"I'm only the mirror that reflects the power," she calls out to him, as he runs away. "I'm not the potentate. You are!" Her shoulders slump in despair, as he continues to run without looking back at her, and she yells to him, "Caleb Brooks, sometimes I feel like slapping the living hell right out of you! He will not be at that lagoon when you get there. Satan has left here and has entered into that young boy's mind, and that unrecognized evil spirit infused Flynn with fear, which urged him to leave, and Flynn abided in it and did leave with his hand in that of Satan's."

"Go to hell, Naomi," Caleb yells, looking back at her, as he continues running away.

"The next time you and Flynn are on that lagoon," she exclaims at the top of her voice, "look into the reflection of the night water, and you will see that you are the real power of life and death on this earth, not me, not the Klan; God has said that your hand and your hand alone will prevail over your best friend's life, as He has proclaimed! You asked about this horse. It's not time for this mighty creature of God to rise into the sky. Not yet. Soon, though . . . very soon, God will command this horse and me to fly."

Sprinting, gagging and out of breath, Caleb reaches the bank of the lagoon. Flynn's new boat is tied to the dock, but his friend is not anywhere to be seen. "Over here, Caleb. I've been waiting for you," Henry calls as he stands a few yards away by the horses and wagon, which is loaded down with the freshly picked corn and recently caught, iced fish.

Wearily, Caleb makes his way to his father and both climb into the wagon.

"He was to meet me here, Papa. Flynn was. Do you think the Klan or Dane saw him on the road and stopped him from coming or worse, hurt him like that thing back there tried to hurt me?"

"What thing, Caleb? Are you talking about Barney?" Henry looks over his shoulder. "That poor boy," he mutters. "Wants so much to be loved, but his pa wants to keep Flynn away from us. Barney, Caleb. They say that Barney has become as strong as a bull, that he is like a living god." Caleb follows Henry's gaze to Barney's swiftly-moving red car.

"Yes, son, Flynn just left. He said you were supposed to meet him here. That's before his pa came and took him away, after that tired boy said he hitchhiked and then walked the rest of the way to the lagoon." Henry examines the sky as he goes on. "At the very moment Barney was putting out his evil hand to his son and Flynn took it, the birds all went wild, and the very sky turned black as night. Both that poor boy and I was so afraid, but not Barney, Caleb. Not Barney. He was right at home and laughing under that dark blanket of evil that covered the heavens. And Caleb, when his father touched him, the boy seemed so afraid, afraid of you, Caleb." Caleb sees Flynn looking back in fear at him from the car. Henry goes on, "I told you that God never gave me a hint that He wanted you to come unto Him, and until He did, I told myself to resist what Naomi was saying about you and our Lord. He did, Caleb. Gave me that hint when the devil made the day sky turn black. It was God who led me to read Flynn's terrified look. Flynn . . . Dear Jesus! It was as if that boy was looking at me with the power of Satan, telling him that I was his enemy, on top of telling you was going to kill him, Caleb."

"Papa, let's not go into Cutterville, not now after this."

"We still need money, son, and there are those in town, even with this dark day frightening them half to death, who are hungry with no money to buy food, and even if we can't sell it, we owe it to God to give this food away to the poor." Looking at the sky, Henry adds, "and that's what I intend to do."

"What about Crazy Walter, Papa?"

"What about him, Caleb?"

"I don't really know why I asked," Caleb replies. "Unless it was to say that he also must be hungry."

Caleb sits in total silence, the weight of the world on his shoulders, as Henry lashes the horse and starts them on their way, to Cutterville, where it's rumored that the railroad people raised hell with Mayor Sipple about the white rioters chasing the blacks away from the train station, and it's said that Mayor Sipple made a deal with the Klan to lay off of the black venders. Now whites have settled down and are no longer taking out their anger on all blacks. For now, they've concentrated on catching and killing only Crazy Walter with Sipple's blessings.

As Henry and Caleb leave, the sheet-like phantom, with its night-dark eyes, waits and watches from the shadows, its eyes on Caleb. Then that substance of evil begins changing into a huge snake.

20

The Viper

Early the following morning, while harvesting their sun-ripened ears of corn, Caleb and Henry move between the tall stocks, sweating profusely as they toil. After Caleb drives the horses and wagon to a new location and stops, he picks up a towel from the seat and dries the sweat from his face, then glances down in surprised. A baseball glove and bat is resting on the wagon seat; at that moment, Henry catches up to him and the wagon and follows Caleb's gaze to the bat and glove, then beams up at Caleb.

"You've been quiet all morning, Caleb."

"Papa, how can Flynn even think I'd have hurt him, let alone kill him?"

"I put that glove and bat there for a reason, Caleb. Take 'em and go to Shadow Grove and join in that game, like the others boys and girls there sent word they want you to do. I'll be okay."

"I can't do that. Play ball with the colored kids and not the whites as well, on that segregated plantation. And especially not until Flynn knows I would never harm him."

Henry finally gives up on trying to persuade Caleb, and after working in silence and plucking countless ears of corn and tossing them into the wagon, Henry, worn out, shakes his head in dismay and again addresses Caleb, who is covered with sweat and frozen in thought.

"Now that Barney has returned and refused to let Flynn or his workers help us, it's hopeless to try and harvest these crops with just the two of us, son."

Angry about all the work he and Henry have done to help on Shadow Grove, regardless of whether Barney hates coloreds or not, Caleb feels that Flynn should have been there for them.

"Excuse me, Papa. I need to cool off," he says, jumping from the wagon with the towel. After Caleb leaves, Henry sees a cloud of dust moving fast down the road toward their property. He climbs onto the wagon for a better view. It's a convoy of trucks, horses and men, led by Flynn, riding hard, shortcutting across the potato fields ahead of the others on his stallion; a huge smile crosses Henry's lips, and now there is a sparkle in his eyes. He looks back at Caleb who is watching from their front yard, where he's bending over and splashing a bucket of water from their well over his glossy head of curls. When Flynn rides up on his horse, Henry jumps from the wagon and greets the dusty blonde boy at a place where the wall of corn plants meet the edge of the road.

Henry hugs the smiling young master of Shadow Grove. "I knew you'd somehow come in spite of your pa."

"He's away and doesn't know I'm here," says Flynn, eyeing Caleb. He continues. "Just Mother and I and, of course, the workers."

The trucks, horses and wagons arrive minutes later, and Sarah's field hands pile off their vehicles, their horses, their wagons and their mules. Leading them is field boss Keith Collins, with his freckled face and kind, green eyes beaming over at Henry as if to say that they were going to get the job done no matter who says they can't. Collins and his men roll up their sleeves and enter Henry's fields. At the same time, a white Rolls Royce pulls up alongside Henry and Flynn. A Texas-size, suntanned man, dressed in an off-white suit and cowboy boots and wearing a light-colored, wide-brimmed, Stetson hat, steps from the luxury car. With him are two other men in dark business suits. For a moment Caleb stands there looking at the trucks, at the workers and at the man in the near-white suit and wide-brim hat. Caleb then quickly dries his head, face and neck with the towel, tosses it aside, and runs back to his father's side.

"What's all this?" Caleb hears Henry ask Flynn, who faces the tall stranger.

"Henry, Caleb, this is Thomas Whittier from Atlanta."

"The same Whittier," asks Henry, "who owns all them grocery stores across Georgia?"

"In the flesh," says Whittier with a twinkle in his eyes. "I've come to talk about your crops, your corn, your tomatoes, your greens, Mister Brooks," says the man of means.

Whittier follows Caleb's surprised gaze to Sarah's workers. Along with the crew Whittier himself has brought along; the workers are hurriedly off-loading line after line of lightweight, pine crates from the convoy of trucks that now stretch around Henry's fields. While father and son look at each other in amazement, some of Whittier's workers break off from the main group and set up an assembly line, a collecting and packing station, while others of their peers quickly go to work in the fields picking the mature crops alongside Sarah's people. Whittier shakes Henry's hand, then Caleb's. "When I make up my mind, he tells Caleb, "I didn't mess around. That's why I brought my best team." Caleb—stunned by the fast-moving events around them—regards Flynn, who winks at him. "I told you, Caleb," he teases. "I also have a brain. Did you think that Mother and I'd not know that you guys needed help? We are the three musketeers, after all, you, I and Henry."

What Caleb does not understand in all of this is Flynn. Is he or is he not afraid of him? Henry is also having difficulty understanding what is happening with Flynn, but does not linger with the thought for long. He faces Whittier and asks, "How in the world? All of these trucks, your crew and Keith Collins and Sarah's . . ." He reaches over and hugs Flynn. "And Master Flynn here. Why would you—"

"The 'why,'" Whittier says, "is the train passengers that travel through Cutterville, and the 'how' is from our local chain-store managers who say that after some of our customers have eaten your vegetables on one of those flag stops in Cutterville and on down the line, from the vendors you sold them to, they don't want to buy ours, most of which are marred by this twelve-state drought in the South and in part of the North. Talk like that, customers not wanting to buy from us, spread faster than a Texas prairie fire." He plucks an ear of corn from the overhanging roadside growth, opens the husk, sinks his teeth into the crisp kernels and swallows the sweet nectar. He beams with delight. When Whittier glances about for a place to discard the partly consumed corn, Caleb takes it from him and places it on the ground among the growing stocks. The excited mogul goes on. "Flynn here says you guys never use pesticides on your crops. What is your secret to growing such beautiful vegetables? And that sky yesterday. Wasn't that strange?"

"God's created the red bugs," Henry nods in agreement and says, "science the pesticides. My bet is on God."

"God? 'Red bugs?'" asks Whittier.

"Ladybugs," Flynn says. He chuckles when a ladybug lands on Whittier's hat. "They eat the harmful insects. There's a ladybug on your hat now."

"I see what you mean," says Whittier, after removing his hat and grinning at the winged lady. He gently blows and watches the lady lift into the air. Replacing his hat, Whittier gets down to business. "Sarah Winthrop and Master Flynn," he begins, then rests his hand on Flynn's shoulder, as if to apologize for referring to Sarah by her well-known maiden name and not by the despised name of Flynn's father. "Sarah," he continues, "still has powerful friends in Georgia as did your grandparents, Flynn, and some of us will never forget how much that brilliant man and woman did for this great state in terms of their contributions to the arts, medicine, and agriculture, but more important than that was their ongoing battle with our legislators to force them into changing the laws and dragging Georgia kicking and screaming into the twentieth century in line with some of the European countries, and out of the dark ages, when it comes to our racial relations here, not that the job is finished. We still have a long way to go yet in this country to make life better for all of our citizens."

Flynn beams with chest-swelling bride when Whittier speaks so well of his fabled grandparents; Caleb smiles at Flynn, as if friends being so close to one another that to praise one about his kin is to praise the other.

"None of the whites in Cutterville," Whittier exclaims, "not even City Hall would tell my agent who you were, Henry Brooks, or how we would could locate the grower of those superior crops when he inquired about you and them over the phone. Even the mayor's office said you had died, that your relatives had all packed up and moved away. That your land was also in a state of drought, but only a fool would have believed that, after the train passengers bragged about your crops." Even as Henry and Caleb's eyes light up with surprise that Cutterville would go so far to deprive them of a living, Whittier goes on without missing a beat. "It was Sarah and Flynn, however, who yesterday contacted me and told me about your troubles in selling these marvelous specimens in that small-minded town, which—if I understand it right—for a while, even refuses to permit you to enter it to sell your produce at the train station. So Sarah and Flynn asked if I would help in getting your vegetables to market. Well, Sir, when Flynn mentioned that you were still alive and here, I let out a yell like a good old Texas boy should, and here we are. My daddy's ninety-eight and still runs the family cattle ranch and a few little-old oil wells in Grand Prairie and never lets grass grow under his feet, so Henry, let's you and I and my accountant and attorney go inside and work out a contract for both of our mutual benefit, while these capable workers load up those refrigerated trucks."

After Henry, Whittier and his two highly paid advisers enter the house, Flynn and Caleb, not knowing what to say to each other, stand there watching the workers swarm through the fields like so many ants carrying boxes, packing them and loading them on the trucks. A troubled-looking Flynn finally glances over at Caleb and upon seeing that deadly serious look from his friend, Caleb is sure that Flynn is going to talk about his fears of being killed by him. Caleb begins kicking at a rock on the road.

"Caleb."

"Flynn." They both say at the same time.

"Go ahead," says Caleb.

"I didn't wait for you at the lagoon," Flynn begins, "Because—"

"I know," says Caleb. "Papa told me. Your father came and took you away. Are you," Caleb carefully continues, gathering his thoughts. "I mean . . . did anything unusual happen to you yesterday at the lagoon. . . . Besides that anomaly of that dark sky?"

"Wasn't that a strange sight? That sky?" Flynn says, appearing afraid.

"What, Flynn? What's wrong?"

"It's just that under that horrible sky, I thought I was losing my mind. Paranoia, I guess. I've never felt that way before. And you, then you saw it too. That was a dumb-ass question. Everyone who has eyes had to have seen that sky yesterday."

"Did you listen to the radio this morning? Everyone is talking about it all over the world it seems."

"Caleb, beyond that frightening day, did you feel anything extra?"

Caleb knows full well where Flynn is going with the question: Flynn wants his opinion about Naomi's prophesy that he, Flynn—after years of probing and putting it together—is going to be killed by Caleb. Caleb knows that whatever he tells Flynn next has to be something powerful enough to take both of their thoughts off of killing one another, yet believable.

"Talking about paranoia," Caleb says. "What I was afraid of on that day were the birds."

"Birds, Caleb?"

"Which is damn right silly, I know. How can a bird hurt you? But I swear I thought they were talking to me. And Naomi, she scares the hell out of me most of the time now."

It seems no matter how hard they both try to avoid talking about their demise, it keeps resurfacing one way or the other.

"Naomi and Mother were whispering about you in connection to that bizarre sky," Flynn tells Caleb. "I'm sure of it, because when they were mentioning your name, and I entered the room they clammed up and were much too nice to me and even spoke of some priest named Father Haas, who they said had been a part of the rescue attempt when my grandparents were killed. Seems that the old priest flew in from California to confer with the archbishop or the bishop—I'm not sure which—in Atlanta about that awful, day-into-night anomaly, and my mother and Naomi went there to greet him, this priest, and wanted to take me along, but I insisted on coming here instead, to help out if I can."

"Flynn, this Father Haas. You're sure he's the same priest who was there when Papa carried your grandfather from the *White Dove*, then carried your grandmother out of the field where she had fallen?" When Flynn nods to him, Caleb's eyes light up as well. The carrying of Flynn's grandparent by Henry, the priest arriving at this time, all added up to him and Flynn facing off against one another. Caleb looks toward his house. "Jesus," says Caleb.

"That's what I'm thinking, too," says Flynn.

"Remember what I told you. Nothing will ever happen to us. Our friendship won't let it."

"But, Caleb, something entered into me that dark day, something that wanted me to kill you, because I was convinced by it that you were out to harm me. And that something in the dark of that day warned me to stay away from you, and it wasn't anything the colonel would have ever said or done to me to make me almost crumble into absolute, bone-chilling fear like I did. This thing," Flynn says almost in a whisper now, while looking down and about the ground, then up at Caleb, chuckling between his words, trying to get control of himself, while suffering from embarrassment over his trembling voice and body. "It was like a Klansman's sheet, Caleb, a thing with a head and feet and eyes like the night. It said if I told you about it, that it would send something to kill me and you."

"I also saw that thing," exclaims Caleb. "Naomi even said it left me to go to you."

Caleb also looks about as if for the creature's reappearance. "Flynn, this is getting too much for us to handle. You're not going to kill me, and this thing that threatened us both, we can fight it together. There's nothing to fear. Say it."

"I have to sit down," says Flynn, tearfully glancing about the ground once more, then walks to Henry's wagon and lifts the baseball bat from the seat to make room, Caleb following.

Flynn suddenly drops the bat and he jumps onto the wagon, his pink lips white and his face gray. "My God, Caleb! Look! It's here. The thing that the sheet said would be sent to destroy me!"

A massive albino sidewinder, with blood-chilling black and red diamond-shaped markings along its thick, scaly body, slithered out of the corn field and onto the road and toward them, a snake twenty feet long with a girth of that of a large German Shepherd. The creature's pink, depraved eyes are locked onto Flynn. Both boys look around for help, but the workers are too far away to notice. Suddenly, the serpent, with the speed of a race horse, charges toward Flynn and the wagon, its forked tongue testing the air as it approaches. Flynn faints, crashing to the ground off of the wagon. Caleb seizes the baseball bat off the ground and positions himself between Flynn and the massive reptile, one with an opened mouth large enough to swallow Flynn whole.

The snake rises up on its tail in cobra style to do battle with Caleb, first, its cold stares, elephantine mouth and its fangs dripping with venom, all primed to kill. It coils itself into a tighter spring position and sails through the air and strikes at Caleb, who leaps back. The snake misses him and lands hard on the ground next to Flynn, who opens his eyes, face-to-face with the monster and freezes. The demonic snake looks up at Caleb then back over at its intended victim and hurls itself at Flynn, who throws up his hands, palms out, prepared to die. With superhuman strength and speed Caleb hits the snake in mid flight with the bat, smashing it to the ground just before it strikes Flynn; and—this time—once its on the ground, Caleb doesn't stop pounding on it until the beast is hacked to pieces and the bat breaks in half. As Flynn just lies there motionless, panting, pale and unresponsive to Caleb's voice, Caleb runs to the well, fills his palms with water, runs back to Flynn and splashes it in his friend's face. Flynn leaps to his feet. "Damn," he exclaims, staring down at the severed snake. "What the hell is that, Caleb?"

"They say some snakes live for years and grow to huge sizes," says

Caleb, "but I've never seen one that looks like this." He feels Flynn's forehead. "Man, you're as hot as anyone can get. Are you okay?"

"I fainted like a damn sissy, if you call that okay."

"You weren't anymore afraid than I was," says Caleb, probing the unusual-looking snake with the broken bat handle, then grimacing and throwing the bloody handle aside.

"Mast-a Flynn," a distant voice calls, "is you gonna help me and Billy Joe or not?"

Brick and Billy Joe are standing silhouetted by the sun next to one of the vans, their big eyes gawking down at the de-bodied snake.

"That the ugliest bunch of mess I done ever see," sputters Brick. "Where it done come from, Caleb, a pig's ass?" He faces Flynn, his troubled eyes begging.

"I can't go with you, Brick," said Flynn, still woozy on his feet.

"But you gots to, Master Flynn. Dane gonna sell it today. That's what he done said."

"Sorry, Brick," Flynn says staring down at the snake, knowing he was that close to dying.

Flynn looks at B.J. and Brick, both boys seemingly ready to die themselves; Brick is actually crying. Flynn faces Caleb. "Brick wants me to go into town and ask Dane to release his car."

"Why?" asks Caleb, his voice trembling belatedly, now, that he's killed the demon from hell. "Brick will only get himself killed showing off in that damn car in front of the whites."

While Brick sadly gazes at the ground, Flynn—wanting to talk about anything or be anywhere else than around that gross-looking nightmare of a snake—finds himself regrettably championing Brick's cause.

"Seems Bruce softened Brick's heart with a paddle against his rear end," Flynn manages to say between his rapid breaths, while keeping one eye on the pulverized snake, his color returning to normal. "Now Brick has decided to give the car to Billy Joe and Claretta as a wedding present. In my condition, I don't thank I can handle Dane Tucker. He can act like a madman at times and can be dangerous." Flynn's pleading eyes focus on Caleb's. "Will you come with us? That is . . . if you don't feel you're needed here to help with the harvest." Flynn glances toward the house. "Or need be inside with Henry and those guys to make sure he gets a fair deal."

Seeing how devastated Flynn is, and how he still wants to help Brick, even in the face of nearly getting killed, Caleb can't say no to him or Brick. "If you and Sarah sent those men to deal with Papa, I'm not worried," he tells Flynn, "but what about you? After fainting, are you sure you want to face Dane Tucker even with my help?"

"I'm fine. And as for those men, you have my word on them as well as Mother's. With this drought covering a good part of the South, Mister Whittier has a lot to gain by being honest with Henry. He needs you guys' crops now and in the future in the worst kind of way."

Caleb watches Collins direct the field workers in a well-choreographed symphony of seamless motion. "I'm certainly not needed here," he says. Wiping the dirt from his hands and face and then from that of Flynn's, Caleb warns. "But Dane, Flynn. You haven't forgotten, have you? We can't just waltz into town like nothing happened between him and Lilly, or that he didn't cut her throat and blame it on Crazy Walter. Dane and the sheriff won't hesitate to cut our throats as well after the beating I gave Dane. But, if you still want to do this for Brick—who wouldn't recognize a favor if it hit him in the butt—then okay."

"Dane wouldn't dare touch us now that Father has returned. Just take my word on it."

After digging a hole and burying the snake in a nearby section of woods, along with the broken bat, the two of them wash themselves off at the well, and then Caleb saddles Old Clara, springs onto her, and with Brick riding double on her with him, and Billy Joe with Flynn, on his horse, the four of them head apprehensively toward town to get Brick and Billy Joe's car from the one-eared madman.

21
The Car Lot

In town, across the square and Main Street from Dane's car lot, as Reverend Miller's church clock strikes eleven in the morning, Billy Joe and Brick linger by his newly-painted, red car. They wait in silence, while Caleb and Flynn confront an angry Dane, who's wearing that tattered, old Dodgers' baseball cap down tightly on his head against a stiffening wind. He glares at Caleb and blasts, "Boy, you got some balls coming back here!" Dane then glares at Flynn. "I don't care who's come with you. Even Barney will agree that you coons have gone too far; and as fer that Crazy Walter is concerned, he can't hide ferever. We'll get his ass. And you, Caleb Brooks, you've gone the farthest of all of you tar babies. You been looking at them Hill sisters when they were naked on that damn land of yours, boy; one of the sisters told me all about it; so don't try and deny it."

"I've looked at worse," says Caleb. "But what does that have to do with Brick's car?"

"What does it have to do with that coon's car!" shouts Dane, after the initial shock of hearing Caleb's uncomplimentary remark about the white girls. "Everything! What good is a car to a dead asshole?" Brick's eyes pop open, as Dane goes on. "And what good does it do fer you to be asking about that car, when you won't be around long enough to see him get it, even if that was possible, which it ain't. You looked at them naked, white girls. So you're a dead man."

"Go to hell," hisses Caleb.

Dane frowns at Flynn, as if to ask if Flynn was going to stand for Caleb's uppity attitude.

"I've also seen worse," Flynn quips, knowing that with the recent developments in his and Caleb's lives that his purpose in the world—pleased with it or not—is light years beyond anything that Dane could threaten to do, dream of, or actually do to him or Caleb, and he lays into the one-eared man. "You see I was also there, and if you're so worried about the Hill sisters, tell their mother to keep them off of other people's property, especially when they're in heat and naked, unless Jayne Hill is looking for a real man for a change, especially over someone

311

your age and who looks like you. I understand you offered her twenty dollars if she would let you touch her breast, and she refused. Is that true?"

Dane runs at Flynn with balled fists and then looks over at Caleb and backs off.

"Brick says you took his money and now refuse to give him his car," Caleb tells Dane.

"So what?" Dane smirks, grinning at the painted car. "That dummy had a good idea after all. Once I repainted that car red, a good, old, white boy begged me to sell it to him, and I'm only waiting fer him to return with the money and it's his." He squints at Billy Joe and at Brick. "The only thing you two are getting is a trip to jail, or worse if I phone Sheriff Richards and if you, Flynn and . . ." He points at Caleb, going on, ". . . this coconut-head friend of yours don't get your dumb-asses off my property."

"You took his damn money, Dane Tucker, now give him his car!" exclaims Flynn.

"Try and prove I took even a penny from that retarded ape," Dane shouts, then glares at Brick. "Now, you're quiet, boy," he yells. "You wasn't so quiet when you put your black hands on Lilly, was you? Called her a whore. Said God would strike you both dead. You may get your wish now."

"I'm sorry, mas-ta Dane," mutters Brick, petrified of the Klansman, while at the same time, recalling how people said Lilly's throat was sliced open and how it was said she had to have suffered unbearably before dying.

"And you might be sorry too, Flynn," Dane warns. "You being Barney's son don't mean spit to me. This is my lot and that car ain't leaving here. It's that ape's word against mine. Brick can take me to court if he has a problem with it."

"That would do a lot of good, wouldn't it," Flynn says, "with him being colored, afraid, unable to read or express himself, and the Klan controlling this town and a certain judge?"

"You made a big mistake bringing them here, boy," Dane yells at Brick.

Brick can see the hanging rope and fire already, taking away his life. The only reason he doesn't give up right then and there on the car and run away, besides Flynn and Caleb being there to protect him, are girls, fat ones, skinny ones, short ones, and nearly bald ones: without a car he won't be able to ride around with B.J. from time to time and have the girls beg him to ask B.J. and Claretta for a ride along with them, and the benefits that will come from that are just too much for the girl-starved boy to ignore, even in the face of Dane's threats. Both boys take cover behind Caleb, who removes a piece of paper from his pocket, paper given to him by Flynn on the way to town.

"The only mistake Brick made was to trust you," Caleb tells Dane. But the dumbest mistakes of all were made by you, two of them: one, we are not violating the law by being on this lot. It's open to the public for the purpose of selling cars. And two, this paper."

Caleb flashes Brick's car receipt at Dane, whose mouth drops open. "Where the hell'd you get that?" ask Dane reaching for it. "Give it the hell to me, boy, and I mean right now!"

Caleb slaps his hand away. The flogging that Bruce had laid on Brick has awakened him to the dangers of blacks putting their hands on or talking back to whites. Brick and Billy Joe gawk at the Klansman, then at Caleb, as if at a man who is—indeed, as Dane has said—standing at his own gravesite and shoveling out the dirt and waiting for someone to open the lid on his coffin and push him into it and it into the grave. Brick, then B.J. fall on their knees before Dane and beg him for mercy for showing up with Caleb. Dane laughs down at the pleading boys. Caleb jerks both of them to their feet. "Stand the hell up!" he yells at them. "Dane's not your damn god!"

"The fuck I ain't them apes' god," yells Dane. "I'm a motherfuckin' Klansman. Get back on your damn knees, you two."

"Shut up!" shouts Caleb, "Before I slap your teeth out of that big mouth of yours."

Dane swings at Caleb, who seizes hold of the one-eared man's hand and twists Dane's arm downward with such force that Dane, as had the boys, goes to his knees, whimpering in pain. Brick and Billy Joe have never seen a black person like Caleb. He not only manhandled Dane, but after now releasing the Klansmen, he also has Dane backing off, pale and afraid and glancing about his lot for someone to help him.

"Nobody is watching," Flynn tells Dane, "so you needn't worry about being embarrassed by us, if that's why you're looking around. Simply give us the car."

"I heard you was one smart-ass, tar-ball, Caleb Brooks," harps Dane, regaining his backbone and pride once he spots several white customers enter the car lot. "Heard you could read and write. But I'll be goddamned if you don't pay in blood fer this! If any of us knew you'd ever hit a white man we'd have killed you in your ma's goddamn, nigger pussy befer you was born and killed her too."

Flynn grabs Caleb when he rushes at Dane, and it takes all of Flynn's reasoning and might, as well as those of Billy Joe and Brick to calm Caleb down once more.

"He's not worth it, Caleb!" yells Flynn. "And you, Dane Tucker, you're not going to kill anyone, and if you don't keep your filthy opinions to yourself, I'll ask the colonel to have someone run you out of town. He won't stand for violence and doesn't think much of you anyway."

"Then you don't know your old man as much as you think, boy, if you feel he'll side with you over me when it comes to them coons. I'm white! They're black! Get it? Are you in so much need of mother's love that you're Caleb's woman to always be around him all the time or what? What are you a man like Barney or a woman like Sarah?"

This time, Flynn lunges at Dane, and it is Caleb who grabs Flynn.

"It's useless to stand here talking to him, Flynn," says Caleb. "Calm down before it's my turn to pull you off of him."

"Caleb, he know the law, Dane Tucker," Brick manages to say. "Can read and everything. And he say that car is legally mine, not yo's. Mine to gets all them girls."

"Them words sound good, but like Flynn said, you Little Black Sambo, this is Klan country and you should know that better'n anyone with your black neck stuck clear out to be chopped off. Booo!" He bellows, causing Brick to jump back. "Judge Chambers will never let an ink spot come before him with a claim against a white person. No court in all of Georgia will ever listen to a nigger, and neither will Barney listen to you, Flynn, if he's still a white man, now that you've come here with these darkys."

Caleb, who prefers to destroy his enemies with knowledge instead of using violence, cooly faces Dane. "Well, here is one 'darky's' message for you and Judge Chambers, Dane Tucker," replies Caleb. "Listen carefully so that my etymology won't go right over your dumbass head. Penal code 487 says that this receipt, handwritten and signed by you, makes clear that you are committing a crime by refusing to return Brick's car to him, and that you will give Brick—the legal owner—his car, and do so expeditiously pursuant to this matter or be slapped with a lawsuit that will stand the hair up on your head." Brick and B.J. immediately run their hands over their hair, as if having actually felt it rise as more angry whites stream onto the lot and gape at them. Caleb continues. "If not a judgement here in Cutterville, then in any federal court in Georgia and hopefully, at the same time, expose the corruption that is systemic throughout this town's judicial system and beyond."

"Hun," mutter Dane, flabbergasted.

"And not only might you end up losing everything you have," Caleb threatens, "for your blatant civil rights violation against Brick Johnson, so might the judge; tell him so for me. I will also look into U.S. Code Title 18, Section 241 and 242 dealing with conspiracy against the rights of citizens, and I will judiciously move heaven and earth to test the rights of every man woman and child—be they white or colored—against yours and the Klan's illegal acts, including alerting them to Miller's church-made drugs, which he sells here and across state lines and those mutilated school kids and others more recent—"

"No one murdered anyone," Dane snaps. "You're bluffing out of your ass! Who can even recall them kids' names that far back, let alone a killing?"

Almost trance-like Caleb abruptly stops talking and stares at Dane's cap, and says something next that startles Dane more than a beating could ever have, and what he says and does also stands the hair up on Flynn, and again on Brick and B.J.'s heads.

Suddenly, as if on cue, the wind howls across the car lot, rattling Dane's used-car shack and sign; the car salesman worriedly watches the door to his office opening and slamming in the wind, and then gawks up at the wind-quivering and battered plastic stringer over his small place of business.

"Somebody can, Dane," Caleb says, also puzzled at the swirling, dusty wind.

"Tell me one person who can, and take him to court, and you'll see how fast he backs off and recalls only the sight of a rope about his neck. Them kids' folks moved away or died long ago!"

"The wind. It remembers everything, including those killings," Caleb says as if being fed the information.

"The wind! You goddamn nigger fool! Then, tell the wind to take me to court. Maybe it too, like big, important you, will make the judge

315

shake in his boots, when it—the wind, mind you—tells him all about them killings." A blast of wind blows Dane's cap off his head; he grabs it in mid flight and hurriedly pulls it on again, but not before Caleb sees something exposed on his brow: a large scar just under his buffeted hairline.

"That mark on your forehead, Dane, that you always hide beneath your hair and cap, what is that?" asks Caleb, immediately piquing the boys' and Flynn's curiosity, their sights on Dane's forehead, also having noticed the scar before Dane had time to reposition his cap: a thick scar, much like the one on Barney's palm, looms in high relief on Dane's large forehead, the mark of the devil. The wind now shrieks in every direction, causing the white would-be shoppers on the car lot to leave.

To Flynn, Caleb seems so sure of himself, too sure. *Was Caleb bluffing Dane?* The blonde boy watches as Dane sweats while keeping his cap in place by holding it onto his head with both hands. What Flynn doesn't know is that Dane has never told anyone the unvarnished truth about his deepest of secrets, not even his father when he was alive, not even on the night of those school kids' death when he told his father that he had fallen off a horse, a scar that—to this day, as it was prophesied then—gives Dane nightmares.

"It came from Geraldine, didn't it, Dane, that scar?" Caleb asks. "Put there by an unknown power, as a memento to your corrupt wickedness."

My God! Dane screams within. *That was her name.*

"Urine . . ." Caleb says, peeling away the layers of the Klansman's innermost secret, even as the wind peels away the shingles from Dane's office building and sweeps the buckets of car-wash water from the roof, the trash from trash cans and scatters it and cans about, while nearly staggering Dane off his feet, as Caleb continues, ". . . Urine, Dane, which came from the girl that you and your animals repeatedly raped, beat and then hanged and burned with those other kids. Her urine did that to you."

Buffeted by the wind, Dane—now in a panic—begins shivering and swearing at Caleb, as Flynn, Brick and B.J.—being buffeted as well—watch in total dismay. Flynn becomes frightfully aware that Caleb is one with the raging wind, a tempest, within himself, which prevents that powerful gale from pushing Caleb about.

316

B.J. shouts to Flynn, "How Caleb know 'bout that girl and that scar on Dane's head?"

"Shhh," hisses Flynn, his finger against his lips, his eyes and ears tuned onto his friend.

Even Dane—like the others—now sees that Caleb is not affected by that uncommon, shrilling wind, and he takes a giant step back from Caleb.

"You," he cries. "You're like her. Like that Naomi bitch! Go away from me, Caleb goddamn Brooks. You're possessed!"

"That ugly, dark night," Caleb continues, grimacing as if caught up in the same suffering as that of the murdered children and, indeed, now one with the wind.

"Caleb, snap out of it!" yells Flynn. "Can't you see you're making him crazy? Us as well!"

Caleb continues, explaining not to Dane, but to Flynn, now, with an almost pleading tone.

"That day at the lagoon when the daylight sky turned black, Flynn, somehow, it all fits. Then and now. Don't ask me to stop, because I can't."

"What fits, Caleb?" asks Flynn, as trash is blown across his face, the car lot and onto the square. "Caleb," shouts Flynn over the raging wind while covering his ears. "Fight it! Whatever this is, the wind and that howling noise, it's doing it through you!"

"This wind," Caleb says, "and that dark sky that was over us in the swamp and here now in town is the same sky and wind that was over those kids that Dane and the Klan murdered, and it's the same sky and wind which was over your Christ—Flynn—when He was crucified." Brick, who loves Jesus, but fears His holy name, steps back from Caleb in alarm. Caleb's words also turn Flynn's blood cold, to say nothing about Dane, who cowers under that fierce blow with Geraldine's name pounding against his brain, her name and those heart-stopping utterances from Caleb.

"He's nuts, Flynn!" says Dane, pushing off one of his cars and gaping up at the sky.

"With those crosses of evil burning and your Klansmen's minds numb from drinking," Caleb tells a panicking Dane, "you and your madmen violated Geraldine as she lay on the ground terrorized in fear and begging for mercy; do you recall how she gave you that scar, Dane?"

317

Dane stumbles back, his hands covering his forehead, his heart pounding, as he's forced to revisit that satanic night of slaughter.

"This girl that you and your friends mutilated, besides those others that night," Caleb says, "this particular, innocent child whose legs you spread apart and got on your knees and poked a stick into her after you and the others—whose grotesque perversion to fecal impaction placing them in the company of Satan—had mounted and sodomized her, this sweet human being whose mother, who is very much alive and still mourns for her, this child who urinated in your filthy face, a stream of hot urine, that the Power—which moves the wind turned into acid, urine as it struck your blemished face, and it forever scarred your forehead to match the repulsiveness of yours and those other creatures' crimes against the world. This girl and boys, it's their voices, back from the dead, that also drives this wind."

"Get him the fuck out of here, Flynn," yells Dane, filled with terror, tipping over trash cans as he moves away from Caleb. "Do it now, Flynn, before he calls down his blacks' evil, dark spirit on us all! He's a African witch like Naomi. You heard him, Flynn. He's insane! I raped no one, just fell off my horse." As the wind hammers Dane about, the spirit of Satan enters his body and he stiffens his resolve against Caleb and yells: "You listen to me, boy! All girls want a dick up their ass, if that's what this is all about. My cow loves it that way. It's the mark of our manhood. Up someone's ass; not all boys want to accommodate girls from the front. This is a sex-starved world, nigger! Everyone knows you get it from a man or a woman or a pig or a cow. Sex is where you find it. That's what makes the world go around, and every one of the coons I ever raped loved it, you hear? Loved it! Loved what I was doing to them. Even in heaven, Reverend Miller says they must be sex. And he tells his members to fuck any way they want to."

As astonishing as Dane's confession is, Flynn keeps his sights on Caleb and thinks:

Is Caleb truly born of God? Jesus, is he?

Feeling the power of Satan in him, Dane rushes forward and head butts Caleb. And, to Flynn's surprise, Caleb does nothing, as if the impact was met by an invisible wall of protection around his body.

"What the hell is going on here, Caleb?" asks Flynn, who is now overwhelmed by what he is witnessing as much as anyone. "Yesterday," Flynn goes on, "turning into night, then the snake and now this business

318

between you and Dane. This talk about the sky and Jesus. Caleb are you saying that Jesus' dying is still being played out by us humans, that this dark sky business will continue going on and off until the end of time?"

Suddenly, the wind goes silent.

"Oh, Lord," cries Brick to Flynn. "Did Caleb do that? Hush up the wind? Did he?"

Brick and B.J. stare at each other, both totally convinced that Caleb is from another place and time, but was he from God or from hell? Neither Brick nor B.J. knows, but one thing is certain, everyone for miles around will hear about what just happened here before the day is out.

"As well read as I am, Dane Tucker, " Flynn tells Dane, clearly trying to bring that morbid exchange to an end with logic, while looking in confusion at Caleb and continuing with "I can count the times I've out-debated Caleb on one hand. If I were you, I'd give Brick that car. Caleb is scaring the living hell out of all of us, not just out of you."

Caleb looks around. Several whites have reentered Dane's lot and are now watching them, including a young white homeless red-head boy, age ten, a small freckled-faced youth with gapped front teeth, a boy who has been forced to grow up before his time, a boy—after having watched Caleb from a distance towering over a frightened Dane, now hates Caleb with all his heart and soul. Dane is a person the young boy idealizes. This ten-year-old child is the boy named Marcus, whom Pennington saw crying over those dead schoolkids years ago, a boy who was then yet unborn and now is very much alive, but by the will of God, if he isn't rescued soon, he will, indeed, be damned to hell, as the wind made known to all who would hear. For now, Marcus sells junk metal on the streets of Cutterville and lives in a cardboard box in one of the town's allies. The young boy always stops by Dane's place of business to pick up old car parts that Dane throws in the trash behind his office. Caleb watches as the young boy, red cowlick and all, hands on his hips, glares angrily over at him. Another boy, watching the sky and pulling a dusty wagon of grimy metal parts, comes from behind the car lot office and to Marcus's side. He also has the fires of disdain burning in his green eyes toward Caleb.

This sixteen-year-old, dirty, pale-skinned boy who appears to be much older, and would better be named Judas—is called Burt. Neither boy acknowledges their last names, either because they've forgotten them or they hate them. Both were raised in orphanages until they ran away together last year and have lived on the streets since. Burt is short, lean and mean. He fancies himself Marcus's controller and takes charge of their junk money, as well as treating Marcus as if a mindless, little girl. Chewing tobacco, Burt spits it on the ground, while glaring at Caleb. Meanwhile, after gawking about the sky in dread, Dane looks at Brick, retrieves the ownership papers and car keys and flings them at Brick.

"Now, get the hell off my lot!" Dane then eyeballs Caleb up and down. "And don't ever come back," he yells.

Billy Joe and Brick quickly leave in the car of their dreams, Caleb and Flynn on their horses, crossing the train tracks into Colored Town and heading for Henry's Land. Because of what happened between Caleb and Dane and the wind, both boys are now afraid of each other and of themselves.

22

Naked in Colored Town

As Flynn and Caleb cross the train tracks and pass through Colored Town, even though they are still gripped in repulsion and astonishment about what they had just experienced on Dane's car lot, both—in a strange way, while having doubts about themselves and each other—are suddenly inspired to be absolutely truthful to one another about thoughts they've previously felt to be too private to share, even between best of friends. Flynn feels secure enough to open with a conversation about intimacy to feel out Caleb—and subsequently—to see if Caleb is still the real, warm-blooded friend he's always known.

"Caleb," Flynn begins, riding along trying to build up his confidence on Caleb's right, "do you remember how Mother and Henry once told us that girls and boys at times have sex before marriage, and that sometimes such behavior might be justified in God's eyes if it's a Romeo and Juliet situation? Of course they never used that terminology, but you know what I mean."

"Yes."

"Well," Flynn says, looking back at the car lot, as if expecting that frightening wind to follow them, then faces forward again, "since you and Claretta never had sex, how did she feel about it, I mean when the two of you were sparking, if you can call it that?"

"After seeing that bizarre event I just went through with Dane back there, are you asking if I'm still human enough to want sex, Flynn?"

Again, Flynn looks back at Dane's car lot and goes on. "The reason I ask is that I'm interested in Earlene."

"Bruce's little girl?"

"Of course I'll wait until she's older. Eighteen, the way Mother says I should, and not while Earlene is just a child."

"Ah!" laughs Caleb, a false laughter to cover his own fears of what happened at Dane's place of business, as Old Clara quivers in her trotting gate. And he also looks back at the car lot, going on, "Good luck. You, whose old man is the Grand Wizard."

"I know. You can't imagine how I feel about keeping it a secret especially from him."

321

"Caleb . . . Did you ever feel anything, I mean beyond when Dane all-out insulted you? On his damn car lot, for a while—when the rest of us were wetting our trousers and thinking we were going to be blown into hell—you were absolutely impervious of feeling that horrible wind or everything else, it seems, back there. Even now you're talking calmly as if it never happened, the same as you were when lightning struck that tree by Naomi."

Caleb—feeling that no one can help him in his present situation of God versus the devil battling for ownership of his mind, not even Flynn—abruptly returns to Flynn's subject concerning Earlene. "It will be as difficult for you to profess any kind of love for her here in Georgia as it would be for me to love or to marry one of the Hill sisters, which I wouldn't do anyway. They're all used up, bone dry. Interracial marriages are a sentence of death."

"But, you, Caleb . . . Look at your complexion. Henry must have married either a light-skinned, colored woman or a white woman, so did you ever ask him who your mother was?" Caleb looks at Flynn as if the remark about Henry having married a white woman, a thing seemingly so remote in the South to both boys, that the entire matter is soon forgotten by each.

Colored Town has its share of half-white blacks. It also has its many layers of desperation, depending on how the sunlight hits it by day or the moonlight by night. Under a dusty sky, caused by that raging wind storm, with the fading sunlight striking the boys and their horses and the neighborhood from the West, the colored community appears to be a quagmire of shingle-less, pigpens, houses unfit even for a dog. Notwithstanding, its broken windows and abandoned old cars, Colored Town is heaven to the young children there, who have no idea that they are poor, as they play with empty tin cans and roll old automobile and truck tires along the earthen streets, while pretending that the tires are the latest cars: Cadillacs, Chevrolets, Nashs, Fords and all the rest.

Several young boys are galloping along while holding onto tree limbs between their legs—in the pretense of riding horses—and, with their free hands, they make lashing motions toward their limbs, which, speeds up their limb horses, to them, the strongest, most beautiful horses in the world, the bigger the limb, the bigger and faster is the horse. When Flynn and Caleb ride through their midst, the dirty-faced children—especially the ones with the tree-limb horses—stop playing

322

and stare up at Old Clara and at Flynn's horse and then at Flynn and then at Caleb, their eyes wide with surprise and soaring hope. For the first time in most of their lives, they've seen a handsome, seemingly, spit-and-polished, colored boy and a white boy riding side-by-side on beautiful, brushed, clean horses as equals, sending one of the children, a seven-year-old boy, dashing for home and calling to his mother through the open front door: "Mamma come quick!"

"What is it, Pee Wee?" a woman's voice calls from within the house.

"It him, Papa, Mamma," Pee Wee exclaims, visualizing a dream that freedom has finally come, a dream which sprung from the stories that his mother has told him about his grandmother and what happened in the show on Christmas Eve a long time ago. When Pee Wee's mother steps from the house onto the porch and into the diminished sunlight, the youngster points at Caleb. "It's the boy that gave me that fish and corn when he was here with his pa. He be the one that that Naomi woman done say come ta give us hope. Naomi, you remember her. She the one you said you and Grandma and Aunt Goldie and Uncle Bootie was in that storm, when Grandma had to walk in the freezing snow without her shoes."

Pee Wee's grandmother has passed on from T.B. His mother, nevertheless, the youngest daughter of the deceased woman, has managed to survive. She's Briana and is sporting a black eye from a beating given to her by her drunken, out-of-work husband. Briana had told Naomi to tell Caleb she loved him, and now she, with her own children, stands on the porch of her ramshackle house staring across the road at Caleb and Flynn as they pass by on the road.

"Hush up!" the boy's drunken father yells, as he comes to the door, his glass of liquor in his hand. "That can't be no Caleb Brooks, not that one who's ridin' with that white boy."

"It has to be Caleb, Sammy," Briana tells her husband. "It's as she said. All of this."

"According to ma thoughts of right and wrong," Sammy says, staggering about, "if that boy be Caleb Brooks, as bright as folks say he be, he'd know all whites is evil!" He looks disapprovingly at his wife. "They're all evil, Briana, and don't stand there lookin' at me like you know everything and I know nothin', or I'll give you another black eye, 'cause Reverend Harris says whites are evil to the bone. Beside, like Reverend Harris also done said, if God was to send us a savior it wouldn't be no Caleb Brooks or any other nigger. It'd be a white man like Jesus or George Washington was."

"But both of them is white," says Briana. "Both Jesus and George Washington, and you just said all whites is evil."

"Don't you talk back to me, woman. That white boy is Flynn Cutter fo' God's sake. Barney Cutter's son. Ignore them two and come on back in the house—like I tell you—or I swear, I'll knock yo' stubborn black ass out cold, girl."

Briana stands there, her sights now on Flynn, and her heart leaps with joy: Naomi had spoken of a boy called Flynn that winter's night when she said, "Get inside and stay warm and pray for Caleb and for the boy Flynn." Filled with joy, Briana's sights shifts to Caleb. "God bless you, Caleb Brooks." Sammy spins her around to slap her, but he's unable to bring his hand down onto her, no matter how he tries. Her husband follows her sights to Henry's boy, who has stopped Old Clara and is now staring back at them. Then the drunken man looks at Briana. Her black eye is gone. Dropping the glass from his hand onto the porch, Sammy sees how Pee Wee is looking down at the broken glass as if at a miracle. Both Sammy and Pee Wee look back at Caleb, then Sammy at Briana and again at his son, as if realizing how horrible a father he's been, and fearing for the loss of his soul he cries. "I'm so sorry, baby," he says embracing Briana and his son. "I'm going to be a better person to both of you. I'm so sorry fo' hurtin' you, Briana."

Briana whispers, "It's a sign that he is the one. That woman Naomi said long ago to Mamma in that snow that the birth of the child will come into the world and love will follow, said that I'd meet him in ma lifetime, and that he will be able to cast out hatred where it eats away at us like a cancer and replace it with love."

"I'll never hit you or drank again, baby," Sammy says. "And tomorrow, I'll go tell Mister Dessen to please give me back my job, that I no longer drank, and God willin' I'll be working again." She kisses her sobbing husband and then watches Caleb and Flynn, once again, go on their way and are swallowed up by the dust. Then, as the family is about to enter their house, that same man who handed out coveralls to Claretta and others blacks, weeks earlier, drives up in one of the factory's truck.

"Sammy," he calls from the open truck window, "Mister Dessen wants you to come back, since you've given up drinking. You start first thing tomorrow, as long as you remain sober."

Sammy looks at his wife and at his son, then at the man in the truck. "How in God's name did he know about me givin' up on—"

"Who knows how those big shots think," calls the man, going on as he drives away. "Maybe someone told him."

"Let's do like the woman Naomi said fo' us to do, honey," Briana—now inspired and filled with the love of God—tells her husband and Pee Wee. "She said pray for Caleb and for a boy named Flynn that they'll not be destroyed by Satan." Briana sets her sights on their neighbors who had ventured into the streets to watch Caleb and Flynn. "Everybody, please pray for Caleb that he walks with God," she calls to them.

The family enters their house, closing the door behind them, against the dust, their hopes soaring.

As Caleb and Flynn leave gawking children and their parents behind, Flynn faces his friend.

"Caleb, about Naomi . . . Even you, now, must give some credence to what she says."

Listening to Flynn and nodding as if agreeing that he has and saying nothing, Caleb's sights are on Billy Joe's car parked by a weed-infested, lopsided house on the edge of Colored Town. He and Flynn stop the horses. Claretta's favorite shoes are sitting on the back of a chair, as seen from the curtainless, front-room window. Flynn looks at Caleb.

"Bruce and his family live in Colored Town, now, Caleb, and maybe that's her father's house," Flynn cautions Caleb, while trying to disbelieve what both of them are thinking: that Claretta is in the house alone with B.J.

"Watch the horses," Caleb tells Flynn, then slides off Old Clara and quietly enters the house, closing the door softly behind him. Parts of the floor, near the door of the front room, is rotting and sagging onto the earth beneath it, the ground clearly visible through the loose boards. An old potbellied stove—on which is a skillet containing two smoking, burned eggs, along with a bucket of coal and a rusty old coal poker—occupies a trashy corner. On that intact section of the floor, Caleb sees something that demoralizes him: a half-smoked corn pipe, filled with a suspicious-looking substance. He walks over, picks up the pipe and sniffs it, then angrily tosses it onto the chair, the over-stuffed chair holding not only Claretta's shoes, but also a depository for her dress. Hearing groaning sounds, Caleb crosses the room, causing the floor boards to squeak.

"Who's out there?" Claretta's voice calls out.

Caleb slides aside a pair of faded draperies and chokes. Billy Joe and Claretta are fully entangled in a broken-down, wooden bed and wrapped only in a sheet. When they see Caleb, they leap out of bed, both still clinging to that sheet. Billy Joe lands so hard on the rotting floor, that his left foot breaks through the wood, and he becomes stuck with one leg above the floor, the other below it up to his testicles.

"Ahh," he cries, as Claretta pulls and he wiggles himself out of the hole; then, stumbling, both Claretta and Billy Joe—sheet and all—dash into the front room. Caleb follows with Claretta's underwear in one hand, Billy Joe's trousers in the other. As Claretta and B.J. cower next to the stove, trembling, B.J. painfully rubbing his testicles below the sheet, and Claretta hugging the tattered material about the two of them, Billy Joe reaches over and grabs the rusty stove poker.

"Everybody knows how strong you and Henry be, Caleb Brooks," B.J. shouts, his light complexion reflecting his reddening, skin-ashen fear. "I'll brain you with this poker, ifin you come any closer. Split yo' head wide open! Don't make me do it, Caleb. But I honest-to-God will ifin you make me."

"Shit!" yells Caleb, glaring at Claretta, who is staring back at him with those cat-like attractive eyes of hers, both out of fear and out of anger. "All this time," Caleb yells at her, as Flynn worriedly listens from the street. Caleb continues blaring at Claretta, "You said you believed in waiting until marriage for us to sleep together." Caleb then turns his rage back on B.J. "And you with that old poker, Billy Joe Maddox, put it down, or I'll make you eat it! And save all that tough talk about splitting someone's head open for Dane Tucker, the next time he takes you and Brick's car!" Caleb points at the pipe. "Jimson! Is that how you got in her bloomers?"

Caleb kicks over the chair on which Claretta's clothing is resting and then kicks the stove, sending it and the eggs traveling across the room and black soot and flames cascading across the floor, setting the house on fire. He throws Claretta's underwear and the trousers at Billy Joe. When B.J. ducks, Caleb grabs the poker from him and bends it in half and then violently hurls it through the window and onto the street, shattering the glass, bringing Flynn on the run into the house. Flynn looks at the burning room, then sees urine steaming from a terrified Billy Joe and puddling about the sheet-covered, naked, black boy's white feet, at a broad-eyed Claretta gawking down at the wet sheet as the last drops of urine trickle from her young man's body. Claretta looks at Caleb and shrieks: "A girl wants to ride in a car, not on a horse or in a wagon, Caleb Brooks. B.J.'s got a real, paid-fo' car that ma brother done gave to us. I need to be loved by somebody with somethin', Caleb, not loved by somebody with nothin'!"

"Papa has land, Claretta!" Caleb yells, Flynn standing by watching in painful silence.

"Land!" Claretta hisses. "You always talk about yo' land like it's better'n a car, even better'n a Cadillac. Well, it ain't! And that old horse of yours. I don't appreciate her name soundin' like mine. A miracle horse is what some calls her, but I say what yo' old horse need is a hospital with a big bed and bedpan."

"Papa and I have the best land around, Claretta. Everyone knows that. And anyone would be proud of that."

Flynn begins stamping out the fire with his feet, while B.J. is too afraid of Caleb to move.

"There you go again talkin' like you white," Claretta says giving Caleb hell and Flynn the evil eye as if having wanted to do so all of her life, then returns to attacking Caleb. " 'Papa and I,' everybody knows you think you too good to say, 'Pa and me.' Who learned you to talk so fancy all the time? Mrs. fancy pants Sarah? Well she might have made them other coloreds study all of them damn books of hers, but not me. Is you in bed with her? That white woman? That why you didn't want to grease yo' rod in me, befo' I became preg—?"

Caleb slaps her, stumbling her back into B.J. and shocking Flynn, even though he is also furious over what Claretta has said about his mother being in bed with Caleb.

"Don't you open that filthy mouth again about Sarah, you little pig," Caleb yells. "What the hell is wrong with you to say such a thing, after all she's done for you and all of us?"

"Caleb," whispers Flynn, glancing about at the spreading flames all around them. "Caleb."

"What!"

"The house is on fire."

"Let it burn!" yells Caleb.

Claretta rebounds, laughing and screaming, the flames now crawling up a nearby wall.

"Caleb!" shouts Flynn. "This place is burning. Claretta," he calls to her, "at least shut up for a minute and get out of here, you and B.J., and Caleb will follow."

"No!" Claretta hisses, then, faces Caleb. "Let's talk about yo' precious land, Caleb Brooks. I says the white man won't let you keep it, that land of yo's, so you got nothin', you and Henry." She points to Flynn. "Ask him. He'll tell you. He's white ain't he? Everybody knows his pa will take that land from you and Henry. Just ask him or your precious Sarah! I dare you!"

"Ah!" exclaims Billy Joe, when the burning side wall falls into the bedroom section of the house.

"Our land will always be ours!" Caleb fires back at Claretta, ignoring the collapsed wall. "And the reason Papa and I still have it is that we'll die to hold onto it for each other and for the women we love." Caleb, now disgusted with himself, throws up his hands. "That was mean of me to slap you," he tells Claretta. "What you said about Sarah." He looks at the drug pipe. "I should have known it was because of the drugs." He gently places his hand against her cheek. "You and Billy Joe . . . don't either of you give into the drugs. Be each other's strength. Okay? Papa and I will help the two of you all we can."

Flynn glances at the flames. "Can we get out of here now?" he calls.

Tears flow from Claretta, and she takes Caleb's hand and says, "Don't be nice to me. I don't deserve it, the way I hurt you and the things I said and felt about Sarah." She faces Flynn. "And about you, Flynn."

Flynn hurriedly nods, accepting the apology; he'll do anything to get them out of there to safety. After seeing each other's unqualified concern for the other, Claretta and Caleb tear up, as the neighbors stand outside in the yard with their strung together garden hoses and spray water through the windows at the flames, inadvertently wetting those inside, as well as the flames, with water. Claretta is soaked to her skin and continues as if the splashing water, the gawking neighbors, or B.J. and Flynn were not there, only Caleb. "I was jealous of you, Caleb, of how Naomi—who folks say is from God—loves you more than her own life, it seems to me. I was also jealous of the love you and Flynn have fo' each other." Tearfully she goes on. "I secretly hated you, Caleb, because of how you was said to be born special and I wasn't. And finally, I was angry with God, because He chose you to be His eyes in this world and not me, even though I prayed on ma knees every night of ma life beggin' God to make me, a woman, His disciple, after I heard the adults talking about you when I was only six. You and Flynn please fo'give me."

"You're forgiven," Flynn says, coughing in the smoke, as the neighbors put out the fast-moving fire, look in at them in disgust, then leave. "Everyone is forgiven, the birds in the sky, the hungry dogs that roam the streets. Now, let's get out of here. Get your damn clothes on, you two," orders Flynn.

Claretta kisses Caleb's hand and replaces it on her cheek and holds it there, her tears streaming. Caleb turns to B.J. "This isn't your fault, B.J. You or Claretta's. It is I who apologize . . . to both of you."

Caleb walks out the door, while Flynn trots to the horses, now tied to a tree. Both boys mount their horses and never look back. Wrapped in the sheet with B.J. and loudly sobbing—with B.J. holding onto his trousers, and their neighbors whisper about how disgusting the two of them are and how they're living in sin, Claretta and her man step onto the front yard and follows their lingering neighbors' gazes, all watching the two boys—one, having seen the poker crashing through the window, and had entered the house to rescue the other, and the other, having been crushed by the girl he thought he adored, and was emancipated from his pain by his white friend's concern and love, Caleb and Flynn gallop out of Claretta and B.J.'s tearful lives.

"I love you Caleb, me and B.J.," Claretta whispers as the house they were planning on buying caves in and crashes to the ground behind them, damaging their newly-painted red car.

At a fork in the road, with Cutterville and Colored Town behind them, Caleb and Flynn stop their horses.

"How did you know that scar was on Dane, Caleb? Did you guess, or was it the wind which accidentally exposed it to all of us? And this Geraldine girl? Urinating on Dane, for God's sake. And why was Dane afraid of that story and of you, even if he did kill them? It was so long ago. He was a mouse, a trembling, frightened, white mouse looking up at a huge black lion who was about to eat him alive. You, Caleb, you were the lion to Dane, to B.J., Brick and to me."

Once again, afraid of himself as much as what Flynn is saying to

329

him, Caleb is absolutely aware that he was manipulated by some unseen power, on Dane's lot, and knows that he has to talk to Flynn about the grotesque world of madness dragging them into its clutches. Now this confession of Claretta's and the way she and Billy Joe looked at him as if he were—indeed—divine. He turns to Flynn and calmly attempts to explain how afraid he is, knowing that it would not be easy.

"Who told you all of these things about him?" asks Flynn, before Caleb can speak, "And about those long-ago killings, Naomi? Did she tell you about them? Tell me, Caleb, because, as God is my witness, now, I'm really beginning to be afraid of you."

"A raven, Flynn."

"A raven? What does that have to do with you answering my question, Caleb?"

"A parrot . . . or maybe the lot of them, or was it Naomi on that horse that possibly somehow caused me to have illusions? Back in town . . . that business with Dane, everything was spinning in and out of my thoughts as if the past moved forward and backward in seconds. Flynn, I actually saw old people, trees and things growing younger, as they seem to be moving backward from our time of life. And that red-haired boy who had that junk wagon on Dane's lot, he still troubles me, and I don't know why. I've seem him somewhere before. Maybe in my dreams. I even saw Papa, Flynn, when he was our age, and when I blinked my eyes, he grew to the age he is now and was going into Pennington's bank."

"This is getting very appalling, Caleb. And you say that in this vision Henry entered the bank? What could that mean? Is Naomi truly from God and you. . . . Who are you, Caleb?"

"I'm who I've always been. Your friend. Please, don't you become afraid of me now."

"Jesus, Caleb. What are we going to do? If it's true that you have special powers, and it seems you do, then I'm really worried about why you were allowed to see Henry in that bank. Could it mean that someone will try and rob it, while he's in there and he is shot or killed?"

"I saw no one shooting him inside the bank, just white people buried up to their knees in the bank's marble floor, and they were all reaching out of that polished marble and grabbing at Papa's legs and his fingers as he walked by them to Mister Pennington's office. That's all I saw inside, but when Papa entered the bank the sun was shining brightly. A second later—it seemed to me—when he came out, again, he stepped into darkness with a frightened look on his face, the same dark sky that was over our land and over Cutterville. I wanted to call out to Papa, but I was taken straight to an image of those school kids' deaths in the past. I saw them beaten, raped, lynched, and burned, and how Geraldine urinated on Dane, as clearly as I see you."

"I'm trying hard to understand you, Caleb, but, my God! And this business about Dane. What did you see in him, when you went up to him the way you did? I mean that so-called photo they say Father showed Dane's pa. You must have also seen it. What was it?"

"If I tell you that, it will profoundly hurt old Amos and Andy, Flynn. Ask your father."

"Jesus! Caleb! Now you're bringing Old Amos and Andy into this nightmare of ours, those two lovable brothers who wouldn't hurt a fly. Get a hold of yourself, or I'm leaving. I can't ask my father. I fear his klan business."

"Get a hold of myself! What do you think I'm trying to do by telling you these things? And, Flynn, this is the frightening part. I sensed that my thoughts held the very key to life and death: Now, Flynn . . . Now is the time for you to say 'My God.' Say it now and try and tell me what this all mean. Explain it to me, Flynn, because I can't, and it is driving me insane."

"Ask Naomi, not me, Caleb. What do I know except that I may end up burning in hell, maybe brought on by that strange mind of yours?" Flynn gazes at the ground, then at Caleb. "By now we both know that there is something extremely unusual about the two of us to say the least. As different from others as Mother and Naomi say we are. What are we going to do about it, Caleb? In God's name, what are we going to do?"

"I'm going out and search for Walter again, in order to feed him," says Caleb. "Maybe that will help me to calm down, Flynn. You can come with if you like. I heard he's hiding in the woods around here. That's my plan for now. As for more than that, Flynn, we live. Live from day-to-day and see what comes of it."

Flynn shivers, forcing himself to logically face the fact that he and Caleb are actually beginning to believe the madness of their existence. He now worries about his friend, more so than himself, as he knees his horse into motion. Caleb calls to him, and Flynn stops his steed.

"Barney, Flynn? Will he give you and Sarah a hard time for being with me?"

"He went to visit his mother, where he stands outside her door all day, pleading with her to talk to him. He's been there twice, but each time she refused to open the door. Only God knows why, Caleb. Father loves her as much as he loves me. For my sake, Caleb, have patience with him. I'll get him to look into Mother's and my religion, and between me, her and our rosaries I'm sure our prayers will change him for the better. Maybe all of this will pass. I'll be okay. And you, too, Caleb. I'll say a rosary for you, as well."

"Pray for yourself, Flynn. Pray, also, that both of us will be . . ." Caleb's voice trails off when he sees a parrot flying by in the sky and then he goes on, ". . . both be protected from whatever this thing is that's happening to us. I love you, Flynn."

"Me too, Caleb."

Flynn continues for home, Caleb the same, only in a different direction.

23

The Betrayal of Christianity

Early the following morning—with the temperature already at eighty-nine and rising—riding on his father's sure-footed plow horse and carrying a bottle of fresh drinking water and a basket of food, Caleb is searching in the swamps and woods for signs of Crazy Walter, as he had promised, in order to care for him. Meanwhile, in town Henry ties Old Clara to a hitching post and walks to the colored entrance of Pennington's bank. He stops and glances up at the bright, blue sky—something everyone does lately, after that blackening sky two days ago. Henry then enters the bank, as Caleb had visualized, a bank swarming with whites who are spread out across its polished marble lobby floor, while impatiently waiting in a slowly-moving, single-line—in order to pickup their government-issued food vouchers from the bank's lone teller. The reason the whites were so hungry and had stolen Henry's crops from his wagon and seized the black businessmen's merchandise from them at the train station was because the food vouchers were late in arriving, and now that they finally arrived, no one is in the mood to wait for them for long. The blacks' pickup day is tomorrow, but for now, white men, women and children in the line near the teller's window jostle and argue about who had reached the teller's window first. However, the moment the whites spot Henry, they stop fighting among themselves and turn their attention on him.

"There's the one who owns all that water, when this town is thirsty," one white man whispers to another.

"Not to mention all those crops on his land," another among those in the line adds, their children listening and learning the art of hating. The children giggle, when one of their numbers pushes Henry on his leg when he passes by him. The adults laugh, causing the children to giggle all the more when they see their parents making monkey sounds and then see them getting on their knees, as if they are short, and mimic the young boy by nudging and grabbing Henry by his legs and his fingers and hands, pulling him this way and that, fulfilling Caleb's vision of whites seemingly reaching out of the marble floor at Henry.

"We ought to kill you, coon man, and take that land from you," a man says, as the lot of them rise to their feet. The man spits on Henry, the others do the same. Henry jerks free of those holding onto him and continues across the lobby, wiping spittle from his clothing with his handkerchief. At the teller's window, issuing the vouchers as swiftly as he can, and having witnessed the harassment, but saying nothing about it, the white teller now looks up from behind his glassed-in counter at Henry, who is lingering on the far side of the lobby near a large, mahogany office door.

"Mister Charles is expecting you, Henry," the teller calls. "Go on in."

"You hear that," someone in the crowd yells, "the coon can go right into the bank president's office while we wait to even get in the line to the teller."

Henry enters the office of the hundred-year-old bank building. Elegant hand-carved ceiling beams and rich, dark, walnut-paneled walls are the first thing a visitor notices. Sitting behind a large, mahogany desk is an old man wrapped in a blanket, while behind him—on that hot day—a fireplace crackles with burning logs. The badly-aged man is Charles Pennington, looking at the ledger books as he shivers. Resting on a pillow near the desk is an aging Saint Bernard, sweating from the heated office. Henry stares out an office window at a Coca-Cola temperature sign and gauge on the drugstore across the street; the outside temperature is now 110 degrees.

"Come in Henry. And close the door," Pennington says. He follows Henry's gaze to the dog and reaches down and pets it. "My second," he says. "She's over the rare age eighteen and holding up just fine," he proudly tells Henry, then adds. "You can trust a dog, Henry. Unlike a woman, they're not after your money." Pennington has the same bald-head pattern as had his father. He's overweight and more than just a little nervous. On his desk is that ledger book, which the old man eases close when Henry glimpses it. "I've known you for some time now, Henry, and we always trusted each . . ." the old man clams up, seemingly in regret, his head held low. He raises his head and goes on. "Look at you. You aged gracefully. . . . While I've grown old faster than you can say . . ." Again, Pennington looks down at the ledger book, then says, "Satan, he was here made of ice and told me to honor Barney's wishes."

"Are you ill, Charles?" asks Henry, when Pennington's voice trickles to a stop. Raising his handkerchief to wipe the sweat from his face,

Henry remembers that spit is on it and tosses the soiled handkerchief into Charles' trash can, and as he does, Pennington looks up at him and mutters, "I've been haunted over all these years now. Did you know that, Henry? Always at night." When Henry just puzzles at him, he goes on.

"That thing. Now, for the first time, it appeared here in my office by the light of day, Satan did." Pennington sobs, his bony hands badly shaking, his voice gagging with fright. "A ghost of ice and snow from that dark night those colored kids were hanged and burned at Old Cutter Bridge and more recently from that day-to-night dark sky that happened over Cutterville. It was made of ice and snow. . . . That thing which came into this office by the light of day from the past, and when it left, a young boy with red hair, a boy who—years ago—said his name was Marcus and said he died because I wouldn't help him and that in the future I will leave his body unburied in the woods through the winters and in sin, if no one saves him by then, Henry. He stood here where that icy ghosts stood, the boy did."

"What boy? What future? What are you talking about?"

"The one who looked over at me for help that night, Henry. God sent him there, Henry, to give me a chance to repent in my older years. This is the year, Henry. Marcus is now born, and he came to me for help, but like that night, when I turn from God and that boy and ran away—unlike the Good Samaritan, out of fear, I also told him to please, please leave this office and my conscious alone." Pennington gawks at Henry with profound fright and goes on. "Then, after the boy left, that thing returned and that spirit melted." Charles stops talking and then says, "Barney, also, left here, not an hour ago, between the time Marcus left and the thing came back. I agreed with what he and Satan demanded of me, Henry. Barney can ruin me if I don't go along with him." Pennington's trembling hand holds onto his dog's collar. "And I did go along with Barney, if not along with God; may God and that boy forgive me."

"What about Barney, Charles?" asks Henry, chills running down his back. "Does Barney's coming to this bank involve me and my boy?" When Charles just sits there sobbing, Henry exclaims. "I'll come back when you're feeling better," Henry says, then he looks down at the floor. He's standing in a stream of iced-over water, freezing the soles of his shoes to it. Stepping back and breaking free of the ice, his eyes widen, he now knows that whatever is happening with Pennington is yet another part of the puzzle that will orchestrate its way into Caleb and Flynn's lives and move them even faster down the road of the cross, but was this redhead boy, Marcus, now another of Satan's weapons against Caleb and Flynn, or was he a sign from God that would help the boys? Henry's words involuntarily tumble out, "Sir, I have to get back to Caleb now. I only came to drop this off to you. I'm sorry you're not feeling well."

Quickly removing a sock from his pocket, Henry shakes out a great deal of money from it onto the desk.

"Here's the thousand dollars out of the twelve thousand I phoned you about that my boy and I made from Mister Whittier. I'm holding onto two hundred for our personal needs. That means Caleb and I have only ten more payments to go, and our land is free and clear."

"Ten payments. . . . Yes. . . . Fifty dollars each," says the banker in a daze-like state. "Do you have to leave so soon, Henry? You just got here," he says looking down at the iced-over floor.

"Caleb and I always eat together and . . ."

Charles stands up and walks to the fireplace, his hands stretched out to the flames.

"Anything I can do to help you before I leave?" Henry asks the shaking old man.

"No one can help," the banker says, looking down at his dog, then at Henry, "Your father, before, he died, never asked me or my father, before me, for a receipt from this bank, a bank which prided itself on its integrity, Henry," he replies. "Father and Mother taught me long ago that a handshake from a banker was his sacred word, and that the hand of God will punish him if he dishonors his God-given duties to live up to that trust." He tearfully looks back at Henry. "I tried to tell Barney and that other thing that I didn't want to do what they were asking of me, that it was against the law of God. Satan reminded me that God is dead, so I did it. Please, Henry. Just leave the money there on the desk, and I'll put it in the book. My God, my God. Just leave it there and leave. Okay, Henry?"

"Okay, Charles."

"Henry."

"Yes."

"Ask Caleb to pray for me."

"I'll tell Caleb," says Henry opening the door, "but if God is white and hates us, as whites say, why would God listen to my boy? But even though I don't understand half of what you're saying, Charles, if Caleb won't pray for you, I will." Leaving the office and passing the booing whites in the lobby, Henry steps onto the street, where people are looking up at the sky. Once again an approaching storm is threatening the town.

On the outskirts of town, Colonel Barney Cutter broods on the porch of his mother's old Victorian. The place is still gated off by a wire fence and remains posted with its deadly warning, but nothing will ever be the same in the old house, nor will it ever be for Barney, who's guzzling from a earthen jug, while firing his .45 repeatedly in the air. Putting aside his firearm, he seizes his mother's small Bible from her porch rocking chair, a Bible which she had sat there and read to him since his early childhood. Barney angrily thumbs through the Holy Book. "Son of a bitch," he wails, "where are the pages that say You loved her, if not me, as she said You did? She said You are all good and Satan is all evil, but You did this to her, not Satan, when You—who was her rock of strength—let her down. I never said goodbye to my mother, when I left a lifetime ago and . . ." He glares at a porch-side window, "You let this happen, now don't turn her black like that on top of it all. She's as white as me." He stares skyward. "Prove that You are God of gods and open the eyes of my mother and make her whole again, as she said Jesus did Lazarus, and I will worship You on my hands and knees for the rest of my days." Once again, Barney looks toward the house for proof that God has heard him. His mother's body lies stiff and blackened of face—as all whites are in death—on her antique bed, just inside the room, next to the window. A receipt from the beauty parlor is resting on her bedside table. His mother never had that broken window across from her bed repaired, and flies have been swarming through it and are crawling over her as she lies on top of the covers in a once-clean, white nightgown, her hair recently groomed, her fingernails manicured and her atrophied arms stiffly at her side, her hands and fingers, like bones—marked with days'-old, dry blood—grip the large family Bible as it rests across her dress and thighs. A blood-stained towel is draped about her throat, the knife of blood—having fallen from her hand—lies on the floor, and there, again, the flies are feeding upon her dry blood. Barney slams the jug against the porch-side window, shattering the remaining glass from the boarded-over window.

"Mother, I came back! You knew I would. Why didn't you open the door and let me talk to you all of this time? I could have saved you. Now that I have all the money we need and our enemies in the palm of my hand and will reclaim this town and reestablish our good name, why did you do it!"

He elbows out the rest of the window glass and boards, rips the huge Bible from his deceased mother's hands, accidentally snapping off several of her fingers. He glares down at the fingers left on her bed; squalling, Barney hurls the Bible off the porch. When it strikes the ground, lightning explodes across the heavens.

"Why didn't You answer me?" he calls to God. "I wanted You to bring my mother back to life so that she can raise my son Flynn to get him away from Sarah's Catholic doctrine. Now I will raise Flynn up to fight his and my holy war against You and to slaughter the infidels who are yet alive and not of Nordic blood: the Jew and the black-skinned ones from India who dare called themselves white; the niggers from Africa who want equality; the Mexicans who invade our borders; the yellow Japanese who failed in their support of Hitler, and the Chinamen who overpopulate our world!" He lifts his arms skyward. "God Lucifer, since God Jehovah on high has turned His back on my mother and on me. . . . I now not only reaffirm my own soul to you, but I also offer my mother and my son's soul to you as well. All I ask is that you also give my boy the same god-like powers you offered me, so that Flynn—not some Africanized, colored boy said to be blessed by God—can rule over the souls, in your name, Satan, instead of in that of God, souls who long for a god to bring them joy, sex and wealth in this world."

As the storm clouds cover the sun, the Cutters' wire gate opens on its own, and a white hearse approaches the house and rolls through the gate to the porch. Towering over seven feet tall, a pale man, dressed in white from his head to his toes, steps from the vehicle. Long white hair projects from both sides of his top hat and over his large, pointed ears like horns, his voice like thunder, as he bellows.

"I've come for the body, Cutter and your Mother will rise again by my hand!" Thunder rocks the forever-darkening sky and once again—for the second time, in the middle of daylight—the dark of night rules over Cutterville, sending its citizens rushing off to church to pray.

Three days later, under a dingy gray sky, in the Cutters' backyard, a commercial driver inches a crane toward Mrs. Cutter's grave with a ten-ton tombstone, then stops, the driver awaiting Barney's signal to continue. For appearances' sake, Sarah is at the funeral, along with Flynn, but she stands a few feet away from the grave with a scattering of Reverend Miller's congregation who were friends of Mrs. Cutter. Naomi, however, is there in spite of Barney telling her not to come. She sits outside the fence in her mule-drawn wagon and keeps a sharp eye on Flynn, who lingers by his father and Reverend Miller's side. Miller and his representative flock—a few of them stroking live snakes and humming—have come to "give witness" to Mrs. Cutter's burial. Feeling that he has to keep intact the image of his mother as a saintly, god-fearing woman in order to absorb Miller's congregation into the folds of the Klan, Barney agreed to let Miller deliver a short speech over the body. As the casket is being lowered into the ground, Miller, Bible in hand, loudly exclaims: "Our beloved sister will rise again in heaven. Blessed be the Lord." Miller sees Naomi staring at him from the road, as if to say his faith has doomed him. Suddenly, Barney yells at the burial crew. The casket—while being lowered into the ground—is bombarded with dirt, which falls on it from the earthen bank.

"No dirt!" exclaims Barney, rushing to the casket—stopping the men who hold tightly to the ropes as Barney gets on his knees and sweeps the gravel and dirt away from the edge of the hole and off the casket with his hands, a confused Flynn looking back at his mother, his eyes clearly asking her what he should do, and getting no indication from her, he stands there and watches his father in total confusion.

"Not a drop of dirt is to touch her casket," Barney yells at the rope handlers. After Barney's wrath, the men carefully lower the casket to the bottom and withdraw the ropes; then, under those gray skies, Barney motioned for the crane to start forward. The grave diggers back off from the hole of fear, their eyes—like everyone else's there—are looking up at that deadly, crane of death, as it and the massive granite monument moves into place. Hand sculptured, the earth-crushing, granite piece is lined up over the grave and slowly lowered toward the opening. Suddenly, the cables snap from that frightening weight, almost tipping over the crane, as the driver jumps free, and the gravestone plummets to the ground. At the last second, as Sarah and others cry out, Barney—who Flynn feels harm will befall, dashes to his father's side—pulls Flynn back from the edge of death. A foot high pile of earth is formed around the grave when the tombstone impacted it and the grave is sealed better than it would have if not for the fractured cables. Barney had ordered that monstrous piece of a mountain to cover his mother's remains to keep the Light of God from penetrating the grave and rotting the flesh of the evil women. The huge headstone is thirty feet high and twenty feet across, as prescribed by a demonic voice, which came to Barney in a dream. The upper section of the firmly placed, polished granite has been chiseled into bull horns; centered between the tips of the horns is a large, eleven-pointed, inlaid, solid-sliver star.

"Father," says Flynn, re-approaching the grave with Barney, both dressed in white hats, suits, ties and shoes and both splattered with dirt. When Barney continues brushing off his suit and doesn't answer, Flynn goes on. "This doesn't look like a Christian grave." Barney just looks at him and walks away and Flynn follows. Then, in the distance, several hundred yards away, Flynn sees Caleb standing by the same bush which he and Flynn had watched his grandmother and was visited by the white doves, a bush from behind which they had escaped when Barney's mother shot at them. A single beam of sunshine breaks through the overcast sky onto the bush, a bush appearing to be on fire under that gray sky with the brilliant light of the sun streaming down onto it, though Caleb doesn't seem to notice, as he stands in that same sunlight beam. His intense eyes beg Flynn to give him a sign that they are still as one, but Flynn looks away and continues along with his father, as the funeral ends, in the gray gloom of day. When Flynn glances back, Caleb has disappeared and the sunlight is gone.

At seven P.M. the same day, in the black community, Reverend Harris stands at his pulpit, his hands folded and resting on his Bible. Behind him is a heavy, ungainly-looking, ten-foot, vertically-hanging cross with its horizontal arms spreading out twelve feet in each direction, over half of the building's width, a cross made from the branches of a dying tree. It hangs from the old church's ceiling beams by two chains bolted to the arms of Christ's symbolic instrument of death. Earlene, Brick, and Claretta are in the packed church with Bruce, who watches his wife, Carrie, approach the front row benches, where church members have asked Henry and Caleb to sit as their honored guest, against Reverend Harris's wishes.

Henry—who had to convince Caleb to come with him and who is so troubled about Pennington's confession, about the dark daytime sky, now waits impatiently up front to see if Harris's message of hope could

340

stem the tide of fear from all people, the blacks and the whites, even though no whites ever come to the colored church. Henry and Caleb stand when Carrie makes her way to them, all eyes in the place now on Caleb, especially those of Reverend Harris's which are filled with contempt and envy of Caleb's growing, unsolicited, newfound standing in the community.

"We all are here to pray fo' God to protect us from that darkness during the light of day," Carrie tells Henry. "We is also here to ask His protection from the Klan, since Dane swears to kill us after he fought with Caleb in the car lot, and we here to keep our kids from worshiping the thoughts of wealth, the joys of smoking reefers and thoughts of unmarried sex, Caleb."

"Why the Klan, Carrie?" asks a young woman leaning forward from the bench behind Caleb. "Them Klan, they is been quiet for awhile and—" She looks at Caleb. "And even with a little fight with Caleb, Dane wouldn't want to kill us all."

"Yes he would," says Carrie, as Caleb looks down the floor. "Yesterday, a whisper done come—as they always do through the grapevine—that Crazy Walker's time on earth is limited, and now it seems that Barney even got all his mean men out searching all over them woods and swamps fo' Walter, Henry."

Carrie's eyes widen, and she reaches over and takes Henry's hand in her and whispers in dread. "Even on parts of yo' land, Henry, them Klan been lookin' fo', po' Walter, from what I'm told by Lana's handyman, who went out to them swamps to give Walker his food and found him gone and on the run." Carrie looks at the young woman behind Caleb and both sadly shake their head, then Carrie confronts Caleb. "Tonight, word was sent to Reverend Harris that because of Walter's big mouth, us coloreds gots to stop worshiping God in our own church or it'll be burned down." The young woman—as well as others sitting behind them—hearing this for the first time—cover their mouths, in dread, as Carrie goes on to Henry. "When Reverend Harris got the nerve to go to Shadow Grove and talk to Colonel Cutter—while young Master Flynn was also in they den listening to his pa—the colonel say to Reverend Harris that he didn't order no burnin' of no church, but he also say that our belief in God done gave us coloreds too big a mouth and head."

"I believe the colonel," the elderly, embittered woman—who was kicked at Marilyn and Lawrence's grave for agreeing with Barney and

341

seems to hate the fact that she was born black instead of white—says from the bench behind them. "We do talk too much like Walter did and brought this down on us, like we doin' right now by talkin' about this, and I just can't believe that Barney would burn our church, either. Ain't he a Christian?"

"Not any mo," Carrie says. "Those who know say he's turned to Satan and away from God, even befo' his ma killed herself." The elderly woman gasps in horror. Carrie turns her sights on Caleb, "Most of the church members here believes this here warnin', about burning down our church—and I still believe in ma heart the threat it mainly comes from Barney—but they say it also done come from the sheriff and from the colonel's young son Flynn, as well, Caleb." Henry watches how Caleb now, leans forward and sits on the edge of the bench, as Carrie goes on. "There are those in this church who hate you for befriendin' that white boy, Caleb Brooks, even knowing what you did to help my man and boy. How in God's name can we call ourselves Christian and hate someone fo' savin' another's life? Heaven knows Satan has entered this house of God, where I thought he never would."

Many in the congregation who hear her words of condemnation look at each other as if to say: "Did you hear what Sister Carrie just said?"

Ignoring the glares of her peers and church members, Carrie continues talking to Caleb, "Some whites and coloreds. . . . They say you did it—saved ma man to make us po' niggers feel that you really are from God. That you just after our money like our preachers is. But I done say to them colored fools . . ." She looks right at the embittered, protesting woman who says they're talking too much, ". . . who done agree with the whites: 'What money!' They hate just 'cause God seems to have favored you, Caleb, over His other children, as He did with Joseph and his colorful coat; the rest of us who didn't get God's praise are like crying, hateful young-ins."

She turns and gives Harris the evil eye, clearly suggesting that he above all hates Caleb. She then goes on. "But I'm here to again thank you, young man, fo' what you did fo' Bruce and Brick." She faces Henry. "Yo' boy and Flynn stood against Dane Tucker and saved ma son and ma man's life. That's why I'll never believe it—till the day I die—that that young Master Flynn had anything to do with threatenin' to burn down this church, as shamefully po' as it is, Barney, yes, but not Flynn."

342

She kisses Caleb on the cheek and leaves. Then, with Harris glaring down at them, Caleb and Henry again take their seats.

"Amen," replies those close-by worshippers who admire Caleb.

The front door is opened, and Naomi enters with a haggard, barefoot, dirty, wild-eyed, on-the-run Crazy Walter. He's glued to Naomi's skirt tail. Shivering, he's wrapped in a filthy blanket and looking about in dread as he holds onto Naomi's hand. Gasping, Harris's congregation begins pointing and whispering as Walter and Naomi make their way to the front of the church. Naomi motions for people to slide aside, then sits next to Caleb and kisses him, while a beaten-down Walter sits and slides even closer to her. As Caleb kisses Naomi on her cheek, in return, he keeps an eye on Walter. Naomi, seeing the worried look on Caleb's face, reassuringly pats him on his knee. "He'll be okay," she says.

"Why'd she bring him here?" church members grumble, gesturing at Naomi and Walter.

"He'll bring the Klan down on all of us now fo' sho', if we give him shelter," someone calls out, then yells at Naomi. "You with that man . . . Is you that woman called Naomi who everyone says is either from Satan or is a witch, or is crazy, which is all the same to us fo' you bringin' him here to this church to be burned down!"

"This house of God," calls Harris from his rostrum, joining in on the attack. "It's fo' His blessed people only, Naomi Bell, whoever you think you are or from, not fo' a fornicator like Walter and you and yo' voodoo witchcraft self. Not welcome here. No, sir. You or him. Take him to Lana's house of sin and let Satan care for you and that man there, a man who opened his pig mouth with that nonsense cut-off-ma-leg talk and almost got us all shot by bringing down the wrath of the Klan on us." Naomi stands up with fire in her eyes; the whispering and the chattering stops.

"Who do you think you are?" she asks. "We're all blessed with something special, no matter how smart or dumb we are, and so that you will realize this, God sent His message to you through Walter on top of that rusty Cadillac, the very symbol of mankind's lustful desires to obtain Satan's fame and riches and not those of God's grace." She gestures to Walter. "Look at him, this frightened, defeated man. He spoke for all of you that inspired day in a way which reached this community's heart." She looks down at Caleb, "Not even Caleb Brooks, at that time, could have delivered such a passionate message or even wished to do so. Not yet, anyway." Again, she confronts the congregation. "Walter's words drove you to such fury that you, for a moment, were as one against the Klan, while crowing like roosters in your defiant dance of joy. Was it God you were prancing about for, or was it for the devil?"

An agonizing groaning of revulsion rises from the congregation.

"Who she thinks she talkin' to," the red-dressed woman, from the porch of wisdom, and now among the congregation with her Jesus-face fan, asks those sitting around her.

Naomi gazes at the section of black-faced women rapidly fanning themselves with those paper Jesus-faced fans, women aware that she knows full well that they are the elbow-flapping, joy-dancing, chicken stutters. Those women lower their heads, when the mixed-blood Naomi continues staring at them and then rebuts the entire congregation, "This man, now hiding in the swamps and woods, sleeping in boxcars and eating garbage with the dogs, has been forgotten by his brothers and sisters, but not forgotten by God. Walter," she says to him. "You have lit a candle for Caleb's footsteps to follow on the dark road of the cross, and have not blown it out to make his way more difficult, by what you did, as has so many of those who worship in this church and are unaware that God is not pleased with them."

Caleb looks up at Naomi as if wishing she were wrong, but now it is clearer and clearer that he is bound to this road of the cross of Naomi's, him and Flynn in every way and now Walter.

"Goddamn you, Naomi!" yells Harris. "Even as much as I distrust the Brooks in this business of saying Caleb is from God, even they got sense enough to know not to bring the wrath of the Klan down on us and on our innocent kids by helping that man. But you! Comin' in here with yo' forked-tongue lies. Out! Get out of here befo' I fo'get I'm a man of God and come down there and kick you out!"

Enraged, Henry rises to his feet. Naomi turns to him: "This is not your fight, Henry. Not yet. You'll need all of your faith and strength for what's to come unto you. At this time, this fight belongs to Walter and to the angels who have come, this very night, to this earth to administer to him during his last few moments on earth." She faces Walter: "Walter's only wish was that he could come here and be with the folks he grew up with and loved for the last time in this church." She takes Walter by his hand. "Let's go, Walter. God will understand that you were unable to speak what's on your heart to this house of self worshippers."

344

As Henry sits again, and Naomi gently guides a traumatized Walter down the aisle ahead of her, the congregation mutters in disgust and shock over Naomi's prophecy that the angels have arrived to visit Walter on earth, because they know that Walter is far from a man of Godliness. Suddenly, as he's leaving, Walter stops, looks back at Caleb and calls out to him. "I also wanted to ask you fo' you' blessin', Caleb. When you get there, remember me, son."

"Get where, Walter?" asks Carrie, rising to her feet and facing him, along with Caleb, who also stands. "Where will Caleb get to?"

"I lived only for sex," Walter tells Carrie, causing a self-serving, I-told-you-so grumble to spread across the church from those who worship sex as much as Walter, who continues talking to Caleb. "After living in the woods without sex fo' all this time I am covered with the dirt of the earth and my own stench, but I feel much cleaner." He gives a sad goodbye look at Caleb. "When you get there, Caleb, what I mean is to Jesus' kingdom in heaven. . . . Ever since I been running, I've prayed that God would fo'give me, and He said that if Caleb—who is Jesus' chosen pupil—does, then I'm forgiven. That's what the angels told me and Naomi. That God said that you, Caleb, has to fo' give me befo' I can go with them to wait with the others until the end of time." Walter nervously faces Naomi. "Is that right, Naomi?"

Naomi nods and stares at Caleb. An absolute hush has fallen over the church, and Carrie sits down on her seat in wonderment. Not a soul stirs, as if everyone has been stabbed in their hearts, all eyes are glued on Caleb, who stands there with such compassion for Walter that it touches all who have eyes to see and a capacity for unvarnished love. If ever a boy felt lost and trapped, it's Caleb. He knows that he cannot be like the politician and skirt around such an all-encompassing request as was put to him by Walter. To do so would be like having Henry—from whom he had received his character—having stood by and watched Lawrence's body burn up in the *White Dove* and to have let Marilyn lie in the calla lilies and rot without having had carried her to the wagon that night, years ago, and into the arms of their and his father's God. And without blinking, and—looking neither left nor right, to test the mood of the congregation—Caleb keeps his sights on the man who—according to Naomi—will soon know what no man alive knows: if there is, indeed, a heaven and a God. And an astonished Caleb finds himself saying, "Not tonight, Walter, you will not ascend into heaven not yet, but within ten days you will close your eyes and remember none of this until you are awakened by Jesus and be with Him." Henry is so moved that he reaches out and takes Caleb's hand with his own trembling one and holds on to it. Caleb looks at his father, at Carrie and at Naomi and a few others and goes on encouraging Walter. "Because of your faith in God, you have been forgiven without my needing to say so."

"My God!" yells Harris, storming from the altar and toward Caleb, as Walter, crying with gratitude, leaves the church with Naomi, and the congregation goes insane with rage and shakes their fingers at Caleb, some now standing, cursing and yelling at him, accusing him of playing God and desecrating God's Holy Name. In dismay, Caleb sits back down again beside his father. Henry's beloved son is horrified.

"Whatever inspired you to say what you did, son, it came from God. I believe that with all of my heart. Don't be afraid."

When Reverend Harris—angrily shaking his finger at Caleb—moves within several feet of him, Henry steps between them, and Harris returns to his pedestal of pride, where he glares out at his standing congregation. "Sit down!" he yells at them. "Who asked you folks to stand up? You're givin' his boy the mistaken impression that he is even worthy of anyone standing up or even cursing him."

When everyone sits again, Claretta stands up, as does Billy Joe, who is with her, Bruce, Carrie and the rest of the Jackson family, including a dozen other church members, all calling out for Caleb to stand up again, raising the level of Reverend Harris's rage. A worried Caleb remains sitting and gazing at his father.

"Naomi said you'll have to save your strength, Papa. Why?"

"You glimpsed the answer to your question when you looked at some of us, including Naomi, and said we'd be there with Walter one day and with Jesus, or the other place, Caleb as we all must, but you still refuse to fully believe. It's time, son, that you take Jesus and what Naomi says about Him and God on faith alone. Even as Jesus told His disciples that we who have never laid eyes on Him will gain a greater reward than those who had witnessed His miracles and still refused to believe and trust in Him. I couldn't have been more filled with God's love for you, for what you said to Walter. Your eyes are slowly beginning to open."

"Papa, we should have let Walter live with us? And Naomi needs our help. She's getting too old to be tramping about in the night and trying to save the world."

346

Before Caleb can stand and go after Naomi, once again the front door is opened, this time by Flynn who lingers there with his pale skin and those penetrating blue eyes locked in on the altar and massive, satanic-looking tree cross; a cold wind blows in around him and rapidly flips the pages of Harris's Bible, the big-eyed preacher gawking down at the wind-blown pages, which stop turning after the door is closed by the usher. On that Bible page, Harris sees one word: "Pray."

"Naomi is an evil witch!" cries Harris, pointing at the page. "She's brought Satan into the house of God with Walter, followed by still another Satan." He glares at Flynn, then at that open page, going on. "It says here 'pray ye sinners!'" Again, Harris glares at Flynn, and again continues. "And Caleb Brooks can't help you! He's too friendly with Flynn Cutter!" He stabs his finger at Flynn. "The next Grand Wizard! Out of this House of God, white son of sin and take that smell of Walter with you!"

A bone-chilling hush falls over the church, as Caleb stands, glares at Harris, then makes his way toward Flynn, a friend that the evil preacher has called the devil, a friend, who now sadly remains at the door of the house of God in shock, looking about in fright, as the usher holds the door open for him to leave. All eyes watch Caleb as he arrives at Flynn's side, places his arm about the blonde boy's shoulder, and they leave the house of the Lord together, followed by Henry.

Under the night sky, Flynn takes in a deep breath and turns to Caleb, who watches him in sorrow. "I wanted to tell everyone not to worry, that I would ask Father not hurt them, but I was afraid to speak in there, Caleb. That strange cross. I was terrified of it."

Henry feels a numbness over his entire body, and Caleb notices the look of dread on his father's face, the same as on Flynn's, who asks, "Does this mean God has turned His back on me, because of Barney's blood in me, Caleb, my fearing the cross?"

"We'll always be together, you, Papa and I," says Caleb. "No one can hurt you or us."

Flynn goes to Henry, who opens his arms to him. They embrace. Henry kisses Flynn on the cheek. Flynn returns the kiss, then looks at Caleb and leaves in his truck.

Caleb's faces his father. "He was saying goodbye with that kiss, Papa."

"I know, son."

24

The Enema

Two hours later, Henry stops Old Clara and their wagonload of vegetables at Sarah's store. "It was a good idea of yours, son," Henry tells Caleb, "to donate the rest of these leftover crops to Sarah." When Henry slides from the wagon and Caleb remains aboard, Henry asks, "Are you coming in or are you going to wait out here in the dark, as if you did something wrong, son?"

"I'll wait here with Old Clara," says Caleb, cleaning off his boots in the moonlight with a rag. Henry rubs Old Clara's nose, gives her a carrot and begins unloading the vegetables. Caleb puts aside the shoe rag and starts organizing the crops for easier access for his father, as Henry—with two bushel baskets of mixed vegetables, corn, oranges and apples—enters the store and begins filling several empty bins with his and Caleb's gifts to Sarah. Not a black face is among the white field hands. They're discussing how Colonel Cutter has radically changed, and he's changed not just himself, but has changed the Grove since his return from his mother's funeral.

"They have the same right to be in here as we do," one of Sarah's workers—Larry Rogers, forty—yells at Sarah's sandy-haired, old, white, female employee called Essie Mae.

"I agree with Larry, Essie Mae," Larry's teenage grand-daughter exclaims. "Colonel Cutter got no right to change the way Mamma said Doctor Winthrop, Marilyn and Sarah had things running here."

"You're a blind old fool, Larry Rogers, you and this child," exclaims Essie Mae, noticing Henry and going on as if he wasn't there. "We have our place and the coloreds theirs . . . in heaven and here on earth. I'm sure that's how the colonel sees it, so what's wrong with that?" She shakes her finger at the young girl. "Children should be seen, not heard. Now, you keep your two-cents worth out of this."

"But Barney . . ." someone cuts in, "he certainly did get mean after returning from his ma's funeral, that's fer sure, but that don't make him the devil like some suggest, or make him wrong about segregation. How would any of you like a half-white nigger fer a child, like that Caleb Brooks is?"

Larry's grand-daughter can't wait to get in her opinion: "Half-breed maybe, but he's smarter far more than any of us."

Essie Mae slaps the girl. "That's enough out of you!" she says.

"Don't you slap her!" says Larry spitting snuff at the spittoon and missing, splattering the floor with spittle, instead. Essie Mae—whose job it is to help One-leg Trout keep the place clean—frowns at the smelly brown spit. It's then that she decides to recognize Henry's presence.

"Henry," she says. "My shoulder hurts. I can't bend down. Be a dear and clean up that mess fer me?"

When Henry looks about the store to sees who else thought that he was suddenly the store's janitor, Old Trout—now feeling right at home as the store clerk with Barney now in charge—chuckles behind the counter, at both Essie Mae and at Henry. Some of the workers, on the other hand, aware of all that Henry has done to help Sarah, them and Shadow Grove, are ashamed of Essie Mae for asking him to clean up Larry's spit, and they turn their backs on the sandy-haired woman and walk away. Henry looks at the spittle, then at the few grinning, lingering whites and lays into Essie Mae. "Your shoulder didn't seem to bother you when you slapped that child," he tells her, close to swearing for one of the few times in his life, even at that, surprising everyone with his sharp-edged reply.

"Don't raise your voice at me!" Essie Mae hisses. "The colonel says the dirty work's to be left to you coloreds, so clean it up, that is while you're still allowed to work on the Grove."

"Go to hell, Essie Mae," blasts Henry. "Clean that shit up yourself!"

Laughter breaks out and, embarrassed, Essie Mae storms into the back storage room and cries. At that moment, Caleb steps into the store to find out why Henry had not returned to the wagon, and the first thing he notices are the white, homeless boys from Cutterville: young, scrap-collecting, red-haired Marcus, in the flesh, with his gapped front teeth. At Marcus's side, his want-to-be-boss Burt, is chewing tobacco while taunting Henry with racial slurs. As Caleb looks at Marcus, for an instant, he recalls that dream-like vision of those dead schoolkids' bodies. Blinking, Caleb frees himself of the disturbing thought. As Marcus and Burt linger by the service counter with Trout, their hatred centered on Caleb, Burt spits his rancid tobacco juice on Caleb's boots. "This is Cutter country now, boy," Burt tells Caleb. "No coons allowed in this store with us whites." As Caleb looks down at the muck on his boots,

Burt again turns and insults Henry. "This old nigger man was asked to clean spit off the floor, boy," he turns and tells Caleb. "He told Essie Mae to do it herself. I can still hear her crying in that back room. Why don't you just be a good tar baby and clean up the floor spit fer me instead." Burt is absolutely sure that Caleb will not attack him in the presence of so many whites, as he had witnessed Caleb attacking Dane on his car lot.

Caleb leaps across the floor slapping Burt so hard that the white boy momentarily sees stars and thinks that he's gone blind and accidentally swallows his chewing tobacco. Burt gags screaming and farting and immediately bends over, his stomach growling and churning in agonizing pain. Even so, Caleb is far from finished with him. He violently forces Burt's head down toward his spit-soiled boots, causing the boy's stomach excruciating affliction. "Nooo!" cries Burt.

"You put it there," Caleb yells, "now you clean that mess off of my boots!"

Wailing and contorted, Burt frantically cleans off Caleb's boots with his bare hands.

"What the hell's wrong with you, Caleb!" hisses Trout, crutching his way on his peg leg and crutches from behind the counter. "Can't you see he's sick? Let go of him. He's just a boy."

"He should have thought of that before he spit on my boy's boots," Henry hisses, then turns to Caleb. "He's had enough, son."

When Caleb releases him, Burt collapses on the floor. The field hands crowd around, trying to help the green-looking boy to his feet, as an angry Marcus sobs, cutting Caleb in half with his young dagger looks of loathing. Once again, Caleb feels that there is something about Marcus, but has no idea that Marcus is the futuristic boy—now born and alive—whom the wind revealed, will die and cry over the dead, of all lost souls throughout eternity if he's not somehow saved during his short lifetime left on earth.

"Help him," Marcus sobs to the whites about him and Burt. "The doctors at the clinic—" The young boy clams up, when he sees that no one—as if fearful of Caleb—comes forward. Marcus turns to Caleb. "The doctors told Burt chewing would kill him one day if he didn't stop swallowing it by accident like he does when he gets falling-down drunk. Can you help him, please?"

Caleb's heart melts. Only the innocence of a child would—at

both—turn to the one who hurt his friend and he hates, and tearfully attempt to save his friend through that person he hates. Caleb shows concern for Marcus, but none for Burt, all the time Henry is waiting, hoping that his son will do the right thing and help Burt. Using a paper napkin, handed to him by Trout, Marcus wipes the brown slime from the hands and mouth of Burt. "You're okay, champ," the ten-year-old child sobs, while trying to help his friend to his feet. "He can't hurt you, Champ. Don't be like Mac Schmeling and let another one of them niggers knock you out. Everybody's looking at you. Get up, Champ."

"Get your hands off me!" Burt yells, nudging Marcus away, as he bounds to his feet and continues yelling at the young boy. "You want these folks to think we're inverts, you crying sissy!"

"I love you, Burt. You're my only friend!" cries Marcus, continuing to touch Caleb's heart. Burt slaps Marcus and pushes him aside, but Marcus run back and hugs Burt about his waist, and Burt draws back to hand whack the wailing boy once more.

"If you hit him again, I'll flatten you," Caleb says, fighting against his feeling for Marcus in spite of his misguided love for Burt. "Now go the hell back to Cutterville, where both of you girlies belong!" Caleb tells them.

"Caleb," says Henry. "Don't embarrass them anymore."

"That's right, Caleb," says Trout. "They learned their lesson, but this may be where they belong for a long time, so get used to it."

As Caleb muses about Trout's remark, Marcus reaches into his pocket and withdraws a cobalt-blue medicine bottle and extends it to his ailing partner. "I found this in the trash," Marcus tells Burt, while drying the tears from his eyes of innocence and Burt groans in pain. "Found it on that farm we last worked, the one that was sold in auction. Take some of it. That farmer said it was medicine that he didn't need no more since he lost everything anyway."

No matter how he tries to forget about both Burt and Marcus, Caleb doesn't want Marcus to end up being slapped again by erroneously giving Burt that medicine. "I wouldn't take that," he explains to Burt, his focus on the bottle. "It's not what you think."

"Who asked you, tar ball?" grumbles Burt, and seizes the bottle from Marcus and squints at the label. "It says here on this label to shake well. Doesn't it, Marcus?"

"You know I can't read, Burt. Don't it always say 'shake well' on bottled things?"

"Shut up, you dumb ass," says Burt looking from Marcus to Caleb. "You want this here coon to think he's smarter than us?"

The ten-year-old boy reflects doubt, while regarding Caleb, as if wondering if Caleb—an ink spot—could possibly be right. He also wonders why Caleb, a black person, no matter how light of skin color he is, would tell Burt not to hit him. That goes against everything Burt has taught him: that blacks are uncaring, even to their own children and would kill a white as soon as look at them. If Marcus has doubts about the medicine, Burt, has none, and he shakes the bottle at Caleb.

"Like I said," he tells Caleb, "this here label says 'shake well,' and don't you stand over there trying to tell me, a white boy, that it don't say that." He backs up. "And I'm not letting you sucker punch me again, so ferget it if that's what you thinkin' on doing."

Marcus sees how everyone is staring at him and Burt. The workers know that Caleb can not only read the pants off of everyone in the store; he can read the legs off of a thousand-leg centipede a hundred yards away in the dark of night. Sarah's field hands stand there in silence, some secretly despising Caleb for his brilliance and wondering what he will say or do to Burt next, which—to them—will indirectly reflect on all of their own ignorance, but Henry steps in and calls to Trout:

"Trout, would you please tell some of these guys . . . instead of standing around here to see a show . . . that they should help me unload the rest of the crops from our wagon for Sarah, so me and mine can get on our way home."

"Bill, George," yells Trout. "No! All of you men," he adds. "You heard the man! Or do I have to call field boss Collins to tell you? All of you get out there and unload Henry's wagon instead of looking at these pip squeaks mouthing off at Caleb and making a damn fool of themselves. Now get!"

As the men and Henry leave to unload the wagon, and Caleb starts for the door to help as well, Burt calls to him and pulls the cork from the bottle, sniffs the contents, and guzzles the bottle dry. He then presses the empty vessel toward Caleb. "I knew you couldn't read." He laughs, "Just knew it. If I can't read a lick, I knew damn well no darky could."

Resting his arms on Marcus's shoulder, Burt giggles on. "As fer us going back to town, the colonel thinks me and Marcus is the type of boys

352

he wants around here to show his son how to survive on the streets, so to speak. At least that would be my guess."

"If he did," says Caleb. "He's as much of a punk as you are."

"Or maybe," Burt hammers back, "he feel it'll make a man out of his boy, instead of letting Flynn niggerize himself around you. 'Niggerize,' I like that word. Made it up just now, all by myself. And, fer your in-fcr-mation, the colonel has already put us on his payroll, so I guess the two of us will go search fer one of them empty houses to live in that Barney says is around here, since some of you coloreds and a few whites moved away fer them factory jobs in town. You're dealing with a college man here, boy. At least—as soon I get my first envelope from this plantation—I plans to attend one of them fancy trade schools in Atlanta. My God!" he abruptly shrieks, again farting and violently doubling over in pure agony.

"If you had as low an I.Q. as that blue bottle," Caleb tells him, as Burt wails without end, "you would know that a small amount of that stuff you drank, even as small amount as a thimble full, was meant to be judiciously injected into a pig's ass once a day to de-worm it, and since you drank the entire bottle, instead of searching for a house to live in, you better be searching for an outhouse to shit in, because shit will soon be coming out your ass and out of your big mouth at the same time."

Laughter thunders from the scattering of women still remaining in the store. Burt drops the empty bottle and frantically spits, ridding his mouth of the bad taste of pig-butt medicine. Trout calls to Caleb as he opens the door to leave.

"I'd like a word with you, Caleb, if you don't mind," he says, hurrying over to Caleb. "I can see now that you're a survivor," he says. "When I yelled at you to let Burt go . . . That is—"

"I would have done the same as you," Caleb says. "What's really on your mind, Trout?"

"Well, as everyone knows, nearly eighteen years ago, the colonel gave me this job when he left this place and—"

"And now you're concerned, because you don't know who will come out on top over this struggle between Barney, Sarah and Flynn."

"Sarah, she listens to you and Henry, and so does Flynn; so if she and Barney should separate and he has to leave here. . . . Well, you know I'm loyal to Sarah, Caleb and—"

"Are you, Trout? Are you loyal to Sarah and Flynn?"

Caleb leaves him standing at the door.

Outside, once their wagon has been unloaded—with Caleb at his side—Henry circles Old Clara and the empty wagon behind the store and by an outhouse on their way home. Inside the four-by-four, foot-wide shack, Burt, his arm swelling from Caleb twisting it, sits on a board with a hole in it over a pit in the ground. "Damn!" Burt spits out in gut-wrenching disgust, while holding onto a bucket and vomiting into it. When Old Clara trots by the outhouse, Burt's bowels explode, sending excrement in all directions. "Oh, God!" he shrieks. "It's coming out of both ends at once! You're a dead man, Caleb Brooks! A dead man!"

25

His Love Embraces the Whore

Having heard about the well-paying factory jobs in Cutterville, desperate, out-of-work, white, war veterans from across the county have steamrolled into town and joined with Cutterville's white citizens against the blacks and are well-prepared in one way—with their war, killing instincts—to do whatever is called for to get the black-held factory jobs. However, with increased armed guards protecting the factory and workers, the veterans, like the ignorant, town whites, have no solid plans on how to do it. Notwithstanding that night, as Miller's church clock gongs nine times and moonlight shines down on the town, six Klansmen—all of them smoking home-rolled-cigarettes and drinking moonshine—are in Sue Ann's tavern across the square from the tire factory and brainstorming on ways to seize the black-held jobs. Also in the modest "House of Joy"—which Sue Ann calls her saloon—are two young white prostitutes smoking and drinking at the bar. The six Klansmen are cloaked in shadows at a table not far from the females: old Hank, Trout, Dane Tucker and three others.

"No more talk about them jobs," yells Dane, then guzzles his moonshine. "I'm burned out talking to you dumb assholes."

"Dane here loves a good fight," smirks one of the toasted Klansmen, nearly falling off his chair. "But just not tonight I guess. Women or children. He'll fight 'em all since his run in with Caleb, when it's Caleb Brooks he needs to hit, instead of yelling at us."

"Shut the fuck up!" yells Dane, weaving back and forth in his chair. "It's fucking Barney you guys should be worried about instead of slinging shit at me." Dane pounds his fist on the table. "Barney prays to Satan just like I told you guys. He worships the devil, you damn fools!"

"And you don't!" hisses Trout, going on. "Worship some kind of devil with all that hatred in you? Bullshit. Besides, that's just a figure of speech to say someone worships Satan. I don't know what gets on my nerves more, you or this talk of Barney going from loving the devil to being the devil, or Caleb damn Brooks being special and having special powers. We all worship the devil. He's called money. Now let's get back to talking about those jobs. I'm tired, tired of talk of Shadow Grove."

Another of the Klansmen, a heavyset slob, squints at the young whores, grins and says, "The only job I care about is the job between a girl's legs to bring us begging for it on our knees. I'm a lover, not a fighter. I say leave the fighting up to those hardened veterans in town. Pussy is what I want to die fer, not be shot by some gun-happy factory guard while trying to get to them niggers in that factory out of it."

"A rabbit is more your speed with your small dick, you damn coward," Dane hisses at the overweight man. "This meeting is about the coons, not about sex. Now shut up."

The big man guzzles his moonshine and grumbles, as the others laugh at him. "Why don't you guys just come out and say what everyone else says, that I'm a fat pig and compared to you guys' dicks mine is a piece of wire. Especially you, Dane Tucker. Your dick is damn big for a white man." He angrily plunks his glass onto the table and exclaims, "You who sit there and say 'this isn't about sex' like you was a saint or something. All the time you can't stop dreaming about them damn Hill sisters, you been after with your ugly face and dick all your damn life. Talking about big dicks, them sisters must have seen Caleb Brooks' snake and liked it, 'cause they must have looked at yours first and didn't like it. They certainly didn't seem too upset when Caleb saw them naked out there in his pa's lagoon last month from what I heard. Now, how do you feel about that?"

"Hey!" hisses Dane. "That's enough! That's old news, and Jayne Hill or her sisters don't like niggers and, as fer Caleb, I'll take care of Caleb damn Brooks at the right time and in my own way."

"Maybe Scott here is right," says half-blind Hank. "Could be the Hill sisters thought Caleb's dick was one of Miller's church snakes, and Jayne tried to kiss its head." Hank laughs, adding. "Either that or Caleb thought Jayne would take money fer him to get a look at her stuff."

Dane glares over at the whores who have forever refused to lie down with him, and he angrily hisses, "Money will make even some white girls these days suck off a nigger rather than be with a white man, it seems to me."

One of the young females runs her fingers across her chest. When Dane stares at her breast line, she laughs at him. "You'll never get any of this, even if you had all that cash everyone been whispering about and thinks Barney brought back with him."

The other men nudge one another and grin. "Poor old Dane,"

teases Cripple Trout, between slurping from a beer mug and too drunk to realize that it isn't wise to mess with Dane, especially when Dane has offered him a share of Barney's money after Trout had seized Metcalfe's lost wad from the boxcar. Dane now feels that it was a big mistake to let Trout drink with them, as the one-legged man crazily jabbers on. "Dane, you're too ugly to get it free, when even a one-legged man like me can gets it from our white women, as well as from them black pussycats across the tracks, and none of us have to break their nose to do it. Maybe Dane should have asked Caleb Brooks how to grow an even bigger dick, while Caleb was beating up on him."

Dane reaches across the table and slaps the mug out of Trout's hand, sending the mug sailing through the air, where it rolls to a stop by the front door. "Caleb's a dead man and Barney's a fool, you stupid old crutch-walker," blasts Dane. "And all of you would be wise to stand with me as head of the Klan and not sit here running off at the mouth."

"Be careful, Dane," says Hank. "Careful how you talk about running the Klan or Barney might cut your face again and even cut you out of whatever he brought back from the war."

"Bullshit," hisses Dane, trying his best to lie to them. "He brought back nothin'! I've already told you guys that more than once. Barney has no money! We'd have seen some of it by now. That asshole said he'd bring back a fortune just to keep us under his control."

"What about the nigger soldier on the train?" a sputtering Trout asks, too drunk to remember that he's to keep his mouth shut about Metcalfe and how he and Dane determined that the gold-toothed man's wad of money was stolen from Barney.

Dane leans forwards and gives Trout a death look, and Trout clams up. As the others look at them, Dane continues glaring at Trout with his eyes of malice for several seconds before, once again, returning to his attack on Barney. "Barney's no leader to have let Caleb Brooks live this long, either. All he had to do is send word from the war. But no! He worried about his little Flynn—that his sissy, weak son would suffer if we killed that nigger and said that he would take care of Caleb, himself, in his own way, when he got back."

"And he will," says Hank.

"Shut your mouth up, Hank," hisses Dane. "Barney's a goddamn fool! Don't nobody sit here and try to tell me he ain't." Dane points out the open window behind them. The others follow his gaze to the protesting whites on the square—veterans included. "Look at them dopes out there crying in their soup 'cause the niggers got them jobs. Them crackers ain't no better'n the niggas, if you ask me. That Jew factory owner don't care about all them idiots harmlessly jawing at his plant fer hiring them people. You guys asked me what we should do to get them jobs. I'll tell you now." He slams his fist on the table. "Burn down that fucking factory! That Jew'll listen to reason, then."

Trout blurts out, "Sheriff Richards says we can't do anything to that Jew's factory without a direct order from Barney, Dane, or he'll arrest the lot of us and—"

Dane reaches across the table and slaps Trout. "Shut up before you talk yourself into your grave. You little, useless, drunken-crippled, piece of shit, just sit there and keep your mouth shut and be glad you don't live in Germany, where, rather than waste food on a one-leg something like you, they'd put a bullet in your useless ass and plant you in their cabbage fields with the ashes of the Jews. What the hell you mean talking when you know you should keep that mouth of yours closed? Not one word about money or anything else out of any of you guys!" Dane pours his and their liquor on the floor. "And no more motherfucking drinks. Sitting there insulting me. No! You will not do that."

Trout goes completely silent and embarrassed, looking about, but no one speaks up for him, and Dane lectures them all with impunity.

"Instead of the colonel staying here killing niggers, he was over there in Europe leading some of Georgia's best young white boys to their deaths fighting our white, German brothers, because Jew money in this country forced America to go to war to stop the Germans from killing them dirty, European Jews. And don't believe this shit about Barney growing stronger. It's a lie to keep us afraid of him."

"What about them army-trained, nigger soldiers we been hearing about, returning to the South with their stolen guns to make war on whites?" Scott, the heavyset man asks, ignoring Dane's warning about everyone shutting up. "What'll we do about them, Dane?" Shrugging. "Just askin' that's all."

"Coons aren't smart enough to sneak guns back home with them from the war," argues Dane. "But, like I've been telling you fuckers fer the last two hours, Caleb Brooks is smarter than we thought. He's somehow found out about our old business," Dane tells them, while glancing over at the females and lowering his voice, going on.

"How many of us who were there are still able recall that girl's name? None of us, but that was her name, and that nigger knew, knew that and other things that only we knew." A troubled look appears on Dane's face, as Scott says "That wind in town and on your car lot. Some say Caleb caused it, Dane? Are you now saying—that because Caleb knows these things that he is like the darkys whisper, that he's another Naomi? 'Cause some of the things I saw that black woman do ain't natural. If you're saying Caleb is like her, and had even a little bit to do with what went on when the sky turned black, and or that God must have told him about that old business, I don't know about the rest of these guys," Scott glances at the others, "but you're scaring the livin' hell out of me, Dane, a man who only lives for love and pussy, not violence and hellfire. If it's true what they say about Caleb," Scott nervously exclaims and looks at Dane's forehead. "My God, what does this mean when it comes to the rest of us? Don't want to be like you with that girl's mark of evil on my head."

"No, asshole!" shouts Dane, covering his forehead with his hair and continuing. "I'm not saying Caleb is like Naomi, and who the hell is she? She's nothing! Nothing, you hear? Henry's half-breed, bastard son is just flesh and bones and can be killed like anyone else, and that fucking, nigger mother of Caleb goddamn Brooks, who they say was fucked by some rich white man in Atlanta, or wherever it was, and was kicked out on her ass—like I told him on my car lot—If any of us Klan had ever thought he'd have ever hit a white man, we would have killed him in his ma's goddamn, nigger pussy before he was born, and that's when the sambo sucker punched me."

"Listen to the brave drunk Klansmen," one of the prostitutes calls to them. "We can hear everything you're saying. Over there worrying about the power of God and who He sees as a saint or gives His blessing to. At least Caleb Brooks didn't kill one of us girls. Cut her throat on that factory dock and raped her. We all know who killed Lilly, don't we, and, then, blamed it on the blacks? And that poor-ass excuse of a sheriff going along with it. Ah! You sure you guys aren't members of Reverend Miller's church of snakes? You sure sound crazy enough to be." Dane is caught off guard by her remarks and momentarily sits closed-mouth and stunned as she continues. "And about them coon soldiers, at least they fought for their country. Did you guys? German brothers ma ass."

"Now you," exclaims Dane, picking up his empty beer mug, threatening to hurl it across the room at the female. "Keep your mouth shut over there before I crush your head like an egg. And go sell your pussy to them apes across the track, if you love the blacks so much."

"I won't be quiet. Barney runs this town, not you. And I despise them dirty people across the tracks as much as anybody does," the whore tells him, "and we girls loves our white boys who fought in the war, and I'll personally give away my pussy free to any returning white soldiers to prove it. They got rid of Hitler, didn't they, and saved the world?"

Sue Ann, the bar owner, enters from a back room. "Why don't all you knock it off," she says. "I could hear you a mile away talking about Barney. Don't you know how dangerous that is? I don't want him thinking my place is where you come to plot against him and—"

Suddenly everyone clams up, as a shadow of death moves into the bar. Barney looms at the open door—the night, dark sky behind him—as he stands there looking over at the young whore who spoke out against Hitler, "Hitler was a man of courage and character." Cutter says scrutinizes everyone and everything, then looks down at the earlier tossed mug, now resting at his feet. The young whore reflects up at him.

"Colonel . . . You're an American, yet you praise Hitler, as if he was faultless in the war."

With Barney is Flynn. He watches in wonder as his father ignores the girl, then gives Hank a knowing glance. Hank returns it with a nod, Dane noticing it and sitting uneasy. Barney then turns back to the whore. "Hitler's only fault was he needed more time to kill the Jews and other undesirables. Otherwise, he might have saved America by stopping those inferior pawnbrokers by the millions, from swarming into this country. Niggers with money that's what they are with their long noses, nigger-shaped mouths, nappy hair and dark skin." Flynn is embarrassed and seems totally out of place in there, as he listens to his father, his head held slightly lower with each racial insult uttered. "Son," Barney tells Flynn, noticing how uncomfortable Flynn is. "The soda pops."

As Flynn goes to the bar, Sue Ann hurries to the counter and withdraws two Cokes for him. Dane watches Flynn in dread. Fearful of what Flynn might have told his father about what he said to Caleb and him on the car lot, Dane quickly condescends to Cutter, blaring out, "You're right, Colonel. The Jews. They was born in Africa, wasn't they? All of 'em."

"So was Christ," says the young prostitute, as if unafraid of Barney, while smiling at Flynn, as he stands near her at the bar; she faces Dane. "Christ was born in Northern Africa with them Egyptian folk."

"Hell, that's different, then," Dane says, trying to appease Barney and making a deadly mistake by forgetting his own words that Barney now worships Satan. He goes on, feeling that he's educating all of them. "The Jews deserve to be cremated and used as fertilizer in Germany cabbage patches. Jesus was white like us. He didn't deserve to be used as fertilizer. Now, shut up over there. The colonel ain't talkin' to you."

Barney turns to Flynn "I'll meet you in the car, son." Sensing Barney's displeasure of Dane, Flynn quickly carries the Cokes outside. When Flynn steps into the night, Barney closes the door behind him and faces Dane. "Doesn't He, Dane," Barney says. "Christ. Deserve to be fertilizer?" Everyone's mouth drops open. To them, it's one thing to privately believe in anything one wishes, but to announce it publicly, especially about not believing in Jesus in the Bible Belt is a shock soon to be heard throughout the town, but Barney's not worried. He knows that people will go along with anything, even corruptness and evil if there's money in it for them, and Barney has more money than everyone has ever dreamed about, and he turns and heads for the door.

"You leaving, Colonel?" asks a nervous Dane. "I thought you came to check up on your boys to see what things are like, well, since you got back. Maybe order us about like you soldiers do in the army and—"

"Caleb Brooks," Barney says, ignoring Dane, going on. "He's not special, and God didn't tell him what happened that night." Barney stands there in silence, the fear projected by him sinking into each and every one there. "And this half-breed boy or Naomi—magical powers or not—has nothing that I can't handle," he warns his estranged men. "The reason Caleb knows about that night is as simple as this: some darky saw what happened, over eighteen years ago, and kept the story alive all this time, but they never brought it to the attention of the law and never will. You see, they—at least—know it's deadly to go against me. And, you, Dane," Barney remarks coldly. "Only a fool needs to show up shouting at his men in the manner of a drill sergeant. A whisper is enough to make the impossible happen, and a glance is all it takes to know what's going on. And age alone does not make a man old or weak, not if his mind assails against it, if that's what you are thinking." Picking up the earlier-tossed mug, Barney holds it between his index finger and thumb and squeezes. The thick glass explodes, causing all to gasp.

361

"Eighteen years ago I lifted Hank's truck off the ground to get to you. That's the beauty of worshipping a different kind of god. I haven't lost the touch." The Grand Wizard turns, walks out the door and into the night calling back, "And the reason your old man killed himself, I haven't forgotten that either."

Once Barney and Flynn drive off in the Cadillac—one of the Klansman whispers, "He's what they say he is. Barney's the devil himself."

Dane slumps down in his chair, as white as a sheet. Sue Ann, slender and in her early thirties, feeling that Barney put Dane in his place, joyfully picks up the dime, which Flynn left on the counter for the Cokes, and flips it into the air, catches it in her hand and happily reaches over the bar and places it in the till. She then rests her right foot on one of the bar stools, lifts her dress and straightens her stocking; slowly, she turns her head and stares over at the gawking men.

"You boys go suck on a cow's tits, 'cause that's all that's going to grease your little dicks this night."

"You one of them white trash who say the nigga's dick is bigger than mine?" fires Dane, glaring at her from his tilted-back chair.

"No," answers Sue Ann, the other two women giggling. "But since we're talking about the coloreds, I been told you think them black bitches got better pussies than us, so go over the tracks to Lana's place, if you guys love that black stuff so much, especially you, Dane Tucker. My girls certainly don't need you breaking their nose like you did to one of Lana's girls. Seem they don't want you over there anymore either, even at double the going price, and they've asked Sheriff Richards to see that you stay away from them and he agreed."

"Go fuck yourself, woman," Dane hisses, as Sue Ann straightens out her stocking. "And don't try your womanly wiles on me by raising your dress as a tease. That means nothing to me, and to prove it, I'll come over there and knock out your teeth. Women should be seen flat on their backs in bed with they legs opened wide, not their mouths."

The two women of the night fall silent. They know that when Dane gets that pissed off when he's drunk, he doesn't play, but when Sue Ann feels she has the best hand in the house, she doesn't back off either. She shifts her other foot onto the stool and straightens out her high-up garter belt. When she does, Scott, with all of that flesh and extra pounds on him, positions his balloon hand under the tablecloth and opens his fly. Dane's vigilance shifts from Sue Ann to the bald man's fist, rapidly mov-

362

ing the table cloth up and down in a desperate try for satisfaction, while locking in on Sue Ann's exposed upper thigh. Dane turns his drunken focus back on Sue Ann, who is unaware of the under-the-tablecloth masturbator in her midst. As she wiggles her hips, while carefully guiding her silky long leg deeper into her rayon stocking, one of the men points at Dane. "Dane," he teases, "you said Sue Ann's wiles didn't move you. Well, look down at your pants. That ain't no hot dog pushing out your fly."

Groaning, the thought of Dane's erection and Sue Ann's leg sends the drunken Scott's hand rapidly whacking up and down under the table cloth. He falls from his chair onto the floor.

"Get out," yells Sue Ann, when the toppled man's sperm splashes onto her new carpet, his penis exposed, while he lies in wasted moonshine and in his own wet pool of ecstasy. "And take that drunken pig with you. Now!"

"I eat pushy bitches like you fer lunch," says Dane, "I'm this close to turning these guys loose onto this place. Just one more word out of any of you bitches. Just one more."

At that moment, Claretta steps from the backroom, and Sue Ann hurriedly covers the exposed drunk with one of the tablecloths. Meanwhile, as Claretta worriedly leers down at the cloth-covered drunk, she removes an apron from her slightly enlarged stomach and places the garment on a barstool. The Klansmen's sights immediately zero in on the dark girl's premature breast, mushrooming themselves up against her blouse.

"I'm ready to leave, now, Miss Sue Ann," says Claretta.

"Thank you, Power of Darkness," whispers Dane, telling himself if Satan is good enough for Barney, who is empowered by him to lift that truck years ago and remain strong, even now, then the devil's also good enough for him as he always wanted and now more than willing to accept as a fact of life. "You've delivered my enemy's lover into my hands."

"Not Satan," Hank whispers. "Barney. He knew Claretta had this extra job. Barney delivered her to us to destroy Caleb piece by piece. Why do you think he asked us to meet him here tonight? Remember that . . . all of you, the colonel runs this Klan and nobody else."

Sue Ann sees how the men are staring at Claretta, and she pulls the young girl aside.

"You can't be finished with them dishes already," she tells Claretta.

"Go back in there and keep cleaning and I'll take you home in the car later."

"Oh, yes, Miss Sue Ann," beams Claretta. "I finished everything. Don't you remember? You said ifin I finished, I could leave early. I gettin' married to ma Billy Joe this very night, as soon as I can get to the church and wash up in they new bathtub that they got there with real hot, runnin' water." Smiling, she points at the door. "I 'spect Billy Joe be outside just a nervously waitin' fo' me, right now. Both our mammas is at Reverend Harris's newly-decorated church to fit me in ma weddin' dress. An all-white dress from the same silk as this blouse," she says touching her chest. "One of the white women that Mamma works fo' gave her a silk parachute her son brought back from the war, and that's what mamma and Johnny Mae cut down, and Johnny Mae made this blouse and ma marryin' dress out of and made it to fit me."

"Sweetheart," says Sue Ann, watching the hungry eyes of the Klansmen. "Now, you listen to me and wait until I have time to take you to the church. I'll just close up early and—"

"Oh, Billy Joe'll do that. Take me to the church. We have a pretty red car now even ifin it is a little damaged from that burning house."

Dane turns ashen with rage, when he hears Claretta mention the car, the source of his beating and ridicule by Caleb. Dane gives a telltale look and nod to his underlings, as Claretta goes on. "And I want to thank you fo' lettin' me earn extra money here," she tells Sue Ann. "Now with the money we earn at the factory, B. J. and I can buy a better house. The one we wanted burned down."

"A silk wedding dress and a house," says Hank. "All of that and a wedding at night, of all things."

"That be right, Mister Hank," says Claretta.

"We keep on top of things like that girl," says Dane, drunk to the point of almost falling out of his chair, "of coons having enough money to buy things. Especially things such as coons owing cars and houses, things that will give them a big head. Right now, however, we're not interested in what comes out of your mouth, just what comes between your—"

"Hush up, Dane!" says one of the ladies of the night. She turns to Claretta. "Just ignore those guys. But, honey, about your wedding. Why at night?"

"Well," begins Claretta, "lots of folk are there right now to help us fix

364

up the church tonight. And lots more gonna be there by the time I get there. Folks all have to clean white folks' houses or look fo' work or work in the fields to survive and got no time in the day fo' attendin' no weddin'. Right now folks there is waitin' fo' me and Billy Joe, Miss Sue, right this very now. That's why I got to go," she pleads, turning toward Sue Ann.

"Listen to that fool," remarks one of the drunken men. " 'Right this very now.' "

Having heard insults all of her life, Claretta politely goes on, trying to ignore the men and focuses on the kind whore. "Folks are busy fixin' all that food fo' the weddin' feast. You girls, and you too, Miss Sue Ann, are welcome to come."

"What about us," hisses Dane. "We got real good table manners"

Claretta continues to the others, "We gonna have a whole roast pig and collard greens, sweet-potato pie and . . . my friends gonna jump rope—and—"

"Did you say jump rope at your wedding?" ask Dane.

"Yes-um, Mister Dane. Since I'm jumpin' the broom, we also want to jump the rope, me and ma girlfriends. They all gots their ropes at the church, even as we speak." Claretta beams up at Sue Ann. "It's a new thing us younger generation members wants to do to breathe mo' energy into stuffy old Reverend Harris's church. He said jumpin' rope is a sin, especially in church, but we plan to do it anyway."

"Nobody jumps rope at weddings, Claretta," says one of the prostitutes.

"They niggers aren't they," Dane says and laughs. "After they jump, let 'em use the ropes to hang themselves and save us the trouble of doing it for them before them two can make more tar babies in a town that's fed up with 'em."

Claretta covers her mouth, then her ears and bursts into tears.

"Animals!" yells Sue Ann at the laughing men. She hurries Claretta out the door and into the arms of Billy Joe, who is decked out in a blue serge suit. "Go," Sue Ann yells to them, then whirls back to Dane. "Don't you ever insult my help like that again or, so help me God, I'll press charges that not even that corrupt sheriff will be able to wiggle you out of. I still have plenty of leverage in this town! Everyone knows damn well that you and your drunken old man and the Klan hanged and burned those schoolkids back in twenty-nine, and more since. I don't care how long ago it was that you killed them, but as God is my witness,

I'll swear in court—along with Caleb, if he still wants to take you and Reverend Miller there—that you punks came in here and bragged about killing 'em during one of your damn drunken rages. And if you put your hands on me or this place, I'll tell Barney that it was you who killed Lilly. Then let's see how long you laugh. If I know Barney, and I do, he already knows you killed Lilly, the woman he once cared enough about to hang you out to dry, especially if he's urged to do so. Now get out of here!"

"Fuck you and God," shouts Dane. "I guess now you'll say that we whites ought to let them ink spots sleep with whites, intermarry, pray and go to church with whites, that we all have the same God? No wonder people like Barney worship the devil."

"Like you all don't by your actions, you son-of-a-bitches?" says Sue Ann. "Don't you get it, Dane?" Sue Ann presses on. "You're a snake in the grass. Didn't anyone get it? There isn't but one God, and me and my girls are sinners. We admit it, but you guys don't believe in Him, only in your damn selves and in the devil if you're a killer! Didn't men feel it besides us women?" begs Sue Ann. "The day the morning sky turned into night and took away our sun, I felt Him, Dane. Felt Jesus." She points to the large bar mirror, "I saw His handwriting on that mirror. 'Pray,' 'pray,' 'pray.' "

Dane hurls one of the mugs across the room, smashing the bar mirror, and staggers to the back door. The rest of the drunks, including Trout—stumping behind on his crutches—and Scott, whom they drag off the floor while tripping over one another, follow Dane into the alley.

"They're going after that girl," one of the whores says.

Sue Ann goes to the window and looks toward Colored Town, then up at the stars and whispers. "God, don't let them catch her. If those men have an ounce of Christianity left in them, please let them remember it and stay away from that child." The two ladies of pleasure sidle up to Sue Ann and hold onto her in dread and ponder over Claretta's safety, knowing that they can do nothing, now, to help her.

Once outside, after first pushing the masturbator on board, the men toss aside shovels and ropes on Hank's handyman truck and climb onto the bed, all thoughts of Christianity having already evaporated from them as quickly as water drops sizzling away on a hot, tin roof. Dane and Hank climb into the cab, and Dane slides behind the steering wheel. "I smell black pussy in the air!" Dane exclaims, driving wildly through the square, scattering the angry job-seeking protestors. Placing his hand on his crotch, he bellows. "Let's get her!"

26

The Horse That Flies

In Colored Town, a short half-mile from Sue Ann's bar—there shielded from the light of the moon by the overhanging branches of a sprawling magnolia tree, Old Clara patiently waits for her masters' commands, while tethered to the Brooks' wagon. Caleb and Henry are also patiently waiting, as they sit on the hard wagon seat, their sights on the road leading out of White Town and across the train tracks toward their present position. The tree, which Caleb, Henry, the wagon and Old Clara are under, is growing on a section of the colored church's four acres, next to a five-foot-high, two-foot-wide, glass-front display box, containing the schedules of Reverend Harris's Sunday church-service. The scheduling box has a large bell on top of it, a bell with a rope dangling from it. Looming a football field away in the background from the display box, from the tree and from the Brooks, is Harris's church. The small, freshly painted building—including the four-foot-high wooden cross atop of it—is in the middle of a treeless field and glowing snow-white under the full moon, as joyous pre-matrimonial music and singing streams from it into the cool night air. On the wagon, Caleb is first to spot Billy Joe and Claretta who—in that red Hudson—after avoiding the whites on the square drive jerking and stalling across the train tracks from the darkened streets of White Town and into Colored Town. B.J., instead of trying to force the impaired car the rest of the way to the church, parks it on the edge of the road near the church's widespread property, and he and Claretta tenderly kiss.

"When Naomi said that two kids would die tonight, I thought she might mean B.J. and Claretta," whispers Caleb to Henry. "Anyway, it looks like they're okay. Thanks for waiting with me, Papa," he says, never taking his sights off of Claretta. "I'm sorry about always troubling you about this Naomi business."

"Lately, she's often been wrong, Caleb. Like the last time she told Sarah that rain would fall on their crops and it didn't and hasn't, but she is blessed in many unexplainable ways just the same, son."

"About Naomi's powers, Papa," Caleb says, again his sights never leaving the girl he loves, "Flynn said Naomi told Sarah that they're leaving her: Her powers, that is if she really ever had any such. Could the power of suggestion have made us all think she ever was special?"

"Caleb, Christ healed the blind, raised the dead, and still most didn't believe in His Godly powers. And where did Naomi say her lost powers was going? To you, son. If you doubt they exist, try using them and find out." Caleb—who has been focusing on Claretta all of this time—turns away from her and faces his father with a blank look on his face, while a distant and happy Claretta is whispering happy nothings into B.J.'s ear, about three hundred yards beyond the bell and church display box. Henry follows Caleb's gaze back to them and continues. "Those miracles that happened in Lourdes, Caleb, had their doubters too. People there couldn't believe what they saw and heard at first either."

"That's a beautiful story," Caleb says, once more facing his father. "Lourdes," he whispers. "Papa, just think how it might have changed the world if it were true."

"A girl, son, named Bernadette, saw a vision of Sarah's Virgin Mary." Henry's eyes fill with hope, and he continues. "You said, 'if it were true,' and I truly believe it was. Think of it. One pure, innocent child turning that town into a pilgrimage center for the world, and it did change the world, but too soon the world returned to its ugly ways, 'cause we humans always forget, even as most of us have forgotten Christ and why He died for us."

"I'm not a cute, lovable, little girl, and this isn't 1860, and Cutterville certainly isn't Lourdes, Papa."

"Tell Him you're bewildered over His glorious gift, Caleb, a gift that Naomi can't hold in trust forever for you, and once she loses it because you refuse it, the gift might not never be returned to mankind, to our dead and alive white sisters and brothers, who many of them, no doubt, were dark of skin, when Jesus was alive, but today, will never know that Jesus is dark indeed, like the good priest said years ago. Many, if not all of Jesus' disciples were good, dark-skinned men to my way of thinking now, and if we don't realize this before we die, what will become of those decent white folks who never accepted this idea of a black Jesus? Tell Him, Caleb, and He will make clear the way for you."

"It's time to leave now," Caleb whispers.

"Son, don't you want to attend Claretta's wedding?"

"Billy Joe and Claretta are happy. That's all that matters now. Let's just go home, where it's quiet, and I can think over these many thoughts you've crowded into my mind, home where I hear the crickets singing and feel the ocean's salty mist on my brow."

"That salty air that you yearn for and that touches your brow is His tears, Caleb. The tears of our Savior, the tears of Jesus Christ."

Henry gently lashes Old Clara, sending her on her way. After father and son leave, B.J. and Claretta laughingly skip along under the stars toward the display box, following the sound of jubilant singing and hand clapping coming from the house of God. When B.J. and Claretta step onto church property—a hundred yards or so before reaching the Sunday-service scheduling box and bell, they spot Hank's truck speeding toward them.

"There's that dark pussy!" one of the men in the back of the truck yells, pounding on the cab roof. The men slip into their white hoods. "We'll scare the piss out of them two hanks and pick 'em clean."

"Run," cries Billy Joe, pushing Claretta on ahead of him toward the display box and the church, nearly another hundred yards beyond the box and bell. "Get to the church!"

Dane cuts them off well before they reach the church-service scheduling box, and the six-man wall of hooded Klansmen swarm from the vehicle and surround Claretta, including the masturbator, who is giggling and hardly able to stand up.

A horrified Billy Joe pleads to the Klansmen. "Please, y'all, Claretta and I gonna get married in the church and . . ."

Dane blindsides B.J., knocking out his tooth, bloodying up his new-bought blue suit. Claretta desperately follows a silent, teary-eyed Billy Joe's longing vigil to the church's warm yellow light gleaming across the darkness of the grassless field at them. Claretta, screams for help, but two of the men grab her while old Hank covers her mouth with his hand. Dane and the others glare at Billy Joe, daring him to react. "Leave her be," B.J. yells, pushing a Klansman away from Claretta with reckless abandon for his own safety.

Dane elbows aside the staggering drunks and confronts Billy Joe head on. "You touched a white man, you monkey-face. Are you following Caleb Brooks' lead by touching us? And what'd you just say, boy?" demands Dane. "Run that by me again. 'Leave her be?' You talking back as well as touching us? You learned that from Caleb fucking Brooks, also? Is

369

that what you call yourself doing? Learning from Caleb, 'cause you saw him whipping my ass?"

B. J. and Claretta—her mouth brutally held shut—sob in oneness, fearing what's next.

"We ain't caused no trouble," cries B.J. "What you want with us? Please take yo' hands off her."

Old Hank glares through the large eyeholes of his sheeted hood and, with his free hand, touches Claretta's breast. She clamps her teeth onto his wrist, and Hank turns her around and slaps her, and when he does, a screeching Billy Joe charges headlong, ramming Hank in the side, with his head, knocking him down, then kicks old Trout off his crutches, and slams himself into several others. Grabbing Claretta's hand, B.J. runs toward the church. Dane leaps into the truck and starts after the two flailing youths, as the courageous boy all but drags Claretta along; they manage to get within a stone's throw away from the scheduling box and bell, while screaming for help; however, the hand clapping and forceful singing inside the distant small building drowns out B.J.'s and Claretta's desperate cries. Dane runs into the two of them with Hank's truck, bashing both off their feet, while bumping into the display box's concrete foundation, cracking it even more than it is already. By the time Billy Joe gets off the ground, limping, and jerks Claretta to her feet, Dane leaps from his truck and quickly overpowers them. As Dane stands watch over the exhausted black teenagers, gasping for air under his hood, the other Klansmen arrive stumbling and tripping, then dance about the terrified couple. Flinging their arms up and down, the intoxicated men mimic the black fan-carrying chicken strutters who had insulted members of the corrupt group during Crazy Walter's cut-off-my-legs speech. The inebriated men giggle at the distant church, a bunch of drunken, little boys seeking the excitement by taunting the building, as if wanting the blacks inside to come out and chase them, everyone except Dane. He continues to leer down at Billy Joe, recalling the humiliation that Caleb had laid upon him; and Billy Joe—sensing the worst—once again looks toward the church windows, so close, but, so far away to B.J. No one is looking out of God's windows to save them. Only the sound of music streams from the building will be a witness to their fate.

"Please, God," whispers B.J. gazing at the stars, "at least You look out Your windows—the way Naomi told Sarah that yo' angels do, and please, God, have mercy on me and Claretta."

"Calm down," says Dane. "We just want a taste of your girl's honey, that's all. Caleb's girl. The girl he thought enough of to want to marry and still loves as far as I'm concerned."

"Leave her be, Dane. I know that voice of yo's, and Caleb, he be special. Folks say so! A good friend of Jesus. Caleb loves me and Claretta. He does. Proved it by the way he cried and then talked with love after he found me and Claretta together. I'm gonna tell Caleb. Ifin you hurt us, he'll hurt you back real bad, the way he did on your car lot."

As B.J.'s sad eyes lock onto Dane's riveting ones of fury, Dane delivers a stinging fist blow to Billy Joe's face, splitting his lip and splattering his blood.

"You gonna tell Caleb nothin'! I run this Klan, not God, not Caleb shitty-ass Brooks, who sits on the toilet and wipes his ass just like the rest of us. He's not more powerful than my hatred of him is, and I got enough of that in me to destroy the whole fucking world!"

A half mile away, his entire world turned upside down—as Henry sits in silence— Caleb is mindlessly yearning to escape into a simpler past. He looks down at initials on the wagon seat, carved there with his pocket knife: those of his, Flynn's and Claretta's. He and Henry sit back as Old Clara, without being guided, pulls the wagon down the unlit road at her own pace for home, her breath rhythmically matching her gait, bursting from her nostrils in the cool, night air. The rocking wagon, the micromoments of peaceful silence between the sounds of Old Clara's exhaled breaths and the reverberation of hooves against the earthen road is lulling Caleb into merciful sleep. Suddenly he opens his eyes and he jumps off the wagon and he races back toward the church.

"Son! What is it, son?"

Henry attempts to turn Old Clara around. The horse refuses to stir. Henry's eyes blink wide open. Standing in front of Old Clara in the middle of the road, blocking her way, is that prancing white horse and Naomi, the two pieces of eagle's feather in her hair, as she sits majestically on the powerful creature, the white steed's penetrating eyes looking at Old Clara, as if commanding her to stand down. "God has granted you your wish to take Caleb's place, Henry Brooks," says Naomi, "but not this night. This burden Caleb must face alone, his first hurtful steps toward his destiny."

"Hurtful, Naomi?"

"Yes, Henry. Very hurtful."

"It's the Light, isn't it, Naomi? What is It having my boy running to? I feel afraid for him. Will he see It, Naomi? Will my boy see the Light that shone down on him and Flynn that winter's night? Will It let my boy's enemies destroy him or Flynn, because Caleb has refused to recognize God in his heart and has not stood up and fought against Barney with all of his hooded evil?"

"Only Caleb's appointment with the keeper of the Light can tell us that, Henry, but tonight, Caleb will indeed battle evil."

"The 'keeper of the Light,' Naomi? What is that?"

"The Thing that was there when Caleb was born, a Thing that witnessed his after birth giving life to the red tree and a thing which Caleb must seek in the end to help him battle Barney; now wait here and pray for your son until the Light of Love, that no man or woman is allowed to see, fades in the sky: Only then can you come for your son. Two young souls will, on this night, rise into the sky in good stead to purgatory, but will be fully awakened from the dead, as they ascend toward the sky, long enough to call out to Caleb to encourage him to kill evil before it grows stronger and kills him."

Henry watches Naomi race that mighty horse toward Harris's church, and then he eases to his knees on the wagon in prayer; Old Clara glances back at him and patiently waits.

At the church, Hank has retrieved a shovel from the truck and is now sneaking up behind Billy Joe.

"Claretta ain't one of Lana's girls!" pleads B.J. to the men that he and Claretta face, unaware of Hank and that shovel of death.

"She is now," hisses Dane, nodding to Hank, who strikes B.J. in his head with the shovel, sending the boy's blood exploding in all directions. Claretta closes her eyes as she's struck in her face with his warm blood. "That's fer being with Caleb, who had the balls to attack me, a white man," yells Dane, going on. "Me! A mother fucking Klansman on his own car lot!"

Claretta opens her eyes and sees B.J. on the ground bleeding from his skull; she collapses and crawls on her hands and knees to her man. One of the Klansmen grabs her by her leg, while Hank and others drag B.J.'s body several yards across the churchyard, so that they might have room to rape Claretta and not be contaminated by Billy Joe's dark, rich blood; they then race back to be first to jump on the stunned girl. Dane stops the oncoming sex-starved men. He leans down and laughs in Claretta's face. Claretta kicks two of the drunks off their feet, then spits in Dane's face. Gasping, Dane falls back, rubbing the sputum from his mouth and cheeks, as if it, too, will turn into the acid which had scarred him so definably during the rape and killing of Geraldine, all of the Klansmen backing off in fear.

After his initial scare, and there is no cutting pain, Dane backhands Claretta across her mouth, picks her up and throws her to the ground, rips off her skirt, strips off her blouse, tears off her underwear and gags her with them. Pull at her thighs as they might, the drunken men can't unlock her strong rope-jumping legs. Dane then drags her kicking and yelping toward the bell and bulletin board. After he gets her there, he yells at his men, "Get me ropes from the truck, you damn weak-ass punks." When the ropes are delivered to him, Dane has his men tie both of Claretta's arms to the nearby magnolia tree, then binds her right leg to the truck bumper and ropes off her left leg around the church's display box, with its truck-damaged foundation.

Dane drives the pickup forward in increments, his mouth watering at the sight of Claretta's shapely nude body, at her powerful, brown legs inching apart, against the truck's might, at her stiff pubic hairs being uncovered all the more in the moonlight with each forward inching of the truck tires, until Claretta's legs are spread to the fullest. Leaping from the truck, Dane fights off the other Klansmen in order to be the first to penetrate Claretta. After they finish with her, and as the inspirational singing continues uninterrupted from the small house of God, and as Caleb—sprinting all out—closes the distance between them, Dane returns for seconds on Claretta's battered body, his groans of gratification assaulting against the young girl's ears, his tobacco-stained lips sucking at her tender breast. Claretta partly chews through her underwear and sets her sights on the sparkling white cross atop Harris's distant church.

"Reverend Harris," she mutters through the tattered gag, "tell God I been as good a girl as I could be." She looks over at Billy Joe's bloody body and whimpers. "Tell Him I'm pregnant with Billy Joe's baby. Tell Him Billy Joe and I thought it was no sin, 'cause Billy Joe and I love each other. Tell Him, Reverend Harris. Tell Him now. Caleb," she gasps in pain, as Dane violently flails atop of her. "Caleb, where are you? I hurt,

Caleb. I hurt all over." She looks at the far-off church door. "Mamma, come help me, Mamma."

As Dane struggles to reach his second climax on the sobbing girl, and the other men tuck in their limp tools of rape and climb aboard the truck, leaving behind a spiritually broken Claretta, tied to the bumper, the tree, and the display box, and gasping for air, Dane hears then sees Caleb yelling and sprinting toward them. Giggling, Dane leaps off Claretta, tucks in his penis, bounds into the truck and starts the motor.

"Nooo," blares Caleb, when he sees Claretta and the ropes binding her to the vehicle.

With Caleb running at them and shouting, Dane smiles down at Claretta. "Never spit on a white man, bitch! Now, Caleb can have what's left of you."

Flooring the gas pedal and popping the clutch, Dane roars the truck forward, pulling down the bulletin board and the bell, dragging parts of the display fixture, the clanging bell and a shrieking Claretta down the road behind the truck, in the direction of the white section of town and pass a shocked, wide-eyed Caleb.

Inside the church, everyone stops singing and listens in apprehension to the sound of the tumbling, clanging bell, and the men of the church order the women and children to remain inside, and they race from the building and into the night.

Meanwhile, outside in the truck, Dane slows down the pickup so that Caleb can catch up to Claretta, all the time Dane grinning with wickedness as Caleb—off balance, flailing, stumbling—grabs hold of the rope that secures Claretta to the truck and attempts to cut it with his pocket knife.

"How does it feel now, Caleb, asshole Brooks!" the one-eared man yells, as the truck continues on at that slower speed, the Klansmen on the bed of the vehicle spitting down at and laughing at Caleb and at a mortified, bumping-along Claretta, whose sights never leave those of Caleb, silently begging him to save her, a girl in shock and now numb against the pain, and not realizing what a devastated Caleb now sees, that she has lost a leg, part of her hand and is gushing blood. As Caleb frantically cuts away at the rope, the men in the rear of Hank's old Dodge begin slinging moonshine from their jars on him, one of them urinating at Caleb to no avail, Caleb ignoring them, while cutting away at that blood-slicked rope, as he calls to Claretta, telling her to hold on.

374

Dane waits until Caleb has nearly severed the rope, then speed off, jerking Claretta's body so violently that the rope snaps, sending her tumbling to a stop against the train tracks and then bouncing back and impacting a nearby Judas tree, knocking off one of it branches, its blooms raining down on her, as the truck continues to speed away. When Caleb, gasping for air, approaches Claretta, blood is everywhere, on the ground, on the tree, and on him and his clothing. He stops and calls to her, and—hearing no reply filled with apprehension—Caleb continues slowly to her and the tree, his teeth chattering, his courage now completely gone. A sight meets his eyes so gruesome that Caleb vomits; he hears Henry and Naomi's voices: "Caleb must face it alone, his first hurtful steps of his destiny."

"Hurtful, Naomi?"

"Yes, Henry. Very hurtful."

Partly blanketed in shadows, Claretta's body is torn in half. Poking through her dark, coagulating blood is her white thighbone looming up at Caleb; her once-smooth ebony skin is stripped from her stomach, the unborn child's arm, broken and bloody, sticking from her torn abdomen, her breasts torn off, her neck broken, her eyes open to the sky. Caleb thrusts his arms up over his head and bellows a Zulu hair-raising cry; the male congregation—having entered the outside and followed Caleb's alarming cry and the trail of blood from the toppled bell—now stand a few feet away from Henry's boy with their black faces and Zulu white, warrior-like eyes fixed downward on Claretta's twisted body, and then those eyes in oneness focus on the one they all now know is their unwilling young leader, and their sights never leave Caleb, their ears are tuned to his painful, primitive cries. Many of them—having been together for generations—recalling their African heritage, remove their shoes and socks and rigidly posture themselves and trample their bare feet on the dusty earth and bounce up and down in place honoring Caleb, as would a jungle tribe before their native chief, and out of the darkness of hatred in the world around them, they become one with Caleb's agony, and with raised arms and clenched fists, their unified cry for revenge is heard for miles around. Then, led by a timid-looking Reverend Harris, the women and children approach the far-flung bodies. Gasping, the youngest of the young ones run wailing back into the church, away from the monstrous sight. An elderly woman takes one look at Claretta's body, grabs her chest and drops to the ground and never rises again.

Ever so slowly, Bruce steps through the wall of men. He takes off his shoes and walks barefooted, as does Carrie. Bruce takes his wife's hand and he and Carrie move to Claretta's dismembered body, where Carrie falls to the ground beside her child's butchered remains and sobs. When Reverend Harris attempts to shield her with his embrace from the view of Claretta's remains, she violently nudges him away. Among those about Claretta is Billy Joe's frightened mother, looking about for her son, and—after realizing that he is missing—she backtracks and finds his body. The woman goes into a state of madness, a squalling, jump-up-and-down, stamping fit. Carrie, however, quietly remains sitting on the bloody soil next to her child. Her gaze shifts to the nearby wall of warrior-like, black, barefoot men, who have their sights on Caleb. Carrie looks up at Caleb with compassion and love, knowing that he had tried his best to save Claretta, and knows how devastated he must feel standing there covered with her blood and seemingly totally drained. Then, as her mother had done when her husband was killed, and her mother's mother before that, Carrie begins smearing Claretta's blood over her face, over her arms and over her legs in the manner of her African tradition, then returns to embracing her child's remains, while never taking her sights off Caleb, Carrie, with all of that blood smeared on her, appearing as if a wild beast.

A tearful Bruce sits on the ground at Carrie's side and mimics her actions, spreading Claretta's blood on his face and holds onto his wife—as she clings to Claretta's remains, and Bruce rocks Carrie in his arms and wearily sobs. Earlene and Brick, hugging and hiding their faces on the other's shoulder, wail in profound sorrow. Carrie looks over at them, then back up at Caleb and she cries aloud. "Tell Him, Caleb. You who loved my child and is bathed in her blood, tell Him I surrender my child and me to Him. Tell Him Caleb Brooks, you who they say have the power of Naomi. Tell God to take me with ma child!"

"No, Caleb," begs Bruce, his bloody hand reaching up and grabbing those of Henry's boy. "We can't live without my wife, me and the kids. Please, Caleb, don't encourage ma God to cause Carrie to die of heartbreak or something else and leave me, or our other children, here alone."

Caleb looks about with concern. *If there is indeed a God,* he tells himself, *then surely God will strike him dead if everyone continues viewing him as their saint.* In spite of knowing of Caleb's feelings, that he takes little stock in the Bible and none in most churches, nearly everyone there continues looking at him with awe and with profound, fearful respect. Reverend Harris, for this reason, even now, glares at Caleb with eyes of hatred, this because he feels Caleb has turned Carrie and the congregation against him.

"Caleb ain't God," he says. "Now, let's get these bodies into the real God's church and pray over them, so we can bury them in our cemetery as soon as possible."

"The law say the coroner first gots to put his mark on papers about them po' dead kids' bodies befo' we can bury them, " says a sad bystander.

"The hell with the coroner!" hisses Harris, for one of the few times publicly condemning a white man. "That damn coroner won't show up until he's good and ready and—"

"Stop it!" yells Caleb, glaring at Harris. "Is that all there is to it? Gossiping about what I am or am not? And then 'let's bury them.' They kill them and you bury them?" he says to Harris, while pointing at Claretta and B.J.'s bloody remains, over the sobbing and wailing voices of despair from the women and the young, the barefoot men gaining courage from Caleb's damning resound.

As Caleb rebukes the preacher, the sheriff's car—lights flashing, sirens blaring—pulls into the churchyard, and Sheriff Richards and his son-in-law, Deputy Snodgress, alight from the vehicle. When Richards shines his flashlight on Carrie and Bruce's faces and sees how Carrie is glaring up at him through all of that red blood smeared on her face, he steps back. "Jesus!" He looks at Snodgress, who eases out his service revolver and holds it at the ready, as Richards goes on with Carrie. "What in God's name are you sitting down there and looking up at me fer with all that hatred in your eyes and all that blood on your damn face like some wild woman?" asks Richards, the sweat pouring from him, as he inches closer to Snodgress after seeing all of these bare feet and angry faces.

"Colonel Cutter," begins Richards, noticing how the barefoot black men now are glaring at him, "said there might be a problem over here in Colored Town tonight. He said his boys paid Claretta to entertain them in Sue Ann's bar." He glances at B.J.'s body, "Then, Billy Joe came into that bar, and because they were to get married, that poor, backwards boy got it in his head to attack Claretta and chased her all the way out here. Barney said if she died of anything, it was from an accident, that's all.

377

From Billy Joe running over her with that new-bought car of his after she had rough sex with them white boys, which—again—she was paid fer."

"Did you examine the car, Sheriff?" calmly asks Caleb.

"What fer, boy? And you stay out of this, boy. Look at all that blood on you, also. Maybe you killed them two?"

"If B.J. ran over Claretta with his car, there should be blood all over it as well," says Caleb. "Again, I ask you. Did you inspect his damn car?"

Everything is suddenly quiet as a grave. Snodgress and Richards look around. All of those angry, warrior-like eyes are hatefully on them now, ready to explode, even the children's.

"Did you, Sheriff?" asks Carrie, looking with eyes to kill at the lawman.

"I . . . I told Dane I'd tow that damn Hudson to the junkyard before I came here," says Richards, as a tow truck is seen in the distance towing away B.J.'s car. "It's damaged so bad it's a danger to leave on the road," Richards exclaims. "Might catch fire. And there *was* blood all over it." He squints at a glaring Caleb, "You folks got to understand that old angry-eyed Caleb over there forced Dane to give up that car with some fancy legal mumble jumble. Congratulations, Caleb Brooks, seems like all of this was caused by you, when you forced Dane to hand over that car to that dumb boy, a car that killed both of them; and now it's on your conscience, not mine."

"Liar," shouts B.J.'s mother, racing away from B.J.'s body and from those trying to hold onto her. She storms up to Richards and points her finger back at her son's body. "You devil!" she yells at Richards "Don't you got no conscience!"

Richards shines his flashlight onto the woman's fierce, dark eyes. "Watch yourself, woman," he tells her.

"Claretta was rope-tied, Sheriff," Caleb hisses, approaching the lawman, the barefoot, black men following. "What kind of fools do you take us for? And take that damn light out of her eyes."

Grumbling, the blacks, as a whole close the distance between them and the lawmen, their fierce eyes cutting into the hearts of the white officers and startling Caleb, who looks around and now knows how the power of words, his words, can so easily move people to violence. Naomi once told him that his words, are not only able to move the black community, into violent action, but also able to move the very mountains if he chose them to do so, as promised by Jesus. Carrie releases Claretta

378

and, covered with blood from head to toe, runs at the white lawmen. "Get out of here, Sheriff Richards, befo' I kill you, you Satan!"

Richards whips out his revolver, and as Carrie's female friends pulls her away from him, the sheriff fires his gun in the air and shouts to Snodgress. "Call fer backup, Reggie, now!"

While Deputy Snodgress radios for help, the crowd drags Billy Joe's mother and Carrie crying, kicking and screaming backwards. "Ma baby," Carrie shouts, "Don't leave ma baby out here with them two, white Satans!" She looks at Caleb. "Kill them two mad dogs, Caleb Brooks," she exclaims, causing Snodgress to gawk at Caleb, while yelling over the patrol car radio for help, his heart racing, as Carrie continues. "Ifin you all that Naomi say you be—blessed, Caleb Brooks—kill Sheriff Richards now with yo' very eyes just by looking at him. He as good as killed ma girl. He be one of them. He and that one with him, in the car, be a Klan too!" She claws back at Richards, as the congregation continues pulling her away. "What kind lawman is you not to know that God is watchin' you, Sheriff Richards? He's watchin' you and yo' deputies!"

Snodgress is profoundly distressed by Carrie's words of their doom, but not Richards.

"God has His work to do, I got mine," says Richards, as Snodgress—from within the patrol car—continues hearing Carrie's haunting words of damnation and with more than a little concern for his very soul reflected on his face; he zeroes in on Caleb's light-brown eyes, eyes that Carrie thinks can kill just by looking at them, eyes that are staring at him. The deputy turns away, as an outraged Richards warns the crowd, "Go on in the church or home now befer my deputies get here! You all know what Deputy Hammer will do to you, you who gave him that name in the first place. To you, also, Caleb, Hammer will break you in two, and that bitch Naomi, as well. That goddamn nigger faker who started all of this in the first damn place, when she came here with the Winthrops. I should have shot that witch in her head at Barney's wedding, then and there and maybe none of this would be happening now." Richards moves to Harris's side. "Get these people out of here," he tells him. "Now!"

"He's right about that," yells Harris. "Both Caleb and Naomi are playin' with fire by sayin' that God is with them, as if He ain't with the rest of us and the whites of this town. Now gather up the dead. Hurry! You heard the man. Deputy Hammer's coming!"

Richards leaves Snodgress at the car on the radio and helps Harris herd the females and teenagers to the church. However, before the bodies can be carried into the building, four cars with flashing, red lights and blaring sirens zoom onto the area. Deputies pile out, hot on the heels of the blacks, clubs swinging. Then—all muscles—and towering nearly seven-feet-tall and weighing over three-hundred and fifty pounds, Deputy Hammer steps from one of the patrol cars, causing the car to dip, then spring several inches upwards. He stands there with his bloodshot eyes, with his specially-made hardwood club, which he calls, his stick of obedience or of death, depending on who refuses to obey him or who is passive and obedient and follows his orders. Those he has mercy on, a broken bone or two for them, that's all. "All of you fairies," he yells to the crowd, "you might as well give your queer souls to Jesus, because your asses are mine. Queers! All of you! I hate queers." Picking out his victims, he sees Brick running to the church and yelling:

"The white devil is here, y'all. The white devil. Run!"

Hammer goes after the retarded boy and corners him shrieking a dozen yards from the church's front door and kicks him to the ground. "Stop that yelling, damn you," he orders Brick, who continues blaring out and calling for his mother, drawing the attention of Caleb instead.

Just as Hammer is drawing back to strike Brick with that club of disobedience, Caleb sprints over and pushes the huge man aside. Hammer is shocked, totally surprised by Caleb's action. While the deputy is distracted by Caleb, wailing at the top of his voice, Brick dashes to his mother—who wrestles free of those trying to restrain her and races to her son. After he falls into her arms she holds onto him, Carrie then stands there with her sights on Caleb and a roaring, Deputy Hammer, who charges at Caleb with his club with the intent of killing Henry's son. Caleb ducks out of the way. Again Hammer swings; this time at Caleb's head with pinpoint accuracy but as a terrified Carrie and Brick hold onto each other and watch, Caleb reaches up and stops the forward motion of the heavy instrument in mid flight with one hand and holds onto it.

"Mamma," Brick cries to Carrie. "Look!"

Deputy Snodgress has also been watching from Richards's patrol car, and Caleb sees him.

"Take the boy out of here," Caleb calls to Carrie, as Snodgress approaches.

After fleeing up the church steps, Carrie and Brick watch Caleb wrestle with the badge-wearing giant, who with both of his oversized hands, is jerking and pulling and unable to out-muscle Caleb, and is stunned by Caleb's unbelievable and seemingly inhuman strength. The towering man turns pale with anxiety, as does Snodgress—who is fighting his own fears about God and Caleb, but knowing that he has no choice but to go to the aid of his fellow officer—somehow manages to continue toward Hammer with his gun drawn and trembling in his hand, Caleb, one-handedly still holding onto the club.

"Let go, you black ape!" hisses an exhausted Hammer, unaware that help is on the way. "You evil demon. What lurks in that evil soul of yours to allow you to hold onto my club like that?"

With no sign of weakening, Caleb maintains his grip on the club, until the snorting and gasping giant burns himself out and goes down on one knee. Seemingly ready to pass out, Hammer releases the club and catches his breath. Breaking the heavy stick in half, Caleb flings the pieces aside. It's then that Hammer reaches for his revolver, but Caleb seizes the huge man's weapon from his holster before Deputy Hammer can get to it. With the revolver in hand, Caleb looks at the approaching Snodgress, some twenty yards away now. Snodgress stops dead in his tracks and gawks about for help. All the other deputies have their hands full and haven't noticed him or Hammer. Horrified and feeling that if he fired his weapon at Caleb, that the invisible power which people say that Caleb has will redirect the bullet back on him, Sheriff Richards's cowardly son-in-law remains frozen on the spot. Caleb tosses Hammer's revolver away, leaving Hammer, Snodgress, Carrie and Brick—back at the church—wondering what Caleb would do next. Henry's boy takes Hammer's hand and helps the exhausted deputy to his feet and walks away, leaving the stunned giant looking over at a perplexed Snodgress, both far less decisive now.

When Caleb passes the church, he sees Brick and a bloody Carrie standing on the top steps gawking down at him. As bizarre as she might appear to others, to Caleb, Carrie—standing there—is a beautiful symbol of someone who was willing to give up her life and die with Clarette. Brick and Carrie, nonetheless, have their own idea of majesty. Her mouth covered by her hand, her and her boy's eyes wide, mother and son stand in shock, as they watch Caleb continue past them, their facial expressions saying what they can't express in words: that Caleb truly is from God.

When Caleb—as if feeling Brick staring at him—looks back, the mentally impaired boy snaps to attention, his shoulders level, his back straight, and legs unbending, he salutes Caleb. Brick is proud to be colored for the first time in his life. Once Caleb continues on his way, Bruce—who has been looking for them—runs up to and hurries his family into the church with the others, fleeing from the club-bearing lawmen.

Something extremely unusual happens next. Snodgress, a church-going man who had witnessed the blacks escape into the church, and thus—to him—the Red Sea to escaped their enemies—now watches them coming out again and—after seeing Caleb defeat Hammer—are standing on the steps and facing their enemies, along with those other blacks who had been scurrying to enter the house of God, all of them standing there with Carrie, Brick and Bruce acknowledging Caleb with their eyes of hope, with their voices, everyone on the steps calling out his name with admiration and love, causing the deputies to pause in confusion.

As Caleb makes his way past these lawmen, they resist attacking him. Snodgress looks up at the stars, which break through the clouds in spots, He's as if seeing the heavens for the first time, and with tears in his eyes, he holsters his revolver and ever so slowly returns to the sheriff's car and finds Richards there. "They learned their lesson," he tells his father-in-law, then gazes up at the moon. Richards studies his daughter's husband, then follows Snodgress's sights to the moon. He looks again at Snodgress and for some unknown reason calls off the attack.

Snodgress yells to the blacks, "Come on and get your dead. It's okay."

Quickly returning to the bodies, the more able men of the congregation wrap the deceased young girl in her wedding dress and B.J.'s remains in a blanket because it's all they had at the time, and hurry them into the church; all the time, an angry Deputy Hammer glares at the blacks, as if blaming all of them for the humiliation laid on him by Caleb. A stunned Snodgress, however, keeps his sights on the moon, which—to him—appears to be growing brighter, lighting up the ground and the white-painted old church, and soon the entire countryside is seemingly illuminated as if from the soft light of dawn. Then, from out of the distant of the lit-up night, a bank of fog rolls in, a thick, swiftly moving, ghostly gray fog—to Snodgress it's like no fog he's ever seen, as it eerily sweeps across the warm earth and encircles those men who are carrying Claretta's and B.J.'s bodies to the church. The main congregation, which remains on the church steps, looks about in apprehension of the suddenly appearing gray, moist haze, the misty cloud now covering them, the church, and the deputies, who stand about looking at one another, then eyeing the thickening oncoming vapor.

"Sheriff," Snodgress says, "are you still so sure about Naomi and Caleb?"

"What the hell are you talking about?"

"The Bible says that Christ told His disciples that they have all powers that was given to Him to forgive our sins. Do you think Caleb and Naomi can raise the dead, can awaken B.J. and Claretta and maybe have God forgive a person's sins? Don't ask me why I ask that, 'cause I don't really know why."

"I'm sure that that woman is full of shit," says Richards. "And so are you. That's what I'm sure about. The only thing that woman can raise is my dick."

Snodgress hears the sound of distant, galloping, horse hooves, along with the sound of young voices laughing for joy. He glances about.

"Do you hear that?" he asks Richards, both blanketed in the fog. "Let's get out of here."

"Are you nuts, Reggie?" asks Richards, walking away. "It's a damn horse, that's all. My little girl wouldn't like that in you, being soft and proving she's more of a man than you are. I'll be with these apes to make sure they remain in that church or head for home. Don't care which, just as long as this trouble ends, and you stay here and keep your mouth shut. Next thing you know, you'll be singing these coon's praises. Yes, I still believe as I do. She's a shithead faker."

No sooner does Richards leave and fade into the thick mist and approaches the loudly sobbing congregation over their dead, beaten and wounded at the church, then the thundering hooves are suddenly upon Snodgress. He looks this way and that, then locates the direction of the sound and stumbles back gripped in hell-bound holy terror. He sees Naomi as clearly as if the fog did not exist, as she charges through the thick, blanket-of-gray haze on that brilliant white stallion; also riding on the powerful creature with her are two fuzzy-looking figures—a teenage boy sitting behind a girl, with his hands about the girl's waist and holding onto her, a girl—who is behind Naomi—her arms about the mystery woman's waist and holding tightly to her as well as to a new-born baby, a jumping rope dangling from about her wrist, all the time Naomi's hair and the horse's mane glowing with fire. The two laughing, young people and baby are totally nude, two young people elegantly beautified in the flaming light from the great horse's mane and Naomi's hair, the girl's pigtails bouncing. When Snodgress blinks, the Herculean horse flashes by and is gone. Snodgress slumps against the Sheriff's car and stands there shaking and holding onto the vehicle's door. "Sheriff!" he yells, bringing Richards on the run through the curtain of fog.

"What is it, now, man?"

"Did you see it?" Snodgress says, gagging, and mutters "It was Claretta." He looks, wide-eyed at Richards. "It was, Sheriff. Claretta, carrying a jumping rope! Her and Billy Joe and a baby. Had to be!"

Richards glances about and exclaims, "You out of your mind! I see no horse no woman. I'll fire you, son-in-law or not, if I find out you been smoking that mind-rot jimson with the Klan or Miller's damn church members. Next you'll be telling me that God raised them coon kids from the dead when we both know them two tar balls' bodies have been carried into that nigger church."

Even as the bodies of Claretta and Billy Joe are laid to rest on the church floor—under the same blanket now—a few feet away from them, behind the altar and that grotesque, hanging, tree-limb cross, Reverend Harris is standing by a rear church window and holding a large, clear bottle of moonshine in his trembling hand. Ever so slowly he places the bottled moonshine on the window ledge. "My, God!" He presses his face against the cold, window glass. He draws back, his heart trumpeting. Outside in the church's backyard, in stunning bright moonlit, alongside the cemetery, Harris sees Naomi and the white horse, a horse—as Caleb has seen it do in the swamp—seemingly dancing on air, a few feet off the ground, while the nude young riders behind Naomi are laughing and singing with her; Naomi's voice rings out loud and clear to her charges.

"Heaven now awaits you, Billy Joe and Claretta, the first of many, who—on this the last day of my powers—are bequeathed to come into God's embrace, and oh, how the world will envy you."

Harris's eyes pop open, his mouth the same, as he sees the white horse rise off the ground, carrying Naomi, Claretta and B.J. and child with it into the sky, and then—faster and faster—it leaves the church, the town, the state of Georgia, and the earth behind. Harris wobbles back from the window, and as he does, he grabs the moonshine and guzzles the bottle empty. The earth trembles, shaking the church, sending the gargantuan altar cross exploding from its chains and crashing to the floor where it shatters into pieces. As those around the altar scream and scatter, Reverend Harris—still at the window—drops the empty liquor bottle and convulses in horror, and with everything that has and is going on, he hears Claretta's echoing voice calling out Caleb's name as the heavenly-bounders disappear in the stars. Harris looks down at the shattered bottle by his feet, as if at his shattered soul; then—from the window—he sees Henry at an isolated area away from the law in his wagon and watches in trepidation as a devastated, zombie-like Caleb, unhearing and seemingly unseeing, stagger aboard the wagon with his father and is driven away in Henry's arms. Harris steps back from the window and stumbles through the shattered cross material, nudging aside church members who are standing about the bodies. He gawks down at Claretta and Billy Joe's remains on the floor under the blanket, the congregation looking at him, as he sobs, bends over and frantically lifts the blanket.

"Are these kids dead under here, or in the stars?" Church members' eyes widen as they look at each other and then at the reverend, and finally out the window at the starry sky. The fog has lifted. Harris drops to his knees as he gazes down at the youths' bodies and agonizingly stretches out his hands to his frightened congregation. "Lord! Lord," he cries aloud to them.

"What is it, Pastor?" asks the porch-of-wisdom, Jesus-fan lady in red.

"Was that a jumpin' rope around that child's waist?" sobs Harris.

"What child?" asked the woman in fear.

"Was I wrong to tell them kids that jumpin' the rope in church was evil?" asks Harris, going on, "'cause they was lookin' at Lana's girls. Was it really Claretta I saw? Was that the Rapture?" He examines the faces looking down at him. "Did anyone else see them three, Naomi, Claretta and B.J. on that horse flying in the sky and calling out Caleb's name?"

"Ohhh," shouts the women in red. "Halleluiah! God save America."

"B.J. and Claretta," someone else exclaims. "On a flying horse?" Everyone there looks out the nearby windows and then down at the bodies, their hearts also thundering with hope that a true miracle has finally happened for them and in Georgia.

"Reverend said he saw them kids!" the red-dressed woman, who seems to have forgotten she had no love for Caleb, bellows, throwing up her hands and wiggling about for joy. "He said they was a-callin' Caleb Brooks' name?" She's now more than willing to get on the freedom train to heaven with Reverend Harris and the rest of the congregation in praise of Caleb.

"When, Reverend? When did you see 'em? Does this mean Caleb is truly from our God?" someone asks.

Harris sobs, "Who is Caleb Brooks? Who is he really besides the son of Henry Brooks? Where did he come from that a important, rich woman like Sarah Winthrop respects him so? What manner of blood runs in his veins that makes him what he is that folks on this earth looks up to him as if he was a disciple of Christ and that Claretta called to him even as she, B.J. and Naomi was on their way to heaven, rising up on the unseen wings of that white horse into the sky."

"They was a-ridin' on a flying horse!" a man—stiff-necking it, prancing about, wiggling and high stepping—yells, repeatedly, as if he is the one on that soaring horse, and spiritually he was, indeed, riding on that horse, as were they all.

"Who is this powerful God of Caleb and Naomi," Harris continues, while sobbing. "A God who can raise her and that horse and them kids into the sky?"

"In the sky?" the old red-dressed, church sister yells, flapping her arms in chicken style. "Praise the Lord! Cock-a-doodle-doo! I'm chicken struttin' to heaven. Cock-a-doodle-doo!"

Some of the members shout, some stand in silence, some kneel beside Harris, some cry, and some laugh for joy. Others celebrate with a vigorous, foot-stamping, rhythmic dance of ecstasy as they prance around the bodies, nearly breaking through the wooden floor with their powerful, frantic excitation which will live forever in their minds and in those of their children who also dance barefoot beside their parents and the bodies.

"It's true," sobs Harris to his followers and to Billy Joe's mother, to Bruce and Carrie, the four of them sobbing together and, with their living children sitting down beside their beloved dead ones. "There is a God," Harris sputters on. "I had eyes but couldn't see. 'Caleb' that beautiful child kept calling out his name, Carrie." He exclaims to Claretta's mother. "'Caleb,' 'Caleb,' she called. Somebody go out there and catch

Henry and tell him or Caleb what I saw. They in they wagon on Thompson Road. I can't help you no mo'. This is mo' than one man can bear."

While several of the congregation race from the church to find Henry and deliver Harris's message to him, others turn their gaze on Claretta's best friend, Pumpkin. Tears flowing down her cheeks, Pumpkin slips into her shoes, picks up her rope from a bench and begins jumping rope in the center of the church crushing pieces of the pulverized altar cross, and as she jumps her words keep pace with the beat of her strong legs and syncopated feet striking the floor as she utters, "Caleb! Caleb! Caleb!" Soon, all of Claretta's girlfriends are sobbing loudly, calling out Caleb's name while also rope jumping alongside Pumpkin. Their voices stream from the church and across the train tracks into the white community, where the deputies have gathered about their patrol cars; everyone on that side of the tracks now listening to the black, voodoo, African, reverberating sounds coming from Harris's distant church, a sound and a church seemingly—to a growing number of whites—now under God's protection. White men, women and children, are all ill at ease alongside the lawmen and deeply concerned for their safety, a few for that of their young ones' souls if, indeed, God hates ugliness; standing along the tracks and listening to the singing which now begins to stream from the black church, a few of the whites even wonder if Jesus, who was born on that dark African continent, was actually white—the way many on the white side of town think He was.

"Now they're calling out his name, Sheriff," Snodgress whispers to Richards, as the call for Caleb is heard over the singing. "And Colonel Cutter ain't the only one who coming back from the war. Them returning black soldiers—like some of the crowd says—will be gun-happy and well trained, and they'll follow Caleb like them black folks over there seem to want to. You said Caleb was timid like his pa, who didn't even question Old Man Pennington when he left them thousands of dollars on his desk, even when Pennington all but spelled it out that Barney was stealing Henry's land. Caleb . . . He can't be that timid with them folks calling out his name like that. I saw how Caleb Brooks handled Hammer, you didn't."

"Caleb's just a boy, damn you, Reggie, A damn harmless kid who plays with Flynn on that lagoon. You want them worried, poor white trash to hear you? You're driving me crazy." he tells Snodgress. Richards angrily guides Snodgress away from the masses.

"You best be real crazy and nervous, Sheriff," says Snodgress, pulling his arm away from Richards's grip, "Even Flynn thinks the world of Caleb, and Sheriff, them lagoon waters out there on Henry's land—where that priest said the soul of God lives—them waters runs dark and deep; and I did see that horse and Naomi. Did see them kids going off to heaven. God's with them, not with the Klan. All that whispering about Caleb is true. Listen to how they call to him. Just listen fer once in your life. They're calling to him when they used to be like sheep and called to God. Who'll keep them blacks from rising up against us whites now? Caleb's different from them other darkys. Caleb's gonna kill us, Sheriff. Caleb's gonna kill us. God knows he is."

The few whites who had stalked after Richards in the dark now stand in the shadows and groan after hearing Snodgress's bone-numbing confession that God is with Caleb.

"Get the fuck out of here, you damn crackers!" yells Richards, when he spots the whites spying on them. "You eavesdropping assholes!" As the whites run away, Richards nudges Snodgress. "Caleb won't kill anybody. If Colonel Cutter doesn't take care of the half-breed—and I mean real soon—if I have to, I'll kill Barney Cutter, his nigger-loving son, Flynn and Caleb goddamn Brooks, deep waters or not."

27

Judas and the Last Supper

Because the law could care less about following up on the deaths or how or when most blacks are buried, the next day, at Sarah's insistence, Claretta and Billy Joe are buried on Shadow Grove. It's one of the clearest days over Shadow Grove in weeks, not a speck of dust in the air. The field hands are gathered in and around the cemetery, along with Bruce and his sobbing family, who came from town with Claretta's friends, with Billy Joe's parents, and with Reverend Harris and his congregation and his choir, which sways side-to-side and sings over the caskets. The blacks from Cutterville, all of whom have heard about Shadow Grove and have marveled at it, are far more curious about Naomi, all wondering about her and her horse rising to the sky with Claretta and Billy Joe, and everyone, to the last man, woman and child—as well as Sarah's workers—have their sights focused on the mystery woman, who never dresses for social acceptance, only for the spiritual needs of the moment. She is dressed in a colorful Afro-Indian-appearing deerskin dress, a brightly-colored, beaded dress made by her own hands. The dignified mixed-blood woman stands beside Sarah with hundreds of small, silver-like bells hanging from her garment and softly tinkling in the breeze, a sound—according to Naomi— that the angels love.

Flynn and Caleb remain apart from one another in the crowd and in total silence; each—however—even with their earlier acceptance that they were different from most people, and that strange things are happening to them, have a worrisome outlook about the gossip of Naomi and her flying horses. Both boys desperately hope its not true, because—if she did fly away on that horse—it would absolutely prove that a higher power has sealed their fate down that dark road of no return and there is no way to escape from it or from their inner terror. Both also have a sense of helplessness over Claretta and B.J.'s deaths and a feeling that they should have done more to save their lives, Flynn from the point of view of the Klan—since he is the son of the Grand Wizard—and Caleb from the point of view of him and Henry having left the area too early, and he hadn't run fast enough and had arrived on the bloody scene too late.

As Flynn stands there at the gravesite his thoughts spiral around Billy Joe:

B.J.—such a pathetic soul—whom they had loved and teased, and now sorely miss.

Even if it didn't happen on a flying horse, Flynn, at least, prays that Claretta and B.J. are indeed heaven bound. Flynn had asked Barney if he had ordered the death of B.J. and Claretta; and Barney, because he truly had no part in the slaughter, had said "No," and Flynn believed his father. Even though Barney isn't there, Caleb, Flynn and Sarah—each in their own way—feel his eerie presence and from time-to-time glance over their shoulders at the manor's windows. After the service, the spectators file by the closed caskets and leave, Sarah, however, has her sights and thoughts on Caleb and Flynn.

Are my sons now mortal enemies, God?

The next morning, as the sun rises over Shadow Grove, Sarah—wearing a sweatshirt and trousers—eases aside the lace curtain of her third-floor bedroom window. She watches Barney speed down the winding drive in his Cadillac and out the main gate. Sarah then turns back to a movement behind the trees she had noticed earlier. Below the window and down by the outside, south wing of the sprawling residence, where it projects at a right angle from the rest of the manor near the greenhouse, she sees Caleb—astride Old Clara—easing the faithful horse out of the tree shadows to the wall below Flynn's bedroom window, while keeping a close watch on Barney's distant car, as it now roars down the highway in the direction of Cutterville. Sarah's heart races as she focuses on her handsome son, his blue jeans fresh and clean, his curly, dark hair sparkling under the sun, his skin like gold. She watches as Caleb leans over in the saddle and lovingly strokes Old Clara's mane to silence her; from her motherly point-of-view, she sees Caleb's action as one taken in order not to awaken other members of the household by the horse's wheezing.

A smile crosses Sarah's face, when Caleb takes a pebble from his pocket and tosses it against Flynn's bedroom window on the second floor of the right-angled wing of the manor. After several strikes against the windowpane, Flynn—dressed only in his shorts and rubbing away the sleep from his blue eyes—moves aside the curtains and looks down at Caleb with a huge smile. When Caleb doesn't smile back, the look on Flynn's face turns deadly serious. He sees that Barney's car is gone and quickly slips into his T-shirt, trousers, socks and shoes, hurriedly makes his bed—a habit he's had all of his life—and climbs through the window, descends halfway down the rose lattice, and jumps the rest of the way to the ground. Sarah, her mother's love causing her heart to race, watches her sons walk to the edge of Manor Hill, Caleb doing all the talking, Flynn, all the listening, his understanding arm about Caleb's shoulder, Old Clara remaining behind, nibbling at the drying grass. Releasing the curtain, Sarah—filled with exultation—returns to dusting the furniture.

On the edge of Manor Hill overlooking the vast plantation and the early rising field hands spreading out across the plain below them, Caleb and Flynn sit under a sprawling oak tree and continue their conversation. Flynn turns to Caleb and asks, "You were there. What did Richards say he'd do about prosecuting Dane and the others?"

"He's sticking to that ridiculous story that B.J. ran over Claretta."

"What about the ropes and the blood on Hank's truck? What did that jackass make up about that?" asks Flynn and then raising his hands in repugnance, "Never mind. They probably washed it off. Once again, I asked Father if he had anything to do with that killing and he—"

"Sarah told me how you had asked him; and your father's answer is easy enough to believe, Flynn, the way Dane has taken over the Klan, or at least thinks he has. But, Richards! No one in his right mind would think that Claretta and B.J.'s deaths were accidental."

"They would if they were white and the ones killed were colored," Flynn remarks, going on. "We all do as long as it protects our race, we whites and the coloreds."

"You're right."

With the sun's warmth streaming down on them, Caleb lies back on the ground and pillows his hands behind his head, and Flynn does the same, both gazing away from the sun's blinding light and looking instead into the soothing, blue.

"Both Claretta and Billy Joe are heaven bound now, Caleb," Flynn says, reaching over and rubbing his hand against Caleb's arm as if to comfort the two of them. "As skeptical as you are, even you must believe that, minus that flying-horse part. But then, after thinking about it all night, so many people said they saw them rising up in the sky with Naomi on a white horse. Some say it had wings, others that it didn't. So I'm quite mixed up about it. But all things are possible with God."

They face the greenhouse and watch Naomi hurriedly returning to the manor, where she enters the kitchen and gazes out one of the windows at them. She steps from the window, washes her hands, slips into her apron and begins preparing the family breakfast. Cradling a large bowl, she whips up an extra amount of pancake mix in anticipation of Caleb eating with them.

On the slope, Caleb and Flynn make the most of their time together while discussing life's twisted turns. "Maybe you're right, Caleb, that it had to have been the fog that made them seem to fly, the same way it made you think Naomi's horse was prancing on air in that swamp, you told me about, but from what I was told, not just Harris said he saw them and that horse fly, the whites in town said that Deputy Snodgress also saw them rising into the sky."

"Seemingly saw them fly, Flynn, would be a more appropriate analogy. Snodgress has been involved in one too many drunken orgies and mindless killings. His guilt must be catching up with him, causing him to see things which aren't there. And that liquor-drinking Harris is likely to say anything to convince his members that he's a living saint." Caleb stares into space, going on. "But, in all fairness to Reverend Harris and the deputy, we were all seeing things, crazy out-of-our-mind things. Even you and I earlier."

"I know."

Sitting up, Caleb exclaims, "If Papa wasn't so insistent on staying on our land and helping you, I'd pack him up and leave Georgia. At times I don't understand why he loves you and Sarah so much, not that I don't, mind you."

"That'll be the day, Caleb, that you'd pack up Henry as if you're the father and he's the child. And you know damn well how Henry can still turn us over his lap and put the belt to both of us if he wanted to and why he loves me and Mother. We're well worth loving." The gaiety soon leaves Flynn's appearance, and he sets his troubled gaze on his friend. "Caleb."

"Yeah?"

"All kidding aside. . . . That white horse that you and others saw Naomi riding with its long, flowing mane, huge tail and feet. We don't own such an animal as that and neither does anyone else in the county. Where did she get it?" When Caleb lies down again in total silence pondering over Flynn's comment, Flynn goes on. "Adults, Caleb, they go through so much hell. Now you and I . . . Do you realize what you just said about packing up Henry? It means we've become the men of our homes whether we like it or not."

Caleb looks at him and then lets his body and soul escape into the sky. Flynn lying on his back, also focuses on a section of billowing whites clouds against that endless blue. Without looking at Flynn, Caleb asks, "Do you still want to soar free like the birds and never grow up?"

"Yes."

"Papa and Sarah, Flynn. Do you remember what they said about this land?"

"When they were our age, you mean? I do, and thank God Collins was here to help them," says Flynn. "He, Henry and mother had to all but run Shadow Grove by themselves."

"You can say that again. Papa," chuckles Caleb. "When he was our age and your mother was only fourteen. Boy!"

"I bet they just woke up one morning and found out they were all grown up, just like that, the way we have now."

"One thing is for sure, Flynn. After the three of them worked their hearts out to save this land and Papa and I our place—with your workers' help—there's no way you and I can ever just pack up and leave, no matter how many times we might wish we could."

"Mother doesn't legally own Shadow Grove. I do now. Did you know that?"

"Yes. Naomi showed me your grandfather's will—sometime ago—and asked if I'd explain it to her."

"Ha!" exclaims Flynn. "That proves it!" He yells toward the kitchen. "Naomi, you don't know everything after all. Otherwise you'd not have had to ask Caleb about the will!"

Naomi looks out the window and chuckles at him. "Lord," she whispers and goes back to her cooking. "Let me always be here with the ones I love in this house, this turmoil, pain and all." She suddenly feels something brush against her and a voice replies. "Your mission on earth will be over in the blinking of the eye, my sister, and we long to have you to return home."

Returning to the window, Naomi sees the boys looking up at a transparent ascending cloud, something never seen by anyone before, a cloud slowly diminishing the sunlight in an astonishing display of light and shade; the curtain-thin cloud is a widespread circle resembling spokes from a city-block-size wagon wheel, down through which the weak sunlight magically streams, shadowing on the boys with its dazzling, lacery, reddish-yellow illumination. Flynn, inspired and filled with poetic exuberance, wants to share his analogical thoughts about the penetrating light with Caleb, but he sees that Caleb's light-brown, hypnotic eyes are fixed firmly on the spoke-like cloud. Naomi intensely watching it all from the window. First them, then the cloud and back again. "Hey," whispers Flynn, fearful of Caleb returning to that trance-like state which happened under the lightning and by the burning tree in town at the square and seemingly even more so now. "Pay attention, Caleb," urges Flynn, trying to diminish his own fears, and going on. "I just proved that Naomi doesn't know everything."

"She knows she will return home sooner than later, and she knows the difficulty that the road to the catalyst holds and who must deal with the end of mankind, Flynn," explains Caleb, his sights never leaving the upward mobile, cloud-burst of spoke-like rays.

"What?" asks Flynn as the clouds slowly break up—as clouds always do—and fade from the sky, leaving the earth blistering under the power of the sun light. "Did you say the end of mankind? Jesus, Caleb, do you realizing what you just said?"

"Yes. We were speaking about your inheritance. Weren't we?"

Flynn is horrified and speculates.

Was it God saying those chilling words through Caleb?

Flynn faces the kitchen window—no sign of Naomi—and then again at his lifelong friend. He's not about to push Caleb back into that dream-like state by discussing Caleb's ghostly, spoken words to him. "About my will," Flynn says. "I was going to say that grandfather felt that it's the man who has the burden of carrying the weight of his family on his shoulders. That's why only the family males are in line to inherit Shadow Grove."

A heartfelt feeling of guilt overcomes Flynn, as he rises onto his elbow, telling himself that he has no right to try and block Caleb's struggle to find himself and God, even if it means that he, Flynn—who ironically believes in heaven and Caleb doesn't would lose everything, the political power promised to him, his land, or even his life by his helping Caleb, if what Naomi says is possible. No, if he truly loves Caleb, then he must help him, not hinder him, in going wherever it is he has to travel. Hoping that Caleb's love for him will always be there to protect him, as Caleb has all of their lives, Flynn again pillows his arms under his head and stares skyward.

"I wish there was a heaven," says Caleb, surprising Flynn. "That's what's important: life without worries, hunger, hating, or killings of children or anyone for that matter." He glances over at Flynn.

Flynn studies Caleb, then finally says, "Sixteen-thousand acres, Caleb, or a million acres, or money by the tons. Not even the colonel returning is really important, when it comes to dying in grace. Caleb, if a person did have money, would it be wise for him to spend it right off, if it's sorely needed?"

"You're talking about your father, right?" Caleb watches Flynn's reaction, both again facing that nagging question and the feeling that their friendship lies in the answer. "It all depends on how much money or if it's stolen or is legal tender," Caleb goes on, "A truck load of deutsche marks, let's say, won't buy a cup of coffee here, at this time, so it would be useless for someone to bring it into this country, providing he or she had a way of doing so—from Germany—without getting caught. On the other hand, if it's U.S. currency and stolen, one couldn't trust banks after so many have failed and the feds are now watching all of them." Caleb ponders at Flynn. "Why did you ask?"

"Do you think that someone who has dirty hands can be forgiven?"

"With what?" asks Caleb, amused. "I mean, this person's dirty hands. What will he scrub his hands clean with, Papa's lye soap?"

"Okay, I'm being abstract. I admit it, but Henry is a special kind of man. If someone learns from him. . . . If your father could teach this person how to make his soap, symbolically speaking; and teach him how to be humble and use it to wash his hands, again, so to speak, maybe this person would learn to be like Henry."

"You mean Barney, Flynn, and the answer is no. Papa would never go near him."

Unknown to them, Barney has returned from town and is sitting on the toilet and watching them from the restroom window. He carelessly wipes himself with toilet paper, unknowingly smearing a bit of feces on his hand. He drops the paper into the commode, stands up, flushes the toilet, and lingers at the restroom window, glaring out at them, his polished fingernails squeezing against his clenched fist, and he leaves the restroom, his hands disgustingly dirty.

Later that evening in the den, Sarah is talking with Naomi, who's busy dusting books on the floor-to-ceiling bookshelves. "He hasn't been my husband for over eighteen years now," she tells Naomi. "I will respect him in every other way, but—as I told him—I will never sleep with him again. Any one of the manor's guest rooms will do just fine for me. Any other questions with that visceral mind of yours?"

"They're here," says Naomi "I best hurry up and finish cooking that dinner, and this time that boy better sit down and eat with us or he'll never hear the last of it."

"And you said you were losing your powers. Certainly not your hearing," teases Sarah, finally hearing the sound of the boys' puttering old trucks approaching.

"I didn't hear that truck, Sarah," says Naomi as she heads for the kitchen. "But more each day, though," she calls back, "I'm reminded that earth is not home, and I'm losing the very last of this eternal volcano in me, this sacred energy that I'm entrusted to hold as its caretaker, losing it faster than I can prepare Caleb to completely take it."

"But you said some of your powers have already been given to him."

"Forced on him, Sarah, but not by me. By Someone whose shadow I couldn't even stand before so great is He."

"The Son of God," Sarah whispers, enlightened.

"He knows Satan is closing in on Caleb and Flynn," says Naomi. "He's spoonfeeding Caleb, otherwise that boy would have been killed by Deputy Hammer. But in the end, if Caleb is to survive, he alone has to embrace God, or Satan will eat him alive."

Outside on the manor's drive, when Flynn stops his Chevy by the porch, both boys alight. Caleb follows Flynn to the manor and then stops. As if feeling the presence of evil all about them, he looks at the darkened backyard, where he scrutinizes the lit greenhouse.

"Come on," Flynn calls, while climbing up the porch step. "They're going to be ticked off enough as it is with you refusing to eat breakfast after Naomi made extra pancakes, and I had to end up taking you all the way to your place, where Henry was, so that the three of us could eat together in peace—as you put it. On top of that, when Henry needs all the rest he can get, and by us going there, we caused him to return here with us, Mother would also jump on us if she knew it." Flynn faces toward one of the worker's shacks. "I hope he get enough rest out there. It's not actually as comfortable as you guys' place, but one day, I'll build new houses for our workers."

"What did you say?"

"I said—" Flynn breaks off his talk and follows Caleb's gaze to the backyard.

"Are you sure it's okay?" says Caleb, his sights still on the greenhouse. "I mean to enter your house."

"Father has to know that you and I will always be friends. Beside, you forget that I'm now the real master of this land. That is, unless you want to wrestle with me to see if I can get you inside, and the winner gets Shadow Grove as the prize."

"And have to worry about the taxes on this place, sheltering and feeding all of your workers," says Caleb laughing, trotting up the steps and playfully jostling with Flynn. "That hardly seems fair. I would stand you on your head and walk you on your ear."

"Why are you looking at the greenhouse?" Flynn asks, as—once again— Caleb focuses on it. "You go on in," he tells Caleb. "I'll join you in a minute."

"I'm not going in there to face your father alone," says Caleb. "I'll wait in the truck." He's well aware that Flynn wants to investigate the greenhouse.

When Caleb climbs back in the Chevy, folds his arms and tries to get some rest, Flynn looks from his closed-eyed friend to the greenhouse and cautiously approaches it. Parked just out of sight beside the glass conservatory he sees Sheriff Richards' patrol car, the car door open, the police radio turned down and chattering about problems in Colored Town, and there, resting on the front seat, near the sheriff's bracketed shotgun, is a briefcase with a letter sticking out of the closed lid. Flynn notices that the stamped envelope is the same type that was used by his father in their correspondence. The blonde boy, puzzling, steps to the well-lit greenhouse window and looks through a worn section of the milky, stained glass. Barney and Richards are inside having a heated discussion. Flynn returns to the patrol car, looks back at the greenhouse, and then reaches into the car and tugs on the exposed part of the envelope; the briefcase cover pops open. Hurriedly Flynn removed a document from the envelope and begins reading it. Shocked by what he reads, he then sees dozens of more such letters inside the briefcase. As the troubled boy scans several of the documents, he hears the greenhouse door open and close. A moment later, Sheriff Richards storms to his car and looks about, enters the vehicle and speeds down a backyard driveway to a rear gate and for town. Flynn moves from behind an oak tree with a handful of the letters in his possession. The greenhouse lights are turned off, and the boy looks about and runs away.

In the spacious kitchen, pots and pans sizzle with food on the nickel-plated, Wedgewood stove. Golden cornbread rising in the oven fills the house with a sweet smell of irresistible dining. In the dark of night, as Flynn approaches his truck, Colonel Cutter makes his way across the backyard and enters the manor's back door and climbs up the rear stairs. In her kitchen, Naomi turns off the stove, her sights focusing on the darkness down the hallway about those back stairs, her ears listening to the squeaky steps, as Barney climbs them to his room. Naomi whispers, "Beware Flynn and Caleb. Beware."

Suddenly opening his eyes, Caleb sits up in the truck seat, and he stares at Flynn. "Well, what did you see?" he asks Flynn.

Flynn's lips are taut and pale. "Nothing," replies Flynn, no longer possessing the letters.

As they enter the manor, and then the den, Sarah is sitting in a comfortable chair and holding a book.

"After supper, it's Latin time, again," she tells them. "Lately, you two have wasted a lot of precious hours away from your studies, especially you, Caleb—on your first attempt—if you want to pass that exam that the senator arranged for you." She smiles at Flynn. "Isn't it marvelous, Flynn, Caleb only seventeen and taking that bar exam."

"I don't feel like Latin today, Mother, or studying books of any kind," Flynn replies. Caleb knows that something is terribly wrong and is deeply concerned about Flynn and attempts to put on a brave face. Sarah studies Flynn and then turns to Caleb when he says:

"I'm not in the mood, either, Sarah."

"Do you mind telling me why you've lost interest in studying, Caleb?" she asks.

Caleb looks at Barney's prize procession, a rebel flag draped across a corner chair.

"I just don't, that's all."

Sarah follows his sights to the chair. "Is that the reason you refuse to—"

"Come and get it!" calls Naomi from the kitchen.

Sarah replaces the book on the shelf. "Then, let's just talk," she tells Caleb. "You, Flynn and I, before we eat. Things being what they are around here, Flynn, do you want to run Shadow Grove in a way that all of our workers and friends feel at home or not? You decide. Don't wait for your father to tell you."

Flynn looks at Caleb and then at his father's flag.

"Where is Father, Mother?" Flynn asks, knowing full well that Barney is either on his way from the greenhouse or, at this time, somewhere in the manor.

"He was tired, and an hour ago, said he was going to his room," Sarah replies.

"I'll just go see if he's okay. I rather not discuss Shadow Grove at this moment. There are thing I need to talk to Father about first," Flynn says completely unaware that it would be a disaster to speak to Barney about what is in those letters.

"He went to his room to rest, not to talk, and it's not every day that Caleb eats with us."

"He can go, Sarah. Now, that Barney's . . . I'll just join Papa and—"

"You're part of this family, Caleb Brooks, and you'll eat with us as you should!"

The moment she says it, Flynn is reminded of just how much he and Sarah loves Caleb and how dangerous it would be to talk to Barney about those letters, and as for Sarah, Sarah knows she's all but told Caleb that he's her son. Her and Caleb's gazes lock. Flynn glances at his mother, and at Caleb. He taps Caleb on the back and chuckles, saying, "Look at you two, and you are family, Mister Caleb, seventeen-year-old, attorney-at-law Brooks. You and Naomi. As much of our family as anyone. And by the smell of that food, Naomi has outdone herself again preparing it." Flynn playfully shadowboxes Caleb. "Come on. I'll personally walk you in and we'll all sit down and—at least—eat this last supper together as a family should."

Instead of using the large, formal Chippendale dining-room table and settings, Sarah has chosen the smaller, intimate atmosphere afforded by the kitchen. As she, Naomi, Flynn and Caleb sit about the smaller table, a table graced with southern fried chicken, mashed potatoes and gravy, collard greens, cornbread and tossed salad, and—for dessert—a golden-crust, peach pie. While sitting there, Naomi notices the kitchen door is being ever so slowly eased ajar. In the darkened hallway, she sees a sliver of Barney's face squinting through the door's narrow hinge-side crack at them, his Klansman's eyes of hatred zeroed in on Caleb. "Everyone hold hands in prayer," she calmly says. Naomi begins the prayer. "Lord, we thank you fo' this meal . . ." While the others' heads are lowered, Naomi keeps a wary eye on that narrow space between the door, ". . . and let no harm come to us this night and let this not be our last supper that we will share together."

28

Lucifer Answers Barney

That night, in the living room, Sarah, Flynn and the Colonel are ill-at-ease playing at a game of cards; Colonel Cutter knows very well that he holds the winning hand.

"You missed a good dinner, Barney," Sarah tells him.

"There will be others" he says, lighting a cigar, then faces Flynn. "Was that Caleb I heard leaving this house, around the time you and your mother finished supper?"

"Yes, Sir," answers Flynn and then adds. "Because Henry knows the ins and outs of laying down the pipeline better than anyone else, even more so than that young engineer you hired, when I went to Henry's house earlier today with Caleb, and I spoke with him about a problem that we have on section one-hundred-and-three of the line, Henry gladly agreed to help and came back with me and Caleb to look at the problem tonight, and after examining that section of pipe, he assured me that it can be fixed, and he'll start on it the first thing in the morning."

"Son," says Barney, lovingly rubbing the top of Flynn's head and hair. "What's all these words about Henry have to do with my question about Caleb being in the house?"

"Since I had asked Henry to help us, he and Caleb are spending the night in Frankie Bogavitch's cabin, since he and his family have moved to Akron, Ohio, to be with his ailing mother. It makes no sense for Henry to have to ride all the way home, only to have to come right back early to-morrow. Henry was much too tired to share supper with us and went right to bed, but Caleb was invited to do so by me. Also, Father, even though he just buried Claretta, Bruce Johnson—who has nothing but admiration for Henry and Caleb—took a day off from the factory and came from Cutterville to help us, as well, when Henry asked him, over the phone, if he would do so. Not only did Bruce say yes, he brought his entire family, except for Brick. Brick refused to take the time off from his job in order to earn money for another car."

"That's all well and good, son, but what's the bottom line? You're talking all around it."

"Our colored help is critical for Shadow Grove's survival, Sir," Flynn says, straightening up in the chair and drawing his father's ire, "as it was in the past with grandfather and is now and I think always will be."

"You think, but are not absolutely sure," calmly reasons Barney, regaining his confident composure, Sarah watching both of them with concern.

"Yes, Father," Flynn says, changing his choice of words and tone of voice, but not his determination. "I think the coloreds, as well as our white workers, are critical for our needs and work well together."

"Why would Bruce do something like that?" asked Barney. "Does he and his family think that voluntarily working here will motivate you, now that the plantation is yours, to permit more of his kind to be buried in our cemetery, or to hire more of them to work here?"

"I'd guess Bruce feels that one kindness deserves another, Sir," Flynn sharply replies, challenging his father. "Earlene is the Johnson's only daughter now since Claretta was killed, and—because she's not permitted to attend school in Cutterville—Earlene still comes here five days a week to be taught how to read and write, and mother sends Amos and Andy in a wagon for her every morning, or one or the other workers. We also arrange to have her taken back home after school. I'm sure that's just one more reason why Bruce wants to do all he can to help us now."

"And our workers, who also attend the plantation school," says Sarah, "insisted on paying for the new books themselves, to show their appreciation of having a chance to learn. Even their children chipped in with their piggy-bank money, Barney. As to why Bruce would leave his factory job for a day to help us, Caleb and Flynn did save his and Brick's life, as you know, and Bruce is the kind of person who will never forget that as long as he lives, and I for one also welcome his help."

Barney withdraws his hand from Flynn's head and leers at Sarah; Flynn feels a cold, diabolical presence all about the room and goes on with less confidence, but continue on he does. "The Johnsons are also spending the night on the plantation in their old house before returning to Cutterville."

"Barney," says Sarah, now that Flynn has opened the door for her, "the school is a good investment morally and financially. We need smart workers who can read manuals, repair tractors and other new equipment which we'll need in the future. As for the school, we built it after you left and—"

"Whom do you plan to teach in that school, Sarah—now that I'm back—the spades, as well?" Barney asks.

Sarah looks from Barney to Flynn. "I didn't ask Flynn, Sarah," Barney tells her, "I heard what he had to say; I asked you. Whom do you plan to let continue attending that school?"

"White and colored children, as well as the adults, when time permits," Sarah replies.

Once more Flynn interrupts, giving Barney very little room to maneuver: "And there will be no more segregation between the workers, Father. I'm sorry, Sir, but that's the way it has always been with the Winthrops, and the way it'll be once Grandfather's will is probated."

In a twisted way, Barney is proud of Flynn's show of leadership, a characteristic trait necessary in Satan's war against God. But Barney is a driven man who hates to lose, and seldom does.

"In the field of battle, son, a few skirmishes are always lost, but not the war. I understand. You're only doing what your mother wants you to do, to follow the habits of your grandparents." He stands, kisses Flynn on the top of his head and walks past Sarah without even a nod of recognition. "I'll turn in now," he tells Flynn. "It's an old army habit of mine, and habits are hard to break. But," he says, smothering out his lit, half-smoked cigar in a nearby ashtray, "as I was saying, with a little practice, one can break or overcome anything." Colonel Cutter leaves the room, filling Flynn and Sarah with dread.

Alone in the master bedroom, Barney—with the winning hand of cards still in his grip—stares out of the open bay window for some time, his angry sights focused on the fogbound school house in the field below Manor Hill, a school surrounded by Judas and thirty-foot-tall eucalyptus trees. Picking up another cigar, the ex-intelligence officer lights a match and forgetfully holds onto it with the flames rising up and engulfing his fingers and then burns itself out while he focuses on the schoolhouse. He tosses the unlit cigar and burnt matchstick aside, without any indication of having felt the pain, picks up his private bedside phone and dials.

"Dane, Colonel Cutter," Barney says puzzling at his intact fingers, then sets his hostile gaze on the school. "About that previous discussion. It's time you earned that life I handed back to you. That's right. . . . After you finish, then do something about that gold-tooth nigger Walter, whose big mouth caused an avalanche of back-talking monkeys to spring up, talk that has infected my family. What? I don't give a good goddamn who you pick to do it, just get it done, and keep my name out of it, and don't make a mess of it as you did Claretta and that Billy Joe in front of the whole goddamn world! No, you leave Caleb Brooks to me. After he's removed from this earth in a less-than-incredulous way—What? 'Incredulous?' You goddamn fool! If you don't know what the word means now, you won't know after I explain it to you. Maybe you should have attended my wife's school with them coons. Just stay the hell away from Caleb. Flynn will forget him soon enough. That's right. Burn it along with those old eucalyptus trees. The oil and flames from them will spread to the building and make quick work of it. Tonight, you hear! Burn it to the ground." After hanging up the phone, Barney bitterly raises his arms and hands over his head and hisses.

"I offer my mother's, my son's, and my soul to you in order to save my boy from his Catholic mother. The blacks are inferior, not our equal that they should eat at my table, the way Caleb Brooks did. Where is the proof that you've even heard me of late? You said that I could count on you. You brought me through the war and tonight said I had the winning hand."

He flings the cards onto the bedside table, where—among those cards which do not slide off the table's smooth surface to the floor—four aces and the joker remain face-up and then suddenly burst into a man-size fireball, the same-shaped fireball which had engulfed and destroyed the *White Dove*. Cutter grabs a towel and rushes to the flames, and he trips and stumbles headlong onto the table, his face and hands in the ball of fire. Jerking back, he frantically feels about his cheeks and then stares at his hands. He looks at the table, at the cards. Nothing has burned, not the table, the cards nor his hands. His eyes open wide, his curiosity thundering in wonder; cautiously he slips his hands back into the cold fire, then out and into it again and again, and out of the fire comes the voice of Lucifer:

"Where is your faith, Barney Cutter? Did I not keep the match flames from harming you? Before the rooster crows a dozen more times over the land, your mother will be risen from her grave, as was Christ from His that you may witness the power of your god, Barney."

"You have! You've heard it! Heard my prayer!"

That night, Burt and Marcus huddle beside Hank's old pickup next to the school, while a drunken Hank waits in the vehicle to offer them a quick getaway, all the time a stiff wind is blowing stronger.

"Are you sure about this, Burt?" asks Marcus. "It's a school where we can learn to read."

"Dane's busying sexing old, rotten-tooth Essie Mae, Sarah's janitor woman who asked Henry to clean up that mess in the store and—I guess—that's why he told Hank to have us burn this damn school fer him. He wants to clean out Essie Mae's pipes and fer us to clean out any chance of them coons ever learning here, them or you, you little dumb ass."

"Do you still hurt, Burt, where Caleb bent you down and made you clean off his shoes?"

"Shut up, stop stalling and do it, Marcus, or I'll throw the leftover gas on you and burn you with that school!" He rubs the top of the frightened boy's head, going on. "Now, go on and dig out the rest of them canning jars of gasoline. Okay? I was just kidding. I wouldn't burn you. You should have seen the look on your face, like I was the devil. I'm your friend. Now, make sure you throw some of the gas on them trees, like we were told to help destroy this school. These niggers out here love barbecuing and we gonna set they souls on fire."

Minutes later, the horizon erupts in a ball of fire, lighting up the night. In one of the workers' shacks, a young white boy, awakened by the smell of smoke, rushes into the field in his shorts and rings the fire bell.

"Fire! Fire!"

Lugging hoes, shovels and buckets, workers swarm from their field-side houses and to the burning trees and school, the brightly combusting, sizzling and popping eucalyptus trees, not only lighting up the land, but raining down skin-peeling teardrops of oily flames from their exploding branches and leaves over and around the school; the workers—including Henry and Caleb—valiantly battle the raging holocaust, but with each lift and fall of the pump handle, less water spills from the old school well.

High up on Manor Hill, Barney sits in the center most rocking chair on the manor's wraparound porch, while smoking his Cuban cigar and watches. At the fire, the buckets of water arrive slower and slower. "Use dirt," yells field-boss Collins, arriving late on the scene. Scooping up dirt with the waterless buckets, the field hands fling the soil onto the building and at the roaring trees, only to have the fine, dusty soil itself explode into flames and cascade onto the building, and onto them as well.

"It looks hopeless," Collins whispers to Sarah, when she and Naomi arrive.

Still, he and the workers attack the school flames with the dwindling water, with the dirt, with brooms, with blankets, and with their faith alone. When Henry and Caleb spot small children near the burning trees and spitting at the flames trying to put them out and—at the same time—flinching from the intense heat of the trees around them, Henry and Caleb drag the youngsters aside.

"Get these kids out of here!" Henry calls to a nearby Bruce, who at, that same moment, sees his last remaining daughter streaking toward the school and the quivering, flame-spitting, front door, a door ready to explode outward from the searing heat behind it.

"Earlene!" Bruce yells, starting after her and tripping over a bucket.

"The books, Pa," Earlene squeals. "We have to save our books!"

"I'll get her, Bruce," yells Caleb to the hobbling man and then dashes after Earlene, calling back to Bruce. "Those kids! Help Papa get them away from the fire!"

Caleb catches up to Earlene and pulls her away from the door, while she continues screaming that she has to save the books. After Carrie and Bruce help Henry clear the children away from the building and trees, they stumble out of breath to Caleb and to Earlene, and both frantic parents seize hold of their hysterical child.

"We just lost Claretta," sobs Carrie, slapping Earlene, then hugging and smothering her with kisses on her slapped cheek. "We don't want to lose you too, baby. God knows we don't!"

Carrie, Bruce and Earlene, desperately hugging one another and crying, gaze at the burning school. Bruce hurriedly guides his family away from the building and the intense heat.

"Us kids got no more money to buy books, Daddy," Earlene sob. "I'm never gonna learn to read now!" Many in the crowd—having heard Earlene say what they all feared, that there is no more money for books—groan and sob. Caleb looks at those sorrowful workers and takes another look at Earlene.

"The hell you won't learn to read," he says, as Flynn runs in their direction from afar.

"Caleb!" Flynn calls when Caleb moves to the smoking school door, kicks it open and leans back as the heat rushes out into the night. While working the water pump with Miss McLeland—the slender, newly hired, white, school teacher—Sarah stops pumping the handle when she hears Flynn's desperate call, and sees him racing toward her on his way to the school. She follows his frantic gaze to the building behind her, where she sees Caleb disappear into the burning structure.

"Caleb!" Sarah shouts, and grabs a bucket of water and heads for the crackling, burning edifice, McLeland follows, both women struggling with a heavy buckets of water. Flynn catches up to them, takes the buckets from them and continues sprinting with the water to the school and enters the building into the mouth of fiery death, a terrified Sarah following far behind and yelling to him. When she and McLeland reach the building, while calling for Flynn and Caleb to get out, many of her workers are there doing the same thing, with the intermitenly falling, flaming, tree branches and the heat staggering them back.

Inside the school, Flynn, seeking out Caleb, deposits one of the buckets of water on the smoking floor and flings water from the other onto the leaping flames. He then picks up the other and weaves and bobs his way forward. Caleb, himself ringed by the sizzling flames, looks back and spots Flynn and yells to him. The blonde boy—now with only one bucket of water left—leaps over a fallen ceiling beam to Caleb's side. As Flynn splashes the remaining bucket of water over their bodies, suddenly—in the middle of those infernal flames, while both of the boys are kicking aside burning chairs, and seems doomed—Caleb sees water, lots of it, being flung over Henry and those men who entered the *White Dove*, while trying to save Lawrence and Marilyn. The roaring school flames draw back from Caleb and Flynn, as if the water in Caleb's vision is demanding that it do so. Then, in a flash the materialized, wet specter is gone, and Caleb and Flynn stand back-to-back facing another wall of advancing fiery death, Flynn, who is unaware of Caleb's revelation, is frightened beyond his limits.

"We're going to die, Caleb."

Both boys are now absolutely in fear for their lives against the subsided but rekindling flames, with the way out engulfed in black smoke and fire behind them.

Outside, as Sarah again approaches the building and the burning doorway, defying the heat and danger, Henry sprints up to the crowd about Sarah and restrains her, as Caleb and Flynn's voices, from time to time, are heard coming from inside the crumbling school. Two men arrive with more buckets of water and are unaware that the boys are trapped inside the school; just as the men are about to toss the water on the side of the building, Henry shouts to them, "Over here!" When they reach Henry with the water, the school's door header begins groaning and buckling. Grabbing the buckets from the men, Henry faces the blazing holocaust. Sarah seizes his arm and begs him to be careful, as others run up to the fire and dampen down Henry with still more water from their half-filled buckets. Henry, recalling the image of his going into the *White Dove*, and sensing that his luck might run out this time, takes a last look of love at Sarah and rushes into the school, while carrying those two full buckets of life-giving water and trying not to spill any of it on the way, the school walls groaning and buckling around him. Just as Henry hears Caleb and Flynn's voices behind a barrier of roaring flames, and is about run through the wall of fire, one of the burning trees topples over and explodes onto the roof, taking out the wall next to it, which nearly strikes Henry, causing Sarah and those outside to step back, wailing in dread for those trapped inside.

"Stay close, Flynn," warns a frightened Caleb with the building shaking from the impact of the tree. "We'll have to get out of here and leave the damn books behind."

"Leave what!" yells Flynn cowering back from the flames. "That's why you came in here? For some damn books and not for some trapped person!"

"Caleb! Flynn!" shouts Henry. "I can hear you. Can you hear me?" At that moment, the fire behind the boys subsides, and a flame-less pathway to the door is visible. "Get out now!" calls Henry.

Caleb suddenly points to three sealed boxes of recently arrived new books in a smoke-filled corner.

"There!" he shouts.

"And here's two more boxes," calls Flynn, choking, "now let's get the hell out!"

Just as they seize the cartons, the wind peels the burning, tree-damaged roof off of the structure and sends it and its shingles sailing skyward and casting down a billion sparks and flames from the tree leaves and shingles and building debris, leaving the boys dodging about and looking up at the dark, open sky of stars; all the time the burning building is shifting, popping out nails, as overhead beams twist and groan and topple down around them, cutting off the way out once more. Outside, Sarah watches the building, wiggling about like an agonized snake, forcing her and her workers even farther back from it, and Sarah cries out, "Mother of God help them!"

The same mighty gust of wind that took off the roof suddenly returns and enters the school and diminishes the timber fire between the boys and Henry, opening a temporary gateway to them, and through that threatening-to-close-again gateway leaps Henry, those buckets of water angled out, held there by the man's incredible strength in his arms, the precious water miraculously never splashing from the buckets onto the floor as he runs. Drowning the boys with water, Henry shoves them through the open ring of fire, as it begins closing once more, and the three of them race gagging into the outside air to the cheers and yelling of, "Thank you, Jesus!"; a moment later, the school windows explode outward around them, splintering the land with a rain of melting glass.

Henry and Sarah run with the boys and the crowd to a safe distance away, just as the entire building implodes. Miss McLeland and several of the male students relieve Flynn of his undamaged boxes and Caleb of all but one of his. Caleb refuses to relinquish the last box—a lightweight one—to anyone but to Earlene, who reaches for it and is hardly able to hold onto it in her emotional state of being, but does, with Caleb's help. Kissing the cardboard container, she goes to her knees with it and sobs with gratitude. Filled with emotions, McLeland gathers the other children around Earlene and they take the container of books from her and places it on the ground. The New Yorker lifts her sights to Caleb.

"Thanks to two boys," she says, "one of whom I once said was too cocky for his own good with his brilliance." She turns to Flynn. "Then there is Flynn, who is forever humble and now courageous as well. Thanks Master Flynn." McLeland takes both Caleb and Flynn's hands into hers, holds her head high, and tearfully exclaims. "We have our books. No one will have to miss a day of school while waiting for another shipment from Atlanta." McLeland—who is a strict disciplinarian—believes in anyone following the rules, and she looks over at Caleb, as if to say she did not praise him as much as she had Flynn, because Caleb is so sure of himself and so strong of will and strength and Flynn is not, and Caleb understands. He smiles at her with admiration, as she goes on to the frightened children. "We'll hold class in the barn and no tardiness or absentees. Everyone be there bright and early tomorrow with your

409

homework finished, your hair combed, and your hands cleaned and your teeth brushed. Now, let's give Flynn and Caleb's parents a moment alone with them."

After everyone steps away with the books and heads for the barn, Sarah—full of anxiety—faces Caleb and Flynn. "Don't ever do anything like that again," she scolds and then holds them close to her. As Sarah wipes soot from Flynn's face, and a few of her workers continue tossing water onto the collapsed building, thunder rocks the land and rain pours down on Shadow Grove. The fires are smothered. Then the downpour stops as quickly as it had started. The workers look at one another with mixed emotions.

"If God put out the fire, why did He do it after the school was burned to the ground?" one of the field hands asks.

"Don't question God's motives," Sarah calls to her workers. "We can always rebuild the school if we have the will to do so, and we do and will! But we will never blame God for the evil around us."

The fieldhand who questioned why God sent the rain too late to save the school walks away, muttering to himself, "I still don't understand why God sent the rain so late or even let it start in the first place."

Naomi knows why. She smiles at Henry, his love for Sarah and that of Sarah for him is never greater, and Naomi sees how Caleb and Flynn are looking at one another with a new and more powerful appreciation of the other, and she cherishes the trust and love rekindling between the white and black workers.

The loss of a few boards is well worth it, she tells herself.

However, will the love between Flynn and Caleb last? A love and hope with a mighty, powerful enemy looming nearby to crush it. Naomi glances toward the darkened shadows cast by a growth of nearby fire-damaged, Judas trees; the trees' elongated shadows are stretching out across the field, shadows that are slowly bending in the direction of the workers and the destroyed school, as if by black, woolly-head fingers and the hand of death, pushed forward clearing the way for that iniquity, a man so corrupted with immorality that the angels flee from his presence, as he and his bat-like thirst for human blood approaches. The closer, and yet-unseen Barney comes the more it seems to affect the whites and blacks, who had fought the fire side-by-side and now cast an uneasy glance at one another. Trout —as if being called to do so—slowly turns and looks at the continuously-bending tree shadows, and then obeying a voice—heard only by him—he begins whispering to the white workers.

"It's the niggers who caused our school to be burned down." The poison words quickly spread among the white workers, who separate themselves from the blacks, each group now eyeing the other with uneasiness. Trout, again, faces the Judas trees, and out of the shadows steps Barney, his cigar glowing red with fire against his ghostly, washed-out face. Driving up in his truck, Hank parks several hundred feet or so away from the raised school house and waits, his eyes locked on Barney. In the truck with Hank are Marcus and Burt. Barney turns his sights on the top of a nearby hill, which overlooks the destroyed school, and Hank drives away. Meanwhile, Sarah, who is unaware of Barney's presence, and recognizing the sudden and unbelievable growing distrust between her colored and her white field hands, calls to them:

"No one here committed this cowardly act of destroying our school, if this separation between you is what I think it is," Sarah tell them, "and there will be no Klansman's lines of hatred drawn in the sands on my son's land! Stop your whispering, you who have just fought that fire of scorn together. Don't stop fighting against the ugly world of disdain now."

Barney's cold eyes of demise focus on Sarah and then on Henry, who goes to Sarah to comfort her. Standing near Caleb, Flynn had not seen his father step from the tree shadows, had not seem the look Barney had given to Hank and had not noticed Hank drive away with Marcus and Burt, no one had. Flynn does, however, notice how Barney is now glaring at Henry and Sarah. When Barney faces Flynn and motions for him to come to him, the young man looks at his mother, at Caleb, and leaves his friend's side, and moves to his father with profound anxiety and confusion. Then, as unbelievable as it may seem to everyone—right after the school fire—another blaze erupts on the nearby hill above the destroyed school. At first it's only a thin line of sparks creeping along the crest of the wet knoll. Then the gasoline-fed sparks run sweeping up a tall poll before bursting into its full, Klan glory: a burning cross.

Caleb grabs a shovel and races up the slope; the black men and teenage, black males follow, seizing weapons along the way: sticks, rocks, shovels and their internal rage, rendering them as fearless as if they were armed with guns. Charging and screaming up the slope behind Caleb and at that burning cross, they terrify the holy hell out of Burt and

Marcus, who had kindled the cross and now—silhouetted against the full moon—run across the hill and escape in Hank's truck. Sarah's black workers hurl rocks at the speeding vehicle, then kick over the inflamed cross and pulverize the symbol of hatred with their shovels, sticks and their feet.

"It was them two white boys who sell junk in town," one of the blacks yells to Caleb. "I'd known 'em anywhere. Don't nobody in this world try and tell me it wasn't them two boys. Ma God, ain't there any white person in this whole wide world gots no heart?"

On the bluff next to the destroyed cross, Caleb's sad-eyed gaze turns downgrade on that which is close to his heart and which can't be stamped out as easily as a burning cross, his friend Flynn, who now seems to be one with his father.

"Thanks, Father, for coming to help us fight the fire. I know how tired you were tonight," says Flynn, desperately hoping that his father is not the architect of the school fire. The blonde boy's blue-eyed deprivation searches about the hilltop to locate Caleb among the silhouetted crowd there and cannot, and Flynn gives in to the will of his father, and they depart for the manor, Colonel Cutter's arm about his son's shoulders.

"I will never be too tired or too ill to make up the lost time between us in order to be with you, my only son," whispers Barney, planting a kiss on Flynn's forehead, going on. "As your Catholic God would for His Son, I would do anything to show my love for you, even unto destroying this world."

As Barney and Flynn leave, a dozen of the children who were pulled away from the fire by Bruce and Henry, and had gone to the barn with Miss McLeland, run from the distant, temporary school house and approach Naomi, as she glares after Barney and Flynn. "Why did the bad people burn down our school, Naomi?" one of them—a little white girl—asks, tears flowing down her pale cheeks.

Naomi gathers in the sobbing children, both white ones and black ones, around her, while an exhausted Caleb and Henry follow the field hands' lead and head to their quarters for a much-needed rest and sleep. "Worry not about the school," Naomi tells the crying children, "But anyone who burns the symbol of His Holy Son's cross—the symbol of Jesus' sacrifice for us and turns it into an unspeakable thing of evil, worry about him," Naomi explains on to the little ones. "This person of evil will

412

surely come to think that burning in the fires of hell is far better than the just punishment awaiting him."

"Do you mean old Hank, Naomi?" a little black girl asks, pointing up at the hill. "'Cause my brother who was up on the hill with Caleb, he say that old Hank was drivin' that truck where we saw the cross burnin'."

"Yes, Louise, old Hank will wish he were dead before this madness ends, but he's only a tool of the one behind this. This, then, is what you should do. Pray for your enemies, that they will not be delivered into the eternal grips of hell." Naomi soul searches into each of the young ones' wide eyes, and teaches on. "Look at one another," she commands them, and the young people do so, gazing at one another with reflection and curiosity, as Naomi continues. "Who is your neighbor?" The children point at one another. "Do you love your neighbors?" When they nod in agreement, she smiles at each of them in turn, and to each she says, by name, "Go home then and also pray that your folks will not teach you to hate your neighbor against the will of God and in favor of Satan because of the different color of your skin." As the children leave, Naomi's eyes refocus on the moving Judas-tree shadows, now tilting in reverse, as Barney and Flynn pass by them. The wise old woman then turns her anxious gaze on Caleb, who has stopped along the way letting Henry continue alone, and is looking back at Flynn and Barney as they vanish into the satanic shadows of infamy. Naomi then catches up with Sarah and climbs the slopes of Manor Hill, Sarah for some deserving sleep, Naomi to pray along with the children that the stars will not abandon them, Caleb and Henry to prepare for another day's trials and tribulations.

An hour after the fires have settled into smoldering ashes and all of the humans have gone, you can hear the stars crying from space, so quiet and so depressed is Shadow Grove.

413

29

Against the Chimney with No Easy Way to Climb Down

The following evening—as the sun sinks low against the horizon and darkness creeps over the land—Sarah, holding onto a rosary, stands at the open guestroom window. Putting her prayer beads in her dress pocket, she looks through her father's powerful telescope and at Little Shadow Place. There is no sign of Henry or of Caleb, only tiny-appearing Old Clara peacefully grazing in the green meadow. Sarah moves away from the telescope to yet another window, an opened one next to her bed. From there, she scrutinizes the pile of ashes that was once their school, the charred remains recalling images of the *White Dove* and how Henry and others risked their lives to recover her parents' bodies; and, now, with Barney living on Shadow Grove, not one of her white workers today would follow Henry anywhere, let alone into a burning plane, or to that school again if it was rebuilt and burned a second time, because to the workers—due to Barney and maybe soon, due to Flynn—the real road to power and success, which everyone desires, does not come from the love of one's neighbor, but instead comes from a willingness to ruthlessly dominate others. Knowing how brutal Barney can be with people who cross him, Sarah would not dare try and convince Flynn to reject his father and his corrupt ways, that and the fact that—as Naomi has already forewarned—it's in God's hands. Sarah kneels beside her bed, removes her rosary from her pocket and prays. "Hail Mary full of grace, blessed are thou among women, and blessed is the fruit of thy womb Jesus. Holy Mary, mother of God, pray for us sinners now and at the hour of our death." She sadly looks over at a framed photograph of Flynn and exclaims on. "Mother of God, I may lose both of my sons. Please ask Jesus, your beloved Son, to give me—the mother of two beautiful boys, and a woman who adores a glorious man in God's image, Henry Brooks—the strength and a sign to show me how to carry on. In Jesus' name I ask. Amen."

The sound of violin music is heard streaming feather light through the window on the soft evening breeze. Sarah rises to her feet and returns to the telescope. She gazes through it at Henry's land. Nothing.

Anxiously, she then swings the scope to the right and onto the road leading to Shadow Grove, and she sees Caleb, six hundred yards or so away sitting beside Henry, who is driving the wagon and Old Clara toward the plantation.

"Papa," says Caleb, placing his violin in its case and settling back in the wagon. "We just left Shadow Grove this morning. I can still smell the smoke on me and in my hair even though I washed myself twice since the fire. You never said why you wanted to come out here again. It'll be dark soon and then, there's the matter of Barney."

"I wasn't sure, son, until this moment. A feeling, Caleb. Sarah needs us."

Suddenly inspired now, Sarah makes the sign of the cross and immediately has Naomi send word to the workers to meet with her in the south field near the barn; she realizes that the whites may protest about being at a meeting with the blacks, so she decides to talk with the whites separately and will have Henry—who is a blessing to come at that moment—speak to her colored workers on their side of the property. However, assuring that the blacks and whites will hear and maintain eye contact between one another, Sarah has also wisely chosen a spot for the whites as close to that of the blacks as possible.

It takes nearly an hour to organize the workers, and when they line up under a starry sky, surrounded by flickering pole torches, Henry confronts the colored workers, and—while both sides of the color line settle onto chairs, benches, stand or sit on the ground—each group glances over the void between them at the other, a stone's throw apart. Caleb sits with Earlene and Naomi in the front row, while Henry holds up his hands, trying to calm the blacks, who are afraid that Barney not only burned down Sarah's school, but that the meeting is about how he will also force them off Shadow Grove, or worse, try murdering them during the night.

"Nobody can hurt you here," Henry tells the sobbing black children. "Every man and woman sitting and standing around you now will put down their lives to keep you safe." Many among the black workers hold onto their children in dread of Barney, in spite of Henry's assurances, while at the same time many of the whites are looking sadly across at the blacks with empathy and with their own arms about their white children, who now also fear Barney and for good reason: they know Barney is not above killing even the whites. Henry points at the barn. "If an animal stable was good enough for Jesus," he exclaims, "then—like the new school teacher says—that barn is good enough for our kids' school, and until the Angel of God or the Lamb of God, Himself, our Lord, comes and warns us to flee as that heavenly Host warned Mary and Joseph to flee from King Herod, who wanted to kill Jesus, and how they warned the Jew to flee from Egypt, we will have no more talk from you parents about takin' these kids out of our school or of leaving Georgia. Georgia is our home for the whites and us."

"Amen!" someone exclaims from the gathering.

Smiling down at Caleb, Henry says, "My boy, as all of you know, is well studied, and he's surely blessed in ways that old King Herod could have ever dreamed of, and—" A thunderous applause for Caleb interrupts Henry's speech. However—after having tried time after time to flee from the public's eyes and from talks of him being blessed—Caleb raises to his feet and acknowledges his father to show the love and respect he has for him, and the black workers give Caleb a standing ovation. When everyone sits again, those who have seats to sit on, Henry continues: "As I was going to say, not even my son understands fully what God wants of him, and no one here or elsewhere, in this whole world, understands my boy, except maybe Naomi." The blacks clap and look ahead at the mysterious woman, as does Sarah and many of her white workers, who have heard Henry's words and have come to love Naomi, and Naomi stands and acknowledges the black workers and then the white ones by waving her hand at them. Afterwards she sits and lovingly gives Caleb a love tap on his thigh.

"My son and Master Flynn," Henry continues, smiling at Caleb and Naomi and then going on, "both boys have been helping me with my English." He glances over at Sarah, and goes on, "So if I sound somewhat smarter than you're used to hearing me—from my last talk to you a while back—rather than a simple pig-slopping farmer, that I am, blame it on them two boys." The children laugh when hearing Henry refer to himself as a pig-slopper, and the adults chuckle, their tension lessening.

Deadly serious now, Henry fixes his stern gaze on the crowd. "There are those who look at my son in awe, but all of us are the 'Calebs' in this world as seen through God's eyes if we love one another, us coloreds and whites." As applause rings through the air, Henry looks toward the white workers to whom Sarah is now addressing, and a few of the whites are taking notice of the man they had learn to love and trust and then

416

turned their backs on in fear of Barney. Henry continues, "Many of us have been murdered, and if we fight back we're sent to jail, hanged or beaten. True enough. But we can't continue reacting in the poison blood of hatred on our part toward all whites either. Don't look at each other so surprised. There are those among us who hate whites as much as they hate us. Hate begets hate, at least that's what Caleb says the Bible tells us. It's us grownups who teach our children to hate, but their clean little God-given, hungry minds—those of the black boys and girls and those of the white boys and girls, working together—that is the stuff of love that will cures us all if we let it!"

Another round of applause breaks out and it continues for some time from the blacks and from Sarah and Miss McLeland on their side of the field. Several dozen of Sarah's white workers are now standing and also applauding. Sarah, however, is troubled. She searches the crowd: Flynn is nowhere to be seen. Hidden from view by the overhanging branches of a nearby oak tree, Flynn is on the roof of one of the black worker's shacks, an outsider on his own land, as he crouches with his back against the brick chimney, his head held low, his bent legs paining him, so motionlessly does he position himself there, his arms folded across his chest and resting on his knees in the chilly night breeze. As the clapping continues, Flynn lifts his sights toward the workers below; and, then, when the clapping stops, he again lowers his head, torn between loyalty to his father's dogma and that of his mother's Catholic teachings which says all men are created equal.

"There are many issues to speak of," Henry tells the blacks while watching Sarah searching over the crowd for signs of Flynn. Henry is doing the same thing, unaware that the tenderhearted boy is only a few yards away, as he goes on. "The bullwhip beatings, the rapes and the hangings, we have to speak of all of these evils. But one thing is clear, we ain't going . . ." He stops and smiles at Caleb. "I should have said 'we're' not going to blame everyone. Sarah Winthrop is not our enemy," Henry reassures them, deliberately not calling Sarah a "Cutter."

"Field Boss Collins or Shadow Grove and God-fearing whites here are not the enemy and neither is Master Flynn. I know there's all this talk about him having Barney's blood in him, but countering that in the boy is the blood of Lawrence and Marilyn Winthrop." On the roof, a soft smile crosses Flynn's lips, and Sarah is deeply moved by Henry's reassuring words, and her love for him radiates on her face, as Henry continues.

417

"Flynn would never give his blessing on burning down Reverend Harris's church in town, or the school here, not the boy we all know, love and trust."

As cheers from the workers echo from the colored side of the line, whites also cheer, whistle and clap, a few of them stepping over the invisible line of hatred and joining hands with the blacks, Sarah deliberately hanging back to encourage all to follow their own heart and not simply because they saw her joining Henry and her dark-skinned workers. Against the chimney, Flynn glances at the manor's master bedroom window, and his heart races in fright. Standing at the window is Colonel Cutter. His blue eyes of scorn targeting the handful of white workers who crossed over to the black side of the field. Cutter picks up the telephone and dials it.

"Henry," Barney says to the listener on the other end of the line in town, while lifting the edge of the curtain for a better look at Caleb's father. "I want his death to be ugly. Ugly, you hear. Then you do Caleb fucking Brooks the same goddamn way. I want their asses nailed to the cross!"

Flynn watches Barney slam down the phone receiver. The frightened boy looks down at Henry, who raises his arms in the air and exclaims: "All of us poor coloreds and whites . . . We've been on our knees too long through ignorance and fear. Now, we stand up against the Klan in a world that won't survive without us loving each other."

"Go to hell!" yells a drunken, old Hank, among Sarah's white field hands adjusting his bifocals, while continuing to shout. "I don't have to listen to this bullshit! I'm going straight to Dane Tucker and tell him all about you damn people out here. Then let's see how willing you coons are to stand up without legs to stand on! We haven't forgotten Crazy Walter with his cut-off-my-legs talk if that's what you people are thinking—that he's still free—and makes you so bold. He'll get his too!" Hank glares at the manor and yells. "And you up there hiding in that big house. That's why I'm going to Dane, because you're doing nothing to stop these fools!"

Hank storms off, followed by several other whites to the old man's truck, and Hank quickly drives away, all looking over their shoulders at the master bedroom window. Flynn follows their gaze there, the room now dark, the curtains unmoving. Feeling the tension in the air, Sarah's black workers begin to glance about in fear and whisper to one another.

Had Henry gone too far? Earlene, however, rises to her feet with so much show of dignity as her young frightened heart can muster that Bruce sobs with pride as she stares at those around her—as does Flynn, from the roof, wanting to see who else will follow Earlene's lead. No one does. The black adults and even the whites who had crossed to the coloreds' side of the field, now look over their shoulders at the whites on Sarah's side of the racial line, as if wanting to go back to them. After Hank's terrifying threat, and feeling that they may be murdered by the Klan for doing so, as had been Claretta and Billy Joe, most of the whites now rejoin those about Sarah, who reflects sorrow and disappointment at seeing this, and Sarah takes a step toward Henry, until he shakes his head, telling her to remain where she is. Henry has yet to play his ace card.

"It's time to stand tall!" Henry pleads, "Stand up. Don't run away."

"We scared," calls an elderly, black woman. "And so are our kids and them white folk. Scared of the Klan, Henry Brooks." All eyes are now on the master bedroom window.

"We don't wants to be hanged," another woman sobs, everyone now looking from the manor house over to Sarah. "Don't wants to be cut up in pieces like Walter gonna soon be, Sarah," the woman sobs. "God knows he's a walkin' dead man, Walter is." As a crushed Sarah looks from the woman to Henry and back, the woman sobs on. "That why nobody in Reverend Harris's church in town wasn't a-willin' to give that po' scared man shelter. They know'd they'd be killed, too, if they did."

Sarah's eyes tear up, and Flynn is also visibly shaken by the black women's, sorrowful confession and again he faces his father's bedroom window, as if hoping against hope for a sign that Barney has some compassion for the colored workers, but the room is still dark, though he can feel his father's presence there. With his eyes also watering up, Flynn refocuses on the blacks, as still another woman among them pleads to Henry. "Please don't ask my child to stand up, Henry. He be all I got left since they done hanged his older brother and pa befo' we moved from town and out here to Shadow Grove, right after them young people in Harris's churchyard was killed."

The woman looks at Caleb, Henry's ace in the hole, and she cries aloud, "Them girls in church who jumped rope over them two dead bodies called out Caleb's name, and Reverend Harris, hisself, done said he saw them dead kids." Stopping she gazes at Naomi and then at Caleb and then talks to Naomi. "And you, blessed Naomi, over there sittin' in

419

the love of God, Reverend said he saw you a-rising up in the sky, said them dead kids was with you and was-a callin' out his name, Caleb's blessed name." From both sides of the field, everyone turns their sights on Caleb. Another woman stands and continues. "We came here—some of us—'cause we thought God was in yo' boy," she tells Henry, "and we thought through Caleb, God would take care of us, but Caleb, he don't seem to want any part of ma God or of us."

Caleb glances about at all of those desperate souls looking from Henry to him. If he remains sitting and doing nothing, it's clear to Caleb that he will destroy the hope that others see in his father.

"Son," Henry calls to him. "Seems it's time now for you to stand up and be counted."

Caleb stands tall and moves to his father's side. From his place on the roof, Flynn continues to crouch, but in spite of the storm of conflict raging within him his very soul swells with pride, and his shoulders rise when he sees Caleb and Henry standing in virtual oneness.

"Tell us, Caleb," one of the religious black women says, "do you believe in God, so that we can put to rest this talk about you can't be a chosen one, 'cause they say you don't embrace our Lord?"

With Caleb now awash under the torch lights, Flynn notices that not only do the blacks sit on the edge of their seats, so does each and every white across the way with Sarah, all waiting to hear what Caleb has to say, if he has or doesn't have a covenant with the Holy Ghost. Now in a stiff stance on the roof, Flynn prays that Caleb, indeed, has a love of Jesus and of God, and thus—at least—separate himself from Barney, who told Flynn, at the lagoon, that he and Caleb thought alike when it comes to God.

"Fear is like being unclothed in a land of ice and snow," Caleb carefully chooses as his first words, going on. "If those of you who stand by your beliefs that God is real, then nothing can hurt you, you who believe the way Papa, the way Naomi, the way Sarah and Flynn believe, that He has prepared a mansion for you, where you will never know hunger, will never feel pain, will never grow old or be cold, even if your enemies strip you of your clothing and cast you out into a sea of ice, even as many of you have heard it said that Flynn and I felt no cold the day he carried me in his arms out of the barn and into the face of a blizzard so long ago now; with your minds you can shield off the freezing snow and even move mountains, according to Naomi and the Bible, and in that sense you who believe are far more stronger than I."

When the applause breaks out, Caleb is surprised, for he had spoken, to be bluntly honest, to empower others, not to receive praise. From his isolation on the roof, Flynn watches a few workers, Naomi and Sarah tearing up, and then he fights back his own tears, as Caleb continues. "Papa, Flynn and Sarah, who is like a mother to me, I love without question." Caleb speaks softly now to the crowd, while unknowingly beaming at his teary-eyed real mother, Sarah, across the way. "The Winthrops—before our time—said that we are all the children of God." Caleb's sights shift admiringly to Naomi, and he praises her with his soft gaze and with his warm smile, caressing her with tenderness and love. "It seems to me that Naomi feels the same way and more: that we are all made of the stars without any diminishing lines between us, and I have not praised her enough for helping Papa to care for me over all these years. Thank you, Naomi." Naomi sobs, her tears flowing. "Naomi believes as she does because of her covenant with her God, so I ask all of you to stand up, not for me, who lack your faith, but stand up in order to grow in strength and goodness, as my father has asked, and your Father in heaven wants. Stand up if you believe in your God, and if you believe in me, even a little after this. For you who have not fully understood my message, then it is simply this: your love for each other is a far greater power than the power that your fears place on you of the Klan. You and I, all of us here are slices from the same loaf of bread. Let's react like it and rise from the heat of the oven as good loaves should, stronger together than apart."

Several more blacks get to their feet and stand with Earlene and with the few whites who crossed over the line to be with the black workers and now remain. Naomi, strangely enough, remains seated in silence, but encourages Earlene and the others to remain standing with a slight wave of her hand when they look at her. This is not the moment for the mystery woman to rise to her feet as she had risen into the sky on her horse. The stage now belongs to Caleb's jurisdiction, and everyone there now seems to sense it: Caleb goes on: "According to Naomi, Jesus says . . ." He stops, reflects momentarily at Naomi and then continues. "Mind you, I did not say 'Jesus said.' That would mean the past to some of us and that He is no longer with us, but Naomi is so sure that after two thousand years since His resurrection that Jesus is still with mankind, with Papa, with Sarah, with Flynn and with all good people, even those

421

in sin—which we all are—so I'll repeat it. The Lamb of God is alive today and He says—" A thunderous applause deafens the ears at the mention from Caleb that Jesus is . . . is now and ever will be alive and with them. Using this sleeve, Flynn wipes the tears from the corner of his eyes, as Caleb attempts to continue against the loud applause, while lovingly beaming at his proud father, at Naomi, who waves to the crowd asking them to stop applauding, and slowly the hand clapping on both sides of the field fades to a stop.

In the darkness of the master bedroom, an eerie light glows red, as Caleb speaks from the heart. "Naomi has told me and Flynn, from as early as we can recall, that if we had the faith of a mustard seed, we could move mountains, so together we can and will move that mountain of hatred between coloreds and whites here and in Cutterville and beyond with the same kind of love that I have for my best friend Flynn and he has for me, for—as a good priest told my father and Sarah—years ago—we are all from the same tree that seeded itself into the world somewhere on the continent of Africa, and all that means is that we are all brothers and sisters. There is no black race. No white. No yellow. No red. Such tagging causes hatred. Learn to live with it," he now demands. "And stop hating one another!"

The atmosphere explodes with horrendous applause and shouts of "praise to God" from the workers. Even though he never said he believed, no one has ever heard Caleb speak so positively of God, of life after death. Ever! And that is good enough for Flynn, as well, as he stands erect, pumping his arm and balled fist in the air: "Yeah!"

Henry steps back into the shadows. This is what he knew Caleb was capable of, what he, as a father, had lived for and had prayed for. High on the roof, and gently rocked by the wind—as are the oak leaves about him, Flynn watches wave after wave of workers follow Earlene and the other's lead and stand, including Naomi. Even the children stand up now, feeding off of Caleb's youthful charisma, everyone there mesmerized by the power of his humility; with Sarah's, black workers now on their feet, a main-body of whites swarm across the field and join hands with them, and—as one family—everyone breaks into song. From atop of his little world of chimney soot and smoke, as he keeps watch on his father's bedroom window, both pride and fear overcome Flynn, proud that Caleb is truly growing up, fear that his boyhood friend is lost to him and that the man who is now Caleb, may be—as he had for weeks feared—taking the first steps toward killing him and Barney, if Barney did not kill Caleb first.

As Caleb stands there with the breeze sweeping through his mixed blood, well-bodied, curly hair, and the torch lights flicker across his golden skin, Earlene takes Naomi's hand into hers. "I want to marry Caleb, Naomi, to stay close to him forever. I love Caleb."

The mixed-blood Kiowa woman searches over the crowd of adoring faces of white and black girls. "You and a dozen others, child," she says.

Earlene follows Naomi's gaze to the adoring girls, all yearning to be held in Caleb's arms and thus in the arms of God. "There are so many of them, Naomi. And you say each of them loves Caleb?"

"Earlene, in the Bible, as Christ passed through the multitude where hundreds touched him, our Lord suddenly called out, 'Who touched me?' There are many who touch us, but only a few in a million with the purity of heart that counts."

"I don't understand. How does that make a difference in the way these girls love Caleb?"

"They don't know what love is. Not pure love. But lust, the same lust which brought down Samson."

"Samson?"

"Yes. There is an outsider here in this crowd with the same kind of lust, even as we speak, a girl possessed by sex. Her sights are also on Caleb, and with everyone looking at him, Caleb can feel her touching him with her immorality." Naomi and Earlene watch how Caleb is glancing over the crowd, a disturbing look in his eyes.

"I'll scratch her eyes out, whoever she is, Naomi."

"Hush, Child. You are no match for the devil, and in God's eyes, she is worth saving, and only Caleb's brotherly love can do that."

"But who is she?" asks Earlene. "I want to know."

Naomi turns and looks at Jayne Hill.

Jayne, her eyes swallowing up the sight of Caleb's tall, muscular body, is standing near the outer edge of the crowd with a tall, curly-haired youth named Leon, one of Sarah's white workers' son, a slender, sex-hungry, but otherwise decent soul of nineteen. "Did you bring it from Miller's church like you said?" Leon asks Jayne, breaking her concentration on Caleb.

"Of course," Jayne exclaims to the naive boy, "That is if you're not too scared to smoke it, or—after smoking it, don't get down on your knees and pray to those statues of yours and ask those so-called saints to give you strength to resist me the next time we both want to do it." Taking his cheeks in her hand, she whispers, "Bark fer me," and then she squints at him as if at her puppy and boldly goes on. "Remember, the only reason I agreed to do this with you is because I've never had a virgin puppy before. Afterwards you have to get me back home befer Ma wakes up in the morning."

"I brought you here and I'll get you back in time, so now, let's go and do it but I still don't see why you insisted on me bringin' you all the way out here. We could have done it in town."

"'Now let's go and do it,'" Jayne, says mocking him, her sights on Caleb.

"You wanta do it or not?" the boy asks, as she continues looking at Caleb. "I'm getting bored."

"Good," Jayne whips, viewing his fly. "That'll make it all the better for me. I like it ready and hard. Bark, bark, bark! Well, come on," she barks at him. "Can you beat it? What is the world coming to? These whites out here are worshiping Caleb Brooks, a nigger. You'll never catch me doing that. Let's get to that barn while I still want to do it with you," she says trotting to the barn.

Meanwhile, in the crowd around Caleb, Earlene tugs on Naomi's arm. "I know Caleb is smarter than all of us, but he saved the books fo' me, him and Flynn. That means he loves me, didn't it, Naomi? And he won't ever change, will he? He'll always stay the same and love me."

Naomi doesn't answer; her sights are locked on Jayne and Leon, as they enter the distant barn. The wise, mixed-blood woman then turns to Earlene.

"Everyone changes, Earlene. Caleb doesn't know it yet, but he's not the same young man who walked into this meetin'." She reflects on the barn, once more, then on Bruce's confused daughter and whispers. "A mountain can't be held by one woman's arms, sweetheart. It's too big, and once Caleb lifts that mountain and bears its burden on his shoulders for all of us, he will never again put it down, because—not tomorrow, and maybe not even by another two thousand years, but too soon Jesus is coming, and it'll be too late then. Caleb's life is now in the arms of his people, the only arms big enough to hold him."

"I'm his people, Naomi," begs Earlene. "I'm colored."

"You don't understand. He belongs to the world. Whites are people, Chinese are people. All came from Africa where God roamed and made us one family in His image. What color is Caleb to you, child."

"The color of honey, Naomi."

"What do you think made him that color, if Henry is as dark as you?"

"I guess somebody white like Flynn Cutter."

"You guessed right, child. Caleb is a mixture of the two extremes in the colors of man. Tonight, pray for Caleb, not for your needs, but for his, not that you might embrace him, but that he might embrace us, for the road of the cross is upon him and Flynn, and may God have mercy on both of them; because even a mighty warrior like Samson was betrayed to the Philistines by a weak, sex-starved woman called Delilah."

"Are you sayin' that even if he has all the power in the world, a woman can destroy Caleb?"

Naomi faces the master bedroom window and watches—yet another—eerie red glow against Barney's window and goes on. "A mountain can be brought down by rain, an ocean dried up by the sun. If Satan is behind it, a woman can destroy the world with her body."

She touches Earlene, quieting her, as Caleb raises one of the torches over his head and then exclaims, "White workers here have never given us trouble, and we have never given them any. The Klan has killed and enslaved human beings in the past with impunity. Now, not only did they burn down the school, they've taken away two beautiful, young lives, Claretta and Billy Joe and will not hesitate to even kill whites, the way they murdered Lilly. Make no mistake about it, Lilly wasn't just killed by Dane Tucker, she was also killed by her hatred, hatred of her brothers and sisters, but I was there, as she was dying and said, 'Come close.' That's all she asked for in the end, a closeness with another human being, a closeness to her brother. So, let's all 'come close' "

As the tears flow, Caleb brings his closing point home with the force of a hammer breaking through a wall of ice. "As for Dane and the Klan, cowards only attack sleeping dogs, and tonight we are awakened, not because of me, not because of any single person, but because of all of us standing up together, and we will not fall asleep again!"

The roar of approval thunders skyward; Flynn looks at the window of Barney's room: the glass is shaking as if in a rage, and with the thunderous ovation seemingly vibrating the glass from the outside and the glow from the inside, the window glass is ready to explode, so deafening is the applause. Sarah now joins her workers around Caleb.

"How will we fight against the Klan?" a white man asks Caleb, "without killing and murdering the same as they're doing?"

As others crowd about Caleb with that same question written on their faces, Earlene whispers to Naomi. "He's so beautiful, Naomi."

"Shhh, child and listen," Naomi tells Earlene, as Caleb answers the how, when and where to fight the Klan:

"We emulate Mahatma Gandhi," he tells them. "We march!"

Catching sight of one of Sarah's elderly lame, white, female residents, whose begging eyes are seeking out those around her and saying that she has never done anything worthwhile in her life, but wants to join the march, Caleb, recognizing this, passionately adds. "You who are impaired shall go with us, if that is what you want, and those who are crippled or too ill even to walk, we'll provide horses, mules, wagons, trucks and cars." He looks at Sarah and she eagerly nods in agreement. He, then, continues. "Those who grow tired on the way and cannot walk the ten miles to town, we who are stronger will carry you on our backs, and if we have to we will carry you back home the same way, because it isn't just the physical bodies we need with us. We are in desperate need of the mental power of those of you who find their strength in prayer. Together we will petition City Hall to rein in, if not fire Richards and his Klan-loving deputies. And any of you who have other demands, share them with all of us as we march."

"Amen!" a choir of voices calls out.

His emotions running high, his arms opened to his son, Henry steps out of the shadows, and exclaims, "There are those out in the world who will wish to kill not just the idea that was planted here to night, but kill all of us, because the devil fears what was said here will spread like weeds all over the world, even as Christianity did, but there is no turning back."

Caleb's heart races with doubt, for unlike the heart that beats within his father, proud and strong, the one which beats within Caleb—in spite of the fact that this night signals to others that he is a man—is yet that of a young boy. He follows his father's gaze to the sea of rainbow faces of those who have now joined hands and are depending on him. Sarah and everyone there weeps when the Caleb turns and embraces his gentle father, determined to do whatever it takes to protect him and everyone else from harm, even if it means he has to die. As the meeting ends, and everyone is returning to their field-side houses, Naomi notices Flynn. He's motioning to her from the rooftop, and she hurries to him; without speaking, he drops Sheriff Richards's documents and letters, bundled together, into her hands, then stands in stoic tranquility, and watches as Naomi glances at the bundle, then up at him, nods and walks away, knowing that this entire business is being played out on the way to the cross, and not to be questioned. Sarah, Naomi, Caleb and Henry have a few words together about tomorrow's marching plans, and then Sarah heads for the manor.

"I'll catch up to you, Sarah," calls Naomi, stopping and showing the letters to Caleb.

"What is this, Naomi?" he asks.

"You will know when you read them."

"Who gave this to you?"

"A lost angel," she says, giving Flynn a worried glance and going on. "An angel whose own letters that he received from his father failed to reflect the man's evil side as do these."

Caleb follows her gaze to Flynn, and as soon as she passes the wrapped correspondence into Caleb's hand, thunder and lightning rock the sky, and both Flynn and Caleb face the manor and see the curtains in the master bedroom ripped from the window, and the windowpane, as if a black hole of death, cracks, followed by howling, wolf-like winds which races across the land, ripping at Flynn, threatening to topple him off the roof. Caleb approaches his friend.

"No!" commands Naomi, "if you interfere now you both will only die." Caleb stops and gazes back at her and then at Flynn, as she goes on. "Flynn must find his own way down and through this storm." As the scattering of workers race to their shacks, Flynn, lost and alone, staggers on the edge of the roof and holds onto the tree branch against the windstorm. Yearning for his friend to lean on, Flynn watches Caleb and Henry, as they regrettably follow Naomi's edict and continue to their assigned quarters. With the wind nudging him about, for the impressionable blonde boy struggling to balance himself on that roof's edge, there's no easy way to climb down again, but somehow he knows he must, and he makes his way feet-first off the dwelling, gripping the brittle clapboards and wood trim as he goes. He quietly walks away, all the more desperate for understanding, for a reason to justify his betrayal of his father. Embraced only by the wind sending its cold fingers of despair running

427

down his back, he no longer feels like a white boy, nor a black one—which he had once told Caleb he wished he were, and as Naomi has said all whites are beneath their skin. To Flynn, he's just someone created by chance to be the color he is, certainly not white, not the color of the driven snow, not white outside on his skin or inside on his soul. How he wishes he could be the in-between color of Caleb instead of someone called "white" and shaped by the hateful past, and by powerful men, and the present politics of his father's money and influence.

Torn between his love for Caleb and the loyalty and love he feels for the supernatural man called "Barney," his head held low, Flynn continues on his way. He looks up. A forgiving Colonel Cutter is standing on the porch step and agonizingly feeling Flynn's pain. He motions for his son to come to him, and suddenly the wind ceases to rage, revealing the power that Satan has given to Barney on earth over mankind. Flynn runs to the house and into the open arms of his father, and they sob together.

"Ma baby," mouths Naomi, watching Flynn embrace the devil. "My lost angel."

"Ahhh," groans the voice of Jayne from the barn. "It feels so damn good. So good."

30

The Long, Gray Line

As the morning sun rises over Georgia, word of Caleb's organized march into Cutterville has spread across the town and beyond, thanks in part to Jayne Hill, who was quick to run to Jerry MacDonnell with the story that started the ball rolling out of control that very night. Because Jayne had informed him that it would be a racially mixed march, MacDonnell's paper had dubbed the marcher "The Long, Gray Line of Protest," horrifying Cutterville's whites, to say nothing about what the headlines have done to towns, small and large across the state, once the story-hungry radio owners learned of the event, towns worrying that their black populations will also rise up. Ironically, again, thanks to Jayne for causing such widespread attention to the march, that gray line—which would have been a couple hundred at best—has swollen to over four thousand and is still growing. All of those other towns which were worried about their black population were partly right. The blacks in those places across Georgia rose up and traveled all night to Cutterville in order to join in with Sarah's workers and to see Caleb in person, after word spread that he was connected to those reported dark skies over the town and surrounding area; Whites, Blacks, Jews, Mexicans and more are arriving all the time, far more groups of people than the citizens of Cutterville have ever seen before. MacDonnell—in competition with outside reporters, who have followed the marchers—rushes about snapping pictures, which he hopes will increase the circulation of his *Sentinel* news locally, but also in cities like Atlanta. Even some white war veterans from out of state—carrying high the streaming red, white, and blue—are parading along with Sarah's plantation workers. Standing on the curbs, the whites of Cutterville—their rocks, clubs, and guns held nervously in their hands—watch in disbelief and hope that the seemingly endless line of protesters will soon end, a line of humanity which seems like a river of damnation striding down Main Street toward the courthouse to destroy them and their town.

Jayne Hill is among the gawking white spectators, her young, wild eyes sparking with excitement, her sisters and girlfriends, at her side, holding each other's hands, giddily taking part in what is to them a refreshing departure in the otherwise boring town.

Suddenly, the smiles leaves the girls' faces when they see the blacks of Colored Town rushing across the train tracks and joining in the march with the out-of-town blacks and with Shadow Grove's field hands, shockingly-awakening the whites who see that they are hopelessly outnumbered on all sides; dropping their rocks and sticks, and putting away their guns, many of the white women and children cry in the face of their worst nightmare, as do Jayne and friends.

Dane Tucker is furious and pushes his way through the gawking white crowd to Hooverville, a tent city—bitterly named, by the national newspapers, to spite President Hoover—a tent city just off the square, where the veterans who had arrived in Cutterville weeks earlier now live, veterans who had peacefully attempted to force the factory to give the black-workers' jobs to them and had failed, and who now stand in silence and watch as their opposite numbers—among the marches—walk by with the American flags.

"You guys just going to stand here like dummies and let them degenerates walk all over this town?" Dane hisses at one of the ex-soldiers. "You boys have guns. Help us ride these nigger-loving punks out of here."

"We fought for that flag, Mister," the ex-leatherneck says, saluting the flags as those carrying it pass by, his fellow veterans doing the same, sending Dane's brain twisting with rage. He storms off, grumbling to himself.

Sheriff Richards and his men are also taken aback by the number of marchers entering the town, and it's not just the numbers of marchers, but their infectious spirit, demoralizing the local whites as if God Himself was injecting the blacks—and the white marchers with them—with unbelievable endurance, seemingly making the more capable marchers—and there are many who fit the description—appear as unstoppable superhumans; for as Caleb had promised, some of the more able workers are carrying the weaker individuals on their backs. Even the horses—with as many as three young people riding on them—prance about full of energy.

The mules pulling the buckboards, loaded down with riders, do so without kicking up a stubborn fuse. The overloaded wagons have come through the trip without breaking down, and the old people are smiling and riding along filled with hope and are reinvigorated as much as the bouncing, strutting teenagers, following the wagons on foot and dancing about to the music in their heads. Caleb and Henry are at the head of the line with the relatively more dignified and quieter group of about a dozen: Sarah, Bruce, Carrie and their surviving children—including Brick, who keeps up with his family this time. Miss McLeland is in a section of marchers behind the leaders and is pointing out different buildings and even a statue of the founding Cutters and teaching her students to spell the name of these sites, as the young people prance about. School was never like this; even Reverend Harris has joined the protesters and has grown a backbone and swears that God is now in him and that he feels right at home with his newfound honesty and humility. Caleb, however, is ill at ease and constantly looking about for Flynn, but there is no sign of him. He turns to Sarah. She shrugs to say she doesn't know where Flynn is either. Among the whites at curbside, Sheriff Richards runs into the street and alongside of Caleb.

"What the hell you think you're doing, boy?" he grumbles looking from Caleb to Sarah. "Were does he think he's taking these folks, Sarah?"

"Nowhere now," says Sarah. "We're here."

The courthouse now looms in front of them, and there—at the top of the building's widespread, twenty marble steps—is the blindfolded Lady of Justice on her pedestal and holding up her balanced scale in her left hand and a sword pointed down in her right. Caleb stops, and the multitude behind him does the same, all standing in silence, as they and Caleb survey the blindfolded lady. The curbside whites watch Caleb with great interest, some of them whispering and pointing at him, others still unaware of who he is and why he's in their town. Then, the curbside whites turn their gaze to the courthouse's doors, which are swung open by two armed deputies, and the lesser god, in his black robe of justice, walks through those two fourteen-foot-high, bronze doors. Hell bent on saving the white race, the man in that robe of justice stares down at the invaders. He's the feared and hated old Judge Joe Chambers, of whom Caleb had spoken when he told Dane on that car lot that he would have the judge and the entire justice system of the town investigated by the federal government. Chambers is sixty-nine and smoking one of Barney's Havana cigars. He tosses aside his cigar and stands between one of the building's ionic columns, his legs spread, his hands on his hips, and he seems prepared to linger there out of the sun and let the marchers roast in the hot weather. Those godlike, towering, ionic, columns which line the portico of the hundred-year-old courthouse are like so many white, vengeful gods, who have never let a colored man walk out of that building with a victory. As Chambers scratches his head and glares down at Caleb from in front of those bronze doors, Barney and Flynn walk from the courthouse and stand beside the judge, Flynn nervously following his father's sights to Sarah and wondering what will happen next. Barney, however, looks away from his wife and deliberately ignores her, opting to challenge Caleb instead.

"Won't you come inside, Caleb," calls Barney. When Caleb doesn't reply, Barney then unperturbedly continues confronting him. "It seems a shame not to offer you a cool mint julep, boy." While waiting for Caleb's response, Barney studies the crowd of marchers who stretch from the courthouse all the way back to the square and down Main Street, the piggybacking, the tired, the young prancing-in-place children, the elderly, the crippled, and the strong. Shocked at the number of the protesters, Barney covers his astonishment with a wicked smile and razor-sharp sarcasm. "After that long walk you must be thirsty," Barney goes on, "the way Jesus thirsted after He was nailed to the cross, so please do come inside and have that drink before you have to turn right around and go back home with these people and maybe turn a few loaves of bread into thousands and feed the lot of them at your place." Caleb remains defiantly quiet and Barney glares at Richards, who is at the foot of the steps reasoning with Sarah.

"Take this boy Caleb and these other folks of yours back to Shadow Grove," Sheriff Richards hisses at her, going on; "Your husband doesn't seem to know how dangerous this business out here is, standing up there like some toy god. This isn't a toy thing, these coons. Not some harmless sword that Barney seems to worship to make him more like your father, who owned that sword."

"Sheriff!" Colonel Cutter yells, "Rejoin your men, Sir. You are dabbling in where you should not. Leave the matter of my wife to me."

Richards glares up at Barney and angrily moves off. It is then, after seeing that small crack in the Klan's armor between Richards and Barney, and feeling that it's the moment best suited for him, Caleb climbs the courthouse steps and approaches Barney and Flynn, and the marchers quickly ring the entire building with their superior numbers. "It is foretold that he will walk into the lion's den alone," Caleb hears the voice of Naomi say. And as he continues climbing the steps, he looks down at her, as she stoically stands next to Sarah watching him with a look of hope. Once he's reached Barney, at the top of the steps, Caleb looks over at Flynn with the same love which Naomi had passed onto him, during his climb. Following the ruling class of Cutterville—including middle-class Sheriff Richards, and two of his deputies, Caleb enters the red brick building.

When Caleb disappears inside the grand edifice, several more deputies attempt to pass through the interracial protesters and climb the steps to the courthouse, but the marchers quickly interlock their hands, preventing the lawmen or any others from entering the courthouse, this to protect Caleb at any cost; and the deputies back off from those stone-cold glaring eyes and determined bodies of togetherness.

Inside the court's conference room, the principle players sit around a large, oak table: Richards, Judge Chambers, Mayor Sipple, Reverend Miller and a half dozen cigar-smoking, concerned-looking men in dark suits representing the state of Georgia; and someone else is there, someone who is a surprise to Caleb, because of the way the town's whites despises him: the Jewish factory owner Dessen, himself. Barney and Flynn sit to the side of the large room, Barney playing down his importance, preferring to give Flynn a military overview of the battlefield. One of the lesser players, a small, troubled-looking man named Roscoe Carlton—wearing a tight-fitting, light-blue suit—sits at the table down from Caleb and worriedly gazes about the room, as if he would rather be anyplace else but there. Caleb seems extremely interested in the man. Judge Chambers, on the other hand, keeps his sights on Barney, the student watching the teacher for incisive head nods and clues. Chambers then turns to Caleb and asks, "What do you want, Caleb? A job? Money?"

"Or is it fame you're after?" asks Richards, leaning out to make eye contact with Caleb, while sitting next to Chambers, a body away from Henry's boy, and going on. "To be called the 'Joe Louis' of Georgia and have the coons beg you to save them like that coon did from that electric chair befer the state fried his black ass? 'Save me, Joe Louis! Save me, Champ,' that coon cried out, as if that Chinese-looking, dumb-ass-so-called 'Brown Bomber' couldn't even save himself if he had to."

"There is no need for that kind of talk," says Dessen, as the marchers suddenly break into song, which permeates the building.

Richards glares at Dessen. "I was just trying to pat this boy on his black back," the lawman says, then faces Caleb. "Caleb Brooks, I'm truly impressed by your organizational skills, boy. When you pick a fight, you pick a big one. With all those singing folks out there, if any of them could read or was a citizen here in Cutterville and could vote, you'd be elected our Mayor."

Mayor Sipple angrily hisses, "Sheriff, you either control yourself or wait outside." He faces Caleb. "Tell us what you're after, Caleb and let's get on with it and resolve this issue."

"That drink which was offered to me," says Caleb, addressing the Grand Wizard. "That would be a refreshing start, wouldn't you say so? I'll have it now." Colonel Cutter smiles at Caleb and leans back, totally relaxed in his chair, as an uneasy Flynn divides his attention between side-glancing at Barney, then squinting straight ahead at Caleb, watching for the slightest reaction between the arch rivals. Caleb smiles at Barney's attempt of disarming him with charm, an approach which Caleb knows will not last. "But water, not liquor which clouds the mind," Caleb goes on. "And, if you would, the marchers would also appreciate some fresh water. So they can save what they have for the walk back home."

"The hell you say," hisses Richards.

"Bring the gentleman his water and some water for us as well, Sheriff," Sipple says, getting a nod from Dessen.

That nod from Dessen to Sipple doesn't go unnoticed by Barney, who knows that sooner or later he will have to take out the Jew factory owner and his influence on the town, as well as taking care of Caleb. When Richards rolls his eyes at Barney, as if to ask if he was going to just sit there and do nothing, Barney lays into him. "The mayor told you to stay away from that church, but you just had to go there and flex your muscle with Deputy Hammer, then make a bad thing worse by insulting these people. Now do as you're told and have your men distribute that damn water to those others outside."

Sipple smiles at Flynn. "And then," he says, "let's hope this young man doesn't break the bank with his demands, Flynn."

After Richards sends word for his deputies to distribute the water among the marchers, he pours some for those around the table. First filling Caleb's glass and then the others, to get back at Barney, a bad mistake. When Richards approaches Flynn and his father with the last two glasses of water, Barney—who will not be served second after anyone, especially after a spade—angrily waves Richards off. Frustrated, Richards returns to the other players and places the refused glasses on the table and flops down in his seat, crosses his arms and angrily waits for Caleb to drink his fill. Finally putting aside his empty glass, Caleb sits back in his chair and says, "About breaking the bank, one would be foolish to even think of doing that. What I want is a political deal."

"Then you come to make peace, Caleb?" asks Sipple.

"I've come with the sword," Caleb exclaims, reaching into his pocket. Richards whips out his .38, jumps to his feet, looks over at Barney and points the weapon at Caleb's head, anxious to pull the trigger, everyone gasping and fearing that Caleb was reaching for a weapon. Flynn jumps up and starts toward Richards, but Barney jerks his son back into the chair. Then colonel himself withdraws his military .45, ready to blow Caleb's head off as well. Caleb calmly continues, "A paper sword," he says with both guns pointing at him now. While Flynn holds his breath, Caleb removes documents from his pockets and places them on the table along with letters and continues. "As I said, what I want is a political agreement. An agreement that Sheriff Richards will recuse himself, not only from this table as an arbitrator, because of his childish demeanor and lack of people skills, but to cut his ties with the Klan." Shock and disbelief reflects on those pale white faces, except for Dessen's.

"What makes you think Richards has a relationship with that organization?" ask Dessen.

"For the same reason I know that Mayor Sipple is also a member of the Klan." Caleb then slides the papers across the table to Mayor Sipple and exclaims on. "It seems that lost paper is the weakness of this town, first Dane, with Brick's receipt on his car lot and now these."

As Sipple seizes one of the papers, he glares down at it and turns ashen, then passes a handful of the documents around the table, including to Barney. The Grand Wizard glares over at Richards and re-holsters his weapons. Richards does the same, then bitterly reflects at Caleb. While the power brokers read the items, Flynn, who knew that Caleb would use the material to discredit his father, is extremely uncomfortable about it just the same. He watches Barney and the others frantically exchange pages among themselves and study them with wide-eyed anxiety, page after page of the Klan's murderous works. Caleb looks over at Flynn, who turns away. After that, Caleb goes on the attack.

"Those papers prove that you men pilfered the town treasury at a time when Cutterville needed that money the most, a crime in anyone's book." Caleb's words sends collective chills around the table. He glances at a beaming Dessen and continues. "It seems your extremely intelligent Sheriff also kept notes which include reaching into the poor whites and blacks' food stamps, and selling them to the local stores for a third of their value, in violation of federal law, but on top of that, the moneys, stolen over the years, shamefully lined your pockets and—more recently—paid for that sidewalk in front of Lana's whorehouse. It's all been recorded, as you can see. I would imagine you all have also seen the mutable references about the people the Klan has murdered, raped and tortured and the court have overlooked, including the recent brutal killing of the boy B.J. and his young-bride-to-be Claretta Johnson."

Barney stands up. "Richards," he calmly says. "Is he right? These papers. They came from you?" When Richards nods, Barney coldheartedly replies: "A sword Sheriff Richards is far from being a toy. It puts asunder not just your soul, but your entire body, from the top of your head down to your crotch."

Richards almost wets his trouser and can only nod and say, "Yeah. My name's on them, but what sword? What are you talking about?"

If Flynn had any doubts about his father being involved with the killing of blacks and even of some whites, he had none now, as the colonel continues interrogating the sheriff.

"Why?" asks Barney, his eyes of contempt squinting at Richards. "Blackmail. Was that it, so that you can run for the senate instead of my boy? Or was it to say that you turned against the Klan to please the northern politicians and their black associates in D.C?"

Richards stands up and grapples at the documents, his worried eyes locked on Barney, Flynn watching nervously, feeling that his father is moments away from shooting, not just Richards but Caleb as well, all of the time Sheriff Richards yelling at the top of his voice at Caleb. "Where did you get those?"

"Who the fuck cares where he got the goddamn papers," shouts the troubled-looking Roscoe Carlton, ready to burst out of that tight-fitting, blue suit. Going on, he shakes his finger at Caleb. "He knows everything, and I don't need to be hit over the head with a goddamn hammer to know it."

When Carlton sees Henry's boy smiling at him, he exclaims, "Don't smile at me, you small piece of dirt in this white man's world." The small, white man then faces Barney. "I have my own damn problems and I don't need to be sitting here listening to this goddamn shit, when I should be at home with my wife, especially if this is going to land us all in jail!"

Carlton suddenly rises to his feet to leave.

"Sit your ass back down," blast Barney, and Carlton does so in a hurry.

Carlton sobs, "Why, when my wife is—?"

"Shut the fuck up," yells Richards, tearing up the documents. "Crying like a goddamn baby, when we're all in trouble here!"

"You're wasting your time tearing those up," Barney says, coming to the table and looking down at Caleb. "Isn't he, Caleb? Wasting his time? And it seems you've managed to cause quite a disruption among us." Taking Richards's gun from him, Barney then nudges the lawman out of his chair and places Richards's revolver on the table and then sits in Richards's chair, looks over at Carlton and whispers. "And you, close your mouth like you were told, and say not one goddamn word more." When Carlton nods in agreement, Barney locks gazes with Caleb. "Caleb Brooks here is much too smart to have walked in here without a way to walk out again, and I mean something in addition to that disciplined crowd outside. These are copies." Barney tosses his paper copies across the table at Caleb who glances over at Flynn, who had smartly made the copies. Barney goes on, as Caleb faces him again. "Do you plan to blackmail us now with the originals, Caleb, beside this political thing you want?"

"I'll kill him with my bare hands," yells Richards charging to the table. "I kept those records and letters to impress my old lady. Ask her. She'll tell you the same. She been bored being alone in the house with the baby all the time and—"

Barney whirls about and slaps Richards across his mouth with the lawman's service revolver, sending him stumbling back against the wall, bleeding besides a shocked Flynn. Barney points Richard's gun at him with the heartlessness of a snake, Flynn leaning away from the lawman in dread, to avoid being splattered with blood, as Barney tells Richards,

"I'm this close to killing you where you stand, so you also keep your mouth shut, while I think of what to do about you and the damage that you've done here and about Caleb goddamn Brooks." He walks over to one of the floor-to-ceiling windows and glances out at the marchers, then faces Henry's boy and returns to Richards's chair. "I ask again, Caleb," says Barney, again placing the gun on the table, "were you going to blackmail these men?"

"I think it's time I said goodbye," says Dessen.

Barney glares at Dessen and coldly explains, "An invited guest remains until the Wizard says that the business at hand is over. You haven't heard anything you've not suspected before. Stay. Unless, that is, it's your intention to insult your host." Having gotten himself unintentionally involved with matters of the Klan, Dessen remains seated, and Flynn remains on the edge of his chair, watching the growing test of wills between Caleb and the colonel, who glares at Caleb with the sheriff's pistol once again in his hand, as if to say it's your move.

Caleb coolly goes on, glancing over at Dessen, "Not all of you, but most of you in this room are corrupt, with blood on your hands." He then faces the others about the table and says. "You know who you are, and up to now, you felt safe, because there has never been proof of your godless deeds to leak out." He looks Barney in his eyes. "I'm not here to try and turn over rocks that are too heavy for me to shoulder, in order to dig up old worms or to take up arms," he tells Barney. "And even with the original papers in my hands, only a child would think that having such was a guarantee of his safety. A wise fisherman knows that a pathological fish, as well as the stream it's in, does not stop a few feet from its source of poison, that—in fact—the fish and stream flows far beyond that starting point, possibly all the way to Washington, where government officials may or may not prosecute the outlawed fish, and—instead—lift it out of the water, clean it up, and toss it back into the stream and permit it to swim free again."

"Tell me, Caleb fucking Brooks," says Barney. "What are you counting on to save your fish now, since it is you who are in the swim of things here and now? God? They say He looks after you."

Caleb gestures at the window. "To answer your question," he tells Barney. "Those thousands of marchers outside waiting for my return . . ." hesitating, he reflects and goes on. "Hopefully they will come in here and tear, if not all of you, then you and a few of your peers to

438

shreds. They're the ones who count on God, most of those thousands outside. I on them." As the men at the table turn their concerned sights on the windows, and Barney stands and looks at all of those worried faces, Caleb continues. "What I want is for people to live in peace with equal rights to work, to love and to help this nation plant the seeds for a better tomorrow between us. A seed based, not on my credo, not on that of the coloreds, or on that of the Mexicans, or on that of the Indians, or on that of the Chinese, or on that of the Jews. It stems from this Christian country's belief that all men are created equal. If that becomes a reality in America, then America—itself—can be saved, because all men will then be judged fairly and equally and we all will benefit from it."

"Just a damn minute," says Mayor Sipple. "You take that preaching back to Africa!"

Barney raises his hand, and Mayor Sipple clams up. Caleb, nevertheless, speaks to Sipple, "It's clear to those who see, and not just look, that the founding fathers meant only that the early, wealthiest, white, Americans such as Jefferson, Washington, Grant—the so-called most highly born—were meant to fall under that umbrella of political privilege of being equal. The seed that now needs to be planted—by you, by me, and by all of us in this world—springs from the hope of the poor who our wealthy citizens have to keep on the bottom rungs of life by renting them as slaves instead of owning them—in order that they, the rich, can maintain their high standard of living, be they white or be they colored whom they walk upon and intimidate and murder."

"May you rot in hell," yells the man in the tight, blue suit as Reverend Miller smiles. Getting to his feet, after taking all that he can, the little man in the blue suit pounds on the table. When Barney—now entertained and also smiling—makes no move to quiet him, the man continues, "You must actually believe the bullshit that folks are whispering in nigger town about you being something special, Caleb Brooks. Do you think that you're a prophet? Do you? Answer me, you young punk."

Reverend Miller joins in: "You're tempting the Lord thy God, by being here, Caleb. "

"You see, I do realize that I am somewhat different from others," Caleb says and gives Flynn a quick glance and then continues. "If I didn't realize that I was born under unusual circumstances by now, I'd have to be blind, deaf and dumb." His eyes again focus on Flynn, but only for a split second, as he goes on, talking directly to Miller. "However, I've never seen God, and I'm not sure there is such a Being. Otherwise, why would He have made so many heartless assholes in the world like you as His modern-day disciple?"

"Blasphemy," shouts Miller, turning to the others in the room. "You all heard this coon!"

"Shut the fuck up, Miller," shouts Barney. "You had your two cents worth. Let's not go on talking about a god from your children's, fairyland books."

"Tell me more about this seed of yours, Caleb," says Dessen, leaning forward, with no fear of Barney or intention of letting the matter drop so easily, his thoughts on the exterminated Jews of Europe at the hand of Hitler. Dessen interlaces his fingers and rests his elbows on the table; next, the factory owner's fingers unlace; his hands press together as if in prayer, his fingers softly touching his lips "Go on, Caleb, does it have a color, this seed of yours. Is it a religion or creed? What power over people will it have if they worship differently from it?"

Again, Barney does not object. In fact he wants Caleb to answer that question, having had pumped Flynn about Caleb in the past and coming up with little or nothing.

"It's not my seed or my wants," Caleb says. "As I tried to explain. It's what the spiritually hungry people on this earth want and need. What they deserve. It's a seed of hope, Mister Dessen," Caleb tells him, a man so willing to listen and Caleb so willing share his thoughts with the honest listener. "A seed where all people love and are loved in return. Of course, it may turn into a political seed as all thing seems to do, but it will not be a seed that flourishes from our Bibles, nor from our religious, our holy temples, tabernacles, mosques, synagogues—which have all failed, seeking instead to seed their own bigoted needs for money: nor will it flourish under hatred which encourages all of us to kill and rape, to conquer other's land, as if we're still in the dark ages."

"Who are you to act like God?" asks Miller as Carlton sits down. "Who gave you the right to infer that we are monsters?"

"Whoever fits this description—as I said earlier—know who you are and will have to live or die with it. You said that I'm no prophet, Reverend Miller. If it's still unclear to you, I'll say it again. I am not one. I have no powers, only some ability which I don't understand; it is you men, around this table, who hold the real power and the means to ruthlessly enforce it against the poor whites and blacks."

Dessen—who had begrudgingly attended the meeting, feeling that it would be in response to some poor, ignorant, black soul barking in the wind without a chance in hell of getting even a bone tossed his way, and now seeing how uncomfortable Barney is, the factory owner sits back in his seat, his thoughts racing:

Who is this Caleb Brooks? Certainly not a meshuggana. No, Caleb is not some insane individual. Even if no one else at the table knows it.

To Flynn, sitting back and listening, if not a prophet—he thinks—Caleb is one lucky person to still be alive in that room. Barney is carrying another pistol on him, one with a silencer. Roscoe Carlton, though, now hates everyone. The man in his tight-fitting suit again leaps to his feet screaming, "Who the goddamn nigger motherfucking, son-of-a-bitching shit do you think you are, you Sambo, to come in here like you're Mister White Almighty—when I have my own troubles—and to talk down at us! We could have your balls cut off and fed to those god-damn, poor-ass, hungry people that you're so worried about. Let them eat you, god dammit, instead of them eating us, because that's what they'll be as good as doing if we go along with him," he yells at Barney, going on, "and recognize them folks outside as equals the way he wants!" Again he faces Caleb. "We'll serve your head to the alley dogs running about in this goddamn town if you don't back the hell off and get the hell out of here, so I can go the fuck home!"

As Caleb focuses in on Carlton, another of those heart-pounding visions slaps him in his face.

Standing up, Caleb crosses the floor and takes Carlton by his hand, Henry's boy's tall frame lording over the small man and over those look-ing up at him, as they sit around the table stunned and watch as Caleb holds the frighten man close and whispers in his ear, "Roscoe," Caleb says. "I understand your frustration and need for extra money to pay the hospital bills and the private doctors and equipment standing by at your wife's bedside." Everyone looks at Barney, their eyes asking what they should do. They're all invisible to Caleb except for Carlton, who is aston-ished more than any of the others, as Caleb continues. "However, Sir, you need not steal from the poor to pay off more bills, not anymore. Your wife has been healed."

Carlton pulls away from Caleb and slaps him while shrieking, "She is dying of lung cancer and every disease under God's heaven, you black faker, you demonic role-playing-son-of-a-bitch! Her bones are like dry

441

spaghetti and break even when she sneezes. The pain she endures! My God, the pain! I'd steal and kill to free her of her torture, and you dare stand there and say that about her. May God Almighty strike you dead and me also for the hatred I have for you, nigger, because without my wife there's nothing left for me! Get out of my sight before I take that gun of Richards's and shoot you to kingdom come and back again into hell, where you crawled out of and came in here!"

The sound of a telephone is heard ringing: moments later, Chamber's secretary rushes into the room and whispers into the judge's ear. Chambers quickly gets to his feet and hurries over to Carlton and whispers to him, as Barney and the others pounder at them.

"She's what?" the wide-eyed man sputters, as he gawks over at Caleb.

Chambers follows the small man's sights to Caleb, then asks, "What did that boy say to you?"

Carlton is too shocked to answer, and Barney studies him, then Caleb and shouts, "You got your agreement, but it's not over, Caleb." Barney physically separates Caleb and Carlton by stepping between them, and confronting Caleb head on. "I have tricks I haven't begun to use yet," he warns Caleb. "Stay away from Carlton, Shadow Grove and my son or I'll hang you from Cutter Bridge. Now do as Roscoe says and get out before I give this gun to him and let him do the job for me."

As Caleb walks out of the conference room, Carlton keeps reflecting after him. Moving down the long corridor, Caleb hears someone suddenly running up behind him, and he looks over his shoulder at Carlton.

"In God's name," he says to Caleb, huffing and buffing, "how did you know? How in God's name did you know? My wife! After being in bed for five years. Just like that! She got out of bed and was dancing about and greeting the servants with laughter and joy. You knew. Knew that she was cured at the very moment you said she would be, Caleb. My God! The doctors were there when it happened, and they say it's a miracle. She's cured." Carlton tearfully gazes into Caleb's eyes, his pale white hand trembling, as he reaches out to touch Caleb, as if touching a delicate angel. "Who cured her, Caleb? Do you know? I'd like to thank him. Was it God?"

Knowing that the man is a staunch Klansman and that it would be like pulling elephants' teeth for him to praise a black man, Caleb knows

442

that when Carlton says he'd like to thank "him" that by "him" Carlton means Caleb.

"It would not be an untruth for me to say I don't really know who cured your wife," says Caleb, while looking within himself, desperately searching for the answer as to who did cure the woman and how he, Caleb, knew about it. "Her faith, I'd say, cured her as much as anything."

Gripped in apprehension, Caleb stands there wondering if there is a God and—if so—why has God chosen him and has not struck him dead for disbelieving so. Carlton runs down the hall in the direction of the parking lot and his car, then stops and looks back at Caleb, "Thank you, Caleb." The little Klansman then continues running toward the rear parking lot, then suddenly stops. Barney is standing in front of him, his eyes filled with rage.

"There is no god but Satan," he hisses.

Leaving the courthouse with the agreement upper most in his mind, Caleb is abruptly troubled by a swarm of personal feelings, such as how his actions will affect Flynn. Without warning, the marchers swarm up the steps and surround him, everyone trying to touch, to talk to him and be close to him at once. Sheriff Richards watches from the courthouse window with Deputy Snodgress. "Barney will be sorry fer hanging me out to dry in front of that nigger," he tells his son-in-law.

"You're lucky he didn't kill you fer having them papers the way you did," says Snodgress, who had climbed the steps with the crowd and had entered the courthouse.

"Not killing me when he had the chance is a mistake he'll live to regret," Richards says.

"Do you think Barney has money like it's whispered?" asks Snodgress. "Otherwise, I think I'll pack up and move out West to Wyoming or one of then coon-free states. It's getting too niggerized here with the tar balls running wild and marching into town on us, with whites and Mexicans and Jews and Chinamen and soldiers. God only knows what's to come next."

"If Barney has that money," Richards says, "I'll find it, and then I'll kill that old fucker."

Filled with dismay, Sheriff Richards glares at the racially mixed crowd and at Caleb who is telling them about the agreement, and they toss their hats into the air and lifts Caleb onto their shoulders. Singing, they carry him down the courthouse steps to the street.

443

While Caleb is being held high, those worrisome, personal thoughts return, thoughts about Carlton's sick wife and how he, Caleb, somehow knew about both the man and his wife. Caleb resolves that he has to accept this phenomenon seemingly forced upon him, that there is nothing he can ever do about it; and, just as he does, a different kind of fear takes hold of him. From his high position he spots Flynn and Barney speeding away in the Cadillac. Then Caleb sees Metcalfe, the black man he and Flynn had tossed off the train. The ex-soldier is dressed in a stylish white suit and sitting in a fancy horse-drawn buggy, his gold teeth sparkling; he's been watching Caleb for some time. Not knowing who Caleb is, due to the distance between them, Metcalfe tips his hat to Henry's boy and smiles across the square at him. "Now, there's one nigger that got some balls," he mutters. "Whatever you did, boy, for that crowd to be worshipping you like that, it had to have taken a lot of damn balls for a black boy to be lifted up on the shoulders by some of them whites over there, a whole lot of damn nerves and in that courthouse of shame at that." Metcalfe then turns his corrupt eyes from Caleb and locks his gaze on the Cadillac. Caleb watches the gold-toothed man rise to his feet in the buggy, when he recognizes Barney, in the luxury, red car, as Flynn worriedly looks back at Caleb. To Caleb, there is no joy in his victory, a victory which may now cost Flynn his life.

31

A Ship without a Captain

Twenty-four hours later, after returning home from a long walk under the warm morning sun, while pondering his and Flynn's altered relationship, Caleb sees Naomi sitting on a horse-drawn wagon and looking down at his mother's grave. He races to her and the house. "Naomi!" he calls.

"You truly love your mother, don't you, Caleb," says Naomi looking from the freshly placed flowers at the base of the tombstone and then at him, going on, "the way you always care for this grave?" She gazes to his grandparents' tombstones, which are well-kept, but without the daily fresh flowers, and she adds, "And not that of your father's parents."

"Papa had his parents, and I had a mother," he tells her, "and now only Papa is here with me. It's my way of letting my mother know I've not forgotten her."

"Even though you've never seen her, you continue seeking her love."

"That's right. Why are you questioning me about her?" Aggravated by Naomi, he walks away. "I have to go help Papa to clear our east field now."

"Seek love from the living, Caleb. Not from the dead which cannot give it to you. You've never seen God, and seek Him not. Yet you go on looking to the dead and to someone you've never laid eyes on to give you comfort and love. Why, Caleb?"

"Why did you come here, Naomi?"

"Henry's not going to the fields today, Caleb," she says, looking over at a butte. "He's up there near God's sky praying. That's the reason I'm here. This is yours and Henry's time."

Caleb pretends he hasn't heard her. Instead, he fixes his gaze on the hill and says, "He shouldn't go near that place. That cave. Those bats. He's fearful of them."

"Yes, but he now faces that which is far more tormenting, that which gives birth to sainthood. As for your fields, this land is yours no more, Caleb. It's been stolen from you and Henry." She locks gazes with the shocked boy. "At the courthouse, Barney told you he had tricks he hasn't used yet. Remember?"

"Liar!" shouts Caleb. "That's impossible! The letter! He knows I have them and . . ."

"Barney is a devious person, Caleb, and you're letting your anger cloud your mind. Even you admitted that those documents, in your hands, were no guarantee to protect you and Henry, and as to those documents, Barney bought space in MacDonnell's newspaper to discredit any story about how he or the Klan had anything to do with killing Claretta and B.J., including that they had nothing to do with the burning of those school kids in the past." She shows Caleb the Cutterville *Sentinel's* headline: "BLACKS FAKED LETTER TO BRING DOWN COLONEL CUTTER!"

"That dog MacDonnell will print anything. We all know that."

"Don't be too hard on him, Caleb. He hasn't your courage to go up against City Hall." Disturbed, Naomi continues. "As for Barney causing the explosion of the *White Dove* and killing the Winthrops, since nothing was in any of those letters and documents which mentioned that Barney had anything to do with their deaths, even Sarah's powerful friends would not be willing to press for Barney's arrest for having a hand in killing Doctor and Mrs. Winthrop."

"But you yourself hinted to Sarah that he killed her parents, and Barney is much too intelligent to have had witnesses to his tampering with that plane."

"That was all that I was allowed to do, hint at it, then and now, so I can't be of help to you in proving anything against that mad man."

Caleb shakes his head in disgust. "How can anyone win against them if they have all the answers, Naomi?"

"Trust the Bible, Caleb. It'll give you the answer to all things and fortify you in the war to come."

"What war? Which Bible? Which should I trust? The one I read to Papa or the one the Klan reads, the one that tells them they can kill us? Our land, Naomi. . . . What you're saying about our land being stolen. . . . Papa just paid the bank thousands of . . ."

"Mr. Pennington was a deviant, wicket man and because of that, he was blackmailed into falsifying the bank books and selling this land." A forlorn look crosses her face, and she goes on. "That poor man is to pay a terrible price for what he has done."

446

"You're dreaming, woman. No white court will ever punish that white banker for what he does to us."

"There is one."

"Please, Naomi, don't give me that stuff about God punishing him." Almost in a whisper, regrettably, his eyes watering up, he looks toward the hill. "Does he know about our land, Naomi?"

"I haven't the heart to tell him." When Caleb turns away, shaking his head, and steps toward the hill, Naomi warns. "Your father is being counseled in regards to the agreement he made with the Light of the World."

"Counseled by whom?"

"By one who was sent by the Father, someone Henry can only hear, but cannot see; only you, Caleb, can see that which your father hears and thinks is of his own voice and thoughts, a thing that his faith along tells him is always there for him."

"Stop talking to me in riddles, you foolish woman. That's my papa. Are you trying to say that he's insane? Please leave, Naomi, and take that unseen thing of yours with you. Papa and I have no need for a God who would play such a cruel joke on us by letting this land be stolen from our family, then—as you as good as said—summons Papa to listen to something, which no doubt will tell him not to worry. To be happy the way the white man will tells him to be after the loss of our land."

Naomi rides off in the wagon, and—while doing so—looks back at Caleb. "As I said, Caleb, only your eyes can see the Spirit that has come through as an angel to be with your father, not my eyes, not Henry's. Go up there and challenge that Spirit of God if you dare, but when the waters of pride swallow you up, and you and Henry's heads are under those pounding waves of despair, a raven will sound the alarm, as it did at your birth, and, then, you will raise up your eyes to the Lord begging for mercy, and Jehovah will hear you. He always does, Caleb and always will."

"If Pennington did this to us," Caleb yells, "the only thing I'll beg God for is the power to kill that corrupt asshole."

"Be careful what you utter, Caleb. Your commands reach even unto the end of the world and can hold back the ocean tides and can move mountains; so irrefutable is this power that God has given to you, the power of life and death, Caleb, the power of life and death. Follow the Light, son, the Light under which you were born, not the one of hatred which you have stumbled into, because you've lost your best friend into the arms of evil."

"'Follow the Light,' you say? 'Be careful what you utter,' you tell me, because it will come true?" he hisses. "Then I say this to you. Show me this Light!"

He gasps. In a bright flash, as Naomi turns away with her arm covering her eyes, Caleb sees Flynn carrying him as a baby into the blinding Light. Trembling, panting and in fear, he backs away from the vision. Stumbling, he looks at the hill and calls to his father, as he had whenever he was afraid as a child. But again he gasps and nearly faints in disbelief. On the hill with Henry is a tall, ebony-colored, winged figure in a flowing, snow-white gown standing majestically over his kneeling father. Caleb turns and runs with the wind.

"There is no light," he shouts at Naomi. "No God! Death to Pennington and his bank! Death to that man!"

At the bank, in town, a zombie-like Pennington climbs onto an office chair and tosses a looped rope over the ceiling beam; dribbling spittle, he slips his head into the noose, steps off of the chair and hangs himself. On the floor, below his thrashing legs is the Saint Bernard, yelping up at him. Next to the dog is Pennington's account book with pages torn out, and next to the book is a photo of the old banker gawking up in surprise as someone snaps the picture of him mounting his dog. Barney has won this round and feels he will continue to do so. Caleb will follow, making Barney god-like over the world.

That night, a few hundred yards offshore, with a billion stars filling the sky over them, and a full moon shining down on them, Caleb and Flynn, while talking aboard their hand-made boat in the middle of the lagoon, have already tied several dozen fish together in their T-shirts and have stuffed them underfoot for Flynn to take home for his workers; the fish are leaping out of the water and into their boat faster than they can throw them out again, but their hearts aren't in it. Now, they sit so closely together that not a breeze can pass between them.

"Are you okay?" Flynn asks Caleb, while rubbing Caleb's back.

"Thanks for coming tonight, Flynn, I needed someone to talk to. Yes, I'm okay. I was afraid your father had convinced you to ignore me."

"Father has received a summons to appear in D.C., concerning the time he was stationed on Corregidor. He seems deeply troubled and is leaving first thing in the morning and might not be back for a week or so. I didn't tell him I was coming here, only Benny."

"That loud mouth?"

"Yes, but he'll keep it to himself, at least I hope he will. Caleb, Henry . . . How is Henry taking it about you guys' place?"

"When I left he was still on that hill praying, where Naomi said an angel was with him."

"And you said you saw it?"

"I saw something beside him."

"Jesus, Caleb, is it the end of the world?"

"He prays all the time now," Caleb laments, "so maybe to Papa it's the end of things as we know them."

"Shall I mention any of this to Mother and see if she can help?"

"No, she would only suffer as much as Papa. Flynn, do you think your father had anything to do with our losing Little Shadow Place? Naomi won't come out and really say, but I know she thinks so."

"I don't know, Caleb, no more than I do about if he had anything to do with Mister Pennington's hanging himself today."

"Flynn!" a voice calls from shore.

Even under the moonlight it's easy to make out that the sixteen-year-old, chubby caller is Benny Hill, Jayne Hill's brother, who all but worships Flynn. He's wearing a short-sleeved shirt with "KKK" hand-scribbled across the chest, has on knee-high trousers and is waving his fat arms and hands about.

"What's Benny doing here?" asks Caleb. "He knows I don't like him."

"Flynn," Benny yells again, "the Colonel brought everyone out here befer he leaves fer Washington tomorrow, to show us that you Cutters now control the water that whites on Shadow Grove and in town need from here! And he says fer you to stay the hell away from that coon! The others are on their way here right now in their slow-ass cars and trucks and wagons, making their way through the trees. I jumped out of our wagon and raced through the woods to get here ahead of them to tell you myself. You're going to be the next Grand Wizard, Flynn! It's to be officially proclaimed tonight!"

Caleb focuses on the headlights of cars and trucks—about a quarter mile away—lumping their way down a tree-lined trail and toward the lagoon, all types of vehicles carrying torch-waving men and a few of Sarah's white workers, whom he recognizes by their torch-lit clothing, workers who have now identified themselves with Barney. Flynn begins rowing to shore.

"You're going with them?" asks Caleb.

"You don't understand," Flynn replies, lifting the oars from the water in mid stroke. "I have to find out more about what—"

"I have ears! Benny said you Cutters control Papa's water. In other words, you're the ones who stole this land!"

"It's that bunch at City Hall whom you should worry about, not me! They took your land, as far as I can tell."

"Dammit! No one can be that lowdown, evil and heartless, not even your father, but he did it. He stole our damn land, Flynn. Wake up! Stop looking at the world through those poetic eyes of yours."

"It's politics, Caleb. It has nothing to do with good and evil. During this drought, the lagoon water gives Henry too much power, political or otherwise for a colored man. They saw that in you when you spoke to them so condescendingly at the courthouse. I wasn't the only one sitting on the edge of my chair listening to you, wondering about all that authority you had to bring thousands from across the state and even the damn country into Cutterville, even now, seemingly at your beck and call."

"Go to hell, Flynn!"

From the shore, with the caravan of Klan vehicles closing in on him, Benny calls to Flynn again. "They're coming, Flynn. Why are you stopping? Come on and get Caleb out of there befer they see him!"

"Your anger is misplaced, Caleb," Flynn—ignoring Benny—says, and continues, "And that deal you made with Cutterville to restrain Sheriff Richards, well, he'll be fired at the end of his term by those men at that table, but not for harassing you and the coloreds or killing them. They fired him because of those documents I gave to you."

"Those bastards," yells Caleb. "I should have crammed those papers up their asses."

"That deal they made with you was to their advantage, not yours, Caleb. As for Richards, with him knowing that he is on his way out, it makes him a desperate man now. Be careful of him. The bottom line to all of this is the ballot box. Now that the coloreds have a right to vote, that political machine in town wanted it to seem that they made that compromising agreement with you, a colored person—the first in the town's history, because they know full well that most of the local coloreds will feel so thankful to the town that they will vote in a solid block for the city bosses. It was all part of a bigger plan to eventually secure a place for me as a senator, with the colored vote taking me over the top. The Colonel only made that clear to me this morning."

Caleb stands up, rocking the boat: "How long did you say you've known all of this, Flynn? About those people, your father or not, going after our land?"

"Since this morning, after Father sided with the others. I just told you that."

"We sit here talking away on Papa's land for hours now and you never said a goddamn word to me about some white assholes trying to steal Papa's property! We had only one or two payments left, Flynn. Only one or two, and that bastard built that damn dock on our property! Get your fucking aluminum piece-of-shit off our water and take that damn dock with you!"

"What the hell could you do even if had I told you, a week ago or now?" says Flynn, rowing to shore once more. "I'm going to them to find out what they're up to next."

"Next! You're Barney's son and in this up to your ass! Isn't that as good as what Naomi's been telling us? That your damn evil bloodline to Barney would bring us to this end? Look at how you're sweating and rowing to be with those animals. Is this why you never came around, so that you'd have time to make plans to destroy me and papa? Are you one of Miller's members now? Do you kiss his snake's head or its ass?"

"How dare you! I'm sweating because I'm afraid of you! Are you now going to kill me through that paranoid mind of yours the way some feel you've killed Pennington?" As Caleb turns ashen with fright, Flynn shouts, "He hanged himself. Am I next? Will you wish me dead, as well, damn you!"

"The hell with you! Papa and I'd die for you. I thought you felt the same about us."

"Then you're a bigger fool than I thought, Caleb Brooks. If we remain friends, the Klan will kill you and Henry."

Caleb violently kicks the side of their boat bashing a hole in the unstable water craft, and then begins flinging bundles of fish over the side, as the cold lagoon water rushes through the gaping hole, into the boat and onto them. "Don't you ever again call me a fool," Caleb lambastes Flynn. "Are you Cutters god to play with Papa and my life this way?"

Flynn hurls the oars and then also, flings a bundle of fish into the lagoon and jumps out of the boat, accidentally tipping it over, dumping Caleb into the night-dark water. Splashing about, Caleb struggles to upright the vessel, Benny frantically calling to Flynn from shore, the trucks and cars nearly upon him and the lagoon now, while Flynn, treading water, yells to Caleb. "Go ahead! Kill yourself, but don't ask me to die with you. It's over! Let go of that damn, shitty-ass boat, Caleb, before it pulls you down with it and you drown your stubborn ass. As God is my witness, our friendship is over!"

"I don't need you or your 'As-God-is-my-witness' or your damn philanthropic gift of Catholicism, which is no different than Miller's or Harris's mindless dogma. Get out of here and take your belief in God with you, yours, Naomi's and Sarah's! But He's not mine, you hear! Your white God is not mine!"

"Why in God's name did He choose you to be His disciple, Caleb?" Flynn exclaims, while bobbing about in the water. "Why in God's name did He choose someone like you?"

A bursting ear-deafening earthquake shakes the entire lagoon, and the water rises upward from the lagoon floor, and falls upon them, and separates them. The overturned boat, along with Caleb still hanging onto it, is lifted into the air by a towering, white, foaming wave, Flynn, cork-screwing about and gaping up at Caleb and their battered boat in horror, the boat and Caleb threatening to crash down on him, and back down the boat and Caleb come, along with what seems like a billion tons of water, which explodes against the surface, washing Flynn two-hundred yards backward to the shore line, where the wave hits, knocking Benny off his feet. Flynn watches in repugnance as Caleb and the boat are sucked below the surface. "Caleb!" he screams.

Frantically swimming against the turbulent water and to the spot where Caleb went down and diving into the moonlit, tumultuous, clear water, Flynn follows Caleb's moonlit air bubbles deeper and deeper into the depths of hell, his lungs crying out for air. Finally, he spots Caleb on the bottom, still angrily jerking and pulling at their sunken boat, the fish escaping from the shirt-wrapped bundles around him. Upon reaching Caleb, his lungs are ready to burst, Flynn deliriously grapples at Caleb's arm. Suddenly, he doubles over, his arms floating lifelessly at his side, his skin turning blue, his eyes gazing lifeless down at the bottom of the lagoon, more dead than alive. Air gushes from Caleb's mouth, as he yells out Flynn's name under that crushing body of water. Seizing hold of his friend's arms, Caleb pushes off the bottom with power from his legs alone, carrying him and Flynn upwards. When they break through the surface into the open air, Benny leaps into the water and swims in their direction. Flynn, meanwhile, is gasping, coughing and sucking in the life-giving air. He then smashes Caleb in the face with his fist.

"You're insane!" Flynn wails out of breath. "Stay the hell away from me!"

As Benny swims out to meet him, Flynn, mortified and steeped with rage, splashes away from Caleb and to shore, where he and Benny are pulled onto dry land by Klansmen and non-Klansmen. Flynn is held close in the loving embrace of his father.

"Are you okay, boy?" Barney asks, kissing Flynn on his forehead.

In the dark of that night, after kissing his son, Barney quickly takes off his coat and wraps it about Flynn, a heavy coat that did not feel the same as had Caleb's lighter-weight jacket, the time Caleb had wrapped it about Flynn in the factory, a jacket that made Flynn feel Caleb's warm, pure love. Barney's coat is one of ice, causing Flynn to shiver all the more and in terror. When torch carriers steps close, Flynn looks at the sleeve of the coat, then down at its length. It's Hitler's coat, a coat steeped in the blood of millions. Showered with admiration from the crowd of whites, the shivering boy feels only dread in Barney's arms. He follows his father's angry gaze to the lagoon. Caleb is nowhere to be seen, and Flynn is guided into the Cadillac under a parade of torches, the barbarous cries of the Klan cementing their allegiance to Flynn, Barney's heir-apparent and future Grand Wizard. As the vehicles move away, leaving the land that Henry once owned unto itself and in the hands of trepidation and obscurity, Flynn is sick, trapped under Hitler's coat of blood, but he dare not take it off, and he never looks back.

32

Death of One Who Prays

One mile from home, on a familiar, red-clay, swamp road, Caleb is walking alone under an early-morning, ugly, gray sky, his thoughts just as ugly and overwhelming him: *Would he have to end up killing Barney Cutter, would his father regain their land, would he—Caleb—and Flynn ever be close again? Would Flynn become the next Grand Wizard? Would Shadow Grove's colored workers be told to leave now that the colonel has gained a god-like foothold on the plantation?* Suddenly all of that matters not; Crazy Walter, riding the rusty bicycle of Lana's handyman, frantically pedals down the road and slides the bicycle to a stop, nearly running into Caleb, this the tenth day, when Caleb said Walter would die.

"I been prayin' I'd find you out here, Caleb, when you wasn't at home," Walter sputters, frantically looking back down the road. "I need money from you or Henry. They after me!"

When Caleb gives him all that he has, a dollar, Metcalfe gawks down at it.

"Oh, shit, Caleb, this won't get me no damn place, let alone out of Georgia."

"I'm sorry, I—Wait! I do have . . ."

Caleb unties a cotton string from about his neck and pulls a small pouch from inside of his T-shirt. Opening the pouch Caleb quickly digs out one of the gold coins which Flynn had given him and hands it to Walter.

"Sweet Jesus, Caleb. Is this what I think it is, gold?" When Caleb nods, Walter tears up. "But gold, Caleb. I ain't worth no gold piece like this, is I?"

"I have another one, but it belongs to Flynn, otherwise I'd give both of them to you."

While Metcalfe is gawking at the precious coin, the sound of a truck is heard. Caleb follows the terrified man's glassy-eyed gaze to a whirling dust cloud on the horizon behind them and speeding their way.

"They found me, Caleb. The colonel, he done left the state today, and I thought I'd be safe fo' a spell, but my God! They done found me! Dane Tucker's men done found me!"

"Take the coin and go," Caleb exclaims. "Leave the bike and get off the road. Through the woods. The truck can't follow you in there!"

Walter tucks the coin in his pocket, and—in spite of Caleb's warning, completely out of control, chaotically, slipping and sliding—he pedals the bike down the road, attempting to outdistance the, seemingly far-off truck. Caleb conceals himself behind the bushes and anxiously watches as Walter—eyes seemingly as large as chicken eggs gawk, terrified over his shoulder at the truck—which is suddenly a football field away—and Walter runs straight into a tree. Sprawled on the ground out of breath, the man with the fastest legs in town watches the truck, now—within striking distance—closing in on him. As if giving up, exhausted and tired of running, Metcalfe just lies there with tears streaming down his cheeks and waits to die.

"Get up, Walter, dammit!" yells Caleb.

When Walter doesn't move, Caleb picks up a rock, dashes onto the road in front of the fast-moving truck, and hauls the baseball-size projectile through the vehicle's front window, shattering it. Hank's old truck careens into a ditch and dips to an abrupt stop. Caleb runs one way; Crazy Walter—breaking out of his near-comatose state—flails the other, across a muddy field and into the woods. Several Klansmen jump from the truck and chase after Walter, while their peers haul-ass after Caleb.

"Caleb Brooks!" old Hank, the lead Klansman, yells, motioning for the younger, faster Klansmen to pursue Caleb. "Kill that half-breed, son-of-a-bitch as well!"

Puffing along with the men who are chasing Caleb, Hank stops, knowing that if Walter has the fastest legs in town, Caleb has the fastest in the county. The others chasing Caleb also soon realize it, as Caleb, dodging bullets and zigzagging through the swamps, leaping over logs quickly distances himself from the Klansmen, who return to their truck and regroup with Hank.

"I'm not going in them water moccasins' damn swamp after that ace of spades the way he runs," one of the men tells Hank.

"He'll get his soon enough," says Hank, sliding into the truck and starting the motor, and going on. "Walter's the one we were told to hang to make Dane look good in Barney's eyes, so let's get my damn truck out of this damn ditch and get after him."

"Hank," ask, Donald, one of the more recent, young Klansmen to join the group, as they push and pull at the truck, dislodging it bit by bit from the ditch. "Why are you siding with Dane, now? Being how close they say you and Barney always were."

" 'Were' is the right word," says old Hank. "When I asked Barney if he had all the money folks says he does and asked him to share some of it with me, since we've been friends fer so long, he laughed at me and said, 'What money?' Then he upped and told me to get lost. That he didn't want to see me again. It was then that I knew—"

"Knew what?" Donald asks when Hank pales and clams up.

"Nothing," Hank tells him. "That's enough talk about things that will get you killed, things that deals with superstitions and stuff none of us understands and might even tear the Klan apart, with or without a leader like Barney. Barney's just interested in killing niggers that's all. That doesn't mean that he fancies himself more powerful than God."

"It's whispered that Trout took some of Barney's money from that gold-mouth coon who was on the O.B.S. local," another of the newcomers says, "and some of the guys says Trout and Dane's been palling up together to get the rest of that money for themselves."

"You're a lot of wet-nose girls, all of you who just got off the potty," Hank yells at the young Klan members. "And you've been told too much as it is. Now stop jawing and push; this truck won't get out of here on its own, and let's catch up to the others and that Walter coon befer it gets too dark to see his black ass out here."

That night on Shadow Grove in his small shack behind the general store, Trout groans in his sleep, a groan reflecting extreme horror. Word had spread fast about how the Klan thinks he and Dane may betray them, and that's why Trout was able to buy those crutches from O'Neal's department store, not with Metcalfe's money, but with money they've already stolen from Barney. Trout has not been able to reach Dane to warn him about this recent accusation, but had planned to once the sun rises. While Trout sleeps a half-smoked pipe of Reverend Miller's firethorn mix rests on his bedside table. Also in the small room are two large, covered, glass cages filled with crawling rattlesnakes, snakes that Trout will sell to Miller's church in town tomorrow. The feel of Satan occupies the living quarters and troubles the younger newcomer among the dark-outlined figures now looking down at the sleeping man. The floorboards squeak. Trout opens his eyes and sees Dane Tucker and four of the new recruits including Donald, who spoke of Dane and Trout palling up to steal Barney's money.

"Dane," shouts Trout, sitting up in bed, realizing that he's not dreaming and that no dream could be as ugly and as angry as Dane appears. "What's wrong? I tried to reach you."

"For what? To tell me how you say you and I are going to run off with Barney's fortune? I have no secrets from these men. You could have told any of them to contact me. Now, it seems some of the boys think that I'm a snake-in-the-grass, trying to shake them down. Damn you!"

"But, I didn't—And we didn't—I mean we—"

"We who? You and Barney? In the past you said you like working fer Sarah," Dane shouts. "Did Barney put you up to saying that you and I were planning on taking that money for ourselves to make trouble between me and the men? Did you go along with him because he promised to let you keep your job?"

A frightened Trout, seeing the handwriting on the wall, looks at the other, grim, angry faces—awash in the moonlight streaming through the window onto them. Dane drags Trout out of the bed by his foot and onto the floor. "Does Barney know we're onto him and his money?" he yells at the terrified old man. "Did you sell us out by alerting Barney?" With Trout groveling at his feet, Dane faces the Klansmen. "This is your first lesson. You can't trust anyone when it comes to money."

"Maybe thousands," one of the young men says.

"And as fer you new guys," Dane turns and jumps all over them, "how can we, the Klan, put the fear of God in them colored baboons and keep 'em in their place if you don't listen to me, when I tell you guys to cut up black bodies and hang 'em where them darkys can see 'em? It's no good anymore to just hang 'em from some tree the way you boys did in Texas, or from a tree where only God knows who'll see the body. From the bridge, the hell home of Satan himself! That's where you hang 'em, from the old Cutter. And that's where you burn 'em, too, so that all the passengers passing on the trains from across the state will see them stinking bodies and know that in Cutterville we don't take no shit from no back-talking niggers. No, sir!" He glares at Trout and hisses, "'Too ugly to get it free,' you told me, when even a one-leg man like you can gets it from our white women! Remember telling me that in Sue Ann's bar the night we kill that Claretta bitch? That none of you have to break their noses to get fucked? Do you! That maybe I should have asked Caleb Brooks how to grow big dicks, while Caleb was beating up on me?" Dane flings Trout's trousers at him. "Get dressed," he exclaims. "The boys found Walter."

"What's that got to do with me, you guys?" begs Trout, his skin crawling in fear of Dane.

"These fools didn't do him right," Dane yells. "I told the dummies to dump the body on Henry's doorsteps and that means the Bridge, a place where he and Caleb can see the fire from their house a half mile away. Now, I've sent their asses back there to get his body."

"Why trouble with them Brooks, when it's the money we want?" asks one of the guys.

"Didn't you see how he and his pa led them discontent niggers and whites into town from across the country and from this goddamn plantation?" hisses Dane. "Yes, we want the money, but first things first. The body burning from the bridge will put the fear of God in those Brooks. And after they piss out blood in fear of us, then we will steam roll over them and they'll wish they were dead befer we'll kill 'em."

"But, Dane," interrupts Donald, "all of us took Metcalfe's body as close as we could to Henry's land without getting shot at by Caleb."

Dane goes into a raging fit: "Are you saying they're afraid of one damn nigger and his pa's old rifle? Now you see why first things have to come first, white men afraid of a nigger. Where will it end? I'll tell you where. It'll end with all of them tar balls running the whole freaking, damn country. What good would money be then, and—?"

"We all know how good a marksman folks say Caleb Brooks is," Donald, again interrupting Dane. "They say Caleb can bring down a eagle a quarter mile away with one shot."

"Dane, I'm too old," pleads Trout, "to go messing around with dead people now and too fragile to be poking around in them swamps at night with one leg."

"You're only old if I say you're old," blasts Dane. "Barney said it first in Sue Ann's bar, and that's the only thing I agree with him on: That the reason Germany wasn't able to whip out all of them low-caste Jews is that Hitler's generals started whimpering and crying about how they couldn't win the war, or is it Caleb or that bitch Naomi that you're afraid of, Trout?"

"Both of them," pleads Trout. "They say old man Pennington had bad dreams befer he killed himself, and I been having bad dreams about

Jews, coloreds and Jesus." He points to his pipe. "And that's why I smoke . . . to forget. Christ was a Jew, Dane. Jesus was a Jew, like the Jews we're supposed to hate and kill."

Dane slaps him. "And that was a slap. Which one hurts the most, my slap or the invisible hand of Jesus? Folks in Colored Town say there are tar babies in Africa talking that old, Hebrew language, even today. Jews ain't nothing but niggers to be killed! So no talk of dreams or mercy fer them folks, if that's what all this bullshit of yours is leading up to."

Dane seizes the firethorn pipe and hurls it against the wall and bellows, "Stay off of that stuff. It makes you crazy!" Studying the cased-in snakes, the one-eared little Hitler goes on. "Crazy or not, one leg or not, you're coming with us, because you know snakes as well as your way around that swamp, and how—in the dark—to make sure we get in and out of there in one piece." Again, he slaps Trout, reducing him to a whimpering child: "And you damn well better not have been about to tell me that in this dream of yours that God was telling you that us whites are wrong to kill them spades, as well as them Christ killers! Enough whites are starting to think like that as it is, so not you!" He hisses at the others as well. "Not anyone of you!"

Trout quickly realizes that his persistence on using God as his shield will get him killed, and he whispers, "No, Dane, like you say. God didn't tell me anything. No warning of any kind." He ends putting in his false teeth.

"Good," says Dane slapping Trout so hard that the old man's false teeth fly across the room and into one of the snake case's ajarred lids.

"My teeth!" Trout cries aloud.

"You won't need 'em, where we're going unless you plan on eating one of them snakes out there." Dane knocks him across the floor, causing the younger Klansmen to look on in fright, as the would-be wizard blasts, "Get the fuck dressed! The nigger's body is almost ten fucking miles from here. I want us to be there when the others return to it, and we ain't getting any closer to it with you crying like some bloody-ass woman about your goddamn dreams!"

A quarter of a mile from the bridge and Henry's land, overweight Sheriff Leopold Richards, along with Deputy Snodgress, their separate patrol cars parked nearby, cut down Walter's body from a magnolia tree, where Hank and the others had hanged him upside down by his ankles, then after he had dangled there, screaming in agony, they had set him afire, and while Walter wiggled about hopelessly trying to put out the flames with his failing hands, the Klan had reached in and cut off his arms, the blistering flames quickly coagulating the blood streaming from his arms and stopping its flow. They then left. Afterwards, the fire consuming Walter's charred head and torso had flickered out before reaching the ropes about his bleeding ankles, and thus, he hung there groaning and twitching for hours before he died. Now as the midnight train from Cutterville rolls through in the distance, Deputy Snodgress steps over Walter's cooked blood—which is spread around the base of the tree—and cuts the rope from the branch. Walter's body hits the ground head first, and the fleet-foot man's skull and neck crumbles as if burned toast; the dollar bill that Caleb had given him is crunched, half-burned between Walter's front teeth, where he had hidden it from the Klansmen just before they caught him. Now his lower set of teeth are precariously anchored in his broken mandible, which lies on the ground—alone with the dollar bill—a few feet away from his shattered head. Snodgress targets in on the money, and while the Sheriff is searching about in another direction, trying to figure out who actually killed Walter, Snodgress picks up the toasted bill, wipes it off on the grass and stuffs it in his pocket, then excitedly goes through Walter's scorched pockets searching for more of the same.

"What the fuck you think you're doing going through that trash's pockets?" exclaims Richards, again facing the scene.

"You never know, Leopold, what a nigger might have, even money."

"Dammit," shouts Richards. "I told you never to call me by that name. 'Leopold.' Sounds like some kind of wild leopard. I'm not an animal. Call me 'Sheriff' if you can't remember what I keep telling you about calling me by that goddamn name."

When Snodgress withdraws his hand from Walter's pocket, and he sees what is in it, his eyes and mouth pop open. It seems that Walter hadn't had time to swallow his gold coin, in order to fish it out of his stool later. "Holy shit, Sheriff," Snodgress says, gawking at the coin. "It's pure gold," Snodgress confirms, biting into the coin with his molars. "Gold, Sheriff."

Richards seizes the coin. "You're my son-in-law, Reggie, and I love my daughter, but don't mention a word of this, even to her, or it'll be all over town about the colonel's fortune in no time. Do you realize that this damn coin is from Germany? See the inscriptions on it? Now we have the proof that Colonel Cutter did bring back possibly a fortune from that country, and by golly, that's the damn reason this Metcalfe boy . . . Yeah, that has to be it. . . . He's been hanging around town to get his share." Richards wipes Snodgress's mucus off of the coin and bites into it, testing it for himself, and then he kisses Snodgress on the lips, so elated is he, and he returns the prize to him. "It's real all right. You keep it. You and I are going to be very rich. Stay here and look around for more of these babies, and see if Caleb and Henry have anything to do with it since we found it out here near their place."

"Sheriff, I don't like being out here alone," says Snodgress, while looking down at Walter's charred remains and scarred over eyeballs, loose on the ground, one of them seem to be looking up at him, the bugs crawling over it.

"What the fuck you mean you don't like being out here alone? You're a damn cop, fer god's sake."

"I've been afraid ever since the night I saw Naomi on that horse. Then, there are the bats." Richards looks at him as if at a pitiful, stupid child. Snodgress, nevertheless, undaunted, goes on, "The snakes, the things you hears in a dark swamp, the wild animals, just waiting to kill us."

"You have a gun. Use it. There's a meeting I have to attend with Mayor Sipple and that Jew Dessen. I'll make it a short one if I can and get back here on the double. Gold, Buddy. We're rich. Go ahead goddamn, Barney Cutter," Richards yells. "Get me fired in six months. With your money, if we find it, I'll quit on my own and live like a king."

"Leopold . . . I mean Sheriff," Snodgress says, then goes on, "if them jobless soldiers in town, and them poor whites attack that Jew's plant—since you're being dismissed soon anyway—would you give the order fer us deputies to fire on them, what the coloreds call our own brothers and sister, in favor of a Jew?"

"Those poor white trash aren't my brothers, the Klan is. You saw how those poor-ass, ignorant whites stood there trembling in their shoes when the coons marched on Cutterville, some even praised Caleb, said he was a saint. So if it comes to the Klan, no, I wouldn't open fire on them; however, putting that aside, let's just say that one always looks out fer himself, even in the face of being fired, because the next boss man is always like the last boss man, and they always check with the old boss man, and nobody cares why you got fired, just that you followed the

461

good-old-boy rules and played the game with the time you had there. That means you're not on the side of the law, not on that of one's neighbors, not on God's, or even on the side of the whites against the blacks, only on the side of the strong. And fer now, the Jew factory man holds all the cards: money. Unless Barney Cutter has more of those gold coins, a lot more, or has cash enough to wrap Dessen up in money and burn him, or you and I get our hands on Cutter's money, we stick with the Jew. And Reggie, think only of the sound of coins. There're no ghosts or avenging spirits or flying horses out here, only the fulfillment of our dreams."

After Richards leaves, Snodgress hears the sound of a violin coming through the chilly night air, a phantom, uncanny, supernatural tune of softness and sorrowfulness emanating from the Brooks' property, a half mile away and setting Snodgress's soul on fire with fright. "Caleb," he whispers.

At the Brooks' place, Henry is in the house, at his bedside and on his knees praying in a world of his own. Caleb—who is outside in the front yard—is praying in his own way, through his violin strings; he's playing "Danny Boy," while gazing about their confiscated property, as if for the last time, the raccoons, the rabbits, and the white-tail deer are silently gazing out of the darkness of the distant woods, all watching Caleb—their pink eyes unblinking, their ears erect—captivated by the transcendental string music flowing from Caleb's heart and from his violin, a gift from Sarah, both the violin and his heart. Suddenly, Caleb stops his performance in mid-stroke. A moment later, the critters of the woods sound off in alarm and the pink eyes disappear, as—all around Caleb—nature's prey stampede for cover; the architect of death has shown its ugly face in the nearby swamp. Caleb quickly steps to their wagon of cotton where he had earlier been saddle-soaping his violin case; he places his violin in the case and locks it. Looking at the house with concern about Henry, he then retrieves his father's rifles from the porch, and enters the woods. He will not pray for divine intervention the way Henry is doing, he tells himself, not and let the Klan come to their home and kill him and his father. No, he will stop them in their tracks, even if he has to shoot them where they stand and end up in the electric chair.

Ten minutes later, after cautiously moving nearly a quarter mile through the woods and following the disturbing sounds of the land creatures, Caleb hears human voices. He conceals himself behind a tree. Just ahead of him, Dane Tucker and his recently sworn-in young Klansmen—their hoods now removed—have arrived in the swamp and are on the train tracks near old, wooden, Cutter Bridge. Klansmen are swarming about through the stream, which parallels the train rails, all ordered by Dane to get in their licks and kicks on someone lying at their feet and begging for mercy, while sending even more of the swamp creatures into alarming fits. With Dane and the others is Burt, who is still sniffing in his snot, then spitting it out trying to clear the pig-butt medicine from his taste buds. Everyone stops kicking and cursing and stands there glaring down at Deputy Snodgress. Trout—hardly able to stand erect on his crutches—would rather have been anywhere than on the train tracks, but Dane has insisted that Trout remain there to witness Snodgress's punishment. As Trout stares down with empathy and despair at the deputy, in that fetal position on the steel-hard railroad tracks and the gravel-and-wood ties, one of the young recruits also gazes down at the lawman with mixed feelings. "He's one of us, Dane," the young recruit exclaims, while listening to the out cry of the swamp creatures and then nervously looking about at the pitch of night, the heavy, moist atmosphere from the thousands of dark, unseen trees and bushes pressing in on them. Sadly motioning to Snodgress, the teenage boy exclaims to Dane, "I thought you told us to wear these hoods and stuff so we could kill a few coloreds, Mexicans, Jews, Chinese and or Jap types on the way out here tonight. People like that, but, Jesus, Dane! We doing this to a white man, the law. The sheriff will never rest until he—"

"Shut up!" hisses Dane. He glares down at Snodgress and then goes on. "When it comes to the amount of money they say Barney has, to get my hands on it, I'll kill my own mom, and that includes the Sheriff, Barney Cutter, or anyone else before they kills us to get that money fer themselves, and—have no doubt about it—Barney Cutter will kill us to keep what's his. Some of you younger guys are fresh from Sunday school, but you better remember that about Barney when you think your prayers will protect you, they won't! Not when it comes to Barney Cutter. He's not like any man alive. He's the devil himself."

"Please, Dane," Snodgress begs. "Can I get up now? My back and legs are hurting me."

Trout's heart goes out to Snodgress. "Those dreams I was telling you about, back in my shack, Dane . . . Every night, the same dream. Pennington wanted to find God in the end and told me about his dreams, as well. But, instead of a ghost of ice and snow, my dreams are about your dead pa, Dane. Even now, I can still smell his rotting flesh. He comes to me at night and writes the words 'pray fer your sins' on my wall and says to love the niggers as brothers."

Dane's head and neck veins pop out and increase with his insane rage; he leaps into the air and comes down hard, splashing stream water onto Snodgress and onto those near him, and he howls, "One mother fucking Sue Ann seeing hands writing the words, 'pray' on her goddamn mirror is enough. Pa would never tell you to love a nigger! Never! You mother fucker! I busted the shit out of Sue Ann's mirror with that beer mug, now you tell me why you insulted my pa, so I can kill you slowly and watch you suffer with Snodgress here. You want-a see what I'll do to you!" Everyone watches in horror as Dane reaches down and loosens Snodgress's belt, jerks the deputy's trousers and shorts below his buttocks and sticks his finger into the deputy's rectum. The mad man removes his finger from Snodgress's buttocks, as a horrified Snodgress—trembling—pulls his shorts and trousers back above his waist. Dane glares at Trout and bellows. "You said you could smell pa's dead flesh? Then smell this, my finger up your nose!" Dane seizes Trout about his throat, sticks his index finger up Trout's nose and holds on, jerking the cripple's head this way and that, causing the blood to flow from the old man's nostrils. As Trout wails in pain, Dane whispers, "Shhh," causing Trout to gag back his groans. "I never want to hear you speak of my pa again as if he somehow is telling you from the grave that what he believed in all his life—the Klan, you mother fucker—and that it is now a thing that is wrong. I never did like your big nose," he tells Trout. "It reminds me of a nigger's lips, and you know how I hate nigger lips. Now, shhh like I told you. No more talk of dreams or any goddamn thing except the colonel's fortune!" He faces the other. "From any of you!"

When everyone falls silent, Dane—removing his finger from Trout's nose—turns on Snodgress with a vengeance. "Where'd you get this gold coin?" he yells, thrusting the coin at the deputy. "You called your damn wife on your car radio and said this coin, and soon many more like it, was the answer to your prayers. Now, make it the answer to mine!"

"My wife is a deputy like me," begs Snodgress. "She wouldn't have told you that."

"She didn't have to tell me. I was in her damn patrol car fucking the hell out of her, when you radioed her with your coded message. It didn't take much to get her to break down that personal code of yours to me, when I told her if she didn't I'll tell you about my fucking her every time you left fer work, her with her big, ugly, fat ass."

"Ahh!" cries Snodgress, looking up at the men, his eyes begging for understanding.

From his place of hiding, behind a tree, Caleb—who is always touched by others' suffering—is not moved by Snodgress's cries of agony: a man sworn to uphold the law and now in bed with all that is evil. Caleb's intense gaze is on Crazy Walter's body, just off of the train tracks and behind the Klansmen. After Dane and the others had returned to the hanging tree to transport Walter's body to the bridge, the Klansmen had found Snodgress there keeping watch over Walter's remains from inside his patrol car, and when a relieved Snodgress stepped from his car, feeling that he was among friends, he had made the mistake of holding onto that gold coin, which he accidentally dropped, and when he reached down to pick it up, Dane beat him to it. Convinced that Snodgress has discovered Barney's whispered-about fortune, Dane had trucked both the deputy and Walter's body to its present location, where the one-eared, would-be leader now plans to hang and then re-burn Walter's remains from the bridge as had been the fate of the young school-kids so that Caleb and Henry would see it from their house and flee from Georgia. Stalking closer behind still another tree and a growth of thickets for a clearer shot, an outraged Caleb, over the brutal death of Walter, positions his rifle, preparing to shoot everyone in sight. Meanwhile, Dane again shows Snodgress the coin. "Is this part of what Cutter brought from Germany, that island?" hisses Dane, as Caleb targets the one-eared Klansman's head, Caleb's finger easing onto the trigger.

"Die, you bastards," Caleb whispers. Shockingly, from out of the woods, a deer crosses thirty feet or so away from Caleb and stops, blocking Caleb's line of sight. It stands there looking at him. Once more—from a different position—Caleb takes aim at Dane, and once again the graceful, white-tailed creature moves into Caleb's line of sight and stops and looks at him. Caleb is dumbfounded, and he stares over the rifle sight and studies the deer. Henry's boy lowers his weapon.

A half mile away, Sheriff Richards, who has been searching for his son-in-law, notices the torchlight flickering in the distance. As he drives his patrol car toward the lights, the night creatures increase their alarming calls all around him. "You'll wake up the dead, you slime," hisses Richards from the lowered car window. "Shut the fuck up!"

With Snodgress sobbing for his life and the animals bellowing from the woods around them, it's impossible for the Klansmen to tell the sounds of those harping cries around them from the ones sounding off about Richards, as once again, Snodgress covers up his head with his arms and hands, warding off Dane's foot blows. "Please," the lawman wails. "I told you I got it from the nigga Walter, the boy your men hanged."

Dane whirls about and faces the men who had helped hang Walter. "Didn't you guys search that coon befer you strung him up?"

"It was all we could do," says one of them, as Dane washes his hands in the stream, "to get pass the stink in order to hang him. I don't think he's taken a bath since the day we had him on the run; we weren't about to go through that coon's pockets. We had no reason to believe he had two cents to rub together, Dane, let alone a gold coin. Where'd a boy like him get a gold coin?"

"It makes no sense to me neither," Dane says and then turns back to Snodgress. "This coin is the work of a white man's mind, not a tar ball's. Try again, Deputy, or die here and now!"

Caleb hears the train, its ghostly, distant whistle crying out from a mile away. The deer dashes away.

"God," cries Trout, filled with dread upon hearing the train; he stumbles alongside the weeping lawman, and, even through he's on those crutches, and knowing he could fall on his face, he tries to help Snodgress off the tracks and to his feet, softening the hearts of the young recruits, and that of Caleb even more, as Trout leans down and jerks at Snodgress's arm and yells at Dane, "You heard the deputy. He got the gold off of Walter. The train's coming! Let him get off the tracks."

"Keep your ass where you stand, old man and you too, Deputy!" yells Dane, when Trout gives up on rescuing the deputy and starts off of the tracks to save himself instead. "Be a man like me!" Dane yells at Trout. Lifting his head, Dane exclaims to the stars. "I'm a man, Pa! Fer once, I'm being a man, not a damn frightened boy who Barney made walk barefoot in that glass and threatened to cut off my other ear. I'm not like the boy who stood by pissin' in his pants while Barney made you blow off your head and since made me pray to God to bring you back from the dead. Now the hell with God! I'm a man, Pa!"

466

With everyone looking questioningly at Dane and Dane at Trout with glaring eyes to kill, Snodgress attempts to crawl off the tracks, but Dane whirls about, whips out a pocket knife, cuts the deputy on his ass, then reaches into Snodgress's sobbing mouth and seizes his tongue, pulls it beyond Snodgress's front teeth and holds onto it with one hand and the knife with the other, the deputy horrified and feeling that his tongue would be severed from his mouth at any second. "It took me shoving my finger up Trout's nose to control him, but he still doesn't believe that I'm his god on earth," Dane yells at Snodgress. "Not Barney! Me! I'm his and your god! Let's see how much pain it takes to make you believe that and force you to tell the truth." The sound of the train is closing in on them, Trout—leaning on his crutches for balance—covering his ears against Snodgress's cry of pain, as Dane jerks and twist the lawman's tongue. Several of the men laugh and ridicule the sobbing deputy, who—besides trying to keep Dane from ripping out his tongue—also grapples at his buttocks to stem the pain and flow of blood.

"Let him go!" yells Trout. "What wrong with all of us? Don't hurt him anymore!"

Dane releases Snodgress's tongue and knocks Trout off his crutches to the ground, then grabs Snodgress by his ear, when he again attempts to crawl off the tracks.

"He's right, Dane," says one of the new recruits, after covering his ears, as had Trout. "Let's release him." The young boy—one of those whose hearts are softened—looks about the darkness. "There's someone out there. I can feel him watching us." When Caleb sees the youngster glances his way, but yet doesn't see him, Caleb eases back into the deeper darkness of the trees, as the boy's sights sweep pass him and focus elsewhere. "God is watching us, Dane."

For the first time, Dane seems afraid and steps back from the deputy. Dane ponders, *Could Caleb be out there?* Burt—the pig-butt medicine not only upset his stomach, it profoundly embittered his heart and now brings back bitter memories of Snodgress: "This deputy's a fool, a nobody," Burt yells and furiously continues doing so, while pointing at the young boy who senses Caleb's focus on them. "Don't listen to this young punk." Burt whirls and continues pointing down at Snodgress. "This one kicked the shit out of me and Marcus whenever we didn't give

467

him a cut from our scrap-metal money. I say kill him, and don't listen to any kind of talk about God this or that. Kill him, Dane."

"In God's name, don't listen to him," mutters Snodgress over his swollen tongue. "I have a wife and family at home."

Dane kicks Snodgress in his side. "If I find out you're double-dealing about where the rest of these coins and gold is," he warns the deputy, "I'll kill you, your wife and your kids!"

Dane has to only glare at Trout, as the old man struggles off the ground, in order to force him to remain on the train tracks, tracks which begin slightly vibrating under the feet of those standing on it; seeing the gut-wrenching apprehension on a trembling Trout's face when he feels the tracks move, the young recruit, remembering how his mother always told him to help others and that God would bless him, the young one—who had sensed Caleb's presence, hurriedly helps the crippled man off the rails, but as the boy struggles off the steel rail with Trout, Snodgress is left on the tracks gawking up at the youth, his eyes begging the boy to also help him, the distant train's speeding wheels of death clearly heard clicking through the cold rails with paralyzing results.

"Let the deputy get up and off them tracks!" Trout yells back at Dane, once he, himself, is free of them.

"Keep your mouth shut, old man, befer I drag your ass back over here," blasts Dane. "I'm not a damn child to fear a fucking train that's not even close to being here yet."

Trout gawks at the train, now slip-sliding into that northerly curve approaching Cutter Bridge, its angular beam of light passing under the bridge oscillating, seemingly accelerating ahead of itself, sweeping over the rail ties like a deadly, diamond-back snake. Limping farther away from the rails with the help of two more of the young Klansman, Trout shrieks at Dane. "You're insane, you fool. You been smoking cow shit too long." Even though the young ones attempt to make him shut up Trout—filled with thoughts of redemption—goes on. "In God's name let the deputy go, or we'll all end up in hell, if not behind bars! He's Richard's son-in-law! A white man, and you're acting like one of those godless niggers, Dane!"

Dane flips open that knife and goes after a yelping Trout, causing the young recruits around Trout to scatter in dread, as the old man tries to run away from Dane, who grabs him and, with one swift move, cuts off Trout's nose. The cripple flings aside his crutches and grapples at his face, his blood splattering everywhere. The terrorized young Klansmen sprint halfway across the field toward Caleb's hiding place before the sounds of the wild creatures cause them to stop and retreat back to Dane, as Trout wakes up the dead with his painful bellowing cries.

"My nose! My nose!"

"Now does it look like I'm joking, or that I'm insane?" asks Dane, picking up the severed nose. "I'll show you 'insane!'" Chewing, then swallowing Trout's nose, Dane turns his eyes of death on his men, as those who ran away and returned shake in holy fear. "If any one of you try what he just did or try to get out of this group befer we get our hands on Barney's money, I'll kill him and his family, so help me Satan! Barney's not the only one who knows how to call on Satan's powers! I'll cut out your hearts and eat them as well if I have to, in order to get that money."

In the bushes, Caleb leans back against a tree, Trout's spurting blood recalling images of Claretta's bloody remains. Covering his ears against Trout's bellowing cry, Caleb watches the noseless man wailing and hopping about on one leg, while his peers stand helplessly by, gaping at him. Trout rips off his shirt and presses it against his face to stop the gushing blood. Dane strong-arms the crutchless, hopping old man back onto the track with him, causing the young recruits to put aside all thoughts of trying to get out of the Klan alive. Henry's son—in many ways as sensitive as Flynn—now backs off and turns to race for home, but stops. "No," he tells himself. "There will be no running home, not with those mad dogs around to hurt papa;" mortified or not, Caleb whirls back around and surveys the oncoming train and then the bloody scene of horror. "Please, God, please find a way to somehow let me and Trout go," whispers Snodgress, knowing better than to attempt to try and crawl off the tracks again, his heart racing, his buttocks bleeding, as he sobs. "Befer he and I bleed to death, God. We're useless to Dane, who refuses to believe me."

Dane repockets the knife and drags a hobbling Trout by his arm and forces a knees-and-hands-down, crawling deputy—at gunpoint—to dog-walk down the tracks toward the oncoming train, the locomotive within a few hundred yards of them now, the other Klansmen goggling at it in disbelief and with heart-pounding distress. Snodgress's wide eyes take in the train, and the deputy goes into a kicking and screaming fit.

"You are as insane as Trout said," he yells, feeling that he has nothing to lose now.

"Quiet, deputy," the professed devil worshipper says, while testing his faith in Satan's power to keep him from harm, as he had Barney, while keeping an eye on the sacrificial lawman and a on a quivering Trout. "I heard you pray," says Dane to Snodgrass, "and I don't think you know anything about Barney's gold," Dane goes on, "or his money, whatever it turns out to be, but I can't let you go running back to the Sheriff and have him put me in that jail of his with all them darkys he got locked up in your pigpen. Not that I'm afraid of them jailed niggers, or that they'd fuck me in my ass, the animals that they are, understand. Anyone can see how brave I am to stand up against a oncoming train on these train tracks and not be afraid like I was afraid to help my pa, when Barney had him blow his head off."

"But that was Barney, not me, who made your pa do that, Dane. Not meeee!"

"Quiet, now," Dane tells Snodgress, "and show me how brave you are, Deputy, you and old one-leg Trout, while I'm showing Pa how brave I am now, even without him here at my side to defend me. Bring on the damn train, Pa," yells Dane, "them blacks all whisper that you're in hell. Then so be it, 'cause Lucifer is all-powerful. I ain't afraid of anything anymore! Satan ain't just with Barney, now, he's with me, Pa, with me!"

"My God!" yells Burt, wishing that he'd stayed behind with Marcus, who was too afraid to come with them. As that switching, to-and-fro, blinding train light streams down the tracks, and fully onto them, onto those standing off the rails, and onto those on the tracks, just ahead of the roaring monster of steel, Snodgress screams bloody murder. Dane, with a grip of steel and laughing, pockets his gun and drags the wailing deputy to his feet and holds onto him and Trout in the center of the tracks, the train's light—truly now—like a blinding snake, lighting up their world and the wide-eyed faces to the three men in its path of immediate demise. Snodgress tries to wrestle free of Dane, but Dane is too strong, for within him is Satan, and the deputy cannot break free.

"Fuck!" yells the old engineer—who's been conversing with his black fireman before finally seeing the three men in the middle of the tracks. Laying on his stream horn, the startled engineer rises off his seat and stares ahead in disbelief, while pulling on the chain of that ear-blasting horn. From his vantage point, Caleb feels his heart racing, his entire body telling him to flee, but once more remains there steadfast, as Dane holds an exhausted, comatose, limp Snodgress in place on the tracks with one hand, while forcing a bloody, nose-less Trout, again by simply looking at him, to remain hobbling beside him. Standing well back from the train tracks, Burt and the other men sweat, their panic-stricken eyes locked on the streaking locomotive, the speeding monster of death now seconds away from the three men, the shrieking horn never relinquishing.

"Do you see me, now, Pa!" cries a wide-eyed Dane.

A new arrival sees Dane from behind a growth of bushes, a stone's throw away; his once-polished shoes mired in the stream water and mud, Sheriff Richards, tripping and falling, is gawking out at his daughter's husband, who is ghostly pale and lifeless looking, and begging for his life, as Dane shakes Snodgress violently and holds him in place. His hand trembling, Richards reaches for his service revolver; it drops from his fingers into the mud. The more he grapples for the weapon, the more his hands shake and the more the revolver slips from his muddy grip, the sight and sound of the oncoming train, its blaring horn impacting Richard's senses, his eyes tearing up, his mouth wide and gasping, the maddening last-second scream from Snodgress, all of these things standing even Richard's blood vessels up on edge from his thundering heart. Caleb's heartbeat also increases, when he sees that seventy-miles-per-hour, six-thousand-horse-powered locomotive roar upon the three men, and those deadly steel wheels lock up, sending sparks flying backward from them. As the train's momentum seems to suck the men into it, at the last second, Dane pushes Snodgress into the path of the roaring death, as he and Trout jump clear. The deputy's body explodes into a wet muck; his torso parts are slammed onto Dane's white robe: tiny pieces of brain, guts, splintered bones and quivering chunks of jelly-like blood substance. Some particles of Snodgress' far-flung flesh slaps against the tree next to Caleb; he looks down at it quivering on the tree bark, and then he feels something warm on him, and looks at his hand: the human sewage on his palm and fingers.

Snodgress's arm is stuck to one of the train wheels and is flopping and flipping back and forth and is on fire until it's pulverized and is gone. While the monstrous steel killer of man slides along, heating up the steel rail, from the locomotive's cab, the man operating the throttle—fifty-year-old hillbilly Parson and his coal-shoveling fireman, Bruno—gape back at the blurred Klansmen along the train tracks, and Parson gets up off of the brakes and lets the locomotive run free. "Just another nigga lynching, seems to me," Parson tells his colored helper. "Keep shoveling that coal, boy. We got a schedule to make up."

With Snodgress's flesh and blood clinging to its clickety-clacking wheels, the boxcars and freight cars rumble over sections of uneven, rails, and their enormous weight causes the steel rails to rise up and down in wave-like motions. When the caboose and its red lanterns flash beyond the torches and men, in the thicket where Richards is hiding, the lawman gags and chokes back the urge to vomit. Racing to his patrol car with his hand covering his mouth, Richards—shaking off pieces of his Deputy's body—climbs into his vehicle and speeds away, knowing that there is no way he can report Snodgress's death, not even to his daughter, when he's a member of the ones who killed her husband. Recklessly speeding down the road, Richards tells himself that he needs time to calm down, time to put together a plan, and regardless of his son-in-law's death, he will not be detoured, will not be denied the gold, even if he has to kill everyone in town in order to possess it and thus Satan have strenthened his hold on all of the money worshipers.

As Richards heads for Cutterville, Dane pushes a bleeding but grateful-to-be-alive, crutch-hobbling Trout ahead of him and the others.

"Now you show us the safe way out of here," Dane grumbles again, violently nudging the one-legged man for good measure, as they cautiously travel through the night and swamp.

Stalking them, Caleb feels both fear and relief that they are leaving. Trout, now petrified on his crutches and sobbing with his shirt tied about his head and that missing nose, also feels pain and fear. Not only does Trout have to fight the pain clawing at his face, he begins to sweat with a greater concern, a deep-seated feeling that he will never leave the swamps alive. "You ain't going to kill me once I get you guys back to your truck, are you, Dane?" Trout manages to squall, between wailing with that stabbing agony and the urge to tear off his very face in order to make the blade-sharp throbbing go away. "I mean Barney, Hank and I are friends, but that don't mean I'll tell Barney how you're after his gold. And about God, Dane, I despise Him as much as you do now. Ahh, I hurts so bad, Dane."

"Keep your mouth shut about us and you got nothing to fear," Dane tells him, going on, "If I wanted to kill you," said Dane, "I'd have push' you into that train as well. "The rest of you guys," he tells the others, "we'll come back here fer a few days, to catch us one of them coons that we missed tonight in a trap with their good-heartedness, when they come through here with food and looking fer Walter and instead discover the deputy and nigger's bodies and try to bury that tar baby, or even both of 'em."

The minute they reach the truck, Dane cuts Trout's throat. He glares at his men, who climb onto the truck bed without a word. Dane enters the cab and speeds into the night, the men on the truck bed holding onto their dreams and the truck's sideboards and trembling, trying to decide who was worse, Colonel Cutter or Dane, the thought of Barney's money now thought to be in the millions, keeping them glued together and willing to stick it out, while leaving Walter behind, crumbling and charred, and Snodgress in pieces, and Trout on the ground struggling to stay alive. As Trout lies there wheezing in his own blood and seeing Lilly's death flash before his eyes, and with those eyes tightly closed, he suddenly sees a glowing light, turning the blood in his closed eyelids an intense bright blood red. It's a powerful light, streaming about him and from someone standing over him; he can feel the person's shoes touch against his leg. Opening his eyes, he sees Caleb all aglow, looking down at him.

"It's so bright. Let me touch the Light, as Lilly had asked. I was there and saw you and her together."

Caleb turns and runs away. "Not again," he cries. "Not another Lilly! No more lights and people dying when I come too close to them."

"God forgive me," calls Trout, then nothing. Everything turns black and he dies, his call for forgiveness dies with him.

Later that night, coon hunters come across Trout's remains and deliver the body into town, never knowing that Snodgress and Walter's bodies are less than a mile away. Trout is buried in an impoverished grave site and virtually forgotten.

33

The Eviction

Less than six minutes later, sprinting like a frightened deer and leaping over a stone fence and onto his father's lost domain, Caleb runs to the house, places the rifle on the porch and falls panting onto his knees. He glances at the hill, leaps to his feet and doesn't stop running until he reaches Henry, who is again on the hill and on his knees praying.

"Papa, Dane killed the deputy, Trout, and Crazy Walter. He's the devil, Papa. Dane Tucker is the devil! And I didn't kill any of them! Why didn't I kill the bastards?"

"It's said we must love our enemies," Henry gazes up at Caleb. "Especially you who are what you are." Henry stands up, his focus down the slope on their front yard and house. "We're you followed? Did they see you?"

"No, Papa." Caleb tells Henry, horrified and carefully studying his fearless father and then exclaims, "Why? Papa, you're not afraid of them! Is it your belief in God?"

"Yes, son. With all my heart," Henry embraces his son. "My love for God only increases the love I have for you."

"Why can't I believe like you and Flynn, Naomi and Sarah? Like other decent, kind people." Henry holds onto his trembling child. "The day you and I entered Colored Town in the wagon to sell our goods at the train station, Caleb, and Crazy Walter made the speech that got him killed, I told you that God hasn't given me even a hint that you are what Naomi and Sarah seems to want you to be; now, you ask why you can't believe the way the ones you love do. Maybe it was my fault for what I told you that day. I was wrong. Caleb, when that dark sky covered daylight, and you—after being in that trance—told Flynn that the darkness was a continuation of Christ's death on the cross, I was beginning to believe, son, now, absolutely, without a doubt, I'd bet my life that God is operating through you to show the world something very different from the way we think today, or think from the days of old. Maybe we shouldn't expect you to be like other disciples, even as the apostle Paul wasn't at first. Do you know who he was, Caleb?"

"No, Sir. I don't recall reading anything about him to you."

"I never ask you to. It was your grandpapa who told me about Paul, that Paul was a mighty Jewish warrior who murdered, raped and pilfered with the worst of them and refused to believe that Jesus was the Son of God, as didn't many of the Jews, which encouraged the crucifixion of our Lord back then, but later Paul accepted Christianity with all his heart, and did more to spread the love of Christ around the world more than any other human being alive. That's who Paul was, Caleb, someone much like you, and absolutely unlike God's other loving children, like Sarah and Flynn and Naomi."

"And you, Papa," Caleb interrupts. "And you. You are one of His loving children, too."

Henry again embraces Caleb and continues, "God knows you're beyond us all in a way that's important to Him. As good as we may be to our families, to our neighbors, or as much as we attend church, we mostly turn a blind eye on seeing others as God does, as our brothers and sisters. God made you to honestly question even His existence. But the one thing you clearly have, that most of us don't, is your love for people—regardless of their color—which has to please our Lord. You showed that love even for the ladies of the night, like Lilly, who God blessed by simply letting her touch you the way she did and die in grace. That's what I now think."

"Not for the Klan, Papa. Not for those violators of the human spirit, not for the godless churches and preachers do I have any compassion, and Flynn, Papa. He loves people regardless of their color, so why has God signaled him out to be killed by me, the way Naomi says?"

"Do not question His purpose, son. He's the Lord thy God!"

Suddenly, from the caves above them, the bats swarm into the night sky, their wings from hell drumming and hedge-clipping through the air, as they travel in their nightly search for blood.

"Dear God," whispers Henry, embracing his frightened son, Caleb's sights on the bats. "Let my boy see the Light and not be afraid of evil before it's too late."

Early the following morning, as Henry and Caleb sit at their kitchen table eating breakfast in grim silence, Sheriff Richards and a deputy enter through the screen door. Richards slaps down several sheets of papers on the table, accidentally knocking over the coffee pot.

"Judge Chambers signed these papers and says this land is no longer yours, Henry."

When Caleb is about to confront Richards for storming into their house, Henry reaches over the table and takes his boy by the arm, silencing him and then hands the coffee-stained court documents to Caleb. "Read it for me, Caleb."

"I know Caleb's got a big mouth the way he talked up a storm at the courthouse," says Richards, "and caused me to get my notice, but that's okay. There are plenty other towns in the South who will welcome my kind with open arms, but, as to those pages, I can't understand most of that mumble jumble on them. What makes you think Caleb can?"

Caleb scans through the half-dozen pages in quick time and exclaims, "It says we failed to pay the mortgage, Papa" The lawmen gawk at him, as he goes on, "Also, Papa, our land's been appropriated by the town for back taxes. All based on damn lies," hisses Caleb.

"Is it legal, son?"

"It's an injunction from the court with absolute terms of perpetuity." The sheriff and his deputy stand with open mouths as Caleb hurriedly fans through the pages and explains on. "And, Papa, it says we can't sell, give away or make possible the transfer of any water from this land without the town of Cutterville's written permission." Sadly, Caleb looks up from the document and at his father. "We've always been protected by the Winthrops, but to violate this order and give Sarah any of the lagoon water would now be judicable to your enemies, Papa, and you could be imprisoned the way the court system works in this state."

"Juda what?" asks the deputy, glaring at Caleb. "What'd he just say, Sheriff?"

Caleb looks at Richards, who closes his mouth and quips. "Boy, you are sure full of surprises, aren't you. As good as they say! Can out-talk white folks and read like one of them damn, white, college professors."

"Why do you waste your time trying to insult me, when you just lost your deputy, Sheriff Richard?" Caleb exclaims, glaring up at the lawman, who steps back completely stunned that Caleb should know about Snodgress, when even the town hasn't learned of his death yet. "Are you so cold and heartless," Caleb continues, "that not even for a moment you can't or won't warm up with a little compassion for others after losing a son-in-law and running out on him, the way you did?"

Richards's eyes widened; he's a threatened man and now desperately wondering how in the hell Caleb knows that he was in the woods and ran off leaving Snodgress to die. He glares at Caleb, as if to kill him with his angry thoughts alone. "You were there, weren't you, boy?" He jerks the papers from Caleb and flings them on the floor. "Chambers says as long as you pay your rent, you two can stay on here until all of the paperwork's legalized." Glaring at Caleb, masking his fears with harsh words, he adds, "I'd have kicked you and your smart-ass mouth out on your black ass. Does that answer your question as to how heartless I am?" Richards glares at Henry in a way that asks him if he approves of Caleb endangering their lives by mouthing off that way. Henry ignores him, while cleaning up the spilled coffee. "The next time you sneak around and spy on a white man, Caleb Brooks, I'll personally cut off your balls, Sarah your protecting angel or not!"

"Don't talk to my boy as if we're one of yours and Miller's mindless snakes," Henry shouts and approaches Richards. "You've served your papers. Now get out!"

Richards's eyes are like daggers with his hatred for Henry, and Caleb lays into the lawman. "And if you want to glare at someone so badly, the way you're looking at my father, do as he says and get out here before I take the gun from both of you and kick you out there, where you should be looking for the killers of Claretta and Billy Joe, Walter and your deputy, as if you don't already know who they are. Remember I still have the originals of those letters, all of them, regardless if your Klan-controlled newspaper says that blacks falsified them or not! There are experts who can testify as to the genuineness of your handwriting." Caleb leers at the young deputy. "Watch out for this man that he doesn't get you shot, then leave you to die alone, as he did Deputy Snodgress. Now, get your white asses out of here! Now, damn you!"

The lawmen leave, with Richards kicking the screen door off its hinges, his young deputy now eyeing him with suspicion. After the lawmen leave, Caleb faces Henry:

"What about Walter, Papa? Shouldn't we go out there and bury him?"

"Only once it's safe to do so, Caleb. We all know how them Klansmen lays in wait to kill anyone trying to recover the bodies. For now, I'd like to know who and why someone drove poor Mister Pennington to kill himself and then steal our property."

"Maybe Flynn and the colonel stole it," says Caleb, picking up the court papers and tearing them into pieces. "Flynn knew about plans to take our place away from us."

Henry is devastated over Caleb's accusation about Flynn. "Naomi said it was Pennington, son. Him and that dog of his. I'll pray for him. I know you don't believe in prayer, even when you and Flynn pray together, but I want you to pray with me. If not for us, then for Flynn and Sarah. They're also in danger now."

They hear a car racing toward the house and look out the window. It's Barney's red Cadillac. Sarah dips the luxury vehicle to a stop at the fence, after seeing the dislodged kitchen, screen door on the ground beside the house; sliding from the car, she sprints along the house, steps over the screen door and into the kitchen.

"Thank God you two are all right," she says, embracing Caleb, then going to the table and sitting by Henry. "I just heard about your land," she tells him. "We'll fight this in court. I couldn't ask Barney about your land, once I was informed about it, because he had already left for the Capitol. I swear if he had anything to do with you losing Little Shadow Place, I will divorce him, Catholic or not, may God have mercy on me, and I will sell all my belongings to recover your land, if we fail in the courts."

"You're not selling anything or saying anything to that man about my place, Sarah. He'd only deny it, and you'd put yourself in more danger than you already are. And there will be no talk of divorce. You made an oath to be Barney's wife until death, and you will not break your word to God, even if I have to die to stop you."

"Please don't speak of you dying, Henry." Sarah gazes over at Caleb, her eyes asking him to also tell Henry that they wouldn't know what to do if he should die and leave them. When Caleb looks with love at Henry and nods, Sarah continues justifying why she should leave Barney.

Caleb walks outside then runs in the wind. Up the hill and down again, he runs, sprinting past Old Clara—who watches him from the meadow. The faster he races along, the more despair seems to follow.

When Caleb returns home again, the sun has left the sky, and the moon rules the night. He sees Henry kneeling in prayer on the hill behind their house. Caleb takes Henry's Bible from the porch and climbs the slope to be with his father.

34

The New Disciple of Christ

Bruce Johnson—upon hearing that Barney would be gone for another week and that Henry still needs help—has not forgotten his promise that he would always be there for Henry, Flynn and Caleb for saving his and his son's life. Bruce has taken a few more days off from the factory in order to work with Henry on the pipeline. Now, he, Carrie and Earlene drink from one of Shadow Grove's water kegs, after returning from placing the pipeline, survey stakes—along with one of Barney's young engineers—to Henry's embezzled property. Putting aside his backpack, his stakes, and hammer, Bruce leaves his family a few yards behind and approaches Henry, who is shoveling dirt with other blacks in one of many knee-deep trenches throughout the fields, which are too steeply banked for the engineers' heavy-duty equipment to handle. Included among the men with Henry are the aging, white-haired Amos and Andy brothers. Everyone is in relatively good spirits, because Sarah has written to her father's friend in Washington about Henry's place, and Henry is sure that Little Shadow Place will be returned to him, and is more determined than ever to get the pipeline finished and to his land before winter. When Bruce reaches the ditch, he clears his throat and gawks down at Henry, terror reflecting in his brown eyes.

"What's wrong?" asks Henry, glancing up at him.

"Henry, me and Carrie . . . saw 'em. It was awful. Out near your place, when we was on our way to get some of that sweet drinkin' water from your well." As Bruce mutters on, the diggers in the trench with Henry stop working and take note. "Near the train tracks off Old Spring Road," Bruce goes on, gagging, his knees shaking. "Blood everywhere. It was like ma po' child Claretta's bloody death happin' all over again befo' ma eyes: all over the place that blood was. Ma God! And even pieces of his flesh. Where is the love, Henry? Where is the love?"

"Don't tell me you took your family near that bridge," exclaims Henry.

"I knows you told us not to go that way, that the Klan had killed them, but somehow with Carrie a-talkin' away—as she always does and me a-listenin'—we walked right upon it. Me and Carrie and that young engineer. Thank God Earlene was a-pickin' flowers behind us a piece and didn't see it. It looked like a butchered hog, what was left of him, but it was his body, Henry."

"What body?" asks a seven-foot-tall man—also in the trench. "I ain't heard about nobody bein' killed lately. Crazy Walter?" the lanky man goes on. "Was it him? Was you saying they finally killed him out there, Crazy Walter?"

"Night before last," Henry sadly says to those around him.

Bruce takes in a deep breath, the other workers waiting with open mouths for him to speak and adds to their fears. "I was afraid to come out of the bushes and get any closer 'cause of them two white boys around that body with them other Klan, y'all," Bruce sputters.

"Then they didn't see you," says Henry.

"No! God help me and mine ifin they had. Even that young boy engineer knew to be quiet when I told him to be. He's somewhere now on Shadow Grove still throwin' up. Poor soul, packin' up his things and is going back to Denver today, he says."

Henry studies Bruce. "You said the Klan and two boys?"

"Good God," one of the diggers whispers. "Two boys? You mean children? Children joinin' them Klan? Lord, we don'ts got no chance of ever outlasting them killers and hope their hearts soften in their old age, not with them kids a-joinin' them, now, to carry the hatred forward."

"It was them two from town who sell scrap metal, Burt and Marcus," Bruce exclaims.

The young boy that Naomi says that God revealed to her before he was born, and said that he has to be loved or he'll end up in hell for eternity, Henry ponders.

Excited, Bruce goes on, his eyes wide, his voice cracking, "And that youngest boy was a-cryin' as they shoveled up the deputy's body parts and put 'em in old Hank's truck and drove what was left of that po' deputy away. They left Walter fo' the wild pigs to finish him off, I guess."

"The deputy!" an elderly man says horrified. "You sayin' a lawman was murdered out there too? Beside Crazy Walter?" He gawks at Henry and exclaims. "Oh, no! Now they gonna blame one of us fo' killin' him."

"Not if it's like Bruce says, that the Klan took his body away," Henry tells them. "Caleb and I have good reason to believe that Richards wants to cover up Snodgress's death to protect his interest in some money that Flynn mentioned to Caleb."

"That po', little Marcus," says the tall man, "I liked that boy."

Bruce timidly looks over his shoulder at his family and adds, "That Burt boy, Henry, was forcing the little one to help them load that slimy, smelly gunk that was left of Snodgress on they motor truck, and that Burt fellow told that little one called Marcus that it was a practice drill for Marcus to learn to kill coons, and that if Marcus went on crying or threw up, that it was Dane who killed the deputy, and that Dane would kill Marcus fo' being a sissy."

Old Amos and Andy—up to now, having remained at the end of the ditch in total silence and unnoticed—had turned ashen and had leaned back against the earthen bank, looking with anxiety and in sorrow at one another every time Dane's name was mentioned, and they continue painfully doing so, as Bruce goes on. "The other body was Crazy Walter's, like Henry said, and that Brut ordered the little one to piss on Walter, and when they all left in Hank's truck, a million flies followed that truck and its smell of death like a cloud, y'all, like a dark cloud."

"Po' old Crazy Walter," someone whispers.

"Fo'get about Walter," says an elderly man, "he brought this on hisself and on us, when he knew they'd kill him and maybe a few of us fo' talkin' out of line the way he did in town."

Bruce nods in agreement and continues, "I never liked that loud-mouth man, either, but after them Klan and boys left in they truck, it was then that I knew, in ma heart, that Walter was my brother and far braver than I ever will be—like Naomi told us all at Reverend Harris's church—I don't want to be one of them that Naomi says will ends up with the goats in hell because I worshiped a Cadillac instead of havin' love fo' ma brother. I buried him in spite of my fears, while Carrie kept Earlene and that scared engineer away. I just couldn't leave that po', colored man that way with the flies eatin' what the wild animals left and layin' maggots on him."

"You did right," says Henry, " 'cause Sheriff Richards . . . not even that Atlanta coroner, who comes to town whenever there's a white killing, don't give a damn about comin' all the way out here for some poor, colored's body, one way or the other."

"You sho' it was the body of the Sheriff's son-in-law, Bruce?" Andy asks, stepping away from Amos.

"It was his body right 'nough, Andy. After them Klan left, I found his badge and his blue-black, white hand with his wedding band still on his finger, that five-and-dime-store ring he was so proud of and showed off to the whole town, even to us coloreds, the day he married Richard's tramp of a daughter."

One of the black trenchers looks over his shoulders and whispers, "You can say that again! His wife thought she was too good to even speak to us, and told the deputy not to speak to us either. Said we all had too small of brains to work in Dessen's factory and make that kind of money over whites."

"Well, I buried that badge and hand right in the same grave with Walter," Bruce says defiantly. "At least now Walter's equal to a part of that white deputy." Bruce looks back at Carrie and Earlene, well out of earshot from them. "Ma woman got so sick and upset after seein' both them bodies, especially that white man's body," he says facing back around, "we thought the baby was a-comin' out of her right then and there."

The tall man stares at Henry. "Bruce said Snodgress died near your land, Henry." The lanky man looks around and goes on. "Is Bruce just sayin' he heard that white boy braggin' that he helped kill the deputy just to protect you?"

"What the hell's wrong with you, Alexander?" Bruce exclaims at the thin, towering man. "After Sarah taught Henry to speak as good as any of them, don't you think he's know how to express hisself? If Henry killed that man, he would have told us, nigga!"

Henry leans against the ditch wall and shakes his head in sorrow. "A bullet—even one from an elephant rifle like mine—doesn't tear a man apart like Snodgress was, the way Caleb and you, Bruce, described him. No, I didn't kill him, but my poor boy was there and saw it all, like I told some of you." Henry goes on, "It was Dane. He pushed Snodgress into the path of the train."

"I thought I knew Dane Tucker as well as any colored could," whispers Andy, actually crying and struggling back to his brother for moral support. "But now I tell you, Dane Tucker is a madman. My God, a madman!"

"As for my boy," Henry tells the others, as the sobbing brothers continue quietly speaking between themselves, at the end of the trench, as Henry goes on. "I thought I had comforted Caleb, but he's still troubled by the sight of that slaughter and washes his hands several times a day after parts of Snodgress's body got on them."

Amos and Andy again look at one another, climb from the trench and run away, trying to hide their tears from the men and not to vomit, their lifelong secret tearing them apart.

"Why them two running away like that?" asks one of the trench men, as he watches the brothers fleeing across the field.

"Afraid of the white folk killin' white folk and them next, I guess," says Bruce while watching the brothers enter their plantation shack and close the door behind them. Bruce turns his sights back to Henry. "But why them white folks now killin' white folks like that, Henry?"

"Guess it's all that talk about the colonel's gold," one of the trench diggers says, looking at Henry for confirmation, then over his shoulder and whispering. "Maybe that deputy was out there thinkin' you knew about that gold, Henry, the gold that that Metcalfe fellow been talkin' about in town. And Snodgress was killed over the gold. I wouldn't put it past Dane to do that. Kill fo' money."

"Metcalfe better stop talkin' so much 'round white folks befo' they kill him, too," says Bruce. He glances back at his family. "Carrie wants to move to San Francisco. Thinks folks in California be mo' civilized, and I agree. Come with us, Henry. You and Caleb befo' they kill you. You done already lost yo' land. California, that's where the real gold is . . . In California where it never rains, and the grass is kept green with money."

"Yeah, Henry, leave while you can," says another worker nodding in agreement. "Even if you move away, Sarah'll give you a fair price fo' yo' land, once the courts return it to you."

Henry looks over at Sarah, sitting on a nearby rise, under a tree in the shade with Caleb.

"Don't mention any of this to Sarah," Henry cautions Bruce and the others. "Caleb and I haven't told her of these killings. She's got all the problems she can handle right now."

"Let's hope God doesn't wash His hands of us pitiful, po' humans, Henry," Bruce replies, "befo' yo' boy can help us the way that Naomi done says fate done thrown his way."

Bruce sets his old sights on the distant manor's kitchen window. Naomi is behind the glass with a bowl of water. The others follow his gaze to her. She places the bowl on the window shelf and begins washing her hands in the water; then she backs away from the sun-reflecting glass, and as if absorbed into the shadows of eternity, as if—to some of them—a signal that they are facing the end of time.

"Mo' and mo'," the tall man says gazing at the heavens, "it seems that God is preparin' that retribution that Reverend Harris say gonna be called down on us, but I ain't afraid. I'm a good Christian and only hate white folk who hate me."

As concern reflects in all of their eyes, the men turn and study Caleb.

Resting in the sunlight, and with the wind blowing through his and Sarah's hair, both a well-suntanned Sarah and also Caleb, smooth of sparkling skin, gleam under the tree-defused heavenly light, and Caleb seems at peace for one of the few times since Barney's return and Flynn's withdrawal from their friendship. "And that's how the rabbit lost its tail," says Sarah to Caleb, sitting at body-length from her.

"Why did you tell me that silly story, Sarah?" asks Caleb, trying to hold back a smile, as he toys with a dying dandelion. "When I was too young to know what hatred was, Sarah, and Colonel Cutter came back from one of his army trips and asked Flynn to wear a Klans-man's outfit that Barney had ordered made for him, and Flynn cried. Barney ripped apart Flynn's books of poetry and made him stand in the corner for hours in that little boy's Klan's outfit, and later, when I told you about it, you made Flynn and me feel better by telling us that same rabbit story." No longer smiling, Caleb glances at the barn, some yards away. "Is Flynn being forced to wear one now, Sarah? A Klansman's robe? Or is he doing so willingly?"

"He's been asked to do so by Barney, Caleb. But not a robe, it's something more menacing in its diguise: a business suit more befitting a young senator than sheets, but a garment of shame just the same. A United States Senator is a noble calling, but not if he is wearing sheep's clothing to cover his fangs of blood, and I'll make sure Flynn remembers that. Is that okay with you?"

"Sure, Sarah. It's okay."

"And, Caleb, I don't really know why I told you that story, just now, unless it's your turn to make me feel better about you and Flynn and how the two of you have grown apart." Caleb turns away, his sights on his working father and the diggers a tenth of a mile behind them.

"Caleb," whispers Sarah, retrieving a new law book from the grass at her far side and handing it to him. "This is from me and from Flynn to you."

She watches Caleb tightening his grip on the rare leather-bound first-edition law book. Caleb then faces the barn. Flynn and overweight Benny Hill are standing high on the hay loft by the open loft door while holding onto pitchforks and watching him and Sarah.

"Flynn," asks Benny. "You've fergotten Caleb, now, haven't you, like your pa told you to when he left fer Washington?"

Flynn doesn't answer; sweating, he wipes his forehead on his sleeve, and returns to pitching hay down to the horses and cows through a hole in the floor. Benny, however, remains at the loft door, scoffing down at Caleb.

"I would like to buy something for you, Caleb," says Sarah, worriedly glancing up at the loft and at Benny, then back at Caleb. "Something special that's just from me. How would you like a new violin, and—"

"I don't think I'll ever play again. It doesn't seem right with our land's gone, with the killings and—"

"What killings, Caleb?"

Caleb had forgotten that Henry doesn't want to trouble Sarah with news of more killing at this time. "I just see no sense in pretending to be content by playing, that's all."

"Live for the future, Caleb, not with all those murders from the past, and would you refuse to continue making the music with Flynn that the angels in God's heaven love so much?"

Stirring about, Caleb again fixes his sights on Henry and the workers behind them. "I'd like to talk longer, Sarah, but Papa and I are paid to work, not to sit and converse while others work."

"Caleb," Sarah whispers, reaching over and stroking his hand, her blue eyes engaging his sandy-yellow ones. "You and Henry are not just field hands that work here. You're more than that, much more. One day, God willing, I'll be able to explain everything to you. Stay, Caleb, awhile longer." She taps the ground with her hand. "Here. Sit by me. We've had so little time together, you and I." As Caleb slides closer, Sarah goes on. "Closer. Sit closer, Caleb."

On the hay loft, Flynn puts aside the pitchfork and returns to Benny at the loft door. "Why the hell are you spying on my mother and him, Benny?" He follows Benny's angry gaze to Caleb, who is settling next to Sarah, their arms brushing against one another. After settling in, Caleb smells the sweetness of her perfume feathering into the warm air and awakening his memory, a perfume Sarah had searched for and had repurchased for over eighteen years and protected in a thumb-size, airtight, crystal perfume bottle and has sparingly used: a popular fragrance given to her by Henry when she was only fourteen, a sweetness which Caleb clearly recalls, having smelled it as a young boy when he was being held in Sarah's arms.

"My mother wore that same perfume, Sarah," whispers Caleb, startling Sarah. "I have no picture of her face in my mind, but up to age five, I smelled it and still recognize it." Sarah sits there near tears, as Caleb goes on. "Did I ever ask you if you knew her, Sarah? My mother? Papa always changes the subject when I mention her. It makes him sad, so I try not to ask him much about her anymore."

Sarah breaks down and cries, and Caleb is profoundly touched and wants to embrace her, but knowing that she is the wife of the Grand Wizard—can only sit and watch.

So does Benny. "Is she crying, Flynn? Your mother?" Flynn remains silent, his sights on Sarah, as Benny goes on. "What the fuck did that coon say to your mother to make her cry like that, Flynn?"

"Hey, man," says Flynn. He nudges Benny away from the loft door. "That's none of your business and between them!" Flynn hesitates and looks back at his mother and at Caleb before returning to his work.

Sarah dries her eyes on her handkerchief and whispers, "I'm sorry, Caleb," she says and then faces Henry, then Caleb. "You see, I happened to know that your mother loved your father very much, and he loved her with his entire soul, and I know that she loved you, and—"

"Still, Sarah. Papa still loves her as much today as he did then. Sometimes I hear him in his room praying for God to look after her, even though she died a long time ago."

Sarah squeezes his hand with so much love and compassion that even the birds in the surrounding trees break into song. "Now," she says, "where was I? Oh, yes. The rabbit."

"No more rabbit stories," Caleb says, erupting into laughter as she tickles him. "You're as bad as Papa, Sarah, when he tickles us and tucks me and Flynn into bed. We're not babies anymore."

"You are . . . To me. I held you in my arms when you were—" She quickly covers up the mistake by adding. "Once, that is, when your mother handed you to me."

"She did? What did she look like, my mother, Sarah? I know she was light complexioned, and at times—when I go to town—some of the whites and colored call me a half-breed, but that's okay. My mother . . . Was she kind like you and was she—"

"She was," begins Sarah, overwhelmed, having opened the door to that intense inquiry. She whispers, "I promise you that I'll always defend you and Henry."

"Papa and I do not wish for anyone to be harmed or die for us, Sarah," says Caleb, getting to his feet. "That's what happens to whites who speak up for colored. Maybe even to the wife of the Wizard. But I can take care of me and Papa. Besides Papa's rifles, I've purchased a revolver. You might want to protect us with your connections, but Colonel Cutter isn't dead, just out of town. Barney's voice, with or without a telephone, reaches from Washington to Flynn, even as we sat here talking. That's why Flynn is always with Benny now. Benny is a Klan through and through. Now talk is that the Klan not only wants our water and land—they've obviously already achieved that goal—they'll not be satisfied until they kill us."

"Sweet Jesus, Caleb! Don't even think that. Flynn and I would never let that happen!"

"When you read those stories to us, Flynn used to suck his thumb when he was afraid. He no longer sucks his thumb, Sarah. If Flynn follows the colonel into the Klan and leads those men against me and Papa, I'd not hesitate to kill him."

"Will you help me to my feet, Caleb?" Sarah asks, trembling, filled with unbelievable and earth-shaking dread, white of arms, face and lips.

Caleb guides her upward and Sarah walks away, totally lost and speechless. High in the loft, Flynn stops pitching hay. He—along with Benny—watches his mother and then Caleb as he runs back to the ditch to rejoin Henry, the law book left lying on the ground, its pages blowing in the wind.

The following day, Shadow Grove's men work late into the night on the pipeline. Henry notices Flynn several yards away in the dark, defying Barney's order that he's to stay out of the fields. The blonde boy can hardly hold onto a muddy bucket of water, which he has been pouring into the steeply-banked ditch to soften the ground, as the men there dig, and then he would dip the muddy water from the trenches if things got too sloppy wet for the workers. Exhausted, he stands there, not only dirty but very much alone. That part of the ditch is close to where Caleb sat with Sarah and said he would kill Flynn if he attempted to harm him or Henry. Flynn looks at the nearby law book that he and Sarah bought for Caleb; the book is covered with dust and dew. Henry looks behind him at Caleb, his shirt tied about his slender waist, as he shovels dirt out of the ditch onto the bank, the sweat dripping from his young, muscular body. It's clear to Henry that Caleb knows Flynn is standing across from them, but Caleb refuses to look up at his friend. Flynn, however, gazes over at Caleb and then quietly disappears into the shadows.

As night falls, Henry continues ripping into the earth with his pick, viciously attacking a section of hard soil, the sounds of his pick—striking rocks and those of others attacking the same line of rocks in the endless section of trenches—is heard near and far over the night-dark land. Soon, one-by-one, the worn-out men pack up and meander for home, lighting their way with their lanterns and dragging their tired bodies along. From the manor's rooftop widows' walk, Sarah watches her home-bound field hands and then turns her attention to Henry and Caleb. Henry now knows, from Naomi and from an undeniable feeling, that his days on earth are numbered, and he's determined to finish his work before his time is up. Caleb—who will never leave his father's side, not if it means leaving Henry alone to work his heart out—continues matching Henry's might, stroke for stroke with his pick, their ditch illuminated by other's left behind, glowing lanterns, the Brooks' grunts and picks seemingly neverending.

Out of sight, at the front of the manor, a spanking brand-new Rolls Royce drones up the tree-lined drive to the manor, and Barney alights, carrying several expensive gift-wrapped packages in his arms; he enters the house and hurriedly climbs the winding staircase to Flynn's bedroom. Noticing Flynn's dropped, muddy shoes, his muddy shirt and jeans, Barney then looks at Flynn asleep on his bed, in his underwear, totally exhausted, the mud still on his hands and face. Barney places the gifts on a close-by chair. One special gift he carries to Flynn's piano and leans it on the keyboard; it's a rare, handwritten manuscript of Beethoven. Having had a difficult time in D.C., Barney had desperately attempted to return home early to be with his son. Now, with the hallway light seeping in behind him, in the semidarkness of the room, the man, who loves his son more than his own life, stands with a glow on his face, as he marvels at his beautiful, blonde, fair-skinned boy. He turns from Flynn and begins picking up his worn-out son's soiled clothing and drops them into Flynn's nearby clothes hamper. Looking about, Barney is filled with elation. Every day, the room tells him a bit more about Flynn: Flynn's books of poetry—which Barney now appreciates—books of philosophy, works by Homer, a carefully hung tennis racket, and—finally—Flynn's baby grand piano near the open window—a piano that, when Flynn's satin fingers plays it, the music soothes Barney's soul. He had tried all those years that he was away to have other children with different women, but it was not to be. Now, even his sexual desires are gone. They've been replaced by his boundless passion for wealth and power and the interminable drive to control the world through occult forces and give it all to Flynn.

In church, Reverend Miller often speaks of one's cup running over for those who are blessed to be a member of his congregation. For Barney, Flynn is the only cup to hold his abundance of love. Feeling that he must compete with God for Flynn's love and admiration troubles him. Barney's heart races with rage every time he sees something on Flynn's bedroom walls, something which he tries not to look at when entering the room: fourteen stations of the cross, plaques symbolizing the fourteen times Christ fell under the weight of the world—that infamous cross—on His way to His crucifixion, in order to save mankind from Lucifer.

Barney knows he could ask Flynn to remove the symbols of Christ, but it would not be wise, not at this time, anyway. He glances at Flynn's bedside table and stepping to it, he lingers there looking down at a glass and wood, framed photo carefully positioned to face Flynn's bed, a photo of Barney proudly wearing his colonel's uniform. Smiling, Barney picks up still another framed photo from the table, a more recent one of him and Flynn jokingly pressing their cheeks together, as they playfully grin into the camera. Carefully replacing the photo, and smiling all the more, he turns and stands by the bed, and strokes Flynn's soft hair. The sound of Henry's pick draws him to the opened window, where he glares down at the conscious black man.

He starts to close the window and to walk away, but instead catches a glimpse of Sarah on the house's projected, side-angled widows' walk. After following her sights to Henry, Barney quickly makes his way from the room, leaving the window open. When the bedroom door snaps shut, Flynn opens his eyes, rolls over and then goes back to sleep.

Sometime later, in the ditch, Henry gazes over at Caleb, who is also asleep on his feet next to him leaning against the ditch, the shovel still in Caleb's hand. The gentle man reaches over and takes the shovel from Caleb, removes the shirts from around the exhausted boy's waist, eases him out of the ditch and onto the ground and covers him with the shirts, then goes back to work.

"The day's finished, Henry," says field boss Collins, tired and disheveled looking, suddenly appearing over the ditch on his horse. "We can't help Sarah if we work ourselves to death. Go home and sleep in your own bed tonight for a change, and get plenty of rest like the others." He glances down at Caleb. "Wake up Caleb from that damp ground before he catches his death of cold. We'll start again in two days. All of us need the time off, and we'll win the fight against this drought; and, as God is my witness, we'll also fight together to get your place returned to you. Okay?"

Not until Henry—after nodding in agreement—awakens Caleb, and both he and Caleb extinguish the lanterns and walk away from the ditch, does Collins leave, stirring his horse to the barn, where white pigeons, roosting on the barn roof, are awakened and look down at him, and then at the Brooks. From her private world on the manor's roof, Sarah whispers, "You won't let the workers give up on the pipeline, and I won't give up on reclaiming your land for you, as God is my witness. Take care of yourself and my son, my love."

In the shadow of one of the several sprawling house's chimneys, Colonel Cutter glares out at Sarah, then down at Caleb and Henry. Sarah—unaware that she's in extreme harm's way—continues watching as Henry, several paces ahead of Caleb, can't wait to get to their nearby wagon and onto its half-load of cotton. When Caleb—bringing up the rear—passes the law book, he stops and looks down at it, his heart melting with the image of Flynn also sadly looking down at the rejected gift of healing. Wiping his hands on his trousers, Caleb picks up the precious book, takes out his handkerchief and brushes it off and carries it with him. At the wagon, Henry moves aside Caleb's cased violin—from where Caleb had left it on the wagon from the time he had stopped playing it and picked up the rifle and had ventured into the woods to defend Henry. As Henry climbs onto the cotton, up on the roof, ever so slowly, Barney moves toward Sarah, his fingernails digging into the palms of his clenched fists, his eyes oozing with loathing. A profound quiet comes over Shadow Grove. Neither Henry nor Caleb seems to notice anything wrong, as Old Clara shivers, shaking her head and flapping her ears, a sign to Caleb that she is only ready to go home.

"The old girl knows the way, Caleb," murmurs Henry from the soft-laden, wagon-load of cotton, as Caleb arrives and places the law book next to his violin case. "We'll unload this cotton tomorrow. Toss the reins over the seat, and come sleep by me, son. Sleep at ma side while I can yet say you're still my little boy, who gives this tired soul so much gladness in these times of sadness for Sarah and for—"

"Sarah. We really love her don't we, Papa? Out of anger, Papa, I told her I'd never play my violin again." When Henry, half asleep, doesn't answer, Caleb smiles. "Go to sleep, Papa." He whispers. "I'll watch over you for a change." as Henry drifts off to deep sleep; Caleb looks at Old Clara. "Home, Old Clara," he calls, setting the faithful old creature into motion, and then removing the back-rest section of the seat and sitting with his long legs dangling beside Henry's head, Caleb retrieves his violin from the case and begins to adjust its strings.

On the roof, Sarah senses someone behind her and turns around, then gasps. Barney knocks her down, sending the white pigeons rocketing off the barn roof and into the night.

"You nigger-loving bitch," Barney hisses, yanking her to her feet. "If it wasn't for our son down in his room, I'd throw you off this goddamn roof right this goddamn, fucking minute! Does Flynn know you lowered yourself to that nigger? Does he?" He slaps her and then drags her to the far end of the roof and to an attic entrance door, away from the main section of the house, under which are only spare rooms. After entering the attic with her, he pulls Sarah to his demonic-inspired room, quickly unlocks the solid, oak door with the old key he retrieves from under the floor board and pushes her inside the darkened quarters, where she stumbles back against Hitler's Nazi coat hanging on the wall. With moonlight sweeping into the attic from the opened roof door, a stunned Sarah sees a large photo of Adolf Hitler hanging next to the coat. There is also a small altar in the room with a miniature, star-pointed, bull's horn the likes of his mother's grave marker.

"If you scream no one will hear you," he hisses. "Earlier, I arranged a meeting in town, but now I'm going to move that goddamn meeting up, right up to that nigger's grave! This business of you sneaking around with Henry Brooks is over: His land and that fucking son of his. Over, you hear! And you will remained locked up here until I get back, and when I do, Caleb half-breed Brooks will be motherless, fatherless and dead."

Barney slowly closes the door, as if to terrorize her all the more, his eyes of death glaring in at her, the half moonlight and part pitch enveloping a horrified Sarah, as the door shuts. Sarah fears for Henry and Caleb as she listens to Barney's key turn in the keyway, locking the door firmly behind him. As Barney replaces the key under the floorboard, down in his room, Flynn sits straight up in bed. He had heard a struggle on the roof and thought he has been dreaming, and, now, speculating over it, he turns his sights to the window and the sounds of Caleb's distant violin strings weaving themselves magically though the warm night air and into his room: "Danny Boy." The tune is not only the favorite of Henry's, it was the love of Doctor and Mrs. Winthrop's hearts. Flynn slips out of bed, goes to the window, gazes into the moonlit night and sees Caleb playing while traveling over a distant hill in the wagon. The accomplished blonde teenager hurries to his bathroom, washes his hands and face, moves to his piano, sits, slides aside the rare manuscript and begins playing "Danny Boy" while focusing out the window at Caleb and Henry, as do the plantation's workers along the wagon's way—men, women and children—listening and watching from their shack doors and opened windows on the hot night, and now being soothed by something more rewarding to them than immediate sleep, the sounds and sights of musical love, as Old Clara, her head low, ever so gently tugs the creaking wagon up the dry-grass slope and across the ridge, Caleb traveling backwards playing "Danny Boy," silhouetted against the full moon.

In the downstairs den, Barney sits in his swivel chair drumming his fingers against his desk, while holding onto a briefcase. He stops drumming and listening to Caleb's violin and Flynn's stirring piano performance, neither boy realizing what Barney does, that it's a haunting, lyrical message between two brothers; as Barney's blood boils, he senses that someone is in the room looking at him and whirls the chair about. Standing just inside the open, sliding doors, by a table, on which is a pitcher of ice water and a glass, Naomi glares over at him.

"You know, don't you, Naomi? Somehow you know. I can feel it. That strange mind of yours knows that I found out about Henry and Sarah. That's why you're here." He leaps to his feet and shoves the heavy desk to one side, sending his pens, papers, and the telephone falling to the floor. "My dutiful Sarah is Caleb's mother, his nigger no-good, bastard mother!"

Upstairs—after hearing muffled voices and the desk sliding, along with the phone crashing to the floor, Flynn is filled with anxiety. He stops playing and begins hurriedly slipping into dry clothing. Downstairs, Naomi is anything but afraid. "Lucifer has deepened his hold on you, Barney Cutter," she tells him. "But if you know about Sarah, it was meant for you to find out by Someone far greater than the devil to hasten you onto the road of the cross in the battle of your life. Flynn is staying away from Caleb, because he thinks you'll hurt Caleb. Why destroy your son and push him into the arms of the father of hell along with you? Where is Sarah, Sir? What did you do to her, damn you?"

"None of your goddamn business, bitch!" Barney shouts. "Tell me, old woman, does my son know about Caleb or Henry and Sarah?"

"He does not."

"Good. You keep it that way. Not a word from you to him. I'll tell him at the right time. Who else knows of this? Answer me!"

"No one else, and as for you and your 'right time,' you mean when you feel it will bring the highest degree of hatred of Caleb and Sarah to Flynn before you kill them and me. You sadistic, damn devil! That's when you'll tell him."

Barney slams his fist onto the desk, exploding two of the legs, and the impact of his blow causes the desk to topple onto its long-side edge. Without her full range of power, Naomi steps back from Barney's might, her eyes wide and reflecting fear for the first time. "No one!" he hisses, "and I mean no one must know about this interracial shit outside of this house. I will not permit the Winthrop name and Flynn's future, as a political giant, to be crushed by this scandal."

"The Winthrop name," says Naomi, lowering her voice. "I will never cast a shadow on the good name of Doctor and Mrs. Winthrop by mentioning this to Flynn at this time—but not because of what you want." She glances at the massive den doors, slides them together, and goes on. "If those two beautiful boys—the way they feel toward each other right now—if they knew they're brothers they might not ever—"

"Brothers! You black ape! My son will be the Grand Wizard and unite the entire Klan nation and become a well-respected U.S. Senator and president of this country, and you are never again—if you value your life—to ever speak of them as brothers."

"He will never be president of this country," exclaims Naomi. "That has already been decided and belongs to a poor, humble newsboy. And if Flynn lives long enough to cast off this evil spell on him and does so, he will become a senator, the humble boy's right hand. It is so written and so it will be, otherwise, all is lost."

Whipping out his .45, he points it at Naomi, then he replaced the weapon in his shoulder holster.

Barney knows that he cannot kill Naomi in the house, and there is no time to take her elsewhere.

Naomi exclaims, "What kind of evil-possessed men are you people to teach children to lust for human blood, like this boy Burt, who bragged about killing poor, Crazy Walter and that deputy? Is that what you want for Flynn? Answer me you son-of-a-bitch! What kind of men are you?"

"I'm he who prevails over all weak, simple-minded, sons-of-bitches, nigger fools like you, the sleepers of this world!" Barney eyes glow red with rage, causing Naomi to back away even more in distress. "Wake up, Naomi and join the race for wealth and power in this godless world." He shakes his finger at her. "You were gifted by God and yet work as a common maid. You who still have some power and much fucking worth left in you, bitch! Lucifer would give up a hundred million of his followers for someone like you and welcome you with open arms and shower you with wealth, even as he will generously reward me and my son."

"My Lord said it first. Get thee behind me, Satan. I will never betray my God."

The power of Satan rises up out of Barney's red eyes, and the force of Satan slams Naomi backwards into the wall, cracking the plaster. She then feels about her eyes.

"My God," Naomi gasps, striking out at the Klansman with her arms and hands, as a cloudy, white membrane seals itself over her pupils. "I can't see!" As Barney laughs at her, Naomi stops grappling and calls out, "My Lord, with Barney having this kind of power, Caleb can't take him on alone, not against him, Dane, Flynn and the devil, and now that young boy Burt, the duplicate of one of Reverend Miller's snakes, but with Your help, I'll fight Barney Cutter tooth and nail at Caleb's side, blind or not. Guide me to this mad dog, Lord, that I might choke the life out of him."

"Burt! That poor-ass, sweet-smelling, street-walking punk!"

494

"Yes, the rotten, sick boy you invited here to work on this good land to be an example for Master Flynn, you cursed-dog-of-a-man!"

Naomi blindly charges toward Barney's voice. He steps aside, he the cat, she the mouse. "For your information, Burt or that Marcus boy doesn't work here anymore. I fired their stupid asses, making a damn fool of themselves by letting Caleb Brooks get the better of them in the store in front of half the damn plantation workers."

Again, Naomi rushes forth and falls over the desk, and her hand lands on the telephone breaking her finger. Seizing hold of the phone, she hurls it in the direction of Barney's voice.

"You stupid, black, old fools!" he says, catching the phone in midair, preventing the long cord from snapping. While Naomi struggles to her feet, Barney puts the phone aside. "Now get the hell out of my sight before I put my foot right up your ass," he tells her, "and take you to the roof anyway, and guide you over the side." Barney moves in and slaps her. "You've spoken your last damn speech in this house about Caleb or anything else. 'Chosen one' my white ass!" He slaps her again. "Say that you reject your God!" he hisses, again slapping her. "Say it!"

Even as she had taken the same kind of slap from the German, years ago, Naomi takes the beating without muttering a sound, and, suddenly, her eyes clear up, her finger heals, and she sees again, causing Barney to cease battering her, and now he steps back, as she focuses those intense eyes on him. "Out of your own mouth," she says. "You have called Caleb what he is, the 'chosen one,' the new Disciple of Christ." Naomi holds her hand against the side of her face to soothe the pain, and goes on. "And so that you will know that heaven's eyes of justice are locked onto you, Colonel Cutter, when you kill Burt—as I say you will and in the manner of that which befell John the Baptist, Jesus, Himself, will forgive Burt his sins, but your gruesome act will send the doves of peace flying from the roof of Flynn's red house of blood and from Shadow Grove, never to return until you are dead."

Barney points at the Winthrops' family Bible, resting on the table beside the pitcher of ice water, and he hisses. "John the Baptist, you say? You people don't own God, no more than my mother did! Reverend Miller has found countless passages in that damnable, so-called Holy Book, which praises men like me for saving the human race, Paul for one!" He retrieves the phone off the edge-resting desk and hurriedly dials it.

"Move it up an hour!" he says after a voice answers on the other end of the line. "What? I don't care how damn late it is. Everyone! Be there! Tell Sheriff Richards if he wants me to save his job for him, I want him and his men . . ." he again scowls at Naomi and then continues, ". . . to show those black apes in Nigger Town just who the hell they're fucking with by taking those factory jobs away from our kind. No! I'm no longer concerned about how Sarah feels about those people! Show them darkys that I'm back and that their demigod, Caleb Brooks or all the protest marchers in this goddamn world won't be able to help them now! Have Richards burn down those nigger-town houses." He slams down the receiver, his blue eyes of rage cutting into Naomi, who has covered her mouth in shock after hearing that the homes in Colored Town are to be destroyed. "You heard right, woman, the coons are doomed! And neither will anyone be able to help Sarah now," he tells the alarmed woman.

"Sweet Jesus," she exclaims, "you wouldn't hurt all those people or Sarah. Not your wife. Not Sarah?"

"Well, I'll be damned," Colonel Cutter says. "The witch seems to be human after all. She actually didn't know that I had it out with Sarah and gave her what she deserved. What'd God do, clip those holy wings of yours, or are we whites just too dumb to know when we've been duped? You're a con woman, Naomi Bell, a goddamn good one. It wasn't you who told me through some miraculous insight of yours that I found out about Henry and Sarah, it was I who opened my big mouth and told you. It seems I'm the only one with the power around here, the power of life and death from Satan, not you, now, or Caleb from God!"

Upstairs, after having tried to listen and make out what Barney and Naomi were yelling about, and having failed, Flynn nervously begins tying his shoelaces—which he had deliberately left untied and now slowly ties them, hoping that the trouble will be over before he ventures down stairs, as the yelling continues from the den.

"Yes my wings are clipped as was said they would be," yells Naomi to Barney, "and I've lost most of the power that was entrusted to me. And yes, you snake in the grass, you have the upper hand over this simple woman, but what powers I had are mostly in another's hands now, the hands of someone who doesn't want them or realize what he has is also the awesome energy of the sun over life and death. That's why in my moment of weakness—for the second time—I failed my God and doubted if Caleb could survive you and yours, and I was blinded by my lack of faith, but if that lethal force of thunder and lightning that's now pent up in him can be brought to life, he will be more than a match against you and Satan whenever this loving, innocent, unwilling, manchild decides to call upon it. And when you meet this 'chosen one' on the battlefield along the road of Christ—God willing—Caleb will kill you. Now, what have you done to my little girl, you white, son-of-a-bitch! Where is Sarah? Tell me, or," she shouts, pointing at the Winthrops' Bible, "I swear on that Holy Bible, power or no power, I'll scratch out your eyes!"

When she rushes at him, Cutter points at the Bible and exclaims, "Show her your strength, my lord and king!"

The large, two-thousand-two-hundred and sixty-six-page heavy, leather-bound Bible explodes off the table and hurls itself across the room, knocking Naomi backwards off her feet. When the Holy Book bounces off of her and hits the floor next to her, it erupts into flames and Naomi frantically rolls away from it and staggers to her feet once more.

"Bring on your Caleb Brooks!" exclaims Barney, grinning down at the Bible and then picking up his briefcase.

Naomi turns ashen as she watches the Bible being consumed in flames, and she whirls back and faces Cutter, her awesome sights boring into him. "May the Lord strike you down that you may linger on your bed near death with bed sores and maggots crawling out of your flesh, so that you may painfully suffer in the thoughts of the evil that you and your Klan and the devil have done to this world."

"Money controls this world, Naomi, and I have lots of it." He opens the den door and yells toward the staircase. "Flynn, get dressed and get down here!"

"Money," Naomi hisses. "Satan needs tons of it—the thing that he promises you, ever since he tried to tempt Jesus by offering our Lord the wealth of the world, money is the one thing God will not let him create. So he needs evil souls like you lusting after it to work tirelessly to earn it for him, in order that he can use it to spread his malevolence, while God's love is based, not on the worldly things of life, but on humility and pure love, which is everlasting."

Naomi picks up the pitcher and pours water from it onto the Bible, smothering the fire, Barney pushes her aside, but Naomi drops the glass pitcher, shattering it, and she doggedly scratches her way back in front of him, her sights locked on the key strung about his neck, the key that locks the door to his control over his fellow human beings, his and Satan's millions. As she reaches at him for the key, Barney violently slaps her hand away. With her face distorted in pain, grunting and groaning, trying to summon up even a small amount of her diminished power, Naomi again reaches at him, and when she does, Barney—once more thinking that she is trying to choke him—bites down on his lower lip, rises up on the tips of his toes and draws back with the steel-lined briefcase to flatten her for good, and as he draws back his arm and hand to deliver that deadly blow, a spark arcs from Naomi's fingertips to the key, jolting the Grand Wizard back on his heels. Stunned, but not out, Barney stumbles forward again and, this time, he slams the full weight of briefcase down on her shoulder, and Naomi falls back in agonizing pain, groaning.

"Flynn!" Barney yells. Then, he sees Flynn, who is standing at the foot of the staircase and looking wide-eyed in shock at the two of them. "Come on, boy, you're going with me."

"No, Flynn! It's your mother! Stay here and help me find her."

"Father!"

"There's nothing wrong with Sarah, son, that a little quiet won't cure," he scolds, daring Flynn to disobey him, then faces Naomi, causing Flynn to turn absolutely anemic. "When I get back, I want you out of this house, Naomi, or I'll personally hang you by your neck, so help me your God!"

"There is no help from God for you!" yells Naomi, raising goose bumps on Flynn's arms. "This day," she warns, "when you enter your ancestors' evil town of Cutterville, and your feet touch the courthouse property of shame, Reverend Miller's church clock of vice will begin tolling the midnight hour, signaling your last days left of absolute power on earth before you face your living nightmare."

"Who is my damn living nightmare? Who else has the power, but me?"

"Caleb!" she screams, shocking Flynn with that explosive response. "That's who, and he will either kill you or be killed, but, now, that fatal battle can't be called off even for Flynn's sake, even if all of us involved prayed to God that it could." She gazes from the destroyed Bible to Flynn, then quickly looks away from him, as if from evil, and admonishes him by condemning him through Barney. "It's you and yours you must worry about now, Barney Cutter, for Caleb will show no mercy on you or

Flynn if . . ." she gazes down at the desecrated Bible, "he decides to pick up this Holy Gauntlet thrown down by you."

Flynn has never been so afraid in all of his life. Even when almost drowning, while attempting to rescue Caleb, he knew no such fear. Now he trembles at the sight of Naomi and fears for his entire family during that heated exchange. Colonel Cutter guides his son to the front door, all the time Flynn continues glancing worriedly back at Naomi, as he stumbles from the house and is driven speedily toward Cutterville in his father's symbol of money and power, the new Rolls Royce car, a car—to Flynn—permeated with the smell of death. When the dust settles, Naomi slowly opens her hand and looks at her palm. The key to the wine cellar is firmly in her grip. She looks about then runs screaming through the house. "Sarah! Where are you, child?"

35

The Clock Strikes Twelve

At the courthouse, inside Chambers' private restroom, Dane Tucker is conversing with the badly-aging, old judge—who hardly hears him. Chambers hasn't slept for more than four hours at a time since hearing the news that Carlton's wife was cursed and possibly by Caleb. Now, Chambers wonders about his lifelong participation in the separation of the races, or if Mrs. Carlton's recovery was a stroke of luck and had nothing to do with God or with Caleb. As Chambers scrubs his hands in the sink near an open door—which is marked 'Private,' when viewed from the outside and the courthouse lobby—the tired old adjudicator knows that it would be political suicide to even think that Caleb Brooks is from God. Drying his hands with his monogrammed towel, Chambers walks Dane to the door and pauses. "I'm not at liberty to comment on any of that," he tells Dane, attempting to be polite. "I'm sorry, but you'll have to ask Barney yourself about what he may or may not have. I've never heard of Barney having money, a lot or a little. I can tell you this, though, Barney's lit a fire under all our butts tonight. So stay away from him is my counsel. He's never been this agitated, ordering us, including the senator, to meet here tonight. Goodnight, Dane. There's much work to be done. Barney and a lot of important people will be arriving soon."

"Not all of us," hisses Dane. "He left me out of that meeting, me and people like me, the common white folks, the foundation of the Klan, the ones affected the most by you higher-ups at these secret gatherings."

"Who the hell do you think you are," blasts Chambers, slinging the towel on the floor. "You couldn't even shine the shoes of these powerful men coming here tonight." He looks down at the towel. "Now, you pick up that towel, Dane Tucker, and get the hell out of here, and never let me see you again unless it's before my court, and I have to sentence your dumb ass to life imprisonment."

Dane picks up the towel, hands it to Chambers, and storms into the lobby. He bitterly looks back at the exhausted judge, who slams the restroom door in his face and locks it. Backing up, Dane stumbles over a scrub bucket of water and nearly falls on the wet floor and then trips over Burt, who is behind him, and, finally, does fall. Burt—who had just been given the job as the courthouse night janitor by Chambers, as a favor to Barney, who sensed that the young boy would be useful if kept close—hurriedly helps Dane to his feet. "I'm so sorry, Dane," he says. "I heard what that old goat Chambers said to you. You and I are just as good as they are."

"Get your damn hands off me!" Dane screams, shoving Burt away. "I'm not like you. You're a dumb, white cracker, ignorant, piss-ass, dick-sucking, toilet-cleaner!"

Dane elbows Burt off his feet and onto the floor, and then storms from the building, climbs into one of his second-hand, car-lot vehicles and roars into the night, passing swarms of hood-wearing Klansmen, club-carrying white civilians, and armed sheriff deputies, who are chasing coverall-wearing, black factory workers and black, non-factory workers down the street and out of Cutterville, as parts of Colored Town burn.

"I am somebody!" Dane yells as he drives away. "Somebody! Not no damn nobody!"

A half hour later, the smartly dressed armed state motorcycle police are everywhere and are truly the "somebodies" with their legal powers of life and death in their holsters to shoot and kill, and their badges proudly on their chests authorizes them to brutalize and to terrorize even over the local law in Cutterville. These elitist officers ignore the blacks' cries for help, as they flee by them and down the street, chased by the mob. The well-trained motorcycle officers have but one thought in mind: to protect an official-looking black limousine, which they roll along ahead of and behind, a limousine that comes to a smooth stop on the courthouse's red-brick, horse-shaped driveway, and has the state flags of Georgia mounted on its front fenders, a local tradition to honor its passenger and signaling an even bigger "somebody" is present. A tall man, wearing a dark suit, steps from the limo and enters the building.

When Colonel Cutter drives down Main Street with Flynn and passes the square, the town has settled down again, and the fire department can be seen fighting against the flames across the train tracks in Colored Town. Barney makes no mention of the fires, and Flynn can see that his father is purposely ignoring the burning, colored homes, and Flynn doesn't mention the fire either, although he wants to. Driving his new Rolls Royce onto the horse-shaped drive, Barney parks in front of the limousine, the state police quickly recognizing who he is and clearing their motorcycles out of the way to make room for him. Once he has parked the car, Barney looks over at Flynn, who is sitting silently in the front passenger seat, his shoulders stooped, his hands between his legs.

"You want to talk about it?" asks Barney. "About that business back there with Naomi?"

"You'll be late for your meeting with all of the questions I need to ask."

"They can wait," says Barney. "After all, you're my son." When Flynn sits there in a profound hush, Barney taps him lovingly on his thigh and says, "As you wish. This meeting, Flynn, is vital for both of us, son and might take all night. But I don't want you returning home just yet. We have to talk first. I've left the car keys in the ignition; start the motor and turn on the heater if you get cold. But switch off the ignition before you get sleepy and close your eyes. Okay?"

"Okay, but what is it that we have to talk about before I can go home, Sir?"

"When I return, we'll discuss it. I want you to hear it from me, not from your mother."

"Was Naomi right? Is something wrong with mother? You didn't hurt her, did you?"

"Are you afraid of me, Flynn?"

"No, Sir."

"Then stop calling me, 'Sir.' I'm your father, not your commanding officer. As I said, when I return, I'll explain everything. I can tell you this much, though. It concerns Caleb."

"Caleb? Is it about what people say? How he and Naomi are from God? If so, he isn't—"

"That boy? Of course he isn't from God. What makes you think I would think that? That would go against the very foundation of a superior white race. The only force in this world is infamy, like Roosevelt realized from the fanatic might of the Japs, and they would have won if not for Hitler being so stubborn. My point, Flynn, is this: this world now belongs to your father. That's enough for you to know for now."

When Flynn just sits there, Barney, clutching his briefcase, slides from the car. The moment Barney's feet touch the driveway, Miller's nearby church clock begins striking the hour of twelve. A bleached-out look crosses Barney's face, and he stares up at the gonging timepiece, recalling Naomi's prophecy:

502

This day, when you enter that evil town of Cutterville, and your feet touch the courthouse property of shame, Reverend Miller's church clock of evil will begin tolling the midnight hour signaling your last days left of absolute power on earth before you face your living nightmare.

Barney squints at a lone figure on a horse in the shadows of the corrupt church. Flynn shades his eyes against the courthouse's driveway lights shining into the car, and studies that figure: it's Caleb on Old Clara. The blonde boy sits up in the seat and looks from Caleb to his father and the state police, all following Barney's sights and looking at Caleb; several of the state lawmen take out their revolvers. Flynn watches his father with mixed emotions; Barney seems less confident now, as the clock continues to ring out the hour. Naomi's prophecy looms large in both father and son's disquieted minds, that Caleb would kill Barney. Caleb turns and rides into the night. Flynn follows his father's return sights to the clock. After watching a troubled-looking Barney continue through the line of state police, shaking their outstretched gloved hands and then entering the building, Flynn looks again at the tower clock, at the dark distance which has swallowed up Caleb, and shivering, he lies down on the rich leather car seat, rolls into a fetal position, covers the exposed side of his ear with his hand against the deathly clock's relentless reverberating, closes his eyes and sucks his thumb.

My friend, Flynn's mind whispers through his tangled thoughts. *Where are you?*

In the courthouse conference room, where Caleb had earlier hammered out his so-called agreement to reel in Sheriff Richards and his clandestine deputies, some of the same men are present, except for Dessen and Carlton. The place is filled with cigar smoke and a confusion of overlapping voices. The impressive, tall man who stepped from the limousine is United States Senior Senator Tommy Feddermann, seventy-one, with flowing white hair and with a the face of a loving grandfather; Feddermann quietly sits to the right of Barney at the large table, around which are several others, including Judge Chambers.

"Who ordered those fires extinguished in Colored Town?" asked Barney.

"I did," says Feddermann. "It was bad timing, Barney. There's an election coming up soon, and I don't need D.C. and the world breathing down my back over those burning shacks."

As the loud grumbling goes on, some in favor of raising Colored

503

Town and others not, acknowledging only the main players, Barney clears the air and gets to the point of the meeting.

"We can't all talk at once," he tells the lesser players, who immediately go silent, as Barney goes on. "If those fires can be put out, I'm okay with that. They've gotten the message by now"

"I hope this won't take long, Barney," says Feddermann. "I have to be in Macon—"

Cutter pours a stack of money from his briefcase onto the table. Feddermann excitedly gathers in the cash. "You've already given us our share," Judge Chambers says reflectively, on how Caleb predicted the recovery of Carlton's wife, and keenly aware that the angry, little man is not there, and having possibly turned his back on the Klan to save his soul. Chambers feels that the more money Barney pays them, the more Satan has his hands on his soul, and the heavier the price they all will have to pay to God when they die. "Now, what's this money for?"

The senator doesn't question the gift and extends a document to Barney. "As promised," he says. "Rescued from Pennington's vault, even as the feds swarmed all over that place, but Pennington . . . that damn fool. Suicide of all things. At least Sarah has her land deed free and clear from his bank, now, and we doctored the bank files, reflecting the final mortgage payment with the money you gave the accountants to pay it off. It's a bit unorthodox but perfectly legal in the public's eyes."

"Not Sarah's," says Barney. "My son's. This deed and Shadow Grove is Flynn's now."

"Absolutely," says the senator. "And it's been settled about Flynn, as well. He'll become an apprentice under my wing and when I retire it's all fixed with the Governor for him to step into my shoes."

After placing the deed in his briefcase, Barney says, "Now, let's move onto the matter of this upstart Caleb Brooks."

Feddermann interrupts Barney and faces the other men, while passing out shares of the money to them. "Barney sweetened the pie with this hundred thousand, because I arranged to get the deed for him." He looks at Barney, like a man not satisfied with the hundred thousand or anything else, "But—the money aside for now—let's thank about this business of Caleb Brooks for a minute. We may be opening a larger can of worms than we realize by letting the Klan kill that boy at this time. Caleb's name is even being mentioned back in Washington by religious fanatics and Northern political darkys, some of whom have sizable influence due to their longevity with the black voters maintaining them in office, like this Powell character in the House." He faces Barney.

"Let's say we let Caleb's father, who can hardly read, I'm told . . . Henry, right . . . run for a meaningless local or state office and win. Then, by carefully picking a chosen few more key, controllable coloreds like him, and putting them in office, we can capture the black vote throughout this state instead of trying to repress it in these changing times. The Senate can't go on forever blocking that anti-lynching and segregation bills, Barney, not after the war and that monstrosity dealt by Hitler to the Jews, with the world's eye now on this country testing our resolve, when it comes to freedom for our black population."

"We just tried that with Caleb. It failed. Now we influence the coons' votes with intimidation like always," says Barney. "Now let's get back to what I want to talk about: Caleb Brooks' downfall before his reputation gets totally out of hand. You said it yourself, Senator: he's even known in Washington, all because of that damn sky turning black and these fools talking about Naomi and Caleb coming from God."

Chambers, after gaining courage from the senator, now asks, "Why do you keep this woman as a maid in your house, Barney—if—as you say, she is the catalyst behind this growing fever to anoint Caleb as a little Jesus?"

"Because I don't legally own Shadow Grove!" hisses Barney. "And it seems you're suggesting that I have no control over that black witch-of-an antagonist—or over my son, or his mother." Barney slams his fist onto the table. "Or are you starting to believe that Naomi is from God? Now, there will be no more talk of Naomi, Caleb or his relationship to Flynn, as if Caleb walks on water or that Naomi's shit smells like roses, not here, not around this table, and not to me!"

"That's your right, Barney?" says Senator Feddermann. "You're the anointed one here. The savior of mankind and now with all that money."

"Who else will save this country from a sea of growing black ink and Mexican brown?" asks Barney. "Tell me! What's behind this kind of talk that we're having now?"

"Barney," says Feddermann, after getting the eye from the lesser men around him, "What's all this about you worshiping Satan? I could care less if you worship a dog, but with this country's credo based on Christianity, is it wise to openly profess a belief in a lesser god?"

"Who or what I worship is nobody's fucking business, but I'll an-

505

swer that question this one time and never ask me again. Money! That's what I worship."

Those around the table take in a deep breath and nervously chuckle now. Each of them have been voted into office by the Bible belt, but it could not have happened without spreading the fear that the baby-making blacks were gaining fast on the whites in the population race, and neither would it have happened without money to spread the message of hatred across the state and the country, and it seems Barney has lots of it to spend, now, and Tommy Feddermann sits there thinking that Barney has a little too much money, but—like the rest of them—lacks the courage to challenge him in an all-out battle for more of it.

Out in the courthouse lobby, mopping away, Burt sees Flynn approaching the building and how the state police officers are shaking his hands with the same respect they had given to the colonel. The young janitor's heart races; his dream of prominence is to be like Flynn, and own a big, fancy house and cars like the one that Barney had and the newer one he now owns; the sight of Barney's son overwhelms Burt, and in spite of the fact that Flynn had sided with Caleb on Dane's car lot, the rag-tagged young janitor tells himself that Flynn's relationship with niggers will change for the better now that the colonel has returned, and that in no time, Flynn will be as much a nigger hater as he is. After convincing himself of all of these things, Burt—bowing and grinning—hurriedly opens the door for Flynn. "Saw you and the colonel drive up in that shiny new Rolls Royce and how them there state police shook your pa's hand and now yours. Boy!" he exclaims, wiping his palms on his trousers and shaking Flynn's. "I bet them gun-totin' state cops don't give you Cutters no trouble. No, Sir! None at all!"

"I need to use the restroom," says Flynn, "if you don't mind."

"Use the judge's," says Burt. "Nothing's too good fer our next young senator."

"How do you know that? The colonel would never have told you anything about it."

Timidly, Burt looks at the judge's open restroom door. "It's over there," he says, "I just unlocked it to clean in there, that's all. Honest. Just to clean. The judge's restroom's over there, Master Flynn."

When Flynn enters the restroom, he notices another door, behind which—unknown to him—is the judicial conference room. As Flynn

506

worries about his mother and about Naomi's fight with Barney, he finds a needed distraction in examining Chambers' restroom floor, quite unlike any publicly financed restroom that he's ever been in; the floor is of polished Italian marble. Even the judge's sink has gold-plated facets. Flynn then moves to the judge's toilet with its velvet-covered seat, and he wonders if it meant that Chambers is as soft as the seat cover appears to be and as his father had said the judge was. After opening his fly, and exposing himself, he reaches down to lift the covered toilet seat, but hears his father's voice and withdraws his hand from the seat. He glances up. Barney's voice is coming from an air duct: "Caleb is dangerous. What else do we need to know?" Barney's bitter voice is heard saying.

In the lobby, Burt—mop in hand—sidles to the side of the ajar restroom door, sets his sights on Flynn's penis and then follows the startled boy's gaze to the air duct and listens as the voices continue: "Wait a damn minute, Barney," hisses the voice of Feddermann. "I'm a damn U.S. Senator, not some goddamn hatchet man."

"You're what I say you are!" shouts Barney.

Inside the conference room, Senator Feddermann looks at the others around the table and goes on. "This isn't Corregidor, Colonel! No Japanese bombs are falling on our goddamn heads to confuse us like you did that special, detail of colored soldiers on that damn piece of worthless land that this damn country lost to the Japs! I covered for you in D.C., then and this last week, when the committee called you back to the Capitol and questions came up, again, about what happened to that money on that island of hell, but what you now ask is out of the question for all of us. Be reasonable, Barney. What did I just tell you? After our victory of the Japs and Germans and those damn Wops and condemning them—as did the rest of the free world—as evil powers of mass murderers, how can we keep on with the business of lynching the coloreds and have reporters running around the country telling Americans and—I might add—the rest of the world that we're a bunch of senseless animals killing them coons? We can't. Not anymore."

"Don't lecture to me!" hisses Barney, pounding his fist on the table, once more. "You're confused as to who's in charge here, Tommy!" Barney tells Feddermann.

"Go to hell, Barney!" Feddermann hits back, "Again, we're not confused over who was in charge on Corregidor of burning that army payroll to keep it out of the hands of the Japs and didn't burn it; and why in

God's name did you send Flynn those coins? Seems some colored boy called Crazy Walter got his hands on one of them and was hanged by this hillbilly Dane Tucker. Now, the whole town's buzzing about there's gold in Cutterville and says it came from you, Barney, so don't talk down to me, not with the possibility of those rumors getting back to Washington, and the committee, once again, calls you before it!"

"Then we pay them off, dammit! This is not about a few coins or about my son who now knows he made a mistake by giving them away." Again, Barney beats up on the table, this time with his palms. "Be direct, Tommy! Spit it out! Nobody in Washington cares about a few, damn, gold coins. Is it the money? Is that what you want? More of that damn army payroll?"

"Ten goddamn million dollars, Barney," says Feddermann, pushing his extra share aside. "Where's the rest of it?"

Someone at that table, in the dimly lit room and curtained in all of that cigar smoke, sheepishly says, "We all know you did a fine job in getting the money into the States, Barney, especially with the little help that Tommy could give you at the time with the seals on those bags, but, like I said, you pulled it off and—"

"Don't patronize me," says Barney with a no-nonsense, deadly edge on his voice. He throws a pitcher of water across the room. In the restroom, Flynn jerks back in shock at the sound of glass exploding against the other side of the wall, as does Burt listening in the darkened corridor. In the conference room, silence rules until Barney again speaks. "Who else dares demand from me?" he shouts. "I have enough on all of you to bury you, if it comes to that! Who else!"

"I, for one, am too old to worry about having more money," says Chambers. "Poor Pennington. Got caught with his fucking dick up that dog's ass or pussy or whatever it was to him, and, of all things, at the bank. Seems it was Jerry MacDonnell, Barney —a friend of yours—and his cameraman, who came in through that open door after someone got poor Pennington sexually aroused and drunk enough and too much in a hurry to get back to his northside residence with his dog and, instead, stopped by the bank with it and forgot about locking the damn side door behind him."

"Or did he forget to lock it?" asks Feddermann, going on. "An intelligence man would be able to open that door. Those pictures were snapped and later sold to you. To you Barney."

"Yes, and the town benefited from it with the land I gave it. Henry's land, all of it except the lagoon and the easement to it. That water will irrigate Shadow Grove and my mother's old place. Cutterville can have enough of it to get it through the drought. Okay!"

"That water comes at the right time, Barney. The town really needs it," Mayor Sipple says, speaking for the first time. "And the citizens will build a monument to you." With a smile, Sipple picks up his money and says, "Then it's settled."

Judge Chambers picks up his share of the money and says, directing his remarks to Senator Feddermann, "Barney's been more than generous about sharing this extra money with us, including Pennington's share, so let's get on with the vote. There's too much left to discuses then to waste any more time on fruitless issues about the money or if we should kill Caleb Brooks. It should have been a done deal the minute Barney mentioned killing that half-breed trouble maker." Chambers, in the best tradition of being a politician, turns to Barney. "You ask me if I'm starting to believe in Caleb and Naomi. I hope this will make it perfectly clear to you where I stand. That boy, coming in here with those letters and demanding that we capitulate to his wishes, as if he were one of us, no, he's not God." Chambers stares Barney in his eyes and says. "Kill him." The moment he says it, a cold chill runs down the judge's back.

"All in favor of killing Caleb Brooks," Barney adds, "say 'Aye.'"

The "Ayes" follow one after the other, then Flynn hears his father's final decree: "Let Richards do it. And while he's at it, have him kill Henry, too." Shocked, Flynn accidentally urinates on the toilet seat.

In the conference room, Feddermann says, "I guess it's for the best. If you all think Henry and Caleb are uncontrollable, we certainly can't have a black man controlling that water, not with the enormous, potential political power that it represents, while whites and Cutterville go dry. And now, as we all must from time to time, I'm ready to compromise. As old Joe Chambers over there as good as said, I can't take it with me, so dammit. I'm okay with the money I have."

Flynn stands frozen in disbelief and then, after realizing that he's wet the judge's seat cover, and making no attempt to clean it up, he hurriedly buttons his fly, runs through the lobby and out the door. Burt peeks out from behind an opened office door down the darkened hallway, his mop in his hand, his wicked eyes watching as Flynn speeds away in the Rolls Royce. Reentering the restroom, Burt eyes the wet toilet seat, touches the moisture with his finger and puts his finger in his mouth and sucks it. As he does, he listens below the air duct for a moment and then hurries to the lobby and dials a desk phone.

"This is Burt," he says when a voice answers on the other end of the line. "Let me speak to Dane. What? I don't care how damn busy he is, masturbating himself is more like it. I'm not just some poor-ass, white trash like he thinks. Let him know who he's dealing with. Tell him I have information to sell him, and if he wants to know about what it is, he'll not only come to the damn phone, he'll crawl on his knees to me to get it and he better not try doing to me what he did to Snodgress or he get nothing. Tell him that!"

The following morning, Sunday, Sarah is wearing dark glasses to hide her bruises. Shadow Grove is nearly deserted but for her and Collins, resting on the panoramic, front porch in two of the wicker chairs, while gazing down-slope at a new school foundation.

"He never did seem to notice the foundation," she says, going on after much small talk.

"Oh, Barney noticed. He's just waiting to use it against you in his own time. Leave him, Sarah," say Collins, getting to what Sarah won't face. "He doesn't deserve you. Striking a woman like that and threatening to kill Henry and Caleb and you. Why, for God's sake?"

"Collins, I can't speak of why he wants to kill me, Henry and Caleb, or even leave him in spite of what he is; even Henry knows I can't break my vow to God, especially now that Flynn has found himself a father. May God help us both, me and Flynn."

"What did you tell Henry, Sarah? About your fight with Barney, or that he threatened to kill the three of you? Jesus. On top of Henry losing his land, this had to come along. Barney has lost his mind, if you ask me."

"Naomi has already warned Henry and Caleb about Barney, but I've told Henry nothing about Barney fighting with me; he would confront Barney, and that would only get him killed for sure, and you, Keith . . ." She gazes in his kind green eyes and continues. ". . . there is nothing that troubles me that I need to bother you and your family with either, but I do thank you for caring."

"We're all family here," says Collins. "There is no need to thank me fer anything."

"You were there when I was born. You were there when Father and

Mother died, and when I married Barney, when Naomi, Henry and I planted that red tree, which is growing so proudly now." She gazes at the distant, thirty-feet-tall red tree and then looks away from it and goes on. "You worked your heart out when the school was burned down, to help rebuild it."

"The colonel hasn't returned from that meeting he and Flynn went to last night. What's going on there, Sarah, if you don't mind me asking?"

"He told Flynn that the assembly might take all night. He should return soon."

"Speaking of Flynn. Did he go into Athens to Saint John's with the others?"

"After arising early this morning, and seeming to be deeply troubled, he said he had to find . . . Dear God," she says, suddenly standing up. "Caleb has never believed in Naomi's abilities, and—I'm sure he has ignored any warning she's given to him and Henry. My God. Caleb. With Henry attending church in Athens, he's alone on Little Shadow Place." She faces Collins. "Flynn said he had to find him. That's why Flynn was so worried this morning. Go on to church with your family, Keith. I have something I must look into before Barney returns."

"Are you sure, Sarah; he said he would harm you?"

"Where I'm going, Barney won't follow," she says. "Please, before you leave saddle the fastest horse we have in the barn for me."

"Where, Sarah? Where are you going that he won't follow?"

"To the Light, Collins, to where the Light of Love shines and evil retreats."

In town, under early-dawn blue skies and bright sunlight, the power brokers leave the courthouse. As Miller's church members are entering their house of prayer, just across the street, Cutter worriedly looks up at the church clock, then about for his car. Judge Chambers approaches and hands Barney a set of ignition keys. "Burt said Flynn left for home in your car last night, Barney, and Burt suggested you use mine, so here. It's unlocked in the parking lot. Have one of your workers bring it back when you can. The boys will give me a ride to the north side. Flynn must have misunderstood you."

"Yes," says Barney, with disappointment, fire and anger in his eyes, "he must have."

511

Under state police escort, the others leave Colonel Cutter behind, pondering and reflecting up at the church clock. He then quickly walks to the courthouse's parking lot, at the rear of the building, and slides behind the wheel of Chambers' Packard. The minute he does, a gun cracks him on his head, and the cold barrel of a .38 is pressed against the back of his neck. Bleeding about his skull and groaning, Barney looks into the rearview mirror and into the face of Dane and a grinning Burt.

"Relax, Colonel Cutter," says Dane, reaching over the seat and retrieving Barney's .45 from his shoulder holster and going on, "Because you haven't killed Caleb yet, and are losing the battle for Flynn. Satan is with me, Barney, I feel him in me as sure as I'm breathing, and because he's in me to test us, one against the other, your powers—if you have any after he said he took them from you—can't hurt me and I can't hurt you with any help from Satan, only with this gun."

Somehow Barney knows it's true.

Dane laughs and says, "Nothing will happen to you, which is more than I can say fer my pa, when he begged you fer his life. I guess you know Burt here. Seems—as he said—it was you who got him the job as courthouse janitor and invited him to join the Klan." Dane follows Barney's rear view mirror, vengeful sights to Burt and says, "Burt here's been on that job fer only a day, but already he's tired of cleaning toilets. I told him I'd get him some of that money of yours from Coug-er-dore or whatever name that island was Burt heard you politicians talk about in that courthouse. Now let's get out to Shadow Grove and see if I can convince you that it ain't worth dying fer all those millions. And Barney, with this town still full of them state police and that important senator from D.C., take your time driving, you hear. We don't want to be stopped fer speeding in Judge Chambers' car, do we? Now get going."

On Little Shadow Place, while fully dressed, Caleb is lying on top of his covers, staring up at the ceiling, when he hears the sound of the repaired screen door being slammed opened, followed by Flynn's voice as he the runs into Caleb's room. "Caleb, they're going to kill you!"

"What?" says Caleb, leaping out of bed and onto the floor.

"Where is Henry, Caleb?"

"In Athens, at church with the others. Who's going to kill me?"

"Get out of here! These men, Caleb! I couldn't sleep last night. And this morning, I've been driving around in circles for hours trying to decide what to do. You can't fight them. No one can. They have the colonel's money—millions, Caleb! To use against the coloreds, including against Henry and you."

"It's true, then. What that soldier on the boxcar said. The colonel's money. All true."

"So what? Go to Athens. Find Henry and keep on going! You've nothing left here, anyway!"

"Papa will never leave here. No matter who says it's not our land anymore. Flynn! Barney's duffle bags. Where are they?"

"Why are you talking about his bags? Leave!"

"His money is in those bags. It has to be. The bags we spoke of months ago, the ones you said were locked. I can open them to make sure his money in there, and I'll use that money as a trade-off for everyone's safety. Where are they?"

"You're asking me to betray my father, to steal his money for you? How can I do that?"

"You can and you will, Flynn Cutter," a female voice is heard saying behind them. Turning around, they see Sarah standing in the doorway. She's holding onto a horse whip, and wearing those dark sunglasses. Dressed in an equestrian outfit, she hurries into the room. "I'll leave my horse here," she says tossing aside the foamed-up whip as her exhausted horse trots by the bedroom window and into the meadow and grazes alongside Old Clara. Flynn almost cries as he gazes at her.

"Did he hurt you, Mother, the way Naomi said? Is that why you remained in Naomi's room with her and wouldn't talk with me last night or come out of that room this morning and why you're wearing those glasses, to hide your—?"

"Let's not worry about me," Sarah tells him. "I see that you drove your father's car here, now drive it and us to get that money, and—as your grandfather would have said if he were still alive and here—'don't spare the rubber!' "

A short fifteen minutes later, Flynn roars the Rolls Royce onto Shadow Grove, bouncing it through the main gate and fishtailing it to a dusty, dipping stop at the barn's rear door and everyone jumps from the car—even as it is still dipping up and down—and to the ground.

"Father has the only key," says Flynn leading the charge toward the huge, opened, rear, barn door. "We can't break that reinforced door down in the time we have left before he gets here."

"In here," calls Naomi's voice from within the barn. When they rush inside, they see her at the wine-cellar door with Barney's key in her hand. "I've been waiting for you," the mystery woman—reflecting her battle scars from Barney—says, as Flynn, near tears, looks, bewilderedly, at her battered face and then at his mother's face and finally at the key. Naomi goes on, "It's vital that you open this door and not me," she tells Flynn. "It will be a strong move against your father's control over you and Sarah."

Still with some nagging doubt in his mind about his father and what is going on about the money, Flynn looks over at Caleb, takes the key and hurriedly unlocks the door. Rushing inside, the blonde boy leads Caleb straight to the stacks of duffle bags and then to the opened bag over to one side of the room. Flynn angrily shakes the contents of that bag onto the floor, and countless paper-strapped U.S. bills fall to his feet, ones, fives, tens, twenties, fifties, and hundreds. As the others re-pack the bag, Caleb locates an old, plantation truck and backs it through the rear door, and everyone feverishly begins loading each fifty-to-seventy-pound bag of money onto the old vehicle. Tossing off her dark glasses to work more efficiently, in picking up some of the strapless, scattered cash, Sarah smiles over at Flynn, who takes one look at her black eye, then nods to her as if that is the last straw needed to convince him, and he tosses the bags onto the truck even faster while holding back his tears of anger against his father. "Pray that Barney thinks this money was stolen by outsiders while we were in Athens, where we are all going after loading these bags," Sarah says.

"Then that best be right now!" Naomi tells them, turning to Caleb. "Leave what's left, Caleb, and take off! The rest of us in that fancy Rolls of his! He's here and in the judge's car!"

From the barn window, they see dust and the Packard, zipping down the road toward the main gate. "You guys go ahead!" Caleb yells. "Not a bag will be left for him to use against innocent people. I'll load the last few. Go!"

With Sarah and Naomi in the rear seat holding onto each other, Flynn roars the Rolls Royce down a back road and heads for Athens, the massive barn concealing their presence, as the luxury car squeals around outlying structures and goes airborne over bumps in the road.

514

When Caleb tosses the last bag onto the truck, he notices a battered, cobweb-covered, globeless red lantern on the floor near one of the wine racks, a lantern under layers of dust, dust now being blown off by the wind entering the barn. Caleb turns away and looks out the window at the oncoming Packard and dashes to the truck, but something turns his attention back to that old lantern, and he runs to it. Moments later, he drives out the back door in the faltering truck and heads for his father's land. Beside him is the dusty lantern, bouncing about on the seat, the open-bed truck laboring under the weight of nearly a quarter ton of bagged money. Caleb and the truck disappear over the hill behind the barn, just as the Packard dips to a stop in front of the lofty red structure, which Naomi had earlier called "The roof of Flynn's red house of blood," and from high up on the barn roof, scores of white doves nervously scurry about looking down at a dazed Colonel Cutter who is pushed out of the car, while looking up at the doves. Barney is elbowed into the barn, Dane —with his gun pressing against the ex-intelligence officer's ribs, Burt just behind.

"Don't forget who told you about all of this," Burt yells. "I want my share of them millions." Inside the house of hay, Barney runs to the open, cellar door and into the room. "It's gone!"

Dane slams Barney in his side with the revolver, doubling him over in agonizing pain.

"Fuck you fer this, Satan!" shouts Dane going on. "No! It has to be here," Dane wails. "I can't be poor any longer!"

Barney, in a raging fit of pain, glares up at the high barn's ceiling and bellows, "Why am I defeated by this small man and this pain, Satan?" Shocked by the eerie sound of Barney's voice calling out to Satan, Dane—who said that he was protected by Satan, and had cursed Satan, along with Burt—backs off in numbing apprehension, both his and Burt's eyes wide, as Barney is suddenly energized with incredible strength, the shirt about his chest begins ripping apart as if by some unseen force, while the material along his arms quiver in waves up and down, as if from a gale blowing beneath them and filling Barney with endless electrifying world-shaking vigor. He whirls about and glares down at Burt and kicks him backwards into Dane, and both Dane and Burt go down hard. Satan has backed Barney, but Dane gets off a shot on the way to the floor, striking Barney in his midsection. Cutter—with a hole in his stomach, but with the power of Lucifer doesn't flinch or fall;

and, seeing this, when he hits the floor, and after his revolver has sails out of his hand, as does the .45 he's taken from Barney, Dane leaps to his feet and races screaming out of the barn, leaving Burt on his own, Dane's voice calling back: "He the devil. Run, Burt!"

Before Burt can even blink his eyelashes, Barney seizes the .45, and as Burt sits up and finally blinks and wails in horror, Colonel Cutter fires a round into the young boy's chest. Dying in that sitting position—as had Lilly on the factory's dock—and with the sound of Packard's chattering tires ringing in his ears, as Dane speeds away, Burt sees the hole in Barney's body where Dane had managed to shoot him. Burt then looks into Barney's eyes and knows—as Dane had said—that he's at the mercy of the devil himself. Quietly, the young boy whispers "Mamma," leans quivering back onto the floor, curls in a fetal position and spews blood. While in that curled position, Burt's distorted eyes focus on three doves settling on the outside window ledges and looking into the barn at him. The dying young boy hears Naomi's curse: *And so that you will know that heaven's eyes of justice are locked onto you, Colonel Cutter, when you kill Burt—as I said you will—your murderous act will send the doves of peace flying into the sky and Jesus will forgive Burt of all his sins.*

Barney follows Burt's lackluster sights to the window and fires a shot through the glass. The white birds fly off the ledge and back onto the roof with the others of its kind, as if knowing that the prophecy has not yet been fulfilled for them to fly away. Barney begins frantically gathering up the few left-behind bills from the floor and stuffing them in his pocket, and only when he's collected all of them does he return to Burt, who is wheezing and petrified of dying.

"You're not dead yet, boy?" asks Barney. He placed the .45 against Burt's head, and the fading boy moves his tobacco-stained lips, but cannot bring forth a sound, so weak is he. His young boy's sights return to those of his happy past, as those eyes look to the window and sky beyond, and they beg to something that only they can see, and with his dying breath, Burt manages to whisper, "Caleb Brooks." A single shot rings out, sending the boy's body recoiling backwards, and still the doves do not fly off the roof, as Naomi had said they would. Burt continues to clings to life, his body twitching and quivering, his begging sights still focused on the sky. "Satan," cries Barney, "don't let Naomi's God do this thing to me, after you made me invincible from this gunshot and now lack the power to kill this boy, even with this .45. Give me strength so that I

516

might continue teaching my son to love only you and not Caleb Brooks or Sarah and her Christian ways."

"Then do as I say," a ghostly voice is heard, causing the entire barn to shake, and the doves outside to frantically rise a foot or two off the roof, only to land again in apprehension, from the nearness of the devil; Following instructions which Satan has given to him, Barney picks up a sickle, walks over to a wide-eyed Burt, lifts up the boy's head by his hair and decapitates him, even as John the Baptist had met his demise, and Burt's headless body groans one last time and dies, sending the white doves rocketing into the sky, leaving Shadow Grove behind.

Again, Naomi's voice is heard: *You have finished killing him, and now may God strike you down—as I have prayed that He will—that you may linger on a bed of sores with maggots crawling out of your flesh and think of the evil that you and your Klan and the devil has done this day and the yesterdays to the world.*

Barney is suddenly gripped in pain from the gunshot, and he wails and staggers about in madness, his hands covering his ears against Naomi's righteous voice.

Later that evening, nervous and intimidated by thoughts of his father returning and finding his money gone, Flynn drives Barney's car through the trestle gate and onto the plantation; at the same time, the field hands are trickling back to Shadow Grove from Athens in their wagons; some of them—having arrived minutes earlier from church—are standing in front of the barn and its open doors, fearfully peeking inside and weeping. After Flynn speeds to the barn and stops, he can smell the scent of death, and he lingers behind in the car, while Naomi and Sarah slide from the Rolls and enter the massive structure. Sarah sees Burt's headless body and gasps, her hand covering her mouth. As do the workers, Sarah focuses on the blood trail that Burt left behind him; his will to live and his involuntary muscles—even without his head—had caused Burt's legs and arms and fingers to crawl and pull his body several feet and had positioned the remains within two feet from reaching the brilliant light of day just beyond the open door. Almost as frightening to the workers and to Sarah, is her husband Barney—who with the hole in his stomach now oozing blood—is stumbling around in the middle of the barn with his arms swinging back and forth in his promenade of mindlessness and muttering. Sarah runs to the general store to phone for the doctor and for Sheriff Richards. When Flynn sees his mother flailing past the car, he climbs from the Rolls and quickly enters the barn and stares down at Burt's body. He almost steps on Burt's head, and wobbles back with his eyes closed and groans. He then opens his eyes and sees everyone looking at him. Flynn then follows their gaze to Barney, and the young man slowly approaches his incoherent father, when everyone else is afraid to do so. When Barney sees Flynn standing before him, the devil speaks through Barney to farther separate Flynn and Caleb. "Caleb," Barney yells in the demonic voice, as the workers listening to it tremble in fright. Grumbling on, Barney bellows.

"Don't kill Burt. Not like that, Caleb. Not with the sickle. He's just a boy. No!"

Flynn drops to his knees and embraces his father's legs and holds onto them.

"Forgive me, Father," he cries and then yells. "Why, Caleb! We let you have the money. Why did you do this to my father? Why did you kill that boy Burt?"

"Hush up, child," says Naomi. "Caleb didn't kill anyone!" She looks from the bloody sickle and at Barney. "The devil killed that boy, the devil and Barney."

"No!" yells Flynn, half out of his mind, gazing back at the bullet holes in Burt's head and then at the head-less body and finally focusing on the sickle a few feet away from the corpse. "Caleb bought a pistol! He told Mother he bought it! Caleb shot that boy and he cut off his head!" Flynn leaps to his feet, picks up the sickle and begins whacking it against one of the horse stalls, terrifying the onlookers and horses alike. "Caleb!" he shrieks. Barney—trapped between the power of God and that of Satan—is a man more akin to a zombie than a human being, and when Flynn spots Barney's bullet wound, he drops the sickle and, once again, falls on his knees before his father and shouts, "Father." Barney squints down at his son: a black-widow spider at her mate, not knowing if he should protect Flynn or eat him. When Naomi attempts to ease Flynn away from the madman, Flynn pushes her backwards. "Father was right," he blasts at her. "You people won't stop until you kill us all!"

On the loft, Dane, having doubled back with several of his new, armed recruits, including Jayne Hill, is listening behind a stack of hay, the same place where Chad had jumped from in his attempt to kill Caleb, and had met his violent death, at the hands of Henry, seventeen years ago.

"Caleb goddamn Brooks," whispers Dane, now feeling that Satan has forsaken him. "That coon has all of that fucking money. I want one of us out here at all times to see if Flynn recovers that money befer we go out in them snake-infested swamps looking fer Caleb, who ain't going nowhere once the Sheriff gets wind of this and boxes him in."

"Remember," whispers Jayne to the half-dozen, money-hungry, young rebel Klansmen with her and Dane, "I gave you guys a ride back out here, just a mile away, when Deputy Hammer spotted Dane in the judge's car and came after all of you with that new big nightstick of his and you guys ran off like a bunch of girls leaving the car in the middle of the road. I gave you that ride, knowing that Hammer will break my skull, like he would yours, because you said I'd get my share. Now, I want my share of that money and to be part of the watch teams to make sure I get it. I don't trust none of you anymore than I trust that crooked Sheriff."

After Sheriff Richards arrives with the coroner, and Burt's body is taken away, and the workers sweep up and wash the blood off the ground, and the barn is quiet and empty, once more, Dane eases up from behind the haystacks. "The rest of you guys beat it and use the back roads. Don't let these folks see you coming or going." As the others begin climbing out an open rear loft window, Dane stops Jayne from following them. With his hand on his fly, he says. "You want money? Good. You'll get that and more," he tells her, still terrified from his run-in with Barney and praying that the man won't recover, while looking Jayne over and running his hands through her hair. "I'm a bigger man in the Klan than Barney can now ever be. We all saw how he's lost his mind down on that barn floor, and was given that shot of dope by his doctor and taken to the house by doc's nurse and Flynn. I was there when Pa and the others hanged and burned them nigger kids, years ago, and I helped light the fires and threw books on their bodies, while one was still alive, and I even pissed on 'em. Now, while you and I take the first watch . . . tell me again what it is you said you wanted . . . Money? How 'bout lots of it, thousands, if you do the right thing and take the first watch all night with me?"

"You're so damn ugly."

He passionately kisses her neck. "Reverend Miller once said that all of you Hill girls are hellbound, and you and I know you could care less, as long as money's involved. Money, Jayne. Maybe even millions."

With a wicked look in her eyes, she smiles, and Dane rolls her onto her back and mounts her in the hay.

36

A Young Girl's Cry for Help

Sarah and eighty-year-old Doctor Schmidt stand on the manor's porch talking in the noon shade. "Is Barney going to be okay, John?"

"There's no other way of knowing, Sarah, and no way to explain why he hasn't responded any better after nearly two weeks in the hospital. That's why we brought him home, as Flynn insisted we do. Even more astonishing about Barney is the fact that he received a fatal stomach wound and lost ninety percent of his blood, and the man, at his age, is even still alive. And Sarah, the carotid artery which supplies blood to the head and involves the aorta and the coronary arteries is—"

"It's eight in the morning and I haven't had my coffee yet. I'm a student of Latin, John, not of medicine. In layman's terms, what are you saying?"

"That Barney's stomach wound severed his main artery. By all accounts, he would have been dead before he hit the floor, but not only did he not go down. . . . Oh, my God. Who is this man, who calls himself your husband, Sarah?" Sarah is gripped in fear, recalling Naomi warning that Barney has the unbelievable power of Satan within him. She pales, as Doctor Schmidt continues, "His stomach wound, Sarah . . . where once the maggots infested his wound, and how they got there only God knows. After I removed his bandages, this morning, to my astonishment, his wound had healed completely, not even a scar. I've sent all of his blood work to the lab in Atlanta, and every one of the tests comes back normal. His blood pressure is an amazing hundred and twelve over sixty-eight, his heartbeat is a phenomenal forty beats a minute, the rate of an expertly-trained, super cross-country runner; his temperature is ninety-eight point six, the same as ours. His eyes follow movements in the room, he reacts to painful stimuli, but he can't seem to talk or actively move beyond blinking and tracking with his eyes. I've never seen anything like it in my life. It's as if your husband is being held in that lethargy state against his will, Sarah, by something that is moving heaven and earth to keep him there." Sarah looks at the front door and at Naomi, who is standing behind the screened-in portal and holding onto a tray with two glasses of liquid on it. Doctor Schmidt follows Sarah's gaze to Naomi, and studies her, and then Sarah's disturbed look. "Let me know anytime, day or night, if Barney is able to move or says anything. This is one for the journal, and—I have a feeling—a case which shall change the way we look at medicine. If he lives, we in medicine can study him for years to come."

Sarah turns ashen, knowing that the world could change into a place of wickedness if Barney lives. Then, Naomi, her battered body mostly healed, carrying the tray and glasses, steps from the house and approaches them. "Would you care for some iced tea, Doctor? It'll be no trouble to get another glass."

"No, thanks," Schmidt replies. "I have to go. Naomi, if you can, look in on my nurse once in a while and give her a break from Barney's bedside. I'm sure she would appreciate it, but make sure you give only clear liquids, tea or broth to Barney . . . No solid food for him at this time. If you have any doubts, then let the nurse feed him. And, now, about Flynn, Naomi, either you or Sarah . . . Try and convince the boy that Barney's condition is not his fault, and that he can't help his father by staying at Barney's bedside the way he's been doing. Flynn needs to get his rest before he, also, falls ill. He seems unwilling to listen to me."

When Schmidt leaves in his aging, black 1920 Ford, Sarah and Naomi move to the porch's wicker table where Keith Collins is waiting. Across from Collins, resting on the table is the colonel's briefcase with the paid-off property deed lying beside it, along with a copy of the Cutterville *Sentinel*. As Collins and Sarah sit in the cool shade, Naomi places the glasses of tea on the table for them and then reenters the house. Sarah fingers the precious deed, as if unable to believe it's there. She then turns her attention to the *Sentinel's* headline: "Cutter traumatized! By God, By Naomi, or by the devil?"

"Thanks again for coming back from town on another of your days off, Keith," Sarah tells him. "I know that you, Ruby and Pauline have so few moments together lately."

"My time is your time, Sarah. You know that. I'm just glad that Flynn is okay, after going through with what he saw in the barn."

She glances across the table with a look of insightful gratitude.

"Keith, the sheriff said now that the investigation into his deputy's death has been closed, that he would probe the killing of Crazy Walter."

"I heard about it, Sarah. He declared that Snodgress's death was an accident, and not the work of the coloreds, thanks to your connection which put pressure on him, and not any equal justice under the law on his part or the goodness of that town."

"It's been two weeks since he promised to start that investigation, Keith, and not a word about Crazy Walter yet. When you were in town, did you hear if he's made any progress?"

"No. Richards also said he'd reopen the case of these massacred school kids. You might as well look for a fifty-year-old needle in a haystack, with him possibly on his way out of office. That's not like the Klan, even with the pressure, to make such an offer. Why would he do that?"

"It's the notoriety. After my contacts pressured him, they also contacted their associates in the media, and Walter and Snodgress' killings have recaptured the imagination of the northern, radio stations, which have sent several of their reporters here, and they're putting a lot of pressure on City Hall, as well as are the one or two out-of-town newsmen who are still here traveling about Cutterville and asking questions about that unparalleled event of our daylight sky abruptly turning as dark as night. Also, with Barney ill and Richards expecting him to die, let's face it, he feels he can hold onto his job and does what city hall and the county tells him and is simply putting the best face on this mess for the newsmen."

Sarah again fingers the deed. "This land. Free and clear. It's like a beautiful dream and a nightmare all in one, not knowing if the money that paid off our debts might have been somehow tied to those who murdered those kids, long ago, including killing that boy Burt, the deputy and Walter. Thank God Caleb was cleared of killing that poor boy. But no one even mentioned Barney as a suspect."

"We don't know that the colonel had anything to do with it, Sarah. Not absolutely sure. Don't be too hard on yourself or on him. About Barney, what did the doctor say about him?"

"Only time will tell."

"Richards cleared Caleb of murdering Burt and shooting Barney. Flynn, Sarah. Does he still think that Caleb killed the boy and tried to murder the colonel, as well?"

"Flynn doesn't know what to think about Caleb, Keith. It's as if he's trapped in time along with his father. He seems not to know that Naomi and I are even alive."

Keith turns his sights to Naomi, who is—once again—standing behind the screen at the front door. Sarah stares at the mixed-blood woman; Naomi is staring off at the horizon. Following Naomi's gaze, Sarah and Keith see a black horse and rider—a good ten minutes away and seemingly the size of a human fingertip—moving fast across the skyline and toward Shadow Grove's trestle gate, through which, at that same moment, Sarah's workers—who had left the land to work in Dessen's factory—are returning to the plantation by wagons, on horseback, and on foot. Most of them are her ex-black workers, carrying their belongings on their heads as they had when they left and now joyously streaming to the general store singing the same song they had the day they had walked away, but with much more vigor and purpose in their voices, knowing that they are now returning home. Sarah watches them in total silence and then whispers, "Just like Bruce and Carrie have left that evil town, more of them are coming back every week now from that factory."

"They're fleeing the Klansmen in town, Sarah, after their homes were burned to the ground, but some of those with your workers are the unemployed whites from that evil place and have come here looking for jobs, and more than a few of those whites down there in that line even openly criticized you—just like they did Mister Dessen—for hiring coloreds in the first place."

"I was aware that they were coming, Keith, and have made arrangements for them. He sent them to me. All of them. God has sent my family home to be with us."

Among the questionable whites is the Hill family. Mrs. Hill is wearing an ugly, white lace collar, homemade, burlap dress and is pining for her husband, not realizing that her lack of self pride is the reason he left her in the first place. Her son, Benny, and her three daughters, including that unpredictable Jayne—in a tight-fitting dress and red shoes—are close by her side. Jayne is wasting little time in looking about for Sarah's young male workers, as she scrutinizes the landscape with her catlike eyes, as if—if not those of Aphrodite, on the prowl for fresh meat—then a lion on the hunt to kill off young men through sex for the joy of it. Collins studies Jayne, as she and the others pass below Manor Hill toward the general store for their housing assignments. "I hope those whites town's folk don't cause trouble here with our colored help," he says, then gazes about the cloudless sky. "Speaking of trouble. We were getting plenty of rain, but now, it's been weeks since the last drop hit the ground."

"Almost as if something is punishing this land because of his illness," whispers Sarah.

524

Preferring not to get involved with the religious entanglement concerning God, the devil, Barney, Naomi and Caleb, an entanglement which Keith thinks about but keeps to himself, even though he knows it is fast spreading throughout the country by way of the radios, the newspapers and too soon, Keith feels, by something called television, where one can look at people acting inside a radio type box, flooding the town with unwanted visitors, which troubles him. He smiles when he thinks how absurd that is to think that people will be able to see human beings inside a radio and he continues with both feet on the ground. "If the rain fails to come, the way it's failed in the past, we'll not be able to help ourselves, let alone the returning workers, this land paid off or not. And besides, Sarah, we can't get that lagoon water with the town holding onto Henry's deed, the way it is, and even if Barney had a plan—as it's whispered—to get Cutterville to release that lagoon water to Shadow Grove, it's meaningless if he doesn't recover, so don't put all your trust in God to feed all of us this winter."

"He's real, Collins. God is real, and He works in mysterious ways. Henry and I both know it. Even Henry's land. If I can't get his land returned to him, in His own time, God will return that land to Henry and give us all of the rain we will ever need. He wants us to have faith." She places the deed into the briefcase and goes on. "I've leaned heavily on you these last few months, you, Henry, Caleb, and Flynn. I only wish Shadow Grove didn't have so many needs. I want to offer you a raise, but besides not knowing if it is blood money, I'm not sure to whom it belongs."

"Flynn said it's in the millions, but no one else here knows that but me."

"If we can't trust you, whom can we trust?"

"I hope Caleb and Henry have hidden that money well, and that it doesn't get them into something even farther over their heads than it has already. There has to be powerful people out there with knowledge of that kind of cash, people willing to kill in order to recover it." When Sarah studies him with the look of fright in her eyes, Collins spells it out for her. "With the Depression still showing its ugly head in this country and the world, Sarah, with millions Barney—with his drive, and if he survives—could politically control this state."

"Or the world, Keith. Him and Flynn with a powerful benefactor's help, but as I was saying about giving you a raise, maybe . . ."

"About that raise, Sarah, we'll deal with talk of a raise when the time's right. All the money in the world won't buy a ticket for me, Ruby and Pauline to heaven when we die. You been more than a boss to me and mine; you've given us a home, a home to be proud of, not just a job. I only wish there was more I could do about our water supply." Beaming at her, he adds with a twinkle in his eyes. "Unless it's like you said when you were fourteen—kick those fat politicians right out of their chairs and out of office and then run for sheriff, myself."

Sarah forces a smile. "I did say that, on that train from New York, just before the death of my soul looked in at me from that train's corridor, and Naomi closed the door in his face and renewed my hope. You'd make a damn good sheriff, Keith. I'd back your election all the way." Sarah is momentarily overcome with emotion, then strokes his hand and adds: "Now, I need you to go into Cutterville."

"All right," Collins prompts with a smile. "What fer, to kick Sheriff Richards' rump?"

"No," she says with a smile and goes on, "to speak to Mr. Dessen."

As she's talking, Collins glances at that oncoming, distant horse and rider, over halfway to the gate now, and thundering along. Again, he dismisses the rider and faces Sarah. "Why would Dessen, the man in the middle of this trouble in town, want one of us to speak with him?"

"He phoned and offered to sell us some surplus water pipes at a good price," she tells him. "He also said he was humbled by our struggles out here."

"Humbled? That man?"

"Yes, humbled. He suggested that I wait until we get the pipes, and, then, once we receive them, I could pay whatever I feel is fair, so to get a head start, while you were returning from town, I had Bruce organize the workers into teams of wagons to go into Cutterville today and begin bringing the first of the pipes here as soon as possible, now that Barney is sick and our supplies are running low."

Below the hill, with the sun slowly rising in the eastern sky, workers and a dozen wagons, tethered to paired mules and horses, are lined up beside the red barn and are manned by many of Sarah's most trusted, steadfast workers, mostly the ones who had faithfully stood by her after the others had left to work in the factory—whites and blacks, who now patiently wait, all looking at the porch and at Collins.

"Well, then," says Collins, finishing off his tea. He reflects on another of those dark clouds moving in on them and says, "I guess I better get these wagons to town befer Dessen changes his mind about selling those pipes."

"Look, Keith," Sarah says, with hope reflected in her eyes and a smile on her face, as she waves toward the barn. Collins sees Bruce waving at them from one of the wagons.

"This is the last time I'll be able to boss that lovable old pig-headed guy around," Collins says. "He and his family are all packed. Did you know that? Packed and ready to strike out in the morning."

"I know," says Sarah, "for San Francisco. I offered them some money to tide them over until they get on their feet in California, but Bruce said between Brick, him, and Claretta they had earned more than enough at the factory and insisted on helping us this last time before leaving. May God bless him, his wife and his children. Carrie wants to raise Brick and Earlene on the West Coast. They have in-laws there. I can't blame Carrie, after the death of Claretta, but I'll miss them."

"We all will," says Collins stepping from the porch. He hesitates, glances at the dark cloud for a moment, then slowly turns to Sarah and says, "We'll see you later."

All the time, that distant rider on the horizon is still coming fast, as if to reach the manor house with a sense of urgency. At the reins of one of the mule-drawn wagons, Ruby, Collin's wife, and Pauline, sixteen, his daughter, had returned from town with him and had stopped off at the barn to talk with neighbors and friends, while Keith had gone on up the hill to speak with Sarah. They wave to Collins as he approaches. Bruce Johnson, wearing a straw hat, is in the mule-drawn wagon next to Collins' family. Sitting close to Bruce is Earlene, and next to her is Carrie, who is still depressed over Claretta and Billy Joe's deaths and now that of Crazy Walter's. Bruce stares at her with concern. His wife's stomach is large with their expected child. On the wagon floor is a picnic blanket and a basket of food. Earlene has packed her own canning jar of delight, and she takes the large jar from the basket and guzzles the honey-sweet lemonade from it, then sticks her tongue out at Brick, who isn't going on the trip to town in order to spend as much time that is left with his buddies before he and his family move to California. Brick lingers by the barn, squinting out of one eye against the blinding sun as the workers prepare to leave, a handful of his friends standing with him. When Collins climbs into his wagon, Bruce calls to him.

527

"It's good to be workin' fo' you again, Field Boss, even ifin it's only fo' today. Carrie done made fried chicken, potato salad and cornbread and iced tea fo' yo' family and us to eat on the way."

"Good!" exclaims Collins. "We could eat a horse!" He glances at his wife. "Ruby didn't have time to prepare us anything."

"We knew she wouldn't have the time," says Bruce, "when Sarah told us she was sendin' word to have you hurry back and take charge of the wagons."

"Thanks, Carrie," Ruby calls to her.

"Thanks from me, also, Carrie," Collins tells her. "I love Ruby to death, and I was worried that she'd feel that she let me and Pauline down by not feeding us, even though it wouldn't have been her fault."

Ruby leans over and kisses Collins on the lips, causing Pauline and Earlene to giggle.

"Hush up with that gigglin', you two," scolds Bruce. "Earlene, you've seen yo' ma and me—and you, Pauline also done seen yo' ma and pa—kiss lots of times befo'."

"But never a white man and woman, Daddy," says Earlene, causing those on the other wagons to laugh, going on. "And I still don't know why we can't go in the truck. Please, Daddy. It'll be more fun, so I can watch you shift the gears and learn to drive."

Ruby and Collins smile at one another. "Those new-fancy motor wagons aren't worth spit," Collins tells Earlene. "Don't give a good dang what Mr. money-bags Ford says. It takes a team of sure-footed horses and mules to pull loads of steel pipes over these back roads to here."

Earlene guzzles even faster from her lemonade jar, her sights locked on her mother, who scolds, "Stop drinkin' that stuff, child," and then whispers, "you knows how it makes your insides act up."

"What about you, Mamma? With that baby so big in you, yo' bladder will act up, too."

"Hush up, child. I'm the mamma here, not you."

"Honey," says Bruce eyeing Carrie. "Maybe you should stay behind with Brick."

Carrie shakes her head and exclaims, "I got to be goin' places and doin' things or I'll die thinkin' about my po' Claretta and Billy Joe. I'm okay." Carrie looks over at Collins. "Come on," she calls to him. "Let's hit the road while me and mine are here to help you guys. Like Sarah said, it'll take y'all several days and trips to get all them pipes from town to here as it is." She turns back to Brick. "Now stay out of trouble and brush yo' teeth, after Johnny Mae feeds you at her place, you hear? All of you youngins be good, 'cause you knows yo' folks will let Bruce tan the lot of you ifin you gets out of hand."

From the porch, Naomi and Sarah watch the wagons pass beyond trestle gate, and then they see that fast-moving horse and rider—a young boy—sliding to a stop at the wagons, the boy frantically talking with Collins. Again, it's Peter Scott. Peter's deceased father was the sandy-haired teenager, Jeffery—who with his freckled face, lips and clenched, white knuckles—had stood beside Henry the day Barney crowned Flynn with thorns and Barney had declared Flynn the Klansmen's god. Peter's father had run screaming into the field, alerting the white and black workers that Dane wanted to hurt Sarah and take over Shadow Grove. Now, the dead man's son has surely inherited the same traits. From the porch Sarah and Naomi see him brushing his sandy hair from his face, as he points to the south. The two women look at each other, as Collins and Bruce quickly break off from the other wagons and head due south. They watch with concern as Peter then rides full-out in their direction and up the winding drive, leaps from his horse and runs onto the porch. Meanwhile, taking a shortcut up the side of the slope, dozens of curious field hands have followed him. They now wait anxiously by the porch, anxiety hanging in the air over them, especially over Jayne Hill, who is among the curious workers and has her own reasons for concern; she listens with dread to Peter's frantic explanation:

"Sarah," the exhausted teenager says. "I saw one of them boys who burned down our school. The one named Marcus. Out there with a Klansman, the one who's a deputy sheriff, as well as a Klansman."

"Slow down, Peter," says Sarah, "so we can understand you."

"They're on Henry's land and drinking moonshine and making more firebombs, just like the broken glass ones we found at the school, after it burned. Heard 'em say they'll come back tonight and burn the barn next. Just told Collins! He and Bruce went after them to make them tell them about the people behind our troubles, especially about Dane Tucker and what's he doing it fer."

Jayne sees all of that money she's dreamed about suddenly vanishing before her eyes, and she covers her mouth with her hand, turns and steps away from the others. Naomi watches the panic-stricken girl recklessly run down the side of the hill and into the general store.

"What is it, Naomi?" ask Sarah, seeing a worried expression across Naomi's face.

"I'm not sure, Sarah," says Naomi, targeting the store with her keen sense of suspicion.

Sarah then stares at Collins and Bruce's distant wagons, an even graver expression now on her face. She looks at the other wagons, now going in the opposite direction and knows that while Naomi may have lost her divine authority, she has not lost her ability to sense danger. Something unspeakable is going to happen to the workers, but with her wagons going in two separate directions, Sarah has no idea where it will happen or to whom. Which should she send riders after to warn or to stop?

"Nothing, Sarah," counsels Naomi. "I see nothing that you can change or should try to do so. Fate. We can't change fate, Sarah."

After Peter's conversation with Sarah, she thanks him, and he and the workers make their way down the winding driveway. Stepping from the store once more, and leaning back against the doorway with her arms folded across her chest, Jayne studies the returning workers, then smiles when she sets her sights on Peter, who's leading his horse.

"That was a very brave thing you did," she purrs, "to come back and tell Sarah about that Klansman and Marcus."

"You're the girl who ran down the hill."

"Then, you noticed me, "she says. "I knew you would. All the boys notice me a little bit."

"I was just wondering why you were running away, that's all," Peter tells her, as those with him go on their way, leading his horse to the field. "Are you sick or something? Is that why you left?"

"Mommy's inside the store signing us up fer a house out here, and I just wanted to be with her," Jayne lies, gestures at the store and continues. "They might have killed you—those who burned down the school, but you all but caught them single-handed and deserve a reward."

She takes his hand and walks to the barn, all the time, her two younger sisters, shaking their heads, are watching them from the store window. Once they reach the barn, Jayne guides Peter into it and closes the heavy doors behind them, leading Peter into a world of half-gray, mystical, lacy light of day weeping through the open spaces in the barn's walls, the smell of fresh-cut hay and animal dung in the air. She takes a nervous Peter past the horse stalls to the nearby hayloft rungs. Stopping, she kisses Peter on his lips. When they continue on and reach the rungs, an irritated stallion in the stall next to the rung is spooked by their sudden appearance and rears, slicking the air with its deadly front hooves, Jayne reaches into the corral and calms the mighty creature with the touch of her hand. "How do you know how to do that, calm that mean critter? And how come you know your way around here so well?" Peter asks. "You just got here with the others from town, didn't you?"

"One question at a time," says Jayne. "You sure you want to know?" "About handling horses? When I was twelve, I used to go out in the field and stand under this big stallion that my pa kept fer breeding, and I would reach up and jack it off, and you should have seen all of that sperm explode all over me." Peter stands there in total surprise, as she continues. "As fer knowing my way around, I know a lot about a lot of things. I'm Jayne so let's keep our questions to names. And you, what's your name?"

"Peter."

"Peter . . ." she whispers. "I like that name fer two reasons. I'll just tell you about one of them and reserve my judgment on the second reason fer a bit later: As fer the first reason . . . You're named after the disciple that Jesus built His church on. I heard that the Catholics say Peter was the first Pope. Do you think you could be the head of my church, Peter?"

"What church is that? I'm Catholic, like Sarah."

"The one down here, silly," she says cupping her hand over her crotch.

"Oh!"

"By the way, Peter," she says climbing the rungs ahead of him, as he shyly tries to look up her dress, "about Barney . . . Apparently you've lived out here fer sometime. Is he going to die, the colonel? And, Peter, do you know if anyone here has heard talk about him having money, and Flynn did he find—" She abruptly stops talking and looks down as Peter becomes suspicious, while climbing behind her. "We can talk about the Cutters later," she says, like a fisherman in fear of losing his catch from the net. "Did you know you'd make a good-looking soldier? There are plenty of soldiers in Cutterville now, who know how to take care of business. My second reason fer liking or disliking you will depend on what kind of soldier you are. Do you know how to take care of business, Peter?"

"I think so."

"With a name like 'Peter,' let's hope so," she tells him.

In Cutterville, Jayne's so-called soldiers of opportunity have taken care of business by greatly expanding their tent city on the square across from the factory, as well as in a field around Sue Ann's bar. Nearby, Dane—wearing a sidearm—is recruiting anyone who can walk or talk, including a handful of angry Hooverville veterans in their dirty uniforms, ex-soldiers who had refused to fire on the marchers and their American flags, but now—with their families hungry, their hungry children crying—they are willing to join hands with the Klan.

"We'll get the rest of them jobs back fer you!" Dane yells to the whites from atop a hay wagon.

As a loud cheer goes up from the gathering, old Hank—restraining a vicious dog named Tramp—with a rope about its neck, approaches and whispers in Dane's ear, causing Dane to withdraw his pistol, check out the cylinder, and then he and Hank—along with the dog—climb into Hank's truck, a truck now fitted with a weapon's rack, containing a double-barreled shotgun, and a rifle across the rear window. Hank—driving the truck as best he can—squints through his thick bifocals and roars off at thirty-five miles an hour and complains, "Jesus, Dane. Jayne called the bar from Shadow Grove. Anyone could have taken her message, and put two and two together, and our secret about Barney's money would be all over town by now even more so than it is."

"Tell me again her exact words," says Dane, now that word's leaked out about Barney's millions. "Are you sure that she meant Marcus?"

"She said one of them boys who had burned down Sarah's school is out there on that coon's once-owned land with that deputy, the one who likes boys. She had to mean Marcus, as pretty as he is and as horny as that deputy is, if you know what I mean. She said Collins is going after them. Jane is worried about getting her share of that money if Marcus talks, and so am I. Sarah still got a lot of political pull, maybe even more than Barney does, and—if that young kid gets caught and scared and he talks, not just to Collins, but to the courts while the colonel is in a coma, or whatever they say he's in, and can't reach Judge Chambers . . . well, you know what you said that judge said to you about locking you up in jail fer the rest of your life if you ever show your face befer him again. We're up shit creek without a paddle. Talk is Barney and them politicians are out to get all of us, anyway, especially you, fer nosing about in Barney's business, about his money and trying to take over the Klan."

"Oh, shit!" screams Dane bracing himself, as Hank narrowly misses an oncoming car. "Stop this truck, you old son-of-a-bitch, befer you're the one who gets us killed. I'll drive."

Back at Shadow Grove, wearing that burlap dress, which swishes about as she walks, Mrs. Hill hurries from the store and loudly exclaims, "Why didn't you two tell me this befer now." She glares at the barn, then looks down at a wooden bucket of water next to the door, water placed there for the workers to wash their dirty hands before entering and handling the merchandise. Mrs. Hill seizes the heavy, five-gallon wooden bucket and shouts, "I'll wash that sinful girl's mouth clean of any more desire to place them lips of hers on a boy's parts where God never meant for her mouth to be, even if I have to drown her." Leaving the younger girls at the store, wide-eyed and nibbling on suckers, while watching from there, Mrs. Hill storms to the barn: "Jayne Hill, I told you to stay close to your sisters while I got us a house. Don't try lying to me anymore, or you'll burn in hell! You got that boy, that your sister saw you with, in that barn and in your pants?"

Lying on her back in the hay loft, while smoking some of Reverend Miller's jimson-firethorn mix, Jayne is drowning in an exciting sea of lust, not in water, as Peter slowly disrobes her. "Take it all off," she whimpers, "and yours too. I want my legs, just like my mouth, where I want you to put it, held wide open."

Once he removed Jayne's clothes, the over-excited young girl throws the drug pipe out of the nearby open window—out of which Dane had ordered them to climb while spying on Flynn. In an emotional, uncontrollable, drug-driven, sexual frenzy, Jayne frantically tears off Peter's shoes, socks, trousers, shorts and shirt. Feverishly tossing his clothing aside, she guides him onto his back and mounts the groaning teenager, and as a wide-eyed Peter gawks down toward his chest at her, she nibbles at his breast, then his neck and shoulders, while quivering in primitive pleasure; he attacks her with kisses and groans, in return, with his surprising stamina and animal magnitude, matching her stroke for stroke. Suddenly, the nervous stallion is heard rearing and kicking at its corral, and—then—clamoring, huffing and puffing up the rungs with that heavy bucket of water, Mrs. Hill glares down at her surprised daughter and a shocked Peter; she splashes the entire bucket of cold water onto them, splitting the young lovers apart. Peter bounds to his feet, fighting off the insane woman's vicious attack, as she hammers him with that deadly bucket. Fighting for his life, he accidentally knocks her off the loft; the shrieking woman lands on her head in the stall of that stressed-out stallion, which thumps on the fallen woman's limp body, as she lays motionless below its rearing hooves. Jayne leaps off the loft and into the stall, nudges the horse aside, drops to her knees and sobs beside the trampled woman. Her mother's mouth is jarred open, her false teeth shattered on the earthen floor, her unseeing eyes slowly turning gray and rolling back in her head. Mrs. Hill groans, then slumps into deathly silence. As a bumbling Jayne cries, "Wake up, Mommy," and violently shakes her mother's body, Peter, looking down from the loft at the dead woman, trembles in fear. Panic in her eyes, Jayne glares up at her skin-soaked, naked lover.

"She's dead, Peter. Mommy's dead!" shrills Jayne, hugging and smothering her mother with kisses, while intermittently howling up at a terrified Peter. "You killed her, Peter! Ah! Ah! Ah!"

Hearing Jayne's horrified cry, a dozen women and men—and children—rush from the fields to the barn. Peter looks out a nearby window and sees them coming. Grabbing up what he thinks is his clothing, he jumps out the rear window with the garments, unknowingly taking Jayne's dress, petticoat and underwear with him. Once on the ground, when he realizes he has taken her garments, he tosses them aside, slips into his wet trousers and runs shirtless and shoeless up Manor Hill to the trees to hide; and there, to his surprise, he runs right into the arms of Naomi. "I didn't mean to do it, Naomi. Honest I didn't," he says on the downhill side of the slop, while looking up into her eyes. "I don't want to go to jail. I didn't mean to kill her."

"Hush, child," says Naomi hugging him with all of her compassion and love. "No one here knows you did anything wrong." Sadly Naomi faces the barn and goes on. "And Jayne will never tell."

"She will, Naomi. She will tell. I broke the law and will be punished."

"Whose law, son? Man's or God's?"

"Man's and God's, Naomi."

"David killed the giant and heaven rejoiced, Peter. The angels rejoiced. They rejoiced!"

Unable to understand her message, Peter sobs, "I'll go to jail, where my pa told me men there do ugly things to young boys like me. She will tell. You didn't see the look she had in her eyes. She said I killed her mother. They say you know everything, but you're wrong. She will tell! Please tell God I'm sorry."

"Jesus has said to His disciples 'Whosoever you forgive shall be forgiven.' I'm a woman, Peter, as was His mother Mary. Our tasks, as women, are to raise His disciples with love, so that they, in turn, can give our love to the world. That what you ask me to do—to beseech God to forgive you—is up to Caleb alone, now, but his love for you young people will not allow him to destroy you by turning you over to the corrupt law because of Jane Hill and Satan's handiwork." She holds the sobbing boy close, as he—in turn—clings to her and cries like a baby. "Trust me, Peter, when I tell you that not on this day or any day after this will anyone hear Jayne Hill's mind or her voice ring clear enough to blame her mother's death on anyone but on herself, and, at that, not for very long."

When the men, women and children enter the barn, including Jayne's sisters, they look into the stall at an insane, wet, naked Jayne crawling about her mother's body.

"You killed Mommy, Mary Jayne!" yells the next oldest sister. "You killed Mommy!"

"Oh, God," shouts one of the women, as several of them—fearful of entering the stall with the convulsing horse—grab several horse blankets from other stalls and hold them in front of the corral to shield the naked girl from the gaping eyes of the males. "Did you kill your mother?" the woman yells, looking over the blanket at Jayne. "In God's name, girl, you're naked as a jaybird! Who helped you kill her? A boy! Is there a boy in here? Did you kill your mother, child?" The horse kicks at the opposite wall from them. "Get out of there, Jayne! Now!"

With the male workers—young and old—peeking under, over, and around the blankets at Jayne, the females—the black ones and the white ones—firmly take charge. "Out! You men out! Back to the fields. You youngins, too. This is women's work."

Before the males can be chased out of the barn, Jayne climbs onto the stall's railing and scurries along its narrow edge to the rungs, which she leaps onto and climbs to the loft. Wailing, she slips into her red shoes and then looks about for her clothing. "I can't find my dress!" she screams. The women, trying to clear the men from the barn, are stunned, as are the men and children, when suddenly Jayne—under the influence of all of that smoked, drug mixture—stands on the edge of the loft and flails her arm over her head. She yells, "I can fly, Momma." She sails off the loft and onto the horse's back. The stallion crashes through the stall gate, and naked except for her shoes, her skin pale, her eyes red, Jayne and the horse hit the outside ground in a flash, scattering and toppling workers, who watch in horror as the wailing teenager clings to the swift creature's mane and rides at breakneck speed across the potato field of laborers and heads in the direction of the only place she ever found peace: the lagoon and Henry's confiscated land. "Caleb!" she calls. "They say you understand. I as good as killed my ma! Please be home, Caleb. Please. I need you!"

"Somebody phone fer the law and get the field boss here and catch that girl, and I mean now!" hisses Old Ben, now going on ninety, is the same old man who Dane and Chad harassed on the day he left the plantation store, and threatened to tell Barney that Dane had eyes for Sarah. Ben yells on, "That poor child has lost her mind, the same as the colonel. God help us. Satan now has his evil hand on all of us."

From the manor porch a shocked Sarah and Naomi—who having returned to the house after comforting Peter—watch Jayne riding across the horizon, as men, already saddled up in the fields, and having heard the cries of horror, go after her. "Who is that child, Naomi?"

Naomi's voice rings with finality. "She's someone who those men will never catch. Jayne Hill, Sarah, those drugs . . . First her voice and then her mind will leave her. That's what Peter Scott fails to understand, as I told you. Jayne Hill is being chased by her own devil, and she can't escape it, but she'll keep trying, and she'll ride that poor horse until it can't run no more."

As the sun's rays creep across the landscape, making way for the morning, Jayne and the horse, foaming from its mouth, clip along past workers' children returning from fishing with their bamboo poles and fish slung over their little shoulders, the young ones' small, innocent eyes gawk up at the naked girl and then blink in disbelief over their shoulders at her, as that swift horse and she—screaming bloody murder—flashes by them and on down the red, clay road. They watch with open mouths and bulging eyes, as she guides the powerful creature onto a meadow of drought-resistant flowers and sprints it parallel to the woods, then up slopes and down the other side, viciously kicking the mighty beast in its side with the heels of her hard, red shoes, forcing the exhausted stallion to run faster and faster, pushing it to the end of its endurance, as it begins foaming about its entire body, the drugged girl riding now in search of a brother's love and understanding. "Caleb!" she continues crying out on the wind.

"Whoa! Did you hear and see that?" asks one of the young boys. She's looking for Caleb, and girls can ride as good as boys after all, when they're in a hurry, even when they're naked."

Five miles from Shadow Grove, halfway to Henry's land, and in the soft light of day, Jayne jumps the horse over a waist-high, stone wall, near the edge of the woods; the exhausted stallion lands with a thud, breaking both its front legs, sending Jane flying head-over-heels to the ground. Staggering to her feet and delirious, she attempts to pull the suffering creature off of its side, but then hears the sound of the rescuers' horse hooves approaching and runs into the woods. When the riders come upon the downed horse, they're not alone. The children are riding on the horses with them. "I told you this was the way she went," one of the tots says, then tearfully gazes down at the fallen horse. The lead fieldhand remains with the suffering horse; the others ride a short distance away with the children. Shortly after, a gunshot rings out.

"Jayne!" the men and children call against the wind, once the shooter returns to their side.

Two miles later, and stumbling along in the woods, jumping from shadows, from the sound of birds, from slithering snakes and even from rabbits which cross her path, Jayne flails onto Henry's lost property and dashes screaming toward the lagoon. Afraid and confused with the landscape seemingly spinning all around her, she recognizes the boys' paint and boat shack and runs to it, opens the door and falls inside onto the floor, and there, on her stomach and too weak to get up, she cries, "Mommy! Please don't be dead."

She grabs her throat, her voice cracking, and then she can speak no more, only grunt. Crawling across the floor, she makes a bed of the boys' old newspapers, wraps herself in one of their paint-stained shirts, curls into a ball and falls into a deep sleep.

37

The Tower of Babel and the Face of Tears

At that moment, as fate would have it and Little Shadow Place degrees hotter with each hour that passes, several hundred yards from the tree-lined lagoon and boat shack, white chickens peck away in the Brooks' emerald-green, front yard. Caleb—with Sarah's permission—has managed to collect a load of sooty but usable wood from the school fire and has neatly off-loaded most of it from a mule-hitched wagon and onto a pile by the porch. In spite of the fact that they might be forced to move off the land at any time, Caleb stubbornly plans to build a roof over the porch so that when Henry sits outside in his rocking chair, he can do so out of the pounding sun. However, when Caleb sees his father sitting so despondently on the porch, all thoughts of building the roof are momentarily put aside in order that he can honor his troubled father by reading to him; after going to the porch and picking up Henry's old Bible, Caleb finds a suitable passage which has always puzzled Henry: Genesis nine: the passage about the "Tower of Babel." After reading from it for only a short time, Caleb looks over at Henry, who sits pitching to and fro in his rocking chair and—Caleb thinks—is pondering the meaning of the Biblical message.

"It's okay," he says to Caleb. "I've heard enough for now." Studying his domestic fowl, he goes on. "There was a time when I never believed my chickens would ever amount to anything," he whispers, "but they ended up winning a blue ribbon and were called the best crop of chickens this side of the Mississippi River. At one time, I think I loved them chickens and wouldn't kill a one of them for us or anyone else to eat. Remember? But there's nothing on earth that's so precious that we lose sight of God over it, because only in Him are we worth anything. It's time for me to remember that." He beams at Caleb. "And stop crying in my soup over this land."

Attached to the porch railing are a group of oscillating, gas-filled balloons. Henry watches Caleb lower the Bible and toy with one of the round, bobbing, rubberized worlds of color. "I had them balloons blown up at the carnival in town to give to Flynn, when he visits us," Henry says.

"The gas is leaking from them, Papa." Henry stares into space. Caleb goes on. "Flynn is eighteen now, Papa. Balloons are for children. He won't come here. We should get rid of these balloons."

"I raised him like my own child, Caleb, raised him like I did you, and Flynn will come, even like he came with that rich, Texas grocery-store man in that big fancy car. The boy must have forgotten about his eighteenth birthday, that's all."

"But, that was months ago, and you're worrying yourself into forgetfulness and confusion about him."

"Like you are, as well, son? At least the confusion part."

"I guess so, but for what? Flynn doesn't care. He refuses to even answer the phone when I call."

"It would be far too dangerous for you and him to be seen together or heard talking with each other on the phone, at this time, as long as all that money's on the loose. Lord, Caleb, I didn't know that much money was in any one place in the whole world. Just think of the good it could do fo' the poor folks in town, even fo' Sarah's workers in them small shacks on her land." Henry rises to his feet. "I guess I best be on ma way up there now."

"You're still going? To help then with the ditch, after saying we would not, then doing so, and again saying no more, when he killed Burt and we finally decided we won't work for that man? That will put you in danger as well."

"Not today, it won't, Caleb. Barney hasn't gotten any better. I truly believe Naomi's right. God is holding that man in bed against his will, and as for my going there—regardless of how many times I might say I won't—in the end, I always go the way Jesus would want me to; to help others."

Henry turns deadly silent. Caleb knows why. It's because Henry feels that he, Caleb, has no faith in the power of God.

"If you feel you must go," Caleb compromises, glancing at the rifle against the porch railing, "then take your rifle with you. Those Klansmen won't stop at just trying to frighten us, now that Dane has all but wrestled the leadership of these animals from Barney."

"And Flynn, Caleb. Isn't there a kind word you want me to say to him from you?" Henry ask shaking his head at the rifle.

"If you see him tell him I didn't kill Burt or hurt Barney."

"In his heart, he already knows that, Caleb. And, son, I don't need that weapon," Henry says pointing at the rifle. "The way I'm to leave this world has already been set in stone, and it isn't from a bullet. This much I've been told."

"Papa. No talk of you taking my place on Naomi's mythical 'road of the cross.' Okay?"

"About that money, Caleb . . . The last time Sheriff Richards came out here, he told you he didn't believe you had anything to do with Barney or Burt and that you shouldn't worry, that he'll investigate more and—"

"He's full of it, Papa. We both know he suspects that we have the money."

"Good," says Henry. "Now, you're talkin'. And that's the reason we're not in jail. Richards is no fool. He's hoping we'll get careless and lead him to that money." Henry steps from the porch onto the grass. Picking up a bag of corn kernels from the lawn, the kind soul begins tossing grain from the bag at the chickens, which snap up the kernels in a feeding frenzy. Caleb places the Bible on the porch railing, then looks back at it and calls to his father. "If nothing else, Papa, your Bible and just the thought of a loving Superior Being Who watches over us is necessary, because if not for that, people would have even far less respect for human life, so never mind what I say about churches and Bibles. The way you look at life makes you what you are. Someone that Flynn, Sarah and all of us love."

"That Tower of Babel story, son . . . Now is the time to tell me what you think it means."

"The Bible describes so many odd goings on," Caleb replies. "The Babel story is but one such aberration: people building a tower to reach heaven, but were stopped short, when God caused the workers to speak different languages. It seems simple enough to me: There are things that belong to God and those that belong to man, and the two can't mix unless God, Himself, invites man to do so."

"That's actually right, Caleb. Now I see it, and it helps, helps me accept the loss of this land."

Stepping off the porch and looking about the landscape, Caleb exclaims, "This land is still legally ours. If I have to take some of that money of Barney's to buy it back, I will, no matter how much of a sin it's said to be. I'll do it, even if it means never speaking to Flynn or Sarah again. Then everything will be as it was, this land and us, and not one thing will ever be stolen from us again."

"That I would never let you do, Caleb, steal, not even to save my life, let alone land. That's not how the Bible teaches us."

"You're my Bible," says Caleb. "My living Bible which loves and fears, Papa. You're my life's blood that keeps me alive, and if you say so, I will never again speak of stealing, but oh, how I'm tempted to do so."

"That's beautiful, Caleb, about me being your living Bible."

The prized chickens suddenly run about Caleb and Henry's feet.

Caleb glances up and breaks for the porch, grabs the rifle, races back to Henry and faces the heaven. A chicken hawk, veering and swooping, its beak and razor-sharp talons open, is circling overhead, then plummets toward them. Caleb follows the hawk through the rifle sights, as it sweeps in a blur across the front yard and passes them within seconds of its prey. Aiming, now, just ahead of the bird's flight path, Caleb begins slowly squeezing the trigger. Suddenly Henry reaches out and lowers the rife barrel, taking away any chance of Caleb killing the graceful, winged predator. The bird's talons find its mark into Henry's prized hen's back. The hen clucks in consternation, as Caleb watches the powerful bird swoop higher and higher, through the sky with it, as hen and hawk become a black dot against the white clouds and blinding sunlight, leaving a trail of white chicken feathers drifting down from the blue onto the emerald lawn like snow. Slowly, Caleb turns his sights from the sky to his father.

"I could have brought it down with one shot, Papa."

"Something put us to the test today, Caleb, and it also took away one of the things I had too much pride in, my prize-winning hen, and it seems that whoever did this also took away something you love."

Looking at his father, Caleb wonders what was taken from him by the hawk.

"Jesus told us not to hold onto worldly goods, son, and God has also tested us when He allowed our land to be taken, especially from you, who believed that this land would always protect you. Maybe He or Jesus sent that hawk to show us that there is nothing that can't be taken from mankind. Don't drop your guard, Caleb. The Prince of Darkness is near and he will use every trick in the book to pull you into his camp, including the love of this property, if he has to. And it won't be a gun or rifle that will protect you and Flynn from him. It will be love. Put that instrument of death away. Caleb, take Old Clara and go ride with the wind at your back and find your way to God."

Reluctantly obeying his father, Caleb leans the rifle back against the porch railing. He removes his boots and slips into his porch-side tennis shoes, then prepares Old Clara and climbs into the saddle with a towel; wiping the sweat from his brow, he then removes his jacket—and not knowing if he'd be back before the cool of night—he stuffs the jacket into his saddlebag and watches Henry climb bareback onto his plow horse and ride across the fields and countryside toward Shadow Grove.

Caleb pushes the towel into his saddlebag with the jacket and rides the faithful horse alongside the porch, reaches out, pulls a red-stringed balloon from the rail-tied bunch and fixes it to his saddle horn, all the time his sights are fixed on Henry. "I love you, Papa, and I pray that your God will always protect you," he says, then canters Old Clara in the direction of the lagoon. Once on the north shore of the vast body of water, with the balloon bobbing up and down from his saddle, Caleb stops a short distance from the boat shack and looks at the opened door, swinging back and forth in the wind; as he sits in the saddle conjuring up images of him and Flynn arguing there, he's unaware that Jayne Hill is sleeping nude inside the tin shack on the bed of newspapers. Caleb turns his attention to the thicket and the land along the bank, where he angrily scrutinizes Flynn's new boat by the dock, then sends Old Clara into a gallop away from the boat, the shack, and the unwanted memories. Racing old Clara along the shoreline—and having no idea of how to go about searching for his father's God—in frustration and perspiring, Caleb reaches back, removes the towel from the saddlebag, slows Old Clara to a walk, wipes the sweat from his face and neck, sticks the towel half in and half dangling out of the saddlebag, and then glares at the wind-bobbing balloon, and punches it. "Too good to come and visit Papa. Is that it Flynn? Damn Barney. Why did he ever come back?"

Once more, as fate would have it, at that very moment, back at Caleb's house, Flynn drives up to the picket fence in a plantation truck, climbs from the cab and walks onto Henry's porch. He looks at the balloons, fingers a tag on them, which wishes him a belated happy birthday. Smiling, he knocks on the door, enters the house and quickly comes out again. "Where is everybody?" he speculates to the wind. Studying the grave and then looking back at the balloons, he steps from the porch with them, picks a handful of nearby wildflowers, and carries them and the balloons to the side of the house and places the flowers on the fake tombstone of Caleb's mother. Tying the balloons to the slender grave marker, Flynn looks down at the mound of earth. "You'd have been so proud of Henry, unknown lady, and his land. Mother prays every night that it will be returned to him, and I've prayed each night that Caleb didn't do it. I don't need to tell you what it is I hope he didn't do, because it makes me sick to even think of it, and since you're Caleb's mother and in heaven with Grandfather and Grandmother, you already know what I mean."

Glancing about the land, gripped in profound sorrow, and realizing that without Henry and Caleb there with him, the beautiful property is an empty shell; the blonde boy touches the tombstone with his delicate piano-playing hands, then walks to his truck and leaves the house and Henry's land behind.

On the south side of the lagoon, unseen by Caleb, due to the cattails and trees about both sides of the shoreline, Carrie and Earlene in their wagon, and Ruby and Pauline in theirs—having had clearly heard and understood Peter's frantic message to Collins about the deputy and feeling the danger all around them—sit in apprehension, as Collins quietly manipulates his lead wagon through the trees, Bruce and his family following close behind in his. Collins spots the rear end of a pickup sticking out of the undergrowth ahead of them and raises his hand. He and Bruce bring their mules to a stop and cautiously climb from the wagons. Collins faces his wife and whispers, "Ruby, you and Carrie ride out of here with the girls at the first sign of trouble. Deputies are sometimes armed, even when off duty, and this one is mean to the bone."

Collins and Bruce arm themselves with fallen, club-like tree limbs and approach the truck and a dying campfire. Marcus—sporting a black eye—and the deputy are fast asleep on the ground. Collins' fears are well founded. The man with Marcus is Deputy Hammer, the one who terrorized Reverend Harris's parishioners the night Claretta and B.J. were slaughtered, the same deputy who called the black congregation queers and said he hated all queers. Wearing blue jeans, a white T-shirt and low-cut tennis shoes, and without his service revolver, Hammer snores as if a pig, as he sleeps stretched out on his back. Several live frogs are tied to the shrubbery with strings about their legs, while their siblings have been turned to charred nuggets on a steel rod over the campfire's glowing, but dying embers. Moonshine jars, firebomb bottles and wicks are scattered about.

Collins angrily kicks Hammer on the leg; and because everyone knows how powerful Hammer is, Collins cracks him over the head with the heavy limb. The drunken man staggers to his feet and runs wobbling toward his truck, as if being chased by the ghost of his past. While Collins chases after the confused, intoxicated deputy, Bruce plants his foot on Marcus's chest, pinning him to the ground. Next to the boy is a tattered, small Bible, its front page open with the words from the boy's deceased parents: *"To our son. Love, Ma and Pa,"* a message his folks had written there just before placing him in that orphanage, where he met Burt. Deeply moved by those words and by Marcus's young face begging up to him in fear, Bruce angrily looks over at the truck-bound deputy as if wanting to kill the man for taking advantage of one of God's children, a boy that could have just as easily have been Brick. No one there or anywhere else—except Naomi—knows that Marcus is the boy who God permitted banker Pennington's son, Charles, to visualize crying in a futuristic death scene over those dead children before Marcus was even born, but Bruce is the first to show him love, cracking opening the door a little for the boy's survival, but that crack is still a far cry from saving Marcus's soul, who is crying—even more desperately—for someone to love him. With his swollen black eye half closed, he continues staring up at the huge black man towering over him and wails as if a trapped animal. Meanwhile, Collins catches a stumbling Deputy Hammer at the truck and breaks the tree limb over his back, taking the fight out of him and then throws the deputy hard against the fender.

"You fucking pig," he bellows, slapping Hammer. "What else were you going to destroy with those goddamn bottles, the rest of Shadow Grove, as well as that innocent young boy?"

"I didn't burn that school!" bellows the deputy. "I was on duty."

While Collins confronts Hammer, Bruce questions Marcus. "What's this man up to out here with you and these bottles and fuses, boy?" asks Bruce, as if a looming, avenging black angel over Marcus, putting the fear of God into the drunken boy.

Marcus spills his guts: "He made me drink with him and he said he'd be the first one to find all that money that's whispered Caleb has out here and said even if we didn't find it, we'd burn down the rest of Shadow Grove and look big in the eyes of the Klan. Said he's give me some money—more than Burt ever did—if I let him mess with me. When I said no, he beat me and then he passed out."

"Why didn't you run away after he passed out, son?" asked Bruce.

"I don't have a home to go to, Mister. And I needed a friend now that Burt is dead. Please, Mister colored man, don't hurt me."

Collins pushes Hammer into Bruce's grip, permitting Marcus to roll free of Bruce's foot.

"Hold onto this trash," exclaims Collins. "Until I see what's in this truck he's in such a hurry to get to. And Marcus, you stay put!"

"Yes, Sir, field boss Keith Collins," bawls the scared boy with his sights on Bruce.

"Take your black hands off me, boy!" hisses a stumbling Deputy Hammer, spitting in Bruce's face. Bruce backhands the defenseless deputy and nearly knocks him unconscious, then holds onto the gasping man with a grip of steel, causing both of Marcus's eyes to open wide as he gawks at the kinky-haired black man. *Only a black angel would dare hit a white cop*, the young boy thinks, picking up his Bible and holding it close.

"You don't tell me nothing, man," Bruce shouts at the pie-eyed Hammer, then glances over at Marcus and back. "Even the devil couldn't do mo' harm than someone molestin' our kids, and you a married man with kids of yo' own."

"Let him go!" demands a voice behind them. Standing yards away on the road, aiming his pistol at Bruce, is Dane Tucker, and there with him—next to his truck—is Hank, with his rifle trained on the females, who are prisoners between the two men. Hank is also holding onto the vicious, barking, and lunging Tramp, which Ruby fears will cause Hank to accidentally discharge his rifle and kill one or all of them in the line of fire. Without entering Hammer's vehicle, Collins—his hands raised—returns to the scene. Bruce quickly releases Hammer, and when he does, Marcus runs yelping to Dane's side, while Earlene having consumed all of her lemonade—nervously wiggles about with her legs crossed and sobs. "I gotta pee, Mamma!" Carrie glances at her daughter, as if asking, *Why now?* "I gotta pee real bad," Earlene sorrowfully adds.

"Ma baby's gotta make wata," Carrie says to Dane, while trembling in dread of him.

"Hun?" says Dane gawking back at Earlene.

"Please," Earlene begs, wiggling about.

545

"Then pee!" Dane says, eyeing her crotch. "Do it here where I can keep an eye on you."

"Get yo'self over to them cattails, Earlene," yells Carrie, casting aside her fears in defense of Earlene now. "Go on and be quick about it."

Carrie turns and looks at Dane as if to say he'd have to kill her if he attempted to have Earlene urinate in front of the men. She turns to Earlene and watches her last born run twenty yards or so away to a patch of shrubbery near the lagoon; and, as Pauline sobs in Ruby's arms, a worried Carrie prays that Earlene will have sense enough to keep on running and maybe find Caleb or Henry, but Earlene has no intention of deserting her mother and father. Half-hidden behind the underbrush, she lifts her dress, lowers her underwear and squats. However, as she lowers her underwear, she notices Hammer running to his truck, open the glove compartment and seize his service revolver. The attractive, black teenager rises out of her squat, desperately trying to squeeze off the flow of urine in order to run back to her father, but can only helplessly watch, as her discharge has its own powerful way. Bruce also sees Hammer sprinting back toward him with that gun. In spite of being only half finished urinating, Earlene pulls up her underwear, and tripping and falling, she flails toward her father, wetting herself as she runs. "Daddy!"

"This black motherfucker hit me!" the deputy yells to Dane, while getting in Bruce's face, once he arrives, all this time, Bruce—knowing his time has come—is watching his daughter screaming back to him, and he yells to her:

"Go back, baby. You don't want to see this!"

On the opposite side of the lagoon, Caleb angrily bursts the balloon just as a shot rings through the air from the confrontational side of the vast body of water, causing Old Clara to rear.

"It was only the balloon bursting, old girl," Caleb tells the stunning chestnut, but knows, down deep, that it was a gunshot—the murderous tool of the Klan—and no amount of wishing that it wasn't will change it.

On the other side of the water, Earlene wails headlong into her sobbing mother's outstretched arms, as Bruce stands shocked with a bullet in his shoulder. "You didn't think I'd let you die so easily, did you?" Hammer asks, wobbling about the black man.

From his side of the lagoon, as a lone sparrow flies across the sky above him, Caleb rises up in the stirrups and looks about, trying to locate the direction of the gunfire in the echoing irregularity over the lagoon and land. The sparrow knows, as it continues on across the water and on pass Bruce and the others—leaving them behind—as Earlene sobs and reaches out for her father. Bruce is hardly able to remain standing upright and limps about with blood streaming down his arm; the loving man, his eyebrows painfully arched downwards, shakes his head with a look warning his child to be quiet and not to draw the attention of the men to her. While Marcus watches in disbelief, and Ruby holds onto a hysterical Carrie and onto an enraged Collins, at the same time, jerking on her husband's shirt sleeve to keep him still, while a fearful, sobbing Pauline restrains Earlene.

Caleb eases Old Clara to the water's edge and listens to the screams intermixing and echoing continuously in all directions across the water.

At the source, Earlene breaks free of Pauline and races to her stunned father.

"Daddy!" she screams. Old Hank tosses his rifle and the lunging dog's leash to an ashen Marcus, and grabs Earlene by her hair; lifting her into his arms, he fondles her bra-less breast through her clothing.

"Fuck her, old man!" Hammer exclaims and then laughs. "Do it so we can all watch you try to get it up! Ha! Show her that even though her sister's boyfriend, Billy Joe, could take it out and put it in his back pocket, like they say, that it ain't the long of it, it's the wideness of it, in your case, the limpness of it!"

"Don't y'all hurt ma baby," Bruce begs. "Yo' problem's not with her . . . It's with me!"

"You got that right," says Hammer, firing pointblank into Bruce's head.

"Ahhhh! Ahhhh!" screams Marcus, followed by those of the females. Collins goes totally pale, as Bruce falls back against a maple tree and thumps to the ground near a granite slab, his blood streaming onto the harden rock. Earlene bites Hank's hand and breaks free of him and races to her father.

In the boat shack, Jayne sits up on her bed of papers, the sound of the gunshot still ringing in her head. Badly sunburned, she looks about for something to wear and notices a straw hat on the floor with Caleb's name on the inside sweat band. Slipping on the hat to protect her face, the blistered girl stands up, finds one of Flynn's old paint-stained shirts, and slips into it.

At the campsite—not satisfied with shooting Bruce in his arm and

547

head—Deputy Hammer fires into Bruce's body again and again, and now, standing over the dead man, he fires again. That final round of gunfire causes Old Clara to rear and topple Caleb. The old horse bolts, leaving her young master behind. Caleb wades into the water and moves aside cattails. Then, as his sights sweep along the opposite shore, he spots Hammer's truck, Dane and the others through the distant treeline. Using the cattails for concealment, Caleb silently breast strokes among them as long as possible, knowing that if he tried to run along the land to reach the other side, he fears he'll be spotted by the Klansmen. After feeling it was safe to do so, he parts the cattails, and goes into an overhand stroke, kicking with his powerful legs, ankles and feet, as he smoothly swims across the lagoon to the massacre.

Jayne—wearing Flynn's shirts and Caleb's straw hat, held in place by the hat strings tied about her neck—runs from the shack and down the shoreline. She sees Caleb in the water. Daring not to enter the lagoon with her blistered skin, her shirt flopping in the wind exposing her nudity, and not knowing about the danger of being spotted by those on the other shore of the water, she holds the straw hat on her head, and runs—as fast as she can in those red shoes—the long way around the lagoon, keeping an eye on a fading-in-and-out-of-sight Caleb as she goes; and it seems God is with her, because no one on the other side has spotted her.

A mile down the road leading off Henry's land, Flynn had stopped his truck at the sound of the first gunshot, and, now, baffled, he sees birds swarming skyward behind him from the trees around the lagoon and he swerves the truck around.

Unaware that Flynn or help of any kind is on its way, crying hysterically, Carrie wrestles free of Ruby and sinks to the ground with Earlene beside Bruce's body; groaning in that deep-rooted, ghost-like custom of her grandparent's African heritage, Carrie cradles the bloody body of her loved one in her arms for the second time in less than a month. When Hammer dances about Carrie, Earlene and Bruce's body, giggling, Collins, in an insane rage, blindsides the deputy and throws him head-first into the campfire's hot ashes, sending Hammer's gun flying out of his hand and onto the grass. As the deputy—howling—runs out of the glowing embers and jumps about beating out the cinders on his clothing, Collins dives for the lawman's service revolver, but Dane steps on the weapon, and Collins, on his belly, looks up into the barrel of the one-eared Klansman's .38, the females screaming at the top of their lungs.

"Why!" exclaims Collins. "Bruce didn't deserve to die!"

"You all been nigger-rized too long if you ask that," Dane yells. "You all got to die."

"I'm going to get me some pussy befer we kill this one," says old Hank, grabbing Earlene again and having trouble seeing through his eyeglasses which are knocked lopsided on his head, as he tries to hold onto a kicking and wailing Earlene. Suddenly, Carrie, with the power of a mother's love, pregnant and all, bounds to her feet and leaps onto a shocked Hank's back, jarring his glasses completely off of his face. The wild woman attacks Hank's neck and shoulders with her fingernails and with her teeth, and as Dane—shocked out of his mind—glances over at Carrie's heinous attack on old Hank, Collins—still on his belly—reaches up and seizes Dane's gun arm with one hand and Dane's testicles, through his trousers, with the other.

Hammer—having slapped out the cinders on his clothing—zeros in on his fallen gun now at Collins' feet. Collins sees the deputy stooping and reaching for the revolver; and—while managing to maintain a firm grip on a squealing Dane's arm and testicles—Collins kicks the gun into the glowing embers. Hammer tries to fish the revolver from the hot ashes with the roasting rod, but Pauline runs in behind him and pushes him back into the heated residue. When Hammer storms out of the campfire, this second time, surging with blinding rage—embers on his clothing or not—his only focus is Pauline, and without mercy he lifts her off her feet to toss her head first into the campfire. As Pauline calls to her father for help and, at the same time, desperately clings to Deputy Hammer's shirt, preventing him from tossing her into the fire, Carrie and Earlene knock old Hank down and join Ruby in an attack on the deputy, pounding him with sticks and kicks to his groin and buttocks. As Hammer fights back, releasing Pauline, and throwing the females about like so much trash, bullets explode from the gun in the embers, causing the mules to break free from their tree-tied ropes and run away with the wagons. When the deputy ducks to the ground, with bullets flying everywhere, Ruby pulls the girls from the fray. "Get out of here!" she yells.

"To where," sobs Pauline, watching the mules run away. "The wagons are gone!"

Ruby hears the welcomed sound of the train. "The bridge! Run to the bridge!"

When the girls run screaming for the distant bridge, Ruby nudges Carrie after them, then turns her sights on her struggling husband and Dane, who is about to break free of Collin's painful hold on him, all the time Hammer hugging the ground with his eyes closed in fear of getting shot, Ruby dashes to Collins and Dane, but Carrie—instead of running away with the girls—stands there sobbing down at her fallen man.

"You have to live for your unborn baby, now, Carrie," calls Ruby as she races forward to help Collins. "Run, Carrie! Run for your life!"

Carrie flops down, hugs Bruce's body in her arms and talks to him. "You ain't goin' no place without me, you hear, Bruce Johnson? We be together too long talkin' 'bout heaven, and I'm comin' there with you! Me and our unborn child." She begins gracefully undulating her arms, wrist and fingers as if to fly.

As Ruby runs shrieking to Collins—who is in the fight of his life against an upright and better positioned Dane—Dane jerks free of Collins and fires his gun skywards while falling onto his back. Collins leaps to his feet and sprints to his oncoming wife. Dane rises up and shoots, striking Collins between his upper, right arm and his side, but Collins and Ruby continue running, Ruby having no idea that her husband has been shot. Dane rips Tramp's leash and the rifle from a petrified, wailing Marcus and then glares at a half-blind, crying Hank, who is yelling for someone to help him find his glasses. Spitting in Hank's face, Dane slaps him and shouts: "You ain't worth the paper you wipe your ass on, you sex-starved, old fool." He tosses Hank's rifle to an awakened Hammer. "Go after the girls," he yells. "I'll get Collins and Ruby! And get those damn keys out of the trucks so they can't double back and sneak out of here in them. No one leaves here alive! If they do and reach Sarah, we're all dead!"

Hammer sprints to his truck, then to Hank's as well, removes the ignition keys and races in the last-known direction that the girls took, while Dane, along with Tramp leading the way, sprints insanely after Collins and Ruby. Marcus, who is left behind with Hank, watches with open-eyed dread, as the old man—crawling on the ground—locates his glasses, gets to his feet and takes out his penis, shakes it, and moves in on Carrie, who continues sitting in the lap of the earth, next to that granite slab of blood, while rocking her man in her arms. Hank—with his corrupt sights set on Carrie's bulging breasts—hustles to her side and kicks her in the stomach; Carries topples backward looking up at him, while gripping her abdomen in piercing pain, pain which would have killed her and her child outright but for that granite slab, which Hank's foot had struck its edge as much as it had Carrie, reflecting most of the impact. "I ain't never had a pregnant bitch befer," Hank tells Carrie, shaking his penis at her

Marcus gags at the sight and turns away, and, as he does, he sees a bright beam appear around the lagoon shore, and from out of the water a light emerges traveling on two feet, then runs upright to the camp site. Carrie sees even more than that: a tall, human figure, silhouetted in the center of the illumination, as it zeros in on her and Hank, and she continues to marvel at its approach, even when Hank drops his trousers and shorts and falls to his knees beside her pregnant body and begins ripping off her dress. Marcus recoils in holy terror, his eyes disbelieving what they see. It's Caleb in the center of that blinding beam and suddenly upon Hank. It's too much for Marcus's young brain, this sight of Caleb Brooks, a phantom which overcomes all of the white boy's young reason to dismiss it as just his fears; all of his young life he's been taught that coloreds are just doormats for the world to walk on and not something from a world of ghosts. The boy lets out an ear-piercing shriek, and when he does, Hank turns around. The old man's eyes slowly look away from the red-haired boy—and up at Caleb and out of that blinding glow, reflecting down on Hank, comes the campfire's metal rod. "Whaaa!" Hank squalls, when the hard metal impacts his body—charred fogs and all, and before he can react, the metal rod explodes itself again and again against his back, bending the rusty shaft in half, and then Hank sees stars as a flurry of Caleb's powerful fists sledge hammer against his face, breaking his jaw, sending him flopping to the ground and onto the granite slab. Soaked to his skin, outlined in the dazzling light, while Marcus jumps about wailing, Caleb kicks Hank away from Carrie and Bruce. He squats and claws at the eight-hundred-pound slab. Hank shakes all over, as he lies on his back and watches Caleb, and even though he knows that it would take five men to lift that chunk of granite, he's also keenly aware that with that bright light about Henry's half-breed, inferior son—a light coming from Caleb's body and not that of God's—that, he, Hank, is seeing the impossible happening before his eyes. Terrified to his bones, the old Klansman knows, white man or not, Klansman or not,

551

that Caleb is determined to crush him with the monstrous portion of a mountain, and when Caleb manages to lifts the massive body of rock over his head and targets him with it, Hank's fears explodes with a howling yell for help, and he throws up his hands and closes his eyes. Marcus lets out a girlish squeal, races for the road and leaps into Hank's truck, locking the door behind him. As Caleb grimaces under the incredible weight of the granite, the glow about him disappears and the wind stirs itself through his curly hair and through the tree branches above him. Battered and bleeding, Carrie points up at the maple tree leaves. "Wait, Caleb," she says. "An angel. In the tree, Caleb . . . It has a face of tears. . . . Bruce, Caleb. It's my Bruce. He says don't kill Hank, that God has His special plans fo' that man." Weaving under the weight of the granite, Caleb's tormented muscles tremble, and he gazes in disbelieve down at Carrie.

"He tried to kill and rape you," Caleb forcefully exclaims.

Carrie flutters her arms like the wings of a dove, as if again trying to lift herself off the ground and leave the earth behind, her eyes locked on the tree and leaves and then on Caleb and finally on Bruce's body across her lap. "Bruce says you're to bring rain and love to this and Sarah's land and to all of the earth, not hatred and meaningless killing, Caleb, which this world has far too much of. Hank is not the one you must destroy, son. Bruce says Barney is the one and that Barney will soon awaken from Naomi's curse with a vengeance. You are the Rain Bird, Caleb Brooks. Bruce says that's one of several, earthly-given names that will be given to you around the world from this day on."

"Listen to her, Caleb," begs Hank.

"Shut up, you damnable, old fool!" Caleb yells. "Did you listen to all those whom you lynched and butchered!"

Caleb prepares to kill Hank no matter what Carrie says or thinks she sees in the tree.

"He's watching you, Caleb," Carrie whispers.

"How can a dead man watch anyone? He's dead, Carrie. Bruce is dead."

"Not just Bruce, son. Him. God is watching you."

As he had as a child, whenever God's name was mentioned, Caleb looks to the sky, but this time, instead of feeling nothing, a tingling feeling runs down his back; and, bellowing, he heaves the slab aside, splitting open a nearby tree. Dropping to his knees beside Carrie, he sobs. Hank looks over at the split tree, at Caleb, jumps to his feet and—limping in pain—he skips and hops his way to his truck and tries to get inside.

"Open the goddamn door, you little pussy!" he yells at Marcus, while jerking on the locked door. Once the frightened boy releases the lock, Hank bounces inside, locks the door behind him, slaps Marcus and desperately looks for the ignition key. Failing to find it, he lays on the horn and yells, "Help! Somebody help! Caleb is insane. He's going to kill us!"

When Caleb angrily turns his attention to Hank and his truck, Carrie holds onto his arm. "Save ma child, Caleb," she whispers. "The angel done said our boy Brick, our girl Earlene and this other one to come will be in the hands of ma sister now."

"What other child, Carrie?" ask Caleb, having never known that Carrie is with child. "What sister?" he goes on to her. "You're an only child."

"The child that He will deliver into yo' hands, Caleb, and then into that of my sister. . . . The world . . . it overflows with all of my sisters, Caleb. Millions of them. My sisters."

She dies holding onto Caleb's hand, and as he loosens her grip and covers her exposed body with the pieces of her torn dress, his fingers are abruptly soaked with warm, amniotic fluid, and a baby boy slips from Carrie's birth channel into the safety of Caleb's hands. He slowly rises and steps back and he gazes in silences at the wailing infant, who cries without being urged to do so, and then, suddenly, sunlight shines all about them and increases by the second, while a pair of white doves circle overhead, serenely gliding in the breezes. In his truck, gripped in pure pain and fear, and half out of his mind, Hank, as well as Marcus, gawk out the window at Caleb, at the baby and at the bright sunlight and the glowing doves around Caleb; and both he and Marcus turn ashen upon seeing the sensorial sight. "Earlene or this baby," Caleb calls, looking about in sorrow. "Whom do I save?" The wind stirs the tree and its leaves trickle down on Carrie's body, and, in a bright flash, millions upon millions of leaves explode from around the woods and lagoon and are sucked aloft into a mighty updraft, escorting the fuzzy-looking soul of the dead woman's spirit as it rises skybound and confronts the white doves, which leads the living soul into the clouds, where voices are heard:

"Welcome home, Carrie, you and Bruce. Here you will sleep among us and others until He comes and awakens us again."

"Marilyn. You and Doctor Winthrop. Both of you made it, too. I'm so glad fo' y'all."

"Yes, Carrie, we made it," Doctor Winthrop's voice says. "And down there is Caleb, our child's son, the color of tomorrow, the re-blending of God's creation. Isn't he beautiful? We must go now. Bruce is waiting for us."

The voices fade and only the sound of the lightly blowing wind, the sound of drifting-back-to-earth leaves, and the joyfully singing of birds are heard. Seeing and hearing all of this, Hank pounds on the truck's horn and wails, convinced that he has lost his mind, Marcus, sobbing, dreading the loss of heaven.

"Did you see that, Marcus?" Hank asks. "Was it real?"

Marcus is too busy looking at the sudden appearance of Old Clara to answer, the only thing that appears real to him at the moment, as the faithful horse trots up to Caleb, the towel on which Caleb had wiped his face hanging from her saddlebag. Gunfire echoes from within the woods, causing Marcus to flinch, but not Caleb. Shivering from his swim through the lagoon, he snaps out of his stupor, and cradling the newborn with one hand, he removes the towel from the saddlebag with the other and wraps the newborn and afterbirth in the soft cloth, then removes his bulky jacket from the saddlebag. And so that Carrie's rich blood will drain downward into her infant, instead of out of it and possibly back into the placenta, Caleb places the towel-wrapped infant in the saddlebag with the afterbirth at the highest point on the towel.

"You're in the hands of fate, now, little man," he says, slapping Old Clara on her rump, sending her racing for home. In the surging, cold wind, and shivering, as the clouds cover the sun, Caleb tosses off his wet shirt, slips into his jacket and then glares over at the big-eyed Hank and Marcus. Sprinting full out, he dashes right past the truck, without giving it and them a second thought, and follows the sounds of gunfire, leaving the gawking Marcus, Hank and vehicle behind. Hank leaps from his battered Dodge and runs in the opposite direction of Caleb, wailing for his life, Marcus right behind him. "Wait fer me, Hank!"

A quarter mile away and speeding in his truck toward the gunfire, Flynn sees Old Clara—her saddlebag and baby unseen on her opposite side—charging down the middle of the one-lane dirt, road directly at him. "Jesus," Flynn exclaims, his hands gripping the steering wheel, his foot hitting the brakes. He swerves, as Old Clara leaps right over the top of the oncoming truck, lands on the road behind it, and flashes on down the road without missing a beat. Flynn careens off the road into a tree.

In the woods, while following the sounds of alarmed birds, Caleb spots Deputy Hammer taunting Pauline and Earlene next to a gully. He's holding Hank's rifle on them with one hand, and pointing at his fly with the other.

"Give me what I want and I'll let you live," he tells them. "The black stuff first."

"No, you queer," shouts Pauline. "We won't let you touch us."

"I deal with both boys and girls," Hammer says, blasting the ground at the girls' feet. "So what?"

Pauline and Earlene see Caleb racing in behind Hammer, and they watch in astonishment as Caleb lifts the deputy up by the seat of his trousers and throws him, rifle and all, six feet down into the gully and a waist-deep stream of water. Both girls rush into Caleb's arms, kissing him about his hands and face, as Hammer frantically searches about the muddied water with his hands trying to locate his weapon.

"The bridge, Caleb," sobs Pauline, pulling Caleb away from the stream. "The bridge!"

Hurrying toward the bridge and the sound of the train, the girls run holding onto Caleb as if he might suddenly disappear, one of them on either side of him. When they reach the old structure, Pauline—in a near state of collapse—sobs in despair: her parents are nowhere to be seen; instead, far down the rails from them and occupying the train tracks, which curve under the old, Cutter's namesake and toward Cutterville, is a lingering, steam-gusting locomotive, jerking forward an inch or two and then settling down, while blocking their way across the tracks with a endless line of jerking, and unpredictable open-top boxcars, making it too dangerous to try and cross between those jerking, steel wheels. The boxcars are loaded down with cotton, some of which is being blown off the top of the freight cars onto the girls and Caleb by the wind. At the controls of the locomotive, the restless engineer, an impatient, old, white, swearing man, whose friends call "Parson," goes on playing with the throttle. With him is the black coal stoker, Bruno, the same two and train which killed Snodgress. Back at the boxcars, Collins and Ruby suddenly appear, running out of the woods and to Caleb and the girls; both parents sob when they arrive, kissing the girls and Caleb. A sad-faced Earlene steps back from the others and looks about. "Where's Mamma?"

"God," yells Ruby, staring at the line of box cars and fearing that Dane will catch up to them. "Please, God, let this train stop fussing around and take us out of here!"

Caleb points to another train crossing atop the bridge. "This one here can't continue until the one on top comes down the slope and clears out in front of it," he tells Ruby, while also looking about for another way around the train. As the engineer in the lower locomotive begins inching his train and line of boxcars steadily forward in anticipation of the upper train clearing five hundred yards ahead of it, Ruby spots Dane and Tramp running their way with a drenched Hammer using his removed shirt to dry off his rifle as he runs, his bitter sights on Caleb.

"They're here," cries Ruby.

Caleb—motioning for the others to follow—climbs between one of the cotton cars and, once safely on the other side, reaches back to help the females through. The frightened women—after eyeing the train's inching-forward wheels—then hearing Caleb's words of encouragement reaches out, and as he leans toward them—one by one—they take his hand and cross over the couplings and between the creeping freight cars. Collins—enduring his pain—brings up the rear, and then everyone races up the hill behind Caleb. While the locomotive on top of the bridge slowly moves down the slope in the direction of the lower tracks, Collins and Caleb run across the top of the bridge to one of the slowly moving train's boxcars, which is adjacent to a red-placard, tanker car. Then, with the help of a black hobo and that of his white partner, also running across the bridge to board the open boxcar—but coming at them from the opposite direction—Caleb and the hobos lift the females into an open door, with the hobos easily entering next. Below the bridge, Hammer fires his rifle up through the ties at Collins and Caleb, who are running just in front of that tanker car. Several of Hammer's and Dane's bullets strike the tanker, sending an acrid-smelling fluid gushing from the hundred-thousand-gallon rolling time bomb and onto the tracks, thoroughly soaking the old wooden landmark, as the tanker crosses it.

In the lower locomotive, Parson and Bruno are unaware that the inflammable fluid is raining down onto the tracks behind them and onto a section of one of their cotton-bearing boxcars. They are, however, aware that someone is shooting up at the bridge, and looking toward the rear of the train, they see Dane and Hammer—who continue firing up at Collins and Caleb. Then, as the locomotive from the top of the bridge emerges in front of the cotton-hauling one and heads for Cutterville, Parson cries out to Bruno. "My God, boy, stoke us up! If those fools back there come this way, we're not waiting fer old number six to clear out ahead of us. I'll back our ass out of here in full throttle, and God help those two crazies if they get in the way!"

On top of the bridge—as their open boxcar approaches the end of that old structure and the downhill marker—Caleb looks at Collins and recognizes the pain reflected on the field boss's face, and Caleb carefully helps Collins aboard and into the outstretched hands of the frightened hobos and traumatized females. Even in pain, however, Collins insists on being the one who reaches back for Caleb, but Caleb stops running. "I can't leave Papa alone with Dane!" he calls to Collins, as the train and boxcar rumbles on by him.

"Caleb, behind you!" yells Earlene, pointing at Hammer and Dane now on the opposite end of the bridge. Before Caleb can turn and run, Hammer raises his rifle and fires. Grabbing his head, Caleb falls off the span.

"Nooo!" exclaims Dane. Collins and the females also scream, as Caleb explodes facedown onto the lower train and into the load of fuel-soaked cotton. Dane, holding onto Tramp, blows his stack at Hammer: "You fool! He's got those millions!"

Hammer gapes down, as Caleb lies motionless in the cotton. The deputy explodes, "Why didn't the fuck you tell me! You said millions! Sweet Jesus. Let's get down there and see if he's still alive!"

As soon as the descending caboose passes in front of them, the lower locomotive pulls off, spinning its massive wheels, expelling sand from its inner workings onto the slippery, steel tracks and picking up steam as it tailgates the lead train, Parson and Bruno gawking back at Tramp, Dane and Hammer, charging down the slopes, both men yelling at the old engineer to stop the train. Shaking, Parson removes a bottle of moonshine from his jacket pocket and guzzles from it.

"You ain't gonna get drunk and run into old number six are you, boss man?" asks Bruno.

"Shut your dumb-ass mouth, Bruno, and just shovel that coal!" hisses Parson. "I do the thinking around here, not you! Hell no, I'm not going to run into number six, you dumb ass! And I'm not drunk or feeble minded as you might think. I drink because I feel a cold coming on."

With the cotton train rolling along faster with each turn of its wheels, Bruno spots Jayne running from out of the nearby woods on his side of the tracks and alongside the boxcars, while holding onto that straw hat of hers and looking back over her shoulder, judging the speed of the boxcar onto which Caleb fell, as it approaches her position, the girl increasing her speed. The old black stoker watches her flailing with all of her might; and he silently encourages her on, *Come on girl. You can make it.* As the boxcar threatens to overtake and pass her by, the crafty black fireman steals a glance at the engineer, who is looking back at Dane and Hammer from the other window, and the old stoker reaches up and eases back on the throttle and unnoticeably and skillfully slows the train just slightly, and he quickly returns his sights toward the half-naked, white girl, as a huffing and puffing Dane, Hammer and Tramp trail her and the train: "Where the hell did she come from?" Dane yells, as he and Hammer, as well as a smiling Bruno, watch as Jayne grabs hold of the steel rung of Caleb's boxcar and climbs onto the top, where she sees Caleb lying face down and bleeding. She quickly turns him from his face to his back and holds him in her arms. Running down the tracks behind the caboose, an enraged Dane and Hammer, reloading as they run, open fire on the boxcar; one of the bullets ricochets off the side of the cotton-soaked car, creating a spark and setting the fuel-soaked cotton on fire, sending smoke and sparks skyward.

Springing to her feet, a panic-stricken Jayne takes off her shirt and desperately tries to beat out the fire, and as she battles the flames seemingly forever, a sudden blast from a fire extinguisher swamps out the raging flames, limiting the burn to the corner of the massive boxcar. Jayne looks up into the face of Bruno, and the tall black coal stoker looks down at the young girl's nakedness and then over at Caleb—who begins to groan. Bruno gazes toward the locomotive, as Jayne slips into her shirt and hugs it about her body and seems ready to give Bruno hell for gawking at her the way he had. Facing her once more, the huge black man places his finger against his lips. "Shhh," he whispers, as she attempts to talk. "No need to explain. Boss man saw the smoke comin' from the cotton, and sent me back here to put out the fire." He looks down at Caleb as if thinking that Caleb and Jayne were runaway lovers, and that the Klansmen were trying to murder them both. "Get off this train as soon as you can, little miss, so boss man don't see you two. That po' boy is a dead man already ifin I ever did see one. If this po' man didn't have trouble feeding his own kids, I'd take him home with me, so help me God."

When he gazes down, Caleb is looking up at him, and as Jayne watches in amazement, Caleb takes Flynn's gold coin from the bag about his neck, and mustering all of his strength, reaches out and places the coin in Bruno's hand. "I've been looking for someone who needs this," he says, in a state of shock, seemingly unaware that Jayne is there, and going on. "Thanks for helping me." When Caleb again sinks into exhaustion, Bruno jerks back from him, trembling in fear.

"Who is this boy?" he asks Jayne. "He touched me! He has the feel on his hands. The feel! He has it!"

Bruno looks at the confused girl, at the coin, unaware of it's worth, then leers toward the locomotive. The kindhearted man leaves, glancing back from time to time at Caleb, while skillfully jumping from boxcar to boxcar on his way back to the locomotive and to the job of being ignorant, shoveling coal and keeping his mouth shout about Caleb and Jayne, and about the coin, like the boss man says a good, old nigger always should.

"You naked, sex-starved bitch!" Dane bellows, as Jayne and the train fades in the distance. "I said we'd share the money with you. I'll kill you! So help me, your fucking God. I'll blow your nigger-loving head clean off! That money belongs to me. Not to you! To me!"

That night, fearing that if the bodies are found they would draw far too much attention and questions from the northern reporters, in town, at so critical a time in the race for Barney's fortune, Dane orders his men to dispose of the bodies of Bruce and Carrie in a place where he thinks they will never be found, and as they carry out his commands, he climbs a telephone pole and cuts the phone lies. When the others return from disposing of the bodies, Dane is waiting for them. Marcus still seeing that image of Caleb lifting that eight-hundred-pound slab, as something from hell and fearing for his life, now sees the one-eared Klansman as his personal savior with Burt dead. He follow Dane's enraged sights to the horizon lights from Cutterville, as Dane triumphantly shouts, "Now try and call here to warn Sarah, Jayne, goddamn, Hill! Trying to help that fucking, goddamn dead Caleb Brooks! Cutterville won't protect you. I'll find you. You're in my territory now." He glares at the men. "That damn girl must have been bewitched by Naomi to do such a thing! We ain't them coons brother's keepers!"

His heart racing, Marcus fingers the Bible in his pocket, and he turns his sights on the shimmering surface of the moonlit lagoon, the words "His brother's keeper" ringing in his ears.

Suddenly, a rifle shot blast a hole in one of the truck windows, scattering the Klan; then a second shot sends the hat flying off Hank's head; everyone leaps into their trucks and speeds away. Henry steps out of the darkness, the barrel of his rifle still smoking. "God wants my boy to love our enemies, but He doesn't expect the same from me, like He didn't from David. I'll blow you folks to kingdom come if you ever come back here. Get the hell out!" he yells. "And stay the hell out of here!" He then looks about. "Caleb, son, are you out here? Where are you!"

38

The Riot

That night, Sarah and Naomi stand over Flynn as he lies in bed with a bandage on his arm and a small cut on his forehead. "Doctor Schmidt said it's nothing, Mother, but you and Naomi keep fussing over me. Have you heard if anything is wrong with Henry or Caleb? Old Clara. The way she was running like that and leaped right over the truck. It was unbelievable." He looks at Naomi; she's smiling. "How, Naomi? You're smiling. How is that possible for a horse to do that? She's not a holy horse like the white one that so many people are still saying rose into the sky with you and Claretta and Brick. Is she? I was driving nearly forty-five miles an hour right at her."

Sarah—who had not witnessed Naomi flying on that horse and doesn't know what to think about it, even as Flynn doesn't, regardless of his some-what-I-believe questions about it now—waits anxiously for Naomi's answer, which may prove once and for all that the mystery woman is not just an unusually blessed person, but is actually a real angel.

"Maybe," Naomi says, beaming at them. "Like a gifted human being can do powerful things, or even an evil one can—such as lifting a one-ton truck off of Dane Tucker and one-handedly dragging that misguided soul from under it—when the power of adrenaline flows in his veins, our Lord—or the devil—certainly can also permit an animal to do like wise, if He feels it's to show the glory of His Father." She goes to the window and stares into the night and mutters. "A horse that is still on the run, until God sends it home to affect us all in His own good time. So—now—let us not waste this moment thinking about me or who I am." She turns to Flynn. "You were asking about Henry and Caleb."

"Henry was here earlier," Sarah tells Flynn, "but he went home to see if Caleb has returned." Down the long, carpeted hallway—in the master bedroom, while lying on his sick bed, and as if having heard Caleb's name mentioned—Barney begins rolling his eyes and groaning. Sitting up in her chair, his nurse puts aside one of Flynn's books of poetry and she watches Barney with growing apprehension, as his bed wiggles and he continues groaning and twitching, the way he has for weeks, but even more so now. Meanwhile, resting in his bed, Flynn suddenly sits up.

"Did you feel it, Mother?" he asks. "My bed and the earth were moving."

"I felt nothing," Sarah says. "Did you, Naomi?"

"Yes," she says and turns away, gazing out the window into the dark. Sarah knows that no amount of urging will compel Naomi to answer if she chooses not to, and she is keenly aware that if Naomi refuses to reveal what she sees or feels it's because by revealing it, it would strike absolute terror in them of things about to come.

"What is it, Naomi?" Flynn asks. "What do you feel?"

When Naomi doesn't answer Flynn, Sarah glances beyond Naomi and out the window. Flames are rising in the dark sky over Cutterville, but more than that, there is a green glow coming from the direction of Mrs. Cutter's house on the edge of town, a green glow growing stronger, and again the earth shakes. This time, Sarah feels it, and she faces Naomi and her eyes, not her voice now plead. Naomi carefully replies, "Collins and the others are cut off in town," she whispers, "and now Caleb is missing." Naomi focuses on the direction to Mrs. Cutter's distant house then returns to the bed. "Pray, Flynn, as you've never prayed before. Satan has awakened the queen of darkness from her deep sleep."

In Cutterville, as the land continues shaking, stray dogs are in the backyard of the Cutter house, following the smell of the fresh scent of death and digging at the depraved woman's grave. A sudden, sharp jolt of the earth cracks the massive tombstone and opens up a wide fissure in the ground, releasing a solid black wall of billions of flies out of the evil woman's burial site, startling the half-starved dogs. Lightning flashes across the heavens, and a zigzagging bolt of electricity slams into the tombstone's silver star, splitting the grave marker into two halves and sending them crashing to the ground, and out of that pit of hell—as the ground rumbles and shakes—upwards soars a green, glowing, and bloody, horrific, winged monster, and as it rises skyward, it shakes off the stray flies from its body, and gobbles them up, flies which, up till then, had been feeding off of the creature's rotting flesh. Their tails between their legs and yelping, the dogs flee, looking behind them and up at the sky, as the winged horror leaves Cutterville behind and heads straight for Shadow Grove.

In downtown Cutterville, gunshots ring out, and store fires rage out of control. Firemen battle blazes whenever the violence subsides enough for them to do so; in Colored Town, however, in houses that survived the first riot, blacks are left to their own devices to extinguish their own fires. A young mother runs from her burning apartment with two children in her arms. Once outside, she wails skyward for God to send Christ back to earth to save them, as He said He would one day, and as she shrieks, a raven flies out of the smoky, dark sky over Colored Town and looks down at the woman and her two children, whom she lowers to the ground and are now running down the middle of the earthen road beside her and sobbing.

Flying on, the royal bird soars over Cutterville's train yard, and the black, winged specter focuses downward on Caleb lying face-up in the boxcar of cotton, his hands at his sides, his skin ashen and pale, his eyes open and unmoving, staring up as if at nothing. Jayne, on her knees—and fearing that Caleb has died with his eyes open—is shaking him and sobbing, as she had for her mother. She sees the raven glide in front of the full moon and begin circling in a downward spiral, fourteen times in all, always with its sights on Caleb; and each time it circles, the circle grows tighter and closer, and the closer it gets to the boxcar and to Caleb, the more his color returns, and he begins groaning and stirring about.

"You're moving, Caleb," Jayne cries somehow regaining her voice. "You're moving about and groaning. You're not dead." With the moonlight shining down on her and Caleb, Jayne realizes that there is a connection between Caleb and the raven, and she follows his sights to the bird of life, and watches in wonder as the color fully returns to Caleb's golden skin, and then she marvels at a moon-cast, shadow—from a nearby tree. The shadow is moving slowly from the tree to the boxcar, angulating onto the cotton, and onto Caleb, the tree branches, and now the tree trunk forming—what appears to be—a black shadowy cross over Caleb's body. The mixed-blood boy's vision sharpens, and his gaze meets that of the raven and then he focuses on Jayne. When she—in turn—looks from him and back to the sky, the bird is gone, she faces Caleb.

"Thank God you're okay, Caleb. I thought you were—" Jayne clams up, as danger all around the boxcar is heard closing in on them.

Having burned several stores and ransacked them as a protest against the blacks for the loss of their jobs, the white looters race through the train yard to join others of their kind rummaging there and all along Main Street and the square. "Kill the nigger factory workers, and if the law won't help us kill 'em, we'll do it ourselves, and let's burn down all of that damn nigger town, once and fer all, like the colonel asked us before that senator, nigger-loving Feddermann opposes it, and that Jew factory as well! Cutterville's dead anyway unless we get those jobs! Burn it!" The rioters yell as they run past the boxcars.

On the square, hundreds of jobless whites armed with guns, knives, and clubs—instead of firing on the guards who, so far, haven't fired on them, and feeling that the guards will not retaliate with gunfire if they only throw rocks at the building, the crowd does just that; they hurl stones and rocks at the factory instead. But then, several of the rioters become bolder and begin scaling the factory wall and are beaten back by the plant's security, which is reinforced by Richards's deputies.

Factory workers—some of whom had been cut by flying glass when rocks sailed through the window on the third floor—get in on the act by heaving worn-out, old re-capable tire casings from the plant's windows down onto the rioters; who, in return hurl a rainstorm of stones at the windows, inadvertently cascading down tons of glass and billions of razor-sharp slivers of glass onto the street and onto themselves and their families. Cut and bruised, the enraged Cutterville whites fire a couple of rounds at the building and then make a hasty retreat behind the veterans' tents. Under Richards's command, his deputies and the plant security storm from the brick structure and attack the rioters in Hooverville and burn down the tents, sending the veterans and their loved ones fleeing into the night. Having stayed out of the fray, for the most part, then seeing their homes burned to the ground, the ex-soldiers take up arms and join the jobless wolf pack, forcing Richards's deputies and Dessen's guards back to the factory, and from behind the plant walls, the deputies and guards shoot down the oncoming ex-soldiers, enraged, gun-firing citizens and the Klan.

Four blocks away in the train yard, Lugo Robb, an old, club-carrying, railyard cop—while keeping an eye on the flames rising in the moonlit sky over Main Street and over Colored Town—hobbles down the train tracks muttering to himself. "They ought-ta send all them coons back to Africa, is what I say." Stopping suddenly, he shines his flashlight on the cotton car which he had been told had been set afire; he sniffs the air and—being the curious old man that he is—he painfully follows the burned fuel smell up the boxcar rungs to the top, with his arthritic limbs and legs agonizingly slowing him down all the way. Once on top, he flinches back in dismay. Jayne is squatting next to Caleb and fanning him with her straw hat, trying to quicken his recovery.

"What the hell," the old man yells at her. "What in God's name! Jayne Hill!" Jayne's jimson eyes stare up at him. "What in the hell you doing up here with that boy, girl?" he goes on. "A nigga and a half naked—What the hell's wrong with you in here with him? He's colored!"

The old man nudges Caleb with his foot, and Caleb slowly sits erect. "He moved. Caleb! You sat up!" Jayne sobs. "That bird, Caleb. In the sky over us. The shadow of the cross and . . . Did it cure you? Did it?"

"Hush up, girl, with that drunken talk!" Lugo snaps. He squints at Jayne as if she's totally bonkers and then looks at the rag she's tied about Caleb's head, a large piece of the already-scant, scorched shirt, which exposes her hairy crotch as she squats by Caleb. "Close them legs of yours, girl! Ain't you got no pride?" The old timer asks, shining his light on her exposed, hairy, hill of Venus. Jayne quickly closes her legs and goes from squatting to kneeling beside Caleb. The watchman points his flashlight on the charred remains of the burned cotton.

"Did the two of you kill your mother, as I heard, and then burn this cotton to try to somehow escape the law by doing so? Stay here. Both of you," he blasts, "while I send fer Sheriff Richards. He needs to handle this, not me. God only knows what this world's coming to. A coon and a half naked, crazy-ass white girl, who killed her own flesh and blood."

"Get up, Caleb," sputters Jayne, shaking and tugging on him, her mind still half-fried from that horrible barn experience of her mother's death and made worse from smoking those drugs, her voice again cracking under the strain. "We got to go. The sheriff's a murder—ahhh."

"Who are you?" Caleb asks, while looking over at her, as Lugo stumbles back, startled by Jayne's sudden out cry of pain.

"Don't give me that bull, boy!" Lugo snaps. He lifts his billy club to give Caleb a piece of it. "You don't know each other? That what you trying to make me believe?" He gawks at Jayne's torn shirt, then at Caleb's fly. "By God, you raped this child. Didn't you? You got her on some of you darkys' reefers, and you took advantage of her. Destroyed that poor child's mind."

"Shut up, old man," says Caleb. "I'm trying to remember who she is."

Now, afraid of Caleb's sudden show of strength, the watchman, with his club in his trembling right hand, reaches out to Jayne with his left, trying to entice her away from Caleb.

"That nigger's dangerous," he whispers to her. "Talking back like that! Don't be afraid, girl. Come over here to me. Your own kind, and—with your help—I'll beat his head in if he makes a move at us."

Jayne hisses at Lugo, while grunting and holding her throat and unable to speak.

"Sweet Jesus, she grunts like a pig," the old timer blares. "What in the hell did you do to this white girl, you black baboon? Did your filthy, black dick go in her mouth?"

"I said shut up," Caleb yells.

"He's on reefer, that's fer sure," says Lugo. "Now I know who you are! You're that Caleb Brooks." Shaking his club, he inches toward him. "That's right! Richards offered a reward fer you as well. You better do the right thing and come with me. Both of you. Now!"

Caleb pushes the old man's hand away, and Lugo blows his whistle; when Caleb hears that blaring whistle it sends the pain once again hammering against his skull and he clamps his palms over his ears. When it doesn't stop, Caleb bowls over Lugo, leaps from the train, hits the ground, increasing the pain in his head, and falls to his knees. Holding onto her straw hat, Jayne descends the rungs half of the way, then jumps, landing on the ground beside Caleb and also sending excruciating pain along her leg from that head-over-heels horse fall. As she groans in agony, Caleb staggers to his feet and lopes into the night. "Caleb," the white girl yells. "It's me, Jayne! Don't leave me here. Dane'll kill me."

Caleb stops, squints back at her, then at Lugo, blowing that silly whistle and painfully guiding his old bones down the cotton-car rungs.

"Jayne? Jayne Hill?" Caleb asks, backtracking, and helps her to her feet, both keeping an eye on Lugo, halfway down the rungs now and still blowing his whistle.

"Caleb," Jayne sobs, her voice again momentarily viable. "They say you have it. That money or gold. Whatever it is. I'm not interested in it anymore. Can you believe me? That bird in the sky. I'm sure it came from God. Destroy it. Barney's fortune before the devil has it destroying all of us, you, the coloreds and us whites!"

"Gold," shouts the old railroad cop, lumping off the freight car.

"Help me catch him, somebody," he calls to a white passerby. "That white girl says the nigger has Barney's gold!"

"She's naked," calls the white passerby, shocked beyond belief.

"Are you crazy," exclaims Lugo to the passerby. "Fuck her nakedness. It's gold I'm takin' about! Gold! Gold, you hear!"

The frail-looking, male passerby takes one look at Caleb's powerful frame, and gold or no gold, he runs away, as do Caleb and Jayne, who limps along clinging to Caleb's hand.

"Come back here!" Lugo shrieks. "That gold! Where is it?"

While running with Caleb, as best she can, Jayne—her hat flopping about on her head—feels something warm dripping onto her wrist and looks down at it.

"Caleb, you're bleeding again!"

39

The Boiling Point of Death

At the factory, as well as on the square, blood also flows; blacks—met with violence on their way to work, bloody and beaten—flee back across the train tracks to a burning Colored Town, even as Caleb and Jayne run blindly toward the square and harm's way, the old railroad cop, driven by thoughts of untold wealth, trying to keep after them, but running out of gas. Turning into an alley at the rear of Dessen's sprawling plant, the teenagers take refuge behind one of several, seven-foot-tall, wide, wooden crates lining the alley walls, where they lose their old pursuer.

Nearby, whites on Main Street are breaking into the stores and stealing everything in sight. In the safety of the dark byway, Jayne repositions her lopsided hat on her head while leaning over, fighting for her breath, the jimson still mightily holding onto its control over her. As Caleb studies the disheveled-looking girl, she covers her slimy mouth and sun-peeled, dirty face with her forearm. "Don't look at me, Caleb. I'm uggg," she tries in vain to finish her sentence, her voice painfully falling apart. Trying to clear his own head, Caleb turns away from her, the crashing sounds of glass, the screams echoing off the alley walls, the re-sounding, sporadic gunfire all scrambling his thoughts even more. He steps from behind the crate and observes the square; what he sees sickens him. The rioters are charging the factory and firing on it with guns and rifles. Opening fire from the factory wall, the deputies and guards shoot into the rampaging crowd, mowing down the rioters. During that bloody one-sided battle, a drunken woman, nicknamed "Battle Ax Betty," after seeing others fail to do so, attempts to scale a section of factory gate.

"I'm a woman," the drunken woman yells to one of the guards, looking down at her from atop the gate wall, as she claws her way up the ten-foot-high gate, while ranting insanely. "And Southern men don't mistreat their women folks. I'm climbing over this wall and I'm going to whip you guards' butts if I have to, to make you stop shooting at us."

She's cracked over her head by the guard, when she reaches the top, and he throws her screaming back onto the sidewalk, tightening the riot-ers' resolve to win at any cost; a few of then drag the woman behind a truck, and there, alone with others of their peers—from behind cars and wagons—they once again open fire on the factory. At that same moment, the railroad cop stumbles into the midst of rioters near Sue Ann's bar.

"Gold!" Lugo yells. Slowly, the gunfire ceases. For a moment, no one in the crowd speaks.

"What gold?" one of the Klansmen finally asks. "Barney's gold?"

"Yes, Barney Cutter's gold!" gasps the old man, out of breath.

Word spreads faster than the blazing store fires around them and the square, and soon even the screaming and breaking of the windows stops, all ears listening to the railroad cop, even the distant deputies and security people scrutinizing and straining their ears from the factory walls fifty yards away.

"A nigger boy and a half-naked white girl, Jayne Hill," a teenage boy—who is standing near Lugo—yells to those at the back of the gathering, after hearing some of the detail. "Caleb. The one Richards was asking about. He got Barney's gold. Heard it with my own ears!"

"What about Jayne Hill?" asks Reverend Miller, coming to the front of the crowd. "This railroad cop says the black ape has her, a white girl. Shouldn't we save her from a fate worse than death if she's his prisoner and he rapes her?"

"Barney must be dead," says Battle Ax, joining the others and rubbing the top of her head. "Ferget about that young, white bitch. There will always be another girl like her around, but my God! The nigger boy stole Barney Cutter's gold instead of us here in town getting our hands on it."

In the alley, Jayne creeps up behind Caleb and peeks out at the whites swarming about Lugo, who is exciting them all the more with his tale of gold and his wild hand gestures and dancing old feet. Suddenly a dozen camouflaged trucks roll down Main Street and onto the square, and hundreds of armed National Guardsmen pile off the government vehicles with fixed bayonets and corral the stunned troublemakers.

"Lay down your weapons," demands the captain in charge of the homeland soldiers.

On the commander's orders, in oneness, the guardsmen take aim at the mob, and the rioters' weapon begins hitting the ground. A minute later, the Cutterville firemen drive onto the scene and fan out, hosing down the burning stores. From the factory's main gate, an angry Sheriff

Richards, along with his deputies, weapons drawn, push their way through the subdued mob.

"Mister Dessen offers his thanks fer your fast response," Richards tells the National Guard commander, then faces his fellow citizens. "Are you drunken fools ready to listen and go home now? Are you, you dumb assholes!"

Richards' tone of voice to the white looters actually gives them no concern. They've been through the exercise before during coon killing and know that, even though Richards is upset with them, they are safe, with him as their father figure, and he knows that if they weren't all so drunk, they never would have gone up against the plant guards, or against him and his deputies. However, some of the teenage rioters have less faith in Richards's ability to keep them out of jail now; they shed tears for having broken the law, their sights on those rifles and fixed bayonets of deadly seriousness.

"Do you need our assistance in jailing those people, Sheriff?" asks the guard commander.

"That won't be necessary" says Richards. "We're all family here. Fighting for the same cause." He turns to his deputies—all six of them—and says, "I want everyone's name that's out here." Still shaken over having had to fire on the crowd, the deputies are slow to act, knowing that some of the rioters are members of their own families or friends and neighbors. "Now, dammit!" Richards exclaims. "So we can clear these streets, threat the wounded, and the rest sent home. The factory's not interested in pressing charges and neither am I."

Old Battle Ax storms up to Richards, spraying spittle on him and yelling, "You can't use that damn badge of yours to get rid of us. You just don't want us listening to Old Lugo here about that money and gold or whatever it turns out to be! You want it all fer your damn self."

"Go the hell home, Battle Ax," Richards tells her. After quickly taking note of the Guard's captain, "Befer you're sorry. I won't mind locking your dumb ass up."

The woman who dared climb the factory wall stands there glaring at him, her hands on her widespread hips, her drunken legs wobbling from her nasty fall. She spits on Richards.

"That's fer you letting that guard throw me off that damn fence and on the goddamn, hard sidewalk."

"It was the gate, not a fence, you old fool, and private property, and you shouldn't ever been on it!" Richards yells at her and jerks out his night stick, grabs Battle Ax by her arm and stick-whips the white woman, until she breaks free and runs screaming into the night.

"A drug user," Richards says to the satisfaction of the National Guard commander.

"The hell with all of this," someone among the rioters yells. "If what old Lugo says is true, let's give 'em our names and get after the nigger and save that white girl—like the reverend thinks we should—and maybe get ourselves some of Barney's gold while were at it."

"Jayne Hill," yells Richards, giving up on trying to keep the captain from hearing about the gold—a thing he needn't worry about, because none of the guardsmen seem to have noticed or cares about such. Richards, however, having learned days ago that Jayne had teamed up with Dane to steal Barney's fortune and exclude him, is beside himself. "The first one who goes after that coon and girl will answer to me!" he yells. "Those two are police business! Now give your names to the deputies and go the hell home. All of you!"

Knowing that—like Battle Ax says—Barney wants everyone out of the race for Barney's money except himself, the old railroad cop mutters, "Guess I did my duty. I'll get back to my trains."

"You, come with me," says Richards, dragging the old railroad cop to the relative privacy of the factory wall. "What's this about gold?" Richards hisses.

"A nigger boy was on my train," rattles the old man, pointing to the distant freight yard. "That colored boy, Caleb Brooks. He was with that half-naked Jayne Hill. The gold everyone's jawing about. Sheriff, that's all I know. He was talking to her about it."

"Then I was right," mutters Richards. "Out there when I told him to stay put and see if Henry and Caleb had anything to do with—" Richards clams up and gives Lugo the evil eye, as if to say you didn't hear what I just said, did you? Lugo completely misses the point.

"Out where, Sheriff? And who is this 'him' person, Sheriff? Does he have the gold? I won't tell anyone. Just want to know, that's all."

"Caleb damn Brooks and Jayne Hill," Richards shouts. "And you, you old fool. You got all these folks jabbering about that gold—as you put it—because you opened your big mouth and planted the idea in their dumb heads. There is no gold. No money! Get the hell out of here and no more of your mouthing off about gold or anything else. If I didn't have a plant meeting to go to, I'd run your old ass in fer starting this riot."

"But Sheriff, I didn't start any of this."

Richards kicks the elderly man in his rump and then reenters the factory. Lugo angrily returns his trains, where he happens into Bruno, the black, locomotive, coal stoker. "What the hell are you doing here so late fer, Bruno?" asks the old watchman, as the large stoker beams down at him. Before Bruno can answer, Lugo hisses, "I guess you heard about that nigger boy and white girl and want some of that gold that that boy's said to have? Just ferget it. You'll only get the sheriff's boot up your ass. Get lost befer I arrest you and charge you fer starting this damn riot," the old, want-to-be-a-real cop says. "Charge you like that asshole tried to charge me, of all things."

"Was that boy who they after, called Caleb?" asks Bruno. "Caleb Brooks, who everyone now sayin' 'praise the Lord' fo' his bein' born? The one who tells Colored Town that Jesus is comin' back? At least that the way I heard it said. Is he . . . Caleb Brooks?"

"Shut up! And get your black ass out of here like I told you."

"Yes, Sir, Mas-ta railroad cop," Bruno tells him. "But you don't believe a colored boy could possibly have gold, does you, and on top of that be smart enough to set this whole town on its ear like this? That would be like sayin' that Jesus really is colored like they say, wouldn't it?"

"You poor-ass people. You have no imagination, Bruno. That's why that boy will be caught and you'll always be shoveling coal, and never have two cents to rub together or anything else of value. A black Jesus, fer God's sake. What will you people think of next?" He points to a starving dog. "Why, that's like saying that dog there can drive one of my trains."

After Lugo goes on his way, laughing, Bruno studies the stars and whispers. "When I thought he was dead, and he touched ma hand, and I found a renewed love fo' You and Jesus, I never thought another person in the world could make me feel that way, especially a colored person." He looks down at his balled fist, opens it and stares at the gold coin. Scratching his head and grinning, he says, "When I get back to Atlanta, I'll start takin' the kids and the little lady back to church, but fo' now, all I can say is I'll be damned," and then he quickly add, " 'Cuse me, Lord, fo' lettin' that curse word slip out, like that, and 'cuse me again fo' what I feel and just gots to say next. Gold and a white girl too. Caleb Brooks you just keep on keepin' on boy, whoever they say you be. There's something powerful in you, and there's hope fo' us so-called dumb coons after all." The big man chuckles and swaggers on down the tracks to catch the next train back to his wife and family.

From the alley, Caleb spots Collins moving across the square, well beyond the guardsmen and the crowd; with him is his family and Earlene close at his side. Collins and the females had waited out the riot with the help of Sue Ann in her bar, and now hurry to the factory gate. Once there, Collins has trouble convincing the guards to permit him entry. "Dessen invited us here!" he yells in pain, the guards threatening to shoot him if he doesn't back off.

Dessen—in his office, after hearing his name being battered about from the gate—looks down from his office window and orders the gate opened. No sooner is this done and Collins and the females begin entering, then gold-toothed Metcalfe—wearing a silk top hat, a dark suit, a pair of highly polished shoes, and riding in his fancy, horse-drawn buggy—comes zipping down Main Street straight for the factory gate, a handful of white men and women on foot, chasing after him with clubs and rocks, as he lashes his foaming horse with a whip, the guardsmen chucking at the sight of it. "Come on, horse," Metcalfe yells to the stumbling creature. "Don't fail me now!"

After Collins and the females enter the gate, and the armed security guards begin closing it behind them, Metcalfe, his wobbling horse and buggy flash onto the factory yard behind the field boss and the females. Metcalfe smiles down at the guards and shrugs. "Any port in a storm," he tells the not-so-pleased uniformed men. An erratic exchange of gunfire breaks out—causing the guardsmen and the ex-rioters on the square to duck. The lone shooter is one of the men among those who had been chasing Metcalfe; and his poorly aimed shot was meant for Metcalf, as seen through the gate, not for the National Guard.

"Hold your fire!" calls the commander, once his men shoot down the white sniper a half block away. Meanwhile, Metcalfe parks his horse and buggy in an area where several other unemployed blacks—who had been caught up in the crossfire on the square—had found shelter from the ranting whites behind the factory wall, thanks to Dessen. The blacks are anxiously waiting out the riot in order to get back across the train tracks to check on their burning homes, but not Metcalfe; he's in no hurry to leave, not just yet. His sights are on Collins, Ruby, Pauline and Earlene and then on Dessen, who has been waiting just inside a nearby, factory door for the shooting to stop. When it does, the Jewish man steps from the plant and runs crouched over to Collins.

"Who is that white man with them two white woman folk and that colored girl?" Metcalf asks the blacks about him. "And that one who just came out of the factory, the one them guards listens to, the one who commands that kind of god-like authority?"

"That first one be Keith Collins, Sarah Cutter's field boss, the one with them scared females. And that other man you might best call him god, 'cause he be Mister Dessen. Them there guards better listen to what he say. He owns this here whole plant and a good part of this here town."

" 'Cutter,' " exclaims Metcalfe. " 'Sarah Cutter,' that's her field boss and her name?"

Metcalfe climbs off his buggy, his wicked eyes and ears fixed on Collins, who is squatting on the ground, totally drained, while conversing with the Jewish factory owner.

"You picked a fine time to show up," Dessen tells Collins.

"Sarah!" Collins gasps, flinching in pain. "You have to warn her, Mister Dessen."

"Warn her how?" Dessen asks, then adding. "The phone lines are down. The only way to her place is overland, and I haven't a man to spa . . ."

Grimacing, Collins slumps over, clutching his side. "My God, honey!" screams Ruby, noticing his bloody shirt. "You're bleeding to death!"

"I'll alert Doc," says Dessen, then faces the deputies and security men. "Some of you men get over here and stand by to help bring this man inside."

As Dessen hurries into the factory, and several guards attempt to help the females with Collins, Richards approaches and waves the men off. "Let me see that wound," he tells Collins.

"Ahh!" Collins yells, as Richards roughly handles him.

Richards looks at Collins and starts walking away. "You'll live," he says.

Collins grabs the lawman's wrist and holds on. "Send word to Sarah," he pleads to Richards. "Warn her about Dane and the others."

"Dane killed Daddy," sobs Earlene, with Metcalfe watching and intensely listening, as Earlene shrills on. "And Caleb fell off the bridge, and we can't find Mamma! Please tell me Mamma ain't dead, Sheriff. Please say you'll look fo' her and Caleb."

"Shut up, you ink spot," Richards yells at Earlene, as Pauline and Ruby glares at the man and—if their looks could kill, Richards would be dead, as he continues with his insults to Earlene. "I wasn't talking to you." He faces Collins. "Sarah and her plantation as good as caused this trouble by treating her blacks like equals, sending the wrong message to our coloreds in town, if you ask me. She's on her own now that Barney's on his death bed. The bastard thought I'd fall fer his bullshit of offering me my job back if I did a certain favor fer him. I'm facing my last days here. I know that. I've been in the business of politicking long enough to know that that asshole would have gotten me fired no matter what I would have done to help him, and I hope he dies a thousand times over."

Metcalfe's eyes sparkle as he inches closer to Collins after hearing that Barney has an enemy in Richards and is extremely sick; the other blacks around him and his buggy attempt to stop him.

"You best stay put, boy," one of the black men warns. "You in Georgia now, not back in one of the northern cities that yo' big mouth, all this time in Colored Town, been braggin' 'bout. That's white man's business over there." When Metcalfe shrugs them off and continues toward Collins, the blacks ease back into the shadows, shaking their heads in anxiety.

On Shadow Grove, Sarah and Barney's nurse also stand back in the shadows, the shadows of the open door in the master bedroom—the nurse seemingly ready to toss in the towel, turn and run, as she and Sarah—with more than a little fear reflected on their faces—watch Barney thrashing about on his bed. "It's as if he's being urged to do so," whispers his nurse. "By something that only he's aware of, Sarah." Unknown to them, outside—in the dark of night—that winged creature from his mother's grave is circling high above the house. The two women slowly approach Colonel Cutter, then stop. Restrained with padded, leather wrist and ankle straps and tiedown padded ropes across his middle to hold him in place, Barney continues twisting and tugging, trying to break free, his eyes open, his sights staring at the open window at the night sky.

"Doctor Schmidt says to give him more Demerol," the nurse explains to Sarah, as they ease to Barney's bed, the nurse explaining on. "Doc said to see if that calms him down. But giving him anymore could be dangerous, with him as old as he is and acting his way. I just don't know what to do or what is going on with your husband, Sarah, and Doctor Schmidt will be out of town until tomorrow."

Sarah looks back at Naomi, who enters the room and stands behind them at the door, a frightened look is on Naomi's face as she follows Barney's sights to the window and the sky beyond. Then, the ground begins moving; the house shakes, and Naomi can only stand by with the nurse and Sarah, as they brace themselves against Barney's bed, hoping that the earthquake will soon pass, and then it does, as quickly as it had started. Sarah shivers with a tingling fear of what she sees reflected in Naomi's eyes, eyes which says Satan is about to enter the house.

At the factory, after the earth stops shaking, within the security of the walls, while Metcalfe lingers nearby, Ruby has had enough of the sheriff, who has returned to Collins in an attempt to seek out information about Barney.

"Get away from him!" Ruby yells at the lawman. Picking up one of the rioter's tossed rocks, she flings it at Richards and then faces the deputies and guards gaping down from the walls at them in surprise of her action. "Isn't there a man among you who will take a message to Sarah?" she calls to them.

Richards angrily walks away, eyeing Metcalfe, who steps in and removes his top hat and lowers his head in respect to Ruby. "This Sarah . . ." he says. "Is she his wife, the wife of Colonel Cutter? His old lady?"

At that moment, the factory doctor and Dessen run to them with help and a stretcher. Ruby hurriedly answers Metcalfe. "Yes, yes," she says, looking back at him, as she, Pauline and Earlene walk beside Collins, now being carried to the brick building on the stretcher by a white-coat bearer and several uniformed guards, under Doc's instructions.

"You're a colored man," Ruby desperately calls back to Metcalfe, while trying to keep up with her husband and those carrying him. "Please warn that wonderful woman, who is as kind to coloreds as she is to whites." Ruby gazes at her groaning husband and then, taking two or three quick running steps to keep up with the stretcher bearers, again looks back at Metcalfe. "Sarah needs to know that Dane killed Bruce and . . ." She glances at Earlene's troubled face and does not say what she feels in her heart: that Dane has also murdered the young girl's mother. "Tell Sarah that Caleb may also be . . ." Breaking down in tears, Ruby struggles on, ". . . be dead. Tell her that the Klansmen who Barney hired to work on Shadow Grove may want to kill her too. The Grove. Go there and warn her."

"I asked about Barney for weeks," yells Metcalfe, as Collins is carried through the factory door, "but everyone clams up. I'll ask someone how to get to this 'Grove,' and you concern yourself no more."

A short time later, on the far side of the square, away from the guardsmen and the mob, Dane and old Hank sit in his truck and watch as Richards runs across the square to them and leans against the battered vehicle's door. He leers through the opened window at them, and when he does, Dane asks, "Is that the soldier-boy coon your deputy said you were concerned about?" Dane gestures toward the back of the factory, as Metcalfe leaves through a rear gate with his rested horse, pulling his fancy carriage, while an upset old Hank smashes a mosquito on his pale arm.

"He was asking too many damn questions about the colonel to suit me," Richards tells Dane. "And Ruby told him to warn Sarah about you killing those tar balls near that lagoon. I was surprised when my man told me you were in town, Dane," Richards says, looking into the truck at old Hank, still slapping at mosquitoes and going on. "I'm curious; why are you here? I thought you were going to stay out in those woods until you located the money and then report back to me."

Dane knows that Richards is desperately searching for answers and has no clue about the Barney's fortune, and would cut his throat in a minute if he had to in order to get that cash for himself.

"Not that I'm not grateful," says Dane, "but why did the mighty Sheriff Richards decide to come to me with this information, since you seem to feel I might beat you out of that money and or gold by my letting Jayne in on the deal? By the way, have you seen her about town?"

"No. Not a hair," Richards says, as Dane glances about and toward the crowded square. "You asked why I'm telling you this," he tells Dane going on. "Barney, he pushed me too damn far in that damn courthouse, when he made me look like a fool in front of the committee. Me! The goddamn sheriff of this county. Made me serve Caleb goddamn Brooks like I was his niggra maid; and as fer you, remember—like you said—I am the 'mighty sheriff.' Now don't you get the thought in your head to try and screw me, you hear? I expect to get my share of that money, no matter who learned of it first or finds it first. You remember that, Dane Tucker. Remember it well. Now, stop jawing and stay on that coon's black ass. He's one slippery character. Talk to him. Don't kill him. He knows more about this business of Barney and what he may or may not have, more than any of us in this shitty-ass town." Smiling, Dane drives away, leaving Richards to ponder.

With the gunshots no longer ringing out in the square, from their place of concealment, Caleb and Jayne watch as two white men with soot-blackened faces and wearing dark clothing—while gaping over their shoulders and about—enter the unlit alley with crowbars and a cable cutter. One of them is also lugging a considerable length of rope about his shoulder, as they again glance about, and then run down the alley to the factory's murky-looking discharge pipe, where—with their dark clothing and blackened faces—they blend into the dark night. Using the cable cutters, the Klansmen quietly open a hole in the fence along the alley river. Putting aside the cutter, one of them ties the rope to a fence post, swims across the river with the free end of the rope, secure it to the drainage pipe's walkway rungs and motions for his partner to make his way across to him. Carrying both crowbars, the partner quickly enters the water, struggling he pulls himself and the tools of destruction along the rope and across the deep water to the factory pipe and its parallel dock. Minutes later, they swim back without their tools. On their way out of the alley, dripping wet, they pass the crate, behind which are crouching Jayne and Caleb. His temple still bleeding and still confused and dizzy, Caleb and Jayne listen to the white men laying out their plans, as they leave the benighted passageway and enter the light of the square.

"Whenever we block off that factory, they say that that Dessen Jew's young-ass, college-attending, supervisor son sneaks coons in the plant through that stinky pipe," the one Klansman tells the other. "With the guardsmen here until things cool down, this might be our only chance—like Richards says—to get to that Jew where it hurts. In his fucking pocket!"

"What if there's a blowout while were in that damn thing?" asks the other.

"Richards' is the one who told us the factory don't flush it except on the third Friday of the month. That's two weeks away. He's in that damn Jew's office even as we waste time jawing about this. Do you think he'd let that Jew man run that water on us while were in that pipe?"

"Hell, no! He'd kill the motherfucking Jew first."

"Well, then, let's do what the sheriff wants us to do and be done with it. While them guardsmen are watching fer trouble to come from the outside, we'll be inside surprising the hell out of them black workers and Jew nigger lovers, and once that Jew's nigger-hiring place disappears, a sympathizer of ours from Detroit says he'll build a car factory on that land and hire a thousand of us whites and not one nigger, unless it's as a janitor. That's what Richards says."

After the men's voices fade, several of their numbers approach the alley and linger at the entrance as lookouts, leaving Caleb and Jayne boxed in. Fighting against his dizzy spells, Caleb studies the shadowy factory, waste pipe seemingly a goodly distance away. "If those guys are right," he tells a shivering Jayne, "that they can get in the factory through that pipe, maybe I can, also, and get some help and clothes for you, coveralls or something, and you can warm up, then get out of here and make your way back to Shadow Grove somehow to be with your sisters and brother. Wait here out of sight until I come back. We're in enough trouble without some white man seeing you like that and with me, the way that whistle-blowing fool did and chased us. Okay?"

"Okay."

Jayne is dreadfully afraid that Caleb will leave her behind, and that Dane will arrive in town, find her and cut her throat before she can be "saved." After seeing that bird revive Caleb, the thing she dearly wants to do now more than obtaining all the gold in the world, is to repent before facing her God. With deep concern, she watches Caleb—in his lighter-colored, reflecting clothing—stumble to the fence, crawl through the Klan-made hole, swim to the huge pipe and climb the half-dozen rungs to the pipe's narrow walkway. The gate that has always sealed off the tubular aqueduct's entrance, from everything except small birds and bugs and had sufficiently permitted the factory discharged an easy flow through its horizontal and closely-fitted vertical bars into the stream, has been pried open by the Klansmen, their crowbars on the ground where they left them, the six-foot, round, rusty gate dangling to one side of the entrance on its twisted hinges, a gate with a warning sign of extreme danger hanging from its rusty bars. Caleb mulls over that warning for a moment, then waves back to a worried-looking Jayne and enters the huge cylinder of breathtaking stench, his thick head of hair a foot or two from brushing against the top of the large tube. No sooner does Caleb enter the pipeline, than the Klansmen return—a good dozen of them, a few slipping into blackened hoods, while others in their midst remove their secreted weapons from beneath their long, dark overcoats. Jayne watches the men as they silently move past her hiding place with the presence of blind hatred and death about them, causing her skin to crawl.

Arriving at a rear, factory window, one of the factory's inexperienced supervisors, Dessen's twenty-year-old son, Curby, notices the men's movement in the dark as they make their way to the river and pipe; however, feeling that it is only one or two of several homeless people—who often sleep in the alley—and that the fence is in place, separating the alley from the plant, Curby simply keeps a watchful eye on those moving shadows and doesn't sound the alarm, but then, the young man's mouth drops open after an overhead cloud clears out and moonlight floods into the alley; stunned Curby watches the Klansmen toss off their long coats, lift their guns, their unlit torches, their gasoline, and their dynamite over their heads, and wade shoulder-deep into the river, then pull themselves across, using the rope as support. The young supervisor stands there gawking out the window, as the would-be assassins climb the rungs to the walkway and finally light their torches and enter the drainage facility.

Dessen's son then turns around and races through the plant toward the second set of those endlessly rising steel stairs, opposite of those on the far, freight-elevator side of the factory, down which his father and the supervisors had descended when they spotted a wet Flynn and Brick in the plant. Dodging forklifts and jumping over pallets of rubber, gasping for breath, Curby rumbles up the nearby, steep steps two and three at a time, then stops halfway up to catch his breath, the workers lingering at their machines watching the young supervisor finish his climb, the air growing hotter with each laborious movement of his spent legs, as he scrambles across a catwalk toward his father's distant, ceiling-high office.

Inside the office, Dessen is addressing a half-dozen men, including

580

Sheriff Richards, the plant supervisors and several other men wearing expensive-looking brown suits. Everyone is attentive to Dessen's and the sheriff's every word. "I say fire the bastards," Richards tells Dessen. "The courts are on our side, and you and this town don't owe them blacks anything."

"This isn't Germany with its cremation ovens," snaps Dessen. "And because the South was built on slave labor, I'd say we owed them every thing rather than nothing." Discouraged by Richards' approach to the problem—and unaware that Richards is inwardly thinking of him with disdain—Dessen looks at the others. "Let's find another solution," he tells them, crossing the room and gazing out a window with a bullet hole in it; Dessen scrutinizes down at the destroyed Hooverville tent city. "Maybe this trouble wouldn't have happened," he says, "if we'd have invested a millionth as much in our returning veterans as we had in the war."

"Take it easy, Brian," one of those well-dressed men in brown says. "The guys in D.C. did the best they could for our fighting boys. The money just isn't there. Not now anyway. Maybe we were wrong in agreeing that giving coloreds jobs here would help the town and Georgia's image and that we'd benefit from more European tourist trade to recover from the Depression, a town where even Americans yearn to visit a city where everyone is treated fairly."

"We couldn't have been more right," says Dessen. "And in the future if a certain party can't control that mob outside, as well as his men, when it comes to all of Cutterville's citizens," he faces Richards, "we'll not wait to fire him and will immediately find someone who can. All of this spilled blood, children without their fathers and wives without—"

Storming into the office and fighting to catch his breath, Curby rushes to his father's side.

"I saw them. In the water!" he exclaims. "They've entered into here with guns and gasoline, and there's no telling what else they might have!"

"Who?" Dessen asks. "Who entered where?"

"Members of the Klan. Moving into the pipe chase. It has to be the Klansmen! Who else would . . ."

"The guardsmen will never get into those pipes or in here in time to stop them," says Krause, Dessen's foreman.

Dessen slams his fist onto the desk, lowers his head and groans.

581

"Dammit, I didn't ask for this war against my plant!" he says, then turns to Richards. "Rejoin your men, Sheriff, and seal off that damn alley so no ones else gets into those pipe and those damn internal pipe chases."

Pale, sweating and afraid, Richards is in a panic. He has been caught totally off guard and had no idea that Curby had sense enought to watch the river. He had turned completely pale when he heard the young man giving away the Klan's position and now feels he's betrayed the Klan's trust.

"What is it, Richards?" asks Dessen, watching the man.

"Those poor men," says Richards, almost involuntarily.

"If you must worry about someone," foreman Krause angrily responds, "pray those animals can't locate any of the two-way pipe hatches and get in here before we can flush them and the rats back into the sewers where they belong. Now, you do what you were told to do and get that alley sealed off from the public, now, or do I have to do it for you!"

Sheriff Richards storms from the office—not with anger, but with the hope that he can get to the pipe in time to warn his fellow Klansmen to get the hell out of it. Once he leaves, Krause looks at the ceiling, as does Dessen's boy. "Maybe we should pray for those men," Curby says, while gazing at the river of sizzling, insulated, ceiling pipes.

"Would you pray for a miracle, Curby?" asks Dessen. "A miracle to part the Red Sea and gloriously save this factory? Is that what you think will happen? That Moses, leading a league of angels, will arrive on chariots of fire and drive those madmen out of those pipe chases? Praying is the concern of rabbis and fanatics." When an embarrassed Curby looks around at the others in the room and doesn't answer, Dessen pats him on the back, as if to say that he apologizes and that it's okay for him to think the way he does. Then Dessen faces the others. "I've invested over three million dollars in this plant. I'll not stand by and watch it destroyed." He nods to his foreman.

Krause lifts the receiver of a red phone and dials with Dessen's contingency plan on everyone's mind. An anxious voice on the other end answers. Krause looks over at a reluctant Dessen, who is absolutely devastated by what's to come from his decision.

"Charlie wants to know how many do you want him to open," Krause says.

"This action has been cleared by the governor himself, Brian," says one of the men in the brown suits, hanging up on other phone. "The plant is far too vital to the region's recovery and that of the state to have it destroyed. It's evident that those men plan to commit arson. Punishable by whatever means. The law is fully behind you."

Dessen looks at Krause and says, "All of them."

Krause repeats the message over the phone and hangs up.

It takes fourteen men to open the seven mammoth steam valves which occupy key positions on the walls throughout the plant; even with two men to each valve wheel, the job to turn and open them is a laborious one, the workers, all eyes and holding their breath, stand by their stations and watch, as the values are slowly cracked open, the building reverberating from the rush of pipe-directed boiling water, the factory's machinery temporarily brought to a standstill.

"There's enough p.s.i. behind each of those back-flow-prevent valves to drive a hundred freight trains," someone among the workers at the disabled molds now whispers.

The office and the entire plant falls silent, all attention on the heavily insulated ceiling pipes, pipes releasing ever more of their blistering energy with each turn of the valve handles, diverting the explosive, skin-peeling, blistering, water of fire from the twenty-ton presses, the tire molds and the massive boilers, sending it barreling, instead, through the pipes and toward the main waste lines, toward the intruders and toward Caleb, who finds himself lost in one of the two man-size, chase pipes, which Dessen's engineers call them. Those two main, passageways are just twenty feet apart, far less than the distance from the chase entrances to the broken gate which is eighty yards away. From the right chase branch, agonizingly slow, stumbles Caleb, his hand against the slimy wall to support himself, his head in a spin. A hundred yards or so ahead of him, in the left-side chase branch, their torches flickering and lighting their way, the Klansmen gaze up at a hatch atop the pipe; steel rungs in the chase wall lead up to it.

"There's one of them trap doors," yells the lead Klansman. "The way the coons get in. Shoot the blacks, then destroy that Jew plant! Who has the dynamite, and be damn careful with that unstable stuff, unless you guys want to be blown out of here. It's as old as shit. Get up here with it, and after we enter that factory and you light the fuses, throw the damn dynamite at those expensive presses, and we get the hell out through the factory's emergency doors up there and in a hurry!"

Suddenly, the pipe beings to tremble, and a line of wall-mounted, water-sealed, electrical lights flash on and off, followed by a siren, pounding its deadly warning against the Klansmen's ears. Then, the unthinkable happens: the men hear the gurgling, sizzling water of death shaking the massive, metal chase pipe, thumping and expanding it this way and that as the boiling water races in their direction. The hissing scalding vapors arrives first.

"Run!" someone yells. Dropping their weapons and torches, the men bolt toward the river-outlet pipe and gate, everyone trying to get ahead of the other, while gaping back over their shoulders, slipping, tripping and falling. The dreaded sound of boiling water following and growing louder, sending hundreds of squeaking rats ahead of it and into the midst of the Klan; to many of the fleeing men, the lives of their loved ones do not flash before their eyes, but instead they see what they will witness after death: Judgment Day. To one or two of them—who realize that anything is better than dying a horrible death, and that they would gladly give up hating and killing and let their children play with whomever they please if they could be saved, the realization comes too late.

Squalling, the men's hearts race, their breathing comes in rapid gasps, but so slowly do they and their legs seem to move, and those who find themselves at the rear of the pack are shrieking for the others not to leave them. Never has that much force and water been flushed into the pipe chase before, and the carefully designed waterproof, workmen's electric lights—mounted on the wall every thirty feet or so and able to withstand the discharge flow under normal conditions—explode one after the other as the boiling, pipe-made river thunders through the chase and slams into those screaming in the rear. Bellowing, the Klansmen just ahead of the surging demise attack one another, all now trying to scramble through the pipe side-by-side, greatly slowing their wailing retreat. The sizzling water impacts them full force, ripping the clothes off of some and not off of others; and in a flash all of the electrical lights are gone, the footsteps are silenced, the screams are heard no more, only the sound of the rushing water is heard, roaring headlong through the dark on its way to Caleb.

40

A Race for Life

As the blistering water races his way, Caleb, still lingering at that right branch, is hit in the face by a hot stream of steam. Then he hears the turbulent, scalding water thundering, not just from the Klansmen's side of the pipe, but from his side as well, and he sprints for the open gate, the scorching water vapors scratching at his back. Tearing roof-high through the quaking monster of concrete and steel—now foaming, hissing and gurgling—the water from hell incapacitates those unfortunate, trapped Klansmen's corpses, leaving parts of the bodies stuck to the sides of the pipe's electrical light fixtures, their skin and muscles cooked into the metal, their bones, alone with boiled rats and bits and pieces of their remains blasted on down the line ahead of their disintegrating bodies and right at Caleb, as he reaches the opening and dangling gate.

From her place of hiding, Jayne sees Caleb dive headfirst into the murky fast-moving river and disappear. Swimming under water, he can still hear the roaring liquid demise following him, and he is horrified, but he would be even more so if he could see what is about to impact him from the pipe: a seven-foot-wide, funnel of boiling, twisting, tubular-demon of rage roars out of the pipes like a living-consuming monster—within this funnel of unforgiving water are the spinning, trapped bodies of most of the Klansmen. It's all that Jayne can do to keep from screaming and attracting Sheriff Richards's attention to her, while he—just thirty feet or so away—and she, behind the crate, watch in torment, from their different vantage points. Several of the Klansmen, who are miraculously still alive—are quivering and tumbling as if inside the see-through belly of a giant tubular whale. When the boiling liquid strikes the river's cold veneer, both it and the rapidly moving river explode, along with one of those old sticks of dynamite, setting off a firestorm, blasting away that tubular out-pouring water's funnel-like hold on the dead and dying, sending the trapped bodies airborne and then sucking them and everything in its path below the surface with it. Downstream, gasping for air, Caleb pops to the surface, just as more bodies are blasted out of the pipe and splattered all over the place, some landing hard into the tumbling waves around him. Henry's traumatized boy dives back into the black, churning ferment, seeking cooler currents. The one or two Klansmen who were trapped within the deadly flow and survived, did so with their clothing ripped to shreds, with their white skin now blackened and peeling off their ivory bones, and would have been better off dead.

As Richards runs to the fence and sobs at the sight of his dying comrades, those shrieking cries from the slowly dying souls bring the crowd, along with Reverend Miller, charging past the deputies, at the alley entrance, and to the fence. One of those entering with the crowd is a cowboy named Jason, wearing a red scarf about his neck and riding a cattleman's pinto horse, his rope of trade dangling from the horse's saddle. When Jayne sees him and his horse through a hole in the crate, she glances at the river, where Caleb went down, says a silent prayer and once again fixes her anxious sights on the gangling cowboy, as he leaps from his mare, a few feet from her place of hiding, and runs to the river's edge where he joins the others in shock and prayer, a sorrowful offering to God for the dead and dying men, for members of their families, and for their friends floating bloated upon the water of defeat. It's then, with everyone's back to her, that Jayne—now, with no concern over her near-nudity—sidles from behind the crate and mounts Jason's horse.

Henry has told Caleb to call upon God when he has trouble that he can't handle. Downstream from Miller, and those praying for the deceased, Caleb is suddenly caught up in an underwater rip tide, brought on by the exploding dynamite, and goes tumbling and turning among several bodies. Unlike the time his strength alone saved him and Flynn from drowning in the lagoon, Caleb is exhausted, and God is the farthest thing from his mind. If he's to die, he tells himself, so be it. Nonetheless, he stubbornly fights on, and it takes all his strength to break out of the turbulence and struggle to the surface, where he splashes about, gasping. Just when he thinks he can't hang on any longer, a lifeline is tossed to him. There on solid ground, astride Jason's horse is Jayne. When Caleb grabs the rope, she quickly wraps her end about the saddle horn and knees the horse, dragging Caleb ashore into a world gone mad. Hearing Jayne calling to Caleb, Jason looks back and sees her on his horse.

"Come back with my critter," he yells, running at her and Caleb.

With an eye on the charging man, Jayne slides back onto the horse's rump, seizes Caleb's outstretched hand, and with a great deal of effort on her part, and a last-minute burst of energy from Caleb, Henry's boy swings upward into the saddle in front of her. Jason, however, arrives before they can escape, and he seizes Jayne's shirttail, while stabbing at Caleb with a hunting knife. Caleb kicks him in his face, but the man manages to hold onto Jayne's shirt, and as he falls backwards, the shirt is torn off the terrified, screaming girl's body and almost topples her off of the horse. Thoroughly physically and emotionally drained and undressed, pink of blistered skin, with nothing on but her straw hat and red shoes, Jayne wraps her arms about Caleb's waist, and holds on for dear life, as they gallop out of the alley, flashing through and around shocked veterans and below factory workers, who gawk down at them from their shattered windows. A man steps in front of Caleb and the pinto, his arms spread. "Stop, Nigga, and hand over that naked white girl!"

Caleb sprints the horse right over the old timer, leaving him on his back, cursing the day that blacks were ever born. Maneuvering between the factory's open-mouthed security men and stunned guardsmen, who jump aside, Caleb swoops the horse on down Main Street, around houses and—to avoid a sudden-appearing blockade—jumps it over a low fence and right into an old white woman's backyard—the woman who trashed the wagon and tried to shoot Flynn from her second-floor window and on the square—crashing through her clotheslines, just as she has gathered up enough courage to come outside and take down her laundry now that the gunfire has ceased. The sudden and exploding appearance of Caleb, naked Jayne and the horse sailing over her fence, sends the woman yelping and tripping back onto her house, where she stands peeking out the window at the riders and wets herself.

Finding himself trapped at one point behind still another house, by a high wooden fence, Caleb races the horse recklessly back past the clothesline woman's residence, guiding the horse onto and across her porch, sending her diving behind her couch. Caleb—his keen eyes looking this way and that for a way out—sprints the horse back onto the street, where he jumps it over a toppled wagon, one which was pushed over by the crowd to block his way in order to capture him. Too little too late. Caleb leaves them behind, gawking at his escape. Leaping the horse over the hoods of cars, past burning stores and shocked firemen, Henry's calculating son successfully crosses the train tracks into Colored Town, where the blacks have sadly managed to put out their own fires, and when the devastated, depressed citizens see Caleb with the naked, white girl holding onto him, another fire flames up, that of pride and passion in the entire black community; the blacks jump up and down cheering, especially the teenage boys, as Caleb and Jayne also leave them in the dust. From the undamaged whorehouse's porch, Lana and a handful of her callgirls, including Mellow Yellow, watch as Caleb and Jayne disappear under that cloud of rust.

"Now, that's my kind of man," Mellow Yellow says. "A nigger who finally knows what he wants and gets what he can't have. If that white girl enjoyed it so much that she gots to hold onto him butt naked in order to be ready to get it again, he must be as good as he looks. Somebody please . . . please remind me to give that beautiful boy some free pussy the next time I see—"

"That's what you said about Crazy Walter and now he's dead," Lana exclaims. "You leave Caleb alone with that jinxing, yellow ass of yours. You hear? They say he's from God."

On the edge of town, Caleb suddenly goes limp. Jayne slides her slender frame onto the saddle with him, her crotch up against his back pockets, her legs and thighs locking in around his thighs to help hold him in place. Reaching through his arms, she seizes the reins. Further securing Caleb on the horse, she uses her knees, squeezing them against Caleb's waist, her elbows locked onto his sides. Switching the reins into one hand, she uses the other to remove her straw hat, and she places it firmly on Caleb's head, hoping against hope to slow the blood from his bleeding scalp, all of this going on while she yells for the horse to run faster, as it and she carries Caleb into the uncertain night. The frightened girl knows she cannot take Caleb to his home, because Richards' deputies and the Klan will be waiting for him there. "Caleb!" she painfully forces herself to yell, blood trickling from her mouth and across her lips, as her jimson-brittle throat cackles as if made of glass. "Don't die! Please don't die like Mamma did!"

At Little Shadow Place, after Richards and several armed men have left and are satisfied that Caleb is not there, on his porch, Henry rocks back and forth in his old chair; suddenly, he springs to his feet. Old Clara is charging down the road to the house; Henry runs onto the lawn and to the faithful horse, as the newborn wails in her saddlebag. When the horse stops next to Henry, he lifts the crying infant into his arms and looks to the sky. "What does it mean? Somebody tell me what this all means."

588

At Shadow Grove, if Barney could talk at that moment, instead lying speechless in his sick bed, he would have let the world know—the way Henry has to God about Caleb—that with every beat of his heart, he loves Flynn, who is at his bedside, bandages and all. The nurse enters the room carrying a gallon jug, a cloth-wrapped package, and a four-foot length of clear, plastic tubing; smiling at Flynn, she places the tubing and package on the bedside table and the jug on the floor next to the bed. She carefully opens the packet, exposing sterile, latex gloves and a sterile, number-seventeen Foley catheter. Turning back the bedcovers, she opens the fly of Barney's pajamas, slips her hands into the gloves and begins washing the Colonel's penis with a pasty, white, germicide solution, lubricates and then pushes the lubricated catheter into the comatose man's limp penis and slowly through his urethral canal and toward his bladder, causing Barney to groan.

"Hey!" exclaims Flynn, having never witnessed her doing that before, as Barney continues moaning from the painful procedure, the nurse—ignoring Flynn's outcry—continues squeezing his penis and pushing the well-lubricated tubing deeper into him. "Don't ignore me!" hisses Flynn. "Get that out of him!"

"Doctor's orders, Flynn," she says, going on. "If I don't catheterize him, he'll end up with far more bed sores with his incontinence."

"I know he wets the bed," pleads Flynn. "But he's a proud man and wouldn't like you handling his body in that way. Beside, he's had no more sores for weeks now." Flynn studies his father's distressed expression. "I apologize for yelling at you," he tells the nurse, going on. "I know you have to change his bedding night and day, but I'll help, and I'll wash and massage his back a dozen times a day if needed, and with daily massages and lotion he'll keep improving, you'll see."

"Young man," she says, "I'm trying—like you— to make sure he has no more of those awful bed sores, and you . . . with you helping with your father night and day, the way you do, has worn you out, and that's not good at all."

Undeterred, Flynn goes on, "Between the two of us, that should keep his skin healthy, but I won't permit you to put that tube in him."

"You're the boss," says the nurse, pulling out the tube and putting it onto the tray. "He's nice and dry now. And you, young man, just had an accident yourself, so go back to bed and rest a while. I'll call Sarah or Naomi if I need help."

"Thanks," says Flynn, leaving with—to him at least—the grotesquely equipment. "I'll just get rid of this."

After Flynn leaves the room, closing the door behind him, the woman—who has no devotional calling for her profession, flings the covers back over Barney and glares down at him in repulsion and thinks:

Pride of what? Your old, wrinkled-up dick? What good is it to you now, old man? Even with all of that money they say you have, you're too damn old to fuck anymore.

She returns to her chair, lights up a cigarette and begins reading a book, never realizing that Barney is watching her, those old, satanic, blue eyes are filled with murderous rage, a rage growing stronger all the time with a need to kill her.

41

The Forsaken Daughter Returns

Late the following evening, as the sun moves into the West, Henry, after waiting all morning for Caleb to return home—and feeling that he can't wait any longer without informing Sarah—arrives on Shadow Grove carrying the baby wrapped in two of Caleb's old baby blankets and wearing a homemade diaper folded together from one of Caleb's baby shirts. Sitting tall in the saddle on Old Clara, Henry spots Flynn and a handful of white boys, including Jayne's brother, Benny, gathered around a nearby log. He points Old Clara in their direction, as they toss pocket knives at the log. It's one of the few times that Flynn has left his father's bedside and it sorely tells: he appears tired and gaunt. When he sees Henry, Flynn quickly jogs over to him. The kind-hearted man looks down at Flynn's pale complexion and then at his bandaged arm. "Are you okay, son? Sarah phoned and said you had that truck accident involving Old Clara. I'm sorry I didn't come sooner."

"Just a bruise," says Flynn, glancing about, as his friends linger at the log staring across the field at him, Henry and the baby. "Is Caleb . . ." begins Flynn, glimpsing behind Henry. "Where is Caleb?"

"Then you haven't seen him either?"

"No, I haven't . . . Henry, that baby."

"I have no idea where this child came from or who it belongs to, but only Caleb could have placed this newborn in Old Clara's saddlebag. Why? That's what's troubling me."

Abruptly, the workers, Flynn and Henry find themselves shaken by the trembling land, which then stops. "It's doing it again," says Benny, trotting over to Flynn and Henry.

Henry becomes extremely uneasy; he looks at the baby, then down at Flynn, both sensing that the quaking is more than a mere act of nature, not with the sky turning suddenly into night, as it had and now with the baby showing up and Caleb missing, and all what's happened in between. Finally, Flynn has the nerve to speak of it.

"Earthquakes happen in places like California, Henry," he says, almost in a whisper and unwilling to shoulder his fears of the events alone and hoping that Henry will shine some light on it with his wisdom.

"Does this shaking have anything to do with me and Caleb?" He glances at Benny, who gets the message and returns to the other boys. Flynn steps closer to the horse and Henry, whispering. "Does it, Henry? With God, the way Naomi has said it would one day?"

Henry leans down to Flynn, as Old Clara prances about. "Stay close to your mother," Henry instructs Flynn. "Stay very close to Sarah. This child had far too much blood on it for a natural birth to have happened. We're dealing with the work of the fallen archangel now, is my guess, not with God or things dealing with earthquakes. I'm sure of it. It's Lucifer, himself."

"Is it the end of the world, Henry?" asks a frightened Benny, stepping back to them—after eavesdropping on part of the conversation between Flynn and Henry. Benny gazes fearfully up at Henry. "Is the earthquake a sign that Satan is here to take me away?"

Unseen at Henry's back, traveling through one of Shadow Grove's dusty fields, an eighth of a mile away, Metcalfe is arriving under the pounding sun, in his buggy. Guiding his horse through Sarah's east field and past her startled cabbage pickers, who hardly notice him with the earthquakes on their minds, the man with the golden smile stops at the general store, and once there, tips his dusty top hat to the two Hill sisters and several other young girls with them.

"Where can I find Sarah Cutter, miss?" he asks the older of the sisters, while fanning himself with his hat. "Thank God this earth shaking business has stopped, wouldn't you say?"

The teenage girl obviously still grieving over her mother's death and concerned about Jayne's whereabouts, as well as the quake—without speaking—timidly points to the store. When Metcalfe goes to the building, he stands there holding the screen door open, while looking inside and watching an attractive teenage black girl named Ressie Mae humming a harmonious melody, while replacing can items back on the shelves, after they had fallen off during the shaking. Seemingly undisturbed by the earth's swaying enigma, the young girl finishes her task, picks up her English book and then plays with a cat in the corner, at the same time keeping an eye on Metcalfe, who she knew was watching her from the moment he opened the door; to her, Metcalfe is one of those unprincipled colored people from Cutter town, who are always out to get what they can from anyone who is dumb enough to let them do so, him with that white man's silly-looking hat. Metcalfe turns his sights on a troubled-looking Sarah, who is across the room working behind the counter, in place of Trout, and cleaning up a small amount of glass from the floor.

"It's not like Trout to go away on his crutches in the swamps and then get himself killed," she tells Ressie, then notices Metcalfe in the doorway.

With the screen door slowly closing behind him and the sunlight steaming into the store and silhouetting him, Metcalfe walks over to Sarah, who squints until he comes into focus.

"Would you happen to be Sarah Cutter?" he asks.

"Yes, I'm Sarah."

"Metcalfe, Ma'am," says the grinning, gold-toothed man, removing his hat when he reaches the counter. "I have a message from Mister Collins."

"From Keith?" Sarah asks, greatly relieved. "Are they okay?"

The screen door opens again, and Dane hurries into the store, observes Metcalfe with disdain and smiles at Sarah. "Hello, Sarah. Of course they're all right," Dane tells her. "Collins couldn't depend on this boy alone to get the message to you, so he sent me as well."

Sarah finds herself recalling how Dane had vowed to harm her the day Barney crowned Flynn with the firethorns and wonders if he still feels the same way. "Dane Tucker," she says, "you haven't set foot on this land since only God knows when."

"I know. I'm sorry about Barney," Dane says, as old Hank, who hasn't returned since angrily leaving Sarah's night rally, watches through the screen door. Dane goes on. "I was wrong in blaming Barney fer what happened to my family all these years. How is he? I know he's in some kind of coma, but what caused it?"

Sarah sees Naomi nudge her way by Hank and enter the building, then stops next to a display of flatware, and, the part black, part Indian woman, toys with a meat cleaver, her sights locked on Dane.

"Mister Cutter is about the same," Sarah tells Dane. "And, Dane, I'm so sorry about your mother. You know, of course, that Barney's mother passed as well." Once again, the ground trembles, rattling the cups and glasses on the shelves and then stops. "It's been doing that for days now," says Sarah, who then faces Metcalfe, as he braces himself against the counter and had expected the worse. "You had a message for me from Collins?" she asks the dark-skinned man.

593

Dane steps between them. "I think one of your workers fainted in your field across the road, Sarah, and I think the others were asking fer you."

"Fainted," exclaims Sarah.

"Must be all that hot sun and dust and fear of the earth shaking," says Dane.

Ressie, seemingly knowing what Sarah will say next, looks at her English book as if it were gold itself, then at the men and takes her book with her as Sarah turns her way and says:

"Grab some ice and napkins, Ressie," calls Sarah, heading for the door. "I'll be right back, Mister Metcalfe. You and Dane." Sarah stops at the door and looks over at Naomi. "Naomi, will you fix a cold drink and maybe some fruit for them. It's a long ride from town to here and back."

As Sarah hurries from the store with Ressie carrying the ice and napkins, Naomi calls to them. "I'll be coming with you," she says, then mutters, glaring at Dane, " 'cause I ain't fitting nothing for no Klansman." Metcalfe is totally taken aback by Naomi's bold attitude. Dane, however, is livid. He stands there gawking at Naomi with enough loathing to kill her with his mind alone. Metcalfe smiles at both of them, now highly amused at Naomi's balls and the aggressive, womanly way she returns Dane's stare.

"I know you don't like me, Naomi," says Dane, as she turns to leave the store, "but don't you leave this store until you do what your master told you to do: fix me and this man something to drink and to eat or else—"

"Or else what?" hisses Naomi. "You'll kiss that colored man's behind, 'cause that's what you seem to be doing. What happened to 'this boy?', 'this coon?' " She then eyes Metcalfe. "Careful, my brother, when the Klan starts calling you a 'man,' they're either afraid as hell of you, or you even more of the devil than they are, or have something they want."

She tosses the cleaver aside. For a moment there, Naomi had touched a nerve in Metcalfe, opening him up to the stark realization that he's not the brightest black person in all of Georgia, after all, not with Naomi's sharp-edged tongue cutting Dane down to size the way it did, and more than that, he's beginning to feel that the Klan may be even more of a threat than he had surmised, with a person such as Naomi putting up such a survival defense.

"What I want of you, bitch," Dane yells at Naomi, "is that you give

594

me what you were told to give me, those refreshments of Sarah's. And you can serve it to us over there." He points at the tables lining the wall by the windows, going on. "And keep your fucking mouth shut, and after serving me—by all means—get the hell out of here and join Sarah in the field. I'd like a moment alone with this man, you half-Indian bitch."

Seizing the meat cleaver from the display, Naomi flings it under-hand at Dane causing Metcalf to duck; the force of that Kiowa throw buries the tip of the heavy blade an inch into the oak post next to Dane's head, causing him to stumble back from the post and cleaver, a now shocked Metcalf comparing her skills of tossing a blade to his of un-der-handing his razor at Caleb on the train.

"May God forgive me," Naomi tells Dane. "But you can eat horse shit and drank cow piss as far as I'm concerned, but you ain't gonna eat it or drank it at no table of Master Flynn and Sarah's. Stay away from Sarah and Master Flynn, or this half-Indian bitch will relieve you of your scalp!"

To Metcalfe, all of those rumors that Naomi is from God are put to bed; there is no way an angel would curse like that, if so, he tells himself, there must be room in heaven for most of the people on earth. He smiles as Naomi walks over, locks the cash register and storms out the door with the register's key tucked in her pocket. Dane slowly turns around and sees Metcalfe grinning at him.

"What the fuck's so funny," Dane shouts. "That bitch and Sarah will be back soon. Wipe that smile off your damn face and let's talk money."

Palpitating with rage, Dane sits at one of the tables, motioning for Metcalfe to occupy the chair across from him. "So, Collins sent you," Dane says, his voice stammering with residual rage toward Naomi, as he and Metcalfe sit facing down one another from across the table. "To do what? Collins, what did he want you to do?"

Metcalfe nods, exposing his teeth with his wicked grin. "The man named Collins told that crooked sheriff in town that you killed lots of colored folks in some woods, and his wife sent me to tell Sarah, but her man didn't send you. Is it true? You killed them folks? Never mind. I know all about how you folks lie about everything."

"You're the boy who was with Barney in the war. The one who lost that money on the train that Trout found. That's who you are. You didn't leave town, just been staying low. And now you're here as the sheriff always said you'd be sooner or later. We know a lot about you, too, you see. You got to be broke and hungry like all poor coons hereabouts, since you lost all of that money, so let's stop the bull, and you sell yourself cheap to me, so I can lay a dollar or two on you and you can buy food and eat. Now, tell me all you know about Barney Cutter."

"You can kiss my ass. That's right. I'm here, and now you've gone from calling me a man, to calling me a boy."

"Kiss your ass, you say? Well, you are a boy, if you think I'd do that. Kiss your black ass! Listen . . . are you as corrupt and evil as Naomi says you might be, evil enough that we can talk man-to-boy without letting God or race get in the way of common sense?"

"That depends on how much sense you're going to make when you talk, doesn't it?"

"I'll up the price. How would you like another gold tooth to keep that mouth of yours closed and you living and breathing?"

"You mean keep my mouth closed like you told that old Naomi woman, to keep hers closed or you'd what? Kick her in her ass? Or closed like two gentlemen of the South—keeping their mouths shut on both sides of the table, when it comes to money, without the ass kicking—where we can come to some kind of civilized agreement, such as one scratching the other's back?"

Dane glares at Metcalfe, who is watching Hank spying in on them from the screen door, and Dane chuckles, leaning out, eyeing Metcalfe's hat, white starched shirt, once-highly-polished, now dusty shoes, and his neatly ironed trousers. "You don't look like a person who would turn down an offer of money because of a few remarks about colored folks," Dane explains, "or just because a few coons were hanged, thieves even the blacks I talked to were glad to see die."

"Coloreds like that Walter," says Metcalfe. "Like that Bruce and his pregnant woman—"

"Wait a minute!" yells Dane. "There's no proof the Klan or I killed any kinky-head folks or anyone else, except some no good punks, like I said. You watch yourself. You're stepping on dangerous grounds."

"I don't give a good goddamn about those dead folks," exclaims Metcalfe. "A bunch of ignorant damn dead niggers don't put bread on my table." Metcalfe slaps his hand on the table. "And I see there's no bread, no drinks, nothing on this table from you either, except a lot of talk about nothing! Now it's your turn. Put up or shut up."

Dane leaps to his feet, Metcalfe the same. Before Dane or Hank—who rushes though the door toward them—can get to him, in a flash Metcalfe whips out a straightedge razor and presses it against Dane's throat. "Now this is a brand-new razor, and I hate to dirty it on you," he tells Dane. "And talk is you already lost one of your ears by talking back. Now, you sit your stupid white ass back down in that motherfucking, goddamn chair, and get used to the idea that you're nothing to me anymore than those dead niggers are, no matter how white you are." Dane looks over at Hank and eases back into his chair. "Now that we've stopped all this fucking around the bush," exclaims Metcalfe, giving old Hank the evil eye, then re-pockets his blade and sits. "What kind of money will you put on this table? Not tomorrow. Not later in the day. Now!"

"I told you. I'm offering another gold tooth," says Dane, finding himself trembling and outmaneuvered by the black man and then realizing that if he's to keep the Klan in fear of him, it will not do to have Hank witnessing him being manhandled by another coon, especially after Caleb kicked his ass in public the way he did. "Listen," Dane hisses at Metcalfe. "You don't go around threatening to cut white folks' throats. You just don't do that and live, not down here, so here's what I'm willing to do beside let you live if you sit there and keep your mouth shut."

Metcalfe glances over at old Hank, and—because the old man and Dane had entered the store without their weapons, and had left their truck parked on the side of the highway—in fear that Sarah's workers, seeing Hank's old truck, would not have let them enter, and both had climbed a fence to make their way to the store—Hank now cautiously inches back by the door, but remains in the store and stares with unbridled hatred at the black man, who is able to keep Hank offguard and at a distance by out-staring him. Metcalfe then continues with Dane.

"You were ready to shit in you pants when that colored woman threatened you with her butcher's knife, so you remain seated and keep your stupid mouth shut, or as I said, and you were too dumb to get it, I'll put my foot right up your white ass, Dane Tucker. You're not dealing with one of these Uncle Toms down here, now." Hank rushes toward the table, his bony fist balled, ready to fight, with Dane's help, of course. "I'll break both your arms, old man," Metcalfe warns, springing to his feet and pushing aside the table for maneuvering room. "Back the fuck off, and if you don't I'll cut you from head to toe before you can say 'God bless Robert E. Lee!'" Hank stops in his tracks, looks over at Dane and—for the second time—retreats, as Dane waves him off and Metcalfe angrily belittles Dane. "You two dummies. Without your damn sheets, what are you? A blind man would have spotted you two morons following me in that poor-ass truck of yours. I can't get out of here with that money without your help, not even ten men could carry it."

Hank's interest piques; he steps closer while asking, "Ten men to carry out what? Money? We thought Barney had maybe a thousand or so dollars or a bit of gold, but if it takes ten men to carry it . . ." Suddenly, Dane slams his hand on the table and glares at Hank, and the old man, realizing that he's belittling himself before Metcalfe, a coon, steps back, saying. "We don't need you, boy. We'll find that gold and—"

"And what?" blisters Metcalfe, scrutinizing Hank, "You two," he says. "With what seems like over a hundred workers of the colonel's—or Sarah . . . who cares who they really work for, him or her—out there in the fields, they'd cut your throats, once they find out what you're up to. Even if you dummies even knew where to start looking or what you're looking for, we'd need each other. Isn't that what someone high up in your group told you? And you guys didn't work all that hard to corner me. And isn't that why I'm still alive and kicking, because this nigger knows what you guys can only guess at? The who, where, and how about that money?"

"And gold?" asks Hank, his hands going up, his palms turned out, signaling that he's not trying to make trouble, as he steps even closer and gibbers on. "How much gold, do you know? And how much money?"

"Not gold, asshole. Money! Oh, it's real enough. I've not only seen it, I've done something that you poor-ass crackers can only dream of doin'. I've smelled, touched and wiped my black ass on one of the hundred-dollar bills that Barney has, just to see how it feels. And another mother fucking thing, you assholes are so dumb that you think you can buy me off with a couple of dollars, when you been trailing me and been looking at my wagon and horse, knowing that they cost more than you can earn in a year."

When Dane rises up to protest against being called such lowdown names, Metcalfe slaps a hundred-dollar bill on the table, and Dane sits back down, and Hank's old eyes enlarge, as both stare at the money.

"Want to touch it, smell it," ask Metcalfe, going on, " 'cause I know you spent all of that cash you found of mine on the train, almost spent it faster than you found it, on drugs, on moonshine, and on them cheap-ass colored women in town." Dane—all eyes—reaches for the money. Metcalfe retrieves it and says. "And I still got enough left to wrap you up and burn you in it, even with the loss of my roll on that damn train, so don't talk like some mindless hillbilly to me. Talk like a man, like somebody willing to die to get his hands on big money, 'cause that's what it'll takes fo' us, you me and your men—a willingness to die for it—to get out of here alive with it!"

At that moment, Sarah returns alone. As she moves to the tables, Metcalfe pockets the money. "Everything seems okay, Dane," Sarah says, noticing the concerned look on Dane's face, then studies Metcalfe's look of superiority as he stands there towering over the one-eared Klansman. Sarah sees how the table has been moved aside and watches Hank quickly realign it. "I accidently walked into them" he tells Sarah.

"That message you were going to give me from Collins," Sarah asks Metcalfe, puzzling between him, Hank and Dane, as a dozen field hands enter the store.

"Yes, Ma'am," says Metcalfe with a moment of uncertainty reflected on Dane's face.

"About that subject we were discussing," says Dane, now smiling at Sarah, then at Metcalfe. "I'm sure some folks I know will be glad to help you find a dentist to get your tooth, even all of them filled with that gold filling."

"No one pays my dental bills for me," says Metcalfe and then chuckles. "We're in America. The streets are paved with gold, haven't you heard? A man should be able to sweep enough of it off the pavement to pay a million dental bills. If you agree that this is America and that's possible just nod your head."

Hank almost chokes, fearing that the loud-mouth black man has given them away to Sarah, or that Dane will blow his top and spill the beans. Hank's eyes widen with expectation, but Dane nods in agreement, and both Klansmen anxiety attacks lessens, as Metcalfe grins at them, and then faces Sarah and says, "Mister Collins said he got cut up a little in that riot in town, and a doctor's looking him over. Said he'd be back as soon as he can."

Dane takes in a deep breath, and Hank breathes easier, and Sarah slumps against the wall. She goes to the window and views the smoke still lingering on the horizon over Cutterville.

"Yesterday, our wagons were turned back," she tells them. "By a contingency of the National Guard, who informed them that the road into Cutterville would be blocked off until their main force arrived and put down the trouble in town. Are you sure? Collins and the others are okay?"

"As good as gold," says Metcalfe eyeing Dane up and down.

Flynn enters the store and is shocked to see Dane and Metcalfe there. He glares at Dane.

"Son," says Sarah, "Dane came by to offer his regrets about your father's illness."

"Flynn," Dane mutters, gazing down, then up again, "any misunderstandings between us in the past, if you can, I'd like to forget them. I'm here to follow you, if and when you step into your pa's shoes."

Sarah is clearly disturbed by the thought of Flynn joining the Klan, but makes no mention of it in front of the visitors. If Sarah is disturbed, Metcalfe is downright shocked, when he recognizes Flynn as the boy who helped throw him off the train. Flynn now scowls at Metcalfe. "And you, Brutus," he defiantly says to Metcalfe, "did you also come to offer Caesar your loyalty or did you come, as well, to slaughter him?"

"Flynn!" exclaims Sarah.

"I'm sorry, Sir," Sarah apologizes to Metcalfe, then to Dane.

"No apology necessary," Metcalfe tells Sarah and then chuckles at Flynn. "Oh, no, young man," he says. "I didn't come to slay Julius, or Augustus, or anyone else, or to offer loyalty or anything else to you." Metcalfe sees Dane gawking over at him and goes on. "I will say this, though, that on that train I didn't know you was a Cutter, young man. But I'm not sorry about what I said to you. Besides," Metcalfe continues rubbing his head, "I ended up getting the worst of the deal from you and that other young fellow, wouldn't you say?"

Sarah looks from Metcalfe to Flynn. "Collins sent word by Mister Metcalfe and Dane from town," she informs Flynn. "Collins and the others are okay."

"Mother, I need to talk with you in private," says Flynn, guiding Sarah from the store, as Ressie reenters the building with her English book and the register key, unlocks the cash register, leans with one elbow on it and keeps a close watch on Dane, Metcalfe and Hank.

600

"We're not here to steal your pocket change, baby child," teases Metcalfe, "Relax."

"Don't touch nothin' you ain't gonna pay fo'," Ressie tells them. "I don't trust no city slickers, don't care what color they be." She suddenly covers her mouth, looks down at the open English book, pages through it and says, " 'They are'," then hurriedly leers up at Metcalfe again and exclaims. "I don't care what color they are."

Outside in the twilight, Flynn sadly faces his mother. "It's about Caleb and someone's baby," he tells Sarah, deep concern reflected in his blue eyes. He leads her to Henry near the back door of the store, where Naomi is standing under a shade tree cradling and bottle-feeding Carrie's newborn, a bottle which Henry brought along. With his apprehensive mother stepping to Henry, while scrutinizing back at Naomi and the baby, Flynn—feeling like the most unlucky person in the world—goes to Old Clara and strokes her nose to ease his pains, maybe even to do as the young children often do, to rub some of Old Clara's perceived magic off onto him, which he feels he surely needs.

You're lucky to be a horse, he thinks to Old Clara. *Being human is too complicated.*

"You're lucky," Flynn hears Naomi tells the infant. Flynn looks over at her, she at him, and then Naomi goes on talking to the helpless baby. "If anyone besides Henry would have found you, they might not have known what to do, but he did just fine in cutting your cord and feeding and keeping you clean, safe and warm."

While Naomi mothers the child, Sarah and Henry exchange frantic thoughts. "Maybe one of the colored families that's heading north to find a better way of life didn't want it, and Caleb found the child by the roadside and sent it home on Old Clara," Henry says.

Sarah breaks down and sobs, "No mother would throw away her newborn, Henry."

Naomi calls to them, "The time will soon come, Sarah, when mothers will cast out their young like garbage, but this is not yet the time. This baby has come out of Carrie's body, as you will see once you look at it."

"My God," exclaims Sarah, going to Naomi and viewing the newborn. "It is so, but where are they? Carrie and the others. And Caleb." She points at the store. "That man in the store said that Collins and the other are okay, but something is terribly wrong." She turns to Henry.

"Form a search party," she tells him. "The child does belong to Carrie and Bruce. Anyone can see that. Look for them, Henry. Caleb and Carrie. Sweet Jesus, haven't we suffered enough? Now this terrible thing is upon us. Carrie would never leave her baby, not unless—"

Suddenly, Flynn spots Jayne—in still another of his shirts, as she darts between the trees and across the edge of the field to her mother's recently assigned cabin, her youngest sister running with her. At the rear of the small house, the young Hill sister waits outside, while Jayne, who had earlier spotted Dane and Hank entering the store and had chosen to enter the rear of the shack for that reason, climbs through the shack's back window, and as her sister stands watch outside, inside the small quarters, a sobbing Jayne, feeling that she's left her sisters and brother without someone to watch over them, and the drugged girl, now loaded down with guilt, enters the bedroom which her mother had lovingly planned out for her and her two sisters. She doesn't know it, but for now, her siblings are not alone, as she grievously thinks. Until Sarah can locate the children's runaway father or—failing that—decide what to do next with the family, the plantation workers and Sarah take turn caring for the mother, and fatherless, fragmented children. Jayne's clothes are draped across a straight-back chair, her sisters having already put their things away; also in the room are two twin-size beds—one of which the younger girls share—and one other, which Jayne was to have, rests in a corner with only a mattress on it, mattresses delivered by family friends from their old house in town. When Jayne sees her mattress, she backs away from it, as if from Satan himself. "No," she whispers and then groans. She continues. "I don't need you. Stay away from me." She quickly tosses off her tar-stained shirt, slips into a floral-pattern dress, steps into a pair of bloomers and puts on dry socks and shoes, purposely keeping her sights away from her old mattress.

Rushing to a nearby dresser, she opens the drawer, finds and removes a bottle of iodine and stuffs the topical medicine in her dress pocket, but then she sees a book of matches in the drawer, and sweat pours from her brow. Slamming the drawer shut, she turns away and starts to leave, then whirls back around, opens the dresser drawer, seizes the matches and runs to her bed, jerks the mattress sideways, reaches into a hole in it and pulls out a pipe, spilling some of the pipe's contents on the floor. Dropping to her knees, Jayne frantically sweeps up the weedy material with her hand and re-packs it into the pipe. She bounds to her feet and—with her hands shaking, the young girl lights the pipe and puffs away. She had told Caleb she would give up the sin of lusting after money, but not after drugs, which—at the moment—is the most powerful god on earth to her, as her body, as well as her guilty mind scream for as a relief, relief afforded only by the joyous smoke of love entering deep into her lungs, giving her a profound feeling of ecstasy and a purpose for living. The wind blows through the window and causes another door in the shack to swing open. Jayne glares into the small room, where her brother Benny's clothes are draped on the family couch, a couch in the front room where he's assigned himself to sleep, too afraid to sleep in their dead mother's bed, which is set up a few feet away from the couch. Jayne finds herself being drawn to the room. After she enters that front room, she gawks at her mother's rococo brass bed, at the dresser and at her mother's bentwood rocking chair, rocking gently in the wind from another opened window. On the chair is the paper Jesus-faced fan from Miller's church. Jayne turns ashen, her sights drawn to the wall above the chair. A framed plaque hanging there turns her blood cold. A sign within the plaque was put there by her sisters after the death of their mother. It reads: "Thou shall not sin, nor drink of liquor nor smoke." Jayne's lips tremble and turn bloodless. Alongside the dresser is a small storage room, used as a closet, its door open, revealing her mother's ugly, dark, raccoon coat, her white-lace-collared, burlap dress, in which she had met her demise. Sarah's workers had refused to bury her in that ugly dress, so it was left hanging there for Jayne decide what to do with it. Suddenly the wind blows the dress off its hanger and onto a small table, sending a glass-framed picture of Mrs. Hill onto the hard, wood floor, shattering the glass. Jayne staggers and screams.

"What's wrong?" calls her sister, lifting herself up to the window ledge to look inside.

"Stay out there!" Jayne shouts. "The devil's in here."

To the drug-induced girl, the dress seems to rise up out of the glass in the wind, floating through the air with an image of her deceased mother in it: the dead woman's gray face, her waxy, pale hands and her buttermilk-colored, heavy, varicose legs are clearly seen through the teenager's distorted senses; as the dress moves toward her, in the wind, it asks: "Why, Jayne? Why?"

"Mamma," Jayne shrieks, dropping the pipe and running from the dead woman's dress and leaping out the window and into the arms of Flynn and those of her younger sister.

"Ahhhh!" Jayne continues shrieking, momentarily believing that she's jumped into the arms of her dead mother.

"It is you," Flynn says and then faces Jayne's sister, "Patty said you asked her where you guys live. She said that you wanted get some clothes. We've been looking everywhere for you. You missed your mother's funeral."

Flinging her arms about Flynn's neck, Jayne gags and groans, trying to speak, the freshly smoked jimson and firestone mix taking its final toll on her voice and mind. Flynn sniffs the odor coming from her breath and clothing.

"Dimmit, Jayne Hill, as if the plantation didn't have enough to worry about. Carrie's baby. And Caleb missing, and now you've been smoking that damn stuff." He faces her sister. "Don't just stand there, Patty. Go and get Benny and your sister so you guys can take care of Jayne before she kills herself. She already appears half dead. I've got Caleb to worry about."

As Patty races off, and Flynn walk from the rear of the house and Jayne follows him, gesturing and pointing, trying to tell him about Caleb, and grunting every other word, she sees Dane leaving the store with Hank and gaping over at her. Flynn tracks her terrified stares to Dane, as the Klansmen look around, then quicksteps in their direction. It's clear that the two men feel they can easily take down both Flynn and Jayne with strength alone.

"What's wrong, Jayne? Why are you afraid of him?" asks Flynn.

She grabs Flynn's hand and sprints with him by the way she came, through a section of heavily wooded trees. After running for a few minutes, she arrives at a wagon, which is partly concealed in the thicket, and she collapses against it, a wagon, which she had discovered in the swamps, along with its two mules, hours earlier. Flynn stares at the mules. "Those are our mules and wagon," he says, as Jayne gasps for air. "My God! What's wrong with you?"

She sees Dane and Hank running after them, and she bounds onto wagon, slides aside Carrie's picnic blanket, reaches out and pulls Flynn aboard, lashes the mules and drives away with him, leaving Dane and Hank behind swearing at them.

Nearly an hour later, the tired mules reach Henry's seized land; all the time, Flynn has been continuously attempting to converse with Jayne, but she's only been able to make incoherent sounds, always pointing to the way ahead of them and trying to force the mules to run faster. At one juncture, in their travels, Flynn had attempted to take the reins from her, but she had fought him off. Flynn now sits back in the seat going along with her, hoping that when she gets where she's taking him, maybe they'll find Caleb and everything will then make sense. As they approach the south shore—a half mile from Old Cutter Bridge, near where Dane and the others killed Bruce and Carrie—Jayne sees a straw hat floating on the lagoon, a hat like the one she had been wearing and had given to Caleb.

"Hat!" she manages to wail, leaping from the moving wagon and splashing into the lagoon.

"Jayne!" Flynn yells, seizing the reins and stopping the mules. "Is Caleb in there? Is that what you're trying to tell me?"

Flynn catches her knee-deep in the water and nudges her back to shore. "Stay the hell put! You're too damn crazy to be of use in here and will only drown."

Jayne watches Flynn swim to the hat and frantically dive. Underwater, he spots a body near his and Caleb's sunken boat. His first thought is that Caleb had returned to try, once more, to rescue the craft, and had drowned; then he notices that the body is weighed down with rocks and ropes, and his heart races out of control. An arm of the corpse is waving back and forth in the underwater currents and seemingly beckons for him to come closer. Petrified, Flynn thinks of turning back, and only his thoughts that it is Caleb gives him the courage to continue. When he reaches the body, he quickly removes his pocketknife and cuts through the binders; after the last rope is severed, the bloated corpse, casting off bubbling gas, zooms to the surface. When Flynn starts his upward swim, he notices still another body on the bottom, that of a woman and his wide eyes reflect his horrendous dismay. It's Carrie. Jayne sees him pop to the surface, wailing in agony, then suck in a lung full of air and dive again. Unable to contain herself, Jayne enters the water and swims to the corpse and rolls it over; it's Bruce Johnson, his open, unseeing eyes looking at her. She screams and wildly splashes—all arms and thrashing feet and legs—to shore, where she falls face down, gagging and feverishly breathing. She loudly sobs when Flynn pops into view next, panting and gasping and holding onto Carrie's soggy remains.

Nearly an hour passes and Flynn desperately wants to get the bodies back to Shadow Grove as fast as he can in order to join in the search for his friend, but with Jayne totally out of control, endlessly crying and gagging and unable to assist or speak, it has taken the sensitive young man nearly the entire hour to swim back and forth, tugging Carrie's body a dozen yards or so before swimming away from the floating body and resting on shore and fighting to regain his endurance before returning to Carrie's remains. Finally, after depositing Bruce and Carrie's bodies onto the wagon—side-by-side, on their backs—along with the waterlogged straw hat, which he places on the front seat—Flynn, nearly worn out, tucks the picnic blanket around Bruce and Carrie's corpses, then climbs into the rig, takes the reins from the whimpering girl and heads for Shadow Grove, and although Bruce and Carrie have been dead for some time and their blood should have coagulated, it seeps bright red onto the blanket. As they travel, Jayne sits there staring at Flynn's rope wrist bracelet. "Henry made it," he says, mistakingly feeling that the half-insane girl was actually seeing it instead of mindlessly focusing on it. She looks away, and sadly focuses on the straw hat, which lies between the two of them. Her eyes wide; she picks up the hat and gawks at it. Bruce's name, not Caleb's, is on the inside band. As if a bolt of lightning it hits her: Caleb is not also in that lagoon! She leaps to her feet, spooking the mules, then sits down, stands up and sits again and begins grunting, clearing her throat and grunting some more; excited beyond belief, she gestures trying to talk, to tell Flynn about the hat, about Caleb.

"Sit down, Jayne. You'll be okay once I take you back to Mother and the others. Some of the men will return to the lagoon and search the bottom again. God, don't let them find him in that water. Let me find him instead and alive," he tells her.

Jayne frantically gestures toward the cattails and the lagoon's distant north shore, and when Flynn doesn't stop, she seizes the reins and turns the mules in the direction of a road leading to the north shore. Flynn regains control and redirects the mules toward his land. Jayne springs off the wagon and runs in the direction of the distant shore, motioning for Flynn to follow. "Come back, Jayne! They're all looking for you. I have to get the bodies home and find Caleb!" Jayne goes her own way, Flynn the same—looking back over his shoulder sadly—without her. After reaching the north shore, the out-of-breath, frantic girl stumbles into the boat shack, and as she had prayed and hoped—she sees Caleb lying on the bed of paper and wearing his straw hat. Then Jayne sees Caleb's bracelet on his wrist. Recalling Flynn's rope bracelet, she runs to Caleb, removes the bracelet from his wrist and races outside, waving it in the air from the surrounding bushes and across the vast body of water and at the wagon and Flynn, who now appears as a quivering, shimmering speck of dust, fading fast against the gloomy horizon, as the light runs away from the dark and night approaches. Jayne sprints to the Brooks' house and pounds on the door, pushes it open, enters the quarters and runs through the house looking for Henry. No one is home as before; crying, she races back to the boat shack and removes Caleb's hat and dabs iodine on his scalp wound, then takes his hand as he lies there. *If not yet*, she ponders, *Caleb will soon surely die.*

A quarter mile away, Flynn cries aloud, "Caleb, where the hell are you, man?"

42

The Blanket of Blood

On Shadow Grove, with the sun's last light fading below the horizon, creating an orange-grayish atmosphere between earth and sky, night and day, Dane—after having spotted Jayne and Flynn riding off together—now knows that not only had Jayne tried to rescue Caleb—who Dane feels is surely dead—she had to have witnessed the killings of Bruce and Carrie, and it's only a matter of time before Flynn returns with her and the news that he, Dane Tucker, orchestrated the Johnson family slaughter, which will give more credence to the rumors of him being one of those having had a part in the deaths of those kids who were burned at the bridge in '29, a crime that again looms in the foreground because of the northern reporters still hanging about town and sniffing out the story of the darkened sky and about Caleb and Naomi supposedly being blessed. Jayne had been told about other Klan killings, and there is no doubt, to Dane, that she will spill her guts out to the reporters, if for nothing else to be paid for the story, if she fails to get any of Barney's money. Working against the clock, Dane has entered the manor and is in Sarah's bedroom, on the second floor and roughing through her dresser drawers, looking for clues to the whereabouts of Barney's fortune, a letter to Sarah from Barney, a key that seems out of place, maybe even one of those hundred-dollar bills that Metcalfe had shown him. After discovering nothing that points to the money, a frustrated Dane goes to the bedroom window and checks out the darkening landscape below the hill. Sarah and Henry are still in the distant field organizing the search party, which has now added bloodhounds to their numbers, their torch lights flickering, the flames dancing in the breeze. The one-eared Klansman resumes his search, his fingers coming to rest on a pair of Sarah's silken panties and remaining there momentarily. Leaving the room, Dane cautiously heads down the dimly lit hallway, toward a light coming from an inward-facing, partly-opened bedroom door, where he peeks in at the nurse asleep in her chair. When he glimpses Barney in his bed, Dane steps back and takes in a deep breath, his eyes wide with apprehension. He sneaks another look into the room. The Grand Wizard is wearing a white nightgown and is propped up with white pillows in a sitting position, while surrounded by cold, sterile-looking, white sheets. Barney's dazed, blue eyes are open and looking straight past the door at Dane. Dane's legs are unable to hold him up and he goes to his knees. Barney's unsettling gaze—however—never varies, his eyelids never blink, as Dane—from that kneeling position— once more gawks in at him.

The motherfucker is in a coma, just like them rumors say he is, Dane thinks, easing to his feet.

Shocked, he glances at the nurse. Hoards of flies are in the room, and in her sleep, the nurse sporadically fans at them as they buzz about her face. Dane hurries past the open door; what he doesn't see is that Barney's so-called comatose eyes are following his movements. Colonel Cutter's demerol-impaired sight then switches to a grotesque form standing in the shadows behind that inward-positioned door: the wrinkled face of a foul-smelling creature with bleached lips and straggly, long, lifeless, gray hair, a female thing with bony fingers, scaly arms, and dried-up tits, and with feathers stemming from her head and flies swarming about her body, as she lingers in the shadows of the door, consuming the flies.

"Turn away, Barney," the thing whispers. "I'm too horrifying to behold."

"Who are you?" says Barney, speaking for the first time since falling into his coma-like state, the nurse continuing to sleep through it all.

"I'm your mother, son."

Leaning toward her and away from his pillows, pale and alarmed, Barney's eyebrows twist downward, his hardened eyes reflecting dismay. "It is you," he says. "Your voice is the same, but your body. Who did this terrible thing to you?"

"Lucifer, son. He is so beautiful, more so than any woman, once he lets you see him as he is. But when I told him that to me, as your mother, that you were also beautiful, he went into a rage and turned me into this appalling thing. God, Barney, He has also made His jealousy known. God has caused the Appalachians to stir in order to awaken those pitiful souls out there that the end of time is approaching." Barney closes his eyes against the revolt of seeing his beloved mother deformed in such a way.

"Get up, son. Our lord, Lucifer has sent me to help you break out of this spell over you and set you free to fulfill his promise to make you and Flynn rulers over this world. Now, Barney. Now is the time for Flynn to rule at your side, with Caleb lying in despair; now, son. Satan promises eternal life for both of us, along with Flynn, and that every man, woman and child on earth will be at your son's beck and call to do with them as he wishes until the end of time, including giving Flynn the power to enslave Caleb, if he should somehow come out of this alive.

"Caleb, Barney, he's unknowingly growing stronger, even as we speak, and Satan now needs both of us to destroy him, so that Caleb's influence on Flynn will die with him." As Barney slides from his bed, his mother smiles, "Our lord and master says that you must go to Henry's land to watch and wait. You must wait, Barney. Remember that, because he has said that God has even blinded him on where your money is, but he counsels that if you do as he says and patiently observe those now on Henry's land, others there will lead you to your fortune, money needed to begin your control over this world, and he will also personally be there to help you kill Caleb." When Barney approaches with open arms, his mother warns. "Stay back, my son. If you come closer, it will be like embracing the flesh of a billion skunks and gazing upon the Medusa." She begins crying. "I begged Satan to deliver me from this hideous body, from these feathers and despicable smell; he said first you and I and Flynn have to prove worthy of his gifts of everlasting life, power and fortune. My God, son! I can't wait that long to be normal again."

As the nurse continues in her restless sleep, Dane makes his way down the third-floor hallway, approaching a closed door. Seeing the room light streaming beneath it and into the hallway, he slowly opens the door and glares at Metcalfe sitting on the edge of Flynn's bed and grinning over at him with a small, metal box on his lap. Metcalfe breaks open the box with his razor. "Gotcha," he quietly says. Metcalf plucks up six gold coins from the box and gives half of them to Dane. "This is what a soldier should die for, not in a war dying for thirty-five fucking dollars a month for his damn country," says Metcalfe. "Gold, man. Gold!"

"Jesus," whispers Dane. "Is this better than sex, or what? Now, where's the rest of it?"

"I tell you the time," Metcalfe hisses, "and right away, you ask me how to build a clock."

"You're too smart fer your own good, boy and fergetting that you're just a tar-ball to me."

"It takes one to know one," whispers Metcalfe, grinning down at the coins in his hand.

"What's that supposed to mean, monkey boy?" asks Dane, pocketing the coins. " 'It takes one to know one?' "

"You really and truly don't know, do you?" says Metcalfe. "The rest of us can take one look at each other and know what side of the bread we're buttered on. But instead of buttering your bread on the toasted side, you smear it on the damn, gummy, sticky, Wonder-Bread side."

"What's he talking about?" asks Hank, appearing at Flynn's bedroom door behind them, then stepping inside the room and picking up Flynn's tennis racquet and ball. "They say these things cost money," he grins. "I could pawn 'em right, Metcalfe?"

"Dane here's," Metcalfe answers, "done lost his ability to see, even when he look in the mirror. That's what I mean, as if you're smart enough to understand." Snickering, the black man then faces Dane. "Have you ever let a colored man get close enough to get a good look at you?"

"Hell no," hisses Dane. "And I ought to cut out your nigger throat, you black ape. Again, hell no. What fer? Except fer you, fer obvious reasons, otherwise I wouldn't let one of you monkeys get within a hundred feet of me.

"Unless he happens to be Caleb Brooks," says Hank, "when he beat you up."

"Shut the hell up, both of you and stop talking in riddles to me or money or no money, so help me God, I'll shut you up fer good."

"Oh, but you won't. Money is you guys' god, same as it is mine. And you won't even think of killing me until we locate, then escape with it. I suggest you look in another part of this big-ass house, while I finish searching in here."

Dane steps to the door, jerks the tennis racquet from Hank and nudges him into the hallway. "I told your ass to wait at the store and keep an eye on Sarah and her workers."

"I was just concerned about you guys, that's all," whispers Hank.

"Concerned," says Dane, slapping him with the racquet. "I'll show you concern. You thought we'd find that money and run out on you. Now, get back to that store, trying to kiss up to that nigger."

Hank hurries down the staircase. Once he reaches the second floor, he see a ghostly, green light flickering on and off from down the hallway and from the open door of Barney's bedroom, which he had earlier passed, right after Dane had done so. It's only now that old Hank realizes that he still has Flynn's tennis ball in his hand. Afraid of Barney's whispered, ghostly powers against anyone trying to steal anything at all from him, Hank places the ball on the landing and—looking back over his shoulder—descends the staircase and quickly leaves the manor. After hearing the front door open and close, Dane looks into Flynn's room at Metcalfe. "Damn peckerwood Hank," he tells Metcalfe, "we stand to make millions and he wants to steal a damn tennis racquet." Dane tosses it onto the carpeted floor, and then glares at Metcalfe. "You said money is my god and that it's just as much your god, so to keep you from planning on making your gods happier than mine with more than your share of what we find, you let me know the minute you find anything. You hear?" Dane goes on his way, stepping with a bit more spirit in his gait, the thought of having millions on his mind.

As the heaven completes its journey into night, the search party is in full swing. Nearly a hundred of Sarah's field hands hold onto their torches and are unaware of Flynn, as he rides slumped over in Bruce's mule-drawn wagon now slowly traveling under a full moon. While approaching the field hands, Flynn's panic-stricken voice of sorrow resounds against the wind. "Dead! They're all dead!"

One by one, the workers stop what they are doing and focus on the moonlit, fuzzy-appearing mules and wagon, at first seemingly traveling without a rider, while melting in and out of the masking presence of dark leaves and trees, encapsulating it. When Flynn, his wagon and the mules pass beyond a field of wheat and enter the moonlit field of cabbage and beans and clearly come into view—his yellow hair blending into the moonlight, the pride-bound workers trained to recognize the familiar voice of their young master, hear Flynn's voice clearly rings out. "Dead. They're all dead."

More and more workers from other fields, near and far—who are too old to search for Caleb—soon hear the passed-along calls from their peers that Flynn is in trouble, and they also—with their eyes like white marbles of despair—focus on the distant wagon and Flynn. The nearby cabbage laborers notice it first, the bloodstained blanket awash in moonlight and flapping in the wind, adding an eerie credence to the teenage boy's clarion call. Involved in a shouting match of questions and answers, at first, Henry and those in the search party, several hundred yards away, do not hear Flynn's cry of despair. Astride Old Clara, Henry is facing the difficult task of organizing Sarah's racially diverse, torch-carrying search party, some on horseback, others on foot, all having had asked and still asking Henry and others a thousand questions on how and what area the search for Caleb should cover. Sarah and a dozen wives and girls are passing out the last of the hot coffee and doughnuts to the several teams, while Naomi stands nearby cradling Carrie and Bruce's well-wrapped newborn infant lovingly in her arms.

"If you find Caleb, fire three shots," says Henry. "Otherwise, we meet back here at midnight."

At the manor, Dane hears the panicked roar of workers' agonizing voices, and he stares out the sprawling residence's, second-floor window and sees what appears to be the very ground moving in waves under the moonlight, as—in a mass of oneness—the field hands swarm to Flynn and the wagon. Once Dane realizes that it is Flynn aboard the wagon, he runs from the house fearing for his life, leaving Metcalfe on his own. After loping back to the general store, Dane sidles up to Hank, who is busy adjusting a bullwhip about his waist and belt, a whip of obedience—named after Hammer's Club—a whip that Hank had hidden under his shirt, and which he was afraid to even try to use against Metcalfe earlier in the store. "I'll lash their eyes out if they come after me now," he tells Dane. "I told you. You should have let me bring that shotgun with us from the truck. But no, you said you wanted us to appear as friends to these folks out here."

"Shut up, you damn old fuckhead!" hisses Dane, as both merge back into the shadows of the store and Metcalfe runs up and joins them, watching the events unfold in the field around Flynn eighty or so yards away.

"What the fuck did you run out on me for," Metcalfe hisses at Dane. "Left me in that damn house to be trapped alone, you bastard?"

When those in the search party see the wagon, Henry and Sarah look at one another. Then Bruce's mules and wagon comes to a stop in the cabbage field as waves of workers stop in front of it blocking the way, workers too afraid to go any closer upon seeing the bloody blanket.

"They're dead!" Flynn cries. "Someone killed all of them!"

When Henry hears Flynn's sorrowful cry, his hopes sinks to the bottom of his stomach.

"That's Flynn driving that wagon!" exclaims Sarah. "Jesus! What is he saying to them, Henry?"

"Caleb," yells Henry, focusing on the blanket. "Ma boy ain't under that blanket of blood, is he?" Dropping their torches, their coffee and their doughnuts, those who have dedicated themselves to find Caleb swarm toward the wagon, with Henry leading the way, sprinting Old Clara through a cotton field and on to that of cabbage, whizzing by the slower runners, still on their flailing way to the young master.

More then a little uneasy, Hank turns to Dane and says, "The trucks and the guys are nearby if we have to get the hell out of here, Dane." When Dane makes no attempt to answer, Hank goes on, while eyeing Metcalfe with contempt, as if to say he's not welcome to come with them. "If that girl told him about—" Hank stops, glares at Metcalfe, then continues in a whisper to Dane. "If she told him about, you know what, then we're up to our ass in doodoo."

A look of despair falls over Dane. He's fully aware that sticking around could cost him his life at the hands of Sarah's angry workers, but then, there is all of that money. He looks over at Metcalfe, and knowing that Metcalfe can hear him, and caring less, he quips, "I'm not leaving and let that coon get his hands on that money by himself."

Metcalfe's thoughts, on the other hand, are far from worrying about Dane. He's smiling. His excited sights are locked on Henry and Old Clara, as horse and master skillfully dodge through the crowd as one body, while rapidly closing in on the wagon. "Look at that old nigger man ride that goddamn beautiful beast, will you," he says, going on. "It's as if that man and that creature are one as an arrow, shot from a bow. Don't anyone ever try and tell me again that there ain't no goddamn colored cowboys in this here stinkin' country! Look at him! No peckerwood can ride any better than that. Go man, go with your bad-ass self!"

"Are you nuts?" asks Dane, glaring over at Metcalfe. "If what I think is in that wagon is, and you stand there praising that coon Henry and his damn horse, that nigger man will team up with them brain-washed po' whites and kill us."

"Look!" says Metcalfe, walking over and excitedly nudging Hank as Henry leaps Old Clara over field-side stone fences and brings the old horse to a sliding stop at the wagon, then bounds off of her and onto Flynn's buckboard. Henry quickly lifts the blanket and gasps at the sight of Bruce and Carrie's side-by-side mutilated bodies. Dane and the others have crushed the corpses' skulls with rocks. Henry covers over the disturbing sight, and as those nearby who had witnessed it stagger back, one of them, a young boy, faints as Henry's watery eyes turn skyward.

At the store, Hank gawks at Dane. "We had 'em weighed down with rocks," he says. "How in the hell did that weak-ass Flynn Cutter find 'em and then get 'em here?"

"More important than that," Metcalfe adds, proving his ability to switch sides in the blinking of the eye (Henry now as much an enemy as Dane and Hank), "did that Jayne Hill tell Flynn and this Henry about you two?" Dane and a tight-lipped Hank gape at Metcalfe. "Don't look so surprised that I know about you," Metcalfe replies. "I'm not from God or magical like some of you southern whites and all of them dumb, black fools say that some black boy—who the Klan fears—is. I only stood out-side Sue Ann's bar window at night, listening to you hillbillies talk about everything from wanting to kill that boy and Jayne girl to wanting to rape her. This Caleb person, I guess, stood outside God's window and got all his dirt on y'all, according to the way some of you go on about him. You damn, sick crackers. Now this business of what's in that wagon. I can guess you killed someone, but why in the hell did you leave them out where they could be found, and at a time like this?"

Hank whispers to Dane, "Are you sure a colored person doesn't have God's ear, Dane, I mean someone like Caleb? He should be dead after he fell off that bridge!" Hank glares at Metcalfe, going on. "Could God be with that boy, like some say, after all?" Hank looks at the wagon. "Will God hear their cries, those workers' and come after the killers of them two coons?"

While the cries of agony continue from the workers at the wagon of death, Metcalfe just laughs as a dumbfounded Dane gawks at old Hank as if he'd like to rip off his head. The golden-mouthed, black man ex-claims, "You goddamn, motherfucking, all-white, mighty Klan! Never, you hear! God is not and never has been on the side of a dumb nigger! Take my word for it." He glares at Dane, adding: "Otherwise our light-skinned niggers wouldn't be trying to pass themselves off as white all the time."

"What does this talk of coons passing fer white got to do with the fact that we're in trouble here?" shouts Hank. "Let's get out of here, Dane. I got a strange feeling about Caleb."

Dane blares, "Caleb Brooks is dead! Shot clean through his head and went tumbling off of Old Cutter Bridge and onto a damn train. Dead, I say. That boy is dead! Again, if he's dead, where is his so-called

God's protection? This is a white man's world. Both of you idiots get it through your heads. No more talk of Caleb."

"Let's not wait around and find out whose world it is," says Hank, whispering to Dane. "Them boys waiting in the trucks fer us brought word from Richards . . ." He looks at Metcalfe, lowers his voice even more and nervously goes on. "That damn Caleb Brooks . . . He's alive."

"Still alive!" exclaims Dane. "He was shot in the goddamn head! What the fuck do you mean alive? He fell off the damn bridge! Saw him do it with my own eyes!"

"Shot in the head," says Hank, "fell off that damn bridge and is still alive, Dane," Hank says, no longer whispering. Metcalfe stands there, astonished by what he's hearing, as the field hands continue to flow to Henry and Flynn, and while they do, Hank explains on to a disturbed Dane. "Caleb was seen riding through town on a horse with a naked Jayne Hill riding on it with him. Something protects that boy. Something no white man wants to believe could. Maybe it's not God, maybe it's even Satan, himself, who watches over that boy."

Dane slaps Hank. "Don't you dare say Satan protects him. Satan protects only me now!"

"I'm getting damn tired of you slapping me all the time, Dane, and you're as crazy as Barney with all this talk about Satan, Dane. Stop slapping me! I'm a man, not—"

Dane draws back and slaps him again, this time across his mouth. Metcalfe's head tilts to the side, his eyebrows arched, as he studies the two of them and steps back, shaking his head, as if to ask what has he gotten himself into.

When Dane draws back to slap Hank once more, the old man throws up his hand to protect himself and exclaims, "Okay, Dane. But whoever Caleb is, after being shot in the head, falling off that bridge, that boy was blown out of that factory pipe with our men. All of 'em killed, Dane. And, again, he's still alive! Alive, Dane!"

It's clear to Dane by seeing the way Metcalfe is scrutinizing them that this latest tale of Caleb is now even puzzling the gold-mouthed, black man as well. Dane realizes, also, that Metcalfe is no fool, with or without Metcalfe now concerned over Caleb; and, like Caleb, it seems it won't be easy to make Metcalfe disappear, but after they find the money, with the help of Satan, die both Metcalfe and Caleb must, along with Hank, who—to Dane—is becoming niggerized.

At the cabbage field, after all the wailing and frustration, shouting and anger dies down, Henry lingers, totally drained, on the wagon beside the bodies and stands in silence, his gaze fixed on the stars. Shifting his sights, he stares at a terrified Flynn, who has been tearfully waving for Sarah to stay back every time she ventures forth from the crowd to stand by him. Flynn, the legal owner of Shadow Grove and supposedly now the "man" to turn to when one is troubled, does not want his workers to see him crying in his mother's arms, even though they, themselves, are wailing in dismay. Knowing that Flynn has to be worse off than anyone else over the deaths, Henry moves to the front of the buckboard and sits on the wagon seat beside him. With his strength and awareness of what and who he is, and that it's okay for a man to cry, he rocks Flynn in his arms, even as mothers and fathers, among the field hands, cry and rock their children in their embraces.

"They were out there in your lagoon, Henry," Flynn says. "Jayne, she took me there. She thought it was Caleb in the water. But it wasn't Caleb, Henry. It wasn't. Caleb's not out there under that cold water like they were . . . like Bruce and Carrie . . . is he, Henry? Is Caleb out there under that water?"

In the front of the line of her workers, a few feet from the wagon, Sarah is in no hurry to disturb Flynn and Henry, as they talk between themselves, knowing that if it were Caleb under the blanket, Henry and Flynn would have told her with their sights instead of focusing on each other. But was it Carrie? Sarah can hardly stand up thinking about that blanket of blood and she sets her sights on it.

"He'll be found," Henry tells Flynn, his eyes also watering up. "He'll be found and he'll be okay. I have a bargain with God. I'm to go first, years before my son."

"You?" asks a teary-eyed Flynn, looking up at Henry. "No. What would we do without you and Caleb? Mother and I? No, you're not going anywhere first or last, Henry. Caleb's alive. And yes, we'll find him. Just like you said. You'll see. And you and he will live a long life here on Shadow Grove with us. This will be your 'Little Shadow Place,' now."

Stepping from the workers, who are crying and kissing her hand in a show of loyalty, Sarah moves to the rear of the wagon, Naomi now close behind with Carrie's baby. The workers who are surrounding the rig shuffle back, clearing a path for them.

"Stay back, Sarah," Henry warns, when he notices her and Naomi.

"Don't look! It ain't Caleb! It's Bruce and Carrie. Ma God, woman! Stay where you are. It's an ugly sight, not even for a man's eyes to see!"

Shaking in dread, Sarah climbs onto the rear of the wagon anyway, and lifts the cover from the bodies, then drops the blanket and turns away ashen and sobbing with both hands covering her mouth, leaving Bruce and Carrie's remains only half covered from the waist down. As Sarah cries out in rage, those workers up close who had already viewed the remains—when Henry had first uncovered them—now also screech in terror, not in sadness or in rage, but in disbelief and heart-felt fright. When Henry had lifted the blanket, Carrie had been placed next to Bruce on her back with her rigor mortis arms locked at her side. Now she's lying on her side and has her arms wrapped lovingly about her man; and as these nearby workers gawk and groan in incredulity at the astonishing sight, Flynn follows their hysterical gaze to the corpses.

"I didn't put them in there that way," a stunned Flynn says. "I didn't have them hugging that way."

Without a cloud in the sky, blackness covers the moon, as if to hide the night light's face from the mutilation of two of God's children. Afraid, as the sky continues unusually darkening for that time of night, Sarah climbs into the front of the wagon with Henry and Flynn. Henry steps aside, permitting mother and son to sit together, to hold onto one another. As Henry watches over Sarah and Flynn, a member of the search party—field-boss Collins—approaches him from the wagon's far side; Henry leans down, and the kind man whispers. "Do we stay here a while longer, or is it a go to get the search under way with the information we have, Henry?"

"Soon," says Henry. He feels, as sure as there is a God, that Flynn will have a nervous breakdown in the face of what he's been through, if he doesn't help him conquer this shocking moment, and he agonizingly looks back at Sarah and Flynn, while speaking to Collins. "After I'm sure Flynn will be okay, then we finish detailing the plans and go and look for my boy."

Now all eyes are on Naomi, who steps closer to the wagon with the newborn; and, without looking at Carrie and Bruce's remains, she reaches her free hand over the side of the wagon and repositions the blanket over the bodies.

"What could have caused Carrie's arms to do that, Naomi? To hug

Bruce?" ask Tootie—one of Sarah's white, female farmers, age forty-two, unmarried and childless.

Naomi remains silent. However, she then nods with a smile at Tootie, as if telling her that she, Naomi, knows who has, indeed, placed Carrie's arms about her man. Every fieldhand there follows the mystery woman's sights to the first star to reappear in that night sky, a star—which seems to all—that is more than a heavenly light in the sky: to them, Naomi is looking at something far beyond all of their reach and out of reach of the murderous hand of the Klan. Sensing that God is in Naomi—even though they've heard she's lost her powers—one by one, the women—not the men—tired and dirty, the blacks and the whites, lower their heads and take each others' hands, their children doing the same with other youngsters, and they do this to openly respect Naomi, regardless of what is said about her, a good woman of God, a woman called Naomi once with the awesome power of God or now just one of them. As the women lower their heads and hum, "Some of you are asking what caused Carrie to embrace her man," Naomi begins. "Don't always look for the answer from others, or want to be told that a miracle caused our sister to embrace our brother; that would be like asking Jesus to raise the dead every time we need proof to convince ourselves that He is truly the Son of God. Jesus limited His miracles that we would follow His teachings out of love for our fellow man with our faith alone, without seeing a miracle every other day, which would even cause a monster like Adolf Hitler to fall on his knees before God and worship the all-powerful Light of Love. There are enough Hitlers in sheep's clothing among us today. We need no more."

Essie Mae, the sandy-haired old, white woman, who asked Henry to clean the spit off the store floor, stands afraid in the shadows behind the crowd without a word.

Word, however, spreads in rapid succession across the field, and the adjacent ones—to the stragglers still on their way—about Carrie rolling over and holding onto her man, even in death. To them Naomi who never looked at the bodies, but instead up at the sky with stars in her saintly-looking eyes, seems to have known everything. What was she gazing at, many ponder: At God? Was Naomi regaining her powers?

From the wagon, Sarah studies the faithful servant woman and sees how Naomi is inundated with tears, something Sarah knows Naomi would never do if she had her powers or if they were being restored, because, to Sarah, angels have no need to cry. Long ago Naomi had informed Sarah, on that ship from Germany, that the Spirit of God which came before them, had nothing to do with her or Sarah, that is was all about Caleb, and that all powers would go to him to test man's love of God against the temptation of Satan, and it seems Caleb's time is truly at hand. Naomi is sure he's still alive, but keeps it to herself for God's purpose to be fulfilled.

Sarah holds Flynn even closer, knowing that he is part of God's equation: the possible evil side with Barney's bloodline in him, the side that might have to kill Caleb or be killed, but is Caleb still alive? Tears flowing from her eyes, Sarah looks at her man; Henry's tears are also flowing at that moment with the same horrifying awareness about the boys.

"Surely, with your beautiful humanity, Henry," Sarah says, while holding tightly to Flynn, the crowd listening to her every word, "if you speak to Him as Caleb's beloved father, God will give us a sign that He understands a mother's love for her children, and that no matter how old they are or who fathered them, to her, they will always be her babies, crying out for her to always be there to protect them, even if it means giving up her own life for them, as Carrie and Bruce have for their child."

Many of the listeners having heard Sarah plead to Henry about her "babies," and knowing that Sarah has only one child, feel that she's confused, and that Sarah is thinking of Carrie and Bruce's newborn as her own, a newborn crying in Naomi's arms without a mother's love. Sarah softly goes on to Henry. "My babies. I can still hear them crying in my womb, even back then, as if they knew this day would confront them."

"The men and I have to leave now, Sarah," whispers Henry, his mind-set having shut out the presences of all others and wanting with all of his heart to hold the love of his life in his arms, to kiss and to comfort her, and to protect Flynn.

Holding tightly to her son, Sarah nods to Henry and then faces her crew. "Everyone," she exclaims, "will you please join me in a prayer for Caleb's, Henry's and the safety of the men who are going with him to find Caleb?"

Sarah kneels on the wagon, and the workers kneel in wavelike motion, one row after the other across the darkened fields. As Flynn remains seated in confusion, Naomi remains standing with the crying newborn in her arms. Then, as the workers silently pray for Caleb and the searchers' safety, Tootie, Sarah's intuitive fieldhand, inexplicably gazes at the sky, a sky now filled with stars and a bright, full moon. Turning her sights from the heaven, Tootie slowly looks at Naomi and then rises to her feet. With her hands extended, the childless woman approaches the crying baby and a puzzling Naomi, everyone looking up from their prayers and watching the event unfold. Naomi smiles and gives Carrie's child to the white woman, who sings a lullaby, quieting the infant into restful sleep. "Is this Carrie's baby, Naomi, like they say?" Tootie asks. "It sure looks like her and Bruce."

"Yes, it is, Tootie. Born for our beloved Savior's express purpose, as I now realize."

"His purpose, Naomi? Then you still can hear Him? Can hear the words of God?"

"It's easy, child, even as Sarah and I heard Him when He spoke to us on that ship long ago."

"He spoke to you and Sarah back then, when she was only fourteen?"

"Yes, Tootie, and so can all of you hear Him. Just listen with your hearts."

Lingering by the store, Dane ridicules Naomi. "Listen to that stupid fool telling them dumb white crackers to listen with their hearts," he tells Hank. "A heart got no feelings."

Metcalfe—as fate would have it, the same as Hank was, has come from a higher class of people—startles both Hank and Dane with what he says next, "A tiny baby," he begins, "and that does seem to be what that colored woman is holding over there. A newborn has more brain cells in its newborn heart than it has in its little head, putting more mystery in the Divine Works—that made us—than we can ever understand." When Hank and Dane gawk at him, Metcalfe blares at them. "What are you dummies looking at? You don't know a damn thing about me, to look at me like I don't know shit. This asshole, gold-mouthed, colored man attended Howard University until the damn army drafted me. I was somebody up to then, just a damn private after then, but that's the army's loss. I went from wanting to save lives and pleasing God to killing Germans and Japs. It was then that my old lady left my ass and the drugs and drinking got me screwed up. Ah! Imagine me coming up with that theory, that the heart of a newborn has brain cells. My professors said I was a genius, but could do nothing, back then, to help me through my troubles and keep me from being drafted. Yes, I also once had a heart, and I've lost more of my mind than you honkies will ever have if you live to be a hundred and sixty. I tell you this so that you know I'm the superior one here and not you two apes."

Dane just stands their laughing at Metcalfe, but Hank is so troubled upon hearing Metcalfe's story that he feels that the blacks are rising up like a flooded Mississippi River with their learning to drown out the white race, but if he thought he could escape that feeling by gazing at the field, he finds out that he is sadly mistaken, as Naomi seems to add to what Metcalfe has said.

"But a heart is only a muscle, Naomi," Tootie says. "A muscle to pump blood, not listen, so how can we talk to God with our hearts?"

"Is it only that?" Naomi asks, gazing about at all the nodding heads of workers who agree with Tootie. Naomi goes on, "Is it easier to say to a dead man 'Get up and live' or is it easier to command to grow brain cells,' especially in our children, who shall lead the way into tomorrow with their hearts as much as with their brains." Naomi faces the wagon knowing that the workers must pray to build on their faith. "We will not cry any longer for Bruce and Carrie, which is a natural, self-serving thing to do. They will live in one of many mansions, to never want, to never grow old, to never suffer again." "It's Caleb we must cry for now, here among the living. Pray that he is all right." She looks at Flynn. "Pray for him and Flynn who are needed to save us all."

"Naomi," Tootie asks, whispering as not to disturb those again praying for Caleb and now for Flynn, as well, her eyes sparkling with kindness and hope in the face of the horror and despair before them, "because Sarah asked for a sign that will tell her that God understands a woman's love for her children, and I prayed for so long for a child of my own, could this beautiful baby be a gift from God to me and a sign to Sarah that He understands us women in a man's world?"

"If Caleb were here, he would tell you so, because only he now holds the disciple's key to God's heart, if he accepts it, that is, but I will say 'yes.' God wants you to have that child." She beams at Sarah, going on, "And in this way, He's also telling you, Sarah, to hold onto your faith in prayer."

Kissing the black infant, as Sarah tearfully smiles at her, Tootie starts across the field to her plantation shack, chatting to her new baby. She stops and glances back at the racially mixed, mystery woman. "If no one objects and God is willing, I'll take Earlene and Brick, too," she says. "They need me now. And, Naomi, so does Jayne Hill, her sisters and brother. I have enough love for all of us."

"Yes, they do need you," replies Naomi with a huge grin on her face, then looks at Sarah, receives a nod from her and continues. "Sarah will have to build you a larger house." As Sarah tearfully continues nodding in agreement, a frightened Brick gets off his knees and runs through the crowd screaming for Tootie to wait for him, and when he reaches her, he looks at his newborn sibling then hugs the white woman about her waist, and he cries in her apron, much the way Flynn and Caleb—as children—had done with Naomi. Naomi breaks down in tears upon seeing this in a hopeless world of despair. Then, from out of nowhere, a comet streaks across the heavens and is gone as quickly as it had appeared, Sarah watching it all the way. A bone-gripping quiet settles over her and over all who witnessed it, sending their hearts racing, some of them out of joy, others out of alarm waiting for the earth to—once again—shake, not knowing if the streaking light in the sky is a good omen or a prophecy of doom as Flynn shivers.

Without warning, an electrical storm racks the heaven, setting the manor aglow. The prayer for Caleb now over, Sarah turns her son over to an anxious Henry. Flynn's blinking blue eyes are slowly drawn to his mother's fearful expression as she sets her sights on Barney's bedroom window, the fierce lightning seems to be emanating from there, striking out at the heavens, etching itself about the window of Barney's room. Flynn trembles. Then, as Henry again sits beside him, Flynn turns away from the sight of his mother and that of the manor and seeks out Henry's kind eyes of courage and love to feed upon. When Flynn, once again, follows his mother's line of sights to the house, Henry does the same, to Barney's window of hell fire. Henry places his strong arm about the shivering boy. Turning away from the manor, Sarah listens to her son, as he struggles to find his own voice and his courage: "I never want to grow up," Flynn whispers to Henry, "not to be forced to take a part in all of the killings, the raping and the hatred. All of it inspired by adults."

Henry looks toward the search teams, and he holds Flynn even closer, while Sarah tearfully looks down at them with profound and heartfelt reverence for the gentle, loving, black man and the love he shows for her son. As the blonde, sensitive lover of poetry continues shivering—with all of the mass confusion going on—no one has noticed that he is soaking wet until now. "Someone bring a warm blanket," Henry yells to the crowd, scarcely able to make himself heard over the dry, rainless thunder and lightning. "And hurry before Master Flynn catches his death of cold."

"I'll get do it, Mister Henry," shouts Benny, raising his hand and quick-stepping away and then breaking into a sprint to the store.

"Barney wants me to fill his shoes, Henry," Flynn exclaims, again glancing at the manor window, the workers trying in vain to hear what he's saying over the thunder, as he goes on. "He wants me to run Shadow Grove for the benefit of the Klan and to become a senator, and I want to become one, Henry, a senator. I really do, to do good for everyone, instead of becoming an evil combination of Grand Wizard and U.S. Senator, but lately I've been having these dreams of the power offered to me, of girls fighting over me, of being showered with money, all that I'll ever need, now that father has so much of it and even more to be given to me beyond what he has. Once I even dreamed of having you and Caleb lie on the ground, so that I can walk on you to keep the soles of my shoes from touching the earth. I don't know who I am anymore. Was I born to be like Barney, Henry? Was I?" Flynn asks, his teeth chattering.

Knowing that he must leave Flynn and search for Caleb, Henry is torn between the needs of the two boys he loves as much as he does Sarah. "Where are them dry clothes?" he calls over the crowd, causing the workers to look about for signs of Benny's return, a few of them rushing off to find him, as Henry again speaks to Flynn. "You're too beautiful inside and outside," he tells Flynn, wiping the tears from the young man's eyes, "to ever be anything but good, dreams or no dreams." Driven more than ever to find Caleb, Henry glances up at a tearful Sarah and, with a nod, signals for her to reclaim her son, but as Henry rises up, Flynn—flinching under the lightning—holds onto the black man. "You're Flynn Winthrop, not Flynn Cutter," Henry tells him, as Flynn again eyes the manor. "And this evil that going on got nothin' to do with you. You got as much of Sarah's blood in you as you do Barney's. You're not like that man. Don't let the thought even enter your mind. I'd bet ma life on your goodness. Sarah Winthrop raised you right." Henry nods to one of the workers then whispers to him. The man then leads Old Clara to the wagon by her reins. When he brings Old Clara alongside the wagon, Henry gives Sarah a looks that she has to obey, and she takes his place beside her son. The frightened boy releases Henry's arm. He then reaches out to his mother. "Where's Caleb, Mother? Has anyone even seen him?"

Sarah looks at Henry. "Find him, Henry," she sobs. She turns to the crowd, while clinging to Flynn and calls out, "The sheriff won't lift a finger to search out these killers of Bruce and Carrie or to look for Caleb, but if it takes every man, woman and child on my payroll and every cent Flynn and I have, we will make those who did this pay! And we will find Caleb!"

"Clear the way," shouts Benny, running back from the store and through the crowd with not only two blankets, but with a pair of coveralls, underwear, a shirt, shoes, socks, and a towel. As Sarah's workers pick up their farming tools, their hoes, their shovels, and some their torches—relighting them—and clubs to join in the search for Caleb, Flynn—ignoring Benny and the clothing—stands up and faces Bruce and Carrie's bodies.

"Mother, they can't be left like this. Not like slaughtered animals. They're already decaying. With or without the proper documents, I want them buried on this land . . . Tonight."

"The coroner could care less about issuing his precious death papers fo' color folk, anyway," a black woman calls out to Flynn, a fact often repeated by blacks. "So while the rest of y'all out lookin' fo' Caleb, us women folk will bury po' Carrie and Bruce after we prepare their bodies here on Shadow Grove."

"On ma land," says Henry, jumping off the wagon and into the saddle and onto Old Clara.

"Cutterville owns your land now, Henry," says Flynn. "They may not permit—"

"Bruce loved my place, Flynn," Henry says. "To him and Carrie, it was God's promised land to His people in bondage, where Bruce said he could look up and see the stars clearer than on any place he's ever known. Before they decided to go to California, both him and Carrie told me they wanted to be buried on Little Shadow Place and that the casket lids be left open as long as possible when we carried them to their graves, so that, no matter which one of them dies first, even in death, or in the light of day—because Naomi long ago said so—they would be facing them stars. My land will always belong to the Brooks. God willing. We bury them there."

"But what about us who'll be left here alone while the men are away?" asks Essie Mae, not knowing which side she wants to be on. "The Klan is like a snake and you never know when or where they will strike next, especially if you take sides against them."

Addressing her as well as the others who fear the Klan, Henry exclaims, "Every one of you heard what Sarah said about making the Klan pay, and we all know how she hates violence. She would never say it as boldly as I would, so now I want to add something more; tell yourself this: if you love Sarah, if you love this place, if this is truly the place you call home, then put down your hoes, your shovels and your fears and pick up your guns and hunting rifles, as some of you already have, and someone bring me a gun as well! And you women who remain behind, arm yourselves. If the snake wants to kill you with its poison, you kill it first! A handful of the men will remain here to fight beside you if it comes to that, and we all pray that it won't."

The workers' roaring approval pains the ears of the young. "Kill the snake! Kill the snake!" the crowd cries aloud, which can be heard, even over the lightning and thunder. To Naomi's way of seeing it, it was not Sarah's voice which needed to be heard over the rumbling heavens. God, instead, had let Henry's anti-Klan voices resound loud and clear to all. Henry reaches into the wagon and strokes Flynn's arm.

"I have to go with the search party," he tells him. "Stay close to your mother and oversee the moving of Bruce and Carrie's bodies to my place for burial. Sarah and Naomi know how the bodies should be arranged on the trip there."

"Nobody's going to search for Caleb without me," Flynn commands, jumping from the wagon, drying away his tears and slipping into manhood.

"Okay," says Henry, his heart gladdened with pride upon seeing Flynn coming into his own. Henry then faces the man to whom he had whispered at the wagon. "I'll take my section to the coast and search there," Henry tells him, as he turns Old Clara toward the west, while eyeing Dane at the store. "If Caleb is anywhere out there, Old Clara will find him." He faces Flynn. "Be careful, son. Caleb never trusted Dane Tucker. Now suddenly he shows up, maybe lookin' for your father's money."

Standing in the shadow behind several rows of workers is Metcalfe. He had slithered into the crowd to hear more of what Naomi had been saying, but instead, had put most of his attention on Flynn

"I will," Flynn replies. As Henry rides away, Flynn completes the drying of his eyes on his sleeve, and surging with love for Henry, he whispers. "You also, Papa, be careful."

When Metcalfe hears this from Flynn, the black man's all-consuming hatred of whites is shaken to its very foundation.

43

Barney Awakens

Once Flynn watches Henry leave, which does not go unnoticed by Metcalfe alone: Benny who—longing for a father to love and feeling that his runaway father will never return—looks from Flynn to Henry and sees the pure beauty in knowing the kindhearted man. When Flynn takes the dry clothing from his want-to-be-a-Klansman friend and hurries to the barn, Benny trots along at his side. At the store, another Klansman has joined Metcalfe, Hank and Dane: It's Hammer, Sheriff Richards' deputy, in his civvies, with the campfire burn scars still clearly seen across his arms and face. He's extremely angry because of those burns, which have driven him to have an even more powerful hatred of blacks, feeling that if it hadn't have been for the coloreds what he went through and now witnessing would never have happened: whites turning against whites to help search for Caleb especially irks him. Hammer leers over at Metcalfe, who is standing next to Hank, two bodies away. The deputy knows that with Sarah's workers all around them and entering and leaving the store to pick up additional weapons and torches in order to join the search teams, it would be a deadly mistake for him to even think of attacking Metcalfe verbally or physically in front of the anti-Klansmen field hands. However, Metcalfe sees how Hammer is leering at him, and, for one of the few times in his life, the gold-toothed man is glad that whites like Sarah and her workers are among her black ones and are all around them. After seeing and listening to how they reacted over the deaths of Carrie and Bruce, and how they worry about this Caleb boy; he feels reasonably sure that none of the plantation's whites will harm him, even if they find out he's after Barney's money, not after seeing how they went to their knees in prayer, but the business of Caleb troubles Metcalfe to no end:

Caleb Brooks. Who the hell is this goddamn boy?

Hammer guides Dane and Hank away from the crowded store, all three looking back at the gold-toothed black man.

"What in the hell is this nigger doing here?" asks Hammer.

"I say who is with us and who isn't," hisses Dane. "Now, get in that damn buggy of his and show him where we're camped on the highway. Then wait fer my signal, like you were told."

Metcalfe climbs into his buggy, followed by a reluctant Hammer. As they sit side-by-side, hope rises in the gold-toothed man. *Maybe Dane and Hammer will cut each other's throats*, he thinks. Metcalfe and the angry lawman ride off into the night, leaving Dane, Hank and the plantation behind. Meanwhile Flynn and Benny have entered the barn, where Benny's thoughts about being a young Klan member weigh heavily on his mind. "I know Caleb never liked me," says Benny, looking sad-eyed at Flynn, "and fer good reason with me wanting to join the Klan, but I want to help look fer him. We can talk about me and you being in the Klan later. Okay?"

Flynn doesn't answer him, and—instead—continues walking within the barn toward a stack of hay. Benny trails behind, following with his head low. While Flynn undresses on the far side of a haystack and slips into the dry clothing, baffled, he looks back, over the stack at Benny. "Are you sure you want to do this? Put aside your hatred and help search for him?"

"I'm sure."

"And I mean search as if you were searching for your own brother, not a colored person."

Benny, his head momentarily even lower, his eyes gazing up at Flynn, hesitates and then repeats Flynn's demands, "As if he was my brother," he says, raising his head and looking Flynn in his eyes.

"Okay," Flynn tells him. "We'll search together, now go and tell all the guys in your club to get their hunting rifles and find us some horses and join me here at the barn."

"I hope it's not too late," Benny calls back on the run. "Everything from mules, trucks and horses were taken by the search party except fer the wagons and mules that'll carry the bodies and the old folks to Henry's place."

Lurking in the shadows outside the barn door, old Hank and Dane watch Benny running into the night. Adjusting his bifocals, Hank whispers to Dane. "There goes your plan of tricking Flynn into helping us find that coon. Flynn and Caleb are like two peas in a pod. You heard what he told Benny. 'Like brothers.' These whites and blacks out there all want to be brothers and sisters now. Everybody here has gone stark naked mad. Flynn's going to help lead the search party fer Caleb. We could be in big trouble, even if Jayne didn't seem to tell that poet-reading, white, nigger-lover about us. And even if we locate the colonel's money, if it's even on Shadow Grove, we might not live long enough to get off this land with it, once they find Caleb and put two and two together. Caleb is one smart nigger, Dane. Even I have to admit that, now, and them extra twenty men and Hammer waiting in Hammer's truck fer us won't make a spit's worth of difference, not against Sarah and Flynn's armed hundreds, and certain not because Hammer is with us with his reputation fer kicking butts, not after everyone knows how Caleb beat the shit out of him at that nigger church and Collins took him down an inch at that lagoon."

Dane keeps his sights on Flynn, who has stepped from behind the haystack and is sitting on a bale of hay drying off his feet, then slipping into his socks and shoes.

"It takes more than words to stop being white," Dane whispers. "It's inborn in whites, even in them ace of spades, to remind them that they're black and should hate us. You'll see how we stick together like white on rice, when this is over."

Dane pats old Hank on the back. "As fer Caleb, if he's still alive, we'll find him sooner than he thinks. I have a plan."

"What about Barney?" asks Hank. "Him and the powers he has and the way he'll come after us, especially after you? Living after being shot like that, when old Doc said he should be dead. I'm more afraid of the colonel than of God or Caleb right now. Do you have a plan fer Barney?"

"Barney is as good as dead," hisses Dane. "With my own eyes I've seen him in that deathbed of his. A zombie couldn't be more dead. Now go get your truck."

"Ahhh," hisses Hank, his heart almost leaping out of his chest. He sees Barney standing at the bedroom window and gazing down at him.

"Who's out there?" calls Flynn from the barn, as Dane is about to follow Hank's sights to the manor.

"It's me," answers the one-eared Klansman then, looking over his shoulder at the manor window: nothing. Barney has disappeared. Entering the barn, Dane exclaims to Flynn. "I want a word with you, Flynn . . ." He turns to Hank, who is still outside gawking up at Barney's window. "Go get the truck, Hank." Hank hurries into the night.

In Barney's bedroom, the nurse awakens and gasps; she bounds to her feet, brushes the flies off of her, looks about, and screams. Barney is standing naked at the window and once again looking down on the massive barn and at Hank, who can easily be seen walking to the main gate.

"Colonel Cutter," the nurse calls to him. "Get back in bed and put on your robe."

"You're dismissed," Barney tells her without turning around.

"Sir," she firmly objects, slowly approaching him. "You've been so sick and the Demerol is confusing you. You can't—what I mean is, I know you're a colonel and an important man, but Naomi . . . and me. Dr. Schmidt left us in charge of you. You must get dressed and back in bed."

"Why! So that you might insult me again?" he says. Hearing the anger in his voice, she stops in her tracks. He exclaims on. "That you might feel disgust at the size of my penis once more? That I'm too old to fuck? Even with all of my money I'll never get it up again. Isn't that what you were thinking?"

"Naomi! Where are you? Master Flynn," she calls in alarm, knowing that Barney can read her mind. It's all true: Barney sleeps with the devil, she tells herself.

Barney whirls about in a rage, and lightning slams across the sky and thunder rocks the house. The man's hair stands up on his head, his appearance that of someone awakened from the dead, his once infertile penis many times as large and throbbing up at her. His inhuman eyes focus on her crotch, and his blood pressure rises with everything else, his penis growing. The nurse stands there gaping down at it and screams. She stumbles back as she follows his gaze to a nearby table. During the time she had been sleeping in her chair, Barney had gone downstairs to the den and had removed Doctor Winthrop's old Civil War sword from the wall and now it rests on the table, alongside Hitler's coat. "Get out before I kill you!" he tells the terrified woman.

She runs yelping from the room and down the hallway past her guest quarters, leaving her luggage and everything else behind. At the staircase, she trips on Flynn's tennis ball, sending it bouncing down the steps. Descending the winding staircase by leaps and bounds, she catches up with the bouncing ball and is out the door and in her driveway-parked car and speeding away from the manor before the ball hits the foyer floor. She looks back at the house and nearly runs into one of the driveway oak trees. Screaming, the terrified nurse misses the tree and speeds on through the main gate and is sucked up in the dark of night, with no intention of ever returning again, not even for her clothes.

631

While Benny searches about the plantation for transportation and young people to help find Caleb, inside the barn Dane—with full knowledge that he can choke the life out of Flynn—is growing impatient with small talk, as he attempts to feel Flynn out. "So, you're going to help look fer Caleb," he says, as Flynn, also tired of talking, is finishing tying his shoe strings.

"That's right," Flynn replies standing up and looking about for Benny and the others.

"But you can't go against your pa and his belief in the Klan fer some nigger, my friend."

"I'm not your friend, Dane," Flynn angrily replies. "And when did you start worrying about what my father wants or doesn't want, and why was Jayne so afraid of you, when we saw you at the store?" Sensing that it's dangerous to be alone in the barn with Dane, Flynn walks from the structure. "And why were you chasing after us?"

"Me and Hank thought you were in trouble," Dane says, following him. "Any fool knows that girl is nuts. You can't believe anything she says." Everywhere he looks, Dane sees dozens of Sarah and Flynn's left-behind workers milling about within calling distance to them, while searching for a ride either to Henry's land with the bodies or to join those looking for Caleb, still far too many workers for Dane to attempt anything drastic with Flynn.

"Did Jayne lead you to them bodies?" Dane asks Flynn. "Did she say who killed 'em?" Flynn just stands there looking about for Benny to return; he knows full well what Dane wants: Barney's fortune. "Just tell me this," hisses Dane. "Do you want to honor your pa by joining the Klan? Yes or no!"

"Excuse me, Dane. I have to get a horse and join the search."

"Why," ask Dane. "Hank'll be right back and you can ride with us."

Once Hank finally reaches and passes through Trestle Gate, he glances back at the manor and turns pale and freezes. Barney, clearly visible and still nude, continues watching him from the bedroom window, the lightning reflecting green off his eyes of hell. Hank runs the rest of the way to his truck, and if it were not for the fact that he is almost as much afraid of Dane as he is Barney, he'd have driven out of there, as he had witnessed Barney's nurse do and is now speeding down the highway in her car, and still screaming, but he knows Dane would hunt him down for the rest of his life if necessary and burn him alive if he ran out on him.

In the master bedroom, Barney slips into his clothing, puts on his shoulder holster and checks his military .45, not that he needed it now with half of Satan's gift of power surging through his body and growing to its full potential; the weapon is simply part of his sadistic joy, a toy which he will use as a first step in terrorizing his victims before finally destroying them with his satanic might. He turns off the lights—so as not to look upon his mother—picks up Hitler's coat, and leaves the room with the gun, the coat and the sword. The monstrous figure of his mother moves from behind the door and across the darkened master bedroom to the window and glares down at the barn, at Dane and then at Flynn her son's beautiful, young boy, the grandson she had hated when she was alive and mortified. Now, those vindictive eyes of death reflect even a greater hatred of him, as she hisses like a snake at him in spite of what Satan wants. She then hurries to a set of bay windows overlooking the rear of the house and watches Barney climb into his Rolls Royce and race the car down a back road, toward Henry's land, guided by his need to kill. A bitter appearance crosses her face. Deep in her heart of stone, she knows that her son no longer loves her, and that she has to be extremely careful or he will also kill her. Suddenly, the church-going woman—who raped and defiled her own son—begins mutating even more, the feathers painfully wiggling out of her flesh. Flinging her arms up and down, she cries out in anguish. "It's too painful to go on with this inflection, this battle between God and Lucifer." Suddenly her body explodes out a blur of feathers, and she smashes open the window and flies out into the night sky and continues to mutate into the very things she hated, a half-human bird, and now with the head of a blood-sucking bat with teeth as sharp as razors, this because she angered Satan by hating Flynn, his choice to help defend Barney. Her purpose now: to follow the Roll Royce to Henry's place, as the glass from the destroyed window seems to fall in slow motion to the ground, catching the attention of several workers, wondering what had caused it to fall.

44

The Baptism of Blood

Outside in the dark of night, while Dane impatiently waits alone a few feet from the barn door for Hank to return, he also hears the window crashing to the ground and looks toward the manor house for some time, as if sensing a far greater evil there than even that of the Klan, as the bird lady's shadow of death flies unseen over him in the dark sky. Meanwhile, Flynn, still ill at ease, and waiting by the store for Benny to return, watches several of his mule-drawn wagons rolling by in the near distance, carrying old men, women, and dozens of children on a slow ride behind the Johnson's funeral procession. The corpses of Bruce and Carrie have been removed from the death wagon and now lie on the two love doors, which have been reverently removed from the Johnsons' plantation shack under Sarah and Naomi's instructions.

The bodies have been placed onto the doors in the manner in which Bruce had asked Henry to do, on their backs, so that he, Bruce, and Carrie can face the heavens, and now the sky is filled with stars. The deceased husband and wife—their mutilated faces and bodies covered with sheets of thin, lacy, see-through material to help conceal the brutality inflected on them—are carried parallel to one another on the shoulders of Shadow Grove's tallest and strongest men, men who had volunteered to remain behind as pallbearers, four of them on each side of the doors and one on either end, moving on emotionally inspired silken legs in perfect step with the rhythmic, spiritual singing of the white and black field hands alike. Those workers, who were looking for a ride to the burial land without success, now run and join with the ones who are walking behind the wagons. And soon an oscillating line of humbled humanity from age fourteen to seventy strings out behind the lofty held eternally sleeping couple.

A dozen torch-carrying women and Sarah, instead of riding in the wagons, walk with the men who bear the burden of holding high Bruce and Carrie's body on the ten-mile trek ahead. The hard-working, common people of the earth who continue on the journey on foot behind and ahead of the stretcher bearers do so in the spirit of brotherhood, carrying their torches in their calloused, sweaty hands, lighting the way of hope and love for what Naomi says is the necessary coming of a new family of mankind. That awe-inspiring line of stately humanity—the elderly riders in the wagons, the pallbearers, the torch carriers, the singers, the walkers ahead and the walkers behind the procession—steadily climb a hill and are silhouetted against the full moon. With the dark, undistinguishable hill below them and the night-starry sky above them, it appears as if those in the procession are actually and truly walking across the face of the moon in the sky, their heads, their torsos, their slowly moving arms and legs sharply defined, colorless and darkly silhouetted by divine design and as if held in space by the hand of God. Flynn can't take his sights off of them. When those who are carrying the bodies grow fatigued, other men are instantly there to take their place; the corpses never tilt, the line never stops, the songs never ebb and the road to the promised land is never in doubt.

As that parade of hope fades in the distance, Flynn leans against the side of the store and looks about the land in a renewed state of depression. A rejoicing Dane, on the other hand, is now at the barn, and looking in at one of Flynn's wet socks, which Flynn had tossed onto a hay stack after he had changed into dry clothing. The sound of a motor is heard, and Hank drives up to the store and stops by Flynn.

"Isn't Dane with you, Flynn?" he asks, climbing from the truck.

Flynn doesn't answer; his focus is on that vicious dog, Tramp, which is tethered on the truck bed beside several four-by-six, wooden planks. Two of the planks are around eight feet long; another two are twelve feet in length. When Tramp begins sniffing at Flynn, the teenager steps back as Dane moves to the truck. "Stop it, Tramp," he yells. "Flynn is a friend." He looks at Flynn and again suggests. "Ride with me and Hank, Flynn. We can search fer Caleb together. It'll be faster with the truck."

"No, thanks," says Flynn, then looking away, when he hears the sound of horse hooves moving toward them. Two of Shadow Grove's young men—one black, the other white, both in their late teens and armed with rifles—gallop on their horses from out of a potato field in a late charge to join in the search for Caleb. Instead of torches, the young men are carrying flashlights, flashing them on and off testing the batteries. As they ride toward him, Flynn waves them down. One of them is Peter Scott, whom Naomi has convinced that Mrs. Hill's death is not his fault and that he will not go to jail. "Your horse and flashlight," Flynn tells the black rider, who stops closest to him; as the black youth climbs from the saddle, and—feeling that the master of the land will need his rifle—he hands it to Flynn, who says, "Only your horse and flashlight." Flynn then looks back at Dane and then again at the black youth and cautions. "But keep that rifle handy."

The young rider stiffens his holds on the weapon and looks over at Peter, who is also contemplating at him, both sensing that something is wrong. The black boy then hands the reins and flashlight to Flynn, gives Dane a glance and faces Flynn. "Is anything wrong, Master Flynn?" he asks, following Flynn's second gaze to Dane.

"You're new here," says Flynn to the light-skinned boy. "What's your name?"

"Tony Bruner, Master Flynn."

"No one is master here," Flynn tells him, while climbing into the saddle. "I know it's difficult with the colonel about, but call me Flynn." Once in the saddle, Flynn glances down at Dane. "Did you kill them, Dane? Bruce and Carrie? The way you killed Lilly? Henry thinks so."

Tony and Peter again tighten their grips on their weapons.

"Gentlemen don't kill people," says Dane, anxiously eyeing the two young workers, and thinking about ways to overpower them.

Flynn looks at Peter. "Have you seen Benny, Peter?"

"Not since he was at the search party with Henry."

"Once he returns," Flynn tells Peter, "give him your mare and flashlight. Tell him to meet me where he last saw me and Caleb. He'll know where it is, and keep these so-called gentlemen here until Benny and I get a head start on them, then see that they are escorted off this land."

"Listen, Flynn," says Dane, dreading the thought of possibly losing sight of Flynn, even for a minute. "Let's you and I talk this over, one white man to the other and—"

Flynn angrily points at Dane. "If this one or his flunky gives you any trouble, kill them."

Peter and Tony's eyes pop open. For Flynn to have said what he did about killing the two Klansmen was akin to the moon telling the stars to get out of its sky. Peter takes aim at Dane, and Tony follows Peter's lead, his rifle targeting old Hank, as Flynn gallops away on the horse. Dane thinks even more about overpowering Tony and Peter in order to follow Flynn, but Benny and a dozen armed, teenaged males arrive running to them on foot. Benny is given Flynn's message, takes Peter's horse, his flashlight and charges into the night after his friend, all of the teenagers now with their weapons trained on Dane and Hank.

"Shit!" says Dane.

In time, Dane and Hank are allowed to leave in their truck, a fuming Dane doing the driving. When they drive onto the highway, Hank glances at a group of trees where Metcalfe's horse and buggy are half hidden in the thicket. Dane turns the headlights on then off, and out of the tree shadows motors Hammer's five-ton dump truck, carrying two dozen or so armed, hooded men. The truck rolls in behind Hank's old Dodge and both vehicles are driven onto a seldom-used dirt road and continue down that unpaved surface without headlights or a sound from their occupants, the fear of their own greed and that of their partners killing them for the money uppermost in their minds, to say nothing about their anger on how long it took Dane to get to them.

"If Caleb is alive, like the men say," Hank is first to speak of a worrisome possibility on both his and Dane's mind. Giving a quick glance at the double-barreled shotgun and rifle tied down to his weapon's rack across the vehicle's rear window, old Hank then goes on, "What if Flynn finds Caleb and the money first? We don't even know where to start looking."

Dane studies the distant column of flickering torchlights of the funeral procession, down the dirt road almost three miles ahead of them. "We have three possibilities," he says. "One, we wait along this road fer a hour or two, then catch up to them funeral marchers on the coast where the nigger Metcalfe heard Henry tell them searchers that if anyone could find Caleb it would be that old horse of his. Second, between them wailing coons and them dumb-ass, white fools with them and them dead bodies, Caleb will pop up, and then we'll kill him again. That's if it's true he's still alive, like they say. My bet is it's my third choice, the place that Flynn told them two punks to send Benny, the same place where Flynn—with all his book smarts—let slip out and almost drowned with the nigger, the night of the caravan, when Colonel Cutter went out there to that lagoon, and Benny ran ahead and warned Flynn to get away from that spade. Yes! That's where we search! That damn lagoon."

"But, Dane, that means goin throught that god-damn swamp area. Could Flynn be that dumb, and how can we track him at night?"

"Barney always says, you always got to have a backup plan." Dane holds up Flynn's sock. "It's wet, but it's not too wet fer Tramp. So once we reach that general area, Tramp's nose will do the rest."

Ten miles later in the moonlit swamp, a mile from Henry's place, Dane stops the truck within sight of Cutter Bridge and alights, and just as he had thought, he spots fresh horse tracks. Hammer, driving the dump truck and excitedly looking about, stops behind them. Dane's plan is to drive the more capable dump truck himself, when they leave again, hopefully hauling away Barney's millions, gold or cash, he doesn't care. The hooded men eagerly jump from the truck bed and look to Dane for guidance, but it is Hammer who speaks to them first.

"Make sure we kill everyone if any of us are unmasked," Hammer says, "or them F.B.I. boys from Barney's D.C. friends will track us down to hell and back if anyone lives to tell them who we are!"

"We kill no goddamn body," hisses Dane, "til we know who can lead us to Cutter's gold and money. I'm in charge here, not Hammer! Now, take 'em off."

Hammer, Marcus, Reverend Miller and twenty-six others remove their hoods. The men stare at the thirtieth Klansman, who slowly removes his hood; he's Metcalfe.

"He'll cut our throats," wails Marcus, the youngest person there.

"Close your mouth, boy," says Dane to Marcus, "befer you swallow a bug instead of a dick. Your girlish ass is here because Hammer seems unwilling to let you and your young stuff out of his sights."

"Fuck off, Dane!" hisses Hammer going to Marcus's side, wondering if Dane really has satanic powers like Barney. "He's twice the man as this coon you brought with us."

At least this coon ain't bending over to let that young boy stick his dick up my ass, you lowdown white, motherfucking, crooked cop cock sucker, Metcalfe wisely ponders to himself.

"No, that little punk isn't better than this coon," yells Dane. "Marcus'll shit his pants the first time someone fires at us. You fuck the hell off, Hammer and keep your inverted mouth shut." Dane turns to the men. "And that goes fer all of you. The nigger's unarmed! I got rid of his razor and everything else he might use against us. Instead of talking about what you don't like, get ready to kill or be killed. Sarah's workers are all around us searching fer Caleb and just waiting to cut our throats! We need all the help we can get, even from this nigger, and if it comes to us having to fight fer our lives past Sarah's coon-loving workers . . ." He points to Metcalfe, ". . . that boy's going to be given a gun. Get that in your heads now and be done with it."

Metcalfe—a prideful man—keeps his mouth shut.

"Let's all pray," says Reverend Miller, "that God is with us in this mission and will understand why we had to use one of His cursed ape creations to assist us in our just war against Satan and Sarah Cutter, who, if she gets control of her dying husband's money—which I'm now led to believe is in the millions—she will use some of that money to build a Catholic cathedral of statues for her fellow worshipers in my town and overshadow me in my small church; she will, even more so, educate and encourage the apes of this world to feel they are equal to us."

As the others ignore him and discuss their search plans with Dane, Miller looks up and sees a shapeless thing flying through the sky high above them. Fear unlike any he ever known before strikes at the heart of the corrupt preacher, and he vomits as the others step away from him and his slime. He leans back against the Dodge, shaking in distress. The cursed Mrs. Cutter, her feathers reflecting in the moonlight, her bat-like eyes and head growing even larger, looks down at him. Miller cries aloud. "My God!"

"What the fuck's wrong with him, now?" shouts Hammer—he and the others, glaring at Miller. "First he throws up. Now what? Pissing in his drawers?"

Miller slumps down against the truck tire, his right hands trembling and holding onto the Bible for dear life, his left hand and finger pointing at the sky. They follow his upwards broad-eyed gaze, and by then, the bird creature has flown into a dark cloud and seen no more. The corrupt preacher gawks over at his peers. "At those kids' funeral, Naomi—with those eyes of hers—was as good as saying to me that my soul is doomed." He gawks at the sky, going on. "Something in me says we're all going to die, Dane. That thing in the sky . . . I want out!"

"People in hell want ice water, you drug-using fool," hisses Dane. "You, I guess, need a goddamn reefer to smoke, like the niggers, fer courage! You're in. You stay in! Flynn said Caleb had that money. If he's alive, let's find him. If he's dead, let's bury him and all of these goddamn, holier-than-thou rumors of him once and fer all, god dammit, but let's get that damn money at all cost, even if it means killing those of us who now want to back off. The rest of you back in the truck, check your weapons and stay put until I return fer you." He turns to Hammer. "You're in charge until I return. Make sure no one leaves. The way everyone is so damn jumpy around here, we'll be shooting each other before long. Hank, you and Tramp, on foot, with me."

As Dane untangles the heavy-duty weapons from the Dodge's window rack, the distant sounds of the search teams' bloodhounds permeate the night air. Tramp challenges back at the barking hounds with drawn-back lips and moisture-dripping sharp fangs. Hank retrieves a bowl of chickens' blood from the back of the Dodge, as well as a jug of moonshine. He places the bowl before Tramp, which quiets the dog as it slurps up the blood, Hank, also, slurping the moonshine—doing his best to calm his own fears—which Miller's outrageous remarks had not helped.

"How in the hell'd them searchers get this far out so fast?" mutters the frightened, bifocaled, old man, sorrowfully looking over his glasses at Miller, a look that tells Miller that he, Hank, is also thinking about leaving. As Hank guzzles from the moonshine jug, Dane whirls from the truck and snatches the jug from him and violently smashes it on the ground. "I warned you about drinking! We need clearheaded men to get out of here, not drunken fools!"

When Dane again returns to the truck cab and jerks at the window-racked weapons, Hank swats at a mosquito, which is swarming him, and he smashes it on his arm and yells, "Get out of there. We don't need you squitas drinking my blood and getting drunk off of it. We need clear-headed bugs on our side to get out of here alive." He sees Dane glaring at him from the truck, old Hank harps. "These squitas will eat us alive. Let's ferget this coon boy, Dane, and get out of here right now. Even if I'm drunk or sober, it's like Reverend said, we can't win. Those barking hound dogs, Henry and all of them armed men got me about to piss in my pants."

"Take it out, leave it in, or blow up like a balloon. Idiot! But don't trouble me with your stupid shit!"

"You know I can't pee or show my dick in front of other men, Dane." Hank looks at Deputy Hammer and goes on, afraid to point out that the strong-arm man is attracted to males, and instead Old Hank targets Marcus. "I ain't no fairy fer you to tell me to 'take it out, piss and get it over with' like I was Marcus over there."

Marcus lowers his head at Hank's remark. The young boy has never been sodomized or pressured by others to do so, except for Deputy Hammer, who was turned down, and Marcus had only—occasionally in a drunken state—been fondled by Burt, but he knows no one will believe him, that his profound need to be loved did not cause him to fully prostitute himself in order to receive that most cherished human need, affection, and the young boy remains with his head held low and is silent, but growing weaker in his resistance to selling his body and willfully raping and killing with each passing day in order to belong to a family, Klan or not. Hammer places his arm about the boy's shoulder: the forbidden fruit which he lusts after—and having failed to get it—makes the wait all the more worthwhile. "That's okay," Hammer tells him. "Every one of these guys has done far worse in their lives than you. Fucked everything from cows and dogs to dead people. But you'll be rich soon, and you're young enough to outlive these old fuckers and to enjoy it."

"I want to go home," whispers Marcus.

"And I really do got to piss, Dane," whimpers Hank.

Stepping from the truck with the rifle and shotgun and two ropes, Dane kicks Hank in the leg, tosses the ropes about Hank's shoulder and then places Flynn's sock next to Tramp's nose.

"Jesus," gasps old Hank—under the weight of the ropes—his bladder acting up, as he crosses his legs and dances about as had Earlene by the lagoon of death.

Dane once again exclaims to him. "Piss in your pants and bring your ass on, you old fool. According to the way my dog is sniffing around, Flynn must have passed through here minutes ago."

"What the ropes fer, Dane?" calls Marcus, thinking the worst, having seen his share of death and desperately not wishing to see any more.

"To hang both Flynn and Caleb, side-by-side," says Dane, "Hang 'em fast and high, once we get that money."

Untying Tramp from the truck, Dane again dangles Flynn's sock before the excited dog's nose, and while the others climb back in the dump truck, under unusually, tight surveillance by Hammer, as well as under the bright moonlight, Dane carrying the shotgun—a revolver in his waist—Hank the rifle, with the ropes dangling about his shoulder, go on their way. Using the extra bright moonlight, they follow two sets of those horse hooves and two sets of human footprints leading the horses, one pair of the prints causing Tramp—trained not to bark in the hunt—to frantically sniff about them until the horse hooves and shoe prints disappear on firmer ground, but Tramp's nose successfully continues tracking over the soil, while excitedly jerking Dane into a trot, Dane's heart beating with expectation, while a reluctant Hank, nervously looking about and lagging behind, feels that at any moment, they'd be struck down by lightning. He's heard that Naomi has predicted a special punishment for him and his kind in this world. Suddenly Dane stops, signaling back for Hank to do the same, as Dane now touches Tramp to continue to keep him quiet, Hank's fears quickly fade away, replaced by thoughts of riches spinning about in his head.

"Did you hear that?" Dane whispers, as Hank eases close to him and helps quiet Tramp, and Dane adds, "Voices. I heard voices."

A short distance ahead of the stalking Klansmen, and clearly seen under the brilliant moonlight, with the distant sounds of the hounds in the background, Flynn and Benny—who had quickly caught up to Flynn—continue leading their horses on foot, while shining their flashlights about and—from time to time as quietly as possible knowing that Caleb's enemies might also be out there—calling out Caleb's name. The boys end up in a clearing of flowers within easy sight of the Old Cutter Bridge, where they spot what looks like blood on the ground; tying the horses to a tree, they thoroughly examine the underbrush.

"It was in this direction that Jayne was pointing earlier," Flynn tells Benny, a dozen feet away and looking about. "She must have been trying to tell me all the time that Caleb was—"

Charging out of the underbrush and pouncing on them are Tramp, Dane and Hank. Hank points his rifle at Flynn and holds back Tramp, as Dane jumps all over Benny, whacking him to the ground with the butt of the shotgun and the fat boy stays down.

"You fucking Judas," Dane shouts at the overweight boy. "You and your goddamn sister betraying me by siding with the enemy. Flynn is a nigger lover! Are you? I warned your sister I'd kill her fer that betrayal at the train, and I'll do the same to you. Now get up and make yourself useful, before I shoot you where you lay." Benny, however, remains downs. Dane doesn't spare Flynn either. He backhands him momentarily forgetting about Benny. "Hurry and go get the boys, Hank," Dane orders, adding, in the returning veteran's vernacular "The eagle flies. This is payday." While training that double-barreled shotgun on Benny and Flynn, Dane again yells at Hank. "And don't stop til you get there, while I keep an eye on these two assholes. That money is as good as ours."

"I don't even now where we are," says Hank, "leave alone which way to start back to the truck. I'm all turned around and lost, and you still haven't let me stop to pee yet."

Dane's mind snaps. "Ahhh!" he punches Hank in his mouth. Flynn lunges at Dane, but pays for it with a blow from Dane's weapon landing hard on his arm, and he staggers backwards, stumbling over Benny, but somehow remaining on his feet, his mind fired up, forming a hurried-up plan, even as Benny—still laid out on the ground, without moving his head or his body—peers up in fear at Flynn and is about to get to his feet, but when Dane turns and glares at Hank, Flynn nods for Benny to stay put. Dane, however, after glaring at Hank, moves toward Benny with that shotgun; Flynn yells at the one-eared Klansman:

"You're one one-eared ugly asshole, Dane Tucker!"

Dane runs back and delivers a fist blow to Flynn's face, and this time Flynn falls against a tree and then to the ground, where he cries out in pain. Benny—remaining flat on his belly, his head to the side—is watching and afraid, not knowing what to think. Should he get up to help Flynn or stay put, as Flynn suggested.

"My leg! You've broken my leg!" Flynn screams.

"His leg!" yells Hank, then eyes a tree-shade-covered Benny against the moonlight. Benny quickly closes his eyes and lies perfectly still. Hank exclaims, "And that one's knocked clean out cold." Hank points over at Flynn. "Now, Flynn, he can't walk, and soon them searchers will surely find us with him slowing us down with a broken leg."

"You stupid motherfucker," yells Dane at Hank. He then glares angrily at Benny and visually examines him from a distance and again verbally attacks old Hank. "You brought this on, you and your need to piss. You asshole! Now you keep an eye on these two while I go get the guys, and if you fuck up in any way while I'm gone and let them two escape, I'll make you wish you never were born. Dead or alive, unconscious or with two broken legs these motherfuckers are going with us to help find Caleb fucking Brooks if I have to make you carry the two of them on your stupid, goddamn back. I'm getting tired of you, Hank." Dane says angrily and storms into the night, leaving Hank behind with Tramp.

Not far away, the old Cutter Bridge had been closed down for the time being, so that it can be decontaminated of the spilled fuel. Up on the structure, Jayne Hill stands on the moonlit bridge's train tracks while pinching off her nostrils against the acrid smell of explosive fuel which has soaked into the span since Dane and Hammer had hit the tanker while firing up at Collins and Caleb. No longer thinking clearly, Jayne never returned to Henry's place to seek his help for Caleb, her distrusting mind now telling her that Henry is Dane in disguise. Jayne had been scouting the area for signs of wild game, and had heard the trucks arriving. She had climbed atop of the old wooden structure in order to get a better view of the land, and she now glares down at Dane as he's returning to the Klansmen. Her hands stained with blood, Jayne—who hasn't eaten since the death of her mother—is carrying the remains of a rabbit, which she has been eating raw. When Dane passes out of sight below the span, she turns her sights in the opposite direction and sees Hank, Flynn and Benny in the moonlit clearing five-hunded yards or so away. *Is that Benny?* she wonders. *My little brother?*

At the clearing, Hank keeps his rifle aimed at Flynn, the searchers' distant, howling hounds frightening Hank all the more.

"What are you afraid of, Hank?" asks Flynn, who cautiously remains on the ground a few yards away from Benny. "That the colonel will make you pay for this? He will, you know. You were his friend. Now you want his money."

"Shut up you sickly punk, or I'll break that other leg of yours," Hank hisses, full of vinegar and the stuff of manhood now that Dane isn't lording over him. The nervous old man ties Tramp to one of the trees, and while keeping an eye on Flynn, he angrily shakes the ropes off his shoulder and then kicks Benny. "Wake the hell up, boy!" When Benny opens his eyes and sits up, Hank tosses one of the ropes to him and orders him to tie it about his arms and legs, and after Benny complies, Hank drags him by the rope with one hand to still another of the nearby trees, Benny helping out by scooting along on his butt to save his skin. Hank then ties the loose end of Benny's rope around the tree trunk, checks Benny's handiwork, tightens down the knots about the boy's extremities even more, and hurries back for the other rope and ties it about the same tree, while all the time pointing the rifle at Flynn. "Now you get over here, befer I blow a hole in your tender privileged, white ass," he screams at Flynn. "And I don't care if you have to crawl. And fer your information, I'm not afraid of anything! Not of you or Dane or Barney."

"Not even of Caleb?" asks Flynn, knowing full well from a few Klan members who have confided in him, that Hank is deeply troubled by the thought that Caleb is a blessed child of God.

Hank pales, but quickly recovers and aims the rifle directly at Flynn's head, his finger easing toward the trigger. "Move it, nigger lover, befer I move you with a bullet."

After Flynn—groaning—hops on one leg over to Benny, Hank orders the blonde boy to sit on the ground beside his heavy-set friend which Flynn does, knowing that old Hank has unknowingly outsmarted him; and that his plan of pretending that he was hurt, in order for him and Benny to overpower Dane and Hank, by surprise, is now for naught. After having Flynn tie himself to Benny, and then inspecting them both again, and painfully tightening down their rope knots, Hank, his hand pressed between his legs, gawks about and runs to a distant bush, steps behind it, rips open his fly and begin forcefully trying to urinate, the potent mixture of salt, alcohol and water—and his long-ago-developed stricture in his penis causing the urine to trickle agonizingly through his urethral canal, his insides ready to explode, and he groans in anguish while his bladder gradually empties. Removing a flask of moonshine from his pocket, he takes a hurried gulp. Hank smiles jubilantly, and talks to himself, "He thought he destroyed all of it, but I outsmarted that one-eared, little Hitler, me and my flask. Hey!" he yells, waving the mosquitoes away from his penis. "You fucking bugs ain't gonna get no free lunch here."

As Flynn considers him and Benny being eaten by Tramp or shot in the back by Hank, in their precarious position, tied up on the ground like two dumb little kids, Benny sees a darkened figure moving in behind the tree behind them. Flynn sees Benny's wide-eyed gaze and starts to turn about and see what Benny is looking at, but before he can, the hand of that shadow reaches from behind the tree and covers Flynn's mouth. As he struggles, he sees the person's other pale white hand. In it is Caleb's bracelet. Once the hand is removed from him, Flynn quickly turns his head, and he gazes up at Jayne's frightened, sunburned face, her white finger now against her parched lips, her eyes on Tramp, who is growling at them.

"Hush up, dog," yells Hank, parting the bush and looking out at them and seeing only the boys and Tramp. He returns to passing his high-octane urine. Jayne steps from behind the tree once more, and from her pocket, she tosses the bloody rabbit to Tramp, and as the vicious dog devours it in chunks and gulps, Benny's sister jerks against the rope to free him and Flynn with absolutely no results. While Benny gawks up at his disheveled sister in near shock, and she looks down at him in sorrow, Flynn attempts to softly converse with her, but she puts her hand toward her opened mouth and shakes her head, signaling that she's unable to speak.

"In my pocket," whispers Flynn. "My knife."

Minutes later, Hank buttons his fly and looks over the bush at the tree. Jayne, Flynn and Benny are gone. Only the severed ropes remain, along with a guppy-looking Tramp, seemingly smiling over at Hank, its mouth ringed with rabbit's blood. Sickened, Hank sees the trucks and Klansmen arriving. He farts.

"You let them get away," screams Dane, when he sees the severed ropes and how a terrified Hank is gawking from the cut ropes to him. Dane leaps from the cab onto Hank, pounding him to the ground. "I should have let them folks kill you when they caught you fucking their cow, you cow fucker!" He yells at Hank.

"It wasn't my fault I had to piss," sobs Hank over the wild beating he's taking and the barking of Tramp.

"You was the only one willing to clean my bleeding feet—like that whore cleaned the feet of your sorry-ass goddamn Jesus, Hank—when Barney walked me through that glass, and I loved you fer it, but now you got to die fer this. You may have cost the rest of us millions!" The Klansmen step back as Dane whips out his pistol.

"A chance," screams Hank. "A chance! Like Barney gave you."

"You want a chance, you nutty fruitcake, talking idiot!" Dane hisses, removing five cartridges from his revolver and spinning the chamber, then pressing the gun barrel against Hank's skull and pulling the trigger. Hank flinches at the sound of the dry click. On the side, watching the madness and sobbing, Marcus removes his small Bible from his shirt and extends it to Hank, who seizes it from the frightened boy and kisses it in rapid succession, tears beading from his now squeezed-shut eyes. Dane again spins the chamber, as the others watch in total horror and disbelief as this time, Dane presses the gun barrel into Hank's mouth.

"You ask fer a chance," Dane hisses. "I'll give you one more. Isn't this how your good old motherfucking friend Barney did Pa? Showed him some kind of picture and made him put the gun in his own mouth and blow his own head clean off! Pray, you bastard! Pray now, but it won't help! There is no god to save you but me, and I won't!"

"Fuck," Hammer says, grappling with Dane. "It ain't like he's a coon. He's white, man." Dane points the gun at Hammer, who pleads. "If you shoot any of us, that fucking search party will be all over our asses like fleas on that crazy-ass dog of yours. Shut him the fuck up, why don't you, befer his barking attracts them searchers instead of trying to kill one of us?"

"You're one lucky man," Dane tells Hank, while closely studying his dog. "I guess it's not your time to die, due to the deputy using his head, not your God, our Hammer over there, 'cause even a blind man can see I lost my mind and was ready to shoot you into hell and back."

As Dane puzzles at Tramp, and then in the direction that the dog is barking, Hank opens his mouth and makes another mistake. "Anybody got any extra newspapers or leaves?" he asks, getting to his rickety legs. "I think I shit ma pants."

Dane cracks Hank across the head with the gun butt. He then turns back to Tramp, frantically barking and lunging against his tethered rope toward the lagoon, the direction which Jayne had led Benny and Flynn. Dane looks toward the lagoon and laughs. "Good boy!" he says. "I can feel it. Flynn has led us to him. He's out here, too, Caleb's out here too! Tramp is telling us all! We won!"

Inside the boat shack, Caleb is sitting on a wide box to one side of the small space, with a bandage hanging loosely from his head; a nearby kerosene lantern is casting its weak light around him, as he rests stooped over and in silence on his and Flynn's large tool box. He hears the door squeak open, and looks up into Flynn's, Jayne's and Benny's delighted faces. While Benny and Jayne stick their heads outside for a quick look around to make sure they've not been followed, then secure the shack door behind them, Flynn stands there gawking with opened mouth at Caleb in disbelief and joy at seeing his friend alive. He then hurries to Caleb, sits at his side on the box and gives him a bear hug. "We've been looking all over for you, man. Why are you here like this?"

"Trying to stay alive," says Caleb, "Which I doubt I will if you don't stop hugging and shaking me like this." Flynn releases him and touches Caleb's forehead and bandage. "A bullet did that," Caleb tells him, "Luckily it bounced off."

"Who shot you?" asks Flynn. "Was it Dane?"

"Jayne said I fell off that damn Cutter Bridge, that is, when she was able to talk." Caleb looks at the frightened girl and abruptly gets to his

647

feet. "I did fall off of it! And Dane, Flynn, he and one of Richards' deputies shot me. My God, Bruce and Carrie . . . they killed them. Dane and Hank and that deputy killed Bruce and Carrie. And that newborn baby, I put it in Old Clara's saddle bag. Is it—"

"Old Clara delivered her to Henry the way you wanted her to do, as for Dane—" He abruptly stops in the middle of his sentence and watches a mortified Jayne tremble and groan at the mention of Dane's name; Flynn rises to his feet. "I knew something was wrong when Dane approached me at the barn," he says, "and so did Henry, even before that."

"Papa," exclaims Caleb. "Are he and Sarah okay? Dane wants to—"

"Both are okay," says Flynn, "but Dane tried to get me alone with them in their truck tonight. I think they would have killed me, and Benny too if Jayne hadn't come—"

"Jesus!" says Caleb, while glancing at Benny with empathy. "You and Benny as well? They must want to kill us all."

"Why?" asks Benny. "I didn't do nothing to them."

"The money," says Flynn, ignoring Benny. "Dane's after it. That's why he's here."

"Here? He's here?" Caleb questions, while removing the dangling, dry-blood bandage from his head.

"He's somehow found out that you and Henry hid all of that money out here on your land," Flynn says, and continues. "Where is it, so that we can move it and—"

"You mean all this talk about your pa's money is true?" Benny asks.

Jayne suddenly puts her finger to her lips, silencing everyone. They follow her gaze to the door. As a train's ghostly whistle shrieks in the distance, the tin door is eased open and the robed and hooded Klansmen rush in, Hank ahead of the others tugging on Tramp's leash to restrain him. Dane nudges his way to the front of the pack with that mean-looking, double-barreled shotgun, his eyes of madness on Jayne. "What did I tell you, bitch!" he screams at her.

Jayne runs to the corner of the ten-foot-by-ten-foot shack. She trips over the newspapers and falls to the floor, then desperately covers herself with the yellowing newsprints. The one-eared Klansman pulls the trigger and blasts her and the papers through the shack wall, leaving Flynn and Caleb in shock and speechless. Even Metcalfe turns away, but Benny pounces across the floor and pounds on Dane's chest, howling and bellows, "Noooo! My sister! My sister!"

"That's fer helping Caleb!" Dane yells at the gun-blasted girl and then backhands Benny, staggering him backwards. Raving on, Dane trains the smoking double-barreled shotgun on Caleb. "What protects you, boy?" The one-eared Klansman squalls at Henry's dismayed son. Metcalfe looks on in surprise, that this is the Caleb that everyone is afraid of, the boy who whipped his ass on the train.

"You get shot in the head," Dane continues yelling. "You fall of the bridge and live. A white girl like Jayne Hill, who hated you niggers until you came along, risks her life to help you. They say you were trapped in the factory pipe and was blown clean the hell out with our men, and while we lose half our members to that one damn, fucking incident, you manage to live, somehow." Dane kicks over the toolbox and shouts. "Every last one of them good white men in the motherfucking pipe die, but you lived, damn you!" He smashes Caleb in the stomach with the butt of his shotgun. "That money! I heard Flynn in the barn! He said you had it. And we heard him again, just now, ask you where you hid it!"

"You!" exclaims Flynn. "You were in the barn! Then it was you who killed Burt and attacked Barney!"

"And I'd attack him again," bellows Dane, spitting on Flynn. "And I hope your old man dies and rots in hell! He killed that boy, not me!"

Reverend Miller holds onto Flynn as he struggles to get at Dane, Tramp barking without end. Dane lifts the barrel of the shotgun toward Flynn. Clearly, Caleb knows that Dane is moments away from killing the blonde boy, and so does Flynn. Caleb steps beside his friend, which infuriates the one-eared man.

"If you pull that trigger, you better hope the spread kills me as well, because if you don't I'll shove that shotgun all the way down your throat."

Deputy Hammer sides with Caleb and warns a hysterical Dane. "What the hell's wrong with you, Dane, anyway, to even think of killing either one of them at this time, when we're all so close to becoming rich? Snap the hell out of this dumb-ass way of thinking. Now that shotgun blast had to have been heard around the damn world by them searchers!"

Dane whirls about and yells at Hank. "Go get that goddamn robe, and tie off Tramp on the truck. He's driving me crazy with all that barking! Do it, Hank, without messing up this time, you goddamn, motherfucking moron or you'll take Flynn's place. I got to kill somebody. I just got to kill one more fucking somebody befer this night ends. Just got to!"

Even though Flynn motions to Benny to keep quiet, the overweight boy sobs as he gazes at his sister. "She ain't never been baptized," he whimpers. "Mama never had time to get my sister baptized," he now wails at Dane. "Now she never will enter heaven."

Dane follows Caleb, Benny and Flynn's bewildered gazes to Jayne's twitching feet, sticking half in and half out of the shack wall, and the one-eared madman blasts the girl's body again, blowing off her leg, causing Marcus to scream and Benny to faint.

"Now she's baptized in blood," bellows Dane. While his men point their guns at the boys who stand there in repulsion, Dane reloads the weapon and presses the shotgun against Flynn's stomach and yells at Hank. "Now, Hank, do what I told you!" Hank grabs Tramp, and drags him from the shack and returns moments later with the colonel's Grand Wizard robe. Dane steps back from Flynn seizes the robe from Hank and throws it at Flynn, who catches it on the fly.

"When Jayne took you away in that wagon to that damn lagoon, we went through your house and one of us found that robe among other things in your room, where Barney no doubt told you to keep it," Dane says glancing over at Metcalfe as if to say it was he who discovered the robe and coins and not he—Dane, and Dane will never forgive him for finding them before he had.

Dane bitterly goes on, "Why? To give you time to see if you had balls enough to wear it? To let you have time to think about joining us. Now, your time is up!" Dane flashes the three gold coins that he got from Metcalfe at Flynn. "How many more of these goddamn coins do you have?" Flynn stands there in silence—wondering who will die if he doesn't tell Dane what he wants to know, but more important, he knows they might die even after he divulges what the madman wants to know.

Meanwhile, Dane continues to lay into Flynn. "Put that motherfucking robe on! And once you or coon-head Caleb over there lead us to that money or gold, and I don't care which one of you does the leading, you continue wearing that robe with respect and pride and show your nigger and poor white cracker workers the power of the Klan by getting us past them fools of yours or die like Jayne!" He thrust the shotgun at Flynn and shrieks. "Into that robe, motherfucker and into your father's shoes, now!"

At Henry's house, as the workers make preparations to prepare the bodies inside the modest, front room, they use Henry's tools and hammer two nails into the wall and then string a line from wall to wall, onto which they hang several sheets, dividing the room in half with Carrie's body on one side of the sheeted-off area and Bruce's on the other. Outside the house, Sarah—wearing one of Henry's aprons, after having planned to help wash and aromatize Carrie's body, and then was sent outside by Naomi, because she, Sarah, could not take it anymore—now nervously strolls back and forth in Caleb's flower garden, saying her "Hail Marys," and as she does, from out of the night, Henry rides up fast on Old Clara and climbs from the saddle at her side.

"Any word on Caleb on this end?" he asks.

"Not yet," Sarah tells him, putting the rosary into the apron pocket.

Henry looks at the house and the empty wagons. "How many male workers are inside?"

"Maybe thirty or so of the older men, not counting the women and children, waiting in the bedrooms and kitchen," Sarah replies. "The others have left to join in the search for Caleb. Why do you ask?"

"Are any of the men armed?"

"A few are. Henry, you're frightening me talking this way."

He hands Sarah a .38. She stares down at the weapon as if stunned by its very presence, so he presses it firmly into her hand. "Caleb bought it for his and my added protection, as you know. I hope you won't need it, but if you do, use it. Some of your workers out there, among the searchers, don't have Caleb or your best interests in mind, Sarah, people like old Hank for one. One of your stragglers saw him leave the plantation in that old truck of his with Dane Tucker."

Sarah tearfully gazes into Henry's eyes, as if recalling how so much time has been taken away from the two of them, and, as she does, her breathtaking beauty fills him with love, while she obeys him and slips the heavy revolver safely into the apron pocket.

"My old apron kind of swallows you up, Sarah," he tells her, knotting and adjusting the apron's shoulder straps on her as best he can, his otherwise steady hands trembling. She places her hands on his and steadies his nerves, and they both knot the straps together and then

651

stand gazing into the other's eyes. "Sarah, what would I do without you; if anything ever happened to you—"

"You'll never have to worry about that, my love. I will never leave you, Henry. Not in this life or in the next. Never."

"Oh, God," Henry says, "I don't understand." His voice drops to an unsure whisper. "Why does hatred hold so much power? Where is the supremacy of goodness and love in this world?"

"Henry," Sarah responds, kissing him on his lips, "It's here, Henry. Love is here." Tears blurring her vision, she continues. "You're bigger than the hateful people of this world. Caleb took after you. He's intelligent. He's strong and resourceful. And he'll come back to us. God knows he will. He was not born to die this way."

"He's also black, Sarah," Henry interrupts. "Our son is black. That's why they will hunt him down, if he's still alive, and kill him. They fear his intelligence, Sarah. I know this but he's also black."

Sarah whispers, "His soft footsteps will reshape the world— Henry—if and when he and Flynn walk together, side-by-side. And they will. Henry, they will."

"Sarah, what good is it to be smart or strong if you're black in a white man's world? Black like me and our boy?"

"Yes," she agrees, "you're black. I wouldn't have it any other way. It's the source of both of our strengths, strengths that will get us all through this."

Their gazes lock and they embrace in a tender kiss. "Sarah," he exclaims, holding her at arm's length. "Since Barney never had the chance to tell Flynn that Caleb is his brother, we should tell them ourselves. They need know now that Barney does." She tearfully nods, and their hands slide apart, as Henry says, "I have to continue the search." He swings into the saddle, leans down and kisses her again and gallops away on Old Clara. When Henry rides past the side of the house, two black grave diggers, brothers Amos and Andy, with their mule close by, tip their hats to him and he to them. Once Henry comes into sight again, on the far side of the house, Sarah watches him until neither the faithful old horse nor Henry can be seen any longer.

"I love you, Henry Brooks," Sarah whispers. "Come back to us, you and Caleb. Flynn won't say it in front of his father, but he needs you and Caleb as much as I do."

Having regained her composure and her innate Winthrop strength,

Sarah reenters the house, a house packed with wall-to-wall people, a handful of them preparing the bodies of Bruce and Carrie in the incensed and sheet-divided room. Naomi steps from a group of praying women and takes a revitalized Sarah in her arms. "Are you and Henry okay, Sarah? I saw him leave."

Sarah gazes out one of the side windows to the road, past Amos and Andy busily digging the graves on the soft, earthen lawn and then Sarah silently confronts her trusted servant woman. "I would never tell him with all of our worries, but I couldn't live if I lost Henry and Caleb, Naomi, even though I told Henry he would go on living if I died." Sarah moves to the windows and lowers the shades.

"You can't shut out danger or that ugly world out there by lowering the shades, baby," Naomi tells her. "That world we all fear must be brought into the light by facing it and all its evil, not hiding from it, because if we don't face it we'll forever live on an earth gone mad until Jesus returns, but with people like you and Caleb, maybe the rest of us will be worth harvesting when our Lord returns."

"And Flynn, Naomi. People like me, you, Henry, Caleb, and Flynn."

"God willing," Naomi replies, suddenly sensing danger, and knowing that even as she had not warned Sarah's parents about what she felt on the plane, because of God's will for her not to, Naomi knows that she cannot warn of what is now moving down the road and toward the house, a danger that God knows will place Caleb's feet firmly on the road of the cross.

45

The Road of the Cross

Rolling through the night to Henry's house, their headlights turned off, comes the trucks and the blood-ravenous Klansmen. Inside Henry's place of devotion and passion, as the sounds of the workers' sorrowful voices—singing time-honored spirituals—stream from the dwelling, Dane and his hooded men bring their trucks to an easy, slow stop a stone's throw away from the Brooks' front yard; alighting from the vehicles and—leaving Tramp behind muffled and tied on old Hank's truck bed—the robed men sneak up behind Amos and Andy, and while Dane presses his knife to Amos's back, Hammer forces a blade against Andy's neck. The two siblings stare in disbelief at the Klansmen, who now surround them, especially at the colonel's gold-threaded, white, silk grand-wizard's hooded robe, which both have seen before, not knowing that it is Flynn who is now wearing it. The sinister Klansmen chuckle when the brothers gawk at Caleb, who, with his hands bound behind him, is being led backwards by a long rope, which—in turn—is tied to still another part of the same rope about the presumed, young, new disciple's wrist, a rope that Hank is angrily jerking, stumbling Caleb into the midst of the shocked grave-diggers.

"What's your, name, old man?" Dane asks Amos and then glances through the large, hooded, eye holes at the house and its shade-lowered side windows.

"Amos, Sir," Amos sputters.

"Tell me, Amos," asks Dane. "Is Henry inside?"

"He just left, Sir. Gone lookin' fo' you, Caleb."

"I'm the one asking questions," Dane says, chuckling and amused. "And this here boy gives the answer to Caleb as if I didn't exist." He tells his men. No longer amused, he lifts the lightweight Amos onto the brothers' mule and hisses at him. "Then you go tell Henry you found him. Tell him if he wants to see his precious reader alive again, that he better come back here with that gold or money. Don't care which one it turns out to be. Alone, you hear? Tell him to come back alone."

Amos digs his heels into the sides of the old mule and rides onto the road a few yards or so and then stops.

"What's that coon stopping fer, Dane?" asks Hank.

Dane follows Amos's troubled gaze back at his frightened brother. Marcus stares with concern as well, at Hammer, who's snickering, with that knife now slowly cutting into a groaning Andy's double chin. "Please don't hurt him, Hammer. I can't take anymore killings," the young boy sobs.

Andy tearfully looks over at Marcus and nods, his old eyes saying, "Thank you," and as he nods, Hammer cuts the old man's throat and pushes him into the open grave.

Dane covers Marcus's mouth with his hand, as Marcus screams. "Hush up, you sissy. You want them folks inside to hear you?"

Beaming at Flynn, Hank says, "Welcome to the Klan."

Wailing, Amos knees the mule and it gallops away with the squealing old man. The Klansmen then turn their bloody sights on Henry's house and the singing old people. No one has heard them.

Inside the dwelling and on their side of the sheets, Sarah's female workers have wrapped Carrie's body up mummy style and are fastening the last safety pins in place, Sarah doing her part and braving it out with them. The men have also completed preparing Bruce's body in the same style. Naomi suddenly steps from behind the sheet and raises her hand, stopping the singing. The field hands follow her gaze to the front room, and Sarah hurries to Naomi's side, just as the door is kicked off its hinges and onto the floor. Klansmen storm into the house, blasting glass-framed pictures of the Brooks' ancestors off his walls. Glass and plaster rain down on the living and on the dead alike.

"Stay put!" shouts Dane, blasting the ceiling—this time—with his shotgun and bringing those who are trying to escape out of the windows and the back door to a halt as he reloads. Forcing everyone onto the floor, women and children are ordered to form an outer circle around the men, creating a human wall between the outnumbered Klansmen and Sarah's frightened, but enraged and unpredictable elderly male workers. While the hooded men seize all weapons, Naomi holds onto as many of the children as she can and tries to reassure them that they will not be killed. Furious about the large numbers of whites there, Dane has other ideas and wants to kill them all, even the children. He takes Hank's whip from him and—while precariously holding onto the two-barreled, death weapon with his free hand—Dane blindly lashes out at several of the white workers. "Nigger lovers!" he yells, drawing their blood.

Sitting on the floor near Naomi and the children, Sarah withdraws the revolver from her apron and fires four shots at the intruders and yells, "Stop it!" as everyone ducks to the floor.

Once the Klansmen get off the floor, including Flynn, and realize that no one had been hit, and Sarah sits there with the gun dangling from her hand and stunned that she had attempted to kill someone, Dane tosses the whip back to Hank and takes the revolver from her and exclaims. "Why!" He focuses on the white workers, "Why! Jayne with Caleb and now you along with Sarah Cutter!" He hands his shotgun to Hank and slams Sarah's revolver to the floor, picks up the nearby hammer and viciously batters the .38 until the weapon's handle shatters, the other Klansmen ducking in fear of the gun accidentally discharging from the impact. When Dane tosses that hammer aside, his men breathe easier. Then Dane sets his sights of death on Sarah. "You bitch!" he yells.

Poor, elderly Essie Mae, in the midst of all of that danger, thinks of how she had worried about who she could force to clean up the spit from the store floor; now she would gladly do anything, even clean out the outhouses to be safe in Sarah's warm, sweet-smelling store again and performing her assigned duty around joyful, laughing people.

At that moment, Reverend Miller nudges a backward-stepping Caleb from the porch and over the toppled door. He pushes Caleb, and the hands-bound boy falls backward to the floor and lands near Sarah.

"Caleb!" she cries and reaches over to untie him.

Hammer aims his gun at her. "Keep away from him or I'll kill you and him!"

"You will not!" hisses Dane, shoving Hammer aside. "I'm not telling you again. I'm in charge here."

"Dane Tucker," yells Sarah. "I'd know that voice anywhere, as well as some of you others. Take off those hoods, you filthy cowards!"

Dane jerks off his hood, his eyes of madness locked onto Sarah, who feels that she has just killed everyone in this room by exposing Dane, and she watches in dread as the rest of the Klansmen remove their hoods, except Flynn and Metcalfe, who remain back in the shadows, fighting his own kind of battle: the one in his head, were he's recalling his mother's words to him as a child of how evil comes into the world only by the white man's hands, and that if coloreds become evil and go against their own kind, there is a special place in hell reserved for them. Metcalfe recovers from his stupor, when Flynn, yelling in rage, flings off his hood, including Barney's robe, as Sarah and the workers stare up at him in shock.

"Dane threatened to kill me if I didn't wear that trash," Flynn tells his mother.

Having handed his shotgun to Hank, an outraged, totally unbalanced Dane—recalling how his father was forced to blow off his own head and by a Cutter—seizes Sarah's battered gun from the floor, and the wild-eyed corrupted-minded, one-eared man hisses at Flynn, "Die with your nigger-loving dead grandparents and let it be with your mamma's damn gun, you asshole!" Dane pulls the trigger several times, but the battered revolver—even though it has two bullets remaining in the chamber—fails to fire. Dane hurls the firearm at Flynn, who ducks, and the .38 sails through the shade and window, scattering glass over some of the sitting workers.

"You damn pig!" yells Flynn, to Sarah's horror, fearing now for both of her sons' lives.

"Ahhhh!" screams Dane, as several of his men restrain him.

"The money!" shouts Hammer to Dane. "Remember the money and don't blow it now, or I will kill you my damnself."

"Satan," screams Dane. "Give me the money, now!" He pulls away from his men, jerks the shotgun from Hank; the Klansmen around him fall back, when Dane whirls about and points the weapon at Hammer, everyone screaming.

Dane—realizing that he is losing it—stumbles across the room, pushing Flynn aside. He leans his head out the busted window beyond the broken edges of glass and gasps for his breath. "Where are you Henry goddamn Brooks!" he screams, ripping off the shade of the window and flinging it at the workers. "Where are you Henry? I'm waiting!" he shrieks.

Less than a half mile away, not wishing to signal others with gunshots, in fear of arousing the Klan, a dozen men leave Henry and gallop off to round up the rest of the search party—carrying Henry's urgent instructions with them. Now, the loving man stands impatiently beside Old Clara, a horse that seems able to sense that Caleb is in grave danger and paces about as restlessly as Henry is. With Henry, four other horsemen anxiously listen to Amos while trying to make better sense of what he trying to tell them, as he sits sprawled on a log crying and repeating himself over and over. What Henry wants to know, and is not getting from Amos, is the number of Klansmen with Dane, their weaponry, how many are guarding outside and how many are inside. Taking in a deep breath, Amos sobs, "He cut his throat, Henry. I saw him do it. Hammer. The deputy sheriff. He cut ma brother's throat."

"We can't let you go back there alone, Henry," a good friend of Henry and of Bruce, among the four, says almost in tears.

Henry looks at the man, and says "They got my boy and Sarah, Flynn and Naomi. If all of us go charging in there, many innocent folks will die, including the children. No. I have to try and find a way for the rest of you to get to those guys without bloodshed if possible."

"My, God, man," one of the four says. "Tell me . . . who? Who, Henry, will back you up in that house? Dane'll kill you fo' sho' ifin you go back there alone. You know he will."

"God will," Henry tells the four of them. "He's always told me He will."

Henry leaves his gun behind, climbs into the saddle and gallops Old Clara into the wind.

"God be with you, Henry Brooks," whispers Amos. " 'Cause you'll sho' 'nough need Him. The devil hisself is at yo' place. I felt his presence as I rode away, and that's fo' sho'. The devil, Henry. He's at yo' place just awaitin' fo' you to show up."

Back at Little Shadow Place, the Rolls Royce is parked next to a fifty-ton, sprawling old oak tree—twelve-hundred feet down the road from Henry's place in the pitch of night—and sitting behind the wheel of the car, Barney Cutter's wicked eyes are locked on Henry's distant house, as he waits for Satan's counsel, as his mother has told him to do, but his patience is fast growing thin; he is, after all, Colonel Barney Cutter, and why should he wait? If Satan wanted him to do so, Satan himself should have told him instead of sending the message through that creature, a thing that Barney, no matter how much he tells himself he should love as his mother—cannot and will never accept as part of him!

Inside Henry's house, Caleb lies on the floor and seems helpless to escape his predicament. When Flynn moves toward him and Sarah, Dane steps in front of the sensitive blonde boy.

"Stay where you are, you punk asshole," Dane tells Flynn, "or I'll not wait fer Henry to get here. I'll burn you alive." He glares at Hammer.

"One of you guys, who I will let remain nameless, so as not to dignify him, had the balls to confront me. Nobody better interfere again."

Flynn confronts him, anyway. "Stay where I am for what?" he hisses. "So you can lure Henry inside and shoot him down, you dog!"

As Caleb attempts to free his hands, to his and Flynn's dismay, the sound of Old Clara's sprinting hooves are heard. Not just those inside hear Henry's approach and are reacting to it; Barneys sits up in the car and watches Henry bring the horse to a stop, leap from the saddle and hurry into the house. After entering, Henry sees Sarah and the workers sitting on the floor staring up at him, the Klansmen's gun pointing down at them. His sights cover the entire room in a flash, from a terrified-looking Sarah, then to Naomi and then at a chalky-white-faced Flynn, who is standing in a corner with one of the Klansmen pressing a gun against the worried boy's side. When Henry sees Caleb—his wrists still rope-bound behind his back—standing near the kitchen door with Dane pressing his revolver against Caleb's head, Henry nearly loses it. Henry's fear is quickly held in check by the tremendous joy of seeing that his son is alive. Caleb yells to him, "Behind you, Papa!"

As Henry turns, Hank leaps from the porch behind him and cracks him on the head with a military .45, dropping Henry to the floor. While the women are screaming, and the Klansmen fire at the ceiling forcing them back to their sitting positions on the floor, Hank—who had told God to go to hell and had made up his mind that that is where he will end up anyway, no matter what, laughs and dances backwards away from Henry and almost falls against Caleb and Dane, who has that pistol nervously held against Caleb's head. In the blinking of Hank's eyes, Caleb violently rams Dane against the piano, knocking it over, shattering the piano keys and the violin atop of it. When Hank turns around to look at the commotion, Caleb leaps into the air and kicks the old man right through the wall and into the kitchen, sending the half-blind man's eye glasses and his .45 flying and the sound of breaking dishes, wayward pots and pans echoing through the house. After Caleb lands on his feet, Dane slams him to the floor and points his gun down at him, his finger squeezing back on the trigger. Metcalfe steps between Dane and Caleb. He looks down through his hooded-eye slots at Henry, then at Henry's boy. The man with the golden smile is no longer smiling. He removes his hood, his black face ringed with sweat. A gasp rises from the workers and Dane is strangely amused with this enough to withdraw his aim on Ca-

659

leb, and he laughs as Metcalfe belittles everyone in sight. "Now you know!" a morally confused Metcalfe hisses at the white field hands, while maintaining his body between Dane and Caleb. "We're all Klansmen! Whites and coloreds alike, all rotten to the core with or without a sheet! Take a damn good look while you at it!" Metcalfe faces down Dane. "And you, you dumb ass! Caleb's the damn goose that lays the golden eggs!" Dane pounds his free-hand fist against his scarred forehead, about to completely lose his mind, and then trembling in rage, points his weapon at Metcalfe's head. "You other fools," Metcalfe calls to the gawking Klansmen. "Dane is totally insane. Are you going to let him kill all of us one by one and end up with all of that money? He's forgotten that we need all the men we can get to pull this off."

Suddenly charging out of the kitchen, ranting and covered with plaster, Hank stumbles toward Caleb, who continues to lie helplessly on the floor between Dane and Metcalfe. "Dane or somebody give me a damn gun," Hank yells. "Let me kill this spade, please, Dane. Please let me kill him." When Sarah hears Henry groaning on the floor and knows that he is not dead and is recovering, she crawls over and wraps her arms about Caleb to protect him from Dane and Hank. Dane pulls Sarah to her feet, and jerks her about and as he does, Naomi—sitting with the children and up to then having remained silent—is mortified as Dane seizes Sarah. Naomi sees Hank's fallen .45, which is within easy reach of Flynn. Her keen old eyes lock in on Flynn, but he's tearfully looking at his mother, fearing for her safety and desperately trying to think of a way to save her and the others, and he hasn't noticed the firearm, the weapon of death that no one else as of yet has spotted.

Please, God, Naomi reflects skyward: *I know it's not allowed, but one more favor.* She then glares at Flynn. *Look at me, son. In God's name. It's Naomi. Look at me.*

Flynn slowly turns and looks at her and he follows her gaze to Hank's .45 in the loose plaster at his feet. Pushing aside the Klansman guarding him, Flynn seizes the weapon and draws down on Dane.

"Mother, move away from him!" Flynn yells, fanning the .45 to and fro between Dane and the other Klansmen.

Groaning, Henry open his eyes and stares up in disbelief: the Klansmen's guns are all pointing at a terrified Flynn. "Keep that gun on Dane, Flynn," yells Henry, sitting up. "As long as you have him in your sights, them others won't shoot."

Hammer blasts Henry in the arm, and his men shoot two of the workers who rise up to attack them. Pandemonium follows with the Klansmen firing into the workers, wounding several. "The next one is through Henry's brains if you don't drop that gun, Flynn!" Dane blares, crutching behind Sarah. Flynn drops the gun. Hank picks it up and goes after Caleb. Dane releases Sarah, seizes the gun from Hank and tosses it to Marcus. "Marcus!" he yells. "See if you have enough balls to hold onto that! We're all falling apart under the fucking stress of that money. It's partly my fault. Don't lose your damn focus now!" Dane backhands Caleb. "Where's the damn money! Your pa had to have told them field hands out there in them woods with their guns and knives to come in here after a certain time. Now, you tell me now!"

"I'm not telling you shit," Caleb hisses. "You'll kill us all anyway."

"Everyone, do like Caleb says!" yells Henry, in pain. "Even if you know nothing about that money, don't even tell these mad dogs your names! Caleb's right. They'll kill us anyway."

"Get Henry on his feet!" bellows Dane, once more seizing the bull-whip from Hank.

Two of the Klansmen pull Henry to his feet, strip off his shirt and stretch out his arms. Dane cracks the whip across Henry's bare back, and the flesh-eating leather draws blood from Henry, who stubbornly suffers in silence from the stinging whip and from the bone-crushing torture put upon his entire body by the gunshot wound, as the Klansmen—aggravating him all the more—pull against his arms with all their might. When Dane draws back to lash Henry again, Sarah screams: "Stop it! The money's in the cave! I have one of the keys! Promise you won't hurt Henry anymore or anyone else and you can have it. All ten million."

"Ten goddamn motherfucking million," exclaims Deputy Hammer, then whistles and scratches his head with a huge smile on his face. "If she thinks that much about the nigger," he says, "let her have him and these worthless others." .

"Fer once I agree with you," says Dane, dragging Sarah to the destroyed front door and stepping over it.

"I'll kill you, Dane Tucker, if you hurt her!" yells Henry. "If I have to rise up from my grave, I'll drag your white ass in it with me, and cut out your damn evil heart, you one-eared bastard!"

Laughing, Dane grins victoriously at Henry. "Rise up from your grave," he exclaims. "That would be a hell of a trick, and when I return you just may have a chance to prove it." He gives Hank an evil, knowing glance and then faces the other Klansmen. "Watch these nigger lovers," he tells his men. The one-eared Klansman then pushes Sarah out the door. "That money better be there, Sarah."

Outside, heading up the hill, Dane suddenly stops. Sarah follows his apprehensive sight over his shoulder and down the road to a deep darkness beyond where a green glow radiates from the pitch of the trees there. "Hey, wait fer me," calls Hammer, causing Dane and Sarah to focus on him, as he runs toward them. "I'm not staying behind with those idiots," hisses the streetwise deputy, adding, "and give you a chance to walk away with all that money, Dane."

"You think I can carry ten million?" yells Dane. "You're a bigger fool than I thought if you think that. Or maybe you figure Sarah here can ask Naomi to turn her into a camel and carry it on her back! But then, if it's there and it's the millions like she says, I'll need your help to at least get it out of this cave she's talking about, so bring your sorry ass on, and keep that big mouth of yours shut for a change."

Excitement builds as they walk westward on the hilltop, where Sarah leads them to a spot about a quarter mile away, to one of three caves on the slopes, this one overlooking Cutter Bridge. It's also a place where wild firethorns and occasionally jimson weeds thrive. Hammer almost steps into a pit, in which dozens of the thorny firethorns and several jimson plants are flourishing, side-by-side. Dane grabs him. "Careful, man. We're not on the streets of Cutterville now. They say holes like this one are the devil's kitchen, and once you fall in it or even get that pure drug scent from these uncut plants up your nose, it'll take you weeks to think clear again, and you can bet that this bitch Sarah's not going to warn us of these holes, or help us in any way if she has anything to do with it." Dane sees Sarah cover her nostrils with her handkerchief, when passing the pit and plants, and Dane covers his nostrils with his hand, Hammer the same, as both men momentarily contemplate the pit, a dark, fourteen-foot-deep, twenty-foot-wide hole with steep walls, walls impossible to climb out of, without help, once having fallen into it. They then move on, catching up to Sarah and impatiently nudging her along ahead of them.

On the Brooks' porch, Hank kicks aside Henry's rocking chair. "Bring 'em out!" he yells. Six of the Klansmen drag Henry and Caleb from the house, both father and son now with their wrists bound in front of them; the Klansmen tie them by their wrists' ropes to the sturdy four-by-four porch railing, and then all six of the Klansmen violently jerk on the well-constructed railing to test its strength, then walk away, gathering up one of the longer four-by-fours that Caleb had hauled from the burned school and had piled by the porch to build Henry's porch roof. They carry that long post with them to the rear of the house as Metcalfe pushes Flynn onto the porch. Flynn's hands are not tied, because Metcalfe feels he is greased lightning compared to Flynn, and could easily take Flynn down if he even blinks wrong. Besides that, Miller, who steps from the house next, is now carrying Hank's rifle and has it trained on Flynn, and it seems, also on Metcalfe. When Flynn hesitates at the porch steps and looks down at Caleb and Henry, both Hank—who storms from the house—and Metcalfe nudge Flynn off the porch and steps.

"Papa, Flynn is so afraid," says Caleb looking over his shoulder with great concern for Flynn, then back at his father's arm. "You're still bleeding, Papa."

Henry doesn't answer. His sight is on the hillside where Dane has taken Sarah; then the gravely worried man glances over at Flynn, who is being spit on in the middle of the lawn by Miller, who also waves his Bible at the teenager. Henry faces his son.

"There's something Sarah and I have wanted to tell you and Flynn, Caleb. It's about who you and he are and—"

Hank steps back onto the porch. "Tell him in the next world, Pops," he says, cutting Henry's rope from the railing with a pocket knife and pulling Henry to his feet by the severed end. With the aid of three other Klansmen, Hank jerks a resisting Henry off the porch. Miller, using the rifle barrel, nudges Flynn on to the side of the house by the fake grave. Old bifocaled Hank also does his part by forcing Henry around the side of the dwelling, where Henry stops and listens as Caleb calls to his out-of-sight father from the porch: "What are they going to do to you, Papa?"

Jerking on the rope, Hank can't budge Henry, who anchors himself firmly in place as he tries to tell Caleb—without endangering Sarah and Flynn anymore than they are already—that Sarah is his mother. "It's empty, son," Henry shouts.

"What's empty, Papa?"

Flynn stops and looks back at Henry, then follows Henry's sight down at the fake grave. Miller whacks Flynn across the wrist and pushes him on his way. Then, several Klansmen help Hank drag Henry on into the backyard. On that cool night, the weather abruptly turns unusually warm, and Henry's muscular body begins to excrete a passionate sweat, a sweat with the scent of roses about it, and the crickets stop their mating calls, and the stars cover themselves with dark gray clouds, as everyone around Henry smells the rose fragrance, but do not know from where it comes.

At the cave—a thousand feet above the bridge and the train tracks— as Sarah unlocks the gate which leads into a moist, cold tunnel, she looks back at Dane. "Remember your promise, Dane. Please don't hurt Henry anymore. Just take the money and leave us in peace."

"You got my word," exclaims Dane. "I have no intention of laying a hand on Henry, not even Barney, as long as he remains out of the picture on his deathbed and I get the money."

Down the road, Barney Cutter has other ideas and his patience is at an end. He curses the night and Satan, as time drags on. Slowly the intolerant, Grand Wizard leans forward in the car seat and, through his growing, unique powers, he senses something and sets his sights on a darkened cluster of oak trees, a horse's gallop or so away. There is yet one other forgotten player in the race for his money: Concealed in the growth of trees and thicket, between Henry's house and the bridge, Sheriff Richards sits in his patrol car with his binoculars trained on Deputy Hammer atop the distant, once-again, moonlit hill with Dane and Sarah. With loathing eating away at him, he watches Sarah swing open the cave gate. "You goddamn little snake-in-the-grass," he mutters, his focus on his deputy. "You'll pay for trying to cut me out."

While Richards is consumed with anger from afar, at the cave entrance, just before entering the gate, Sarah hears pounding sounds traveling on that hot wind with the smell of roses on it, streaming their way. Sarah stands there in fright listening to that hair-raising hammering echo until Dane pushes her into the cavernous hillside ahead of him, followed by Deputy Hammer, who looks about the outside darkness, then locks the gate behind them. Sheriff Richards—once again having watched the three of them—turns his field glasses on Henry's sideyard. The pounding sounds are coming from the Klansmen, who had chosen the post, from Caleb's wood stack—which will make their project stand higher and better seen—over one of the ones they had trucked in and now are nailing spikes into two of those planks, one from Hank's truck, the other from Caleb's stack. The planks are laid out on the ground in the form of a cross. Richards, again, refocuses on the cave, where he's now absolutely sure the money is located. He checks his pistol and smiles.

Inside the sinister cave, bats by the hundreds of thousands swarm in and out of the towering murky ridges above the three intruders. The darting, sweeping, squealing bloodsuckers' acrid-smelling excrement stifles the nostrils, and the sounds of their wings wildly scissoring through the darkened air sets Hammer into a panic. "I hate 'em," he exclaims, "those satanic winged devils. Isn't there some fucking light in here?" As they feel their way through the dark, Sarah—who also fears bats—locates, by touch, and hastily lights the first of a line of miners' lanterns with matches which—along with the lanterns—have been placed every hundred feet or so along the way by Henry. Dane takes the first of those lanterns from her and carries it, while she and Hammer light their way along the path of lanterns. Finally—still in the lead, Dane following close behind her—Sarah lights the last of the lanterns and blows out the match. She looks down; at her feet is the half-full, five-gallon can of kerosene, which Henry had purchased from her store and had used to refill several of the glass-globe lanterns. She recalls the past, the store, the love and workers who gathered there, before Hammer nudges her on her way.

"This is an old coal mine," Hammer then whispers to Dane, while looking about.

Just as Sarah passes by the five-gallon kerosene can, she sees another lantern, one which should never have been placed there, the battered, red one, the one Naomi broke when Caleb was born and when Chad had tried to kill him, a lantern—unknow to Sarah—placed there by Caleb after he reluctantly took it from the wine cellar, weeks ago and—after having brought it along with him and the money and, not knowing why, dropped it in the tunnel and simply forgot about it.

"How much farther?" exclaims Hammer, as the bats swoop in alarm, aggravated by the lights, breaking Sarah's focus and thoughts, bats which should have flown from the cave long ago and had not, kept there by the hand of Lucifer.

"The money is about twenty feet ahead," she says, and not knowing why, reaches for the battered lantern. Dane nudges Sarah on her way.

"Forget that piece of shit. Can't you see it's all fucked up? Since you say we're so close, the ones we already have will do. The money. Lead us to the money."

A few steps, directly ahead, and they arrive at a large opening in the tunnel wall. "In there," Sarah tells them. "Now, let me go."

"No way in hell," says Dane again pushing her, this time into the chambers.

Stumbling, he and Hammer quick step into the hollow behind her, the sound of dripping and running water permeating the air. Their eyes light up when they complete their entry and see Barney's duffle bags neatly piled on wooden pallets in the center of the crater's wet floor. The men put down their lanterns.

"I can smell it," shrills Dane, frantically opening the unlocked bag and shaking out the paper-strapped bills onto the wet floor. "Millions. My God," Dane and Hammer shout one behind the other, and Dane adds. "Millions to die fer!"

Back on the porch, Caleb is frantically scraping his wrist rope against the railing attempting to unravel it; while at the side of the house, close to the backyard by the truck, Henry's wrists have been re-tied, not together, not to the side-door porch railing, but to an affront to God, the wooden project that the Klansmen were so passionately hammering together. Breathing rapidly and gripped in apprehension, Henry is lying face up and nude on the Klansmen's hurriedly made, man-size cross. His wrists are tied to the cross arms, his ankles to the center plank from Caleb's wood pile.

"Is this what my son would have had to face, my God?" Henry whispers, while sweating under the hot wind. "If so, I thank you for letting me take his place on this horrifying stage of the road to redemption, as it was with Your Son, but please, God, give me the strength to endure what I fear is next to come."

You will suffer much, but the angels will be beside you to bypass purgatory and bring you directly home to me, my brother, whispers the voice of Jesus to Henry's ears alone.

Nearby, Miller, who has stuffed his Bible half in and half out of his pocket and is pointing his rifle at a hysterical Flynn, sees the sudden look of peace come over Henry, and the preacher is so afraid, for he feels that that which delivered Henry from the gruesome fear of what's to happen to the black man, and causes even him, Miller, to tremble in terror, was none other but God. However, Miller is determined to put all thoughts of God out of his mind, for he feels that he has absolutely gone too far now to turn back. He watches as Henry looks over at him then at Flynn.

"Pray with me, son." And Henry begins praying aloud, and the beloved, frightened boy joins in, "Our Father, who art in heaven . . ."

The Klansmen laugh at Flynn and at Henry, but Metcalfe—profoundly touched by the sight and the sounds of Flynn and Henry praying together, steps forward, removes his shirt and ties the sleeves around the praying man's waist and, with the length of the shirt, covers the condemned man's nudity. Hank jerks the shirt off Henry, who continues to pray, as Hank yells at Metcalfe. "I'm not finished with this boy yet!"

Then, both Henry on the cross, and Caleb, on the porch, recall Naomi's prophecy: "When the waters of evil swallow you up, and you and Henry's heads are under those pounding waves of despair and hopelessness, Henry will cross over the bridge of life."

"Papa!" calls Caleb, when he hears Henry and Flynn continued praying.

". . . and forgive us our trespasses as we forgive those who trespass against us. Amen." After he and Flynn end the Lord's prayer, Henry calls to Caleb. "Son. Be strong for both of us now."

"You sound like one of them Catholics, praying with this poet-reading white boy," shouts Hank, seizing the disturbed Miller's Bible from the would-be preacher's pocket and waving it at Henry. "Fer thine is the kingdom and the power and the glory ferever and ever amen. That's how it ends in our Good Book, you zombie jigaboo!"

In the heat of that night, when Henry looks over at him, Miller feels the cold fingers of death creeping throughout his body.

"What are you looking at me like that fer?" screeches the corrupt preacher.

"I dread what awaits you," Henry tells him.

Flynn, eyes watering, looks down at Henry and tearfully asks, "Why did God let this happen to you?" The perceptive, blonde boy looks at the madness of Miller and Hank and again down at the goodness of Henry. "Tell me so I can hate God, the way Caleb does."

"Caleb doesn't hate God, son, only God's false prophets." Henry—once again—turns his gaze on Miller. "Those who occupy a high place—at their own risk—in the religious family of man and say they love our Lord, and they do at first, but later, in their moments of weakness, embrace Satan for the riches of this world."

"I don't embrace Satan!" screams Miller. "And neither will I be struck by lightning or destroyed by Naomi and her witchcraft 'clock-strike-twelve talk' that folks say will also destroy my church the way they say it put Barney on his death bed. That was the earthquake, that's all, that damaged my church. The professor I went to said there are only three states in this country were they don't have earthquakes and we're not one of them. That's my guess. An earthquake. That's what damaged my church. Not Naomi and her so-called powers. She never had any power. She ain't God Almighty! She's black and so is Caleb!"

"Dane gave his word!" shouts Flynn, stepping forward, only to be slammed back against the house by Hank. "He told Mother nothing would happen to Henry," Flynn defiantly goes on. "His word. He gave his word!"

"So what?" says one of the sidelined Klansmen, drinking moonshine with the others, now that Hank is in charge. "The coons say Caleb wants be a lawyer. Tell him to sue us."

"You can have Shadow Grove," Flynn tells Hank and Miller, while keeping his gaze locked with Henry's uneasy brown one, Flynn's blue eyes telling Henry to hang on, that somehow he'll save him, and to have faith. "Take all the money and the land," Flynn sorrowfully wails to Hank, "but let Henry go."

"Your land ain't shit with the town holding claim to the lagoon water out here, now that the colonel's as good as dead!" exclaims Hank, taunting Flynn, waving Miller's Bible at him and hoping against hope that he didn't see what he thought he saw in Barney's window, and that Barney is truly dead. "Besides, we're getting all the money anyway. Ain't that what Sarah told Dane? And stop eyeballing that naked nigger man like he was Jesus Christ on that cross. That's an idea! Christ's side was pierced, wasn't it? Right!"

Dropping the Bible, Hank removes Barney's old Bowie knife from the truck, a knife he had recovered after Chad's death. He spits on the blade, slices Henry's side, and giggles, as pearls of dark blood bubble out of the powerful man's pink under flesh and streams down and across his smooth, dark skin, as Henry trembles in agony and Flynn sobs.

"Will you look at that," says one of the newer Klansmen, stepping from the house's side door and onto the scene, joining his peers in a guzzling, moonshine frenzy. "The nigger is the same color inside as we are. I'll be goddamn if he isn't. First time I've ever seen that."

"Ahhh!" screams Henry, arching his back, when Hank cuts deeper into him.

"Papa," cries Caleb, his heart pounding. "What are they doing to you? Somebody! Please! Flynn! Help Papa!"

Flynn goes completely to pieces and wails out of control. Inside the house, under the guns of the Klansmen, Sarah's workers hear Flynn's and Caleb's deep-felt soul-piercing cries for help, and they pray, beseeching God to answer the boys' pleas and help Henry; Naomi, however, knowing that Jesus' time on the cross was agonizing long, even as Henry's must be for a while longer, has her eye on one of Henry's cast-iron skillets on the floor in the kitchen, where Hank knocked it off the stove when he was kicked though the wall, a skillet heavy enough to kill the same as any bullet from as gun. She also sets her sights on a pot of boiling water on Henry's stove, water which had been placed there in an attempt to warm it in order that it could be used to wash their hands after preparing Bruce and Carrie, water steeped with Henry's lye soap. As the water on the stove boils, things are heating to a boil outside, as well.

"Papa," Caleb continuously calls from the porch. "What's wrong, Papa? What are they doing to you?"

Hank yells toward the front of the house to Caleb, "You people sing so loud in church like you own God. We're here teaching your pa he ain't worth spit, that's what we're doing to him, Caleb Brooks, and then we're coming after you to teach you the same, to never put your black, half-breed hands on a white man, and God help you when we get through with you fer even being near that naked Jayne Hill. Never, you hear! Never touch a white man or get nowhere near a white woman, a naked one at that!"

Like the reoccurrence of diarrhea that one contracts and feels has passed—Reverend Miller, gripped in that on-again, off-again fear of losing his soul, gawks down at Henry and then at Flynn, and finds himself sweating in dread, as Hank thrusts several spikes into Flynn's trembling hands, along with Henry's hammer. Flynn is appalled and steps back shaking his head. "No," he screams, flinging the tools of torture to the ground. "You want me to nail him . . . to nail Henry to that thing, with his hammer and those nails! No, you white sons of bitches!"

"What is he trying to make you do, Flynn?" calls Caleb's frantic voice from the porch. "Don't let them make you hurt Papa!"

"Pick 'em back up, now!" shouts Hank to Flynn, slapping him again and again, while yelling at him.

"You got two seconds befer I slap you blind," he warns Flynn. "You're the Grand Wizard's son, not a nigger lover! Pick up that hammer, now!"

Biting against his lip, squeezing back the tears, Flynn continues shaking his head, as Hank slaps him all over the place. Hank then knees Flynn in the stomach and Flynn gags, out of breath, and can only gasp, the world dizzily spinning around him, as he hears the blurred voices of the Klansmen about him, laughing, their mouths open wide, their rotting, teeth yellow, their drunken breath nauseous. A sudden clap of thunder quiets all of the laughter, and Miller looks at the sky, as his diarrhea of bowel-moving dread returns. He recalls the earlier feeling of death when he saw Barney's mother flying in the sky, and he prays that he can hold out without breaking down, and that no one notices his fears; then he sees Henry looking up at him—a look of forgiveness—and all bets are off. When Hank again slaps Flynn, Miller falls apart.

"Stop it, Hank!" Miller yells and then points his rifle at Metcalfe with the intent to kill and Metcalfe knows it. "You pick up them spikes now!" Miller warns Metcalfe. "You do it, nigger. Hold them nails in place, while this bloodthirsty Hank nails them down! Do it, you Jewish-looking bastard, just like they did to Christ!"

"Who the goddamn fuck you calling bloodthirsty?" shouts Hank, ignorantly going on. "You think you're better than the rest of us, you and your fucked-up Bible? Is that it?" Hank picks up the dropped Bible and hurls it against Miller.

Metcalfe reluctantly picks up the spikes, then follows Henry's troubled sights to the sky. The moonlight not only is intensifying, not only that, the moon, itself, seems to be growing larger, as it shines down on the cross and Henry. While Reverend Miller, Hank and his drunken men fail to notice the moon and its seemingly bizarre behavior, Flynn stands frozen facing the lunar light, stunned, his lips moving as if praying. With Miller targeting that rifle and his rigid sights on him, Metcalfe—filled with regret and seeing how uneasily Henry is now looking up from that cross at him—places a spike on the predestined man's wrist. Henry whis-

670

pers, "My brother, do it fast that this bitter cup placed upon me might quickly end."

Gesturing with his fingers, Henry signals for Metcalfe to lean close to him, and Metcalfe does, leaning down on one knee, as Henry whispers: "Save the boys' lives, if you can."

Metcalfe looks over at Flynn, then toward the front porch. The man with the golden smile—who had told old Amos, in the boxcar, that he, Metcalfe, wasn't any brother to any damn, ignorant, Uncle-Tom cowardly nigger—is now crushed and knows that he and this most unusual soul called Henry Brooks are undeniably linked, and that they are brothers.

The gold-mouthed man's hands shake as Miller pokes him in the back with the rifle and he—while still kneeling—holds the spikes one after the other; and Hank continuously slams down the hammer with all the hatred that lives within him. Henry's powerful cries shake Caleb to his knees, as Hank's voice—paralleling Henry's agonizing cries and groans—shrieks, "'Fer thine is the kingdom, the power and the glory ferever,' like I told you. Say it! I want you to suffer fer hours upon hours until you repeat it right befer I have mercy on you and take you out of your misery with a bullet in your head. You who once owned all this land and water and held it over the heads of the whites! Say it, nigger or suffer all night long."

And Henry does suffer, nailed to that cross flat on his back and consumed with unbelievable pain that, he's now aware of, is but a fraction of the overall pain that Christ went through. Flynn stands stooped over, looking down at Henry with soul-wrenching anguish. Tears flowing, he faces the heavens: "God, I'm the one who is unclean and infected with the colonel's blood, not Henry, and I'm unworthy to ask anything of You. But please, God, don't let Henry suffer anymore like this."

A raven passes across the face of the moon and its huge shadow is cast down from the heavenly light and over the cross and over Henry, and Caleb's father takes in a last breath: "Sarah," he whispers and dies.

46

Shadow of the Cross

Having put together his plan of attack, Sheriff Richards now sits in his patrol car pondering, and double checking on the movement of the Klansmen with their burning torches while guarding Caleb on the front porch. Turning his binoculars on the side of the house, Richards sees Flynn sobbing down at Henry on the cross, and takes special notice of two of the men who have joined in the search for Barney's money: two more of his deputies. Still in their uniforms, their sheets and hoods now removed, the deputies laughingly chat with Hank and are fully under Dane's control, with Hank—at this time—acting as Dane's eyes and ears. The lawmen are following Hank's instructions, astride two of the Brooks' farm horses and preparing to patrol the outer perimeter of Henry's property with one hand on the reins, the other on their guns, their eyes always looking about, ready to kill any Johnny-come-lately trying to stake a claim to the money, and Richards knows that includes killing him. When the riders venture out of view, on the far side of the house, Richards checks his service revolver, slides from the car, and then—just as he's about to make his way toward the distant hill on foot with his flashlight, police radio and weapon—he hears the faint sounds of the search party's hounds barking. Retrieving his spy glasses, he climbs onto the hood of his car and then onto the roof, and uses the binoculars to look over the nearby lower tree tops at the search party's flickering torch flames, a half mile or so away and moving with deliberate speed toward Henry's place.

"Dimmit," he hisses, realizing that he has no chance of getting to the hillside and killing Dane and Hammer before the workers arrive in the area. He decides to drive there, even if it now means his car will be seen when he passes the Brooks' house and the other Klansmen. Suddenly, he feels the patrol car dip and sway. When he turns around he faces Barney on the car roof with him. Wearing Hitler's long, black, leather coat, his ears, now, twice their normal size, his eyes a blood red, and his skin slate gray, Barney is death on legs.

Richards whirls about to jump to the ground. Too late. Barney whips out the sword from beneath the coat, and—with one downward two-handed thrust—slices Richards from the top of his head right down through the middle of his crotch. The left side of Richards's body falls one way, the right side the other. It's Barney, who has not waited for Satan's instructions and has been punished with diminished sight, then jumps to the ground, picks up Richards's binoculars, and walks away, leaving the sword and Richards behind, sprawled out prone on top of the patrol car: his right side, his leg, half of his stomach. The left side, including half of his distorted fat cheek rests against the cold, metal roof. One of his arms and parts of his left-side torso sliding down the driver-side door, the front window glass also stained red with his blood. Barney never looks back, and when he reaches his concealed Rolls Royce, he slides behind the wheel and once more, with the help of those binoculars, scrutinizes his son.

"I'll kill you," yells Flynn, lunging at Hank, and Barney, with those large ears, hearing it all.

"Then kill him, son, so that we may be one with him, our lord, after all," says Cutter, feeling Lucifer will forgive him.

High above the bridge, in the cave—where Satan has deliberately, angrily refrained from permitting Barney to go because of Barney's disobedience—lit up by lantern light, Dane is tossing money into the air and exclaiming, "Thank you, master! I am now one with you." While Hammer rolls around in the water and over the cash floating on the shallow watery surface, Sarah is standing in a corner, afraid to move and looking about for a way to escape.

At the house, there has not been a sound from those on the side of the dwelling for nearly a half hour. Then, Reverend Miller—clumsily trying to carry his rifle and extra bullets in his hand and going through more changes than ever now—is filled with misgivings; after having had a horrid hand in Henry's death, he mopes along and approaches the front yard with thoughts of Henry heavy on his mind. Miller's lifelong dream of building a huge church seems unimportant now, his conflicting beliefs driving him nearly insane: It wasn't his fault, he tells himself, that Henry died. Meanwhile, several Klansmen carry Caleb's toppled piano onto the porch, prop it up with Henry's rocking chair and bang on the keys in a choppy marching, chaotic beat, signaling the arrival of Miller and the others from the side of the house, filling Caleb with apprehension. When Miller reaches the front of the residence, he refuses to look at the porch and at Caleb, even when Caleb struggles to his feet and calls to him.

"Where is Papa, Reverend Miller? In God's name, where is Papa!"

Flynn shows up next, heartbroken. His wrists are now tied firmly in front of him, his tearful eyes seeking out Caleb, who is jerking violently against the partially segmented, heavy rope. Metcalfe and then Hank—with his rifle—follow Flynn. "Master Flynn's a good old Klansman," brags Hank to Caleb. "Colonel Cutter would have been real proud of him tonight, the way he nailed your pa to the cross to save his own damn skin."

The look that Caleb gives Flynn—a look that kills Flynn's heart, blaming him for Henry's torture—causes the blonde boy to sink to his knees in despair, and he looks up at Caleb, but before Flynn can respond, it is Miller who breaks down and sobs, gaping up at the sky, and then up at Caleb and the porch. "I thought I would be, but now I'm not proud of what happened to your father. My congregation and I will pray for his soul. Okay, Caleb?"

"The way you and yours prayed in the back, 'Fer thine is the kingdom and the power and the glory ferever and ever amen!'" shouts Caleb, as he's violently knocked to his knees by the Klansman who had been banging on the piano. "Pray for yourself, you bastard," Caleb continues yelling at Miller, his strength ebbing, as he calls out "Papa!" When Henry doesn't answer, Caleb glares from the porch at Flynn. "What did you do to Papa, Flynn, you and Miller? What did you do, you son-of-a-bitch!"

"Shut up, Sam Spade," the piano banger shouts. "You're next you know."

Miller's frightened eyes look from Caleb to the side of the house, as the sound of the sputtering truck is head approaching. A pot-bellied Klansman, clutching and grinding the gears of Hank's truck, runs into Henry's chicken coops, scattering the white domestic birds throughout the yard, as he drives the old Dodge to the front of Henry's lawn. Positioned on the back of the vehicle is the man-sized, upright cross with Henry's body nailed to it. Metcalf's shirt, red with blood, is once again wrapped about Henry's waist. Instead of a wooden sign attached to the top of the cross, as had been for Jesus, proclaiming Him "King of the Jews," a sign is nailed into Henry's skull, which reads: "Jesus don't love no niggers or no Jews." Tramp, tethered to the cross, is chewing at

Henry's feet and intermittently licking up Henry's warm blood. Caleb turns absolutely catatonically frozen in mindless motionlessness and in spirit. Laughing, Hank runs up to the house and throws a bloody piece of flesh onto the porch at Caleb. It's Henry's penis.

Bellowing like a wounded animal, and with a sudden and unprecedented show of strength, Caleb explodes upward, shattering the railing and ripping off his bonds. Old Hank farts, as Caleb, roaring, picks the piano up over his head and slams the quarter-ton, musical instrument down on the four Klansmen—who had brought the upright outside—crushing them, as they cower in a corner of the porch, the violent impact of the shattering piano, a rekindling of Samson pulling down the pillars of the Philistine's Temple, scattering wires and piano keys tearing away a corner of the house. Inside the dwelling, attracted by the racket, the dozen or so Klansmen all run to the windows and look out, and when they do, the old timers, men, women and children, jump all over them, onto their backs, kicking their legs out from under them, biting and pounding them with their fists and seizing their weapons. Outside, after crushing the Klansmen, Caleb leaps off the porch with part of the busted four-by-four railing. He splits open Miller's skull with one blow, then seizes the preacher's repeating rifle and shoots the two patrolling deputies off their horses, as they charge back to the house and toward him, firing their weapons. One of the deputies dies immediately, the other—Gilbert Hawkfeller, only wounded and pleading that he has a wife and three, young children—gets to his feet and stumbles squalling and bleeding into the treeline—Caleb refusing to shoot him in his back—permits him to live. Hank and Metcalfe dive behind the truck. As Sarah's elderly workers tie the Klansmen up inside the house, a few of the sheeted men—having escaped detection—flee toward the doors. Naomi runs into the kitchen, seizes that boiling water from the stove and slings it in the face of one of the escaping killers before he can reach the door, sending him screaming and blind into the wall. The angry mix-blooded woman then picks up that heavy skillet from the floor and looks around for someone else to pulverize. Marcus flails onto the porch, while still clinging to that .45, which Dane had earlier tossed to him. The young boy takes one look at Henry on the cross, drops the gun and faints. Metcalfe and Hank see Naomi and the workers storming onto the porch after Marcus. The near-sighted old man's hands tremble as he frantically attempts to untie Tramp from the truck: "Porch, Tramp!" he yells, "Kill!"

After killing Miller and viciously kicking his body aside and killing still another Klansman, with a shot to his head, Caleb now turns his rage on Flynn, and even with Flynn's hands tied and having no way to defend himself, Caleb knocks his friend to the ground onto his back, then straddles him; and—while sitting on the terrified boy's stomach—Caleb points the rifle at Flynn's face. From the Rolls Royce, Cutter sits up in the seat and, with the fieldglass, watches Caleb manhandle Flynn, and he hurriedly starts the car motor.

"Wait, Barney," a demonic voice says, that of his mother.

"I can't," Barney yells. "They'll kill my boy."

"You will obey me, Barney Cutter," the voice warns, that of Satan.

Lightning strikes, sending that monstrous oak tree crashing down on the Rolls, exploding out its window and tires, crushing the hood and annihilating the winged, silver-lady, hood ornament. The doors are all jammed shut, trapping Barney behind the wheel. "No!" he cries. "Don't do this to me!"

"No!" Flynn cries, as Caleb's finger slides to the trigger.

"Help my boy, Satan!" Barney screams, pinned back in the broken seat, staring over his chest at the house and Flynn, his powers rescinded.

Crouching behind the truck with Metcalfe, Hank—in pure desperation—rises up from behind the vehicle and fires at Caleb, who returns fire under the old vehicle, and as he had the two deputies; and alike with the tin cans while practicing with Flynn at the lagoon, he finds his mark, shattering Hank's ankle, causing him wailing pain. The large-bellied Klansman who drove the truck onto the lawn slides from the cab, and while backing off, fires his pistol at Caleb. Both Caleb and several of the workers on the porch shoot down the truck driver with an array of shots, riddling his body with lead. Finally, Hank frees Tramp, but instead of charging at the porch and scattering the workers, so that Hank can make his escape into the nearby woods, along with Gilbert Hawkfeller, whom Caleb had spared, Tramp—sniffing and snarling, his big head rocking side-to-side picks up Flynn's scent and goes straight for him and Caleb, who turns too late to take on the large, mad dog. Not Naomi. She grabs Marcus's gun from the porch, whirls and fires round after round and manages to blast Tramp just as he leaps into the air at the boys. Howling in pain, Tramp lies down on the soft grass, whimpers and dies besides

Caleb. Marcus, who had awakened and had been lying on the porch, too afraid to move, looks up at Naomi with that gun, and he leaps to his feet and runs yelping into the yard and hides behind a tree, where he finds momentary safety. Remaining on top of Flynn, Caleb yells "You killed Papa!" at the terrified boy.

"Caleb! Stop!" shouts Naomi. "How can you believe that?"

The field hands drag Naomi back into the house, when Hank and the couple of the earlier escaped Klansmen fire at them at cross angles. Enraged over being shot in the leg, Hank, limping in agony, positions himself for a clear shot at the back of Caleb's head and whispers, "Please let me kill him Satan, since God has turned His back on us. Please let me kill that black son of a bitch." When Metcalfe hears Hank asking help from Satan and that God has turned His back on the Klan, Metcalfe—who has been raised as a Baptist by his grandmother—has heard and has seen enough. He eases to his feet and grabs one of the shorter boards off the truck, and bashes Hank across his back. "Ahh!" screams Hank, landing face down on the ground, losing his glasses, but not his rifle.

"You won't get rid of us by cutting off our dicks!" yells Metcalfe. "No, Sir, asshole!"

Dazed, Hank sees Metcalfe's blurry form lifting the board to smash him yet another time, and the old Klansman flips over and pokes the rifle barrel between Metcalfe's legs and fires. Filled with adrenaline, the gold-mouthed man cracks Hank once more, planting him, this time, onto his back and sending his rifle sliding under the truck. Caleb, totally out of control and absolutely convinced that Flynn killed Henry, and seemingly unaware of the events going on around him, presses his rifle barrel against Flynn's mouth, the anger-possessed teenager's finger now in place and easing back on the trigger; Naomi and the workers race off the porch calling for Caleb to stop, a seemingly impossible thing to do now. Metcalfe, however, who vowed—once he was thrown off that train—that he would kill Flynn and Caleb, stumbles from the rear of the truck.

"No!" he cries to Caleb and then looks up at Henry, blood seeping from both their crotches. Naomi immediately stops and backs off to the porch steps and motions for everyone to do the same, permitting Metcalfe—seemingly touched by the Spirit—to continue unimpeded in his act of contrition before God and the angels for his many sins, and the

677

gold-toothed man sorrowfully faces Caleb. "That white boy didn't do it," he sobs to Caleb, who stops his attack on Flynn and listens to the man he had grown to despise. "He was willin' to die to save your pa," says Metcalfe. "God knows he was. I killed your pa by helping them dogs nail him to that cross, not that boy."

Metcalfe collapses, dying on his knees before the cross. Caleb flings aside the rifle and pulls Flynn to his feet and jerks him into his arms and—kissing his cheek—cries. "My God! I almost killed you!"

"Caleb," says Flynn, sobbing. "You didn't know. You didn't know."

"I'm sorry, Flynn," Caleb goes on, sobbing all the more, "I'm so sorry! I tried to kill you, Flynn! I tried to kill you!"

With Hank still unconscious thirty feet away behind the truck, both boys look up at Henry, the sky—which once turned from daylight over Cutterville and the swamp to the black of night—now suddenly changes from the darkness of night to the brightness of day, then fades back into night, sending the workers running about in interpretation.

In Cutterville, having seen the bright light over Henry's land, men, women and their children race out of Miller's church, the church clock clanging without end, and the cross atop the building topples to the ground and shatter into splinters. On every corner, from Cutterville square to the earthen streets of Colored Town, people lament, watching the horizon over Henry's land and wondering what that sudden change from a night sky into a daytime one and back to night again means; then, many of Miller's congregation, and those of Harris's church, feeling that God will deliver them from harm, including from that frightening display of light, return to their churches to pray. Many, however, from both sides of the train tracks now, are convinced that God loves all mankind equally, regardless of the color of one's skin, and they leave the churches and meet at the train tracks where they cross over the rails of segregation and into each others' arms. The whites and the blacks, churchgoers and non-churchgoers, firemen, store owners, factory workers and those Northern reporters have all heard the rumors that the Klan has gone to the swamps to hunt down Caleb. Those citizens of Cutterville and outsiders climb in their cars, their wagons and on their horses—some of them on foot—and they hurry toward Henry's land to join in the search to save Caleb, not to kill him.

At Henry's place, down the way from the house, Barney is temporarily blinded by that light in the sky—and fearful that it represents the power of God—he calls on the devil and he hears Satan's voice calling back to him and the power of Satan begins to slowly re-empower him.

"Now you know, Barney," says the voice of Satan. "By being patient, you have learned—it seems—that your son will never follow in your footsteps to serve me. When Flynn leaves to save his mother, follow him and there you will find your money."

"Yes," says Barney, trying to ward off what he's keenly aware of is to come, the loss of Flynn's life by his own hand, this Satan would demand, and then it comes:

The voice returns, "Your thoughts are open as the breeze is to me. If God can order one of His followers to slaughter his beloved son on the sacrificial altar, instead of a sheep, kill even your son as well as Caleb if you love me."

"You are the only one I have left in my life now for me to love," Barney tells the Master of his soul, "and I will do as you say. But grant me one wish."

"Ask and it shall be yours."

"I know that Flynn loves me. Face-to-face with him, he will tell me so. I'm his father. If I convince him to rethink his relationship with Caleb and love you, will you let him live?"

"I will give the entire universe to him, if he worships me. Tell him that. And for you, who will never have the power to perform miracles the way Jesus has consecrated into His disciples, but it is within my power to make you hundreds of times stronger than any mortal who has ever lived, including Samson. Close your eyes and patiently wait until I fully enable you with my strength. Afterwards, your car will run again. Use it to swiftly move through this night to reach your goal and your money and conquer the world for me, even if you have to destroy it—in doing so—and your boy."

At the house, Caleb quickly unties Flynn's wrists, while continuously apologizing to him. Once free, Flynn looks to the hills. "Mother, Caleb!"

Just then, recovering from Metcalfe's blows, Hank finds his bent glasses, puts them on, seizes the rifle from beneath the truck, staggers to his feet, fires at Caleb and misses. Caleb hands his rifle to Flynn and nudges him away. "Go help Sarah," he yells to Flynn.

"But you have no weapon," exclaims Flynn.

"Go, and take your men with you." Caleb says while looking up at Henry's body. "Papa and I will protect each other. We always have."

As Flynn tosses the rifle back to Caleb, anyway, and races off, Caleb lets the weapon fall to the ground at his feet, his sights on the body of his father. During this time, Hank has removed his glasses, and is frantically rubbing the dirt off of them with his fingers, in order to get a clearer shot at Caleb. Naomi and the others open up on the old man and his truck, forcing him to duck behind the vehicle once more. On the run, Flynn looks back at Caleb and then at Naomi and at a dozen of his workers on the porch ahead of him, some armed with Henry's pots and pans, some with the Klansmen's guns or their own. Flynn calls to them, and several of the field hands toss their guns to him. "No, Flynn," Naomi yells, as he runs by the porch and catches one of the tossed weapons on the fly and continues racing up the slope. When the workers swarm off the porch to follow Flynn, Naomi stops them. "Flynn! Come back!" she again calls, as Hank peeks over the truck, the workers again pin him down with their wild shots.

"Why'd you stop us from going with Master Flynn, Naomi?" one of the field hands asks, with one eye on the truck and Hank. Again, the man asks, this time angrily, "Why did you stop us!"

Naomi lingers there, her eyes focused on the road of darkness beyond the house and at that toppled oaktree. Still pinned behind the wheel of his once-shiny Rolls Royce, Barney is reaching up and lifting the mountainous tree that projects through the car's roof onto him. His enormous upward thrust splits open the car seat, pops out the seats metal springs and brackets; the incredible downward pressure which transfers to Barney's feet, when he lifts the branch and tree, bulges out the bottom of the Rolls's floorboard to the ground, and the floor explodes when Barney heaves the tree onto the road from within the car. Kicking open the driver-side door, Cutter bounds from the Cadillac and drags the tree aside, clearing the way for him to use the road, and a moment later Naomi sees him speeding down the road, and she exclaims to the man who had asked why she had refused to let them follow Flynn.

"You'll all die up there," she says, looking at him and whispering in dread. She again faces the road, the elderly workers following her disquieting gaze, as Barney roars past the house in his battered Rolls Royce, the busted-out floor board sparking as it's dragged against the road, the damaged machine blaring out like a wounded monster from hell. Everyone gapes at the demonic appearance of Barney, who looks neither left nor right, only straight ahead in the direction his son is racing: the cave atop the hill. Yielding to Naomi's wiser judgment and cowering back from the road and from the view of Barney, "Then, who can save Sarah and Flynn, Naomi?" one of the old men asks, adding. "The National Guard? Can they come from town and save Sarah and Flynn in time?"

"Not even a thousand like the guardsmen can stop Barney if Satan is with that man, and Barney has the full power of Satan in him now."

"Then, who can save them, Naomi?" one of the women asks.

They follow Naomi's sights to a wrathful Caleb, who stands there—a few feet away—looking up at the lifeless body of his father, the rifle that Flynn had tossed to him and he had refused to catch still lying on the ground at his feet. Snaking up from behind the truck, Hank gets off a shot at the porch dwellers, then ducks back out of sight. The old people do exactly what old Hank wants: they all open up on him at once, their bullets flying everywhere, striking the trees, the ground and the Dodge truck, filling it with holes, flattening the tires, blasting off the truck's antenna, knocking out the headlights and shattering every piece of glass that the old vehicle had left on it. One by one, the workers run out of bullets. Laughing, Hank stands up and takes careful aim at Caleb, who continues standing there in a daze-like state, suffering up at his father's body, the workers at the house calling to him, begging him to run. With their ammunition depleted, Naomi, with that heavy skillet again, in her hand, charges off the porch at Hank.

"I ain't gonna let you kill my baby," she cries, as the men and woman scream for her to come back, and the children—peeking out the window from within the relative safety of the house—also cry for her to stop.

Hank aims at Naomi's heart, as she runs by Caleb toward him, and she steps on one of those guns that were tossed to Flynn by the workers and falls just as Hank fires; the bullet strikes her in her shoulder, knocking her face-down on the ground in gut-gripping pain. Hank then leers at Caleb, who turns away from the cross and looks down at Naomi bleeding on the ground a few feet away. Henry's boy turns his enraged sights on Hank, who is suddenly terrified as much as he's ever been of anyone in his life; he feels as if he's a mouse against a lion; and utters a desperate, spluttering bluff: "Kiss your black ass goodbye, Sambo," he says, trembling, looking through his rifle sights at Caleb.

Then—from around him—Hank hears the sounds of grumbling, human voices, and out of the darkness and the trees swarms the search party, hundreds of them, encircling him and all targeting the old Klansman with their eyes, their anger and with their weapons. Led by a sobbing Amos, they gaze up at the cross and at Henry, the elder field hands on the porch, all pointing to the cross to make sure everyone sees what the madmen have done to Henry. Then they point at Hank. Collins—his chest medically wrapped and his arm in a sling, Ruby and Pauline—Collins's wife and his grieving daughter, as well as Earlene—Carrie and Bruce's devastated child are among the search party. Dessen is there with his foreman Krause and many of Dessen's coverall-wearing factory workers have gladly given their time to join the search for Caleb; in oneness of purpose, the outraged search party stands there as if waiting for a pin to drop in order to rush upon Hank and beat him to death. Then Hank notices even more of the town's people arriving: a line of headlights flashing by the downed tree that had fallen on Barney's Rolls Royce and he had pulled to the side of the road. To make matters worse for the old Klansman—as those vehicles close in on the house—he can clearly see that the motorcars, the horse-drawn wagons behind the cars, are crammed with Cutterville's racially mixed citizens and Hank knows—like the search party before him, the ones coming down the road, are not coming to save him but to save Caleb. Hank turns his sights back on the search party. With everyone's outraged eyes fixed on him, it seems to Hank that all of mankind has deserted him.

MacDonnell, having known of the search for Caleb, and having beaten the out-of-town reporters to the story—as usual—is busy snapping pictures of Henry with his camera and the enraged wall of humans about the cross. Leaving the porch, Sarah's elderly workers join up with the new arrivals. Naomi is helped off the ground by several of the women who stand guard around her and defiantly yell at Hank, daring him to shoot, as he pans his rifle from them, to Caleb, to the angry search party and back again, not knowing which way to turn next, as the late arrivals from town spring out of their vehicles and join the others against him.

"Ahhh!" cries Essie Mae, as she leaves the house after having been one of those relieved of her duty of guarding those captured, bound

Klansmen. Now she stands on the porch wailing up at Henry's body and the cross, totally crushed, and she screams, "I thought I despised you, Henry Brooks. I'm so sorry! God, who did this to him?" She follows the crowd's sights to Hank. "You! You did this to him! Ahhh!" she bellows charging toward Hank.

The pin has dropped, and in oneness, the crowd rushes Hank, but suddenly, the ground shakes, the windows in the house crack and the modest dwelling sways, sending the children inside screaming out the door and into the arms of their parents. The captured Klansmen, with their hands tied behind them, along with those guarding them, run from the house and sit on the ground under the guns of Sarah's elderly workers, everyone waiting as the quaking stops. Even with the trembling earth and the dread of it by others, one of those in the crowd is so enraged over the killing of Henry that he hardly felt the earth shaking under his feet. He's Edwin, the black friend of Henry who pleaded for him not to return to the house alone, that Henry's dependency on God as a backup would mean nothing to the evil Klansmen and that Henry would surely die. Edwin sets his eyes of rage in old Hank and shrieks, "You're a dead man, Hank! A dead man! I'm going to tear you apart with my bare hands for what you did to that good man!" He sees Henry's chickens running about the land and adds, "And I'm going to feed you to his chickens!"

Naomi cries aloud to the multitude, her good arm raised, as she glances about and stops them. "Hank's punishment has been decided by Someone Whose hands are far larger than ours," she tells them. "Someone Who holds the entire world in His palm."

"God," whispers one of Miller's white church members, some of which are still arriving and gazing down at Miller's body, then at Metcalfe's kneeling corpse at the foot of the cross, then up at the cross at Henry, and gasping.

With the standoff between Hank and the crowd, and with Caleb standing in silence staring up at his father, a white man from Millar's church—in the midst of the others, while keeping an eye on Hank, walks up to Naomi and asks, "Are you talking about God, the real God, Naomi, and when you say 'His hands,' will we finally be able to see Him?"

Everyone listens for the answers with uneasy expectation, and when she fails to answer the man, they follow her sights to the heaven in mystification.

"They're all nuts," whispers the plant foreman Krause to Dessen.

"Are you so sure, Krause?" Dessen asks, watching the sky. Krause's eyes open wide, when he also sees that the moon has turned turquoise blue, and a wave of blue light is streaming from it; Krause staggers back, as do many amid the astonished crowd, as one-by-one they contemplate the moon. Hank's sights are also glued to the blue, pulsating light as it reaches the earth and sends the shadow of the cross and that of Henry's limp body quivering over the lawn to Caleb, where it lingers at the sorrowful boy's feet. Hank's mouth drops open. He and the others watch as the light wraps itself around Caleb with the speed of a whirlwind as had the wind around Sarah on the ship. Then, out of the dark beyond the blue beam, a raven soars into the spinning light with Caleb and hovers over his head. A deafening silence falls over the stunned crowd, as the raven changes from pure black to one with a whitened wing, then glides, out of the blue vortex and through the sky, where it settles atop the cross above Henry's head.

Earlene sobs out of control, one of the black women holding her close and sobbing with her. Earlene begins to pray. Still within that blue whirlpool of silent air, Caleb slowly turns and faces Hank, and immediately the spinning world of light and wind about him vanishes. Hank turns gray with fear and steps back when Caleb approaches him, closing the forty or so yards between them. With the rifle squeezed tightly in his hands, the elderly Klansman quakes in horror, the workers and spectators look at Naomi, their eyes asking her what they should do, but she just watches Caleb with her own uncertainties.

"Go ahead and shoot," Caleb tells Hank, less than thirty feet away from the petrified Klansman now. Caleb stops and points at Henry. "You can't hurt me. You've already killed my life."

As the crowd groans in horror, some making the sign of the cross, others praying, some on their knees, others standing and moving angrily toward Hank, once more Naomi waves then off and tells them that Caleb alone has to find his way to the cross through or over Hank, just one of several obstacles Henry's boy must now face, and the crowd remains silent and still, afraid after that.

When Caleb continues approaching him, Hank—driven by his all-consuming fear—fires point blank at Caleb, and when he does, everyone wails in dread. At the moment Hank fires that weapon, Naomi's head jerks backward, and, astonishingly, the mystery woman's eyes follow the red-glowing, spinning bullet's flight as if it were traveling in slow motion at Caleb. Then, just before the bullet strikes him, from out of the night sky, a black blur of thousands of ravens swoop between the bullet and Caleb; the red-glowing projectile penetrates the ravens' feathery mass of oneness, and it explodes through them and into Caleb's heart, the impact blasting the back birds and their feathers skyward and staggering Caleb backwards. The crowd—shocked beyond words or tears—watch with open mouths as the glossy, dark bird feathers—accompanied by thunder and lightning—rise skyward and then fall back down from the heaven as an inky-black rain, pounding against the land, a black rain which washes over the blood of Henry and Metcalfe and over all those who are there, and gives birth to a single rose, a rose that is pure white from its petals to its thornless black stem, wiggling up out of the ground, causing Essie Mae to whisper within:

It's true. The color that is truly white springs from the black rain. I am that which is near-white, which springs from that which was black.

A gawking Hank watches as the white rose continues rising from the blood flowing between the kneeling body of Metcalfe and that of Henry's on his cross. The white-winged raven caws, looks about the crowd and flies through the dark rain of night and is gone.

"I shot you, saw you bleed!" Hank shrills to Caleb who—once again—approaches him, the black rain lacing itself down Caleb's body, washing away the blood from his wounds, and healing him, the crowd completely alarmed and dumbfounded, Hank nearly going down on one knee, as he trembles, while backing away from Caleb. "You should be dead!" The old Klansman looks from Caleb to the darkened sky of rain and then at the crowd. "You all saw it," he sobs. "Caleb should be dead, and all of this that's happening isn't real; tell me we're all having the same nightmare." Hank drops his rifle: "What in God's name are you, Caleb Brooks?" he exclaims, his knees shaking, the crowd sobbing out of control, afraid of everything and of everybody now, including of Caleb. "Show me your chest, Caleb Brooks," yells Hank. "Show me that you have a wound there where there was none before, so that I will know you are not from Satan and that I was wrong to try and kill you, so that I can ask God fer fergiveness befer I die at your hand."

Caleb lifts his shirt, revealing his golden chest. "There is no wound," he tells Hank. "You ask who I am. I am not even worthy enough to be compared to Jesus in any way whatsoever. I am the person who will remove your clothes and do to you what you've done to Papa," He pounces on Hank, ripping off his shirt and knocking him down. Grappling at the old man's legs, Caleb pulls off Hank's shoes and socks, slapping the pleading, sobbing man when he tries to fight back, kicking and screaming. Hank's trousers and shorts are torn off next. Hank bellows, "My privacy! Don't shame me by letting them see my thing! My thing! My small thing!"

In the pouring, coal-black rain, Caleb lifts the naked man face-up over his head, the rain pounding into Hank's nostrils, into his ears and down his open mouth, gagging him; as Caleb carries the frightened screamer to Henry's picket fence, ready to impale him onto the sharp points of wood, a half dozen whites—who were border-line Klansmen and have come from Cutterville and feel that Hank hasn't done half of the things that he's accused of doing and are not sure he had a hand in murdering Henry, are now horrified at the thought of the man they've known all of their lives being brutally slaughtered that way, against the fence; those terrified whites look about for a place to run and hide, so afraid are they of Caleb now, feeling that next he'll be doing the same thing to them.

Some blacks are also afraid, afraid that Caleb will not kill Hank outright and thus, by not doing so, let the Klan off the hook to continue killing them at will. No longer able to control of his bladder, Hank's urine arches upwards from him, and he attempts to impede it by covering his groin with his flailing hands. Just when Caleb is about to hurl Hank onto a horrific death, the wind howls up through the hole in Henry's crotch and out of his mouth, creating an alien sound, freezing Caleb on the spot, as he listens to the roaring vibrations rolling across his beloved father's wind-blown lips, garbled sounds which Caleb seems to understand, sounds which cause the crowd to shutter in near panic. The wind softens to a breeze and the reverberation from Henry's lips is heard no more. As Hank gawks down at him, Caleb looks up at the petrified white man.

"I'm not going to kill you, Hank," he tells the Klansman, to the seeming relief of Dessen.

"You ain't?" Hank asks, even more afraid now. "Why, Caleb? I killed your pa, and now you want me to live." Hank sobs. "Is it for a worse punishment to come?"

"If this runaway hatred of people, of Catholics, coloreds and Jews is

686

to end in this world," Caleb begins and then lowers Hank to the ground, and waits, as Dessen lifts his hand and wishes to speak to the people.

"If Caleb kills Hank," Dessen takes up the slack and tells the crowd, going on, "it would only cause more of those who hate to murder more of us."

Caleb looks over at Dessen with surprise and admiration that the Jewish man—besides him—had actually heard and had understood Henry's message.

Caleb then looks at Hank. "And yes, Hank," he tells the trembling old Klansman, "a more terrible punishment awaits you, you who would have raped a dying, pregnant woman . . ." The few, doubtful whites who have championed Hank's cause stop whispering among themselves and listen, with shame as Caleb goes on, enumerating Hank's crimes against humanity: ". . . You kicked her! Kicked her in her womb where she carried her child and would have killed her newborn! You helped murder those school kids long ago, brutally raped and burned them, you who once held a respected professorship and position in life to heal the hatred, yet chased down Billy Joe and Claretta on their wedding night, when Dane yelled, 'Let's get her!' And you, old man, added, 'And fuck the shit out of the love of Caleb's life. Claretta, here we come!' "

Caleb looks up at his father. "And it was your hands that nailed Papa to that cross, mutilated his body with that godless sign, suggesting that God and Jesus didn't reign over His people, that He hated them instead, because they were only niggers with money." Yes, old man, I have to believe with all of my heart that you will face something that no one would wish on a dog, but you are a snake, and I am finished with you."

"Yes! It's all true," says Hank. "How did you know? How did you know, Caleb? How in God's name did you know? That and more. It's all true! What you said about me. But Barney, he knows things too. Like you! He does, Caleb! he knows! Barney! He said God does hate them and that Jesus didn't reign over them folk. That the Bible and every thing . . . that it's all a lie."

The supporters of Hank now look at each other and sink to their knees and cry.

In that continuous downpour, someone looks up at the cross. "My God!"

On the board that is affixed into Henry's skull, the words damning him are slowly being washed away by the black rain and are being replaced with the letters "J.N.R.J."

"What does it mean, Naomi?" someone calls to her. "Those letters?"

Naomi—now nearly as divested of her powers as she will ever be—turns to Caleb and asks, "Do you know, Caleb?"

"Jesus of Nazareth reigneth over the Jews," Caleb says as if the age-long truth is written before his eyes for him to read. "The black Jews, even now, roam the African desert to welcome all of mankind home."

Joyously Naomi begins clapping her hands together.

Impossible as it may seem, after all that has happened, the rain, the ravens, the bullet—which Caleb feels missed him, even the letters on the cross is not imperial proof for Caleb's logical mind. In a world where time starts and ends each day and all things in between, and the sun and moon, winter, summer and fall depends on time, it's impossible for him to see how God can be timeless, without a beginning and an end and thus, impossible for Caleb Brook to believe in God, at least to understand the meaning of God. Was it not all of this talk of God that almost made him kill his friend? ponders Caleb, and took away the life of his father?

Naomi faces him: "It will be a thousand times more difficult for you to travel this road ahead of you, son, than it was for Apostle Paul over his entire life, as he passed through hell on his journey into night, before seeing the Light and trying to convert the heathens of this world to Christianity."

It suddenly stops raining, and an aurora borealis takes its place across the sky, the bands of vibrating, swishing colors—in rapid succession—ripple through the heavens, and many among the crowd prostrate themselves before the cross and groan, asking God to forgive them. Those who had run back toward Cutterville, in fear of Caleb, and had lingered at the edge of the treeline to watch and listen, return and drop onto their bellies all about the cross, as well, a cross washed clean by the rain and standing in all of its glory, a cross representing not the man Henry nailed to it, but Jesus who died on it to save the world. Aghast, MacDonnell manages to keep snapping pictures, as Hank plummets to his knees, his head low, his sobs heard around the world. Even Dessen's factory supervisor Krause prostrates himself, as Hank fearfully eyes Caleb and sobs in fear.

"Let me remain here, Caleb, so that I can repent and be a better person. Here, Caleb with you and these others."

Naomi targets in on Hank. "Now you want to repent, after what you see as a miracle from God. It's because of people like you that Jesus refused to make miracles as often as He might have, for as I've said it before, even Adolf Hitler, if he were alive and here this night, would genuflect before our Lord. You are not wanted here, Hank," she tells him.

Hank gets to his feet and stumbles over to her, his hands outstretched in sorrow, many in the crowd who know him saying "But for this night and God, there go I." Naomi leads the naked man away by his hand, while he covers his manhood with the other, Adam being cast out of the little Garden of Paradise. Naomi guides him among those prostrate, frightened souls from Cutterville, and as Hank gawks down at the sight of his old friends, stunned that they no longer wish to even look up at him or admit that they once knew him, Naomi says:

"You are lower than those who once worshiped the snake and whose faces are now to the ground before God, and you will beg to be permitted to dig in the dirt with your nose like a pig in order to escape what lies before of you."

"Kill me, then!" Hank cries again to Naomi, and then—with teary, wide eyes—he looks about at those few in the crowd who do gaze upon him and his nakedness, and all of his false pride leaves him, and he removes his hand from his crotch, clasps his finger together in prayer, humbly exposing himself for all to see that he's a changed man, as he begs, "I want to die rather than face this unknown that you Caleb and even the Jew knows what's coming to me."

Stopping in the midst of the prone masses, Naomi leers at Hank. " 'Even the Jew,' you dare say, even now, as if Jews are so low in the design of things that you, who are the lowest of low, speak of them that way?" she nudges him on his way. "You haven't learned a thing. Kill you?" she exclaims. "You won't pass from this world so easily, Sir," she tells Hank, as he stops and looks at her, sobbing, as she continues to lambaste him. "No person will offer you food or drink, and as you did to Henry with that animal of yours, stray dogs will crew at your exposed heel bone, and flies will feed upon your rotting flesh, and you will live and suffer through this punishment for a hundred and ten years, and reek of a foul odor to signal your approach to all God-loving people on this earth, that they may flee from you and your corrupt soul."

Hank wails, searching about for sympathy, his tears flooding down his cheeks, and finding no pity from the crowd, he refocuses on Naomi with the eyes of his childhood years. "Stop crying," she tells him, "and don't look at me so sad-eyed, 'cause it won't help. This you have brought on yourself." Hank hobbles away and continues sobbing deep into the woods with the bullets lodged in his ankle, and already the flies are invading his open wound and flesh. Once the elderly Klansman's lamenting voice fades in the distance, two of Sarah's workers spot a petrified Marcus hiding behind the lawn tree, and they chase after him. The ten-year-old boy runs screaming into Naomi's open arms and clings to her waist, but Naomi's eyes fill with tears and she shakes her head at him. She knows that this is Marcus's time to spiritually live or die and that what awaits him is that he will also be banned from the community of man and will walk with Satan and Hank, where he will stand by as the ghost of tomorrow—air thin—and witness the burning, tortured, raped deaths of young children across the world throughout all eternity, if no one saves him this very night, a punishment even greater than that of old Hank it seems.

"It's not up to me now to save you, Marcus," she says, as he tearfully gazes up at her, and at the angry crowd, not only unwilling to offer him unquestioned love, because they know him not, but also unwilling to let him live a moment more for his part in Henry's death. "It's up to Caleb and only Caleb, now, not me or this crowd," Naomi tells the frightened, young boy. Her tears freely flow when she sees the little boy's teeth chatter against one another in his all-consuming panic attack and god-awful fear. He looks over at Caleb and his small shoulders droop. His anguished look of despair tells Caleb that the young boy feels that he, Caleb, will kill him. Marcus whirls about and clings to Naomi; she turns him back toward Caleb, while dreading the punishment Caleb might exact on the young boy who has lived in the sin of hatred all of his young life, and—at this moment—Caleb is not in a forgiving mood, not a second time, not after having just given Hank back his life, and Marcus, regardless of his age, is a Klansman at heart. Naomi gently nudges the boy at Caleb. And Marcus obediently walks quickly in that direction while crying with his thumb halfway in his mouth and between his small teeth, the way he must have sucked it when he was afraid and was in his mother's arms. As everyone watches with baited breath, Caleb stands there staring down at Marcus, as if saying "What do you want here with the evil that's in you through and through?" Marcus stops halfway there and turns his head and looks up at Henry and the cross, the weight of that awful scene and that of the world seeming to be too much for him, and his small, childish head tilts back, threatening to topple his youthful body backward and the boy off his feet. He squarely faces the cross.

"I'm sorry, Mister Henry! I didn't want them to hurt you. I'm sorry I'm evil and no longer an innocent child, the way my mom always told me I was. Then I met Burt. I'm so sorry, Mister Henry. Honest I am, Mister Caleb," he says turning back to Caleb. "Will you ask God to fergive Burt? He's the only friend I ever had, and I love him."

Fighting back the tears, Caleb opens his arms to Marcus, and the white boy runs shrieking into Caleb's safe embrace, and he clings to Caleb and Caleb to him, and all those who had cause to hate the boy marvel at the two of them, and from every man, woman and child there, tears flow like rain. Caleb runs his fingers through Marcus's hair, lifts the boy's salty-wet chin and consoles him: "You are yet a child, and can change," Caleb whispers, his tears flowing without end, as he gazes at his father and embraces Marcus all the more and then Caleb dries away Marcus's tears and guides him back into Naomi's open arms.

"Are we to be judged with the Klan?" Naomi tells the pursuers of Marcus. "You heard Caleb. This child's your brother! He needs only to be loved and his and our hearts will heal."

Whites and blacks put aside their weapons and cry with Marcus, holding onto him and onto each other, while sobbing up at the cross and at Henry. Caleb spots Reverend Miller's Bible on the ground, picks it up, tears the Good Book in half and scatters its pages into the wind. While she continues holding onto a still trembling Marcus, Naomi faces Caleb. "You have destroyed the Bible that you despise, Caleb Brooks; yet, it is the true Bible you must still save and cling to, as you did to this young child."

Wiping away his tears, Caleb asks, "What Bible, Naomi? Aren't they all the same, a way to enslave the many by the few, and just another political tool?"

"The true Bible lives in the minds of God's children," Naomi tells him, while pointing out sobbing members of Miller's church in the crowd. "Many who are like Marcus are, at this very moment, still under

Satan's spell in Cutterville and throughout this world. You must awaken the love in them all and—"

"Please, not now, Naomi. No talk of love. Tell that to Papa. Tell him how God loves him but still let him die this horrible death."

"Your tears, Caleb. They were meant to be. They're the healing waters of your soul, son . . . The flowers in God's garden need to feed on all of our tears; they are the salty fertilization of our lives and the cement of adoration to our Lord. Your gentle, loving father, the Winthrops, Claretta and B.J. are on the fast track to heaven and already have a place reserved for them to be with God, while the rest of the world will have to wait for Jesus to summons us to rise. And you must believe that and kill the resentment that still lives within you, and then destroy the evil that is Barney Cutter. Go and help Flynn before Barney kills him and the woman—as a child—you often thought of as your mother. Sarah, Caleb. Go and save Sarah, and yes, I said, 'to summon us to rise,' for I have lost all my powers and will have to die and be raised once more with everyone else at the end of time."

Dessen steps up to Caleb with a long-barreled revolver. "I've made lots of money in my time," he says, "but I never felt life was really worth living unless I had even more money . . . that is until now. I'll go with you, Caleb Brooks. This gun will stop an elephant."

"If Mister Dessen is going, so am I," says the plant foreman Krause, checking his pistol, as more of Dessen's factory workers step forward.

"Barney can't be killed with guns now, Brian," Naomi tells Dessen, while looking at a green glow atop the hill near the far-off cave.

"Why can't he be killed with a gun, Naomi, and if not by what and by whom?" Dressen asks.

"Barney is one with Satan and can only be destroyed by the flames of Love." She turns and gazes at Caleb and says, "The Spirit of God will show Caleb where this Holy Flame dwells."

"How can I leave him like this, Naomi?" Caleb asks, facing Henry and the cross. "How can I leave that trusting, kind man like this?" Caleb approaches his father's body. "I have to get him off of that thing. I have to and then I'll go help Flynn. He took his men with him, didn't he? Even when you told them not to follow him, some did, didn't they?"

"Henry is women's work, now, Caleb even as the body of our Lord was," Naomi tells him. "And that cross of shame is now sacred, as was the one Christ died on. Your work is to the living here on earth, and no, Caleb. Flynn went alone. I couldn't stop him to warn him about his father."

She gives a nod to the women, who tearfully climb into the truck and crowd about the cross and Henry's body. Working together, the weaker sex untie the ropes which hold the cross to the truck, and they lift that heavy cross and the man, lovingly called Henry, off the battered vehicle and into the passionate arms of scores of more females reaching up from about the truck and tenderly placeing the cross and Henry onto his green lawn, Henry's white chickens streaming onto the lawn and staring down at him. When MacDonnell refreshes his camera with film, Amos angrily snatches the instrument from him. "Have you no shame?" the black man asks.

"He's doing God's work," Naomi tells Amos. "The world needs to see these pictures in order to gladden their hearts and soften their hardened souls."

"I'm sorry, Mister Newsman," old Amos says, wiping away his tears of sorrow for his dead brother and Henry, while returning the camera to MacDonnell. The newsman looks into Amos's teary-eyed gaze, then around as if seeing colored people for the first time, then at the whites and blacks working together at the scene of love: the cross and Henry. Captivated by their deep transfixed eyes of remorse, the newspaper-owner-reporter wipes his eyes on his sleeve and resumes his task of taking pictures, as does the Northern newsmen. In spite of her shoulder wound, Naomi insists on personally removing the board and spikes from Henry's head and limbs. Caleb has listened to all of what Naomi has told him and the others about how Barney is protected by Satan and can't be killed by the gun, and—in spite of everything, and with absolutely no faith in a Divine intervention to protect him—he takes the only protection against the Klan that they understand and fear: a gun, Dessen's long-barreled revolver, and as the out-of-town reporters with their fancy cameras flash pictures of him, Caleb races up the hill with Dessen's revolver and is hoping against hope that he's not too late to save the lives of the two people he now loves more than his own life, Flynn and Sarah.

47

A Test of Faith

A quarter mile away from his father's house on the slopes overlooking Cutter Bridge, where Sarah had led Dane and Deputy Hammer, Caleb, sprinting along, is half insane in despair and—while having reflected compassion and indulgence for Marcus—however, now, as he runs, with deep-reaching anger, he plays into the hands of Satan and spews out his hatred of the world. "He believed in You. He loved You, and You let him die! Papa says no man can look upon Your face and live! You have no face, because You don't exist. Do You hear me! Show me Your face, not the Northern Lights, not a seemingly growing moon, which science will eventually explain away. Your face. Show me that You truly loved papa, if You are alive and real!"

Suddenly Caleb trips—losing the revolver—and falls into that deep pit of firethorns and jimson plants which almost claimed Hammer. Landing on the bottom, Caleb becomes hopelessly entangled within the thorny growth.

"Satan is proud of you," a voice calls down to him, "Even Flynn, with Barney's blood in him, and with reason to hate God after suffering as a child from that painful crown, has not given the one called God as much heartache as you have, Caleb. Don't struggle, I'm here to help."

Looking up, Caleb draws back in repulsion when he sees the source of the voice against that dark sky: Barney's bird-creature mother, hovering a few feet off the ground and glowing with the smell of death about her, as she gazes down into the unassailable hole at him and sending down flying bits of grass, weeds and dust from those powerful beating wings. She's now aging fast and covered with filthy, graying and dying, limp feathers.

"What are you?" the frightened boy asks, drawing back even more from the sight of her, the thorns piercing his flesh, and causing his arms, sides and legs to bleed.

"I'm Barney's mother, the messenger of Lucifer, and I've been sent to help you out of the trap where your father's God has placed you, because you have challenged Him, and He wants you dead. Barney is near. Listen to me, Caleb, and join my son and hate God. Because Henry failed to raise you to be humble and to love Him, God will torture your father for an eternity."

"Son," Henry's voice is suddenly heard, infuriating the bird woman, "you were raised to love God, and God has made your road of the cross more difficult for you after my dying in your place so that you can fight Satan head on. You have been baptized in the thorns that now embrace you and draw out your blood, even as Flynn felt their pain as a child. Now, both of you have been touched by this despised symbol of man's injustice to man, which scarred the body of our Lord. Use those painful thorns as your shield and your cross and stay with my counsel. Don't listen to this pleasure-causing creature with her lips of corruption and damnation."

"Papa!" cries Caleb looking about the pit and the sky for his father and totally confused.

"Is he real, Caleb?" asks the bird woman. "Can you see him, your father or God, as you can see me, the proof that I and my master Lucifer exist and are real?"

"Where are you, Papa?" Caleb asks, going on. "Has He hurt you? God. Is He real?"

"Where is your faith, Caleb?" Henry's voice asks.

"I don't know, Papa. If God is with you, tell Him to let you come back to me, the way Lazarus was brought back from the dead, by Jesus, after he was buried. You've been dead less than an hour. Surely God or Jesus will send you back for Flynn and Sarah's sake if not for mine."

"No one ever wants to return, Caleb, to leave the jungles of warmth and plenty, where the fruit and flowers never cease to bloom, and the lions lie down with the sheep, and no man hates another. Earth is a place steeped with the blood of embodied souls who kill to conquer the land and enslave their brothers and sisters; then, after gaining the whole world, the conquerors wait for the cold hand of death to end their misery, and all that they possess and rule is gone in the blinking of the eye for others of their kind to seize upon and continue the carnage. That's why the angels in Heaven marvel at Naomi, who came into the world for you and Flynn and remains there still, even now."

"The hell with him, Caleb," hisses the bird woman. "And the hell with God! Do you see what He and Satan did to me? God will do the same to you and Flynn as well. God let Satan turn me into this goddamn thing that smells like piss, and Satan delays in reversing. Please, Caleb, listen to me, so we both can get revenge on God, who wanted so much for you to love Him, you and Flynn, who are the symbol of the human race's hope to Him before He sends Jesus once more to descend on Judgment Day; but now the two of you can rule this world under Barney and Satan and have all the sex and—"

A bolt of lightning strikes the bird woman, exploding her, scattering her body into fiery particles of flesh, and then into dust. At the cave, a stone's throw away, pulling and jerking on the gate, Flynn sees the explosion and is immediately covered with the jimson and firethorn dust, which was blown out of the pit, the drug dust also now covering Caleb in that deep hole of hell. Wrapped painfully in the grips of the thorns, Caleb can only watch the burning, thunderbolt-struck, dusty remains of Mrs. Cutter's body, as they fall into the hole around him; sizzling and crackling, as her dusty body parts are consumed by the fire from heaven, the wailing female's face, mouth, arms and hands—still intact—reaching and quivering out of the flames, toward Caleb before she is finally disintegrated into nothingness. Then a voice like thunder speaks, causing the world to quake:

"Pride has blinded you to the truth, Caleb Brooks." Then, from the sky, a Light descends and X rays itself right through Caleb's body. He looks down at his hands, at his torso and at his legs and at his feet, and he would rather have been struck by lightning and rendered dead than to see what is before his eyes: bones! He's nothing but a white-bone skeleton. Terrorized, he squeezes his eyes shut against the blinding X-ray Light and then feels himself floating out of the pit and toward the Source of the terrifying glow; trembling before Its pulsating might, he's again confronted by an earth-shaking voice. "You dared ask to see the face of your God, Caleb Brooks? Then look upon my face and die; for no man of sinful pride such as you looks upon the face of his God and lives."

A serene-looking, manly Figure begins forming in the Light, devastating Caleb with mind-crushing consternation, his invisible heart pounding against his fleshless rib cage, his mind spinning, not an eyelash can he blink, nor a limb of bones can he move. "Jesus?" he asks. "Are you Jesus, the Light of the world?"

"Out of your own mouth you have said it, my brother. I am that I am, The Lamb of God."

"Then, God . . . Jesus . . . Is there no God besides You?" he asks the Holy Figure, still in the process of developing.

"He is in Me and I am in Him. In His mercy, He permits you to see Him through Me, so that you may not die for looking upon His divine Presence while mired in your sin of conceit. You were born to fulfill a mission, Caleb Brooks. Have you done so?"

"My God! My God!" Caleb cries aloud. "I've changed my mind. I don't want to see God's face or Yours. I know now that You are Who and What Papa and Flynn say You are, all good and deserving of all my love. Papa raised me the best he could, so don't blame him," Caleb pleads and then goes on but in a whisper to the developing image of God in Christ, whom he continues to see, even with his eyes closed. "Flynn and I love Papa. Do what you want with me, a sinner for not believing, but please, God, in Jesus' name, don't hurt Flynn or Papa anymore than the Klan have already done, the way Barney's mother said You would."

"God has shown me His boundless love, son," Henry's voice is, again, heard. "Heaven's door is held wide for the just, Caleb, but for the sinners you were born, not for me. You, with more honor in you than dishonor, were a test of man's will against Satan. You spoke not out of pity for yourself, but out of your love of Flynn, and for the sickly misguided Klan truck driver who cried out for you not to kill him because he had a family to care for, and you opened your arms and heart to Marcus, and for Lilly, Jayne, Benny and me. He has heard your cry. Listen and you will hear His Sacred Heart of Love beating for you and for us all and your reward will outshine that of King Solomon."

Caleb's own heart begins to reappear, and all of those down the hill around Henry's body and the cross stand speechless looking up at the distant hilltop that is now all aglow in the forever-changing Light, and they cover their eyes and ears against the sound of Christ's beating heart and run here and there wailing and pleading in alarm.

Even in Cutterville, those who had remained in town—be they white or black, and had refused to join in the search for Caleb and, instead, held onto their loathing, be it racially motivated from whites, or steeped with jealousy from one's own kind, such as in the case of blacks who say their's is not jealousy and instead lie to themselves by saying that Caleb is not a gift from God, because, to them, only a white man can be so honored—are also hearing Christ's heart, from Sue Ann's bar, from the Main Street stores, from the factory and, once again, from the church of snakes. Whites join those fleeing from Harris's place of worship—all of those who had remained behind to pray—everyone running with their hands covering their ears, begging for forgiveness, but only a few of them, including both the whites and the blacks, beg for the forgiveness for hating their neighbors, because they know not who their neighbors are.

On the hill of Light, Caleb continues speaking to the voice of his father.

"Will I ever be able to see God's face, Papa? I've sinned so badly."

"God's face and love is everywhere, Caleb. You've listened without hearing and looked without seeing. You've but to open your eyes to see the loving face of God in all of us."

Caleb opens his eyes and looks into the face of Flynn, who is tearfully lying on his stomach and reaching into the pit toward him, the blonde boy's face, white, his eyes reflecting fear, his hands trembling under the changing indigo Light. Caleb stares at his own golden-tanned hands, then at his torso and at his legs. Once again he has a complete body, skin over muscle and bones and made whole. He gazes about. The thorny branches have been lifted from him and now lie scattered on the ground and dead at his feet. Again, he looks up at Flynn and stretches out his hand to his friend and is pulled from the pit of hell. Awash under the Light, both boys are afraid and hardly able to speak.

"Caleb what was that thing I saw flying over that hole and talking to you?"

"Then you also saw it," Caleb says, sinking to the ground and gasping for his breath.

"Yes, but, my God, Caleb, what was it?"

"It said she was your grandmother, Flynn. She and Barney are possessed by Satan."

"Jesus, Caleb. What about me? My God. What does that mean when it comes to me?"

Caleb is so distraught and so drained that he sits there, unable to rise. When Flynn sees Caleb ready to collapse onto his back, all worries about himself disappear, and as he had when he took Caleb from Naomi's arms in the barn, and then carried him as a baby, Flynn helps Caleb to his feet and lifts him into his arms. Struggling, he carries Caleb across the hill to the cave, both covered with the jimson and firethorn dust. As Flynn carries Caleb, the powdered drugs are blown off of them by a prevailing wind which forms a vortex about them and in a flash the vortex is gone, along with the drug dust, neither knowing that a miracle from heaven has made them immune from the effects of the drugs. Exhausted, Flynn stumbles, sending him and Caleb tumbling to the ground within a few feet of the cave. Remaining where they fall and catching their breath, they look back at the skyward Light, which turns into a shooting star and fades into space. Both face the cave. "It's locked. The cave gate," says Flynn, checking his revolver. "We can't get in. Mother is in terrible danger." Flynn follows Caleb's gaze to another side of the hill, then looks at Caleb. "The rifle, Caleb. I gave it to you. Where is it?"

"I didn't bring it and also lost the revolver I had," Caleb says, gazing at the sky. "Come on. I know another way into the cave. Hurry!"

"Jesus," Flynn whispers, terribly afraid, while looking back at the sky, as well, as they race up the hill and away from the cave entrance. "Were you looking at God, Caleb, when I saw you gazing at the sky from that hole?"

Caleb glances about as they run. "Not now, Flynn. I feel him all around us."

"Feel whom?"

"The devil. Your father is here."

"He is?" Flynn asks, looking about in the dark. "Then, Naomi . . . why hasn't she sent our workers, Mister Dessen and the others? I have only this pistol, Caleb. How will we defend ourselves if you think my father is from hell and is here?"

"Naomi says that guns or a thousand men won't stop him, but Dane and Hammer aren't like your father, not bulletproof, and they're the ones who have your mother; so hold onto that gun of yours." Both boys continue running now with an eye out for Barney.

"If Father can't be stopped with a gun," asks Flynn, close behind Caleb, "Then how?"

"Naomi said love. That we should fight Barney with love. Just keep running, Flynn. I don't know what she means either."

They hold onto the other's hand to steady themselves as they run over rocky ground and now arrive at their destination. With Caleb taking the lead, they slide through a tight crevice in a little-known, spring-diminished, muddy hill. Then, out of the darkness behind them, from a section of hillside trees, steps Colonel Cutter—wearing Hitler's coat—his red eyes fixed on them as they slip into the opening. Barney looks at the mud and running water, and then at his coat, a coat that is his covenant to Hitler and to Satan to carry on that madman's work, and Barney doesn't want to dirty it. He turns his sights on the locked cave gate and crosses over the grade and stands before it. A thick cloud covers the face of the moon, and Flynn's father rips the entire gate off of its hinges and hurls gate hinges and all off of the hill.

Below the hill, Naomi and the women having removed Henry's body from the cross and wrapped it in swaddling cloth, are gently carrying his remains to the house, when they see the cave's gate sailing through the sky and watch as it crashes into one of Henry's cotton fields, just missing the women and the cross. The gate then burst into flames, scattering the nearby workers, but not Naomi; her arms crossed over her chest, her eyes squinting, she stands her ground, and—as Henry's body is hurried into the house—she gazes up at the hill and says, "Is that all you've got? Then the boys have a chance, Satan. They have a chance."

Deep within the cave and high on a ledge, a muddy Caleb and Flynn lie on their stomachs and contemplate their chances, as they look through a fissure down a vertical wall of granite to the lower, cold, lamp-lit large chamber.

"Thank God, Caleb," whispers Flynn. "She's alive."

They can clearly see Sarah, Hammer and Dane, however, with the bats darting and sweeping about in alarm because the lantern lights now block their way out into the night and confuse them, and with the creatures' high-pitch shrills echoing off the cave walls, it's impossible to hear what Sarah and her jailers are saying. Then, from out of the darkness, a bat darts at Flynn, and he leaps to his muddy feet sending him sliding backward on the slippery edge, and cascading rocks off the ledge ahead of him as he falls, and seemingly following the rocks to his death down into the dark depths below. Flynn, however, manages to somehow reach out to Caleb's out-stretched hand while Caleb remains on his stomach, anchoring himself to the fissure wall with his right hand and grabs onto Flynn's wrist, with the other just as Flynn's head drops below the ridge line, violently jerking Caleb forward, but Henry's boy's powerful grip holds to the bedrock, and he pulls Flynn to safety. Hugging the solid ground once more and gasping, Flynn is ready to explode with a series of expletives, which always follows a shocking experience, but Caleb presses his finger against his lips and then looks through the opening into the chamber and sees Hammer looking up into the dark at their position.

"What the hell was that?" the deputy asks. "That sound, like falling rocks?"

"Just them bats," Dane remarks, kissing a handful of money. "Now shut up and help me pack this stuff back in the bag and let's get the hell out of here."

"Bats my white ass," hisses the frightened deputy. "If it's bats they must be awfully big. I bet it's that tar baby Caleb Brooks. It must be Caleb. He's alive. I can feel it." Hammer gawks about. "The hell with packing one damn bag! I don't give a good goddamn about them other guys. I fought against that nigger, and I know what he's like from the way he took me down. I'm getting my share and getting the hell out of here while I can."

Above the fray, while Flynn and Caleb are on the move again, making their way down the darkened ledge leading to the chamber, Hammer places his gun on the open bag of money, then he grabs a seventy-pound bag of cash, and three more and staggers under the weight. He sees Sarah racing for his revolver, but refuses to drop the bags of cash, and weighted down with the money, he lumbers to his weapon. Sarah reaches it first, and she blasts him right through the unfilled portion of one of the money bags dangling over his stomach. The deputy lowers the baggage, looks at her in surprise and plops to the ground. Sarah drops the revolver and screams. On the ledge, Caleb and Flynn have heard the shot as they run, however they continue on their way down the narrow footpath, running faster now. There are no openings in the wall to look down on the chamber, where Dane has seized Sarah about her throat and is squeezing the life out of her. "You've always disrespected me, you bitch!" he exclaims, "treated me like I'm a goddamn, fucking tar-baby spade! And now you will help me carry all of this money out of here, or I will put a goddamn bullet in your goddamn head."

Sarah sees a monstrous figure looming up behind Dane; her blue eyes blink in disbelief, and she shrieks. Dane releases his hold on her, turns around, drops the gun and gags, as he stares into the insane eyes of a grotesque, chalky, discolored, red-eyed demon: Barney, a man turning into three things that he worships: an image of Hitler, Satan and himself. Barney wraps his fingers about Dane's neck and with one hand, lifts him up by his throat and holds him there kicking and gagging several feet off the ground.

Reaching into the one-eared Klansmen's pocket with his free hand, that hideous creature which was once Barney removes those three gold coins which Metcalfe had given to Dane and missing the coin that Flynn had given to Caleb, the one Dane had taken from Snodgress. Meanwhile, having backed herself in a corner with no way out, Sarah can only stand helplessly by and watch as Barney looks down at the coins and then at Dane.

"You violated my house and my son's room," exclaims Barney, slipping the coins safely into Hitler's leather coat pocket and going on. On the high ledge, the boys find another fissure and look down in pure panic at Barney, Dane and Sarah. While Sarah watches in repulsion and is absolutely frozen in fear, Dane—beginning to black out—holds onto Barney's arm of steel with both hands, trying to lessen the downward pressure, caused by his own body weight to his throat. Barney goes on. "For years you wanted to know why your old man killed himself." Laughing, Barney reaches into his deep pocket and retrieves that old photo, the photo which he showed Dane's father at the killing bridge, a photo which Dane's old man blew out his brains rather than let Dane and the world see. Posing in the old snapshot—taken in a Texas cotton field—is Dane's much-younger-looking father, standing between Amos and Andy with his arms lovingly about their shoulders. Old Amos was around thirty at the time, Andy twenty-five and Dane's father eighteen. Dane's white grandfather had had an off-and-on relationship with Amos and Andy's widowed mother, and it was from this lonely black woman's womb that Dane's father was born. Half-brothers to Dane's father, Amos and Andy have kept it a secret all of their lives.

"What in the hell's that?" asks Dane, hanging onto Barney's arm, bubbling out spit while he dangles for his life, Barney loosening his grip of death just enough for Dane to breathe and speak. While setting the one-eared man back on the ground. Dane's bulging eyes cannot escape their focus on the photo. "That's Pa!" squeals Dane. "He's got his arms around them coons, one of 'em we just killed. Why's pa hugging them motherfuckers!"

High up, the boys continue on the move, recklessly running down the slippery path and trying to reach Sarah in time, not knowing if she's now facing Barney.

"Your father hung those kids to the bridge with his own hands, Dane Tucker, but if he had his way, he would have killed every coon in town, because then he wouldn't have to be reminded of what he, himself, was every time he looked at one of those offsprings from the apes." Fully aware that Dane is a dead man and that she is next as well, unnoticed, Sarah inches away from Dane and Barney, as her husband continues. "Your father was a white-skinned nigger, Dane motherfucking Tucker! And that Andy nigger boy who Hammer killed and threw in the grave is your uncle, you half-white bastard."

"Noooo!" wails Dane, shaking his head, his eyes expanded to the fullest and his tongue hanging out. "Oh, nooo!" he bellows pounding his fists against his head. "I'm white! I can't be black! I'm as white as you."

Barney drops the photo, and as Dane gapes down and sobs at it, "Pa, oh, Pa!" Barney snaps his neck. Once Dane hits the ground, face down in the inch-deep water, Colonel Cutter moves in on a sobbing Sarah before she can escape from the chamber, his powerful hands targeting her throat.

"I could have made you queen of this world, Sarah, but you dirtied yourself with Henry, and now you must also die, you and that tar ball thing you call your son."

Stopping at another, but lower edge fissure, the boys look through it and see Barney slapping Sarah. "That bastard," exclaims Flynn. He whips out his revolver and fires, striking Barney in the back. Barney doesn't even flinch. He laughs at what amounts to a bee sting, and he looks about to locate the shooter. When he does, Sarah picks up Dane's gun and fires point bank into Barney's chest, and while Barney flinches from the direct impacts, he continues insanely laughing at Sarah now as well, and then he raises his arms and exclaims, "Thank You!"

Barney grins at a confused Sarah and exclaims. "Satan, Sarah. He's given me eternal life!" Dropping the gun, Sarah runs away, screeching for her life, but Barney reaches the exit first and blocks it with his mutated, enlarged body, forcing her to run this way and that with him laughing after her.

"Naomi's right. Guns won't kill him," Caleb says, holding his hand over Flynn's mouth, when Flynn attempts to yell down into the chamber at Barney. Caleb reaches out with his free hand and lowers Flynn's arm and the revolver and whispers, "You might even hit Sarah."

"Together," whispers a horrified Flynn, going on. "Do we have a chance? Do we, Caleb? Can the two of us alone bring down the devil and save mother?"

"We can try, okay?"

"Okay. But, how, Caleb, when you don't believe you're special? What chance do we have to go up against the devil? What can we use to stop him?"

"Flynn, I now believe I do have power, and as to what we can use to stop your father, I'll know it when I see it."

"See what, Caleb?"

"Love, Flynn. I'll know it when I see it. Naomi says only the flames of love would destroy your father. With it, we can take him down."

"Our friendship? You're saying the love we have for each other may work against him?"

"I think that's part of what she meant; now let's find the other part before he kills Sarah."

"Are you sure, Caleb! That's we can take him. That's my mother down there? Are you sure bullets won't hurt him? Maybe Mother missed. She's not a good shot."

"She shot him dead-on, and so did you. You heard your father, who's now playing cat and mouse and taking his time about going after Sarah. He said he has the power of Satan in him, and he does. I feel that power, even now, all around us. Can't you?"

Caleb races on ahead. Appalled, Flynn glares down at his father, eases the gun onto the foot trail and catches up to Caleb, both boys armed only with hope and their love for one another, as bats swoop into the chamber below them. The red-eyed, winged devils swarm about Sarah, darting and clipping her with their razor wings, and threatening to attack her with their bloodthirsty fangs, but stay far away from Barney, who continues his insane laughter. When the boys enter the passageway of lanterns, they hear Sarah's screams for help, and Flynn grabs hold of Caleb's arm, as they continue on the run.

"What are we going to do, Caleb," gasps Flynn. "Just run in circles looking for this unknown thing while Mother is killed?"

Flynn watches as Caleb suddenly stops and gazes down at the battered, red lantern, Naomi's voice ringing in his and Flynn's ears: *Barney can only be destroyed by the Flames of Love. God's Spirit will show Caleb where the Holy Flame dwells.* Flynn follows Caleb's gaze from the lantern to the can of kerosene, and Flynn nods, both boys knowing what to do.

704

A moment later, Sarah runs into the tunnel of lanterns and falls face down, the bats following her. However, movement is what attracted the hunters of blood, and when she remains motionless, the bats divert their attention from her to something stirring just beyond Sarah. In that moment of reprieve, Sarah sees the five-gallon kerosene can that Henry had purchased in her store to fill the cave lanterns. Instead of sitting upright, as it was when she and the Klansmen entered, it's now lying on its side, some of the clear fuel still spilling from it.

Unseen by her, Caleb is a stone's throw away behind her and at whom the bats are now streaking. He intuitively holds up the battered lantern, and immediately those wings of death swoop away from him. While holding onto that lantern, Caleb is suddenly visited by a vision of Chad dropping from the hay loft and knocking it out of Naomi's hand as she cradles him, Caleb, in her arms when he was a baby. Sarah's bloody cries end the eye-opener. She's is on her knees looking up, as Barney towers over her, his shadow independently moving behind him; a shadow with the horned head of Lucifer, wagging its tail as if that of a dog. At that moment, Sarah sees something over Barney's head: Flynn. He's on a fourteen-foot ledge above the chamber entrance and gripping a bucket with one hand, while pressing his finger against his lips, warning her to give no notice of him, as Barney taunts her.

"I guess you're not as beautiful as I once thought," he tells her, unaware that not only Flynn is watching him, but that Caleb is also scrutinizing him from afar. "I won't let you turn my son into some Catholic, nigger-loving freak, you bitch. I'll kill Flynn before I let him worship your God of peace, love and brotherhood."

Flynn is so upset with his father that it takes all of his control not to give away his position to Barney by acting sooner than Caleb wants him to.

"Beware, Barney," that demonic voice again makes itself heard. "Caleb is near and he has the power of God in him."

"Goodbye, Sarah Winthrop," Barney guardedly says, looking about for signs of Caleb, and then back at Sarah, "Because it seems, as they said, that your God has blessed Caleb, after all, I will save my strength to deal with him, not on killing you." Barney withdraws his .45 from his waist and takes dead aim at Sarah, Flynn looking to Caleb, knowing that their plan can't work unless Caleb is ready.

"Barney, asshole Cutter!" Barney hears Caleb yelling out of the dark distance at him.

Cutter withdraws the gun from Sarah's direction, and sets his eyes of fatality on Caleb, as he steps out of the distant pitch carrying the unlit lantern. Barney's evil expression turns uglier yet. "So we finally meet on your road to the cross, but your old man got there first, it seems, and now you will follow him screaming and kicking, you goddamn motherfucker." He glances at Sarah.

"Don't look at her, asshole," yells Caleb. "Your fight is with me, a man. Or are you someone who can only beat up on women?"

Barney looks back at Caleb. "You're going to be sorry your stupid mother ever pissed you out into this world."

Caleb glances at the lantern and it ignites. "You plan to kill me with that piss-ass light, boy?"

As Caleb steps closer and out of the shadows, the lantern's wick begins to glow brighter, to the sound of Naomi's voice, *Only the hands of a disciple can enliven the Eternal Flame as prophesied, Caleb Brooks.* And with those words, Caleb again looks at the wick and the flickering, yellow lantern light transforms itself into a blinding, sapphire flame. Perspiration immediately floods from Barney's face, his fear encompassing him, as he squints against the radiating energy.

He looks about as if for help. "Where is Flynn? I know he came in here with you. Flynn! I'm your father. Together we can defeat the Light! Satan, where are you?"

"Flynn's love is pure," says Caleb, giving Flynn a hurried look, then focusing on Barney, "And the two of us are more than equal to you and Satan."

"Father!" Barney calls out. "Help me destroy this manchild of God, who holds God's lightning rod in his hands, so that I might reclaim the love of my son."

The ground trembles, and the bats swarm out of the cave—regardless of the lanterns' lights that stopped them before—and into the night they fly. Then the devil shows his love for Barney by sending gravel and boulders tumbling from the ridges at Flynn and Caleb. Flynn doesn't know which way to turn or run and sets his faith and his gaze on Caleb, and not a pebble strikes the transfixed, blonde boy or his mother, whose gaze—like Flynn's—is fixed on Caleb, as the rocks and boulders thunder down from high directly at Henry's boy and Barney in a test of wills.

"Drop the lamp and run, boy!" hisses Barney, "or Satan will crush you."

"He will try," says Caleb.

Undaunted by the rocks impacting the ground around him, Caleb is now assured that God truly loves and protects him, even as Satan protects Barney, and when Caleb nods to him, Flynn, from the ridge, yells down to Sarah, "Move away from him, Mother!" As Sarah crawls away, Barney looks up at Flynn, who shouts at his father. "You killed my father!"

"I'm your father!" shrills Barney, quivering, with one eye on Flynn, the other on Caleb and the lantern.

"No!" Flynn shouts, "You're not my father! Henry was my father, whom I loved."

Caleb breaks into the conversation, "And it is the power of his love for Papa that drives the energy of this lamp, Barney asshole Cutter," yells Caleb. "Now, Flynn!" he calls. "Now!"

Flynn douses Barney with kerosene. In total horror, Barney looks back at Caleb then at the lantern, and screams, "Satan, show them your mightiness over them and God! The Light. They have His Spirit and His love!"

"I can't face the Light!" a demonic voice echoes through the tunnel, filling Sarah and Flynn with dread. "Run my son," the voice warns.

Caleb flings the lantern and Flynn ducks for cover, as does Sarah when Flynn yells for her to do so. Barney sees the lamp coming. He turns and flees, and as he does, the lantern strikes him in his back, and he erupts into a blinding ball of fire. Barney runs screaming down the tunnel and leaps through the cave entrance into the moonlight. Stumbling, as his flesh melts from his bones, he falls over the cliff and flails through the night sky high over the bridge. The search party—several miles away and below the hill on Henry's land—see a burning, flailing Barney streaking through the night air, just before his flaming body crash onto his ancestor's wooden structure of horror. The fuel-soaked bridge explodes twisting and groaning in excruciating pain as if some malevolent, living creature, indeed, abides therein, and as the bridge groans and twists, the souls of those murdered school children from years ago rise up freed from Satan's grip and soar with the angels into heaven's lobby of other waiting souls. Immediately after the children escape, the entire bridge drops onto the lower train tracks, taking a shrieking Barney with it. An even more horrendous explosion follows, seen far and wide, and the smell of Barney's burning flesh hangs heavy in the air, as millions of voices can be heard welcoming the lynched children.

The next morning, when the fire finally dies out, under a blue sky, and the firemen's hoses and warm rising sunshine, only ashes remain. Those three coins, which Barney had taken from Dane in order to return them to Flynn, are lying atop the ashes: tiny beads of fused, gold, walked upon by unaware firefighters and spectators; just so much dirt under their feet, gold, worthless to God and to man's mortal soul alike. Sarah, Flynn and Caleb stand at the cave entrance looking down at the destroyed bridge. They then walk hand in hand down the hill to Henry's land, where Naomi and the others await with open arms to welcome in a new day.

48

The Lion Is with God

Under yet another radiant, blue sky, Henry's bronze "coffin" or "wooden coat"—depending on which old-timer lovingly depicts it—enshrined with calla lilies, sits with its cover open in Shadow Grove's cemetery. Henry's body lies inside the white silk-lined casket facing the heavens as if a person of royalty. Sarah—dressed in black—gazes down at him through her tears. She's flanked by Caleb and Flynn, both boys wearing black suits, white shirts, appropriate-colored ties and polished shoes. Naomi and Earlene stand close by, surrounded by Sarah's workers, including Ruby, Pauline and Marcus—who now lives with the Collins family. Having always prayed for a son, Collin's prayers, as have others, have been answered. Among the visitors from across the state, as well as from Cutterville are Dessen, Judge Chambers, white-haired Senator Feddermann, and many high-ranking officials including the little man in his blue suit, the man—Carlton—Caleb had told that his sickly wife had been cured. The road leading to Shadow Grove's trestle gate is packed for miles with folks on foot, in cars, in buses, on horseback, and in wagons, some are the citizens of Cutterville, and workers from other plantations throughout the South. From as far away as Europe people have come with names that are difficult for the locals to pronounce; many of them tourists—milling about the road, among the town citizens, the newsmen and the church officials trying to get a glimpse of Shadow Grove—had started their pilgrimage to the plantation weeks earlier, when news of the daytime sky turning black over Cutterville and over Henry's land had spread near and far. They all have dissimilar customs, color of skin, and speak different languages, but have much in common: they yearn to know about Caleb's God and wish to be close to see and touch Caleb. They've arrived by the thousands, and still coming, a fact which does not go unnoticed by Cutterville's businessmen and the Georgia politicians. Collins is the new sheriff; he and his deputies—both black ones and white ones—make up a skillful team with the state police keeping order in the well-behaved, inquisitive crowd.

On that warm day—in an old truck parked down the road from Shadow Grove's gate—one of deceased, Sheriff Richards's ex-deputies, who was with the Klan at Henry's place and had escaped, sits behind the wheel of his Chevy, while rolling down the truck window and fanning himself with a newspaper. He's Gilbert Hawfiller, whom Caleb had allowed to live and now anxiously watches the growing crowd. His wife, Julie, and their three crying children, two boys and a girl, all under the age of fourteen, are with him in a truck piled high with their household belongings.

"Shut up that damn sobbing back there befer I take a switch to you kids," he yells.

"How is your wound, honey?" the Klansman's wife, Julie, asks, trying to take his attention from his frightened children.

"It's okay. No thanks to that spade I thought was going to kill me. I also cut my damn leg on a piece of sharp tin when I fell off the back of Henry's damn, beat-up horse."

"Caleb could have just as easily have killed you, honey. They say he's a excellent shot."

"There's no place fer us here anymore, Julie," the disgraced deputy tells his wife, then glaring at her, for saying that Caleb was an excellent shot, as she and his children look in amazement at the diverse crowd.

"There would be," she tells him, "a place fer us here with all of our neighbors and friends, if you would swallow your pride and ask fer fergiveness of God and the coloreds like most of our friends at Reverend Miller's church did. I'm sure Sheriff Collins would open his heart to you and—"

"I'll never ask those people fer fergiveness or anything else. Now, you just sit there and shut up and get used to the idea befer I whip your ass again, all of this business of folks coming here is just a cult that's all and no one can change my mind."

On the edge of the crowd, several of the black Jesus-fan women from the porch of wisdom—are listening with opened mouths as the ex-deputy continues to verbally abuse his wife.

"Asking me, a Klansman all my adult life, to beg fergiveness of them niggers. I ought to whip your ass anyway just fer the hell of it."

"Please don't hurt Mamma again, Daddy," sobs the oldest child.

"Shut up back there befer I take a belt to you, as well," he blares.

"No you won't, Gilbert," Julie yells. "Not to me or our children ever again."

She seizes her purse, looks at her children in the back seat and yells to them, "Jerry, Kenneth, Mary, out of the truck. Now!"

As she and the children scramble from the vehicle, Gibert looks at them in shock. "What the hell you think you're doing, Julie? Get back in this truck, okay, or I'll leave you behind." When she doesn't move, he glares at his kids. "You kids get in here. You and your mother will starve. Who will care fer you, but me? Now do the fuck what I tell you and get in here."

The black women move to the Julie's side and one of the women—the one in her red dress—stares at Gilbert. "All of us here in these times will have to depend on the kindness of others," she tells the abusive ex-deputy, "not on you and the devil, not anymore. Hopefully, we learned our lesson" She places her arms about Julie's shoulder, then looks at Gilbert. "These children are our kin. They are far better off without you, who would bring them under eternal damnation with your ugly hate. I gots a big lovely house, they can come and live with me." Julie and her children disappear into the crowd with the black women and with those others who are seeking the love of God.

"I'm not with Satan! I'm not, Julie!" Gilbert suddenly rolls up the window glass. A horrible odor permeates the air; old man Hank is approaching, hobbling along with his walking stick. The ex-deputy hurriedly drives away, passing Hank and crying, "I'm not like you! Stay the hell away from me!"

When the fly-infested Hank—his hair long over his shoulders, filthy and in tangles, his bare feet and lips, blistered and parched, and his scarred face almost beyond recognition—sees his old deputy friend drive speedily away from him—he crosses back into a field away from the people, for he knows that he will be driven away from them if he did not depart on his own. Painfully limping along with that crudely-made walking stick, he talks to himself, as, in that same field, a starving dog, its nose sniffing the air, stalks him, then charges in and nibbles at Hank's bloody foot.

"Because I was a Ku Klux Klan," Hank tells the wind, while stabbing at the dog with his stick, "I walk this road of pain alone. I tried to shoot myself, but my trembling hands can't hold onto the gun. I've taken poison, cut my wrist, even stopped eating and drinking water. Lord have mercy on me. Have mercy on me, an old man, and let me die. Please let me die, God."

Long after Hank and his acrid stench fades from the land, back at the road, in the distance, suddenly there's excitement. An elderly Father

Haas is seen on Shadow Grove, just inside the Trestle Gate, the old priest is gazing down from his horse, while conversing with Naomi. She hands him a purple package and Father Haas reverently places it in his saddlebag, and makes the sign of the cross over Naomi, who then walks back in the direction of the remote manor, having learned in her old age that for, mankind anyway, walking is the best medicine in the world for aging bones. Father Haas leaves Shadow Grove on his horse and carefully make his way onto the road among the spectators. "Father," a powerful-looking black man begins, as the priest draws near: He's the train-coal stoker Bruno, "were you on Henry's land, before coming here, to see where God spoke to Caleb where the officers won't let anyone on his land? And did you bless Henry's casket?" he asks, pointing to the up-sloped cemetery, "and were you able to see Caleb up there? I returned something to him and just wondering how he's doing."

In the crowd with everyone trying to get the priest's attention, are Sue Ann and her girls, standing side-by-side with Lana, Mellow Yellow and the rest of Lana's money winners. The women of the night are all ears, tears flowing down their cheeks as Father Hass answers the white woman's question: "Yes. I saw both Caleb and Flynn. And I did bless Henry's casket and that of Lawrence and Marilyn's."

"I heard that Flynn and Sarah returned millions of dollars to the army," says ex-deputy Gilbert's daughter Mary, who, along with her mother, brothers and the black women—all of whom have made their way to the front of the line with the help of one of the new deputies. As her brothers stroke Father Haas's horse, Mary—who has been brought up in Miller's church of scorn against blacks, Jews and Catholics—looks at her smiling mother, who nods to her with encouragement, and Mary continues speaking to Father Haas. "After Flynn and Caleb saw the Light of God, does that mean because one of them is colored and one is white, that God loves us all and not hate colored and Jews and Catholics or us now like Pa says?"

"They say whites and coloreds get along like sisters and brothers on Shadow Grove, now that that Barney's dead," a black man tells Mary and those around him and the priest, while others in the crowd far behind them are trying their best to hear. The man who has informed Mary about how people live like sisters and brothers on Shadow Grove is Sammy, Briana's husband. Briana and their son, Pee Wee—who first alerted Briana that Caleb and Flynn were riding through Colored Town on their sparkling horse—is there with a changed and loving dad.

"Father," Briana's son calls to the priest, "did Daddy get that factory job 'cause of Caleb or 'cause of you or God in heaven?"

"God leaves much of man's life into our own hands," Father Haas tells the boy. "If your father got a job, it must be because Mister Dessen understands that we all need to work to feed our families." He again faces Mary, from the church of snakes, a girl who had so desperately asked her question, clearly fearing for her soul. "Do you love God, child?" She nods to him and the Father goes on. "God loves all who loves Him."

Sammy has decided to convert to Catholicism and looks at the saddlebag. "Is that a chalice you carryin', Father? The one I saw you put in yo' saddlebag, the one that folks say gave birth to Caleb in the Winthrops' barn?"

"Is it, Father, the chalice, the one the devil called the 'can,'" Someone calls from the midst of the crowd, which moves in closer to the priest and his horse, the caller going on, "If so, it's a miracle. Can you let us touch it?"

"The chalice's job here is complete," says Father Haas. "As for miracles, you've already touched it, and it's touched you years ago in the cemetery—as I see it now in all of you—when Sarah embraced the joy of God by touching Henry with love."

Those in the crowd who are of Catholic persuasions—including many who are not, among which is a Semitic family of three—kneel seeking the priest's blessings. He makes the sign of the cross over the crowd, taking special notice of the Jewish family, which he blesses in a separate motion and seemingly—to those who notice—in a special way. As he had arrived and left over seventeen years ago—when Sarah's parents died in the plane crash—Father Hass leaves on his horse with the chalice and a book of Homer. Once the priest has departed, that Semitic-speaking family, the Jewish man, his wife and their teenage son watch him until he disappears behind the crowd, and then this special family attempts to pass through Shadow Grove's guarded gate and onto the plantation; they're the Lewin couple—Joel and Rebecca—whose newborn Naomi had saved with a miracle on the *Imperator* voyage, the night its bronze propellers went into motion and propelled Sarah out of Stettin Bay and into the future. When the family reaches the gate, Col-

713

lins and one of his black deputies stops them. "Might I help you, Sir?" the black deputy asks, as Collins stand by and lets him handle the family of three.

"Is this where Sarah Winthrop lives?" Joel asks.

"And a colored woman named Naomi?" Rebecca adds. Hearing this, Collins looks from the family to a distant Naomi, now slowly walking her tired bones up the winding, oak-lined driveway. He then turns back to the visitors. "Naomi lives here but she needs her rest and can't be disturbed," he tells them. As the family walks away, Naomi suddenly turns around. Her old hand blocking the sun from her eyes, she stares back at the Lewins.

"We met Sarah and Naomi long ago," Joel says, to Collins as they leave, "and would like to see them once more, but thank you!"

"I'm sorry," says Collins, his voice reflecting his puzzlement, as he keeps an eye on Naomi's reaction to what she sees. "Everyone wants to talk to Naomi, Sarah, Flynn and Caleb."

"It's okay, Keith," calls the graceful voice of Naomi, as she, still squinting at the family, makes her way slowly, then faster and faster, then hurriedly back to the gate.

"It's Naomi," someone whispers from those near the front of the crowded road, and the word quickly spread.

"Naomi. It was her all the time talking with the priest by the gate," the word continues spreading.

All eyes are focused on the gate and the elderly, mixed-blood woman, as she now runs to the middle-aged couple and their son. Stopping within a foot or two of the gate and the family, Naomi tilts her head to the side, her wise old eyes lighting up; a smile crosses her face. "Joel, Rebecca?" she shouts.

"Naomi!" Rebecca calls.

"Rebecca!" again exclaims Naomi, moving to them with open arms, Joel and Rebecca running through the gate to Naomi, each hugging and kissing the other.

"My God," Naomi sobs for joy. "I didn't think I'd ever see you again." She looks at the boy. "This, then, must be Little Joel!"

"He's nineteen, now, Naomi," says Joel senior. "Little Joel, this is the woman who asked God to save your life and forever changed ours." Crying, the boy and Naomi hug one another, as the crowd watches in awe.

"Who are they," a stranger asks Collins. "That family that the priest recognized and Naomi now hugs?"

"Someone who commands the love and admiration of Naomi," says Collins, smiling at the four of them. "And that's more than good enough for any man, woman or child alive."

Among the mass of people, a saddened-faced, handsome, young, white man—age twenty-eight—speaks to his mother: "She's the angel who appeared in the snow and gave me that money and this blanket, Mother," he says, while others listen, and look at the blanket, as he lovingly cradles it across his arm close to his heart, going on. "And I've never been sick again. I wanted to thank her, and show her this blanket and tell her that I'll always keep it near me as a reminder that there are also good colored people in the world, and to tell her that one day, if I ever become important—and I will—that I will be kind to all the people and work with Caleb to bring love back to us all."

"Adam," his mother says to him while glancing at the crowd and whispering. "Be careful on thinking that folks are angels. They say she's a good, Christian woman, but God's angels aren't down here among us. Not yet, anyway."

"Caleb is, and so is Naomi. She is, Mother, a real angel. But there are so many here who want to talk to her, so I'll never be able to."

"But if she's an angel, like you seem to think she is, she'll know how you feel and that you're here, won't she, Adam?" his mother says, not believing a word of what she says and only trying to pacify him.

She blinks in astonishment, when she looks up and sees Naomi stare directly back at them, the crowd following her gaze to Naomi, then back to the young man and his blanket.

"You saved my life, Naomi," Adams calls. "Thank you."

Naomi nods to Adam and his mother. Then, the mystery woman and the family of Joel walk hand in hand to Manor Hill, Little Joel looking back at the dreamy-eyed man with the blanket, smiles at him, then faces Naomi and never takes his sights from the woman who also saved his life, a woman his parents have said is from God.

Adam now holds his blanket even closer to his heart, as his mother beams up at him with love reflected in her eyes. "She knows, Adam." She glances about the crowd and whispers. "They all know now that you are special, because of all of us in this endless sea of humanity, Naomi turned her gaze back to you. Now, I also believe. She's truly from Him,

715

from God." Everyone who hears this utterance from the mouth of Adam's mother focuses on Naomi, including a man on his horse next to Adam, the cowboy Jason, stroking his pinto, which Jayne had stolen to rescue Caleb from the river, a horse that had been returned to him by Caleb.

After having heard everything said by the priest, Adam and others, Jason leans over and whispers to his horse, "Seems you and I ran into this Caleb boy in that alley, and instead of either one of us getting a raw deal that day, we both was a part of history." He smiles and looks about the crowd, then tips his wide-brimmed hat to Naomi, as she and the Jewish family disappear under the canopy of trees, branches and leaves lining the winding driveway to the manor.

"Naomi," says Joel, as they make their way up the driveway, "It's so beautiful here. Does all of this belong to Sarah?"

"She feels that it belongs to all of us," Naomi tells him. "It's what Jesus' death on the cross has taught us: to share with one another, but Flynn, her son, is the master here now, a kind, gentle soul, who writes poetry and plays the classical piano the likes of a pure angel. You'll love him as much as we all do."

Walking under the oak shade trees, Joel is overcome with joy. "For a long time, Naomi," he tells her, "I struggled with the guilt that I would be betraying my family and our heritage if I accepted Jesus as the Messiah." He lovingly beams at his wife, at his son and they at him, and he continues. "Apostle Paul said that 'For us, there is one God and our Lord Jesus Christ.' The three of us now realize that our people have been waiting—in recent time—for nearly two thousand years for the Messiah to come and save us. He's been here and gone, Naomi. It was our races' stubborn pride that kept us from seeing it, and it was only after years of study of the Bible and other historical books that my family and I fully recognized that there are not two Messiahs, one born to die for us and one born of David to live for us. We now agreed that there is but one God and He has but one Son."

Little Joel adds to his father's comment: "Paul said 'Are they Hebrew? So am I. Are they Israelites? So am I. Are they the seed of Abraham? So am I.' " As Naomi kisses him on the cheek, Little Joel tearfully says to her. "And now, so are we, Naomi, true believers in Jesus, the Son of God."

"We read about Shadow Grove in *The New York Times*," says

Rebecca. "About you, Sarah, Flynn and this young man called Caleb, and about the miracles that happened here, and we . . ." She takes her family's hands, and it's the younger Joel who goes on:

"We all decided that we want to live here with you and Sarah," he says.

Rebecca quickly adds, "If you will have us, that is."

"Have you!" exclaims Naomi. "You just try to get away. Blessed be His name. This is both a sad day with the death of our beloved Henry—Caleb's father—sad to some who still don't realize what it means to die and be welcomed into God's heaven, but it's also now a day that fulfills His joyous love for us." Naomi embraces Rebecca. "God has brought the lost tribe of Israel home to the community of man. The world is finally gathering in her chicks."

At the cemetery, several minutes later, as Joel Senior and his family wait with Naomi to show their respect, now that Father Haas has blessed the open casket and has gone, and countless others stand back and also wait their turn, Sarah—with Caleb and Flynn at her side—abides over Henry's remains. "I know you loved the coast, Henry Brooks," Sarah whispers, and then she continues speaking softly to him, "loved the sounds of the waves crashing below the bluffs, the smell of the salty air . . ." She can't go on and lingers in tears flowing from her blue eyes as she gazes down at Henry. The man she loves lies in splendor. Even as God had moved Carrie's arms about Bruce's body, He has made Henry's once-battered body, miraculously whole again, not a mark on his remains. Sarah continues, wiping the tears from her eyes. "I know you would not want me to think of how beautifully God has restored you, the way you will appear in heaven, because you would say that such thoughts reflect only an earthy value. Caleb has told me how—when he was in that pit of thorns—you told him that God loves you and how beautiful heaven is, and that no one wants to ever come back here, but I brought you here to be close to me on this land, which is as much yours as ours."

Sarah kisses Henry gently on the lips. An astonished Flynn and Caleb look at each other. Sarah, then, touches Caleb's golden face and kisses him, while holding onto a stunned Flynn with her free hand. "You were my second-born, Caleb," Sarah tells him.

"My mother is dead, Sarah. At our house in her grave," Caleb replies, absolutely shocked and baffled, the near-standing field hands as

717

well, with open mouths, when they hear Sarah's act of contrition, and even more so as she goes on. "It was necessary to have everyone believe that I was dead to protect you, Henry and Flynn. Now, your mother wants to profess her love for you and Henry before God and the world. I'm not in that cold grave on little Shadow Place. I'm here. Your father and I have longed to tell you and Flynn of the love we had for one another." She smiles at a stunned Caleb. "Yes, Caleb. I am she. Your mother." The nearby workers look at each other, the blacks doing their best to restrain themselves and to keep from leaping up and down to show their rapturous hope for the better tomorrows to come in theirs and their children's lives, feeling that for the first time with Sarah's help, and that of Caleb and of Flynn and the schooling they'll get while living there, there is no task too difficult, no goal too high or too far to reach for them and their families. The whites—some crying with overwhelming elation, a few standing in denial and in shock, not knowing what to think—fix their gazes and hopes on Sarah, who faces a confused Flynn. "Barney was your father, Flynn, but Henry considered you his son and loved you as much as he loved Caleb, this you already know." Crying and dumbfounded by the news that he is Caleb's brother, and deeply afflicted by Henry's death, the blonde boy just stands there looking at Caleb, then at his mother. Taking both of their hands, Sarah goes on, "You and Caleb are both born of me, one white, one colored, but the same in God's eyes."

The workers clap, when Flynn moves into Caleb's arms and they kiss one another's cheek. Caleb, Flynn and Sarah step away to make room for the workers to pass by the casket and say their final goodbyes to Henry. A few feet from the casket, and still overwhelmed by the realization that they are brothers, Caleb's light-brown eyes lock on Flynn's blue ones, both fighting back the tears. Both, in turn, kissing Sarah, then kissing Naomi, who introduces Caleb, Flynn and a surprised Sarah to Joel and his family. As the Lewins, Naomi and Sarah move under a shade tree to catch up on each others' lives, Judge Chambers and Senator Feddermann, removing their hats, approach the boys.

"MacDonnell's and others' pictures have circled the world, as you two can see," Chambers says, with a smile, looking at the distant Trestle Gate and the swarming people and parked vehicles on the lower road. "Those pictures have no doubt given countless millions hope. Hope, Flynn and you, Caleb! Not from the second coming of the Klan's god.

718

Not hope for some slow judicial rules and regulations to do away with injustice, for these things are the work of politicians and are small in the eyes of God and will automatically come when we love each other. Your father's death, Caleb, that's what has rekindled the hope in that which was implanted in mankind by Christ's crucifixion, in the first place, to show us one thing: that we're all one family. Even my wife has volunteered now to go into Colored Town and teach the children there to read and write until we strike down all the laws that keep coloreds from attending our white schools, laws that force people to live across the train tracks. There are still some among us who resist these changes, but these laws will be removed in days, not years. You, Caleb and Flynn, and all of your workers who were involved in the killing of those Klansmen on Henry's land have been expunged of any wrong-doing." He shakes Caleb's hand. "Can you ever forgive this old man for the way I misjudged you because of the color of yours and other's skins, whenever they entered my courthouse?"

"There's room for forgiveness from all of us," Caleb tells him, "and always will be. Yes, of course," Caleb says smiling at Flynn. "I forgive you, the way all brothers must."

Chambers is deeply touched by Caleb inferring that he, Chambers, is also his brother. The old judge faces Henry's casket and then turns and steps a few feet away, his eyes watering up.

"I concur with Chambers," says Feddermann, the Senior Senator from Georgia, as more elected peers approach Caleb and Flynn, including the little man in blue, their hats in their hands. Feddermann goes on. "What's been said here . . ." He gestures to his fellow lawmakers. "We all agree with it."

Mayor Sipple steps over and enters the conversation. "The phones are ringing off the hooks with offers from companies who want to set up shop in Cutterville. Now, suddenly, there is need for more workers and not just jobs for the few."

"Seems the world wants to live in Georgia near the place where God visited earth," calls Reverend Harris, after getting an ear full from among the amazed, nearby workers gawking at Henry's body. Harris, standing tall and wiggling his shoulders, suggesting that he had a part in all of what has happened.

"Our veterans," Chambers continues, "our local whites, our

coloreds are all working side-by-side in Dessen's factory now, and those fire-damaged Main-Street stores are being rebuilt even as we speak."

"Enough of that," says Feddermann. "Get to Henry's land, or I'll tell him myself."

During all of this time, Flynn has been standing by with his hands behind his back and rising up and down on the balls of his feet, and smiling as if knowing what's coming next will gladden Caleb's heart, as it will Henry's, now that he's with God and no doubt being allowed to listen.

"Caleb," Chambers says, clearing his throat, "the colonel took away your land." Handing the deed to Little Shadow Place to Caleb, the old judge again clears his throat and adds. "We're giving your lagoon and your land back to you, free and clear, with a bonus of no property taxes for a generation to make up for our unthinkable disservice to you and your father." He leans over and whispers. "Pray for me, Caleb."

"Caleb, we're ready and eager for you to work with us for the good of Georgia," says the Senator, "and after you finish law school, we want you to come back here and run for a high-ranking state office as well, maybe even take old Chambers' job, since he's as old as dirt and can hardly cut the mustard anymore. And do pray for him and all of us, if you would, you and Flynn." Feddermann, trying to control his own emotions, faces Flynn, and getting a nod from his peers, says, "And, you Flynn Winthrop, with your grandfather's famous last name, my senate seat is ready for you, whenever you're ready for it."

Flynn and Sarah have legally changed their last names to Sarah's maiden name "Winthrop", this in a matter of three days, due to an all-out effort by City Hall and MacDonnell's paper printing a special edition to run Sarah's notification of the name chance, and with that proudly in mind, Flynn nods in agreement to Feddermann's offer. Having satisfied their conscience, the aging senator, Chambers and the others blend back into the crowd filing past Henry's casket as just a half dozen more humbled spectators. Caleb and Flynn return to Sarah, and Caleb hands the deed to Naomi to hold. After the stunned workers and visitors have viewed Henry's body, Caleb, Flynn and Sarah excuse themselves from Naomi and the Lewins and take the short walk back to Henry's casket, where they kneel beside his body, even as a scattering of field hands continue walking by, including Naomi and the Lewins, and viewing Henry's remains. Sarah removes a white document from her purse and extends it to Flynn, who reaches out for it.

"Wait, Flynn," says Caleb.

He looks at Sarah. "Do you mind, Sarah? Before he receives what you have for him . . ." He faces Flynn and adds. ". . . I've been carrying something very special for you." Once more facing Sarah he explains on, "And I would like to give it to him first."

Sarah beams at both of them. "Go right ahead," she tells Caleb. "It pleases me to see you two involved with each other again."

Caleb takes the tobacco pouch from about his neck, opens it, removes something from it, stuffs the pouch in his pocket and hands Flynn the gold coin, which Flynn had asked him to hold for him the night he had said goodbye to Caleb and Henry, a coin that Bruno had heard had belonged to Flynn and had returned. Flynn looks at the coin, at Caleb and almost cries all over again. So moved is he that—through all of his troubles and deadly occurrences, Caleb had held onto the coin, as he had prayed he would—Flynn puts the coin into his shirt pocket without so much as a single word as he then receives his grandfather's document from Sarah, who understands her blonde son's silence and sees it as the full measure of Love for his brother.

"Thanks, Mother," Flynn says and again gives Caleb a loving smile.

"I wanted Henry to give that paper from your grandfather to you, Flynn," Sarah tells him. "Now, I'm doing it here before him in his place. My father left an addendum to his will to be opened on your eighteenth birthday," she tells him. "Henry and I, however, thought it wise to delay showing it to you until we could tell you about your brother, since the possibility of my having other sons enters into the wording of the appendix." She tenderly touches Caleb's face and then Flynn's. "Although it was well known that you would inherit Shadow Grove, Flynn, this is your grandfather's last will and testament that makes it complete."

Leaving Caleb and Flynn alone beside the casket, Sarah returns to the Lewins and Naomi, and she stands at her life-long friend and spiritual teacher's side, both ravishing in the love shown between the brothers. As Flynn reads the legal document, a smile crosses his face. Caleb taps him on the arm and says, "I told you you'd not have to worry about being late to work one day." Beaming, he goes on. "I'm ready to work with you, Flynn, to build the kind of Shadow Grove that Sarah . . ." He faces his mother. "That Mother and Papa dreamed of, if you want my help, whether you run for the senate or not."

"It's a done deal," says Flynn, somberly glancing at the casket, then re-folding the document and returning the favor by tapping Caleb on the chin. "You know how politicians are. I'll run and win, then come back here from time to time and work for you, the next oldest son, which, pursuant to this addendum mother gave me . . . if the oldest son dies or does not wish to own this fingernail-soiling land, it goes to the next oldest boy." Flynn reaches into his trouser pocket and removes something shiny from it. It's the coin that Caleb had given to Crazy Walter and Barney had overlooked, because it was in Dane's shoe for safe-keeping.

"I got it back for you, Caleb, washed nice and clean." Flynn tells him. "Don't ask me how I got it. It's one of those political 'you scratch my back, and I'll scratch yours' thing." As Caleb—filled with emotion—takes the coin, a coin of love, not of greed for gold, Flynn has another surprise: "Shadow Grove is yours, little brother. You know as well as I do that I'll never get used to this place, no matter how many times I wash my hands."

"Caleb," a black boy yells from the group of viewers passing behind them. "Did Master Flynn just say Shadow Grove belongs to you, a colored man?"

"He did," says Sarah, calling to the boy, then smiling at Rebecca and admiring Little Joe and stroking his dark head of hair, going on. "And I'm the lucky one. This is a real family again."

The black workers start off coupling hands with the whites and rocking side-to-side and singing; and when Caleb and Flynn stand up together, and hug one another, a thunderous applause breaks out and continues for minutes on end, even spreading down to the thousands of visitors on the road, who join in clapping and swaying their hands and arms to-and-fro, copying that of those at the cemetery. Suddenly, over the cemetery, dozens of white doves appear in the sky and swoop in a widening circle around the casket, as those on the road and at the grave site watch in wonderment.

"See," Adam tells his mother, while clinging to his blanket and going on, "I told you. The doves know it. Naomi is. She's a real angel."

Naomi watches the doves circle in the sky as if someone has given her a surprise party, and she smiles with a nod of approval. The white birds have returned now that Barney is dead, as she had said they would.

Two short years later, a raven flies over Shadow Grove and looks down at the plantation. Henry's land is now part of the six-teen-thousand-acre plantation and all the land in between with the completed pipeline running from Shadow Grove to Little Shadow Place. As God had promised, Caleb's reward, indeed, outshines King Solomon's in Caleb's time: The once-dry plantation has now become a paradise of green fields and gently rolling emerald hills. Once badly in need of paint, the manor house gleams like a white jewel against the blue sky. In the house, Barney's portrait has been removed, and the Brooks' ancestors' photos have been restored as portraits and now hang beside those of the Winthrops along the spiral-staircase wall and in the large ballroom. One other significant item is in the house; it lies on the foyer's pie-crust-top table, along with freshly cut calla lilies. This prominently displayed item was placed there by none other than Caleb: it's Henry's old Holy Bible. Caleb, with a new, expensive violin—given to him by Sarah—Flynn, at the grand piano is poised to play. Sarah, Naomi, Joel, Rebecca, Little Joel and Earlene are in the room sitting on overstuffed chairs and velvet couches. Sarah turns to Earlene. "How are you and Tootie getting along?" she asks her.

"It couldn't be better, Sarah," Earlene says, hugging her. "And thanks for the new house you had built for us. Brick and I love Tootie. She just like Mamma and tells me not to drink so much lemonade, 'cause you know what."

They laugh together and then Sarah tells her, "You're part of our extended family, now, Earlene. Now go. The vocal . . . My mother's favorite, the way I taught you."

Caleb and Flynn perform Schubert's "Ave Maria," and Earlene—the picture of grace—walks across the room to the boys and sings it in Italian, her voice that of an angel. Outside, as the soulful sound of the young girl's voice, the melodic keyboard fingering of Flynn, and Caleb's deeply moving violin performance carries across the thriving plantation. Milk cows dot the hillsides and workers, blacks and whites joyously labor side-by-side in the fields, as it was once under Doctor Lawrence and Marilyn Winthrop's tutelage, and why not? Field hands now live intermixed in new houses, all with porches and green lawns, the elderly taking it much easier, the white elderly and the colored ones interchanging stories about the old days, as they lovingly hang out the family's laundry in the backyards or watch over tots at play in the front of their houses, or just sit about their houses or bask in the sun. As the mu-

723

sic spreads across the fields, one-by-one, the workers stop what they are doing and listen to the musical measurements of love streaming from the grand hilltop house's open windows. A new and much larger school—for those who want to attend there instead of traveling to town, with grades kindergarten to twelfth—looms nearby with a memorial plaque to Henry on its base. Then, it begins to rain. The workers watch Caleb, Flynn and Earlene dash from the sprawling house and race across Manor Hill's quarter-mile-wide crest, laughing in the downpour. Peter Scott—having been freed by Caleb of all thoughts of guilt for the death of Jayne's mother now—races from the school and to the porch where Little Joel stands watching Caleb, Flynn and Earlene, and—with youthful joy—Scott motions for the new boy to join him in the chase after the big-two men of the land. All of the children then stream from the school with their teachers—Miss McLeland and a dozen other teachers among them—encouraging the young ones on. Marcus—feeling wanted and loved for the first time in his life—is one of the laughing young people who—racing with the wind—catch up to Little Joel and Peter, and the children, alone with Peter and Little Joel, overtake the leaders, a trotting Flynn, Caleb and Earlene. Shooing thousands of ravens into the sky from the summit, as the young and innocent charge across it, the little people stringing out behind the forerunners, and the rain pours down over them and the land in buckets. Naomi, Rebecca, Joel Senior and Sarah, resting in the wicker rocking chairs, watch the parade of love from the porch, along with a hundred or so visitors and several deputies standing on the lower road in the rain and with no intention of leaving due to the downpour.

"Shadow Grove is making it on its own, now," says Naomi. "And there's much happiness in this old house again." A section of the Cutterville *Sentinel* is blown from the table onto the porch and lands at Naomi's feet. She picks it up and sadly scans it with her aging eyes: the headline reads: FINALLY WE KNOW, a small grainy snapshot of Stella Fuchs, as well as others, is displayed with the words: "New Yorkers among Those Found Killed by Hitler." Naomi slowly folds the paper and drops it in a tableside trash can. Suddenly she looks about.

"What is it, Naomi?" asks Sarah.

"He's here, Sarah. Watching over us. Henry . . . Here. Jesus has let him make himself known."

Joel, Rebecca and Sarah follow Naomi's gaze across the hill to Old

724

Clara, who's been retired to her own pasture there. As if being ridden by an unseen rider, the old horse is sprinting in the wind, paralleling Caleb, Flynn, Earlene, Little Joel, Peter and the children, with an aging Pancake who is—also seemingly now blessed with amazing longevity—lagging behind Old Clara and barking as if to say, "Wait for me." Sarah looks over at Henry's old rocker, it's gently moving in the breeze.

"I can feel him," Sarah says. "He's again in the saddle, a lion among men. And all this rain of late, Naomi. Did it come from Caleb or from you?"

"The power's with Caleb, now," she answers reaching beyond the railing and letting the rain splatter against her hand. "And with his love, it goes far beyond what I had or ever will have again, and in his hands, it also has no limits." Naomi sits back in the chair and lets out a tired breath.

"Now I can relax and have that tea with Joel, Rebecca and you. The lion's with God, with Whom everything is possible, Sarah. Henry's with God." It seems that Naomi still has some of her power after all, the same as all loving, honorable people do, who have an ability to sense the presence of God through love. As Joel and Rebecca watch with a smile, Sarah beams at the mixed-blood woman:

"You never did tell me," she says to Naomi, "are you an angel or not?"

"Child, God would not waste one of his angels by making one of this lowly soul."

They knowingly smile at one another, and as they do, the Hollies' singing "He Ain't Heavy, He's My Brother," is heard over the falling rain and across the vast countryside.

"What a beautiful song," says Sarah. "I've never heard anything like it on the radio."

"It's from the future," says Naomi. "Caleb's future, where some will follow him and others will fall by the wayside."

Beyond the wheat fields, the red tree grows straight and tall, its branches of fire reaching for the sky, not a firethorn or jimson weed in sight. Caleb and the others continue sprinting across Manor Hill, as if across the sky, leaving the jealousy, the fear, the hatred of others forever behind them. Parakeets swoop through the rain and over the heads of the young. Sarah's older workers race from their houses to be with Caleb, Flynn and the children. When Earlene tires and drops back among the

725

following runners, Marcus dashes up alongside the leaders. Caleb slows the pace so that the young boy can keep up with him and Flynn, and—immediately—the rain stops, and a Divine voice speaks: "*Come unto Me*," it says, as if from a hill called "Summit." Easing to a trot, Caleb looks over at Flynn, who says, "I also heard it."

Back on the porch, Naomi's gaze is on that highest point of Shadow Grove's vast land, the summit, a quarter mile away from the manor, where the crude cross on which Henry was crucified looms, and many whites want torn down. Naomi's sights shift to a dazzling, white cloud drifting down around the cross and hill. Sarah turns from the sight to Naomi, as do Joel and Rebecca.

"What do you see, Naomi?" asks Sarah. Naomi faces Collins below Manor Hill at the trestle gate.

"Let everyone enter, Keith!" she yells. Minus the reporters, who have all left town, when the gate is opened, the multitude—Keith Collins, his wife and daughter—who had chosen to be with Collins and converse with the visitors—and his deputies—hurry up the slopes and to the summit's baseline.

"Come on, Sarah!" shouts Naomi, taking Sarah's hand and quickstepping off the porch, Joel and Rebecca following her and Sarah to the baseline of Summit Hill. Everyone there has stopped in awe, and the children wait in total silence as Caleb and Flynn—by the foot of the summit's slope—stand apart from the others and focus up at the cross and cloud in trepidation. Half of the newly-arrived crowd are there to debunk Caleb, whom they despise with his golden skin and close friendship with a powerful, rich, white boy like Flynn Winthrop. Mocking, they watch as Caleb and Flynn—as if in a daze—tremulously climb the sanctity of the slopes together, the cloud suddenly growing brighter, the fear rising within the boys and crowd.

With their stiffened body language voicing Flynn and Caleb's misgivings, Sarah's workers, witnessing it, begin muttering in dread for her son and Caleb, as do many others. Naomi tells them not to worry that heaven smiles on the boys. The embittered, newly-arrived spectators disregard her counsel and hold onto their dislike and suspicions of Caleb, as he and Flynn—in alarm—feeling the presence of God all around them, reach the summit, and linger by the cross. They gaze up and gasp. Standing in the cloud, a stone's throw above them, in a flowing, white robe and looking down at them, is Jesus Christ. The brothers' hearts gallop out of control, as Jesus, again, calls down to them, "Come unto me."

Flynn falls to his knees and makes the sign of the cross. "How, my Lord, with You so pure and justly above us sinners as You are?" he sobs, and Jesus opens His arms to him and Caleb.

"Your faith has served you well in the past, Flynn. And with that faith, you can soar." And the boys, vacillating in disbelief, rise up in the sky beside the Son of Man, and the cloud glows with blinding intensity. Below the summit, people groan in terror, in adoration or lie face-down on the ground, or drop to their knees looking up at Caleb and Flynn, who appear to be absolutely alone, as they float in the sky and talk with Christ.

Caleb, his eyes watering, faces Jesus and exclaims: "When Papa died, I said God had no face, but now I know I'm looking at His face."

"Your father is in paradise with Zackary and a blessed few others who wait for my return, Caleb, and—Caleb—Zackary is the man who died on the cross next to me, without having to linger in purgatory for purification, as had not Henry, because of God's love. Long before your father was born of his parents, and before you were born of Henry's seed, Caleb Brooks, you were alive in God's mind, that you might do His will, and—after your birth when you were made known of this—you were filled with doubt, the way my disciples were."

As Jesus speaks, still unseen to them, many of those watching from below reason that it is wickedness that empowers the boys skyward, and they lean back, feeling that heaven will strike Caleb and Flynn with lightning at any minute. Others feel it is an illusion from Satan that causes what they see. While the ungodly ones—below the hill—fill themselves with doubt, Jesus places His hand on a troubled Caleb's shoulder, cautioning him and Flynn.

"There are those who, in their hearts, know that the two of you are from God, but—even knowing this—they will try to crucify you for loving one another as you do."

In the midst of the disbelievers, and being blessed to see and hear Jesus—the same as Naomi—Sarah takes Naomi's hand and holds on, as Jesus goes on to Caleb, "You are chosen over all others on this earth, as Naomi has told to you, Caleb."

The Son of God places His other hand on Caleb. With His hand on either of Caleb's shoulders, Christ—now—leans the weight of His body against Caleb's young might and breathes on him, strengthening him all the more and counsels on: "When you and Henry rode in your vegetable wagon through Colored Town, you spoke of a man strapped in the electric chair, a man who called out, 'Save me, champ!' This condemned man of yours—also named 'Zackary'—did not call out to God, as Zackary of old did from his cross to me and thus to God, but—instead—this modern soul, to be electrocuted, called out to those of earthly fame, those of the theater, of sports, and of riches—even as you did, Caleb—in your own way, by depending only on your mind of science.

"To you, the Bible which serves God's needs and its interpretation that serves the needs of Satan are one in the same: evil. It's only that way if you let Satan control your thoughts. In the wagon, you questioned the very heart of heaven when you said if God put people in hell to burn forever, then God is worse that Satan." Jesus removes his hands from Caleb's powerful shoulders and enlightens him: "It is man's love of evil which sends the children of Light rushing into the arms of darkness, to Satan—the arch fiend of transgression, the misleader of youth—and into the clutches of his hell fires." Christ, then, turns to Flynn. "And you, Flynn Winthrop, with your blue eyes and yellow hair and the long-ago loss of the browness of your African ancestors' skin, but still holds onto the love of your brother, know you that Satan's powers are infinitely greater than any dictator's, king's, or president's with the machines of today and of tomorrow spreading his will around the world faster than the speed of light, eroding away my Father's house. Your task, Flynn, is to become a powerful senator for God's purpose, to help Caleb rebuild the rock on which rests my Father's church. This is why God has given a long life to both of you, even as He has to Naomi."

The crowd is amazed. Caleb and Flynn are once again abruptly standing among them.

Flynn faces Sarah. "He said it, Mother! Jesus did."

"Said what, Flynn?"

"The image, Mother. When He first spoke to us, He told Caleb and me it was His. His blood, His sweat and tears, on the Shroud!"

All eyes face the heaven, filled with hope, all but a few seeing more than just the sky.

The Son of Man ascends into it, leaving the boys to the world: we

728

are all of the black stuff of carbon atoms from the heavens and the stars, and all made from the dark skin of Africa.

The boys have been told many secrets of heaven, which they cannot reveal. To do so would cause mankind to make heaven secondary to his desires of blatantly seeking the pleasures and riches of this world and take his changes with Satan in hell.

This is not the Day of Judgment, not yet.

The Shroud has been found; a guiding Light, left behind by the hand of God.

The End

A Love Song for Melba
"Death Angel"

Death Angel—Who has arisen from the dead with Your love—my friends say You are the custodian over all blame, can cure the lame and will understand. At eighteen and beautiful with a full life ahead of her, Melba died on a Sunday, was buried on a Wednesday with white, casketed flowers draped about her head. She was but a child who wanted to have my baby, the most beautiful newborn she said we'd ever have; now she's gone. She had hurt me and I hardened my heart against her.

At night while I sleep, I feel her presence at my side. When I open my eyes and reach out she is never there. Have mercy, Death Angel—Son of God—and grant me peace; those last days of her life I sent Melba away and drove her into another man's bed. He beat and misused her. In the cold darkness of uncertainty she ran back to me.

"I love you," she cried out in despair as I opened the door, but because of my pride—once again—I sent Melba away. Oh, Wind of the Living Breath, of the Source of Pure Light, she returned to that man's dark house of ill repute that same night and took his gun while he did sleep. She entered his bathroom and turned frame-ward the lock, sat upon his toilet and the trigger did cock.

The thunderous sound shook his house, and Melba's blood flowed from her stomach and across the floor. I can still hear that bullet ricocheting off the toilet, as they said it had, after it penetrated her body and blasted on through that man's bathroom door, a bullet forever ricocheting and echoing through my mind with Melba's voice calling, "I love you, Stanley, I love only you."